THE VILLAGERS

A NOVEL OF GREENWICH VILLAGE

BY

BRUCE ELLIOT

BLEECKER STREET PRESS

NEW YORK CITY

Bleecker Street Press
463 West Street, Suite A323
New York, N.Y. 10014

First published as *Village* by Bruce Elliot, Bantam Books 1982
Reprinted as *The Villagers* by Edward Field and Neil Derrick, Painted
Leaf Press 1999

Cover art by Dennis Selby
Cover design by Diane Derrick
Book design by Dean M. Tsuyuki

ISBN: 978-0-692-00141-7

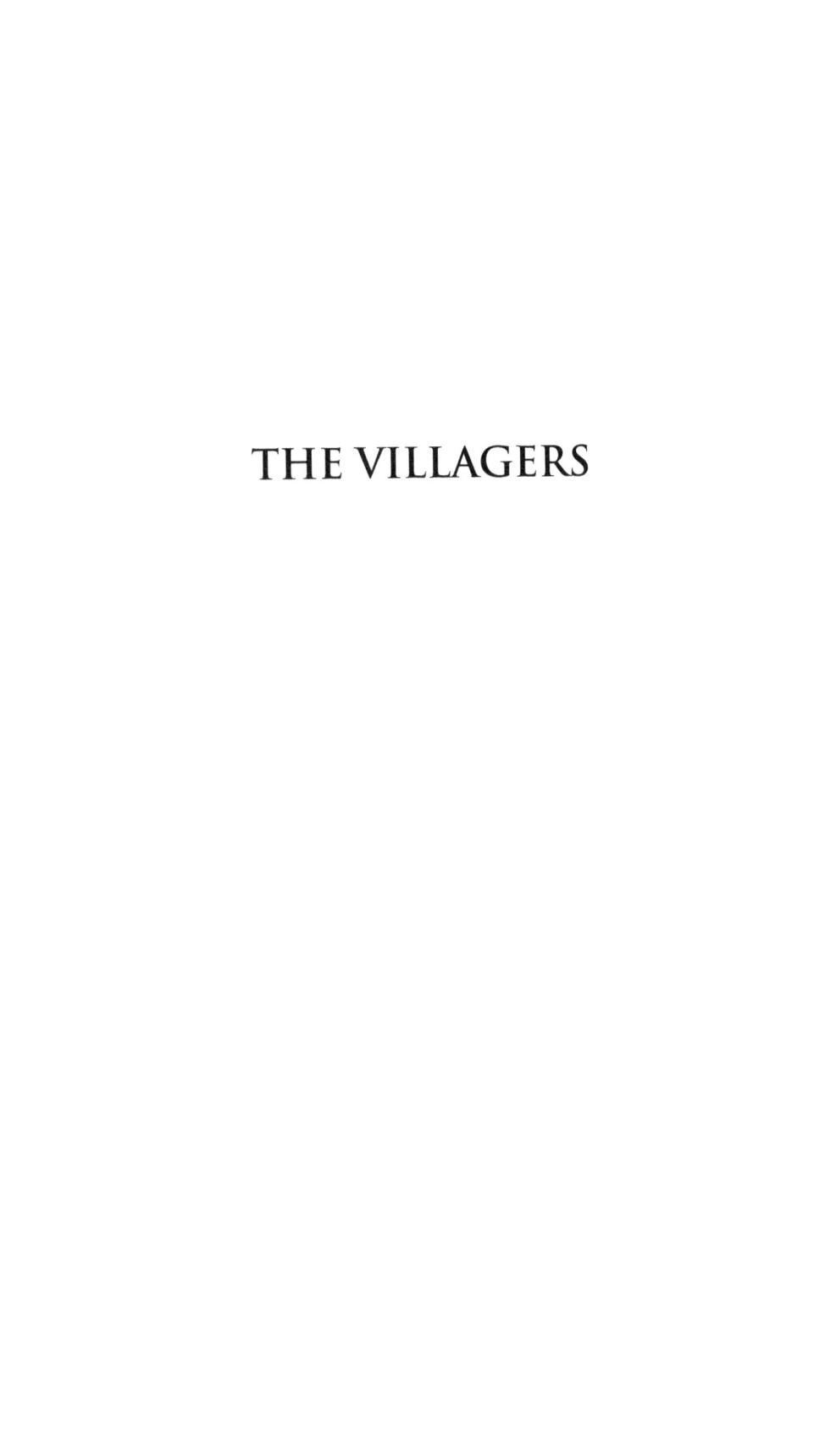

THE VILLAGERS

When you drive into New York City from the west and see the skyline of Manhattan ahead of you across the Hudson River, there's no easy landmark to point out where Greenwich Village is. It's somewhere in that nondescript area of low buildings between the Wall Street skyscrapers and the skyscrapers of midtown.

But Greenwich Village doesn't need any landmarks to give it distinction. It's a neighborhood that has remained almost intact while the rest of the city goes on tearing itself down and rebuilding. In contrast to the rest of Manhattan with its orderly, numbered cross streets, the Village is a confusion of irregular streets, lined with brick and brownstone townhouses, iron railings in front and Dutch stoops leading up to the handsome doorways.

Though it was artists who gave the Village its reputation, there aren't as many living there any more—not since the rents started to spiral up a couple of decades ago. But the Village still attracts the kind of people who want to live in a place where anything goes and no one cares. And for as long as anyone can remember, that's been the Village's story.

But it's not the whole story.

Sometimes, in the hush after a winter snowfall or perhaps on an airless summer evening just before a thunderstorm, when the parked cars are wrapped in shadow and the streetlights cast a ghostly glow on the nineteenth-century house fronts, you might almost imagine a horse and carriage clattering along under gas lamps, in an earlier time, when other people lived there....

BOOK I

1845

1

The parlor windows of the house on Perry Street were thrown wide to catch the breeze. By the light of an oil lamp, two women were absorbed over a planchette table, attempting to contact the spirit world. They sat across from each other, their fingers resting lightly on the back of a saucer that was slithering over the letters of the alphabet painted on the glossy tabletop. The saucer seemed to have a life of its own, as the women's hands followed its erratic movements.

They were trying to contact the spirit of a young woman who had once lived in the old house across the street, its dilapidated presence looming among ancestral trees, ghostly in the moonlight. It had been built a century earlier, in the midst of what was then a tobacco farm.

Before the Revolutionary War, the village of Greenwich was only a jumble of huts at the river's edge, where Indians, escaped slaves, and ne'er-do-wells lived. But the village had encroached on the fields, until all that was left of the tobacco farm was the old farmhouse, restricted to a plot of tangled vegetation, across cobbled Perry Street.

At the planchette table, the older of the two women, gaunt, somberly dressed Miss Swindon, was as spellbound as her charge, fragile, young Fanny Endicott, by the saucer moving under their fingertips. They felt the spirit they were summoning shimmering in the air above them. Both women caught their breath when the saucer beneath their fingers wavered and abruptly stopped. Then, an arrow painted on the saucer's rim began to move from letter to letter, spelling out a message.

"M-E-T   I-N-D-I-A-N   B-Y   R-I-V-E-R," Fanny read off in a breathless voice. "F-E-L-L   I-N   L-OV-E." She looked up at Miss Swindon, her eyes shining.

Although she was twenty-two, with a baby daughter asleep upstairs and an infant son dead two years before, Fanny Endicott looked hardly older than a schoolgirl. Her auburn hair was parted in the middle and arranged in curls on either side of her face. She was wearing a flowered muslin dress, its skirt billowing out over a crinoline. Her voice was shrill with a schoolgirl's excitement. "But how wicked to be in love with an Indian! How could she!"

"Hush," Miss Swindon reproved her gently, "you'll frighten her off."

She had been hired by Thomas Endicott as companion for his ailing wife when they moved up from New York City to the village of Greenwich several months before. Fanny needed constant attention because of her neurasthenic spells, but Miss Swindon had no trouble coping with them. She was not intimidated by difficult behavior, having cared for a variety of invalids in her time. With her wide knowledge of patent medicines, she had perceived immediately that the best thing for Fanny's spells was Dr. Starkey's Magic Elixir, a tincture-of-cannabis remedy she herself found ideal for all kinds of female complaints. By this time, there was no doubt in Miss Swindon's mind that she had become quite indispensable to the Endicotts.

Mr. Endicott had made it clear that he disapproved of the planchette table as hocus-pocus, but Miss Swindon disagreed. She was convinced that spiritualism would eventually heal the imbalance in her mistress's delicate nature that brought on her spells.

Ethel Swindon had introduced many of her former patients to planchette, believing that contact with the spirits would prepare them for the imminent death they faced. But she had never been attached to any of her other charges as she was to Fanny and, unlike them, Fanny was certainly not dying. She had the unaffected sweetness of a child and a pure soul, and it was Miss Swindon's observation that as long as that goat of a husband wasn't around, she never had any of her spells.

Today he was down in New York getting supplies for his printing shop and would not return until later. Whatever Thomas Endicott thought, Miss Swindon saw no harm in his wife talking to the spirits. It made Fanny happy if nothing else, and that was the important thing.

"Ask her about her half-breed baby," Fanny was begging. They had talked to this young woman many times before, but like a child with a favorite story Fanny could never hear it often enough.

Tilting back her head in its embroidered prioress cap that emphasized her beak of a nose, Miss Swindon called out in the awesome hypnotic voice that Fanny loved, "What happened to your baby, Lavinia?"

A breeze from the open windows made the oil lamp beside them sputter and sent crooked fingers of shadow clutching at family portraits on the walls. Fanny shivered with delicious goose bumps as the saucer beneath their hands spelled out that Lavinia's enraged father had his daughter's dark bastard drowned in the river.

"How dreadful!" Fanny said, but her high color showed that she was more thrilled than saddened by the tragedy. "What happened next? Hurry and ask her please!"

In the same theatrical voice Miss Swindon asked the long-dead Lavinia to describe her own fate, while Fanny's eyes sparkled.

As they had heard so many times before, Lavinia's father not only drowned the baby but had her Indian lover strung up on the great oak tree still visible against the sky across the street, its branches blackened by lightning. The unhappy Lavinia had died of a broken heart and was wandering forever, lost in the other world.

Suddenly, the saucer, which had been transmitting the communication from beyond, spelled out "G-O-O-D-B-Y-E," and came to a halt, lifeless beneath their fingers.

"I don't want to stop yet. It's too early," Fanny said, petulantly.

Miss Swindon regretted that her charge did not yet have the proper attitude to the spirit world. It was just ghost stories to her. Fanny might be a wife and mother, but she was still such a child, how could it be otherwise?

"You're not too tired, my pet?" she asked.

"I'm wide awake."

"Just a little longer then," said the older woman indulgently. "Whom shall we contact next, Marie Antoinette or Mary Queen of Scots?"

But before Fanny could make up her mind, steps were heard on the stoop outside, and the saucer came to life again under their fingers, sliding back and forth from the letter M to the letter A.

"Perhaps we had better stop," said Miss Swindon. She knew full well who it was turning the latchkey in the front door, but did not take her fingers from the moving saucer.

"No," Fanny cried, as the saucer continued sweeping from M to A across the table. "It's spelling M-A-M-A, don't you see?" She was too distracted to pay any attention to the door. "Chester's calling me!" This was her first child who had died of yellow fever down in New York.

"Hello! I'm home," Tom Endicott called from the hallway, then came into the room with his package of printing supplies. Not much older than his wife, he was fair-haired and boyish, but wore a perpetually anxious expression.

Miss Swindon instantly took her hands off the saucer, bringing it to a stop. Whenever he came into the house the mood changed.

"He needs me," Fanny was repeating, ignoring her husband. "Chester needs me."

Miss Swindon stood up, her face impassive as it always was in front of her employer.

"It's my fault," Fanny wailed, clutching the saucer to her breast. "I didn't have enough milk. I never should have given him out to that wet nurse."

Tom dropped his package and ran over to her at the table. "It wasn't your fault, Fanny dear. Chester died of the yellow jack, you know that."

She turned on him, her pretty face contorting. "Don't lie!" Her voice took on an ugly edge. She put out her arms rigidly to hold him off as he tried to comfort her. "I know what happened to my baby and I won't be talked out of it."

Miss Swindon was already reaching for a green bottle of the elixir from her reticule.

"But he's dead. Little Veronica needs you now," said Tom, snapping his fingers at Miss Swindon. "Can't you hurry, woman?"

Unruffled, the paid companion poured some water into a glass from a pitcher and measured out a few drops from the bottle.

Fanny was on her feet and pounding the table with her fists so that the oil lamp rocked. Tom snatched the lamp away just in time and put it out of reach.

"I won't stop," she screamed. "You can't make me!"

He took the glass from Miss Swindon, and his arm around his young wife's shoulders tried to get her to drink it.

"No!" she cried, as she wrenched away, striking out at him. And then began the terrible litany of obscenities he had grown to dread.

"Come, Fanny," said Miss Swindon firmly, moving Tom aside and catching a flailing hand to hold it like a wounded bird against her bosom. She took the glass from Tom. "Now, drink this!"

At Miss Swindon's touch Fanny broke off her screaming. Mouth still open, her dilated eyes seemed to focus on the older woman's commanding face. Without a murmur she let the glass be put to her lips and drank it down.

Immediately she was quiet and looked around in confusion as if she had just awakened. Tom put an arm around her and she leaned against him, docile, his own wife-child restored, and he helped her up the stairs.

The crisis was over. In despair that it had happened again, he was furious at Miss Swindon for upsetting his wife with that spiritual nonsense, when he had given her explicit instructions not to. He would speak to the woman first thing in the morning, and this time he was not going to listen to any argument, even if she was the only one around who seemed able to control his wife.

In the quiet of their bedroom, softly lit by a hanging oil lamp, Fanny lay her head against his shoulder. "I'm so ashamed, Tommy."

It was the ethereal voice of the girl he had fallen in love with and it moved him so deeply he had to clear his throat before he could speak. "I understand, my poor love. Why don't you go to sleep now?"

He pulled back the counterpane on their four-poster bed and laid her down gently, curls framing her face on the large goose-down pillow. It was remarkable how quickly the look of frenzy disappeared.

Her eyes were dreamily tracing the intertwined lattice roses on the wallpaper. "I'm such a worry to you, aren't I? I don't know why you put up with me," she said, reaching out for him.

He sat down next to her, pushing aside the billowing crinoline of her skirt, and stroked away the damp hair from her forehead. "Fanny, I wish you wouldn't play that morbid game with Miss Swindon. It always upsets you."

She took his hand in hers, holding it close under her chin. "But I keep thinking of little Chester, Tommy. He was only three months old when we lost him, my baby in heaven." Her lips began to tremble.

He stroked her cheek, gone so pale. "But it's Veronica who needs you now," he said, reminding her once more of their neglected infant on the floor above with only a nurse girl for a mother.

"Veronica?" she said, as if she didn't remember. "Oh, Veronica... yes...."

Tom had hoped that having a second child might erase the memory of their dead son and cure her of the horrible spells. He leaned closer and said,

"Why don't you take Veronica out to the park tomorrow?"

Ignoring this, Fanny kissed his hand. "Poor man, it's you who needs looking after."

He brushed away the last of her tears and his heart began to pound, responding to this rare show of concern. "You do care about me, don't you, dearest?" Through the thin calico of her dress he felt the softness of her shoulder she had not let him kiss in so long.

Pushing his hand away without looking at him, she changed the subject. "We must find a permanent hired girl. Old Mrs. Atkins isn't taking good care of you."

She was rejecting him again. He fell back hopeless across the foot of the bed.

Fanny raised her head, holding down her crinoline so that she could see him. "Is anything wrong, Tommy?"

He didn't answer and stared at the ceiling.

"Don't be like that." She got up on her knees and leaned over him. "I know I haven't been doing my part, but from now on I mean to run the house properly myself."

Seeing her small breasts falling forward against the shirred bodice, he softened, unable to resist pulling her down and giving her a kiss. She giggled and sank against him, letting him stroke the back of her neck. He knew he had to go slowly, not to frighten her. When she allowed him to do this he could forgive her anything, but it was rare that she did. These past two years since the baby died he had gotten so little fulfillment.

Everything had been perfect until then. She had let him make love to her with the docility of a good wife. But after Chester's death she started fighting him off, until he would give up in despair.

Gently, as though it were a game, he maneuvered her over onto her back. Then, leaning on an elbow, he trailed his fingers over her bodice and began to recite the poem she loved. "*I was a child and she was a child, in this kingdom by the sea, and we loved with a love that was more than a love, I and my Annabel Lee....*"

Fanny was actually smiling, a finger toying with his hair. Maybe, Tom thought, this time.... Delicately, he started undoing the buttons of her dress, trying not to breathe too loudly. But her smell of innocence was too much for him and he fell on her, taking her lips hungrily.

Instantly she was wild, fighting him off, hissing, "No, no, no," like a trapped animal.

For a moment he was out of his mind, wanting to force her. She was his wife. She belonged to him. He had a right to her.

But her voice pierced through the pounding of the blood in his ears. If she screamed, Miss Swindon and the baby's nurse upstairs would hear.

He gave up as he always did now, and lifted her back onto the pillow. It was difficult because she was holding herself so rigid, her knees locked against him.

Hiding her face in the pillow, she said in a faraway voice, "Don't be angry, Tommy, please."

"It's all right," he said, turning down the lamp. "Go to sleep."

2

Tom was too agitated to settle down in his study with a book. He took his hat and stepped out into the warm night. The moon had gone behind a cloud and a single gas lamp cast a circle of light on the cobblestones. All was still except for the rasping of insects from the grasses and shrubs around the old farmhouse across the street and the occasional mooing of cows at Hinkle's dairy in the next block.

He hated it out here in Greenwich. It was as desolate as the upstate town of his boyhood that he had run away from. He started walking toward the river, hoping for a breeze from the Atlantic.

He and Fanny lived in a row of attached brick houses that had been built a few years before in the simple Federal style. There were empty lots on either side of the row. Farther along the street more brick houses were going up to the corner. A brook gurgled among piles of building materials before disappearing into a conduit under the street. Houses were being built everywhere in the area now, filling in the last of the empty fields.

But Greenwich was still very much a village on the city's northern fringes, connected by a stagecoach along a rut-filled road down to Battery Park at the harbor. Although New York was rapidly expanding north along Broadway—the main road that ran the length of Manhattan Island—the village remained a place apart, almost a rural backwater where people still kept pigs and chickens.

A lonely dog howled at the night sky and was answered by the yipping of foxes somewhere off in the hilly ground and marshes on the outskirts. Tom shivered.

In the sky to the south he could make out the faint glow of the thousand gas lamps in the city. Lower Broadway and the Bowery at this hour, he knew, were thronged with people filling the saloons and theaters and other night resorts. After months of exile up here he resented more than ever having had to leave the city he loved—and all the more because the move had failed to make Fanny better as he had hoped. In fact she was worse— he couldn't deny it any longer. He was at the end of his rope.

Tom Endicott had grown up in Binghamton, a mill and shoe factory town beyond the Catskills, raised by a strict uncle who owned a print shop. It was a barren childhood and at sixteen he had run off, hitching a ride on a wagonload of shoes to Newburgh-on-the-Hudson where the driver got him on a river barge transporting the shoes down to New York City.

He found an apprentice job as a printer's devil in a large printing firm on Chambers Street and took a room in the house of a dry goods merchant named Slocum who lived behind Trinity Church. The Slocums were the first real family Tom had ever known. All the children treated him like a brother, but it was Fanny, the eldest daughter, he became most attached to.

Sitting together in the sunny bay window of the back parlor, he and Fanny often read the latest work of Edgar Allan Poe. Tom always identified her with the ethereal heroine of the poem she loved the most:

> It was many and many a year ago,
> In a kingdom by the sea,
> That a maiden lived, whom you may know
> By the name of Annabel Lee.

Sometimes while her mother was in the kitchen and her younger brothers and sisters played and shouted outside, Fanny seemed so soft and vulnerable beside him that he found himself trembling with desire for her. When she asked him what was wrong he blushed, knowing that someone so completely innocent couldn't even imagine such things.

Lust had always been a problem for Tom. Once, in his room over the print shop back in Binghamton when he had been indulging himself with an onanistic fantasy about rescuing a virgin tied to a stake, his uncle had caught him at it and beat him with a cane, warning him he was heading for insanity. After that, whenever the urge came over him he tried to resist it, but to his shame he couldn't.

Much as he ached for a woman, the prostitutes he had seen waiting on South Street under the bowsprits of the clipper ships at the wharves repelled him. Only a pure woman would satisfy him, and that was only possible within marriage.

At nineteen Tom decided to ask for Fanny's hand. He was already a pressman by then and his future was secure. But it was with some hesitation that he approached Fanny's father, since he earned barely enough to support a wife.

Surprisingly, the dry goods merchant made no objection to having him as a son-in-law. He even promised financial assistance as long as Tom needed it. He could be of further help to him, Mr. Slocum said, since he was a member of the Tammany Club, a group of concerned citizens who kept watch over the city government to see that it stayed honest and helped business.

During their engagement, Fanny's willing caresses worked Tom up to such a pitch he could hardly keep from pulling her to him in a frenzy. But on the wedding night, when he let himself go after holding back for so long, it was as though he was committing some barbarity against her. Afterward, as she wept beside him, he was ashamed of himself and did his best to comfort her. Still, as a dutiful wife Fanny knew her husband's rights were not to be denied, and from then on did her best to hide her natural distaste for his lovemaking.

After the birth of their first child Fanny didn't have enough milk and had to give the baby out to a wet nurse just as the annual summer epidemic of the fever began. When the infant died, Fanny was guilt-stricken, though Tom tried to make her understand that it wasn't her fault—or the wet nurse's either. Everyone believed the yellow fever was brought in by clipper ships from China. No one gave a thought to the dank wells they got their drinking water from.

Fanny was never the same again. The doctor diagnosed her condition as a severe neurasthenia, and advised that they have another child as soon as possible.

But the birth of Veronica the following year had only made it worse. Fanny showed no interest in her second baby and became adamant about keeping Tom off. Most painful of all, her "irrational outbursts," as the doctor called them, began. In a flash she could change from his beloved Annabel Lee to a stranger possessed by a devil. Those soft lips were capable of shouting the most awful things.

Fanny couldn't be left alone any more. But after witnessing an attack, the woman he found to stay with her quit. Later, even the hired girl left in tears.

It was Fanny's parents, the Slocums, who urged him to put her away. They were afraid no one would marry their younger daughters if it became public knowledge that there was "severe instability" in the family. But Tom would not hear of an asylum.

The doctor suggested that moving up to Greenwich might be the solution. The village to the north of the city was set on higher ground and had long been a refuge from the epidemics that regularly struck New York. Away from the city's hubbub and with plenty of fresh air, the doctor saw no reason why Fanny shouldn't recover from her fixation on the dead baby and in time become her former self again.

The Slocums had shown themselves almost too eager to help the young couple move up to Greenwich by buying the house on Perry Street for them and advancing Tom the money to pay for Fanny's care. In fact, he was beginning to suspect the reason her parents had been so anxious to marry her off to a poor printer like himself in the first place. She must have had a long history of mental disorder and they had kept it from him.

Since he had brought her up here to Greenwich, her parents had all but abandoned her. The mother had only come to see her once, the father never, and her brothers and sisters were forbidden to have any contact with her at all. He doubted that they ever mentioned her name any more.

For a while Tom had tried to hold on to his job at the printing plant down in the city, but coach service was unreliable. Getting there for the night shift was almost impossible, and chancy even during the day since the coach ran through marshy land along the river and the wheels often bogged down in bad weather. He was forced to give up the job, and with additional help from his father-in-law—grudging this time—he made a down payment on a printing shop on Bank Street a few blocks away from his house. But even if he was able to make a living doing jobs on a hand press, as he had done in his uncle's shop in Binghamton, Tom didn't like it as much as working with a crew on the large rotary presses down in New York that turned out books and periodicals.

One of Tom's immediate problems when they came to Greenwich had been to find another companion for Fanny. After asking around, the wife of the German tavern keeper down the street recommended a woman she knew who had cared for invalids before.

Fanny was devoted to Miss Swindon from the start, but Tom had never liked the woman, feeling her sharp eyes on him whenever he wanted to be alone with his wife—and especially when they went off to bed. Miss Swindon was careful enough to efface herself during the times she wasn't needed by keeping to her room, which was next to theirs on the second floor. But even then he felt her accusatory presence.

Fanny's condition made it impractical for them to have much of a social life. They were invited over by the neighbors at first, but Tom always went alone, offering the excuse that his wife was ailing. It soon became accepted that Fanny did not go out, except for church. "Poor Mrs. Endicott's health" did not permit much visiting, and "what a misery it was for poor Tom."

The moon had come out again. At the end of Perry Street the Hudson gleamed on the incoming salt tide from the Atlantic. The river looked as serene as it must have before the coming of the white man. Just a few miles away to the south, ships and schooners lined the waterfront of New York City, but aside from barges, only steamboats or an occasional sloop bound upriver for Kingston or Albany ever passed here.

Ahead of him, accordion music was coming from a small tavern. It was the Four Winds, where he had heard about Miss Swindon from the tavern keeper's wife. Tom was not one to frequent the local taverns, although whenever he went down to New York for supplies he liked to stop in for a beer at one of the vast, ornate saloons on Broadway. But now, hearing the cheerful din, he had a yearning to pass some time among ordinary people to get his mind off his troubles.

He was about to go in, when the swinging doors burst open and four husky Irish seamen hoisted out a sailor whose head lolled down in a drunken stupor. "Into the horseshit with ya, ya limey bastard!" they bellowed, and tossed the sailor onto a pile of manure and straw at the curb.

Clapping each other on the shoulders and soundly pleased with themselves, they pushed their way back inside.

Tom changed his mind. This wasn't his kind of place. He was about to walk on when his arm was taken by a burly young man with a beard and a lion's mane of hair.

"Don't be alarmed, friend. They're all good lads. Come in and I'll stand you a drink."

The man's eyes were gentle in spite of his rough appearance. Tom let himself be led inside. Even if some of the patrons were disorderly, he didn't want to be alone.

The tavern was crowded and noisy and full of tobacco smoke. He immediately felt better. To his relief, he saw no one he knew. He couldn't bear the usual well-meaning questions, the eyes always looking away out of politeness and embarrassment when he put on a good face about Fanny.

It was a humble place compared to the saloons down in the city, poorly lit by a couple of patent lanterns hanging from the beams. The customers seemed to be mostly fishermen and bargemen from the river who lived with their families in the older wooden houses close by along the shore. Seated at one end of the crowded bench along the wall was the accordionist, an old seaman wearing an earring who was playing a rollicking tune called "Blue-Eyed Bonnie."

"Brew for two thirsty bards of the open road, Fritz," Tom's bearded guide called out when they got up to the bar.

It was an odd way to ask for a beer, Tom thought, but Fritz Unger, the big-bellied tavern keeper, seemed to take it in stride and good-naturedly set about filling two steins at the tap for them. Unger recognized Tom and reached over to shake his hand.

Tom's bearded companion took out a snuffbox and offered it, and when Tom declined, took a pinch himself. "My name's Whitman," he said. "By trade I'm a scribbler for the Brooklyn Eagle, but for my soul I write verse."

In his workman's corduroys and an open-necked shirt under the jacket, Whitman didn't look like a journalist, though his speech left no doubt that he was an educated man. In fact, Tom was the only one in the tavern in a broadcloth coat.

"Don't let Walt recite any of his long-winded poems to you, Mr. Endicott," the bartender said in his guttural accent. "It will put you to sleep, I promise you that."

Whitman laughed, his eyes like a friendly lion, and blew the foam from his beer. "Better to put a man to sleep, Unger, than to poison him with your free lunch." He picked up a piece of herring from a dish on the bar and popped it into his mouth.

The tavern keeper shook a fat finger at him and went away to help his stout wife roll in a new keg of beer and lift it up to the bar.

The versifier was delighted to hear that Tom was a printer. "I've been looking for someone like you, Tom Endicott, to publish a folio of my new verse," he said, pulling a sheaf of papers from his jacket. "This is the kind of poesy America needs," the tawny eyes looked into space, "the kind that sings with a big voice."

Tom tried to explain that as much as he liked poetry, it wasn't the sort of thing he printed. He wasn't set up for it yet.

Whitman held the manuscript out to him. "Will you read it anyway? That's all I ask, friend."

In good humor, Tom took the sheaf of papers and tucked it away in his pocket. Then, turning to order another round, he spotted the large painting hanging in the shadows above the bar. A voluptuous nude reclined on a buffalo skin with one arm around the head of the beast and the other holding up a smoking six-shooter as if she had shot it herself. She looked real enough to pinch.

Whitman took in his reaction and laughed. "Like it, huh? That rusty-haired chap over there painted it." He pointed to a young fellow with a droopy mustache at the end of the bar, sketching away on a pad.

As Tom stepped back to get a better look at the painting, the heel of his boot crunched down on the toes of a barmaid coming up behind him.

"Ow! Divil take it!" the buxom girl swore under her breath, plopping down a tray of empty mugs on the counter with a bang. Holding on to the bar, she bent over to rub her foot while Tom tried to apologize, feeling like a fool. But she surprised him by bursting into laughter.

"What are you trying to do to our Molly," Whitman boomed, "trample her to death?"

Tom turned red at the teasing. "I feel terrible...I swear I didn't see her...."

"Pay no mind to that blatherer," the barmaid said, drying her hand on her apron and holding it out to him. "I'm Molly Hanlon, sir. Pleased to meet ya."

She couldn't have been much more than nineteen, Tom thought, with the kind of robust good looks that come from health, rather than Fanny's pale fragility. Molly Hanlon's lively eyes were blue and her black hair was piled up in curls, with the locks falling haphazardly over her forehead.

As he took the warm, damp hand and gave his name, Tom flushed again.

The barmaid laughed. "Whatever brought a gent like yourself in to mix with the likes of us?" she asked, looking him over.

Her familiarity was embarrassing. Tom was always shy with women, not to mention immigrant working girls. And her teasing him about being a gentleman just because he was wearing his city clothes made it worse. He mumbled something about Mr. Whitman having brought him in.

"Oh, I see, it's like that, is it?" she said with a wink at the bearded poet as she picked up a full tray of beers.

Tom's blood was pounding as he watched her move off among the rough men, her ample bottom swaying.

"She's a peach, isn't she?" Whitman said jovially. "Just the kind of woman we need in America." He took a long swallow of his beer in tribute to the barmaid.

Shouts came from the front of the room. The "limey" sailor was staggering back in through the swinging doors, straw sticking to his soiled middy blouse. The four seamen who had thrown him out rushed forward to clap him on the back like an old friend and brought him up to the bar where they ordered him a pitcher of ale.

Tom was feeling completely at home by now and asked Whitman whatever made him come to this out-of-the-way tavern instead of one of the big saloons down in the city.

The poet looked around approvingly at the colorful water rats and their rowdy camaraderie, and answered, "You might say that I come to loaf and invite my soul." Then, seeing Tom didn't know what he was talking about, he laughed. "I mean, I always have a whale of a good time here in Greenwich."

Tom shook his head. "If you were forced to live up here like I do, you wouldn't be saying that." He sipped his beer morosely.

"Doesn't sound so bad to me," Whitman said, his lion's eyes taking on a golden hue. "To my way of looking at it, the village of Greenwich is a wondrous place."

Across the room the old accordionist broke into a polka and two drunken bargemen holding on to each other began kicking up their heels.

"And it's not just half-baked versifiers like me who say so," Whitman went on. "The Indians thought so too." He had done a newspaper story, Whitman said, on the Canarsie tribe who once lived around this part of the Hudson River. What's now Greenwich was part of their land and they considered it sacred ground. Their medicine men came here to have visions, and they held all kinds of ceremonies, from rainmaking to powwows.

"Come now, Walt, I don't believe a word of it, do you, Mr. Endicott?" the tavern keeper broke in, filling mugs with rich, dark brew from the tap and setting them out on the tray for the barmaid.

"I'm not making up the tale, Fritz," said Whitman, raising his voice over the hullabaloo as the two bargemen polkaed around the room. "The Canarsies had a legend to explain it. They hold that their sun goddess was shot out of the sky once by a warrior's arrow. The sky and everything went dark, and you know what? She fell right here on Greenwich. Naturally, being a goddess that little arrow did her no harm."

"Beggin your pardon, lads." The barmaid with the untamable curls pushed her way between them to pick up the tray, her womanly figure in its tight apron brushing against Tom. Whitman gave her round bottom a pat. She slapped his hand off, hoisted up the tray and, turning around, threw Tom a bold smile as she left that made him uncomfortable. For a moment he could hardly concentrate as Whitman went on with his tale.

"The Canarsies' sun goddess was as luscious as that one," he said, nodding with his mane of hair toward the barmaid. "Naturally, the earth god woke up when she fell into his lap—who wouldn't? I don't believe I have to spell out for you fellows what happened next...."

"He fricked her true, is that it, Walt?" said a giant of a young sailor with corn-shuck hair and freckled face who had come up behind them.

"Billy, my boy!" Whitman cried. "You've said it exactly. It lit her up again and sent her soaring back into the sky where she belonged." He swept his sailor friend into a bear hug and the two went into a huddle as the poet bombarded him with questions about the cod fishing season on the Banks.

Tom sipped his beer. It was a silly yarn. He knew damn well nobody but an eccentric poet would ever come to Greenwich for a good time, much less any gods out of the sky. Whitman was sociable enough, but he was a queer duck. Look at the way be was carrying on with the freckled-face galoot.

Tom turned around with his elbows on the bar to survey the room. He caught occasional glimpses of the busy barmaid laughingly exchanging banter with the rough-talking seamen. It wasn't that she was pretty exactly. She was too fleshy for his tastes.

"She's a good girl, isn't she, Mr. Endicott?" the host Fritz Unger said behind him as he rinsed out mugs in a wooden tub. He told Tom that she had come over from Ireland only three months before. But she was hardly off the boat before she had made the mistake of marrying a fellow countryman who turned out to be a brute and beat the life out of her. She was running away from him when my wife met her on the coach coming up from the city and offered her a job. "Such a hard worker, Molly is, and so cheerful," Unger said, shaking out the mugs. "The tavern is no place for a girl like that, but Mrs. Unger is here and it's all we can do for her."

When Tom finally paid up and said good-night, he caught one last sight of Molly across the room, carrying a tray of steins out to the back.

It was as if Molly Hanlon knew he was looking at her. She turned and gave him a wink, before she pushed through a door marked Beer Garden and was gone.

It was nearly midnight. Although the streets of Greenwich were as quiet and deserted as before, Tom inhaled with pleasure the smells of summer flowers and foliage and damp river air. He had drunk half a dozen beers, but he was remarkably clear-headed.

It wasn't like Binghamton after all. Though the glow in the sky to the south was mostly gone now, he didn't need it to remind him that he was on the edge of the city here. And if he didn't work for a big printing firm any more, there were advantages in having his own shop. To begin with, he was his own boss.

He bent over to drink at a public pump at the corner, letting the water splash over his face. It tasted so much fresher than the water down in the city.

He couldn't get over the barmaid Molly looking at him like that. Yet for all her sass, she was certainly no loafer—and she didn't let anyone trifle with her either, that was clear enough. He had to hand it to her. She hadn't taken the easy way out. So many girls who went through what she had would have ended up on the streets.

An idea struck him. He had been intending to go down to the immigrant station at the Battery to hire a girl just off the boat to do the housework. Old Mrs. Atkins, as Fanny had reminded him, was only filling in since their last girl had quit. Was it possible that this barmaid might be interested in the job? He couldn't afford to pay her all that much, but he had no doubt it would be as good as the tavern. Working for a family would be better for her than a public bar. Unger himself said it was no place for an honest girl. He wondered how she would feel about the idea.

As Tom climbed the stoop of his house, taking out his latchkey, he was whistling "Blue-Eyed Bonnie" under his breath.

Upstairs, Fanny was still awake. She was propped up in the four-poster bed, trying to concentrate on one of the spiritualist tracts Miss Swindon subscribed to.

Whenever she was given the elixir, she had the most extraordinary visions. Tonight had been no exception. After Tom had left, when she closed her eyes, she found herself in a gossamer gown astride a unicorn galloping through a faerie woodland, the mythic creature's muscled flanks beneath her. Higher and higher it leaped, until finally she was thrown off into the air in a soaring arc, landing breathless on a pillow of flowers.

She awoke, tingling all over, tears of joy streaming down her cheeks.

This must be the higher spiritual state Miss Swindon had been talking about. Her companion said that when her moral sense was more developed, she wouldn't need to take the medicine any more. But how was she ever going to bring herself to such serenity without it? If only she could become the wife Tom wanted her to be.

Always it seemed to her that there were forces trying to get hold of her she couldn't beat back. She didn't understand why those awful words came out of her that hurt her husband so. She didn't know where they came from. They had to be the devil's work.

Yet, sometimes things seemed so unfair. What the world demanded of a woman was too difficult. Maybe she should never have been a wife and mother at all. But wasn't that God's will for all women?

She was so tired, so confused. This kind of thinking always led her nowhere. There had to be some way of placating these devils inside her.

When Tom came into the bedroom, Fanny told him that she was sorry about getting a headache earlier and that she was feeling much better now.

He was touched as always that his delicate wife didn't remember a thing about what had happened. As he took off his trousers and laid them over a chair, he looked tenderly at her. How fragile she seemed in the light muslin nightdress. He was glad he hadn't listened to her family and sent her away. He was perfectly willing to devote his life to taking care of her.

When he got into bed he put his arms around her to protect her with his gentleness. She looked up at him so wide-eyed, so vulnerable, he had to kiss her. Her lips trembled and he kissed her again.

And then the undeniable feeling rushed over him—he wanted her, the wife who for two years had been little more than a ghost. As he pulled her against him, she started whimpering, "No, Tommy, no."

But this time he was incapable of stopping. He had been a good husband, considerate, faithful, obeying her commands to desist. It was not that he was a brute, he loved her. He wanted her to know that he loved her more than anyone else in the world. He would prove it to her.

He closed his eyes and overrode her protests. "No, no, no!" And as they grew louder, he bottled her scream with his mouth as she convulsed around him.

Only when his passion had exploded inside her did he hear her cries. He lifted his head. "My angel," he murmured, looking down at her as she threw her head back and forth on the pillow with her eyes turned up. "What have I done to you? Why are you carrying on like this?"

A door closed in the hall. Miss Swindon's. Tom swore under his breath and turned down the lamp. Within minutes he was snoring, but Fanny lay awake all night.

3

Tom Endicott's printing shop on nearby Bank Street was in a small two-story brick building originally put up as a bank when a good part of the business of New York City had fled north during one of the outbreaks of yellow fever. But the banks that had taken up temporary quarters and given the street its name had returned to the city along with the other refugees as soon as it was safe to.

The lower floor had an office at the front with windows on the street and the shop in the back, the upper floor being for storage. Along with the hand press and other equipment, Tom had inherited a capable old man from the former owner who was able to do much of the printing work, giving him time to go out and drum up business. Most of his work until now had been handbills for auctions and funerals, and the like. But he had just gotten a job that was more interesting—an anti-slavery pamphlet.

His assistant had been pulling a set of galleys and brought them out for him to check over at his desk with the ink still sticky. Slavery in the South was becoming a big issue, with tracts pro and con flooding the city, though he hadn't paid much attention because of his concern over Fanny. It was a relief to him that the new hired girl, Molly Hanlon, from the tavern was now looking after things in the house. Maybe he could hope that life would take a turn for the better.

Tom started to correct the galleys. He agreed that slavery was objectionable, but he had to be careful about expressing his opinion because the business community was mostly in favor of it. In fact, New York City was profiting slavery. Bankers loaned the southern planters money to grow cotton. Then brokers bought the cotton cheap to sell to the mills in New England.

Now that he had got his first printing job from the abolitionists, Tom wondered if he shouldn't also go after some business from the temperance people. There was even bigger money there. He didn't hold strong views about drink one way or the other. He had once attended a rally down at Castle Garden and found the public repentance of the drunkards highly entertaining. If he could do work for both abolition and temperance, he might be able to afford a second press. Then with a binding machine he could even do private editions of small books.

He pushed aside the galleys and took out the manuscript that queer duck of a poet Whitman had given him the other night at the Four Winds. Tom liked poetry. He sometimes read Emerson and Longfellow aloud to Fanny, though not Edgar Poe any more—Poe was too morbid and apt to set her off. But poetry generally had a soothing effect on her.

Leaves of Grass, by Walt Whitman. His first look at the poem confused him. It wasn't like poetry at all, just long rambling lines without rhyme. It was a pity the man didn't know how to write. Tom had liked him, and he was the one who had introduced him to Molly Hanlon, after all.

It was just yesterday that Molly had come to work for them. Fritz

Unger, the tavern keeper, hadn't been happy about him hiring away his barmaid, but the German had been decent about it and left it up to her to decide. She had immediately accepted. She said she was grateful to the Ungers for having taken her in, but there was always the danger that her brute of a husband would find her. Working for a family would be safer.

The atmosphere in the house seemed to lift as soon as she arrived. When Tom let her in at the downstairs kitchen door, a shawl over her head and carrying a pitiful bundle of belongings, Molly Hanlon might have been any poor immigrant girl just off the boat. But as soon as she threw off the shawl, shook out her black curls and looked around, furrowing her brow in mock disdain, he recognized the impudent serving maid from the Four Winds.

"Who ya been allowin to cook for ya in this pretty kitchen, I'd like to know? It's a bit of a mess, if ya don't mind my sayin so. But don't worry, Mr. Endicott, I'll set it to rights fast enough."

She wouldn't hear of taking one of the little bedrooms on the top floor where the nursery was and where the previous hired girl had slept, insisting that she would be perfectly comfortable with a camp bed set up for her in the pantry. She'd be able to slip out for Mass every morning at five without disturbing anybody. "The kitchen here's the room I mean to make my own anyway," she told him, "and I'll hear no more about it."

When Molly saw the nurse girl trying to induce Veronica to take her first infant steps, she declared that she had to get right to work to fatten up the little tyke—as well as her poor mother. "What they need is to have their blood built up, and it's good Irish cookin will do it in no time."

Her enthusiasm was infectious and Tom felt the burden of the past two years lifting from his shoulders. To help her get started he offered to go to the market for her if she would give him a list. He had sometimes done it for old Mrs. Atkins, since Fanny had never been able to.

"What do ya need a list for?" she said. She could just as well tell him what she needed and he could remember until he got there, couldn't he?

Now, as he sat in the print shop, the poet's manuscript open on the desk in front of him, he admired the artful way she had let him know she couldn't read or write. Even more, he remembered the grace with which she whipped an apron off a hook and wrapped it around her comely body so that her breasts lifted as she reached behind to tie it.

A line in Whitman's manuscript jumped up at him: "....*curves upon her with amorous firm legs, takes his will of her, and holds himself tremulous and tight till he is satisfied...."*

To his shame Tom felt a physical response and shifted in his chair. He wasn't a prig, God knew—behind the barn anything went—but to present this kind of thing to the general public.... He shuddered to think of his innocent Fanny hearing it.

This went beyond erotica—it was smut. Even if a man were fool enough to print such a thing, he would lay himself open to prosecution. In a hidebound little place like Greenwich he'd be run out of town.

The bell over the door jangled. Tom pushed the poet's manuscript under the abolitionist galleys and straightened up in his chair.

A slight young man with a mustache and long hair came in carrying a portfolio. He introduced himself as Albert Cogswell and asked if he could sell him any artwork.

Peddlers of all kinds were always coming into the shop, though not often dressed as outlandish as this one. Under a battered, broad-brimmed hat his reddish hair fell to his shoulders and boyish freckles still covered his face. His scrawny frame was emphasized by cinched-up cavalry breeches that looked like they had seen duty in the Indian wars, and he was wearing beaded moccasins on his feet.

Tom said he was sorry, he didn't use artwork in his printing, and turned back to the galleys.

But his visitor was not to be put off and leaned over the desk. "Come on, man, how can you run a printing business without some illustrations?"

Tom looked up annoyed, and for the first time thought there was something familiar about him. The name Cogswell didn't ring a bell—but that droopy red mustache.... "Aren't you the fellow who did that painting over the bar at the Four Winds?"

The young man grinned and said he had to do all kinds of things to make a living.

Feeling a little less put off by him, Tom said he thought the painting was a fine piece of work.

"You liked it, did you?" Cogswell said, looking pleased. "Then how about me doing a portrait of your wife in oils?" Before Tom could turn him down again, he elaborated, "If not your wife, then your young'uns, your dog, or your mother-in-law—with or without her clothes on. I can paint a flower garden on your dining room wall so real your women will swear they can smell it."

Tom couldn't help smiling at the sales pitch and leaned back in his chair. He said he wished he could use Cogswell's talents for something, but he couldn't afford him yet.

"Wouldn't you use illustrations if you had an engraver? I do engraving too."

"Hold on, Mr. Cogswell, I'm not about to go into anything complicated like that. Besides, the work I'm doing doesn't use any graphics."

"But I could set you all up for it. Look!" Cogswell came around the desk and before Tom could stop him he turned over one of the galleys and with a piece of charcoal began to draw what he had in mind. He said he had picked up a broken shirt-collar press from a dump somewhere that could be adapted for the printing of engravings, and sketched the contraption in quickly with its fat rollers. Next to it he drew in a worktable for engraving the plates, and with a couple of squiggles added himself with long hair holding an engraving tool. "Wouldn't take up much space and hardly cost you anything at all. What do you say?"

Shiftless as he looked, this fellow sounded like he knew what he was talking about. Engraving demanded a high level of craftsmanship. If he actually could do it, it would open up all kinds of possibilities. For one thing, the shop would have a better chance of getting jobs from the temperance people. Their pamphlets were always full of illustrations of drunken husbands beating up their wives and children, and the like. "The trouble is," Tom said cautiously, "I'm already over my head getting started here."

The artist hiked himself up on the desk and leaned toward him. "You wouldn't have to pay me a red cent for the engraving I do for you, Mr. Endicott, if I could use the setup for my own work too."

"You're being a little generous, aren't you?"

Cogswell got up and began to pad about on moccasined feet, stopping only to look in at the old man working at the clattering press before turning back. "I'm not trying to put anything over on you," he said. "But can I show you my work first? I think you'll get my drift then."

Tom nodded, watching as he untied his portfolio and began spreading drawings and watercolors over the desk.

They were scenes of life along the Hudson River. Tom was no judge of art but the rendering of boats and fisherfolk looked as real to him as that nude Cogswell had done over the bar. Tom asked if by any chance he belonged to the Hudson River School of painting that had been written up in the papers.

Cogswell snorted. "Those fellas paint the Hudson like it was still the uninhabited wilderness. I paint it the way it is." He leaned over the desk again so that his scraggly hair fell over his face and, picking up one of his sketches, shad fishermen on the river, pointed out some Indians with tooth necklaces in a skiff. "We still got a lot of Indians around here, I'm glad to say, but it's changing fast. I'm trying to record everything before it goes."

Tom scrutinized another picture showing one of the squatters' settlements that dotted the undeveloped areas of Manhattan. Cogswell had portrayed every sordid detail, including an urchin urinating in the dirt. "Isn't that the shack town just north of here on the river?"

"I grant you it's not your high-falutin Washington Square," said the artist, hiking himself back up on the edge of the desk, "but it's not a bad place to live."

Tom stared at the collection of huts improvised out of sod and packing crates and the hulls of boats, with patches of corn and flapping clotheslines between. "You live there?"

"You better believe it!" Cogswell tapped the sketch with his bony finger. "We got Mohawks, Canarsies, Delawares, and a lot of half-breeds, besides plain mavericks like me who want to live our own way." He pointed to a female figure with braided hair and a pipe in her mouth crouching on the ground grinding corn. "That's my woman."

Tom was aghast.

"She lets me live my life without any fetters on me, not like one of your dang churchgoing females in a bonnet."

Tom tried to conceive of this man bedding down in his shack with a squaw. "Well, I'll say one thing for it," he managed to get out, "you don't have any rent to pay."

Cogswell jumped up. "It's not rent that's my problem, man. It's vellum and pigments and canvas—they cost an arm and a leg." He gathered up his scattered drawings. "I figure if I could run off a hundred prints of these scenes I do, even peddling them for a few cents apiece, say, I'd come out way ahead of where I am now." He slipped the drawings back into the portfolio and tied it up. "That's why I wanted to set up an engraving process for you. When I'm not helping you, I could use it for my own work—even etchings and lithographs."

"But how would you have time for my work with all that to do?"

Cogswell grinned. "Don't worry, I'll do crackerjack work for you—whatever you want."

Tom couldn't fail to respond to the young man's gusto. "Well then, I don't see why we can't give it a try," he said, extending his hand.

After Cogswell was gone, Tom tried to get back to the proofs of the abolitionist tract, but it was hard to concentrate. An hour before, expanding into engraving had been the furthest thing from his mind. The press alone would have set him back a fortune. Converting a shirt-collar press was an ingenious idea. Why, if it worked out he could get bigger jobs, not just this penny ante stuff he was doing now.

He liked Cogswell and had no doubt he was as good an engraver as he claimed. But it was a pity he dressed so freakishly. Looking that way, the man was going to have trouble convincing important people that he was any kind of an artist—no matter how talented he was.

Tom couldn't get over his living in that shack with an Indian woman—lying with her on buffalo skins. It was unbelievable. He gave up on the proofreading and took out Whitman's poetry manuscript he had shoved under the galleys.

> *O young man passing by,*
> *my hand reaches under your clothes to caress you,*
> *and your hand reaches under my clothes to caress me.*

These lines couldn't mean what they seemed to! He gazed out the window, ruminating. A street cleaner was shoveling horse droppings into a wagon, banging the shovel against its wooden side. The poem must be some sort of metaphor for brotherly love, like in the Greeks.

Then Tom recalled Whitman's behavior in the tavern—the way he had thrown his arm around the freckled-faced sailor, their long intimate talk, some of the things he had said. It didn't necessarily prove anything, but all kinds of peculiarities did go on in the world, though until now, so far as he knew, not up here in Greenwich—in spite of Whitman's tale about Indian gods coupling here and leaving a restless spirit behind.

He went on reading:

> *Come share my bed*
> *where we shall lie in a naked embrace*

all night long.

That certainly didn't leave much to the imagination. Did this fellow really think he could get away with writing about such a thing? Even if it were true, it wasn't something you ought to shout from the rooftops. Whitman must be crazy to expect that even an open-minded man like himself would think of publishing it.

Still, one couldn't be sure—it was poetry after all.

He gave up trying to imagine what men could possibly do with each other and took out a sheet of foolscap and folded it over. Dipping his quill into the inkwell, he told the bearded poet from Brooklyn that he would be very surprised if he found any printer at all for the manuscript—it was sure to offend everyone. As a poetry lover himself, he wanted to remind him that poetry should concern itself more with the soul than the body. And as a last piece of advice, he suggested that if he expected to be a poet someday he should set about learning rhyme and meter.

4

On a drizzling, blustery morning three months later, Ethel Swindon in a dark rain bonnet and cape was going down Perry Street toward the Four Winds tavern. She held her umbrella in front of her against the gusts, treading carefully so as not to slip on the wet leaves on the slate walk. Stepping around a pile of bricks, she observed with disapproval the new houses going up in the last vacant field between the Endicotts' house and the corner.

She was certainly not going into the tavern. No respectable woman would set foot in such a place. She had no truck with alcohol in any form unless it was labeled "nerve tonic," which she found fortifying.

Fanny Endicott's paid companion was on her way to see her friend Hannah Unger, the wife of the tavern keeper, in the Ungers' rooms above the tavern. She had some questions to ask about the new hired girl, Molly Hanlon, who was taking over the Endicott household to the point where Ethel herself felt in some danger of being eased out of her job.

To start with, Ethel didn't like her looks. Molly Hanlon wasn't the usual lump of an immigrant who knew her place. She had an almost obscenely overdeveloped figure and looked boldly at all of them like she thought of herself as an equal. Worst of all, that gullible young fool of a husband didn't seem to mind. She even caught him smiling whenever the hussy was in the room.

As if that weren't bad enough, he had gotten her angel pregnant again. Sleeping just next door to them, she could hardly avoid hearing his brutal advances. She could not understand why he didn't have the decency to restrain himself when he knew how delicate his wife was, and that another confinement and delivery risked her tenuous hold on sanity, if not her life.

At the corner Miss Swindon struggled to hold on to the umbrella as the wind threatened to carry it off. The day before, after being confined to her room with one of her sick migraines, she had come down to find Fanny almost hysterical with laughter over some gibberish about leprechauns the hired girl was telling her. It was plain that that one was setting out to win her young charge away from her, unless she did something right away. She wanted to talk it over with Hannah Unger who had found the girl in the first place.

Miss Swindon and Mrs. Unger had worked for the same Washington Square family years before, Hannah as cook and Ethel in her first job as paid companion. But when the family moved away, Hannah married Fritz Unger and went to live with him over the tavern. The two women had kept in touch. Whatever one might say about most tavern keepers, the Ungers were a respectable couple who lived a Christian life—and Hannah would tell her whatever she wanted to know.

If it weren't for the migraines, that hired girl would never have had the chance to get at Fanny. But Miss Swindon had been a victim of the terrible headaches ever since childhood when one misfortune after another had been visited on her. Her irresponsible father had first brought her to live in rural Greenwich in 1812 to escape the yellow jack that had carried off her mother down in New York. The move had ruined any possibility of Ethel growing up in a refined society. Then, in the crash of 1820 her father lost all the money her mother had left her for a dowry. The young vicar who was courting her at the time broke off, and without a dowry there had not been another suitor since.

She climbed the outside stairway to Hannah Unger's door, shook the wet leaves off her skirts, and folded her umbrella shut with a snap.

The rosy-cheeked tavern keeper's wife welcomed her friend warmly—

Hannah always liked a good gossip. She brought in a pot of coffee and freshly-baked plum tarts, and the two women settled down at a bay window with the rain drumming against the glass. Below on Greenwich Road, a team of horses was being hitched to the stage for its afternoon run down to the city. The mud would make it a difficult journey.

"And how is our dear Molly getting on?" Hannah asked in her heavy accent, arranging her plump figure in a rocker and pouring out the coffee. "Such a good worker she was for my Fritz. The Endicotts are lucky to have her."

Selecting a tart, Miss Swindon replied evasively that there didn't seem to be anything the girl wasn't capable of doing.

Her friend missed the innuendo and beamed. She was so glad their barmaid had found a more suitable place. Fritz always said a tavern, even one as respectable as theirs, was no good for a pretty young woman. "Too many temptations," she said, with a significant nod.

Miss Swindon stopped munching to listen. This might be what she was looking for.

"*Ach,*" Hannah went on, misreading her friend's interest, "it's not the way it was when I first came over from Koblenz. These immigrants come without any families. So many wicked people around to tempt an unprotected young girl just off the boat...."

"Are you saying that Molly Hanlon...?"

"*Ach,* it broke our hearts to hear about it, Fritz and me! It was that devil husband of hers. Hanlon! The poor child was black and blue, he beat her so. She had to do what he said."

This was more than Miss Swindon could have hoped for!

"Terrible, it was. The only way she could get away from his fists was to what he wanted. Paint up her face and go down and stand in the doorway across the street where he could watch her from the window."

She listened open-mouthed as her friend told her how Molly had dispatched the first lout who came up and offered her money. Not knowing what to do, she let him lead her away. But when he shoved her into an alley and tried to grab her, she kneed him in the groin, doubling him up, and she ran off. "The next thing you know she was on the coach coming up here to Greenwich. Such a brave girl, our Molly." Hannah's plump body shook as she chuckled. "Another cup of coffee, my dear Ethel?"

But Miss Swindon was already wiping the crumbs of the tart from her lips and getting up. "I've stayed too long as it is," she said. "Mrs. Endicott will be waking from her sedative."

The tavern keeper's wife was disappointed at her friend's departing so abruptly. She had looked forward to a long gossip about the old days.

But Ethel Swindon had no time for reminiscing. She was impatient to get to her employer to impart some interesting information.

Tom was in the shop with an apron over his vest and his shirtsleeves rolled up, setting type for a temperance tract. The raw weather had laid up his elderly assistant with rheumatism. He wanted his first temperance job, an essay on the dangers of alcohol for the working-class family, to turn out especially well so that the temperance people would give him more work. In fact, he was so optimistic he had already ordered a second printing press.

He was composing each page with an elaborately designed initial capital letter like a medieval manuscript, while Albert Cogswell worked on an engraving for it in the back of the shop.

The artist was singing a bawdy version of "Oh! Susannah" as he worked at his converted shirt-collar press, inking the stone in the bed with a roller and spinning the handle to press the paper down against it.

He made the printing shop a lot livelier, the rascal. His talk was as outlandish as his faded cavalry breeches and his patched green coat. His costume never changed except on cold days when he wrapped an Indian blanket around himself. When Tom had first told him about Fanny and her spells, Albert said she didn't sound so crazy to him. In the settlement where he lived over by the river, all the women let off steam like that and no one called it crazy. Some of them even went into trances and spoke in tongues. "You can't mess around with our women. They know what they want and they don't let us forget it."

Tom said that they didn't sound civilized to him, but Albert had only laughed. "Send your wife over to live with us. We don't want our women to be civilized, we want them to be natural."

Tom smiled over his singular new friend and dropped a line of type into the bed. He hadn't done much typesetting since working at his uncle's printshop in Binghamton—at his job down in the city he had mostly worked as a pressman. But he quickly got back into the old rhythm, reaching for the type in the font in front of him and laying the letters into a composing form in his other hand. After a while he could follow the text, hardly having to pay attention to what he was reading.

The rain drizzling outside did not lessen the happiness he felt. His business was flourishing, Albert was proving to be far more helpful than he expected, and Molly Hanlon's presence in the house had lightened the formerly gloomy atmosphere. Now he looked forward to going home to lunch every day. She always had a bright smile waiting for him as soon as he stepped into the dining room, and even after supper, as he sat in his study doing his accounts or reading, it was a comfort to know that she was down in the kitchen, humming away as she kneaded dough for the next day's bread.

Albert came over with a proof he had just pulled and slapped it down over the type font, breaking Tom's rhythm. "How's this strike you?"

Tom was exasperated to see that Albert had been working away on one of his river scenes. "Is that what you've been up to all morning? I thought you were doing the illustration for the tract."

"Pleasure before duty is my first rule in life." Albert grinned. "Once I've warmed up, I can knuckle down to 'The Virtuous Maid Led Astray by Demon Rum.' I'll show her with the devil's hand up her skirts. That'll make those pious hypocrites come in their breeches."

Tom snickered nervously. It was hard to get mad at Albert, even if he didn't think much of schedules and deadlines.

The bell over the door jangled and Ethel Swindon marched into the shop, unconcerned that her umbrella was leaving a track of water over the floor behind her. She demanded to speak to Tom privately, while casting a sour look at Albert Cogswell.

"Do pardon me, madam," said Albert, nearly genuflecting before her. He rolled his eyes at Tom, picked up his proof, and retreated to the back of the shop letting out a war whoop as if wild Indians were after him.

Miss Swindon pretended not to hear. Ordinarily, she said, she would not have considered disturbing Mr. Endicott at work, but under the circumstances she had no choice.

Suspecting she was up to something, Tom put down his composing form, took off his apron, and led her into the office, closing the door behind them.

When she was seated in the chair beside his desk, she wasted no time getting to the point. "I've just seen my old friend Mrs. Unger, and I've heard the most shocking news about the new housemaid. I thought you ought to be the first to know, sir."

He flushed at her gall. He had an impulse to throw her right out, but everything about Molly Hanlon interested him, even gossip.

"I'm afraid your hired girl is not quite the respectable woman we took her for," she began. "My friend, Mrs. Unger, is so naive, her heart goes out to any stray cat. Well, it seems"—she discreetly lowered her eyes—"Mrs. Hanlon confessed to her that she had been a woman of the streets." She looked up quickly to catch his reaction. "It's not the kind of thing I could normally bring myself to mention, but with an innocent child in the house...."

Tom jumped up, ready to show her the door. "That's a damn lie, and why the hell you repeat such a thing...."

She kept her seat, imperturbable. "Mrs. Unger does not lie."

Leaning toward her with his hands on the desk he spoke carefully. "I'm sure your friend told you what she believed to be the truth. But I'm afraid she got the story wrong. Now if you'll excuse me, I've got to get back to work."

Ethel Swindon rose to her feet with a thin smile, adjusting her bonnet and rain cape. "I was only trying to do my duty. After all, she has been doing her best to influence your wife and daughter. If you are unconcerned. sir, I'm sure I don't know why not!"

"Good-day," he said, shutting the door on the meddling bitch who, not at all discomposed, marched off into the rain holding her head high.

This was too much. Tom knew the woman was jealous of anyone who came near Fanny, and was not above trying to besmirch anyone she perceived as a rival! As a paid companion Ethel Swindon might think she was indispensable, but he was going to start looking around immediately for someone to replace her. She had just cooked her own goose!

Sitting in the dining room waiting for lunch, Tom repeated to himself that the vicious story was only a jealous old maid's fantasy. But when Molly Hanlon pushed through the door from the kitchen carrying a steaming serving bowl, her full figure only too evident under the thin housedress, he looked away, feeling a sudden rush of guilt.

"Here's a meat and potato stew for ya, sir. It was my father's favorite dish back home. I hope ya like it."

He smelled her healthy body as she came over to serve him. Whatever had possessed that Unger woman to spread such a tale? With her imperfect English she had obviously misunderstood whatever Molly had told her.

While she ladled the stew onto his plate, the buxom hired girl chattered on. "This morning I was teachin your wife gin rummy, sir. She's a wonder. She picked it right up and beat me every time." She laughed at the memory, her breasts shaking.

Why did she have to wear such revealing clothes? For an instant he saw her standing in a doorway on lower Broadway with her face painted. He shoved his plate aside, unable to eat.

"Ya don't fancy the stew, sir?"

"What were you doing playing cards with my wife in the middle of the morning?" Tom said severely. "Don't you have enough to do?"

She turned pale as if he had struck her, putting down the serving bowl.

But something was taking him over. There was an impudence about her overdeveloped body that belonged in a doorway.

"I only went into Mrs. Endicott's room when I was called," she said, now going red in the face. "She asked me to keep her company."

It was not hard to imagine her making lewd suggestions to passing men. Tom felt himself shaking. "My wife has a companion to look after her."

Her blue eyes darkened with anger. "Miss Swindon was out and your wife was nervous bein alone. I thought I was doin ya a favor sittin with her."

"From now on, I prefer you to attend to your own duties."

Molly Hanlon stared at him, then with a mock curtsy and a sarcastic "As you wish, sir," she turned and swiveled her hips toward the kitchen door.

Rage boiled up in him. She was walking that way deliberately, like one of those women. He saw it all now. She had been provoking him ever since she got here, pretending it was all cheerfulness and innocence.

"Stop!" he shouted, getting up. "Why didn't you tell me the truth?"

She wheeled around at the kitchen door. "What's that?"

He was no longer able to control himself. "I'm talking about your life down in the city."

She walked slowly back, her hands on her hips. "What is it you're tryin to say to me, Mr. Endicott?"

His fists were clenched and his forehead was sweating. "I'm saying that you're not what you pretend to be."

They faced each other like pugilists at a prizefight and she called him a dirty sod.

"Whore," he said, "you're a whore!" The passion for her that he had never faced overcame him. He seized her breasts and thrust her back against the wall, covering her mouth with his.

Just as fast, she kneed him hard in his swollen groin. He backed away, bending over, clutching himself. The pain was excruciating.

"Ya won't have any use for the family jewels if ya try that again, I promise ya," she said grimly, an arm still up in front of her heaving breasts. But in spite of her attempted bravado, tears welled from the corners of her eyes.

He staggered into a chair, trying to get his breath.

She walked over and poured him out a cup of tea, shoving it across to him. "Drink it. You'll be all right."   Like an obedient child he drank, not caring that it burned his throat. He set down the empty cup, looking at it miserably. "I shouldn't have done that. I don't know what came over me."

"Who called me that filthy name?" she asked.

He didn't answer her.

"I know. It was that Swindon woman. She hates me."

He turned to her quickly. "I tried not to believe her, Molly, but I went crazy when she said it."

"It's God's truth," she said quietly, "I was on the streets..."

Tom chest tightened.

"...but I ran away the first chance I got." And then she told him the story of her husband, Hank Hanlon, beating her and forcing her to go out to sell her body. She'd heard he was in prison now for knifing a man in a holdup. "And I hope he rots in hell," she said, but quickly crossed herself.

Tom was quiet for a moment. "I can guess what you think of me."

"Ya wanted to believe her, didn't ya?"

He put his head in his hands. "May God forgive me, I believed it because I wanted you. Both of us being married, there was no other way unless I could persuade myself it was true." He told her how miserable he had been since Fanny's breakdown, how he had hated having to exile himself up here in Greenwich, and how her cheerfulness and vitality made him love her from the first.

Standing beside him, she ran her hand maternally over his soft, fair hair. "We both have our miseries, don't we, Tom Endicott? I'll confess my heart's been out to ya since I first saw ya."

He turned and put his arms around her hips, pressing his face against her skirts, feeling her vibrant life. It was the first time in two years that he was able to give in to the loneliness and misery he had been forced to hide.

5

It was a Sunday afternoon and at the dinner table the Endicott family waited for dessert. Through the dining room windows, the lilacs were budding in the narrow, fenced-in backyard, and the pussywillow bush by the outhouse was already covered with furry catkins. The winter supply of cordwood in the shed along the fence was almost used up. But the circular patch of rose garden in the middle and the ailanthus trees were still wintry bare.

"New York City made a big mistake not running an avenue right up into the middle of Greenwich." Tom said. Wearing his Sunday-best suit, he leaned over and wiped some baby drool off his daughter Veronica's chin. A pinafore over her gingham dress and her hair in long golden curls, she sat in a high chair playing with a drumstick. Molly, who had taken over the care of her from the nurse girl, had fed her earlier in the kitchen, but Tom liked the baby to be at the table with them, always hoping that Fanny might show her some attention. Tucking his napkin back into his shirt, he continued, "That way it would have brought the business up here to our side of Manhattan Island instead of over on Broadway." He looked at his wife whose fragile beauty was enhanced by her impending motherhood. "Fanny, you should see the new mansions over there—and the hotels. I'll hire a buggy one day and we'll go have a look."

"What a sweet idea, Tommy dear," she said, her pale hand stroking the sienna paisley shawl he had bought her from a clipper ship captain just back from the East. "Of course, now that the weather is so mild, perhaps Miss Swindon and I might walk over there by ourselves."

Her paid companion shook her head, reminding her that no walking out was possible until after her confinement.

Fanny made a little frown. "Of course, you're right." But she brightened quickly. "Anyway, it will soon be over and then we'll all go together."

It moved Tom to see her so happy. These past months during her pregnancy she was so much better. Even in her advanced condition she had joined him at table instead of taking her meals with Miss Swindon in her room as she used to. It seemed that this pregnancy was the right thing after all.

"Personally," Miss Swindon said, rummaging in her drawstring reticule for a throat lozenge, "I prefer Greenwich without all that construction going up over on Broadway."

The woman had avoided eye contact with him ever since after he had practically thrown her out of his shop. He was still determined to get rid of her and intended to as soon as Fanny recovered from her delivery.

Her grating voice went on, defying him. "If they'd cut the avenue up this way, we'd have more of that foreign element coming here than we do already. They'd come straight up from the boats. As it is, we can hardly call Greenwich an American town any more."

Miss Swindon shut up abruptly, as the hired girl came into the room with a bowl of peach cobbler. Tom could tell from Molly's blazing eyes what she thought of the woman's anti-Irish innuendoes.

Since the day, months before, when he had lost his head in the dining room, he had controlled his feelings for her, though it had not been easy. He had given it much thought and had come to the conclusion that not only would it be cruel to Fanny, but also wrong to take unfair advantage of the generous-hearted housemaid. He was trying to convince himself that Molly's cheerful presence in the house was enough, but it was torture, as always, to keep his eyes off her as she served up bowls of cobbler at the sideboard, pouring on cream, and setting them around.

With a display of squealing and banging her drumstick little Veronica announced that she too expected some peach cobbler.

"What a little piggie ya are, me darlin," Mollie laughed. "I gave ya more than ya could eat in the kitchen, but oh well...." Without asking permission, she took Tom's spoon and, dipping some cobbler off his dish, leaned over to stuff the child's mouth, and gave her a loud kiss on the top of her head.

Miss Swindon looked askance, expecting him to protest such cheek, but Tom's eyes were following the irrepressible hired girl tenderly as she sailed back to the kitchen.

Fanny, who had noticed nothing, said that she found Greenwich a refreshing change after the ruckus of the city. "And I have my dear husband to thank for bringing me here to rest my nerves. We're all so much happier now, aren't we, Veronica lamb?"

The child looked frightened, not used to having her mother speak to her.

Tom beamed at his wife. It was the first time she had ever expressed any gratitude for all the trouble he had gone through for her. She really was so much better. He told her, and he meant it sincerely, that now that she was feeling herself again, he didn't mind in the least giving up their life down in New York City.

Fanny didn't seem to understand. "Giving up?"

He tried to read her clear brown eyes that were suddenly fastened on him.

"Whatever did you give up for me?" she said.

With a sense of unease, he protested that he didn't give up anything that mattered.

"Don't lie to me. You gave up everything you cared about." Her voice took on the jagged edge he thought he had heard the last of months before. "You do blame me, don't deny it."

"But Fanny, dearest, you have gotten better, so much better...." He trailed off helplessly. He knew with a hollow feeling it was already too late. His illusion of happiness was collapsing like a tent. Veronica threw down her drumstick and began to snivel.

Fanny pulled herself heavily to her feet to face him, her mouth twisting, uglier than he could have believed. "If I am better, it's only that you haven't come near me," and, gripping her protuberant belly, shrieked out, "because of this!"

He moved quickly around to her and tried to put his hands on her trembling shoulders to calm her, but she shook him off.

"Don't touch me! You think I like being in this condition?" She beat her fists against her belly. "I hate it! I'd strangle it in my womb if I could!"

When Veronica started to scream, Molly ran in from the kitchen and picked the child up, rocking her in her arms, as she tried to understand what was happening.

"Quick!" Tom snapped his fingers at Miss Swindon, who was

fumbling in her cluttered bag for the medicine. But he was too impatient to wait. He grabbed the bag out of her hand and dumped the contents onto the table. The bottle of elixir rolled straight to Fanny, who snatched it up and shattered it against the wall before going at him with her nails.

"Get some more!" he ordered, grappling with his demented wife who was clawing at his face.

"I have no more," Ethel Swindon wailed, watching in anguish as her gentle mistress yanked the tablecloth, dumping the dishes of cobbler, the candlesticks, and the contents of her reticule all over the floor.

"There's a bottle in the pantry," Molly said, and rushed to get it, the terrified child clinging to her like a monkey.

Tom tried to hold his wife back as she pounded the table. "Listen to me!" she cried. "Why can't I make anyone listen to me!"

While he struggled with her, Molly ran in, thrusting the medicine into Miss Swindon's hand. The woman filled a glass with water and, with her usual maddening precision, measured out the drops. In charge of the situation again, she turned to her mistress and held out the glass. "Now drink this, Fanny!" she commanded. "Chester wants you to. Do you hear me? Chester!"

With eyes rolled up into her head, the demented creature, breast heaving, looked around as if trying to recollect where she was. Then, in a plaintive voice, she asked, "Chester? My baby?" And allowing Miss Swindon to tip the glass to her lips, she drank the medicine down.

Tom held his breath. As always, the miracle happened. The attack was over as fast as it had begun. Fanny let him help her out of the room and up the stairs.

Miss Swindon followed behind, triumphant, knowing that her position was no longer in danger. However bewitched the young fool of a husband might be by the slattern of a hired girl, he was never going to find anyone else who could get through to his wife at the height of her seizures.

When Tom came downstairs again, he found Molly tucking Veronica into her crib in the kitchen. She asked him how Mrs. Endicott was.

"She's asleep. It's always the same," he said, sinking into a chair at the kitchen table. "God, how she fought me...." For a moment he closed his eyes in utter weariness, then roused himself and asked Molly how she had got the child to sleep so fast.

She sat down across from him. "Ah, it was nothin'. An old Sligo remedy. A few drops of whiskey in her milk. It always works." She smiled down at the sleeping little girl.

"I don't know what we'd do without you." He put his hand over hers on the table.

But the moment was interrupted by a shriek from upstairs, and Miss Swindon ran down to tell them that Mrs. Endicott had gone into labor.

"Go for the midwife, Tom!" cried Molly, jumping up. "We'll manage here until you get back."

But by the time he returned with the midwife, a son had been born, delivered by the capable Molly Hanlon who knew all about such things.

As Fanny lay, wet and exhausted, in a half-doze, Molly handed the infant wrapped in a blanket over to him. "Such an easy birth, it was. It just popped out, the darlin."

Wiping the sweat from Fanny's brow, the midwife said the cannabis drops always made the labor easier.

Tom Endicott looked down at his new son, so red and wizened, feeling nothing. But how could it be otherwise with a neurasthenic wife who despised him, who didn't want this baby, who didn't want her other child? He felt Molly was watching him, wanting to share her strength with him, but he couldn't bring himself to look at her.

6

As Tom had expected, Fanny took no more interest in her newborn son, Claude, than she did in her daughter Veronica. She had never had enough milk for breast-feeding, and this time, as before, he arranged for a wet nurse, a relative of the Indian woman Albert Cogswell lived with, who had just lost an infant of her own to the croup.

He asked Albert if he thought the wet nurse's husband would mind her moving in with them.

The artist laughed. "I don't think so, Tom. You might say she's between husbands just now."

So Phoebe Pagett, a tiny, dark woman, came to take care of both children. Beneath her homespun skirt she was barefoot, but her breasts looked full enough to feed a tribe and that was what counted. Her big, black eyes took in everything. She had hoops at her ears, and her kinky, braided hair led him to speculate that there might be more than Indian blood in her veins. Albert had told him that escaped slaves often were given asylum by Indians. With the baby at her breast and Veronica piggyback tied in a shawl around her shoulders, Phoebe looked like a tiny tree bursting with fruit.

Fanny was slow to get her strength back in the weeks following Claude's birth, and the family doctor recommended a convalescence by the sea. Tom had no more illusions that she would ever get really well, but he hoped the sea air would do her good. He took her and Miss Swindon down to the Battery where he saw them off on the little steamer that made daily trips to the Rockaways, a quiet resort on the south shore of Long Island.

He came back to the house feeling a terrible burden lifted. Moreover, it was the first time he was able to relax around Molly without worrying that someone was looking on.

Phoebe Pagett ate dinner early in the kitchen with the babies, and afterward squatted on the floor bathing them in a copper basin. By the time he got home from work, she was back with them up in the nursery on the third floor.

It was a joy for him to come into the house to find only Molly there. With Fanny and Miss Swindon away, they were free to carry on a lively conversation during his dinner, as she brought the dishes in and out. He even had a wild impulse and asked her to sit down and eat with him, but she laughed and blushed, saying it wouldn't be right. So after dinner, he took to bringing his evening newspaper down to the kitchen where he pretended to read, while she went about cleaning up and baking the next day's bread.

It was a marvel to him that at the end of the day she looked as fresh as when she first brought him his porridge in the morning. Aside from the cooking, she had the whole house to take care of, cleaning and scrubbing and emptying the slops, though with the coming of mild weather she didn't have the ashes to clean out of the fireplaces.

Doing the laundry was no work at all, she said, with all the hot water she needed from a tank in the iron cookstove and the miracle of running water right in the kitchen. The pipe and faucet had been installed several years before by the previous owner of the house when the Croton aqueduct started bringing good water down from upstate.

Running water wasn't the only miracle you could buy these days. There were so many new inventions on the market and everyone was clamoring for them. Tom took advantage of Fanny's absence—her nerves would never have stood workmen banging around the house—to have some gas lighting fixtures put in. When he turned on the gas jets in their petal globes, the parlor blazed with light, a wondrous thing after the smoky whale-oil lamps.

One day, Tom came home at noon to find Molly gone and no lunch in sight. Phoebe was sitting on the grass in the sun in the backyard nursing the baby with a great breast shamelessly out, while Veronica scampered around her. He called through the window to ask where Molly was.

"She gone away. The po-lice took her." The dark eyes watched him unblinking.

He scolded Phoebe for talking nonsense but she stuck to her story. Two policemen had come to the kitchen door and taken Molly off with them. Tiny Claude lost the nipple and went red in the face, but she shoved it back into his mouth and he worked away at it happily. "Look like she in a heap'a trouble."

Tom ran back through the kitchen and up the steps to the street, heading for the police station. But as he slammed the front gate, he saw Molly coming down the street toward him. Without a thought for the neighbors, he ran to her. But she wouldn't answer any of his questions. Her face grim, she walked on back to the house and down the kitchen steps. As he followed her inside, she stood by the worktable keeping her back to him, her shawl slipping from her rich dark curls.

Taking her gently by the arms, he turned her to face him. Her eyes were full of tears. "Molly...dearest, what happened?"

She moved her lips but no words came. Then she was crying, her head against his chest.

He let his arms go around her, trying to ignore the scent of her hair, the feel of her trembling body, whispering to her that whatever had happened he would stand by her.

At last she was able to tell him that her husband, Hank Hanlon, had been stabbed to death in a brawl in jail. She had gone down to New York to identify him at the morgue.

So that was it. How could he ever have imagined she had done anything wrong?

Her head still against his chest, she said, "Sure and I thought I didn't hate that man any more, but now that he's gone it's all come back to me what he put me through."

She asked if she might lie down a bit, and he helped her to the little nook she had arranged for herself in the pantry, where on the wall above the bed a crucifix hung next to some ears of Indian corn. She lay down and he covered her with her shawl.

"I'll go make some tea," he said, but she held him back.

"Don't leave me now, Tom, I'm on a rack of pain."

He understood. In her anguish she wanted him close. Awkwardly, he squeezed himself on the narrow bed with her and held her in his arms.

Still quivering, she clung to him. Her skirts had pushed up and her stockinged leg was soft against him. He was ashamed of himself for his quick desire, but hoped that in her distress she wouldn't notice.

Outside, a window banged open on an upper floor of the old farmhouse across the way and a housemaid called down to a knife sharpener who had set up his grindstone on the street. A wagonload of lumber, pulled by a team of drayhorses, creaked and jolted over the cobblestones.

He lay beside her sick with pleasure, kissing her brow tenderly from time to time. From the backyard, little Veronica set up a wail and was comforted by Phoebe, crooning to her in some Indian dialect.

If this was all that life ever offered him, he would be grateful.

But the voices in the backyard drew nearer and a door slammed as the little nurse re-entered the house with the children.

Coming to with a start Tom jumped off the bed, mumbling that he had to get back to the shop, and he slipped out of the room as Molly sat up and stared after him in amazement.

The next day there was an awkwardness between them. Molly served his meals perfunctorily, avoiding his eyes, and whenever he was in the house she kept herself busy in the kitchen. He was in despair that his obvious desire for her at such a time had offended her.

That night as she set his supper before him without a word he couldn't stand it any longer and grabbed her hand. "Please listen. I feel like I took advantage of you. Forgive me."

"Advantage ya call it?" She pulled away her hand with a hard laugh.

"Any man in Sligo would have given me some lovin when it was clear I was in need of it. But oh no, not you, Tom Endicott, with your Protestant minginess. Ya torture a girl until she's ready to scream and then ya get up and leave her."

"But you were suffering...."

"I was that. That's when I needed the comfort of ya. Haven't ya ever met a woman with red blood in her veins before?"

"You mean you aren't mad at me because I took advantage of you?"

"Stop sayin ya took advantage of me. I'm mad at ya because ya took *no* advantage of me." She turned away in exasperation, looking out at the backyard, which was rapidly getting dark. "That's what I get for fancyin a man of a different sort than me. Ya never know what looney ideas they have in their heads."

He finally allowed himself to understand this unpredictable creature. "What would a country boy from Sligo do now?" he asked.

Her blue eyes mocked him. "Well, he wouldn't be sittin there in front of a plate of cold stew, I can tell ya that."

Tossing his napkin aside, he got up, put an arm around her waist and led her back to the pantry where they fell on the bed. Instantly, her arms and legs around him, she was writhing and gasping for breath. Alarmed that she was having some of kind of fit, he drew back and looked down at her.

Her eyes opened. "What's stoppin ya, my love?"

"Am I hurting you?"

"Hurtin me? I'm havin the time of my life. Get on with it!"

Before this, Tom had only experienced a woman lying passive beneath him. Not trying to understand her frantic behavior he let himself go—he had held back so long.

Afterward, she leaned over him and, with her curls falling damp against his face, kissed him on the mouth. "So ya are a real man after all, Tom Endicott. It's many a day I been waitin for us to ignite. Now maybe you'll be able to show that poor wife of yours how to enjoy it."

Her bringing up Fanny threw him into momentary confusion. "She would never act like that," he said indignantly.

Molly laughed as she sat astraddle him in her loose camisole and stockings half fallen down her thighs, pushing her hair back up with one hand. "Oh, I know you men. Ya go to the hoors or the hired girls for a little real lovin.'"

He simply couldn't keep up with her. "But did you do it with your husband that way?"

"Hanlon? I hated it with him."

"Still, you married him."

"Ah, life isn't always so simple, my pet—ya know that as well as me. When I got off the boat down at the battery, it wasn't all fine ladies waitin there to offer me a position as a parlor maid. It wasn't that way at all. Only madams and pimps and the like—the scum of the earth, come to inveigle country girls who had never been ten miles away from the houses they were born in. A fool I was to trust that bastard but I didn't know where to turn, it was all so new. He knew how to worm his way into a girl's confidence, that one did—may he rot in hell. He bought me a pint right off and even helped me find a room. Greenhorn that I was, scared out of my wits"—she gave a bitter laugh—"I married him. But believe me, my darlin, I never once did it with him like I did it with you just now."

He pulled her down to him, nuzzling against this outrageous, adorable woman, letting her carry him away again to perfect bliss.

The following days were the happiest of his life. He spent every night downstairs with Molly in her little room, where she taught him that a woman could take as much pleasure in love-making as a man. She continually surprised him, not only with the abandon with which she threw herself into it, but with her adventurousness in exploring every avenue of pleasure.

The one thing that bothered him during this was that the little Indian nurse knew what they were up to all the while. Phoebe's dark eyes followed him whenever she saw him going downstairs. One night she actually came in on them kissing—she had come down to the kitchen to refill a sugar-tit, her remedy for quieting restless Veronica. But from the way she backed out of the room giggling, he understood that she approved.

When the letter came announcing Fanny's return from the seashore, he told Molly he was not going to give her up, she had become the center of his life.

"Now listen to me, darlin," she said, as she lay in his arms in the little pantry that had become so dear to him, "there's no way we can go on with it in this house. Your poor wife's already half out of her mind with misery and I'm not going to add to it. It would kill her if she found out we was carryin on under her very eyes."

"We could run off!" Tom suggested.

"And leave those two little tykes who have only you in the whole blessed world to watch out for 'em?"

"I don't care." He buried his face in her breasts.

She pulled up his chin and made him look at her. "Tom, we got no choice but to face it. What we've had has been a blessed thing. We got to remember that it's more than most people have in their whole lifetime."

She was right, of course. They'd been allowed this brief interlude, but now it was over. Tom wanted to cry—there had been a lump in his throat all his life that he couldn't get out, not even now when he was forced to give up the only thing he cared about in the world.

And then they were back. It was worse than he had anticipated. He resented the invalid routine taking over the house again—Miss Swindon rushing downstairs at all hours to get trays for her mistress and continually complaining about the noise "that Indian nurse" and the children were making. Even Fanny's pale fragility as she sat in the parlor with a shawl over her knees didn't seem so heartrending any more after Molly's ebullient health.

He had never told Albert about his affair with Molly, believing that a man damaged a woman's good name even by talking to his best friend about her, but now, needing sympathy, Tom confessed to him the whole thing and how wretched he was.

Albert surprised him, calling him a fool for giving Molly up. There was no reason he couldn't keep both his mistress and his wife happy under the same roof. It worked all the time in the shantytown by the river where he lived.

Indignant at his friend's reaction, Tom said that it might kill Fanny if she found out about it, and she was bound to find out in such a small house.

His friend told him that women were stronger than he thought. "Of course, there's always the chance that one of them will take a knife to the other and you'll end up worse off than you are now, but you got no choice, as I see it. Look, friend, men are natural bigamists. Especially in your case—you got a wife who's no good to you as a woman, where's the harm?"

"But it's immoral!"

"Don't give me that horseshit. If you think a man's got to deny himself what nature means him to have, then you deserve the fix you're in." Albert turned back to preparing a steel engraving for printing, and Tom left the shop disappointed. The way things worked in Albert's squatters' town would never work for Perry Street.

But as it usually does, nature resolved the situation in a way Tom couldn't have imagined. One evening toward the end of June after Fanny was in bed, Miss Swindon had come downstairs in a dark rustle of skirts and announced in her dramatic whisper that scandal was staring them in the face if he didn't do something about that hired girl at once.

It seemed that she had the habit of getting up early to have coffee by herself in the dining room, and for the past couple of weeks she had heard Molly Hanlon being sick every day. "You know as well as I do, sir, what that means—she's with child!" The woman tried to hide her look of satisfaction by rummaging for a lozenge in her reticule.

Tom told her she was talking nonsense. But even as he said it, he was afraid, sickeningly so, that it was true. He wondered how he could have overlooked the possibility of this happening. What a fool he'd been to think that they could get away scot-free. Every pleasure in his life had to be paid for ten times over.

When he heard Miss Swindon's door overhead click shut and he knew that the viper was back in her lair, he ran downstairs.

The air of the kitchen was yeasty with the smell of bread baking in the oven. Molly was on a stool brushing out her splendid mop of black hair, her voluptuous body in a nightdress. It was the same nightdress with the yellow ribbon run through the collar that she had on the night before Fanny had come back, the last night he had been with her. He felt weak in the knees and leaned against the door.

Molly saw the state he was in and, without missing a stroke of the brush, asked him what was wrong. She had never looked so beautiful, so healthy, so full of life. Maybe it wasn't true. Maybe the old bitch had lied.

"What's this I hear about your being sick," he said quietly.

"I'm perfectly well, Tom. There's nothin sick about havin a baby."

"My God"—he put his hand over his eyes—"what have I done to you?"

She brushed the curls up from the back of her neck vigorously. "Just another case of the poor servant girl tumbled by her master, is it?"

"Don't talk like that. This is serious. Why didn't you tell me?"

"I didn't need to," she said wryly. "That old harpy did it for me. But ya don't have to worry, I'll be leavin before anyone's the wiser. Your family won't be disgraced."

He went over and got down on his knees beside her, taking the brush from her hand and putting it on the table. "Will you listen? You know that doesn't mean a damn thing to me. It's only you I care about."

She looked at him, her eyes brimming with tears. "Oh, Tom, I'm sorry. It's nature's dirty trick on women, isn't it?"

He held her hand. They were silent. After a while, he said, "I'll find some way out of this."

"What can ya do, marry me, maybe?" She gave a rueful smile.

"Why not? I'll divorce Fanny. You're more of a wife to me than she ever was."

She patted his cheek and got up. "Thanks, dear. I know ya mean it, but I'm not helpless like her, as ya well know. Havin a baby's not the end of the world." She opened the oven door, and, pulling out the rack, wrapped on a plump loaf of soda bread to test it. "Anyway, these things can be taken care of."

"But that's dangerous!"

"Not if ya have it done right away, it's not." She set two freshly baked loaves on the windowsill to cool overnight. "There's nothin wrong with it. Even the church doesn't call it a sin before it quickens."

He went over and put his cheek against hers. "I won't let you do that."

"All right, if that's the way ya want it, I won't." She searched his eyes. "Now what do we do?"

"I don't know yet, but I'm not going to let anything happen to you."

They looked at each other silently. It was painfully clear to both of them that his attempt to sound confident meant nothing.

Ethel Swindon wasted no time in telling Fanny about Molly Hanlon's pregnancy, adding that the master knew about it too, though he had not shown much inclination to discharge the girl.

But if Miss Swindon was disappointed in her employer's reaction the night before, she was even more put out by her mistress's failure to show any interest at all. She had hoped that Fanny would insist that he get rid of the slut at once.

Tom spent the next morning in his study pretending to do the household accounts, but actually racking his brains for a solution. He even considered the idea of sending Molly off to the shantytown to stay with Albert and his Indian woman for the period of her confinement. They would certainly look after her when he wasn't free himself, but he couldn't imagine his dear girl in one of those shacks among the kind of people who collected there, with immorality all around.

He thought of sending her out west, finding her a job with another family to begin a new life, but her condition made that unwise—and besides, the thought of her being so far away depressed him even more.

He had been sitting for a long time with his head in his hands when he felt a soft hand on his shoulder and a sweet voice from the past recited the familiar lines:

> *"And so all the night-tide, I lie down by the side*
> *Of my darling—my darling—my life and my bride,*
> *In the sepulchre there by the sea...."*

Fanny stood beside him, a robe over her trailing nightdress, her old self. "I know what's bothering you, Tommy, and you mustn't worry any more."

He looked up at her, seeing the gentle concern in those light brown eyes. It was an echo of the past.

"She's a wonderful person and I know you love her very much."

Tom was stunned. She must have fathomed the whole thing somehow.

"We must do all we can for her, Tommy. Find her a room where she'll be comfortable. It won't cost much."

He took her pale hand and pressed it to his cheek. "You're so good...." He was unable to go on.

"And you must spend as much time with her as you like and not worry about me. That's how you can make me happy." Her lips touched his forehead and she departed as silently as she came.

He understood. His love for Molly was the way out for her. She was releasing him from the physical bond of a marriage that had never been right. He saw at last it had been a spiritual love between him and his wife, and now she would always remain his Annabel Lee, the virgin bride he fell in love with.

7

Molly found for herself two small rooms over by the river. They were in a cul-de-sac where cheap housing had been put up for the immigrants. The place was popularly known as Shamrock Alley and was tucked out of sight just behind St. Luke's Church, which the Endicotts attended. The alley was nothing like the other village streets with their tidy houses. The first time Molly took Tom there, it reminded him of etchings he had seen of the slums of London.

The clamor struck him as soon as they turned in past a dilapidated tavern on the corner that expelled drunks night and day. It was another world. Wooden porches ran the length of the rows of connected brick houses, and the two upper floors were reached by outside stairways. The whole thing was like a barracks around a courtyard.

Everybody seemed to be living outside for the summer, leaning over the porch railings, shouting to each other and lowering pails for provisions and beer. Urchins ran around underfoot, pulling at Tom's coat demanding pennies. He was taken aback when Molly picked one of them up, wiped its nose on her handkerchief, and gave it a kiss before setting it back down.

Her two narrow rooms didn't make him feel any better. The raucous voices from outside were clearly audible. A slatternly neighbor woman with dyed-red hair pushed her way in and introduced herself as Mrs. Brophy. Tom didn't want his Molly to be here any more than in squatters' town.

"But don't ya see, love," she said, sitting on a sagging iron bedstead without a mattress, this is just right for me. It's my world. They'll take me the way I am, and there won't be any trouble about you comin by either. I wouldn't feel right about livin where everyone turned their noses up at me. Ya wouldn't want that, would ya?"

He looked out at the alley, dubious, but she came up to him and pinched his cheek. "You've already been so good to me, ya mustn't be a fussbudget now. I like it here and here's where I'll have my baby."

He couldn't insist, because her mind was obviously made up, and he was the one, after all, who had gotten her into the fix she was in. Trying to hold down his misgivings, he left her there, with Mrs. Brophy helping her put the place together.

When Tom got home, there was Miss Swindon pretending to be arranging dahlias on the hall table. Without looking at him, her smirk said it all. She had been waiting for him just to twist the knife. Nobody was going to get away with anything as long as she was around.

He was furious. He went right up to her and looked her straight in her beady eyes. "I'm keeping you on for only one reason—my wife needs you. But if you ever open your mouth about Mrs. Hanlon again, you'll be out on the street with no references. And I'll make damn sure that you never get another job in Greenwich."

She gave the flowers a last plump and turned away, tucking stray hairs under her tight hairnet as if his threat meant nothing to her. But he knew she got the point because for once she didn't talk back.

At first, Tom was self-conscious about leaving the house after dinner to see Molly. He felt that his casual remark about going out for a walk hung lurid in the air behind him, and not only Miss Swindon and Fanny knew what he was up to, but even Bridget, the new hired woman who had replaced Molly. A lumpy old thing, he had found her down at the docks at Castle Garden just off the boat, surrounded by bundles, waiting for a relative who never showed up. She was forever thanking him for having rescued her from the turmoil of the immigration depot. The smell of her cooking sometimes reminded him of Molly. Once he actually forgot and started down to the kitchen—but then he remembered.

It didn't get dark until late and all of Shamrock Alley seemed to be in the welcome party every time he came. Feeling overdressed in his checked trousers, single-breasted frock coat and high hat, he negotiated his way past the tavern where beer drinkers in collarless shirts and caps crowded the walk. He didn't look right or left, as he stepped around the urchins and women chattering in their Irish brogue on the outside wooden stairway. He was sure that everyone was watching him climb to her rooms on the top floor. It was only when he pushed aside the curtain she had hung over her open door and felt her arms around him that he started breathing again.

But making love here was even better than it had been at home. The rowdy atmosphere of the alley made him feel that he had escaped the prison of his house. Sometimes as he lay with his exuberant mistress, he imagined that he was in bed with one of the women who used to accost him on the waterfront. His old fantasy of rescuing pale, helpless maidens no longer aroused him. It was so different with Molly from what it had been with his passive wife, which once he had thought was normal.

When he was lying quiet beside her afterwards, hearing the women on the walkways outside bantering with the men drinking below, he looked at his darling's happy and perspiring face and was disgusted with his sordid fantasies. But Molly told him things about the life of the alley that fired his imagination—about mothers and daughters who went a-whoring together in the shadows of the Gansevoort pier, fathers who slept with their own daughters, even men who considered themselves married to each other. Everything seemed to go on here.

One evening in the fall when they were making love, Molly, beneath him, pushed at him to stop. Out of breath he asked her what was the matter.

"I'm five months along, lovey. Ya must go easier now." She took his hand and ran it over the mound of her belly.

It had been getting bigger without him noticing. In the grip of his lust he had forgotten all about her condition.

"Forgive me," he said, abashed. "We won't do it again, not until after the baby comes."

She laughed and pulled him down to her. "What a queer one ya are. Do ya think we must stop our lovemakin because there's a little one inside sayin, 'Don't press too hard, daddy'? I need ya more than ever now that I'm nearin my term. Ya movin inside me spreads the pleasure around him so he's born happy, and the comfort of it will make the birthin easier."

But Tom was not reassured. He told her he was afraid that when he got carried away he might hurt her as well as the child.

"If that's what's worryin ya, my pet, there are other ways to do it."

"Just what is it you have in mind?" He laughed, nervously, leaning on an elbow.

"I'll show ya." She pushed him over on his back and started to move her lips down his body.

Shocked, he tried to stop her.

"I'm in charge now," she said, and her mouth continued its progress down over him, until he was flopping rhythmically beneath her.

He had always thought that such an act degraded a woman. How foolish he had been. The woman he loved was paying the highest tribute to his virility.

When she lay beside him again, she whispered that it was his turn now.

At first, he thought he had misunderstood. Then the demand astounded him. He could never do that! No man would.

But she continued to caress his belly and rub herself against him passionately. "Go on, Tom." She took his hand and wiped it between her thighs, bringing it back up to his face so that he couldn't help breathing in her heavy woman-smell.

Unexpectedly, a desire to grovel in her like a dog went over him.

As he walked home through the night streets of the village, the only sounds his footsteps on the cobblestones and the steeple bell of St. Luke's tolling eleven, he still tasted Molly on his lips and felt more of the chains that had bound him all his life falling away.

8

Molly gave birth with the help of the neighbor, Mrs. Brophy, on a cold dawn in January, 1847. It was a boy and she named him Patrick.

By the time Tom arrived she was sitting up, a shawl over her nightdress, red-faced but happy, the baby at her breast. He couldn't help but contrast this picture of motherhood with the birth of Claude the year before, when Fanny had taken so long to recover and had no milk and it had taken weeks of Phoebe's nursing to put color into Claude's sallow cheeks.

When Tom showed surprise at her having named the baby Patrick without consulting him, Molly said, "Well, we can't call him Thomas Endicott, Jr., now, can we? I thought it best to name him after my father, who was shot down like a dog by English troopers. So Patrick he shall be."

Patrick was a lusty baby, with a patch of hair black like his mother's. And when she put him into Tom's arms the little blue eyes, which were hardly able to focus yet, seemed to be looking up at him happily.

Throughout dinner the following Sunday, Tom could hardly wait to get away to see Molly and the baby. He had been down to Shamrock Alley every evening since the birth four days before, but this was his first chance to be with them during the day.

It was a tender period between Molly and Tom now, even without lovemaking. She had a chance to tell him many things about her life in Ireland he had not heard before. It turned out that at the time her father was shot, she too was involved with the Fenians who were fighting to throw out the British, and she had run off to America to escape arrest.

It was unbearable for Tom sitting at the table at home listening to the chitchat between Fanny and Miss Swindon about some bonnet they were trimming. Outside, a thin afternoon sun shone on the leftover patches of dirty snow in the backyard. He was able to get away only after Bridget brought in the dessert, a watery rennet custard he detested.

But when he had waded through the slush over to Shamrock Alley and was climbing the stairs, he heard sounds of a party. It was an unpleasant surprise. Instead of finding Molly alone with the baby, a group of neighbors was there, stuffing their mouths with smoked oysters and pickled eggs on hunks of soda bread and washing it all down with beer. Molly in her Sunday best was the center of attention, reclining on the daybed nursing Patrick, with a breast exposed before the company as if it were the most natural thing in the world.

The crowded room was suffocatingly hot, reeking of stale clothes and beer. Whatever had possessed her to ask all these people in? They didn't need anybody else around. He wanted her to himself.

"Ah, there ya are, Tom!" She waved him in with her mug of beer. "Ya missed the christenin but you're in time for the party."

A gap-toothed man in an oversized frock coat seized his hand and pumped it vigorously, assuring him that the little tyke would never want for a codfish as long as Seamus O'Rourke was around.

When the baby lost the nipple and set up a squall, Molly gave her breast a squeeze to test it. To Tom's mortification, a squirt of milk shot into the air. "Nothin's wrong with it, ya little souse," she said. "Then is it the beer ya want?" She pretended to tip her mug to the tiny mouth as everyone roared with laughter. The infant resumed its suckling and everyone in the room raised mugs in salute, joining little Patrick by guzzling down their beer.

Only the blowsy Mrs. Brophy was not too far gone to see how uncomfortable Tom was. She got unsteadily to her feet, brushing crumbs off her lap. "Ah, Molly, I for one have had enough partyin." And raising her voice so no one could miss her meaning, she added, "Sure and it's time all of us was leavin ya to rest."

Everyone drained their mugs in a rush and got up to depart, letting Tom know by their good wishes and back slapping on their way out that they were well aware of who he was.

"Here, now!" Molly cried. "What are ya going for? Tom don't want that, do ya, Tom?"

Mrs. Brophy bent to kiss her on the forehead. "I'll be around to see ya in the mornin, darlin." She also gave Tom a beery kiss on the cheek and allowed as how proud she was to be the baby's godmother, having stood up at St. Aloysius for the christening. Chuckling tipsily, she toddled out after the others.

Molly looked forlorn, a fallen curl pasted to her damp forehead. "Now why did they have to go, I wonder?" She sighed and raised her mug. "Oh, well, here's to the bashful parents!" She winked at Tom and drank it off, leaving a mustache of white foam.

He stared gloomily out at the sooty snow on the porch railing. Those dreadful people. Their own private little world had been ruptured, violated. She had tossed it away without a thought for him or what they had together.

"What did you have to do that for?" he asked, finally able to speak.

She colored in quick anger, "I've had my baby christened, if that's what's botherin ya." She wiped the foam off her mouth with the back of her hand. "I don't want my son growin up to be a bastard, even if you do."

He dropped his head in utter hopelessness.

"Don't worry," Molly said from the bed. "I didn't give away your dirty little secret." She raised the baby to her shoulder and patted its back briskly to burp it. "What kind of a Catholic would people think him with a name like Endicott, anyway? Hanlon's a good enough name for any Irishman—and Irish he's goin to be, if I have anything to say about it."

Tom sank down on one of her wooden chairs, gloomier still. "Everyone knows Hanlon couldn't have been his father. You weren't with him for months before he died."

She laughed. "What an arse ya are, Tom. Father Doherty knows how hard life is for us poor women down here. It's the innocent mites the good man is thinkin about, God bless him." She yawned, settling the baby down beside her on the bed. "Ah, what difference does it make now, anyway?"

She snuggled down farther in the pillows. "Ya should have seen the little devil. Ya would have laughed. He peed all over the father's robe as he was bein sprinkled with the holy water."

After that Sunday, it seemed to Tom that Molly threw herself into the life of Shamrock Alley as if he didn't matter as much to her any more. It was a rare visit when neighbors didn't drop in on them without a by-your-leave. Sometimes, when he arrived, she was standing out on the stairs or even down in the alley, holding the baby on one hip and laughing with what looked to him like very disreputable characters.

He found his visits more and more depressing. Although there were still those moments when they lay perfectly content in each other's arms in the dark as before, she seemed hardly willing to tear herself away from her social life to be with him. When he complained, she told him that he was being a sourpuss again, that she was enjoying not being pregnant and having to be so tied down. She didn't have to be afraid of her husband showing up any more, and she was starting to live free out in the world, as she had always dreamed.

One day when he arrived after work unexpectedly, Molly was nowhere to be seen. He paced her narrow rooms, imagining all sorts of calamities, and was on the point of going next door to ask Mrs. Brophy or one of the other neighbors if they knew where she was, when she rushed in with the baby, her blue eyes shining, and announced that she had found herself a job.

"I won't have to take any more money from ya, Tom. Aren't ya proud of me? That was my idea in the first place when I came over."

He could scarcely believe his ears when he heard that her job was at another tavern, this one on the waterfront called the Blarney Stone, owned by one of Mrs. Brophy's sons. "Just what are you going to do with the baby while you're there?"

"Take him with me, of course."

"Good God! Into a tavern?"

"What are ya talkin about? Them lads were so sweet to him today, he got more attention than your two little ones ever get from their nurse girl and a mother that's too daft to even look at them."

Tom held on to the table trying to control his temper and said that he would not hear of her taking his son to such a place, even if she insisted on working there.

"I'm so glad that I'm not married to ya, Mr. Endicott! Thank God ya don't own me!" She took the baby into the other room and slammed the door after her.

The next evening Tom stayed home. As he sat before the fire in the parlor with Fanny across from him doing her embroidery—Miss Swindon was in her room with a "convenient" migraine—he could hardly hold the newspaper steady, he was so riled up at Molly for defying him. Not only that, but daring to take an infant—his son—into a saloon! Why was she doing it? He had set things up for them perfectly. She didn't need to work.

He had resolved to stay away and let her stew in her own juices for a while. She'd come to her senses fast enough if he wasn't around. In the meantime, it wasn't so bad in his own house. Fanny was better since Claude's birth the year before. In fact, ever since that night she had visited him like an angel in his study, she hadn't had a single attack.

But as the days passed, he felt his pride weakening, and one evening when Fanny asked him out of the blue why he was staying home every night, didn't he have other responsibilities, he could have kissed her with gratitude for making him see how stubborn he was being.

He had been missing Molly desperately, much as he tried to be interested in the latest chapter of the Dickens novel in the Herald. He was more than ready to bury his pride and make up.

By the time he was running up the familiar wooden stairs to her room he couldn't wait to fall on the bed with her and tell her how sorry he was....

But just as he got to her landing, the door to her rooms opened and a thickset workman came out. He was whistling as he passed Tom and headed down the stairs. Tom had an uneasy feeling, but he told himself not to jump to conclusions. He had come to beg her to take him back and nothing was going to stand in the way.

She opened the door to him, wearing only a wrapper and with her dark hair a-tumble around her shoulders. "You here again!" she said, staring at him, as if he were the last person she expected to see.

He pushed her in and shut the door behind him. "Who was that?" he demanded, forgetting his carefully planned speech.

"Who are ya talkin about? Oh, him. Only deliverin a hod of coal he was." She turned to pick up a pile of wash from the chair he always sat in. "It's been so chilly, I don't want the baby to get the croup. Ya want to see him?"

There was a suggestion of gin in the air. With a sinking feeling, he asked what the fellow was doing delivering coal at this time of night.

She gave a vague smile, tucking her hair behind her ears, until Patrick set up a howl from the other room and she hurried in to him where he lay in his cradle.

Her bed—the bed they had shared so many times—was all rumpled. Though he tried to hold back, his sick heart made him blurt out, "You're lying to me. He wasn't here for that."

She looked up from the cradle and snapped back, "Who are you to ask me questions about anything? I haven't seen hide nor hair of ya in days. Ya expect me to sit here all by my lonesome and me a healthy woman, while you're playing lord and master over on Perry Street? I'm makin my own way now."

Tom felt like the breath had been knocked out of him. "So you did it then. You didn't care after all."

She stood defiant in the bedroom doorway, expecting him to come back at her full force, maybe even hit her, as any man she had known before would have done, which would surely have been followed by reconciliation in bed.

But he would have none of her. He picked up his hat and turned to go.

Frightened by his coldness, this unexpected gesture of finality, Molly tried once more to provoke him so that things would turn out all right. "Why don't ya look at me? All right, so I did it with him! But it was only because I was missin ya so. I thought I was never goin to see ya again. If you're mad at me, Tom, then let me have it, but don't just stand there."

He started to open the door and she was over to him, clutching at his hand. "Don't go! It's you I want, my darlin. Only you!" But he paid no attention and pulled away.

As Tom walked off into the darkness below, she leaned over the porch railing and shouted so that the whole court could hear, "All right, then, Tom Endicott, I want no more of you or your money. And get it into your head that my child is a Hanlon and will be raised a Hanlon, not one of your tightassed family!"

When he hung up his hat and coat in the hall, tired to his bones, the little Indian nurse Phoebe was sitting barefoot at the bottom of the stairs in the shadows, whispering to the children, who should have been in bed long before, about old Greenwich prison that used to stand by the river, and how all her family used to watch the prisoners being flogged until the blood ran down in pools and they shrieked for mercy. But best of all was when they led out one of the murderers to be hanged.... Year-old Claude on her lap and three-year-old Veronica at her feet were staring up at her, entranced.

In the parlor Fanny and Miss Swindon were playing planchette, the saucer under their fingers swooping over the painted letters on the table between them, and Fanny's eyes were dancing with an unhealthy excitement, red blotches on her cheeks.

He dropped into an armchair in his study and stared into the dead ashes of the fireplace.

But like the phoenix, the flames soon rose again from the ashes. As the weeks passed, the pallidly tranquil atmosphere of the house that he pretended to find bearable got on Tom's nerves. He was unable to keep himself distracted by the Herald and found himself longing to get out in the evening. Even Fanny was showing signs of uneasiness the more he stayed around.

It was sex he needed. He had never been so honest as to put it so baldly before, but remembering his nights in Shamrock Alley showed him that this was it, plain and simple. Of course, there were prostitutes in the city—thousands of them—but whenever he tried to picture one of them in his arms, it was always Molly's face he saw, and he was enraged at her all over again.

But the rage kept turning into desire. He still wanted her. She could whore around as much as she liked but she could damn well be his whore too.

Once more he went back to Shamrock Alley and climbed the wooden stairs to her landing. Outside her door he heard her laughing and he thought she might be playing with baby Patrick. But when she opened to him, he saw by the smoky light of the oil tamp the coal man sitting in his chair holding a beer. His house of cards tumbled as he understood all at once how profoundly he loved her.

This time she did not try to explain. She stepped out, closing the door behind her. "I'm sorry, Tom," she told him, "but ya got to understand that I meant what I said. Ya may not have seen it, but it was comin to an end between us for a long time. I'm not sayin it was no good, but it's over now. I'll always be grateful to ya for helpin me, but we're from two different worlds, you and me."

The blood in his ears was pounding so loud his voice didn't seem to be coming from him, but he had to get her back. "What about our son?"

"My son, Tom. Don't ya see, the world will never let him be ours? Ya comin here all the time would keep him a bastard, and now he's got a chance to grow up respectable. He's a Hanlon, whose father died before he was born. Ya don't need to worry about him and me, I earn enough at the tavern." She put a soft hand on his arm. "You'll forget in no time." And before he could find anything to say, she slipped back inside her room and shut the door.

Immediately, he had a million things to tell her. He wanted to call after her—no one would ever take care of her as he would...help her...not just money, she would always have him to count on...he wanted her to know how much he loved her—he was ready to beg her on his knees, but the door with its chinks of yellow light around it was closed against him.

For hours he walked the streets, passing through grief, humiliation, and rage, one after the other. He had crawled back to her and she had spit at him. He could see her laughing with that man about the spectacle he had made of himself. It made him sick to his stomach.

That night as he lay awake tossing, with Fanny in her nightcap curled up beside him in her drugged sleep, he pictured Molly and the man going at it like dogs, with the baby—his own flesh and blood—in the cradle right next to them. It rankled that she was getting away with it. The child shouldn't be allowed to grow up with her, his son wouldn't have a chance. But what could he do? He couldn't make a public outcry. Even if right was on his side, the courts were out of the question—it would be too much of a scandal.

He had to get the child away from her somehow, kidnap it if necessary, find an old woman to raise it in the country. She'd never get at it. He would make her suffer.

He saw the door with its chinks of light closed against him and seized the pillow, burying his face in it. It wasn't the child he was upset about. He only wanted to hurt her because she had thrown him out—and the agony was that he still loved her. How was he going to get along without her?

He'd talk to Albert about it. No. He wouldn't understand—Albert would tell him that no woman was important enough to suffer over, one was as good as another, the same old thing.

He had to find someone who would take him seriously. There was the vicar at St. Luke's—you were supposed to turn to your pastor in time of trouble. Impossible. He could never go to that old windbag—he would never understand either. No one could.

He was going to bust if he didn't find someone to talk to. The vicar wouldn't do, but he couldn't get the bell tower of St. Luke's out of his mind, rising over the roofs and treetops of the village.

Although he had never done such a thing in his life or even considered it, he was in so much torment that finally he slipped out of bed and got down on his knees on the cold planks of the bedroom floor.

Instead of saying some prayer he knew by rote, he found himself asking for help in his own words. The old lump in his throat that had been there all his life seemed to dissolve, and when he opened his eyes he became aware of the first pale intimations of dawn filtering in around the drapes and the cool freshness of a new day.

He climbed back into bed and pulled the quilts up against the chill. As he drifted off, he imagined—whether it was a dream or not he never knew—that Fanny had hovered over him and put her lips to his forehead.

After breakfast Tom stepped out, reborn, into a perfect spring morning. He filled his lungs with the salt air from the river mixed with the pungency of wood smoke, fresh horse manure like fermented hay, and the riot of lilacs in the garden across the street. At the corner of Bleecker Street he tossed a coin into the hat of an itinerant fiddler with straw hair like a scarecrow, whose music accompanied the clatter of horses and wagons on the thoroughfare.

He still loved Molly—he always would—and it was going to hurt a long time, but he saw clearly the wrong he had done her. He had lived selfishly and was going to make amends. His higher self was in charge now. He had a great need to find something worthwhile to devote himself to, to fill the place where she had been. He didn't know what that was or how it was coming, but he knew in his bones he would find it.

9

In the following days Tom kept thinking of that moment on his knees and waited for a sign, for he was sure that his prayer had been received.

At the printing shop it was clear that Albert guessed something was up, so without going into details Tom simply admitted that he and Molly were through. Although he couldn't explain it to anyone, he knew that something genuine had happened to him and he didn't want Albert scoffing or calling him crack-brained.

But from then on Albert never let up on him, suggesting one woman after another, usually some relative from his wife's extensive Indian clan who wouldn't cause him any headaches. Tom fended him off—all that was finished for him, he said. He still had the natural desires every man was tormented by, but he was convinced that when he found his path it would take care of everything.

One day, when the bell over the shop door tinkled he looked up from his work and in walked the alderman's pretty young wife, Florence Howells, with Otis Skidmore, the local bookseller. Mrs. Howells had shocked the women's group at St. Luke's, according to Miss Swindon, by urging them to fight for the right to vote. Otis, who had opened his bookshop recently after a year of wandering around Europe, was rumored to be working for the Underground Railroad, helping slaves escape to Canada. Some people even said there was a tunnel in his cellar that led to a landing on the river.

When the couple handed Tom a manuscript they wanted him to print up as a pamphlet for them, he was surprised to discover it was about temperance. He would never connect temperance with people like them. For him, the Temperance Society had always meant his uncle in Binghamton, a fanatical teetotaler who blamed all the evils known to man on drink and the devil.

Tom spread out on his desk copies of the temperance pamphlets he had already printed up, pointing out to them the various layouts and typography.

Florence Howells, who had removed her bonnet to arrange a bunch of violets fastened to it, shook her head firmly. "Oh, my, no! Those look much too stuffy. They give an entirely wrong impression of what we're all about.

We want to shake things up a little." She plucked a wilted violet and tossed it into a brass spittoon.

She and Otis had a different idea about what temperance was all about, she told Tom, as she retied the bonnet under her chin, and they wanted their tract to make that quite clear.

The bookseller, an earnest young man who sported mutton chop whiskers, explained that their object was to attract new blood into the Society and they were banking on their pamphlet to do it. "We hope to get a little controversy going with this thing," he said, slapping the manuscript. "You ought to come to one of our meetings yourself."

Tom told them that even if he wanted to, he wouldn't qualify since he enjoyed a glass of beer now and then.

"So do I!" said Otis enthusiastically, and explained that there were two schools of thought about that in Temperance. His side didn't object to fermented drinks like beer and wine.

"Total abstinence isn't necessary for people like us," Mrs. Howells added. "But for some people it's the only way. We'll never he able to wipe out poverty unless we attack liquor first, because it's liquor, after all, that's keeping those poor wretches down." Embarrassed at her own sanctimoniousness, Florence smiled. "Besides, we have a very good time in the Society. We're not all fossils there, Mr. Endicott. The liveliest people are joining these days. Our group has started holding street meetings and we go all over the city together. Do come, if you can."

When they were gone Tom read over their manuscript. It was unusual for a tract, not one mention of the devil or damnation or any tales about country girls in the city led astray by a glass of beer. The gist of it, from what he could make out, was that the liquor interests were making huge profits off the misery of the poor, and it argued for taxing the booze makers out of existence.

Outside, a milk wagon clattered by, its empty cans banging in counterpoint to the sound of the presses in the back of the shop.

Tom was curious about these temperance meetings. He liked both Florence Howells and Otis Skidmore and there was no doubt that they genuinely wanted to help people. He thought of Shamrock Alley and that tavern spilling out its drunks into the street day and night. Those poor wretches down there led such terrible lives. Molly's face rose before him, telling him it was all over between them, closing the door. He got a grip on himself. He had to do something useful with his life now. Maybe this was it. There was certainly not much else to do in Greenwich.

Albert came out from the back of the shop, buttoning his jacket, and stopped to look over Tom's shoulder to see what he was reading. "More of that horseshit?" he snorted, and sent a stream of tobacco juice into the spittoon as he left for the day. Albert was getting more comissions than he could handle, painting his opulent nudes in the taverns that were springing up on every corner as New York City, swollen with immigrants, expanded northward river to river.

Tom shook his head at his unregenerate friend. There were certain things Albert was never going to understand.

The pamphlet was delivered in time for Tuesday's meeting. On a whim, Tom joined the crowd at Woolsey Hall on Gansevoort Street. Florence Howells, the bookseller Otis Skidmore, and other young members of the Temperance Society were distributing their pamphlet at the door and welcomed him heartily.

After the singing of the temperance anthem, the program did not get off to a promising start. Some itinerant preacher doing the "devil and damnation" circuit pounded the rostrum, warning that in spite of all the social reformers infiltrating the movement, the real purpose of the Society remained the salvation of souls and the redemption of sinners. From a couple of rows off, Mrs. Howells caught Tom's eye and looked up at the ceiling in exasperation.

But Otis Skidmore wasn't having any of it. He bounded up to the stage and declared that they weren't going to get anywhere with such fusty attitudes and that it was time to face the real problem. It was not the drunkards who were guilty. They were only the victims of the liquor interests, backed up by corrupt politicians. Even more important, in his view, it was time the Society woke up to other issues like freeing the slaves and the rights of women.

The scattering of applause from the younger members in the hall was nearly overwhelmed by the loud booing from the old guard.

After the usual testimonials from some reformed tipplers, the meeting broke up with heated discussion on all sides. Flossie Howells and Otis and their friends pushed back chairs and joined hands round, with a lusty rendition of "Onward Christian Soldiers." Tom was about to leave when

Flossie broke away to take his hand and bring him into the circle.

At first he felt awkward, but the enthusiasm of the group was infectious, and by the time they dispersed he was feeling so good that he agreed to meet them for a street rally the next night to take their message directly to the people.

With the encouragement of his new friends Tom threw himself into "the work" as they called it, glad not to have to sit home, miserable and bored with Fanny. It wasn't that he had forgotten Molly, but he was convinced he had found something worthwhile to fill his life with. The only fly in the ointment was his old problem of lust, but he told himself that if he kept busy enough he would conquer it.

One hot summer night he went with Flossie and Otis to hand out leaflets on Greene Street just beyond Washington Square. It was the heart of New York City's red-light district, just out of sight of the fashionable hotels and restaurants of Broadway. The gaslamps had just been lit, but the street was already in full swing. Men, elegant in their high silk hats, gloves, and walking sticks, stepped out of hansom cabs at the canopied entrances of dance saloons and bordellos and, as music poured into the street and barkers called out, pushed their way through the swinging doors.

Tom did his best to keep his mind on passing out the temperance leaflets, but he couldn't avoid seeing the women, dressed in flimsy negligees, fanning themselves in the windows. Through a swinging door he caught glimpses of gaudily done-up women, bells tinkling from their red boots, laughing raucously with men. It reminded him of a picture Fanny had hung opposite their bed in which the flames of hell were licking around just such a scene, while Satan hovered over it all with his pitchfork.

A buxom blonde, sitting on the low sill of a brothel window only a few feet away, was fanning her breast that a flamboyant gold satin dress amply displayed. To his discomfort, she caught his eye and winked, even calling out over the noise of the street, "Hey, captain, ready for a bit of fun?"

"Well, I never!" said Flossie, going crimson. Looking up at the woman in the window, she addressed her directly. "Don't be so smart, miss. Can't you see you're being exploited? You don't have to be here. You could be in some respectable job."

Heavily painted eyes looked Flossie up and down. "I had a job, sister, working in a cotton mill seventy hours a week for two dollars and a quarter. Go peddle your papers somewhere else." And with that she leaned out and tapped a passing gentleman with her fan. The man curled his fingers around it and let her pull him up close for a whispered exchange.

Dispirited, Florence Howells led Tom and Otis down the street through the throngs of men appraising the wares at the windows. "You know, that poor creature's got a point," she said when they had turned onto Bleecker Street and were starting for home. "We're going to have to offer something more concrete than inspirational ideas to get to people like her."

Discouraged by their lack of success, they didn't stop for buns and coffee at the little bakeshop on Bleecker Street that night as they usually did. But when they broke up, Tom was too disturbed to go directly home, so he dropped by the print shop, intending to do some work until he calmed down.

There was a lamp lit in back where Albert was working on his own printmaking as he often did in the evening, but Tom didn't feel like talking. He flopped down at his desk and tried to do some proofreading.

He had never seen a woman looking so debased as that blonde sitting in the window with her painted face and her flesh oozing out of her fancy dress. God, it was degrading how they made you feel.

"That you, Tom?" Albert came out from the back, looking scrawnier than ever in a red woolen undershirt and suspendered trousers. "I usually have this place to myself at night." He wiped his forehead. "Gad, it's a hot one today. It was sure as hell cooler over by the river this afternoon. What a fine place to paint!"

Tom didn't look up, but the artist was in no hurry to get back to his engraving and sat down on the edge of the desk, stroking his drooping mustache. "You know, there's something about Greenwich that appeals to low-down sods like me. Can't put my finger on it exactly, but seems to me there's less hassle here than most places I been, in spite of you and your temperance freaks." Albert grinned, but noticing Tom's hangdog look, asked what was bothering him.

Tom couldn't hold it back any longer. "I thought I'd seen everything," he said, "but tonight we were over on Greene Street and I tell you it was unbelievable. Do you have any idea what it's like there?"

"You old reprobate! Over at the cathouses, were you? Did you have a good time?"

Tom got up, ready to hit him, but his friend eased him back down. "Hold on, old fella. You know I'm a kidder."

Tom sank back in his chair and put a hand to his eyes. "It was horrible, horrible...."

Keeping his arm around Tom's shoulders, Albert said quietly, "It's not so bad, friend. You're just a man like any other. You're horny as hell, isn't that it?"

Tom nodded miserably.

"Can't fight nature, friend. Now that you're through with Molly and with your wife an invalid, a man's still got to shoot his load or he wouldn't be a man. Why don't you let me take you back there? I'll introduce you to some of the girls."

Tom stared at him.

Albert nodded, smiling. "Sure, I know a lot of them. Where do you think I get my naked models from? They're good girls. They know what a man needs. Specially when he hasn't got a woman of his own, like you."

"I know you're trying to help, Albert, but I can't do that." He did his best to explain. "It may be a joke to you, but until I found temperance I didn't know what to do with myself. It gave some meaning to my life and the people are my friends. If I were to do such a thing...."

"Listen to me," said Albert, laying a hand on his shoulder, "this has nothing to do with your work in the temperance. And no one will ever know."

That night Tom went back to Greene Street without Albert taking him there and without any temperance tracts under his arm. And afterward, in spite of his guilt, he told himself it was better to lie with a whore than corrupt another virtuous woman.

From then on he visited Greene Street regularly, and gradually stopped making excuses to himself about it. Fanny could never be a wife to him in the full sense of the word. So whatever the world might think of him if they knew, he was still a man.

1858

10

One wintry evening, Tom Endicott left the print shop early because Miss Swindon had sent word that she was having another of her migraines and was unable to take care of his wife. The task fell to Tom since Fanny couldn't tolerate either of her children for very long, though Veronica and Claude were now old enough to help out. But to his sorrow, their mother's erratic behavior had made them permanently wary of her. In spite of Albert's jibing, it was only his involvement with the Temperance Society that had sustained him these last lonely years.

Tom hardly looked boyish any more and his clothes were shabby, attesting to the fact that for years he had had no woman who cared enough about him to look after his needs properly. Miss Swindon was always coming down with a headache when he was at his busiest. Not only was he needed at the shop, but there was a temperance crusade at Woolsey Hall that night. One of his presses was tied up running off the program that had to be ready in time for the meeting. The other press was printing a handbill for a department store over on Broadway that was introducing an ice cabinet for preserving perishable food, as well as a zinc-lined bathing tub with a gas water heater attached. Tom had heard the heaters sometimes exploded, but these days nothing put off the novelty-mad public from buying up all the new household inventions on the market. Tom himself had installed a brick furnace in the cellar that piped warmed air up into the rest of the house.

On his way home from the shop he stopped for a moment to watch some neighborhood boys sledding on the snow-packed street. It was already dark and the gas lamps threw a nostalgic light over the scene, reminding him of bellywopping in the town upstate where he grew up, one of the few pleasant memories he had from his boyhood. Usually he tried not to give in to such sentimental feelings—there was always the danger that he would start longing for Molly again.

He had only run into her once in the intervening years. That was in the autumn of '52 on one of those crystal-clear days in New York when everything stands out sharp and the colors are intense. The air was so fresh it seemed to have blown in straight from the Catskills.

He had gone to the pushcart market down on Hudson Street to help Otis Skidmore who was making a campaign speech. That year Otis was running for the office of alderman on the Temperance ticket, a post vacated by Flossie Howells' husband when he had been elected to the state assembly.

Tom was passing out leaflets, while Otis on his soapbox was trying to drum up support from the new voters among the immigrants. Across the street a speaker on Irish independence had collected an enthusiastic crowd with a tirade against the English. But Otis wasn't having much luck. No one in the busy street market was paying any attention to him except for some heckling urchins.

Tom had been doing his best to shoo them away when he saw her. She was heading back in the direction of Shamrock Alley, which was not far off. With his heart pounding, he pushed his way through a mob of people busy haggling over a load of fresh fish spread out on the cobblestones.

Until then he had believed that filling up his life with community activities was enough for him. But to his surprise he found himself running after her, everything else forgotten.

As he caught up with her, he saw that she had a toddler holding on to her skirt. His first thought was that it must be his son Patrick, but this child was too small, only two or three. And for a moment he wasn't sure if it was Molly after all, her face was so much fuller and under the shawl her belly was big. But then he realized she must be pregnant.

"Molly!" His voice nearly choked getting out her name.

She turned and her blue eyes looked puzzled under the same untamable black curls. Then she broke into her broad smile. "Why, Tom, ya haven't changed a bit. You're still pretty enough to turn every girl's bead."

He was so nonplussed by her old, sweet naturalness that he dropped his leaflets, and she burst out laughing.

As he fumbled to gather them up, she took one out of his hand and looked at Albert's drawing on the cover of a greedy distiller holding a huge liquor bottle over the open mouths of the poor below him.

"Would it be temperance you're in now? Ah, Tom, ya never could have been an Irishman."

He couldn't stop coloring like an idiot and looked for something to say. "I see you're married again. I'm so glad."

She laughed with the old heartiness. "Ah, my dear, still the same innocent, ya are? A girl doesn't have to be married to have herself a fine family. I'm not made to stay with one man forever."

He looked down uneasily at the toddler in a neatly patched coat and trousers who stared back suspiciously.

"Timothy," said his mother, giving him a yank, "show Mr. Endicott ya got a tongue in your head."

The boy only turned to sniffle against her skirt.

"He's nearly four now, would ya believe it? And another bun in the oven." She patted her belly proudly. "Ya must think I'm a lost soul for sure, but I'm happier than I've ever been. I make a good livin at the Blarney Stone and I got no worries."

Nearly suffocating in the heat of her presence, he stammered that he had to get back to Otis, but she put a hand on his arm, making him tremble.

"Ah, come home with me first and see Patrick. Such a sturdy lad. Nearly eleven years old, would ya believe it? He's a real helper already. I'll say you're an old friend."

But Tom had mumbled an excuse, saying he would try to come by another time, then watched as she strode away through a drift of brilliant maple leaves on the walk, throwing back her shawl and shaking her black curls loose in the breeze until she turned the corner.

That had been more than five years ago, and for a long while after, it had seemed to him that the life he had so carefully constructed for himself was no more than a makeshift. Nevertheless, that meeting had made it clear to him that it was better they had gone their separate ways. Considering how she wanted to live her life, it could never have worked out—not in a million years.

Under the gas lamps of Perry Street, the boys were shouting around him now as they threw themselves down on their sleds. On a pile of snow against the picket fence of the old farmhouse across from his house, some boys playing king-of-the-hill were pummeling each other with snowballs. For a moment he thought he recognized his twelve-year-old son Claude holding the summit against a barrage of snowballs, until he saw with disappointment it was some other boy.

He sighed as he climbed the stoop and stomped the snow off his boots, preparing himself for whatever might be waiting for him in his gloomy household.

After shedding his coat and scarf in the hall, he looked into the parlor where Claude was playing by himself on the carpet. The boy was so engrossed in his game that he paid no attention to his father. He had constructed a prison yard out of cardboard, complete with a row of scaffolds and nooses made of string with which he was hanging cardboard prisoners one after the other, his lips moving as he made up some grotesque tale about it to himself.

When Tom interrupted to ask how things had gone for him that day at the boys' academy, Claude looked up with his mother's nervous eyes and mumbled an inaudible reply.

Tom went up the stairs heavily. He wished he could get closer to his son, especially after his own miserable growing-up with his uncle, but Claude had never responded to his self-conscious overtures. The boy's eyes bothered Tom, so nervous, as if Fanny's trouble might have been passed on to him. Claude had always been frail and still occasionally wet his bed. He needed to get out more, make friends. It wasn't enough for him to help out at the shop on Saturdays as he had been doing lately. Tom resolved to try harder to reach him.

On the second floor, his daughter Veronica's door was closed as usual. She was fourteen but no more sociable than Claude. She spent most of her time after school in her room writing poetry, which she never showed to anybody. He had asked to see it but she always refused.

On the other side of the door Veronica had laid aside her pen and was standing over the hot-air vent in the floor, her eyes dreamy, swaying back and forth as the heat rose under her skirts. Her lips moved as she recited a poem. Like her brother, Veronica had no real friends at school and didn't want any. She preferred not to attract attention, and kept herself as inconspicuous as possible.

When Tom went into their bedroom, his wife was in her chair by the window working at her embroidery. He was relieved to see that she was not in the unstable condition Miss Swindon's message had led him to expect. In the last years her attacks had become more frequent again, which left her increasingly listless. Although she was only in her mid-thirties she looked older, her skin transparent and her hair prematurely gray.

As he changed his jacket, something in her quiet pose reminded him of the delicate girl she had once been, and he went over to kiss her cheek.

But she was not sewing. Her hands lay holding her embroidery hoop in her lap, and she stared vacantly out into the night. She scarcely paid attention to him any more.

After Veronica had helped him get her to bed, Tom sat in his study with the newspaper in front of him. If his children weren't happy it was no wonder, he thought. They didn't have much chance with a mother like that. If only it were possible for him to give them a more normal life.

He let the newspaper drop. He had no interest in the latest Lincoln-Douglas debate, or the fuss over Irish anarchists throwing bombs, or even the slavery issue that filled whole columns.

He could still go to the temperance meeting if he wanted. Fanny was asleep and it wouldn't be any trouble for Veronica to look in on her. But he didn't feel like it—things had been going from bad to worse there too.

Once, in the company of Otis and Flossie, it had been exhilarating to go around the city together fighting for what they believed in. But tonight he would have to disappoint Otis, even if his friend counted on him more than ever to help shake things up, since Flossie had moved up to Albany with her assemblyman husband. And she wasn't the only one of the livelier members who had left the Society. Many of them had deserted for the antislavery cause and the women's movement—"bloomerism" the papers snidely called it.

The fusty old guard in the local chapter was having it all its own way lately, rampaging against sin. Sin to them meantone thing—immigrants. Now that Greenwich had been engulfed by the city, piers were being built along the riverfront offering all kinds of unskilled jobs. What the old guard was worried about was the immigrants coming in to take them, and bringing down real estate values. So calling for a crusade against "vice" was just their way of attacking the immigrants. Things had come to such a point at the meetings there was even open talk against "pope worshippers," by which of course they meant the Irish. Tom didn't like the way things were going at all.

He shoved back his chair and paced the room from the heavy drapes of the bay window to the portieres closed against the drafts, and back again. He and Otis and the others ought to be able to stop those temperance bigots somehow. He was still young, not yet forty, and in good health. But the way he felt, it was as if his hands were tied. He didn't know what to do—about temperance, about his family. Everything was so difficult. If only he could make something happen.

If only he could see Molly again....

11

Tom did see Molly again, but in circumstances he never would have expected—or wanted.

The following Saturday, he was sitting in the shop editing a temperance tract that he and Otis hoped would show up the hard-liners for the bigots they were. Albert Cogswell was off on a trip up the Hudson sketching Indians fishing through the ice, and his son Claude was at the counter to deal with any customers who came in, when the door flew open with a blast of cold air and a street boy about ten or eleven ran up to the desk.

"Are you Mr. Endicott, sir?" the boy asked boldly.

Tom didn't want to interrupt his work and motioned him over to the counter, but the boy held his ground. "No, it's you I come for."

Tom dropped his pen, his attention riveted. Though he hadn't seen this boy since he was born, he would have known him anywhere. The son of his illicit liaison with Molly Hanlon. He was a sturdy lad in trousers belted up with a rope, a patched jacket, and a floppy workman's cap in hand. He had his mother's curly black hair and frank blue eyes—and he was very upset about something.

While Claude gaped at them from behind the counter, Tom pushed back his chair and turned fully to Patrick. "I'm Mr. Endicott. What can I do for you?"

"It's my ma, sir," the boy said in a rush. "The cops raided the Blarney Stone last night and took her to jail. She's told me many times how she used to work in your house and she always said I was to go to you if there was ever trouble."

Tom asked no questions. He told the astonished Claude to mind the shop and, snatching his coat, followed after Patrick, who had already set off in the direction of the Jefferson Market jailhouse.

The snow-packed sidewalks had been spread with ashes, making it possible to move quickly. When Tom caught up with him at the corner, he tried to find out what had happened, but all the boy was able to tell him was that "it was the shithead Protestant temperance people behind it. But why arrest my ma? She never done nothin," he said, and broke into a run as the clock tower of the courthouse came into sight.

At the jailhouse Tom demanded to know from the constable sitting at a desk behind a wooden barrier what the police thought they were doing arresting Mrs. Hanlon.

Pulling on his long mustache as he lounged in his chair, the policeman told him that under pressure from some high muckety-mucks in the Temperance Society they had raided a bunch of taverns on the river on suspicion of harboring anarchists. An anarchist, an ugly customer named Mahoney, had been found at the Blarney Stone and was shot dead trying to escape. "I'm Irish myself, Mr. Endicott, but these anarchists come here to America and think they can take over. You should have seen that Hanlon woman tryin to scratch our lads' eyes out when we got Mahoney. We had no choice but to take her into custody on an obstruction of justice."

Tom paid her bail, and waited impatiently in front of the barrier. He was appalled that temperance was behind this. He knew, of course, that the fanatics in the Society believed that smashing up taverns would solve everything. And it was true that some of them had connections at City Hall. But did they have the police in their pockets, too? It made him sick.

"Ya think they're gonna let ma out soon?" Patrick asked. "I don't want to lose my job."

The boy was sitting on the bench along the wall holding his cap. Tom had forgotten all about him. He went over and sat down next to him and asked what his job was.

Patrick told him that he worked a ten-hour day every Saturday and half a day during the week after school, helping to put in the new sewer system in Greenwich. "The pipes are goin to dump all the shyte right into the river," he said, his eyes shining.

Impressed with the boy's spirit, Tom asked if that wasn't heavy work for someone his age.

It wasn't so bad, Patrick said, and he was learning a lot. Sometimes they even let him hold the plans for them.

Tom wanted to know how he got the job.

"Tammany got it for me. All I had to do was give em my vote."

"But you're not old enough to vote!"

"I don't know how it works myself, but everybody says it's only Tammany that's ever done a damn thing for us micks."

Tom knew that the political organization put the names of the dead on the voter rolls, but this was the first time he'd heard they used childrens' as well. He asked Patrick what his wages were.

The boy said he got a dollar fifty a week and his ma was always telling him she didn't know what they would do without it. "Timothy's not much for workin," he said. His brother who was nine was always getting into scrapes. His ma said it was because he was wild like his dad.

Tom felt a pang at the thought of Molly with other men. God only knew who the father of Timothy was. Recalling that she was pregnant the last time he saw her, he asked if there wasn't another brother too.

The boy said no, only a sister, Nora, who was six.

Tom questioned him about the man named Mahoney the police had shot at the tavern, suspecting he might have been the father of the other children.

Patrick looked down at the cap twisting in his hands. "Danny Mahoney was our best friend in the world. He loved us all so, especially Nora, and he kept us laughin all the time with his jokin. I don't know why they had to... to kill him." His lip trembled.

A door clanged somewhere in the back and a policeman ushered Molly out. She was haggard, her hair tangled and her shawl torn.

"Ma!" Patrick broke into sobs as he ran over to the rail trying to shake open the wooden gate, but the policeman pushed him back and opened it from the inside.

Mother and son threw their arms around each other, his head against her breast—until she became aware of Tom standing there. She glared at him, tears wet on her cheeks. "It's not a vice den I run, Tom Endicott, and I don't relish spendin my nights in a jail cell—thanks to you and your friends in the temperance." Pulling Patrick along, she charged out of the precinct house and down the steps to the street, leaving Tom stupefied.

She couldn't think he had had any part in this! He would do anything in the world for her.

He caught up with her as she stood outside, adjusting the shawl over her tangled hair. "Molly, it wasn't my fault. I swear to God I didn't know anything about it. I didn't have anything to do with him getting shot...."

"Oh, didn't ya now...." She slammed Patrick's cap on his head and hurried off down the street. The boy turned to look back uncertainly at him, and then ran after her.

An hour later, when Tom went into Otis Skidmore's bookstore, the bookseller looked up from a heated discussion he was having with several members of their group. "Where have you been, Tom? Have you heard what happened? What are we going to do about these maniacs?"

"I've got to speak to you, Otis," he broke in, not looking at the others. The bookseller led him into the back and asked what was up.

"You'll have to do without me from now on. I'm finished with the whole goddam thing."

"Tom, what are you talking about? We've got a fight on our hands. We've all got to stand together. We need you."

"Look, Otis, can't you see what temperance has become? It's not anti-liquor any more, it's a bunch of goddam bigots against the poor down there in Shamrock Alley who haven't got a hope in hell of getting out of it."

"But you can't blast the whole movement just because of a few crackpots."

It wasn't just a few crackpots, Tom said, and the proof of its bigotry was that only Irish taverns had been raided. They hadn't touched Unger at the Four Winds, for example. "And in the name of our sacred Society the cops shot a man dead. Can you tell me that that had anything to do with liquor?"

"Well, say that at the meeting tonight! That's just what they need to be told, straight from the shoulder."

"I'm sorry, Otis, I'm through." He started for the door.

"No, Tom!" Otis cried.

But the door had closed behind him.

When he got back to the shop, Tom told his son that Molly was a former hired girl in the family who had gotten herself into some trouble and he had gone to help. But he could tell from the way Claude kept looking at him that his curiosity was far from satisfied.

Tom sat down and tried to work, but he was too upset and decided to close the shop, sending the help and Claude home. He went straight to the Four Winds and belted down his first whiskey since Temperance.

Although he told himself that he was not responsible for the raid on the Blarney Stone, he was miserable that Molly believed him to be part of it. He had to make her listen, but with her Irish temper, how was he going to do that? And he did feel at fault in a way. He ought to have known those moral zealots were up to something. Maybe he could have stopped it.

Without a job, she was going to be in desperate need of money. Patrick's weekly dollar and a half wasn't enough. The least he could do was help her out. She couldn't refuse it, if for no other reason than she needed to feed her children.

Tom's first view of Shamrock Alley after ten years nearly brought tears to his eyes. It had hardly changed, except for a woman with a green sash standing at the tavern door collecting money for Irish prisoners. Children still shrieked as they played underfoot, while biddies with corncob pipes cackled to each other across the railings of the outside porches.

Upstairs on Molly's landing, a little girl with wide eyes and her finger in her mouth opened the door to him. This had to be Nora, the sister Patrick had mentioned.

"She's nappin," Nora said, when he asked for her mother.

He patted her head and walked in. The room was cozier than he remembered it. The shabby furniture was made more cheerful by a bright afghan on the low bed, an embroidered linen tablecloth, and an oval braided rug that covered most of the floor. There was even a shelf of books and a pipe rack that he thought, with a twinge, might have belonged to Danny Mahoney. As the child in her neat pinafore stared up at him, he tried to imagine what Mahoney had looked like.

The bedroom door opened, but instead of Molly a boy about nine came out fastening his suspenders. Showing no surprise at seeing Tom, he held his palm right out and asked in a wheedling tone, "Gimme a dime, will ya, mister? I ain't had nothin to eat all day."

"Timothy, that's a fib, and ya know it," the little girl piped up. "Ya had cod pie and cabbage, same as we all did."

But Tom gave him a coin anyway, and with a whoop the boy slammed out the door and down the stairs.

The little girl tittered. "He's runnin with the Dusters now."

The Hudson Dusters, the street gang that snatched purses. What a difference between him and Patrick.

Tom didn't know whether he should wait. He couldn't just sit down and make himself at home until Molly got up, and after what she had been through he certainly didn't want to wake her. He was about to leave, intending to return later, when there was a stamping of boots outside and Patrick came in, his face smudged from work.

For a moment the boy was startled to see him, then he broke into a grin. "I was hopin ya might be comin by, mister." He hung up his cap and coat, put his lunch pail away, and went to wash up.

There was an odd contraption over the washstand that Tom hadn't noticed before. Above the basin a barrel had been rigged up, with a pipe extending from the top of it and out through the window. The boy turned on a beer cock at the bottom of the barrel, filling the basin with water.

"We gets our water from the rain," Nora said. "Paddy made it!" She looked proudly at her brother who was bent over scrubbing his ears.

Running water was unknown in any of these old tenements. Everybody had to carry water up from the pump out on the street.

Patrick grinned as he dried his neck. "It's not fixed right yet. Lemme show ya." He point out to Tom through the window how the pipe from the barrel was connected to a rain gutter along the edge of the roof. "When it don't rain it goes dry, but I'm goin to put a tank up there."

It was an impressive device for a boy of only eleven to have rigged up, and Tom praised him for it.

While Patrick was attacking his mop of hair with a comb, Tom explained that he didn't want to disturb his mother while she was resting, but that he had brought a little money for them. He took out an envelope and added, "Tell your mother that when she needs more to send you over to the shop."

"We don't want your charity!" a voice yelled from the bedroom.

Molly had been awake, listening to every word. "But it's not charity," he called back, trying to sound reasonable. "I owe it to you for"—he looked at Patrick—"for...back wages."

"Get your arse out of here!" she bellowed back. "We don't want you!"

Tom tried to hand the envelope to Patrick anyway.

But the boy shook his head, faithful to his mother. "I think ya better go," he said. "Ma isn't takin it so good. It's not as though we don't have any money. I'm workin full-time now. I quit school."

On the way downstairs, Tom was racking his brains about what to do, when an old woman lugging up a bucket of water greeted him by name and he recognized Molly's neighbor, Mrs. Brophy. She was shrunken now and the red hair had gone white.

"Ah, Mr. Endicott, ya been to see her, bless ya. I guess ya heard about what they done to Danny Mahoney. Isn't it a shame?"

Tom told the old woman how Molly believed he was involved in it, and had refused to let him help her out.

"I knew it couldn't be you," she said, patting his arm. "But she's suffered a grievous loss and is not to be blamed."

He put the envelope into her hand. "Do you think you might get her to see reason? I want to do what I can."

"She's stubborn as a mule, but I'll see to it." Mrs. Brophy tucked the envelope into her pocket, before picking up the pail and carrying it on up the steps.

On his way home, leaning into an icy wind coming off the river, vexed as he was by Molly's refusal to understand, Tom let himself hope that the old woman would talk her around. The one thing he could do was to send money.

He turned out of the wind onto Perry Street. What a sturdy, nice-looking boy Patrick was, and already taking charge of the family like a man. He wished Claude had some of the same energy, but how could he expect him to be any other way with an invalid for a mother? Patrick had Molly's blood in his veins and that made all the difference.

Was it possible she would never believe he was innocent? He was furious all over again at what the Society had done to her, and was disgusted with himself for having stuck with it for so long.

In spite of Patrick's attempt to keep the family going, life deteriorated in Shamrock Alley. Molly developed arthritis, and gin was finally the only thing that eased her pain.

Her younger son Timothy was seldom home. He was usually hanging out with his street gang, and when he got nabbed by the cops—as sometimes happened—he didn't have much trouble talking them into letting him go—

they were Irish too. By sixteen he was taller than Patrick and passed for a man. He even boasted about his adventures with women—the Hudson Dusters had little mercy on any girl they caught out in the streets in their area at night—and he needled his older brother about still being cherry.

It didn't bother Patrick. After all, he had been bringing the family a regular paycheck for several years already. Since working on the sewer system, he had been getting better jobs through Tammany, laying tracks on the city's north-south avenues for the horsecar lines that were replacing the stages.

There was a girl Patrick liked. Her name was Hester. They looked at each other across the court. But he was too busy to waste his time on any girl. He preferred to spend his evenings improving himself by reading the books, mostly on his favorite subject, science, that Danny Mahoney had left behind.

Molly had given up trying to find work for herself, and got so drunk at the taverns where she spent her afternoons, that sometimes, befuddled, she brought someone back with her. Once Patrick came home to find his sister Nora crying on the steps outside and, in the bedroom, a man into his mother's skirts as she lay passed out drunk. Though the man was nearly twice his size, the shame and horror Patrick felt gave him strength to throw him out. Then he sat down at the table and sobbed, as his mother—whom he could never blame—roused herself to make dinner.

But it didn't take long for the bottle to ruin her entirely. If Tom had come across her, bloated and tipsy, he wouldn't have recognized her, and soon she became indistinguishable from any number of shapeless women in shawls laboring through the streets with their bundles.

1864

12

On a gray winter day, Claude Endicott, was walking crosstown to take the Broadway stage up to Columbia College on Forty-ninth Street. He could have taken the Sixth Avenue horsecar, which was closer to home and the most direct way, but he was in no hurry to get to class and preferred to linger as long as possible on the bustling streets of wartime New York. In the four years the Civil War had been going on, the city had become more congested than ever. It was depressing, Claude thought, not to be part of the greatest adventure of the century and instead have to devote himself to dreary studies.

At Fifth Avenue he had to wait, as a battalion of fresh-faced recruits his own age in new blue uniforms marched by on their way to the parade grounds in Washington Square. Further along, he lingered at the window of an art gallery to admire a painting of the Battle of Bull Run, in which a dying Union soldier was passing a tattered Old Glory to a fellow soldier on horseback.

At college Claude was always drifting off during lectures on subjects like Locke's Theory of Social Credit, that he didn't even try to understand. He preferred to dream of being wounded on the battlefield himself and found unconscious by a southern belle in great hoop skirts, who had him carried back to her plantation by slaves, where she nursed him back to health.

He had started going to Columbia two years before when he was sixteen. He hated college and had tried to enlist, lying about his age. But, still being puny at that time and looking far younger than he was, he had been turned down.

It had caused a ruckus at home. His father refused to understand Claude's wanting to go to war and went into his usual tirade—how he had struggled to make his way up from the bottom and if he had ever had an education he would have become more than just a small-potatoes printer, and here he was giving his son the opportunity of going to college and Claude was ungrateful.

His classmates at Columbia bored him as much as the lectures. He didn't care about punting on the river, going out to beer cellars, or boasting about chasing after chorus girls. He would rather be alone than waste his time like that.

His sister Veronica's idea was that the two of them were different from other people, who were so unimaginative, so predictable, so self-satisfied in their ordinariness. But Veronica could afford to talk that way because she was going to be a poet. He only read books—and dreamed.

As Claude continued his walk across town, even a pastry shop at Mercer Street didn't let him forget the glorious war he was missing, displaying in its window cookies shaped like soldiers and cakes whipped up out of sugar and cream into martial fantasies of citadels with turrets and flags.

Broadway, when he got there, was a bedlam of jostling people and horse-drawn vehicles. New York City was booming with the prosperity the war had brought, its population swelled by people from all parts of the Union come to cash in on the bonanza. Half the men he saw were in uniform and sometimes it almost seemed that as many women were in mourning, which did not in the least reduce the general exhilaration.

Claude had gotten his draft call earlier in the year, after his eighteenth birthday. He had pleaded to be allowed to go, but his father wouldn't hear of his dropping out of college and paid the three hundred dollars to buy him out of the army. He tried to point out to his father the injustice of the draft law. Because the poor couldn't afford to buy themselves out like the better off, that was exactly why there had been the draft riots the year before, and the city had been brought near to collapse for days by rampaging mobs. But because the blocks around Perry Street had been untouched, his father dismissed the whole thing. His father always acted as if they were living in some kind of isolated village, when anyone with eyes in his head could see that Greenwich was just another part of New York City—if more old-fashioned than the rest.

Since he couldn't be a soldier, all Claude wanted was for the war to be over as soon as possible. After the first few years when everything went wrong for the northern armies, it was clear now, with Sherman heading into Georgia, that they were going to win. And just as soon as it was over, he was going to quit school and take off for the French Quarter of New Orleans, no matter what his father said.

He caught sight of the Broadway stage dashing through the welter of wagons and horses clogging the street. All the stages were decorated with scenes of famous horse races or historic events. On the side of this one was painted a splendid picture of the great Indian chief Tecumseh handing over his feathered headdress at his surrender at the Battle of Tippecanoe. But instead of stopping for passengers, the stage driver sitting up on top whipped his frothing team and careened by, splashing slush on everyone. It was always most crowded here around A. T. Stewart's, the city's leading emporium. And if his coach hadn't been full and he needed the fares, Claude knew well enough the driver would have raced a competing stage to the coach stop, creating havoc in the busy street.

But another stage finally came along and pulled over to the curb, the driver so bundled up against the cold only his bulbous nose showed. All the men waiting crowded forward to leap on at the back door, but Claude stopped to help a lady, who, holding her skirts, was trying to step across the muddy gutter onto the step. By the time he got on the stage himself the seven places on each side were filled, and standing on the straw-covered floor holding on to a strap as the coach lurched off, he drifted into a fantasy of his future life in the French Quarter with an octoroon mistress.

He was moving toward the front of the coach to pay his fare, when it came to a sudden halt, throwing him across the lap of the lady he had helped into the coach. He regained his balance, stammering an apology, but with an air of amusement the woman assured him it was nothing, as she rearranged her fox-trimmed coat and muff. She had dark, almond eyes, high cheekbones, and smoothly coiffed hair on top of which was perched a petite Parisian hat.

Claude avoided looking at her, feeling his face hot, but he knew her eyes were on him as he handed a dollar bill up through the slot in the roof to the driver on the seat outside. The fare was five cents, so he was chagrined to find, when the change envelope was handed back down to him, that it contained only forty-five cents. He counted it again to make sure.

Fifty cents was a fortune to let the driver get away with, yet Claude couldn't bear to make a scene after having fallen all over that elegant woman, and anyway it was practically hopeless to shout up to the driver through the slot in the roof. Of course, all the drivers were perfectly well aware of that, and if they wanted to shortchange you, there was really nothing much you could do about it.

He felt a pull at his sleeve and the elegant passenger spoke. "You really must demand your change, you know. You have it coming."

Ready to sink through the floor, Claude said it wasn't worth the trouble.

"But you must," she insisted, and to his amazement she actually stood up and, holding on to his shoulder, called through the slot to the driver to return the fifty cents.

The driver deliberately jerked the reins to make the stage lurch from side to side, throwing the lady back into her seat, and everyone had to hold on for their lives. But when they drew up to the Union Square stop she got right back to her feet, rapping with her umbrella on the roof and insisting that the money be returned.

With everyone staring, Claude looked down at the trampled straw in embarrassment.

To his surprise, the driver handed down the correct change in an envelope. Claude was so pleased he forgot his awkwardness, smiling his thanks to the exotic-looking woman, who astonished him again by saying, "Young man, you must be a poet."

He said that he wasn't.

"But you do like poetry, don't you?" Her almond-shaped eyes smiled at him.

He assured her that he did.

"Well, then," she said briskly, opening her jet-embroidered bag, "you might like to meet some other poetry lovers who are friends of mine."

As the coach drew up to the stop at Madison Square—without a lurch for once—she got up to go and handed him her visiting card. "My evenings are Thursdays. If you have nothing better to do, come by at eight." Gathering her skirts in her gloved hand, she stepped down to the curb on immaculately-booted feet and, opening her umbrella, walked off into a lightly falling snow.

Her name, embossed on the card in gold, floral calligraphy, was Mme. Adele Averbach, and she lived on Thompson Street south of Washington Square. Claude was too excited to go sit in a stultifying lecture hall, so he returned home to get his skates, wanting to feel the cold wind on his face as he sped across the ice, with his long scarf flying out behind him.

When he came back down the stairs in a heavy sweater, a neighbor girl named Elizabeth Cooper poked her head out of the parlor. Ever since she had been a little girl she found excuses to hang around pestering him. She was fifteen now, but to Claude, Elizabeth was still the brat she had always been. Seeing his skates, she asked if she could go too, but he made an excuse and, slamming the door, ran down the steps to the street.

Over the years, the Coopers next door were the only neighbors the Endicotts had ever gotten involved with. Kindly Mrs. Cooper, far from being put off by Fanny's "vagueness"—as most of the neighbors were—sometimes volunteered to be company for her when Miss Swindon was ailing. Professor Cooper, who taught history at New York University on Washington Square, had been active in the fight against slavery before the war and had tried to interest Tom in the movement. But while Tom sympathized with the abolitionists, he couldn't bring himself to join any more organizations after his disillusionment with temperance. Nevertheless, he had accompanied the professor to Cooper Union in 1860 to hear an address by Abraham Lincoln, then one of the presidential hopefuls of the new Republican Party, which had a liberal platform which appealed to the professor

When the Civil War broke out four years before, Professor Cooper was called to Washington to work in the Lincoln administration. While he was away, his wife, also devoted to reformist causes, organized a group of neighborhood women, including Veronica Endicott, to knit wrist warmers, scarves, and gloves for the troops. Though several years younger, her daughter Elizabeth had befriended the reclusive Veronica, and was often in the house next door. What Mrs. Cooper did not know was that the main attraction for her daughter was the Endicott son, Claude.

The war had brought Tom more business than he could cope with. His printer's devil was drafted into the army and with the old man who assisted him retiring, he persuaded Albert Cogswell to work with him full-time on the presses. The Indian shantytown that Albert lived in had been torn down when the piers were built and he had moved to another squatters' area up in the Central Park. Albert had discovered photography and built a darkroom for himself in a corner of the shop. He had even put together a camera from one of Lumière's diagrams. But there was little time for that with so much work coming in—announcements of war charities, drives for winter clothing for the troops, and warnings against "copperheads"—southern sympathizers. They also turned out folders for the government on how to save on scarce food items like sugar and cooking oil needed for the manufacture of munitions, or what the populace should do in the case of enemy invasion—for a while in 1863, Confederate troops had come as close as Pennsylvania until they were pushed back at the battle of Gettysburg.

That was the year of New York's draft riots, ignited not only, as Claude believed, because the poor resented the rich being able to buy themselves out of the army, but also over having to go to war for the liberation of the slaves who would become rivals for their jobs. Thousands of immigrants surged up from the slums, setting fires, pillaging stores, tearing up horsecar tracks, and chopping down telegraph poles. Several city blocks went up in flames. Molly Hanlon's younger son, Timothy, was part of a mob that was smashing windows and looting—and chasing anyone black they could find on the streets. Across from the Jefferson Market police station, a Negro was hung from a lamppost, while the cops hid in the basement to save themselves from the mob that tried to break down the door,

Patrick heard the uproar from Shamrock Alley and saw the light in the sky from the flames, but there was nothing he could do to keep his brother out of it. He had worked hard to hold the family together as best he could, but with his mother deteriorating from drink, Shamrock Alley was no place for his little sister Nora to grow up in, and when she was twelve he found her a job as maid with a family on St. Luke's Place near the Protestant church.

Molly died in the summer of 1864, and Patrick, just past his seventeenth birthday, asked Hester to wait for him and enlisted in the army. By winter he was a foot soldier with General Sherman's forces, poised on the border of Georgia with no Confederate troops left to stop them between there and the sea.

13

Claude went to Mme. Averbach's on her next Thursday. It was nearly nine before he got there, but he hadn't been able to get away earlier. First, there was dinner to get through, which had been delayed because his father came home late from the shop. Then, he didn't want the family to see him slipping out in his best clothes and have to explain where he was going, so he had to keep to his room until his mother and Miss Swindon retired and his father was occupied in his study.

His heart was beating fast as he tramped through the snow to Washington Square. Mme. Averbach's town house on Thompson Street was much grander than the Endicotts', with tall French windows and slim, fluted columns on either side of the classic doorway supporting a fanlight arc of stained glass.

A servant hung Claude's hat and coat on a rack in the hall already bulging with wraps, and showed him into a crowded drawing room illuminated by the dramatic chiaroscuro of candelabra. It took a moment for his eyes to adjust.

Incense hung in the air as if it were a temple. The guests appeared to be talking animatedly in the shimmering candlelight that threw faces into silhouette, yet the sound in the room was strangely muffled, punctuated now and then by high laughter like the shattering of glass.

Mme. Averbach, in a green taffeta gown emphasizing her tiny waist, detached herself from a small group and came up to him. Emeralds glittered at her throat and from her lavishly piled hair. She took his hand. "The young man from the omnibus! I'm so glad you came. Do tell me your name again, I want you to meet some of my friends." She waved a gloved hand holding a fan in their direction.

After the introductions—Claude was too embarrassed to catch any of their names—she said to them, "Didn't I tell you?"

The group studied him curiously while he squirmed.

"You're absolutely right, Adele," said a cherubic man in a flamboyant red velvet jacket. "He's the spitting image."

Mme. Averbach turned to Claude with her beautiful smile. "It's Edgar Allan Poe we're comparing you with." But noticing how uncomfortable he was as the center of attention, she quickly apologized. "How thoughtless I am. I've let our obsession with Poe make me forget you're just in from the cold. Oliver"—she tapped the cherubic man with her fan—"why don't you take our new friend over to the fire and see that he gets some refreshment."

"Quoth the raven, at your service, madam," he replied with a mock bow, and to Claude's relief, led him away.

"We'd all die of boredom in New York without her," the cherubic man named Oliver said, his little eyes darting around the candlelit room as he sidestepped through the guests. "She's made it almost like Paris here. You know, Edgar Poe is all the rage over there." He chattered on about things Claude had never heard about—bohemianism and Baudelaire.

They waited at a crowded buffet table where liveried servants were dispensing drinks.

"Adele said you were a poet, didn't she? I'm a composer myself. You must show me some of your work. Perhaps I can set it to music."

Claude tried to tell him he was not a poet at all, but Oliver dismissed this with a wave of a plump hand. "Anyone who looks as much like the young Poe as you do has to be a poet."

It wasn't only Oliver's red jacket that was unusual, but also his dark, velvet trousers and big floppy tie. With his fat, red cheeks and impish eyes, he looked the picture of an overgrown school boy. Claude thought that even his voice was most peculiar as he spoke. "People say my songs are even better than Stephen Foster's. We're both fugitives from the South, you know. Did you hear that he died of drink at Bellevue Hospital last month?" He handed Claude a glass of a milky-green liquid.

Claude looked at it uncertainly.

"Don't worry," Oliver said, his little eyes twinkling, "it's only absinthe. Baudelaire couldn't have written a line of The Flowers of Evil without it. Some say it drives you mad." He threw back his head theatrically and drained his glass.

Claude took a sip. The liquid had a bitter licorice taste.

"Oh, go ahead. One glass won't destroy your brain."

Claude held his breath and drank it down, and Oliver immediately had their glasses refilled.

As they came up to the roaring fire, the absinthe was beginning to whirl in his head.

Oliver was pointing out a painting over the mantelpiece. "Isn't it a perfect likeness?"

Claude didn't understand. The picture was of a reclining female nude with a blue satin ribbon around her neck and a turbaned blackamoor waving an ostrich fan over her—as explicit as anything his father's friend Albert Cogswell painted for barroom walls.

"It's Adele, don't you see? But then, who bothers to notice a face when the clothes are off?" Oliver tittered.

Daze by the absinthe, Claude stared at it, as the chubby man told him that Edouard Manet had painted it in Paris. Was it possible that his aristocratic hostess, bending toward her guests so graciously across the room, had let herself be painted in the nude? And more unbelievably, was displaying it on her drawing room wall for all the world to see? His face burned from the strange liquor he was not used to.

Oliver was chattering on about how he met Adele in Paris long before she sat for Manet, and what a pity it was that the Civil War had forced both of them—like so many other Americans—to come home, but a good part of her money was invested in Southern cotton and all of his own was. "It was not easy for her to come back here, when you think of the scandal. But as far as that goes, I'll never be able to show my face in Charleston again. I was involved in quite a little scandal of my own." He looked at Claude expectantly, hoping to be prompted to further revelations.

But Claude, who felt mesmerized by the opulently painted canvas, only asked what had happened to Mme. Averbach.

"Adele?" Oliver was visibly disappointed but he quickly recovered. "You didn't know about the trial? It made headlines in all the papers—but of course you're too young to remember and I, alas, am not." He told Claude that Mme. Averbach had been forced by her parents into a marriage with a department store tycoon. "You know," he whispered, "Adele is Jewish, but absolutely blue-blood Jewish. She and her husband simply loathed each other from the start, and before the honeymoon was over he took a lover. But I have to hand it to her, so did she." He tittered.

Mme. Averbach had left her group and was now talking with a tall, well-dressed Negro who was obviously not a servant. Claude wondered if there was any experience she had not tasted.

One summer night at their estate in Saratoga, Oliver was saying, Adele was awakened by a noise on the grounds and, with a little pearl-handled revolver in her hand, went to investigate. How could she know the shadowy figure in the shrubbery was her husband coming home drunk?

There was a spectacular trial, and though she was exonerated, the result was that it was impossible for her to appear in New York society again. "She had to exile herself to Paris, poor dear."

A group of latecomers entered the room, distracting Oliver from his revelations by their loud talk and laughter. A stout man in the middle of them was holding forth in a cloud of cigar smoke. To Claude, it seemed as if the room was stretching away and the newcomers were at an impossibly remote distance from him. He put a hand against the fireplace to steady himself.

"It's Mina," cried Oliver. "Mina Hunneker!"

The imposing figure with the cigar who had arrived was not a man at all. Claude's head was spinning. It was a woman dressed as a man, her hair pulled back tight.

"Come!" Oliver snapped his fingers at him. "You've got to meet her. She's Adele's best friend and the top real estate agent in New York." According to Oliver, the canny businesswoman had made a fortune predicting where the city would spread. Although everyone laughed at the idea that New York could possibly expand any further, she was buying up farms at the far end of Manhattan.

Claude was petrified at the prospect of being face to face with such a formidable creature, but Oliver was pulling him forward. He almost tripped over a low divan where three people looked up, their faces macabre in the firelight.

Surrounded by an audience of male admirers, Mina Hunneker, the hearty woman dressed as a man, had planted herself directly in the brilliant light of a candelabrum. "These suffragettes are the bunk," she was declaring in a deep voice. "All that ranting and raving. They're just rattling their chains."

Her entourage of men laughed and applauded. Oliver danced about trying to get her attention, but she waved him off with her cigar and went on with her diatribe.

"There's no getting at Mina when she's on her soapbox." Oliver leaned closer to Claude. "Don't tell Adele I told you, but she and Mina slept together once."

The words settled slowly in Claude's befogged mind and he tried to put them together.

"Just to see what it was like, of course. After all, what can women do with each other?" Again, Oliver tittered.

Claude didn't understand what he was talking about, but didn't care. The absinthe had submerged him in deep water and he was being swept along by the currents. It was all so different here, so grotesque— and presided over by the lady in the green gown, the magician who had cast this spell. He looked around for her and instead focused woozily on the chalk-white face of a woman with eyes like unblinking nuggets. She seemed to be wearing some kind of nightdress.

Oliver was jumping around from one absurdity to another, but broke off when he saw who Claude was gaping at. "That's Tatiana. Ethereal, isn't she? Never says a word. But what a dancer!" He called over to her, "Tatiana angel, your costume is most fetching!"

The chalk-white face gave a grimace that might have been a smile, then quickly composed itself, the nugget eyes as blank as before.

"What's wrong with her eyes?" Claude asked, as Oliver propelled him back toward the buffet.

"Oh, that's belladonna and lord knows what else she's taken tonight." Oliver stepped over the legs of a man, sprawled on cushions on the floor, who appeared to be asleep. "But what can you expect? She's supposed to be the granddaughter of the Marquis de Sade."

Claude barely knew where he was any more. Fragments of talk came to his ears from people around him, about seances and alchemists and Omar Khayyam. Under hanging braziers of incense, people were lounging on divans and cushions, nibbling sweetmeats set out on brass trays. In one corner, several people were puffing at the serpentine stems of a water pipe, the smoke of the burning hashish bubbling through the water as they filled their lungs. He'd only read about hookahs before in a travel book by Burton who had stolen into Mecca disguised as a Moslem.

"Claude, are you there?" Oliver's voice seemed to be coming through a tunnel. "It's time we got our seats for the entertainment."

Servants were setting candelabra in a semicircle in front of a drapery of purple brocade at one end of the room and people were pushing their seats into the center.

Mme. Averbach swam into view talking to the handsome black man, the jewels on her bosom and in her hair flashing in the candlelight. Claude felt that once he had seen her nakedness, but how was that possible?

Then he was sitting cross-legged on a cushion at the rear of the audience. He looked around for Oliver, but only a stranger sat beside him, apparently bemused by a servant twirling a dark substance on a pin over the flame of a candle. When the substance had the consistency of taffy, the servant scraped it into a long, carved ivory pipe with a glowing coal in its bowl and handed it to the stranger. The stranger inhaled deeply, then passed the pipe over to Claude.

He took it without question. He was being offered one exotic experience after another, and considering the ordinariness of his life until now, he saw no reason to resist.

The smoke he inhaled had an odd sweetness totally unlike tobacco. He held it in his lungs, and after exhaling, sucked in a deeper draught that seared his throat like cold fire.

The stranger beside him took away the pipe. "That will do for your initiation, young man." The voice was so remote it seemed disembodied.

The guests hushed as Mme. Averbach appeared in front of the candelabra. Holding out her arms to the audience, she announced that the entertainment would begin with an original ballet entitled "Hymn to Emancipation."

As a harp began to strum ascending arpeggios, the girl with the nugget eyes waltzed onto the stage, her white gown diaphanous in the candlelight. Veils on her wrists floated languidly as she moved her arrns. Claude could hardly believe that the wraith had transformed herself into such a shimmering butterfly.

The next moment a black male dancer leaped into the light, startlingly naked except for plum-colored tights, and began stalking her erotically. It was Mme. Averbach's black companion.

"Of course, I'm all for Emancipation," Oliver, who had appeared from nowhere, whispered in his ear, "but I have to confess that I miss the old days behind the barn with the slaves."

The girl was pirouetting away from her black pursuer, just eluding his grasp. Then, as if hypnotized, she fluttered on her toes in one spot, helplessly waiting for him.

Claude had never seen anything like it. In the real world it was forbidden. It might end in a lynching.

With the harp rippling to a crescendo, the black man pounced, lifting the haunted girl by the waist. He whirled her around, her head and arms thrown back so that the veils at her wrists brushed the candle flames, until at the music's climax he bent her over in a long kiss full on her mouth.

Claude couldn't breathe as the glistening black body covered the white body. Amid the bravos and applause that followed, Mme. Averbach came forward to embrace them both.

He asked Oliver if the black dancer could possibly be Mme. Averbach's lover. He felt his words coming out like beads widely spaced on a necklace. He was so disoriented he wouldn't be surprised at anything any more.

"Oh, my, no," Oliver said loudly. "Adele is between lovers now. Antoine is Mina's property. She picks him up every night in her carriage after his performance at Purdy's Theater."

"The woman with the cigar?" It was hard for Claude to believe.

"Don't be fooled by her male drag. That one is all woman."

In front of the velvet drapery Mme. Averbach was introducing a recitation of "Ulalume" by Edgar Allan Poe, who she said had once lived nearby on Third Street and to whose spirit the evening was dedicated.

All the candelabra were extinguished and for a moment all was darkness. Then a cadaverous-looking man appeared holding a single candle that illuminated his face weirdly from below. Oliver told Claude that the man had been in jail for five years on a charge of sodomy, adding wickedly, "And he's married with six children, to boot!"

Against a series of bell-like notes from the harp, the elocutionist began the verses of the poem in sepulchral tones. A trance fell over the listeners. The candle wavered and shadows hovered like night phantoms. The ghost of the dead poet seemed to be in the room, wailing out its morbid anguish.

Claude looked around as arabesques of shadow crept toward him from the walls. The magic of the evening turned to menace. Oliver's hassock was empty. On the other side of him the stranger who had given him the opium pipe looked like Satan. He had to get out before he screamed.

With the demons almost upon him, he staggered out into the hall where he searched in a panic through the mass of coats for his own. He was trying to get his arms in the sleeves, when he heard a rustle of skirts and a voice whispering, "Wait, Claude," and Adele Averbach's fan touched his shoulder. An apparition of shimmering emeralds, high cheekbones, almond eyes floated before him. "Come tomorrow for tea," he heard. Then, as the mournful cadences droned on in the drawing room, she vanished, leaving behind the words "Promise me" hanging in the air with the scent of jasmine.

He stepped out into a wintry night. Bells of horse sleighs jingled as they clip-clopped by on the snowy street. The stars overhead cut the night sky like diamonds. He crunched down the icy steps. His panic was gone and he took great ecstatic breaths of frosty air.

14

Claude hardly slept that night. At breakfast in the morning, he couldn't bear to listen to his father's boasting about General Grant's latest victory at Bull Run as if he had been right there himself. What did wars have to do with the important things of life? He felt sorry for his father, who never knew what it was to be young. His mother, who seldom went out of the house, had missed out on life entirely. His sister, Veronica, sitting across from him nibbling her toast absentmindedly as she stared out the window at the snowy backyard, was forever lost in a dreamworld. None of them had ever been alive like he was.

He could tell Miss Swindon knew something was up, the way her beady eyes watched him as she sipped her insipid camomile tea. The old maid would drop her teeth if she ever saw anything like the world he had seen the night before.

Just as he pushed back his half-eaten porridge and got up to go, Elizabeth Cooper, who was staying over while her mother was away visiting Professor Cooper in Washington, startled him by asking out of the blue what he thought of Edgar Allan Poe. Did she have some kind of uncanny intuition? But her schoolgirl eyes were looking back guileless as ever, as she explained she was writing a theme on Poe for school.

With the prospect of tea at Mme. Averbach's that afternoon, going to classes that day was out of the question. Instead, Claude went to the college library to read up on the legendary poet he was supposed to resemble. In a faded daguerreotype he examined the hypnotic eyes that were reputed to have looked straight into hell, and tried to imagine how he would look in the same cape and string necktie.

He even tried to learn a few lines of "Ulalume" by heart, but the rustle of taffeta and the scent of jasmine kept getting in the way, so that he finally gave up.

On his way back downtown, the streets were so jammed with Christmas shoppers added to the wartime congestion that the horsecar was continually held up. The stores and hotels were festooned with holiday decorations, and as the horsecar passed through Union Square, carolers in front of Delmonico's were singing "Adeste Fidelis."

When Claude was shown into her drawing room later that afternoon, Mme. Averbach put down her pen and rose from her writing desk. Her mauve, watered-silk dress with ruffles falling away at the elbows shimmered in the late afternoon light, a light that gave her skin a soft glow and brought out golden tints in her long, auburn curls pinned up at the back of her head. She looked smaller than she had the night before at her salon, more delicate.

"I'm so glad you've come," she said, advancing in a swish of petticoats and extending her hand. "I've been doing my holiday cards, but I have to admit I've been thinking of you all along."

He flushed with bashful pleasure.

Tea was already laid in front of the fire. He started to sit down on a Venetian chair across from her.

"Oh, please, not so far away." His hostess patted the cushion beside her on the sofa.

In the fading light, the naked figure in the painting above the fireplace seemed to emerge from the canvas and hover in the air, as Mme. Averbach poured the tea. Adding a few drops of crème de menthe, she handed him his cup. "Did you enjoy yourself last evening?"

He told her it had been a revelation to him. "I've always felt like a fish out of water until last night."

She laughed as if he had said something witty. "I'm glad you felt at home in our little pond. My friends were all enchanted with you." Her hazel eyes with tiny golden flecks watched him over the edge of her teacup.

He glowed. The enigmatic face in the painting also seemed to be reflecting her approval of him.

"But don't you want to smoke?" She held out to him a small silver box filled with slim paper tubes of tobacco.

His father had read aloud at breakfast an editorial in the Gazette that denounced the cigarette, a recent import from the Orient, as effete and immoral. He took one, and to his delight, Mme. Averbach also took one herself. Then, after lighting their cigarettes with a taper from the fire she leaned back, her classic profile outlined against the light of the bay window, and exhaled a thin stream of blue smoke into the air.

He had hoped there might be something like this waiting for him in New Orleans, but never dreamed it would fall into his lap right here at home. He wanted to tell her how glad he was to be there but didn't want to sound clumsy. "I like your portrait very much," he said at last, daring to refer to something so intimate, so naked. "I think the composition has classical balance." It was a phrase he remembered from some lecture.

For a moment he thought she was going to laugh at him, but she didn't. She didn't appear to find it pretentious. "I'm glad you like it, but you know, it's not just a portrait of me. It's the way a genius of the brush responded to me. Sitting for M. Manet was as fulfilling an experience as love."

No woman had ever spoken so frankly to Claude. "If you don't mind my saying so," he said, "I think Mr. Manet caught your true spirit." He blushed and puffed at his cigarette, not daring to inhale, afraid he might start coughing and make a bigger fool of himself.

"You have such insight, Claude!" She leaned toward him almost girlishly. "That's exactly why I have the painting hanging in my drawing room. I know that some people might not approve, but then don't ordinary people misunderstand everything?"

He was flattered that she didn't include him with ordinary people, and even considered him worthy enough to take an interest in.

"I don't want the world to see me only as a fashion plate," Mme. Averbach said, dismissing her elegant dress with a sweep of her hand. "These clothes falsify what I really am."

Claude protested that he thought she looked beautiful in them.

She smiled. "Naturally, I do what I can to make myself presentable, but they're encumbering just the same. Ideally, I believe, women should wear simple draperies like the Greeks, garments that move with the body rather than distort and conceal. I can understand why many men seek out the company of lower-class women who are less bound by fashion and formality."

Claude was having a hard time following her. Why would any man prefer a lower-class woman to someone as refined as she? His cigarette had burned down and he didn't know how to get rid of it.

"It's such a pleasure talking to you, Claude," she said, tossing her cigarette casually into the fire. "Young as you are, you understand me. Some people might think I display the painting out of vanity, but that's not it at all. I do it quite simply to remind men that I am as much of a woman as those in the lower classes they run after. That painting ought to show them." She laughed and refilled his cup.

He tried to laugh with her, but he was uncomfortable.

She handed him back his tea. "It was only when I woke up to the fact that the morality society expects a woman of my class to follow is artificial and stifling that I was able to throw it off." She pressed his hand. "I wonder if you understand what I'm talking about?"

He was confused. "I'm not sure I've ever thought about such things, Mme. Averbach."

"Adele," she corrected. "And it's high time you did." Leaning closer, she said softly, "In that painting I am as God made me. Does it please you?"

"Yes," he choked out.

Her eyes gleamed with yellow glints in the gathering twilight. "Then why don't you kiss me?"

His confidence shattered. He had never been with a woman before in his life and he was scared to death. He stumbled off the sofa onto his knees, groping for her hand. "I would do anything in the world for you...but it's all so new...."

She stopped him with a finger on his lips. Bending forward, she embraced him tenderly, her breasts beneath the silk pressed against his cheek. "My sweet boy, you mustn't think I'm making any demands on you. We've only just met. You'll come to my Thursdays and I'll play the piano for you at tea. Do you like Chopin?"

He was comforted by the warmth of her bosom. Her jasmine scent was intoxicating. His arms slipped around her and he looked up to find her waiting lips....

Afterward, as they lay in the glow of firelight, Claude Endicott let his fingers run over the flawless body of the odalisque who had stepped out of a painting and made him a man.

The following Thursday he was accepted at Adele's as her protegé and treated as a regular by her circle. Oliver bustled around presenting him as the young dauphin. Mina Hunneker and the cadaverous elocutionist invited him to take part in a tableau they were arranging as a birthday surprise for Adele. And he shared another pipe with the opium smoker. This time no feeling of menace disturbed his euphoria, as a guest played impromptus by Schubert on the Beckstein, while a cageful of canaries was released into the room to fly about trilling.

In her bed that night, Adele held Claude's face between her hands, looking deep into his eyes and said, "You must be careful of opium, my darling. The others are experienced and able to handle it, but it can so easily take you into a world where I can't follow. Believe me, I've seen it happen before."

Holding her close, he scoffed at the notion that anything was ever going to come between them, but the whole next day he resisted using the new, inlaid-ivory pipe the opium smoker had given him.

He visited her every afternoon at teatime, all the while letting his family believe he was still attending his classes at Columbia. When he left his house in the morning, he spent the day with her friends, often drowsing away the hours with the opium pipe until time to see her.

On Christmas Eve his father was visibly annoyed when he excused himself from the family circle around the candlelit Christmas tree—the Coopers were over, the professor having come up from Washington for the holidays—and went to Mina Hunneker's flat on Twenty-third Street to rehearse Adele's birthday tableaux.

And shortly after the New Year of 1865, in Mme. Averbach's drawing room, Claude wore a white robe as the central figure in a series of living pictures entitled, "The Assumption of Edgar Allan Poe into Heaven." Oliver, Mina, and the others in purple, portrayed the Olympians of the Arts welcoming him through the celestial portals. Adele watched from a thronelike chair and said afterward that she felt the poet himself had been in the room.

They decked Claude in garlands and at the end of the evening led him upstairs, the dancer with the chalk-white face strewing rose petals before him, while the cadaverous elocutionist recited, "*0 moon of my delight that knows no wane....*"

As the procession entered the flower-filled bedroom, Adele awaited him in the identical prose of the painting, naked on her bed of white satin with the blue ribbon round her neck.

The group left the lovers in each other's arms, and from outside the door serenaded them with the Bridal Chorus from "Lohengrin," before departing.

As February passed and the warm days of March started melting the piles of dirty snow in the narrow streets, Claude lay in his room on the evenings when he was not at Adele's and sank into the delicious half-sleep the opium smoke induced. No longer was he a victim of the mundane world that had so bored him and driven him into empty fantasy. He didn't need fantasies any more. Reality was in Adele's encompassing arms, and that was superior to anything the world had to offer.

In April, Perry Street was again filled with the scent of lilacs from the garden of the old house across from the Endicotts'. It was finally being demolished to make way for a new row of houses. Sledgehammers were smashing down the inner walls, and timbers were flying out of the upper windows. A team of horses strained against their harness to pull down the sagging outbuildings.

One afternoon, Adele canceled their rendezvous because her dressmaker was coming, but Claude couldn't keep himself from going over anyway for the joy of seeing her lovely body being fitted with silks and satins. As he climbed the stoop to her front door, he anticipated her mock distress at his barging unannounced into her feminine world, and then her impatience at having to stand still until the dressmaker unpinned her, so that she could throw herself into his arms.

When the street door was opened, he pushed past the servant who tried to stop him, and reached the top of the stairs before it came to him that there had been a man's hat and cane on the table below. As he hesitated in the hallway, Adele's bedroom door opened and she came out tying the sash of the scarlet peignoir she always wore at their trysts, and demanded to know why he was there.

"Didn't I tell you not to come until this evening?" she said with unexpected coldness. Her body musk came through the jasmine scent.

He could only stare ar her.

Then, taking pity on his evident shock and confusion, she said in a kindlier voice, "You know, my dear, neither of us ever made promises...."

Downstairs, as the servant closed the door after him, Claude's only thought was his pipe of opium, to blot it all out. He paid no attention to the church bells from all over town suddenly filling the air. But at the bottom of the steps in front of the house chubby Oliver rushed up holding a copy of the Herald with the banner headline, LEE SURRENDERS.

"It's over, Claude! Oh, lordie, Grant's done it!"—his voice was shaking—"I'm a Southerner myself, and if they cut my tongue out I don't care, but this is the happiest day of my life."

Claude looked at him blankly.

The chubby man stopped, immediately surmising what had happened. "My dear boy, it's dreadful for you I know, but it had to come sooner or later. We all knew it would." He put a plump arm around Claude's shoulders. "We've all been through it with her and you have to be grateful for what you get. There's a law of nature—I had to learn it myself the hard way—the strong devour the weak, and she's stronger than any of us."

Claude walked away without a word, oblivious to the people pouring into the streets, the noise in the air as the city went into a frenzy of jubilation. Hysterical newsboys were yelling out the headlines, as their extras were snatched up. Strangers were swigging from bottles and passing them from hand to hand. An accordionist was playing in front of a French restaurant, the waitresses dancing with the passersby. On Washington Square even the rich had come out of their townhouses along with the servants to join the festivities.

Claude moved like a phantom through the jubilant crowds at Jefferson Market, where soldiers were kissing every girl in sight and whirling them around. From every church in the city, bells went on clanging out the universal joy that peace had come at last.

But his pipe was the only thing that mattered to him.

When, finally, he got home and shut the door, the house was empty. Even his mother was out. The rooms were still and joyless in contrast to the frantic activity of the streets. It suited him that way. In his room on the third floor he fumbled with his opium paraphernalia that he kept in the drawer of the bedside table, and soon was sucking in searing lungfuls of smoke.

But the oblivion he craved did not come. His head throbbed from the roar of cannon going off in the harbor and the shriek of ships' whistles in the river, the popping of firecrackers and people shouting in the street below—and everywhere the infernal clanging of the bells, bells, bells. Claude dropped the pipe and lay staring into nothingness.

When the family came home that evening after having attended a thanksgiving service at St. Luke's, Tom Endicott glanced through his mail, which he had overlooked in the excitement, and found a letter from Columbia College informing him that his son had been dropped from the rolls, not having attended lectures since December or taken any exams.

At his wit's end over his good-for-nothing son, Tom took a lamp and stormed upstairs.

He found Claude stretched out on his bed in the dark, his arm over his eyes against the lamplight. What in God's name was the he always lying around for? There was a terrible smell in the room—as if the furnace were leaking fumes through the register. But the furnace wasn't on. Putting the lamp down on the desk, Tom banged up the window to let in some air.

"I suppose it was too much to expect you to be here to go to church with us on this tremendous occasion?" He held his voice steady. "But to actually drop out of college without a word to me! Is that what I bought you out of the army for? Boys without a fraction of your privileges have been dying like flies for four years while you've done exactly nothing."

Claude didn't answer.

"Don't you have anything to say to me, you damn sniveler?" Tom gritted his teeth to hold back his rage.

His arm over his eyes, his son still didn't look at him. "Speak, damn you!"

Claude mumbled, "I know I'm a failure, you don't have to tell me."

"Don't try to wiggle out of it!" Tom's years of frustration overwhelmed him and he began shouting. "I've worked my life away for the lot of you— you, your mother, and your sister. All I wanted was what every man wants, a reasonable family life—and what did I get?" He was stomping around the room, clutching his head. "... a family of misfits! Your mother's the worst of the lot. She's sat there and made a fool out of me for twenty years!"

Claude sat up and yelled. "Don't you say a word about her! You've never cared about any of us. If I'm a failure as a son, what kind of a father do you think you've been? You're nothing but a cold fish!"

Tom was stunned and sank down on the stool in front of the desk. The boy had never raised his voice to him before.

To Claude, his father suddenly looked prematurely old and beaten, the lamplight etching the lines into his face. He threw himself back on the pillow, more miserable than ever. "I'm sorry I said that."

But his son's unexpected denunciation had knocked the wind out of Tom. "You told me you didn't want to go to college in the first place," he said. "I shouldn't have pushed it." Then he added, wistfully, "God knows, I always wanted us to be friends, with your mother ill and Veronica off in her own world."

It was the first time Claude had ever seen the loneliness in his father, and it made him feel that this was someone he could talk to after all. "I quit school because of a woman, pa," he said, and in a rush he poured out the story of Adele and what had just happened. "I don't think I'll ever get over it."

Father and son were both silent. Outside, the noise of the victory celebration was dying down. Down by the Battery, fireworks were bursting in the sky.

It was Tom who broke the silence. "You'll find a way to live with it. I did, when it happened to me."

Claude raised his head and looked at his father.

Tom nodded. "That's right, the same thing happened to me once. I know how you feel." Relieved at being able to talk about something he had kept bottled up for so long, he told about Molly and his illegitimate son, Patrick, in Shamrock Alley, as Claude sat cross-legged, listening intently.

When his father had finished the story, Claude thought for a moment. "He was the boy who ran into the print shop that day, wasn't he?"

"That was him. I've heard he's just back from the war, wounded in the leg at Savannah by a sniper the day Sherman reached the sea."

"Have you seen him?"

"No. I'd like to, but I'm afraid he wouldn't want anything to do with me."

It was incredible. A brother he didn't even know about. This man in front of him—his father—was not as ordinary as he had always thought. "I could go see him, couldn't I, pa?" he said.

Tom considered this. "I suppose so." Then his face lit up. "Why, yes, what a good idea. You go see him!"

It was after eleven before Tom finally picked up the lamp and said good night to his son.

15

As he lay in the darkness, Claude went over and over the extraordinary scene with his father. It was the most amazing confession he'd ever heard. But as the hours of the night wore on, the image of Adele returned to torment him, and in the morning, more hopeless than ever, he saw no reason to get up to face the world without her. The singing of birds and the brilliant sun coming through the drapes only seemed to mock him.

In the kitchen Veronica was preparing a breakfast tray for her brother, having heard the loud voices the night before and knowing how he was always crushed after one of their father's onslaughts.

When Elizabeth Cooper dashed in from next door—she had come to sit with Mrs. Endicott because Miss Swindon was once again indisposed—she volunteered to take the tray up to Claude. She was wearing her school uniform—middy blouse with white sailor collar and navy-blue pleated skirt.

Outside his room, with her heart fluttering, Elizabeth took a deep breath, gave the door a tap, and walked in with a bright "Good morning." Her sleeping prince, who had never paid the slightest attention to her, was lying there with the quilts pulled up to his nose, and from the look on his pale face, utterly out of sorts. She set down the tray and hurried to pull open the drapes, hoping the beautiful spring day might cheer him up.

But his eyes only squinched up against the sunlight, as she set to work plumping up his pillows, letting him know that she was not going to be put off that easily. He scowled at being forced to sit up and was not mollified when she poured out a cup of steaming coffee and handed it to him.

"You might feel better if you drank it," she said, sitting down on a chair and gazing in adoration at the truculent youth with sleep-matted hair. "Go on, drink it."

He took a gulp of the hot coffee, and immediately spit it back, looking at her indignantly.

Thrilled by the long-lashed eyes in the pale face finally noticing her, Elizabeth leaned over briskly to put a napkin in the saucer where coffee had slopped over. "You oughtn't to be such an old grouch, you know. The war's over, it's spring, and if you looked outside you'd see that the whole world is happy."

"Who cares?" Claude muttered, sipping his coffee.

Satisfied at having gotten a response out of him, she sat back. "Why are you so grumpy today?"

He took another look at her, annoyed at her schoolgirl curiosity. "I wish you'd go away. There's nothing the matter."

Elizabeth was not about to retreat, she was enjoying it all too much. She crossed her arms. "Of course something's the matter. You've been acting queerly since just before Christmas."

He looked at her in alarm, nearly spilling his coffee again. "Have you been spying on me?"

"I have not! It's perfectly obvious that something's been going on. You've been putting on your best clothes every day, you've let your hair grow awfully long—why, I don't know—and you've been going around with your head in the clouds." She reached back to straighten the collar of her middy blouse, outlining her young breasts.

Claude was almost embarrassed to notice she was not quite the pesky child any more. Her hair that had always been in pigtails was now tied back loosely, and her green eyes were beautiful. He turned away. "Well, that's all over."

She took his cup and poured him more coffee, in despair that anyone would ever take her seriously. "I know you think I'm still a child. But I'm sixteen now and I'm getting pretty tired of looking on at other people's lives, wishing I had one of my own."

"Oh, yeah?" Claude said. "What would you say if told you I'd been carrying on with a married woman?"

It was the most extraordinary statement anybody had ever made to her. Elizabeth didn't know what to think, it was simply incredible. "That never occurred to me, I must say...."

Claude leaned forward in bed, his elbows on his knees. "I shouldn't have told you, I guess, but you may as well know what a horse's ass I am." And as the girl listened, her heart pounding, he told her how Adele Averbach had used him. When he was finished with the story, he closed his eyes against the pain of it all.

In a state of confusion, Elizabeth went to the window. Below, an ordinary street scene, housewives buying vegetables from a pushcart peddler, the half-demolished old farmhouse opposite quiet because of the holiday for the end of the war. "How awful for you," she said at last, keeping her back to him to hide her burning face.

"I shocked you, didn't I?" He was afraid he had gone too far.

She turned around quickly. "Certainly not! I've heard much more scandalous things than that." Still unable to look at him, she picked up the breakfast tray. She had to get out of there. She had spent over a half an hour in his room alone with him. She started for the door. "I wish there was something I could say to help you, but I'm afraid...."

"Don't go!"

"I can't stay right now."

"But I need someone to talk to."

"I have to get down to your mother." But she stopped at the door. "Perhaps...if you like...we might meet in Abingdon Square this afternoon." Amazed at her own daring, she didn't wait for a reply.

When she was gone, Claude opened the drawer of the bedside table, fitted together the sections of his inlaid ivory pipe, and lit the candle to soften the resin.

While Elizabeth sat reading to Mrs. Endicott, she got over her shock and became used to the idea of Claude being part of a world of depravity. How right it was that the young man she adored had done something so wickedly romantic and, most wonderful of all, who could ever have imagined that he would take her into his confidence?

By the time they were sitting together under the flowering elms in the park at the end of Bleecker Street, she was proud of him for being someone who wasn't afraid of life and actually did daring things.

She asked him about all the details of the affair, unable to hear enough about the lurid candlelit atmosphere of the artistic soirées. "Opium!" she cried, when he told her about the drugs some of the people used there. "How decadent! Did you try it?"

Flushing, Claude denied that he had.

"What a pity," Elizabeth giggled, "I don't think I would have been able to resist." She looked around at the commonplace mothers and children in the park. "Oh, Claude, I do envy you. All my life I've wanted to know painters and writers and people like that. I'd give anything for even a glimpse of Tatiana and that colored dancer."

"Well, it's all over for me now. I'll never go back there again." He posed moodily, imagining the picture of Poe.

"You're thinking about her again, aren't you? There are other women in the world, try to remember that."

"You don't know what she was like," he said. "She was more than beautiful. Every man who ever met her fell in love with her. She's a Circe turning men into pigs." He choked, overcome with self-pity.

"Well, you've got to put her out of your mind," she said in a practical tone. "Go back to your studies and make something of yourself. Someday she'll be sorry for what she did when she sees how famous you are."

He told her it was too late for that. Unfortunately, he had been thrown out of Columbia.

She thought for a moment. "Then why not get a job in a bookstore. You like books, don't you? And you'd meet all kinds of people."

"I could never do that," he said. "I can't talk to people. They make me nervous.

"But what about at Mme. Averbach's salon?"

"That was different."

She thought again. "I know how hard it's been for you and Veronica growing up, your poor mother ailing and all. Of course, it's a far more romantic atmosphere than my house. I love mama and papa, but we're so conventional. If only you got along better with your father, it might be easier for you."

"What a coincidence you should say that," he said, more impressed than ever with the amazing understanding of this girl who had always been a child to him until today. "My father came up to my room last night. He was in a snit about me getting thrown out of school, but the strangest thing happened. He told me that years ago he had an affair with another woman too, and would you believe it, he said I have an illegitimate half-brother living not six blocks from here."

"A brother! And illegitimate—that's absolutely lurid! I'd give anything to have an illegitimate brother. It's part of being an artist."

"I haven't got used to the idea myself," Claude said almost cheerfully.

"Aren't you dying to know what he's like? Maybe he's an anarchist. Why don't you go see him?"

"He's Catholic, I know that for sure."

"All the better! Mme. Averbach was a Jewess, like in Ivanhoe." Elizabeth sat back, sighing with the wonder of his revelations. "I think you should write a novel about it all. Everyone would want to read it."

Her enthusiasm made him smile.

"Don't laugh," she said, her bold green eyes chiding him. "It's the perfect way to get over a tragic love affair, and when you meet your brother it will open up a whole new world to you."

"Will you help me write it down?" he asked, suppressing his smile. His life was beginning to seem less tragic to him already.

"Of course, I will. I don't have your imagination but you can dictate it to me. I always won prizes for my penmanship."

She might still be a schoolgirl, Claude thought, but she was very sensible.

When he got home, Veronica was in the parlor covering a lampshade, busy with parchment and scissors, spectacles perched on the end of her nose. In her prim, starched dress and hair pulled back in a bun she already had the look of a spinster, though she was not yet twenty-one. Since finishing her studies at the Greenwich Academy for Young Ladies, she had taken over the work of running the house.

Though it had been some time since brother and sister had had a real talk, Claude sat down and asked her what she thought about Elizabeth's suggestion that he get a bookstore job and live a more regular life.

"I used to think I wanted to be like other people too," Veronica said, snipping off a length of brown ribbon, "but the more I've worked on my poems, the more I've come to see what a blessing it is to just be yourself."

That sounded like sour grapes to him, Claude said. Deep down, didn't she really want a normal life too, maybe to get married some day? Hadn't she ever been in love?

Veronica fitted the ribbon around the lampshade. "Of course I expect to fall in love, but when I do, it will be in my own way and my own time. I'm not in the least worried about it." Having tied a big bow on the lampshade, she patted it with satisfaction and gathered up her materials.

Miffed at her complacency, he thought she needed a jolt. He told her about their illegitimate brother, Patrick.

Veronica was unimpressed. "That has nothing to do with me," she said firmly, and walked past him down to the kitchen.

His sister was like a creature under a rock, refusing to come out into the light. There was no way he was going back to that himself. He had wasted too much time already.

Claude spent most of the next few days with Elizabeth. They walked around the reservoir at Forty-second Street, and rode the ferryboat across the Hudson to Luna Park in Weehawken, and sat in Abingdon Square, the tiny yellow flowers of the elms falling on them like powder, while she read to him from Hawthorne's short stories.

She was forever asking him to describe for her again the Thursday evenings at Adele Averbach's, and he was beginning to feel proud that he had been part of such an exotic world. The only thing he didn't tell her about was his opium habit. Whenever the pain of Adele came over him, and it was not quite so sharp any more, he took a pipe in his room. By the time his supply of opium was finished, he wouldn't need it again and planned to give it up.

In the middle of reading one of Hawthorne's stories called "The Prophetic Portrait," in which a beautiful couple get married and go off to Europe on their honeymoon, Elizabeth put down the book and asked why the two of them shouldn't get married too. Claude was so taken aback he laughed, never having considered such a thing—and besides they were too young.

But when she pointed out that they were a perfect match because she understood what he had gone through, it didn't seem such a bad idea. Wasn't her healthy optimism the best antidote to Adele? Besides, what else did he have to do?

Their life together would be dedicated to the arts, she declared. He would become a writer, and although she hadn't settled yet on just which one of the arts she intended to pursue—she was so interested in all of them—she too would be an artist of some kind.

At the Endicott dinner table that night Elizabeth piped up that she and Claude were thinking of getting engaged as soon as she finished school in June. Of course, she hadn't told her parents yet, they expected her to go to Vassar, but she would talk them around.

Veronica and Miss Swindon looked on dumbstruck. Fanny smiled vaguely, not really taking it in. But Tom couldn't have been more pleased, once he got over his surprise at how quickly his son seemed to have recovered from his broken heart. He jumped up and brought out a bottle of hock he had been saving for a special occasion.

As the young couple were toasted, Elizabeth preened at having been transformed in a moment from an inconsequential schoolgirl to a grown up bride-to-be.

The next day, feeling better all around, Claude walked over to Shamrock Alley to look for his half-brother Patrick. He had always avoided the area because the immigrant toughs who lived there menaced any outsider they caught in their territory.

The tavern at the corner of the Alley was packed with regular patrons and returning soldiers still celebrating four days after the end of the war. The tavern keeper pointed out to Claude the stairway leading up to the Hanlons. In front of it, Patrick's younger brother, Timothy, a hulking youth with an incipient red mustache, was pitching pennies with some other teenage roughnecks, blocking the way.

As Claude walked toward the stairs, conspicuous in his high collar, plaid college jacket and matching cap, he felt them looking him over, and one of them even spat into the dirt. They didn't move, forcing him to step around them. Climbing to the third floor landing, he was aware that the tough with the red mustache had detached himself from his mates and was behind him on the stairs. By the time Claude stood before the door the tavern keeper had indicated, the youth with the red mustache was leaning against the porch railing, eyeing him, chewing on a toothpick.

Inside the room, Patrick was lying down, resting his leg that had taken a bullet in the battle of Savannah. When he heard the knock, he got up with a grimace of pain and, pulling up the suspenders of his army trousers, limped to the door. He was not a tall young man but he had a stocky frame in a collarless flannel shirt, with the broad face, dark, wild hair, and his mother's blue eyes.

His leg throbbing, it didn't make him feel any better to see the pale, effete-looking young man in fancy clothes standing in the doorway. But when Claude introduced himself, Patrick was staggered. He held the Endicotts directly responsible for destroying his mother. Through her last hellish days, she had railed against Tom Endicott and it had become clear to him that his father was not the dead Mike Hanlon after all.

"You might not remember," Claude said, attempting to bridge the awkwardness between them, "but we saw each other once in my father's print shop."

"I remember, all right," Patrick muttered.

"You do?" Claude said, brightly. "I couldn't figure out what was going on."

"That was the blackest day in my mother's life...."

This wasn't the way it was supposed to go. Claude tried to find something right to say to this thickset, bristling stranger who was nothing like the brother he had imagined. "I'm so sorry about what happened to your mother. I never knew about it until the other night."

"A fat lotta good sorry does." A twinge in his leg made Patrick grab onto the doorjamb.

Claude saw at once he was in trouble. "Look here, you shouldn't be on your feet. Let me help you to a chair."

Patrick stood his ground and said through teeth gritted against the pain, "Was it your father sent ya down here?"

"Oh, no...he didn't....Not really. I came because I wanted to. He had nothing to do with it. I mean, he is concerned about you, of course," said Claude, feeling himself getting into even more of a mix-up. "Look, can't I come in and talk for a minute?"

"We got nothin to talk about." Patrick stepped back to close the door.

Claude tried to hold it open. "I've had a hard time too. Won't you even give me a chance?"

Patrick boiled over. "If you don't get outta here, I won't be answerable for what I might do!"

"But we're half brothers!"

"Ya ask me, there's not a drop of the same blood in us!" Patrick slammed the door and limped back to the table. He was shaking, his feelings in a turmoil.

In his anger against the Endicotts he had never given a thought to this brother his own age. Why did he have to come around now? Patrick didn't want to know him. He didn't want to know any of them, not after what happened to his mother.

He certainly didn't need their help. He may have started out digging sewers, but just as soon as his leg healed, Tammany had a job waiting for him as foreman of a crew extending tracks for the horsecars into the northern reaches of the city. He knew he had a future in public transportation. While he was away at the war, he had thought of ideas for putting tracks in the air and even below the ground that could revolutionize city transit. And he was going to marry Hester—a good Irish girl who loved him—and raise a family, and he would go a lot further than that sad-eyed nincompoop of an Endicott who had the nerve to suggest that there could ever be any brotherly feeling between them.

Outside on the landing, Claude stood dazed by Patrick's reaction. Timothy, who was leaning against the rail with his toothpick in his mouth, watched him and, when Claude finally started down the stairs, followed behind. When they reached the bottom, Timothy gave a whistle between his teeth and several of his pals grabbed Claude and pulled him into an alleyway, where Timothy began to beat him with his big fists. Several people in the court saw what was going on and ran over, shouting.

Patrick came out on the porch to see what the commotion was about. Someone below cried, "Hey, Tim, kill that cream puff!" Forgetting his leg, the young veteran held on to the rail and vaulted down the stairs.

His brother was stomping and kicking Claude Endicott, who lay writhing in the dirt. He pulled Timothy off and smashed him back against the brick wall. With a neighbor's help he got Claude to his feet and they carried him out to the street, laying him nearly unconscious on top of a pile of old clothes in a ragpicker's wagon.

At the Endicotts' house it was Elizabeth Cooper who answered the door. She gave a cry, seeing Claude bloody and battered, and helped Patrick get him up to his room. Veronica went for the doctor while Elizabeth set about washing the wounds and getting some whiskey down him.

When Patrick got back to Shamrock Alley, he found his brother Timothy on the couch, holding his shoulder and groaning. Their sister Nora, who at fifteen was already married and expecting a child, was laying on cold compresses and trying to comfort him.

"Get up, ya blitherin shit!" Patrick limped over and, brushing his sister out of the way, pulled his hulk of a brother to his feet. He grabbed a cap and jacket from a peg and thrust them at Timothy. "I shouldn't be doin this, but I'm goin to give ya a chance to save your worthless arse."

With Nora wailing and wringing her hands, he pushed Timothy, who was protesting his innocence, out the door. At the corner of Greenwich Street, he flagged down a hansom cab and took his brother straight down to the Battery, where he signed him on a freighter leaving that night for Liverpool. Patrick did not heave a sigh of relief until the lights of the ship disappeared out in the harbor.

In spite of his injuries, Claude spent a fairly peaceful night, with Elizabeth never leaving his side. But he never fully came to, and the next day, heavy sweats began, and bouts of unconscious raving. The doctor suspected there might be neurological damage as well as a concussion. Claude's heart had always been weak and the doctor said it would be a while before they would know the extent of his internal injuries.

When Patrick came over to find out how Claude was, Elizabeth asked him in and took him upstairs. For a moment Claude's eyes opened briefly and, hoping he could hear him, Patrick told him what a damned louse he felt like for the way he had treated him the day before.

"As soon as you're back on your feet," said Patrick, "I want you to meet my Hester. You'll be dancing at our wedding, I promise ya...."

A flicker of a smile crossed Claude's face, and Patrick felt the slightest response as he took his hand.

Elizabeth went down to the door with Patrick afterward and thanked him for all he had done. On the way home he thought hard about the remarkable girl with the green eyes, who was ministering to her beloved like an angel.

In the early hours of the following morning Claude went into convulsions. In his delirium, with his arms flailing, he pulled out the drawer of the bedside table, upsetting the contents onto the floor.

Before the doctor could get there, he died, with Elizabeth, Tom, and Veronica looking on. At a cry from behind them, they turned to see Fanny standing in the doorway in her nightdress, her hair bedraggled and tears streaming down her face.

Afterward, the doctor discovered the sections of the ivory pipe and the brown lump of resin on the floor by the bed and asked Tom about it. Tom said that he had never seen it before. The doctor sniffed it, tasted a bit of the resin. After a pause, he said that internal injuries might not have been the only cause of Claude's death. It appeared he had been an opium addict, and with his weak heart, had died of heart failure from being deprived of the drug.

Bells were tolling everywhere on April 16, 1865, the day after President Lincoln's assassination at Ford's Theater, as a small party of mourners walked behind a cart carrying a casket through empty streets to St. Luke's Church. Claude Endicott was buried in the churchyard in the presence of his family and the Coopers, while the shocked city and half a nation were in mourning for the Great Emancipator.

1870

16

Faced with the heady possibilities of the postwar boom, New York City had soon put aside its grief. Tom Endicott's printing business also shared in the general euphoria. Even without temperance jobs, the presses were kept humming. There were circulars for the grand opening of Macy's department store, announcements for the American premiere of Verdi's opera "Aida" at the Academy of Music, broadsides against Boss Tweed— the corrupt politico, head of Tammany Hall, who was bilking the city of millions—and all kinds of other printing jobs. But Tom no longer took much interest in it and left the bulk of the work to his employees.

For a while it was all he could do to cope with Fanny. In the months following Claude's death her behavior became more erratic than ever.

Though the poor woman had never paid much atteation to her son while he was alive, his death seemed to affect her deeply. The cannabis elixir was no longer effective in controlling her outbursts, and in fact produced visions that made her crazier. Even with Veronica's help, Miss Swindon could hardly handle her and had to move into her bedroom to be with her every minute, while Tom slept downstairs on the sofa.

One day, Fanny broke away from her companion and ran up to Claude's old room where she started to fling his things out the window onto the street, shrieking for all the neigborhood to hear, that he needed them in heaven. The time had finally come when Tom had to face the fact that he couldn't keep her at home any longer. Without informing Miss Swindon of his plan, he found a private asylum for Fanny further up Manhattan island overlooking the Hudson where she would be well cared for.

On the day the attendants from the home came to collect her, Miss Swindon went berserk, trying to keep them from taking Fanny away from her, and fought a pitched battle in the downstairs hall, shouting that Tom was the cause of all her mistress's troubles, fathering an Irish bastard to drive his legitimate son to addiction and his wife out of her wits with shame.

Tom didn't even have his friend Albert around any more to keep his spirits up. The squatters' settlement Albert had been living in in the Central Park area had been pulled down to make way for the city's new museum of art and he had gone with his wife to live with her people, a tribe of clam-digging Indians on the eastern tip of Long Island.

Elizabeth Cooper, who always made the house livelier with her running in and out, had also left. She was away at Vassar, the country's first college for women, which had just opened upstate. Although Veronica was still at home, doing most of the housework and cooking herself now, she was not much company. Father and daughter never had that much to say to each other.

With so little to do except for visits to Fanny at the sanitarium, Tom often wished that he could have some contact with his natural son Patrick. At the time of Claude's accident Tom had been impressed all over again with the extraordinary young man. They had spoken briefly a couple of times, though it had been awkward between them. Tom had tried to make it clear that he would like Patrick to continue visiting them, but after Claude's death he never came back.

He couldn't blame Patrick for still resenting him—what kind of a father had he been, after all? The way he had treated him seemed more inexcusable than ever. Why hadn't he insisted on seeing his son all those years, no matter what Molly or the world thought about it?

Tom got news of him now and then through old Mrs. Brophy. Patrick had left his job with a crew laying horsecar tracks, and had gone to work helping to build the first elevated line in the city down the length of Greenwich Street. From his front stoop Tom could see the girders of the structure that already blocked the view of the river. Property values along the route of the elevated were plummeting and people were moving out. According to the Tribune, it was bound to get worse when the trains were rattling overhead, hauled by steam locomotives belching God only knew how much smoke over the area.

Mrs. Brophy had kept him informed when Patrick got married after the war to his girl Hester, and the couple moved to a small flat farther away below Houston Street. But Hester had one miscarriage after another, her health declined, and in the first summer of the seventies Mrs. Brophy told him that she had been "taken by the Lord" after another stillbirth, of childbed fever.

Under the circumstances Tom saw no reason he shouldn't go to see Patrick, but as it turned out he didn't have to....

The end of summer was always the most melancholy season for Tom. That had been when the bold-eyed servant girl came to work in the house twenty-five years before, and for a brief time his life had been transformed. One evening, when an orange moon hung over the row of new houses across the street where the old farmhouse used to stand, there was a knock at the door. He seldom got callers in the evening. When the Coopers came over, they never bothered to knock.

A young man with his cap in his hand and a black armband on his sleeve was standing there. Patrick.

"It's only a moment I need of your time, Mr. Endicott, and then I'll be on my way," he said, with just a trace of his mother's brogue. He was leaving New York in the morning and had something to get off his chest.

He was more muscular than ever, with the broad, open face Tom remembered so well, but his hair was tousled and he looked like he hadn't slept.

Tom stepped back and invited him in.

"I expect you're surprised to see me after so long," the young man said, looking uncomfortable in his workingman's clothes in the front hall where the woodwork had been polished for a generation to a dark gloss.

"Yes," said Tom, who was more than surprised, "but come in, come in."

With a hand on the shoulder of this son he hardly knew, he led him into the parlor, trying to think of something more to say. He had thought Patrick never wanted to have anything more to do with him, yet here he was. He offered him a chair.

"I'll stand if ya don't mind, sir." Patrick ran a hand over his square, unshaven jaw, seemingly as unsure as Tom about how to begin. "I should have told ya years ago, Mr. Endicott. I never even told my wife, God rest her soul, I felt so bad about it."

Unable to make any sense out of this, Tom said how sorry he was to hear about his wife's death. The words sounded stiff, all wrong, but Patrick didn't seem to notice. Twisting his cap as he stood there, he said he was leaving New York because he had made a mess of everything. He had been bad for his wife—not to mention his brother Timothy—and what he had done to Claude was shameful. "I'd like to straighten it out with ya before I go."

Tom tried again to get him to sit down, but the robust, curly-haired young man, who looked so much like Molly and yet so different, ignored him in his urgent need to get out what was on his mind.

Timothy was the one who had done it, Patrick said—he had been with the Dusters. "When Tim heard me yellin at Claude, he got the wrong idea. I never meant it that way, Mr. Endicott. Your boy only wanted to be friends."

What was he talking about Claude for? Tom wondered. The accident had happened so long ago, it was hard for him to make sense out of what the lad was saying.

Patrick went on, explaining that out of respect for his mother's memory he had put Timothy on the boat for Liberpool to give him another chance. "It wasn't right, I know, Mr. Endicott, and now Hester's gone and all...." There was a catch in his voice and he put a hand over his eyes for a moment. "I hardly knew your boy...refused to know him, I mean...it was as though I killed him myself."

Tom understood, finally. That thug of a brother had been the one to give Claude the fatal beating, and it was on Patrick's conscience that he had shipped him out to save his skin.

Patrick put on his cap. "I'll take myself out of here now, sir, and I promise you'll never see nor hear of me any more."

For a moment Tom was speechless, as this lost son, who had reappeared out of the night, started to leave. He had let the world take Molly from him, the most important thing in his life—was he going to let it happen again? He sprang to the door in time to take his son by the arm, pull him back to a chair and force him to sit down. "Now just be quiet and let me say something for a change." Tom stood over him and told him that Claude didn't die from that beating. Claude had had a weak heart and there were other complications that he wouldn't go into now. "And about you putting your brother on that boat, the Molly Hanlon I knew would have said you did the right thing, and I think so too."

Patrick looked confused. "Are ya sayin ya don't hold it against me?"

"You brought Claude back here, didn't you? I'll never forget that."

Patrick was silent.

Tom walked to the window, his back to the young man. The moon was higher now, and brighter. "Claude is dead and all that's over," he said. "What I feel bad about is that all those years you were growing up down there I neglected you." There it was, what he'd been carrying inside him for so long, out in the open. He hadn't expected ever to have the chance to say it to this boy whom he had made a bastard. But now that he had started, he wanted to tell him the whole story of his love for Molly, and he did, without apology and not sparing himself. "When your mother let me know that she didn't want anything more to do with me," he finished, still gazing at the moon, "I used that as an excuse to stay away."

The room was still, except for the crackling of the fire.

Patrick spoke at last. "But ya gave us money."

Tom turned back to him. "Those measly sums? I know it's late in the day, but I've got some money put by and I'd like you to have it."

Looking down at his calloused hands, Patrick said he didn't need anything.

Tom came over and pulled a chair close to him. "I wish I'd done something when there was time. With you going away I won't have the chance." He sighed. "I'm getting old, I guess."

Patrick started to protest but Tom shook his head. "I may be only fifty but it's been a long while since I've had much to live for. My daughter doesn't need me and my wife is in an asylum. I need a friend. No"—he corrected himself—"I mean, I need a son." He looked straight at Patrick. "If it's not too late."

"Ya shouldn't oughta say that, Mr. Endicott." Patrick's eyes had filled with tears. "I been feelin so bad…." He started to sob.

Tom was upset too. He had never seen a grown man I such a state. He fumbled with a bottle of whiskey, poured some in a glass, and handed it over.

Patrick looked up, tears rolling unashamedly down his broad, innocent face, and gulped it down.

"All right now?" said Tom, quietly.

Patrick gave a last snuffle and rubbed the back of his sleeve across his face. He grinned through his tears. "Ya really set me off, sir, but I wasn't expectin ya to take it like that."

Tom poked up the fire, and after a while they started feeling easier with each other. Patrick confessed that his marriage had never worked out very well. His wife, Hester, had been a saint in every way, she never complained, but somehow she always made him feel like a brute. It was like there was no fight in her.

Tom thought what an irony that this boy's marriage sounded so similar to his own. But Patrick was still young—there was still time for things to go better for him. He vowed to help him however he could.

It was his sister Nora, Patrick was saying, who had been the real solace to him since Hester died. She had two little ones now, with another on the way. Her husband, Billy Yates, was in the same work gang as him on the new elevated. "Ya can see the el from here," he said. "Isn't it a fine sight?"

In no time Patrick was holding forth loudly about his work as if he hadn't just been bawling his eyes out. "And that's only the beginning." His hands gripped his thighs enthusiastically and he described a tunnel that was being built downtown for an experimental underground train. "There's the real future for municipal transportation. Can't ya see it, Mr. Endicott?" He spread out his brawny arms. "The whole city crisscrossed with tunnels carryin passengers and freight in every direction, and our streets fit to walk in again." He grinned. "Ah, but I'm bein carried away. Hester used to say, 'Pat, ya only live for them tracks and tunnels.'" Once more, his eyes misted over. "God rest her soul."

Alarmed at the threat of another outpouring of tears, Tom tried to divert him by asking him about his ambitions. Patrick said his dream was to become a construction engineer on the elevated railroad, but that would depend on his getting taken on as an apprentice by the engineers. He didn't have the education they had, but on practical matters he could show them a thing or two if they would just give him a chance.

"Then you won't be going west after all?" Tom was beginning to get an idea.

Patrick frowned. "Well, I'm not so sure. You're makin me feel different about things."

"Look here," said Tom, "I know a couple of engineers on your elevated. It happens they attend my church. Maybe I could introduce you to them on Sunday."

"Go to your church with ya, ya mean?"

The way he said it, it was clear he had never been in a Protestant church before. Tom amended his offer. "I could talk to them about you, if you like."

"Would it be possible, sir?"

Over whiskeys, Patrick told him that he was giving up the flat he and Hester had lived in and taking a room closer to the work site. His sister Nora had asked him to move in with her and Billy and the kids, but it would be too crowded and he wouldn't be able to study his engineering books.

"Why don't you move in here with Veronica and me?" The words popped out before Tom knew what he was saying.

Patrick's jaw dropped. "Here?"

"Why not? There's plenty of room and Veronica's a good cook."

Patrick said he couldn't think of doing such a thing. "It would mess up your life. What would ya tell people?"

"I've a right to take in boarders, don't I?" Then it hit him. "I've got it! Why don't I adopt you?" It was so perfect, he wondered how he hadn't thought of it before.

"Adopt me? But I'm a Hanlon—and a Catholic!"

"What's to stop you from becoming an Endicott and a Protestant?"

"Protestant? But, Mr. Endicott, that means Eternal Damnation!"

Tom was not going to let a little thing like that stand in the way, now that he saw what to do. "We take all the sacraments at St. Luke's, too. You could go to Mass there every Sunday the same as you do now."

Patrick scratched his head. "I'm not the one for goin to Mass every Sunday, I can tell ya."

"Well then, I don't see that it'll be a problem, one way or the other."

By the time they said goodnight, Patrick had agreed to come over the following Sunday and they would discuss it further.

Tom couldn't wait to get things started, and rushed off the next day to consult his lawyer about the legal procedures necessary for adoption.

But on Sunday, when Patrick was back again and they sat in the study with a decanter of port on the table between them, Tom didn't like the way things were going.

In stiff collar and Sunday-best suit too tight for his stocky frame, Patrick was frowning into his glass of wine, as if he were avoiding his father's eyes. "I've given your offer much thought, Mr. Endicott," he finally began, "and I do want to thank ya for it. It's not that I'm a religious man exactly. As I told ya, it's not every Sunday that I go to Mass, but ma was born into the Church, and me and everyone I know as well, so I don't see how it would be right...."

Tom told him that he wouldn't have to give up his faith if he didn't feel right about it. He was still his son. He could come live with them anyway.

But Patrick was adamant. Looking around at the ornately-furnished room, he said he wouldn't feel easy about that, in this kind of place, away from his own kind....

He broke off at the sound of rustling skirts and a lively "Hello!"from the hall.

A girl, whose softly piled hair reflected the russet tints of the chrysanthemums she was carrying in her arms, appeared in the doorway. Her green eyes widened when she saw Patrick. It was Elizabeth Cooper, just back from Europe, and she and Patrick hadn't met since Claude's death five years before.

After graduating from Vassar, she had gone abroad as traveling companion to an elderly widow. The galleries, the cathedrals, even a romantic flirtation in Paris—she had loved it all. But with the clouds gathering for a war between France and Germany, the old lady got nervous and they had come home. Though back with her parents only a few days, Elizabeth had perceived Tom's loneliness and was already doing her best to cheer him up.

She dropped the flowers into a vase on a side table and came in. "You're Mr. Hanlon, aren't you?" she said to Patrick. "It's marvelous to see you again."

Her remarkable eyes had stayed with him all these years without his knowing it. And she remembered him too. Overcome by bashfulness, he could barely stammer a reply.

"Please excuse me," she said, her cheeks flushing, "I can see that you two are having a serious talk, and I don't want to interrupt." Before Tom could stop her, she started for the door at a girlish skip, but got in trouble with her skirts. Turning around to give her bustle a mock slap of disapproval, she threw them a delightful smile and disappeared.

It was such a breath of fresh air to have her back again, Tom said, observing Patrick's high color.

"It's next door that Miss Cooper lives, if I'm not mistaken?"

"Yes," Tom said, playing his hand for all it was worth, "but sometimes she's here more than there—not that I mind."

Patrick studied the ruby liquid in his glass. "It's true I was christened Hanlon in the church, but then Hanlon is not my father's name when ya think about it, so Hanlon's not really my name...so maybe my religion's not my religion...." He cocked his curly head and winked at Tom. "Can we look at it that way, Mr. Endicott?"

17

Patrick's arrival in the house was understandably difficult for Veronica. Although her father had paid little more attention to his reticent daughter than she had to him, he might have anticipated her lack of enthusiasm when he told her out of the blue that Patrick was to come live with them. She was not scandalized—she had known of her half-brother's existence for years—but she was not happy about being forced to share the house with a semi-immigrant from the slums.

Her worst fears were confirmed when the loudmouthed stranger in workman's clothes showed up with a worn carpetbag and stomped up the stairs after Tom to settle in. She couldn't understand her father's sudden interest in him.

Patrick, for his part, found this prim, twenty-six-year-old bespectacled girl with a sheaf of her poems under her arm almost as unappetizing as she found him crude. That first evening, when he came down to sit with Tom in the parlor wearing only his long-sleeved underwear under his suspenders as he was used to doing at home, she picked up her cat and walked out in a huff.

Tom was embarrassed that anything should go wrong so soon. He apologized to Patrick, explaining that Veronica had her mother's high-strung nerves and that until she got used to him, it might be better if he kept his shirt on downstairs.

Things did not improve at breakfast the next morning. With Tom and Veronica in the dining room, Patrick covered his awkwardness by blabbing too much about the technology of the new flush toilet upstairs. "Where I come from, chamber pots and privies are all we got." He tried to laugh, but stopped when he saw Veronica glaring at him.

"People do not discuss such things at table, Mr. Hanlon," she said, forgetting her usual restraint.

Before he could check himself, Patrick shot back "Ya mean ya don't have calls of nature like the rest of us, miss?"

Veronica turned crimson and looked to her father, expecting him to reprimand such vulgarity.

Instead, he reprimanded her. "Patrick is not a Hanlon any more, Veronica. He's an Endicott now," he said quietly, reminding her of the fact of the adoption.

She dropped her napkin and got to her feet. "You've taken leave of your senses, papa. You can't make him a substitute for Claude, no matter how hard you try." Her voice was shaking. "Excuse me...." She ran out of the room.

Things were even more strained when the three Coopers from next door came to Sunday dinner to meet Patrick.

Everyone except for Veronica was happy for him, but even with a natural physical grace, he had not had time to learn their table manners. He tied his napkin around his neck and swilled his soup noisily, while Veronica looked mortified. Professor Cooper tried to ease the tension by asking him about his work on the elevated line.

Swiping his napkin across his mouth, Patrick said that thanks to Mr. Endicott, he had been taken into the engineering office as an apprentice. Planting his elbows on the table, he warmed to his subject. "We're goin to be puttin up elevated railroads all over New York City. Ya know what that means, professor? It means it's goin to bring the city right into Greenwich."

"But I thought we were trying to keep the city out," said Veronica acidly.

"Maybe we thought we could keep the city out," Tom said, taking Patrick's side again, "but this is 1870 and we can't turn our backs on progress."

To everyone's relief, the hired girl walked in with a baked ham on a platter. But when Patrick heard the girl addressed as Kathleen, he took another look at her. Pulling at her apron, he asked wasn't she Big Jim O'Hara's little daughter from the Alley?

The girl looked around in confusion and hurried back to the kitchen.

Unaware of his blunder, Patrick told how Big Jim O'Hara had taken him to the Tammany Club and gotten him his first job.

Veronica whispered to Mrs. Cooper, "He'll be asking the girl to sit down with us next!"

Elizabeth hid her amusement behind her napkin. Veronica was being impossible, of course, but even if Patrick was amost as beautiful as the Adam in the Sistine Chapel she had seen in Rome, he did lack a certain finesse, devouring his food like a bear and scattering bits and pieces around him on the tablecloth. She could understand how lonely Mr. Endicott had been, but she wondered if he might have been a bit precipitous in giving a home to this uncouth young man. Still, there was something about him....

Professor Cooper said that maybe Tammany getting Patrick a job was not a bad thing, but that crook Bill Tweed had driven every honest civic leader out of the organization.

"Mr. Tweed may not be to every one's likin," he said between mouthfuls of food. "But ya got to admit it was a bunch of crooks he threw out, even if they was posin as 'honest civic leaders' as ya call them." He scraped together the remains of the peas and potatoes on his plate. "When my Hester, God rest her soul, was failin, it was Tweed's boys sent a basket of food around. And how would I ever have got my job layin tracks when no one else would hire a mick? They're all crooks anyway, so if they want me to vote for them, why the hell not?" With his knife and fork he stuffed his mouth.

Veronica couldn't contain herself. "But it's the moral issue we're concerned with here, Mr. Hanlon."

Patrick swallowed his food with a gulp and poked his fork at her, "You can talk, Miss Endicott, raised in this house from the time you were born. My mother never sat at this table, she scrubbed the floors here. Shyte on your high-and-mighty moral issues!" Shoving back his chair, he stood up and walked out.

"Oh, dear," said Mrs. Cooper in the embarrassed silence that followed, "we have no right to act superior. But don't worry, Tom"—she put a hand on his arm—"he'll get over it. He needs time to get used to us all."

Elizabeth put down her napkin, saying she'd be right back, and followed after Patrick up the stairs. She had never seen anyone behave like that, but he was the product of a proletarian background, and Veronica *was* driving him to the wall. They had all been rude making him feel that they were ganging up against him. She was going to apologize.

She found him staring out the window in the parlor. He looked quite acceptable in a new, well-fitting worsted coat and checked trousers. She took a deep breath and began, "That was a pretty little scene you just pulled, Mr. Endicott."

He whipped around, eyes blazing, but catching her amused look, he turned back, muttering, "I'm no Endicott and never will be. I don't fit here. It's too hard for a dumb mick like me."

She went a few steps closer. "You were just boasting about how hard your life was over in that slum, or did I misunderstand you?"

Keeping his back to her, he snarled, "Oh, shut up about what ya know nothin of, ya fancy bitch."

Elizabeth was not intimidated. "Is your vocabulary so limited that all you can use is obscenity?" When he didn't reply, she let him have it. "You poor slum kid! That's your excuse for everything, isn't it?"

He turned to see her flushed cheeks and the green fire of her eyes, and couldn't help laughing out loud. "Ya sure you're not a mick yourself? Ya got the sass of one."

Elizabeth laughed back. "Absolutely not. I'm three quarters English and one quarter Scot."

Patrick threw himself down in an armchair, his legs stretched out. "I was wicked in there," he said. "Didn't I just knock them on their arses!"

"Yes, you did," said Elizabeth, "but maybe they needed it."

"Ah, it's not them, it's me. I've got no education. How could Mr. Endicott think I'll ever fit in here?"

She sat herself down on a hassock in front of him. "I've had plenty of education and European travel, and I can't do anything. You can build elevated railroads."

"Still, it's manners that makes all the difference in this world," Patrick said.

"If that's all you're worried about, I could help you there. It's nothing you couldn't pick up in a minute—that is, if you don't mind a woman showing you." Her eyes gleamed at him.

He sat up, rubbing his hands. "When do we start?"

"Well, I suggest that first off you come back to the table with me and we have dessert. But for mercy's sake, don't tie the napkin around your neck, even if it is the best way to keep the chocolate sauce off your tie."

At the elevated construction site, Patrick was the first Irishman to work in the engineering office. If the engineers were a little prejudiced at first, as time passed they discovered how useful he was. Having started at the bottom, he had a practical knowledge that none of them had, combined with a natural aptitude for technical matters.

One day when he had been there nearly a year, his sister's husband, Billy Yates, who was still on one of the work crews, caught up with him outside the office and invited him down to the house. Nora had received a letter from their brother Timothy, who was living in Ireland.

This was as good a reason as any for Patrick to get together with his sister again. Since he had moved up to Perry Street to live with his father, their occasional meetings had been awkward. But it had been six years since he had put his brother on that boat and he was eager to get news of him.

The Yateses lived on Greenwich Street on the second floor of a house picked up by their landlord at a bargain price because of the elevated going up outside the windows.

When Patrick and his brother-in-law came in, Nora was nursing her newborn. She looked worn out after having had three children before she was twenty. His usual bluster failed to overcome her shyness, and seeing the candle burning before a picture of Our Lady on the wall, he was aware of the gulf that had opened up between them. Nostalgia came over him as he remembered the Latin chanting of the Mass.

It was a relief to smell stew coming from the kitchen and have something familiar to talk about.

"Ya don't want any of that, Paddy," she said, when he asked for a taste of it.

"What do ya mean I don't? I haven't had Sligo stew in I don't know how long."

They all felt easier as his sister set out steaming bowls of kidney, potatoes, and leeks before them. When he tucked his napkin into his shirtfront the way Elizabeth had instructed him, Nora tittered. He quickly retied it around his neck and, feeling his old self again, made a show of digging into the stew with gusto.

Her two toddlers stared at him openmouthed as if he were a stranger, but after they finished eating, while Billy stayed on at the table filling his tobacco pouch, Patrick got down on his hands and knees and played with them. They squealed and laughed and crawled all over him, while Nora fluttered around protesting that he was dirtying his handsome trousers on the floor.

Later, when the children were tucked into a big iron bed in the corner, Patrick read Timothy's letter aloud. Their brother was living in Cork, working for a ship's chandler, and had married a local girl. He wrote that there wasn't all that much money in Ireland, but he liked it better than in America because you didn't see any signs like "No Irish Need Apply." "I got into mischief over there because I was ashamed of me being Irish. Nora, I want you to tell Paddy that him putting me on that boat was the best thing that ever happened to me."

Afterward, over tots of whiskey, Billy said, "It's a cryin shame Tim had to leave the country. He could have been workin on the elevated like us."

Patrick said there wasn't that much work back then and, to change the subject, told them about the young lady next door to the Endicotts he was keeping company with. While Billy poured out another round, his sister asked which church the girl attended.

"Ya may as well know right now, Nora, she's not a Catholic."

"Oh," she said, and got up to clear the table, keeping her face averted.

Since she was upset, he thought he might as well let her in on the whole story and get it over with, and he told her that he didn't see himself as much of a Catholic any more either.

Carrying the stew pot, she turned in the kitchen doorway and stared at him.

"Ya don't have to take it that way," he said, My real father wasn't a Catholic. It's not the same as with you and Tim, is it?"

"Is that how ya see it?" she said stiffly, and went into the kitchen.

Although she pressed a packet of her home-baked shortbread on him when he left and said she was ever so glad things were going well for him, he couldn't help noticing that his sister did not urge him to come again soon.

18

Elizabeth Cooper was strolling down Bleecker Street on the arm of her fiancé. It was a Sunday afternoon in spring and velocipedes were going by, some of them even pedaled by women showing bright stockings below their shortened cycling skirts. Elizabeth had given up her original idea of their spending the afternoon at the new Metropolitan Museum of Art because Patrick had made such a face about it. But even if he didn't share all her interests, she was happy. Being together was all that mattered. In fact, it was just their differences that were going to be the strength of their marriage. She admired the unique qualities he brought from his ethnic background, so colorful compared to her own. And once they were married she would tactfully introduce him to the arts, the same as she had taught him table manners. Although still his expansive self, Patrick already behaved well enough socially even for hypercritical Veronica.

Elizabeth waved to two friends passing in a pony cart, wanting to show her fiancé off, in his beautiful pearl-gray suit with velvet trim around the lapels and a dapper bowler hat.

After their wedding in June they were going to live in the Endicott house. Tom had insisted on moving up to the top floor with Veronica where he would have another bathroom put in. Elizabeth couldn't wait to fill those old-fashioned rooms with some new ornamental furnishings that reflected her own advanced tastes. And Patrick was planning to install the latest plumbing and heating devices.

They stopped and Patrick bought peanuts from a vendor. Walking on, Elizabeth reminded him of more people she wanted to invite to the wedding, and would they fit into her parents' garden where it was to be held.

Patrick cracked a whole handful of peanuts at once. "I never heard of gettin married outside a church. Sure it'll be binding?"

Elizabeth considered this. "Maybe you shouldn't have given up your faith. Tom wouldn't care if you went back to it, I'm sure." She told him that she had always adored the idea of Catholicism. It was so aesthetic. The cathedrals in Europe were the most inspiring structures she had ever seen. "We don't have anything like them here."

"I don't know," said Patrick, picking out the peanut shells in his hand and tossing them right and left. "If you're talkin about structures, St. Aloysius is as fine an edifice as I'd ever want to see."

"It's not just architecture. It's the glorious music, the Latin, the incense. Aren't you going to miss all that?"

He popped the peanuts into his mouth. "My ma, God rest her soul, would break my arm for sayin it, but there's a lot of malarkey in it too." The church wasn't all as noble as it seemed, he told her. It was the money from the pockets of the poor that built those cathedrals she liked so much. Plenty of people went to confession on Sunday and sinned the rest of the week, knowing they could get away with it.

But as they passed Our Lady of Pompeii on the next corner, it didn't escape her notice that he crossed himself automatically.

The night before the wedding, Patrick sat up with his father, having a whiskey in the parlor. His fellow engineers on the elevated had given him the bottle as a wedding present. His old work crew had tried to get him to spend the evening with them, but although he had never heard of a bridegroom not going out with the boys before the big event, he felt it was the right thing to stay home, since Tom had done so much for him.

With all the good will in the world, it was always hard to keep a conversation going with Tom. Even after two years there was still a certain strain being alone together. Patrick was trying, without much success, to keep things a little lively by talking about his favorite subject. "I got the idea myself for a subway a long time ago, and here these bloody limeys have beat me to it," he said, referring to the London underground that had just opened. But it was his opinion that it wasn't going to be so easy for New York to build a subway of its own, seeing as how Manhattan Island was solid granite. "I haven't figured that one out yet." He grinned.

Tom asked about smoke in the tunnels. He had been reading the articles in the Herald about the proposed subway in order to keep up with his technically minded son, who had so impressed the chief engineer with his abilities, once he was given the chance. "They say," Tom said, "that over there in London the smoke from the locomotives almost asphyxiates the passengers."

"Nothin to it," said Patrick. "I'd solve that one fast enough with ventilation." And he was carried away with his ideas about building airshafts.

The clock on the mantelpiece struck nine, and Tom couldn't keep from yawning with fatigue after all the wedding preparations that day. It was the ultimate satisfaction to him that his newfound son, who had come up from nothing and already made such a good show of himself, was marrying the perfect girl—a girl almost more of a daughter to him than his own.

Patrick sensed the evening coming to an end and, hoping to forestall it, suggested another drink. "I shouldn't feel so antsy I guess. If I was out with the lads they'd be gettin me drunk and maybe even tryin to get me to one of them hoorhouses over on Greene Street."

Tom blanched at mention of the street he continued to patronize in secret.

Mistaking his expression for disapproval, Patrick reassured him with a laugh that he wouldn't have done anything like that, and reached for his father's glass to refill it.

But Tom put his hand over it and got to his feet, saying he wanted to be up to the mark for the big day. After formally shaking his hand and congratulating him, his father went upstairs.

How different Tom was from the kind of men he had grown up with. He knew that, behind the reserve, his father had a deeper affection for him than any of the lads who were always putting an arm around his shoulders, but could never show it. Even after all these months, there was so much about this new life he had to get used to. He wished he could run over next door to see Elizabeth as he would have any other night—Veronica was over there with her—but this was the one night he wasn't allowed.

He needed a pickup. He started to pour himself another whiskey, then thought better of it. Suddenly, all this gentility was too much for him. He slipped out into the night and went to find his mates.

Albert Cogswell said afterward that the light in the garden on the day of the wedding had been ideal for picture taking. At Elizabeth's suggestion, Tom had asked him to do the wedding photographs and he had traveled in from Long Island especially for it. In a rented cutaway Albert looked almost civilized, his unkempt red hair and beard tamed by a barber's shears and brilliantine.

Instead of setting up his tripod in the parlor and taking the usual formal groupings, Cogswell surprised everyone by trying out an idea of his own, made possible by the new dry-plate photography. He took his tripod and camera out into the garden, and though several of the guests objected to the mechanical intrusion on such an occasion, he set it up in various places during the ceremony and the reception that followed, wherever he thought he might get an interesting picture.

Whenever he called "Stop!" his subjects were to hold still until the image had registered on the plate. Elizabeth loved it. How original to think of photographing a wedding while it was going on!

Albert focused his apparatus first on the latticework bower specially erected in one corner of the garden where the ceremony was to take place. The rambler roses that had just burst into bloom trailed over it and a paper-mache cupid was perched on top.

He got a picture of the bridegroom waiting in front of the bower with old Reverend Hendryks from St. Luke's, whose round steel-rimmed glasses clearly reflected the tripod and camera. Patrick, handsome in his wedding suit, was staring so curiously at the gadget pointed at him he might have been about to step forward to take it apart and see how it worked.

Next, Albert turned his tripod around to snap a radiant Elizabeth on the arm of her father in the rear doorway. She was wearing her grandmother's veil and wedding dress—an Empire gown of startling simplicity, the white mousseline de soie falling free to the floor from the high-waisted bosom, and carrying a bouquet of sweetheart roses, lilies of the valley, and violets. Partially visible behind her was Veronica, her maid of honor, looking like she wanted to die in the elaborately curled hairdo and velveteen dress with flounces and bustle Elizabeth had chosen for her.

With his camera focused on the wedding party under the bower once more, Albert called "Stop!" throughout the ceremony as well, creating a series of charming tableaux. After the bridal embrace, he got Patrick sweeping Veronica into a bear hug with a big kiss, saying, "Ah, Veronica, you're a real sister to me now," as she blushed furiously, delighted.

Billy Yates and his wife Nora, Patrick's sister, were ill at ease. It was the first time they had gone to a wedding without their children, or seen a wedding party without children running about underfoot and the men getting pickled, but this was the strange way the Protestants did it. Billy Yates had a fiver ready, but no one ever passed the basket around like at a regular wedding.

While the guests were being served fruit punch and sponge cake from the buffet table on the lawn, wicked Albert got a picture of a flustered Nora

Yates dipping into an automatic curtsy, having unexpectedly come upon a former employer. Afterward, Elizabeth tore the picture up before anyone could see it and chided Albert for taking it.

In the middle of the reception, while the camera was focused on the bridal couple receiving congratulations, there was a sudden disturbance from the house. A moment later, the back door burst open and a flamboyant young colored woman dressed in the height of Parisian chic tripped down the steps and over to embrace the bride. "Elizabeth, honey! Thank God, I'm still in time!" When Albert yelled "Stop!" the woman, thoroughly professional, turned to pose for the camera, blocking out the bride with her ostrich feather hat.

Then, while Albert slipped a new plate into the camera, the woman turned to a dumbstruck Patrick. "Lizzie," she cried, "where did you find him? He's gorgeous!" She flung her gloved arms around him and kissed him, holding her full lips on his long enough for Albert to get the most sensational picture of the day.

It wasn't until the newlyweds were on the day coach bound for their honeymoon upstate in Saratoga that Patrick finally had time to ask about the colored woman.

"I've told you about her before, Pat. That was the Winifred Beaufort I knew in Paris. Can you imagine, she was a slave until she was fifteen!" Winifred's owner had been a cotton merchant in Louisiana, she said, who raised her as a servant for his daughters. She was with the family in Paris where her owner was doing business when Emancipation came, so she ran off and got herself a job singing in a music hall—she had spoken Creole French from childhood and had no trouble with the language. "That's where I met her," Elizabeth added. "Isn't she extraordinary?"

"Ya didn't go to a music hall! That isn't respectable."

"But of course I did. We saw each other all the time. She was the only American I knew there except for old Mrs. Saltonstall, the woman I worked for." Elizabeth didn't mention to her new husband that a young man named Jean-Paul who was smitten with her had been the one to introduce them backstage.

"Maybe I'm old-fashioned, but I don't feel easy with them coloreds."

"You will, when you get to know her. She's so much fun." She snuggled against him. "In Paris it's the most ordinary thing. You even have ex-slave owners mixing with ex-slaves socially. Of course, that wouldn't happen here."

"Well, I don't like it," he said, looking out at the Hudson River, already shadowed in purple as the setting sun lit the peaks of the Catskill mountains orange.

Elizabeth laid her cheek against his shoulder. "Oh, but things are changing, Pat. Anyway, Winifred's different."

When she planted a kiss on his set jaw, he had to give in to his saucy little bride with her ridiculous ideas. The passengers around them smiled knowingly as he took her in his arms and kissed her.

19

Winifred Beaufort had come back to America on the chance of a job in a music hall. An American theatrical agent working in Paris had given her a letter of introduction to Will Kennedy, a New York impresario, after hearing her sing one night in a little café. With her sultry voice and European style, the agent told her, she was exactly what Kennedy was looking for.

Winifred had not intended to return to America—she was completely at home in France. In her seven years there she hadn't done so badly, in her own eyes, though her ambitions were far from fulfilled. She regularly sang in the chorus of musical revues. She even got to perform alone sometimes in café concerts, developing her repertoire of songs for the day she hoped to be a star. But from what the agent said, it sounded like she might get ahead faster in New York and she decided to take a chance on it.

Her only memories of America were from when she had been a slave in the South. Back then, even in the North, a free black person could be kidnapped and sold into slavery in the Deep South again. But since Emancipation, Negroes had been declared citizens and given the vote, and she had heard show business was receptive to entertainers of her race.

For her interview with the impresario she wore a green shantung dress from Paris with a mauve cape and matching sun parasol, which was smarter than anything even the white women wore at the Broadway Central Hotel where she was staying. But as she approached the theater on Fourteenth

Street, she was somewhat dismayed by the grubbiness of the marquee and the rundown look of the whole block, with brownstones converted into businesses and rooming houses and many of the lower floors into saloons.

After the elegance of Paris, even the finest New York buildings looked measly to her, but Winifred reassured herself that under the glowing lamps of evening with carriages drawing up to discharge well-dressed patrons, it could be a very different matter.

Having been away a few years himself, there was no way for the agent in Paris to know that the area had undergone a rapid deterioration as the city continued its push northward. When the agent had last seen New York, Fourteenth Street had still been very much in the center of things, but that was before Delmonico's restaurant had moved uptown to Twenty-third Street, before the fashionable residences on Union Square were turned into business establishments, and when the Academy of Music was still the only opera house in town.

Will Kennedy was not New York's top impresario, the agent had said, but he could give her the start she needed. Winifred held on to the thought for reassurance as she picked her way through the ropes and props of backstage.

In his cramped, windowless office that was gloomy even with a gas lamp, Kennedy lounged in a swivel chair, polka-dot suspenders over his striped shirt, a bowler hat tipped back on his bald head, appraising her as if she were on the auction block again.

He barely glanced at her letter of introduction, chewing an unlit cigar stub in his mouth. "What's your speciality, kid?" he growled in a New York accent. "Gospel, rag, or minstrel?"

Holding her indignation in check, Winifred replied haughtily that she sang French music hall songs and, exaggerating slightly, since there was no one within three thousand miles to contradict her, told Kennedy her last job was as the star of a musical review on the Champs Elysées.

When he looked dubious, she got up and with a flamboyant strut that waggled her bustle, went over to a battered upright piano. Laying her parasol on top of it, she sat down, and with improvised flourishes on the keyboard sang in French a ditty called "La Demoiselle du Regiment" that everyone had been singing in Paris. As she got to the chorus, she turned to Kennedy and interpolated some "ooh-la-la's", which she knew were irresistible to Americans.

She was in the middle of the verse that always brought down the house, where with rolling eyes the demoiselle of the song describes the succession of soldiers in her arms, when the impresario bawled out that he had heard enough. "That kind of stuff don't go over here. Can you pick a banjo?"

She spun around on the stool and glared. "What do you think I am, anyway?"

Kennedy smirked as he shifted the cigar stub between his lips. "Where do you think you are, anyway? I got a job for you as a banjo picker. You get to sing a chorus or two even." He leaned back in his chair with his hands clasped behind his head and ogled the brown bombshell. The customers, he knew, would eat her up. He could see her already—breasts and bottom bursting out of skimpy rags with a cotton-field backdrop, singing a little jig tune, as a chorus of fieldhands did buck-and-wing around her.

With his checked trouser legs spread wide, she couldn't fail to see that he was deliberately flaunting his excitement. The theater managers she had dealt with in Paris had also expected her to come across. If they were smoother, with the inevitable hand-kissing a lady was supposed to fall for, they were still pigs at bottom. But they never began this crudely. "You wouldn't recognize a special talent like mine if it were shoved down your throat, Mr. Kennedy," she said, pulling on her gloves. She tilted her chin defiantly so that the gaslight caught the sheen of her hair dressed in a mass of braids pulled back into a chignon.

Kennedy had his hands on his thighs. "Take my advice, kid, it's not very often a colored girl gets a chance. When we do minstrel, most of our tootsies are in blackface. I'm doing you a favor offering you anything at all." He got up, tugging at his pants to adjust himself, and came around to put a hand on her shoulder. "You know why I'm willing to take a chance on you, Winnie? It's because you do have something special." He tickled her ear, making a pendant earring glitter.

She shook him off and got up from the piano stool, aware that her junoesque proportions were arousing the dog in him. As she picked up her parasol and gathered her skirts, she told him in her most refined accents that he didn't have as much in his trousers as he thought, and if he expected her to get down on her knees and worship that, he had another guess coming. She turned on her heel and walked out.

He came out to watch her from the stage as she swept up the aisle to the lobby, her skirts held to one side emphasizing her magnificent behind. "If you change your mind," he yelled after her. "I always got a job for a looker like you."

Blinking against the bright sunlight on the street outside, Winifred was seething over that pipsqueak impresario. He couldn't run a flea circus, let alone a music hall she'd want to work in. That bastard in Paris had sold her a bill of goods and she had fallen for it. No one who knew her back in France would believe she had been such a sucker.

As she walked toward her hotel, she realized what a mess she was in. She didn't have a dime to her name and her hotel bill was due. But by the time she got to the hustle of Broadway, things didn't seem so bad. With her voice and looks and a Paris wardrobe in her trunk, nobody was going to keep Winifred Beaufort down.

20

When the honeymooners returned from Saratoga, they expected to have the house on Perry Street mostly to themselves, since in the meantime Tom had moved up to the top floor with Veronica.

But to their surprise and consternation a dinner party had already been arranged for them, cooked by Veronica with Mrs. Cooper's help. The two families joined them at table without being invited, eager to hear about the honeymoon and their plans for the future. Not wanting to hurt anyone's feelings, the couple did their best to look pleased.

After dinner the families followed them upstairs to the parlor, chattering even more animatedly over coffee as their eyes drank in the lovers. The lovers on the other hand had been dreaming of nothing else, since taking the train back that morning, but having an intimate supper together and stealing off afterward to their room.

Gazing at their ripe daughter and virile son-in-law in wonder, the Coopers were reminded that twenty years before, in their fumbling attempts at passion, they had only had a glimmer of what was possible. But after Mrs. Cooper's pregnancy, sex had become less important and they had been distracted by their many liberal causes. They had scarcely thought about it since, until tonight.

For Tom, it was bittersweet to see the children united with the blessings of the whole world. Patrick's merry blue eyes evoked Molly's and the memory of a love that could never be.

Even Veronica felt an odd glow she couldn't account for. It was her first experience of people radiating fulfilled sensuality and it thrilled her. Her goose bumps she attributed to her new fondness for her thickset, curly-haired half brother who was so happy with his lovely bride.

When the newlyweds finally managed to escape to their bedroom, which Veronica had redecorated for them as a surprise, Elizabeth closed her eyes at the horror of the exquisite floral-bouquet wallpaper having been painted over white, stark as a monk's cell. And even more awful the heavy, maroon tapestry drapes with the cluster-ball velvet fringe had been replaced with gossamer curtains that made her feel exposed to the world. Something had to be done at once, but how could she ever change it all back without hurting her hypersensitive sister-in-law?

When the lamp was out and they were in bed, the feelings that they had been holding back all evening were not there. They lay listening to Tom's footsteps coming downstairs to the bathroom outside their door, the cataract as he pulled the chain, the endless gurgle as the water trickled into the tank again, and his steps back up to his room and his shuffling around just over their heads. Then there was Veronica's door opening and her mouse-like tiptoeing down the stairs, followed by her frantic jerking on the chain since the tank had not yet refilled. Patrick muttered that he would make sure the new toilet was installed up there the next day, even if he had to do every bit of the plumbing himself.

No sooner had Veronica retreated back upstairs, than Tom began to cough directly above them, the springs creaking as he shifted in bed.

Patrick sat up and said that he wished they were back in the hotel by the lake where they could have a little peace.

Elizabeth, who was just as upset, still dwelling on the hideous evening, said she couldn't understand how her parents could have been so insensitive, inviting themselves over like that. Her mother had sounded positively asinine gushing about her own honeymoon at Long Branch, New Jersey, which she had hardly ever mentioned before.

"Yeah," said Patrick, "and did ya see how Tom looked at me misty-eyed all evenin? It made me feel queer all over, knowin he was thinkin of my mother. Damn 'em all!" He grabbed his pillow and flung it across the room.

She whispered for him to be quiet, but he was already out of bed, pacing the floor on bare feet in his nightshirt. "What the hell do they think they're doin? We're not a pair of freaks on show like Tom Thumb and Lavinia Bumpus. I'd like to wipe out the lot of them."

"Please, Pat, they're going to hear," she pleaded. But he ignored her, snarling that they were going to move out of this assembly hall. When she didn't answer, he stopped. She was weeping into the pillow, trying to muffle her sobs.

In a moment he was beside her, sorry for his outburst. He had never seen her cry before. All the women he had known from his world wailed at the drop of a hat, but Elizabeth never. It rent his heart. It was terrible. He took his quivering bride in his arms and kissed her face all over, begging her to forgive him. "I'm the most goddamnedest sinner in the world, my darlin."

"Oh, Patrick!" She threw her arms around him. "My love!"

He reached for her breasts, bending down to kiss them. For the first time since the lovers had arrived back home that day, desire overcame all distractions.

As the days passed, the newlyweds kept waiting for the well-meaning but suffocating devotion of their families to wear itself out, but their relations seemed even more determined in their efforts to please. Veronica begged Elizabeth to let her cook for them—it was the one thing she had to offer. So Elizabeth had to put off trying out on Patrick the special little dishes she had learned in France.

Mrs. Cooper expected her daughter, as a young matron, to participate in some of her causes. Elizabeth had looked forward to devoting herself to making a home for her new husband, but her mother shrewdly played on her social conscience, which she knew to be as well developed as her own.

"But dear, don't tell me you can bear to stand by while thousands of horses in this city are being beaten and worked to death every day. And as for the immigrants in their hellish slums...."

Elizabeth couldn't close her eyes to cruelty to animals, or immigrants, or the plight of women, or children in factories, so she found herself giving up her free time and sometimes not getting home until after Patrick did.

Tom's constant solicitude was even harder to take. When he was sitting with his son in the parlor after dinner each night, the minute Elizabeth came up from the kitchen after trying to help Veronica he made a point of jumping up and leaving them to themselves, making them guilty knowing he was going to sit alone upstairs in his room.

When Pat came home from work with only one thing on his mind, to get upstairs and break in on Elizabeth's nap for a few moments of bliss before dinner, Tom inevitably jumped out of his easy chair and buttonholed him about some boring news item in the papers, while he had to stand there and pretend to be interested, not wanting to hurt his feelings.

When he woke up and wanted to hold his wife in her sleepy morning softness in his arms, there was always that knock on the door and Veronica tiptoed in with the breakfast tray and poured out their coffee, her eyes shining in unconscious response to the intimacy that filled the air.

On Elizabeth's birthday, Patrick had promised he'd make it home for lunch by twelve thirty, no matter how busy he was at the work site. For once, her sister-in-law had left them with the house to themselves, with the excuse of taking Tom his lunch at the printing shop. But it was already after one.

Elizabeth had just about given up hope, when through the window there he was bounding up the steps, bursting through the door and, clasping her in his arms, he kissed her hungrily.

Elizabeth was ecstatic. "You did get away after all, Pat. Veronica's made us a splendid shrimp creole."

"To hell with that," Patrick said, hustling her toward the stairs. "I've got other ideas."

"But she's gone to so much trouble," she said giggling, as he pushed her up the stairs.

As they lay disheveled and happy, he idly traced her breasts with a finger, and said, "It's good I'm not a Catholic any more, ain't it? I always used to say if it weren't for the Church I'd fuck all the day long."

In this marriage Patrick had discovered the wonder of sex for the first time. Though he had been married to Hester for nearly five years, she always lay there like a stone, obediently permitting him the exercise of his marital rights, so Elizabeth's joyful response was a revelation.

"You mean you don't think the Episcopal rite is as sacred as the

Roman?" she said as sternly as she could manage. "I wonder if you're taking your new faith seriously." Then, seeing his hangdog look, she laughed and kissed him. "But you're right about one thing, dearest. In our church we don't insist that lovemaking just be for procreation. A husband and wife are allowed…" she blushed, "you know what I mean…whenever they want."

"Ya wicked little slut." He grinned and, giving her a final kiss, leaped out of bed and grabbed his trousers. "Now I'm hungry as a horse. Whatta we got to eat?"

In no time Elizabeth was pregnant. And though they were happy about it, in one way it made matters worse—both their families became, if anything, more suffocating with their attentions. It was even harder to find time to be alone. The irony was that now Elizabeth wanted her husband more than ever. Pregnancy only seemed to increase her randy appetite, though it took her a while to convince Patrick, after his sad experience with Hester, that satisfying it would not lead to a miscarriage.

Tom and even staid Professor Cooper, who was not a garrulous man, talked about nothing else but the coming grandchild. Veronica began to knit little garments, only dropping her knitting needles to run down and get Elizabeth hot milk, which she hated. Mrs. Cooper, heretofore a sensible woman, put aside her committees and causes to ransack the Broadway emporiums for layettes, baby blankets, and an avalanche of toys. She even dragged Elizabeth off to lectures on child care.

One night, matters reached a head when Patrick came home from work to find Tom in the parlor entertaining his old friend Albert Cogswell, who had just moved back to a rooming house in the neighborhood after the death of his wife.

Tom started to get up, insisting that his son come in and have a whiskey with them. But Patrick was ready for him. Nothing was going to stop him this time from rushing straight up to Elizabeth. Holding his ground in the doorway, he firmly declined his father's invitation, and to make it quite clear that he meant what he said, leapt up the stairs.

With his tie off and already out of his jacket, he opened the door, only to find Elizabeth sitting with that colored friend of hers from the wedding, deep in conversation.

Elizabeth looked up, smiling. "Pat, you're home early, or is it later than I thought?"

Patrick's face went hot. "Is it too much to ask to be alone with ya even for a minute?" he barked.

Winifred Beaufort knew a family crisis when she saw one. "I was never here," she said, hastily gathering up her things and rustling across the room to the door,

Patrick was ripping at his collar, red-faced, muttering, "That goddam woman...."

"Don't be upset," Elizabeth said, going over to unfasten his collar. She was sorry that he had come in on Winifred, whom he couldn't accept being in the house. Her friend was usually gone by the time he came home, but the two of them had been so involved in the problems Winifred was having, she had forgotten how late it was.

For several months Winifred had been making the rounds of theaters, vaudeville houses, and even dance saloons all over the city, and had finally been forced to admit that no one wanted to hire a negro entertainer no matter how good she was. Having only worked in Paris where the race situation was easier, she had been completely misled about the way things were in post-Civil War America. "Honey, the only thing they want a colored girl for here is housework or hustling, and I'll be damned if I do either," she had been telling Elizabeth just before Pat broke in. She bemoaned that the only thing left for her to do was to crawl back to that two-bit entrepreneur Will Kennedy, and take whatever degrading part he offered her.

As Elizabeth worked on his collar studs, Patrick went on raging. "Either you and me move out of this house right now or I'm goin to become a mass murderer." He turned his head so she could get at the recalcitrant button. "We'd have more privacy in a boardin house than we have here."

She agreed, with a sigh, that the situation had become intolerable.

"This whole neighborhood is givin me a pain in the ass. I'm goin to be workin farther uptown soon when we finish the line around here. What's to stop us from movin out of here and into one of them fine apartment houses they're puttin up on West End Avenue? They got hydraulic elevators that carry ya up to the tenth floor and gas cookstoves in the kitchen and runnin hot water besides. A couple of the fellas I work with live there. How about it? We'll let Tom have his house back."

"It's true"—she sighed, looking out at the row of Federal-style houses across the street—"some families are moving away. They say Greenwich isn't the same any more." She knew that if Pat had the power he wouldn't hesitate for a minute to tear down all those handsome houses and put up one of the West End Avenue monstrosities. She turned back to him and started unbuttoning his shirt. "I know things are bad, Pat. Maybe we will have to move, but do we have to think about it before the baby comes? I really can't bear it."

He took off his shirt, wadded it up and threw it into the corner, putting his hands on her waist as she unbuttoned the top of his long johns. "Okay, we'll stay for a while. But honest, now, does that flashy friend of yours have to be around here all the time?"

"I wish you'd try to like her a little. She's having such a hard time. Things haven't worked out for her here, and don't forget she was a slave until the war." Her fingers toyed with the hair on his chest.

"Fuck Winifred and fuck the whole lot of em!" He scooped her up into his arms and fell with her on the bed.

"Better lock the door," she managed to say, but Patrick was beyond that.

21

Will Kennedy was mounting a musical revue called Carry Me Back To Old Virginny. It was to be a nostalgic tribute to the Old South that the Union armies had not long before destroyed. This suited the current mood in the North, which was already tiring of the postwar period when idealistic young people had flocked south to help the newly-freed slaves, setting up schools and health programs. It was already apparent the government was not about to break up the plantations and give land to the Negroes. The Ku Klux Klan was riding in the night to force them back into the cotton fields, and all the financial interests in the North tacitly approved.

Winifred's financial situation was so dire, she had to take a job in Kennedy's show. If she had the cash, she told Elizabeth, she'd be on the first boat back to France. But defeated in her search for any work at all that used her talents properly, she numbed herself to what she was being asked to do in the show.

She was the only genuine Negro in a blackface chorus line of happy darkies. With a red kerchief knotted around her head and a ragged skirt that showed glimpses of red-and-white stockinged leg, she went mechanically through the shimmy steps Kennedy had worked out for them.

But in the middle of the first night's performance, as the chorus was rolling their eyes while singing about "Waitin on the levee for the white boys to come," she woke up to what she was doing. She tore off her kerchief and, to the whistles and jeers of the audience, ran off the stage.

Will Kennedy found her in the dressing room wiping off her make up. She threw down the sponge and turned on him. How dare he think she could go along with his filthy myth of happy slave times? It was an obscenity! She knew what it was like to work in the cotton, and stand up on the auction block to be leered at and pawed over by those swine, and be the target of every white man's lust.

Will was knocked on his ear. He had never seen such a gorgeous woman in his life. He couldn't bear for her to walk out on him again. As she put on her street clothes, he pulled her around and shook her hard to make her listen. "Okay, okay, I'll give you a solo."

It wasn't one of her French songs—he wouldn't go that far—but it wasn't all that bad. She sang about a creole from New Orleans, daughter of a white planter and a slave mother, who became the toast of Paris.

On the first night the drunks quieted down and some of them even applauded. Will was dazzled. By the second night, her old confidence was back and she threw in a chorus in French. Will said he'd allow it, if she'd do a little sashaying and high-stepping across the stage, so she did, and it brought down the house.

Stage-door johnnies who hung around after the show to pick up the girls, she ignored. But one night a bouquet with a note in French was delivered to her backstage. "May we pay homage to a beautiful chanteuse and toast her in champagne?"

She was as delighted to meet the four young Americans just back from studying art in Paris as they were to come upon her in provincial New York. All of them talking away a mile a minute, they took her off to an impromptu party at their studio building on Tenth Street, where they kept her singing her repertoire of French café songs until dawn.

As soon as she was able to pay her bill, Winifred moved out of the hotel into a boardinghouse her new artist friends recommended. It was full of show people, and turned out to be at the other end of Perry Street from the Endicotts.

22

For months, Patrick Endicott announced to everyone he met that it was going to be a boy. In June, when Elizabeth gave birth to a girl, he put his arms around his wife as she lay exhausted but shining and told her that it didn't make any difference—he was the happiest man in the world. But Elizabeth saw almost at once that he didn't take much interest in the baby.

It was as if the infant, whom they named Alicia, understood her father's disappointment from the start. But her grandfather Tom adored her, and it was to him, later on when she was old enough to begin talking, that she reached out her little arms and addressed her first word, "Papa."

It got on Pat's nerves to see the two of them cooing at each other. Occasionally he tried to pick Alicia up himself, but she always cried. It was bad enough that Tom was a pain in the neck, now he was taking his child away from him.

Elizabeth was usually busy with the baby when he got home, so there were no more private moments before dinner and he had to put up with his father's unrelenting attentions more than ever.

One night before dinner, while waiting for Elizabeth to finish nursing the baby upstairs, he was relieved because Tom hadn't shown up yet and for once he was able to read the Herald in peace. He was into a story about a small tribe of Indians in California that had been resisting being taken off its land and shipped to a reservation.

Just when he was getting into the details of the latest battle, in which a dozen braves were holding off a battalion of soldiers, the front door opened and Tom came in, visibly upset about something. It seemed that Albert Cogswell's room, which was beyond the el by the river, had been ransacked and his drawings messed up. The room was over a roughneck tavern called the Galway Bay, and Tom had warned him against moving in there, but Albert didn't understand that parts of Greenwich had gone downhill since he had lived here before. Tom had spent the afternoon helping him move his belongings into the unused storage loft over the print shop, which would do temporarily as a place for him to stay.

"The kind of people coming into the village these days...." Tom sank into an armchair across from Patrick and pulled out a handkerchief to wipe his brow. "It's just not like it used to be."

There it was again, Patrick thought, turning a page of the newspaper impatiently. Like all long-time Greenwich residents, his father felt an automatic superiority to newcomers. Nobody else had a right to be here but them. They thought they owned the place.

"The micks are takin over, is that what ya mean, Tom?"

"I wouldn't say that. Who knows who those people are? It just isn't safe over there any more. They're even calling it Murderers' Row."

Ever since he got married, Patrick had been holding back his irritation against his father, but this was too much to take. "That sounds like anti-mick talk to me, however ya slice it," he said, looking at Tom over the paper. "The lads at the Galway aren't a bad bunch. I stop in there for a beer myself sometimes."

Tom heard his son's resentment and backed off. "Don't get me wrong, I'm not saying they had anything to do with it."

Patrick raised his voice. "If ya really want to get a knife in your back I'll tell ya where to go. Go over to Little Italy where the wops are, that's where. I'll tell ya one thing, Tom," he said, shaking a finger at the older man, "those lads are as good as any of your almighty snobs who act like they came over on the Mayflower." He threw down his paper. "Oh, they make ya feel like shyte around here, they do."

Hearing her husband shouting below, Elizabeth handed the baby over to the hired girl. The infant set up a shriek, adding to the commotion, but she rushed downstairs, buttoning her bodice. For months Pat had been threatening to tell his father off. She had begged him not to. It would be too awful. But as she came into the room she knew from his red face and Tom's pallor that the worst had happened.

"For mercy's sake, you two, what's going on down here," she cried. "Please, not before dinner. Veronica's been slaving all afternoon on a gateau amandine."

"Fuck her gateau!" Patrick yelled, jumping to his feet. "I'm sick of all this talk against the micks around here. No one says what they mean and ya never get a moment alone with your wife." With Alicia screaming louder than ever upstairs, he turned on her. "What the hell's that kid squawking for? Didn't ya feed it?" He went to the window and, keeping his back to them, gripped the frame on both sides with his fists.

Elizabeth and Tom looked at each other in stunned silence. "He wasn't attacking the Irish," she said at last, "were you, Tom?"

Her father-in-law, who was in shock at discovering the extent of his son's hostility toward him, mumbled that he certainly hadn't meant any disrespect to the Irish.

"There, Pat, you see?" she said brightly. "And don't worry about Alicia. It's natural for her to cry. She's a baby. I think what we all need is a good dinner." She went over to him and took his arm.

But the significance of his son's outburst did not escape Tom. How could he have missed seeing before this how much he had been in the way?

He waited until the meal was over and Veronica was out in the kitchen getting the dessert. Then, trying to sound casual, he told Elizabeth and Patrick that in all the fuss over Albert's getting robbed he had forgotten to tell them his news. He would be moving out soon. He had decided to share the loft over the print shop with Albert.

The young couple's eyes met guiltily like children discovered in a shameful secret. This was not lost on Tom, though he talked on briskly. He and Albert were about to embark on a new project, something they had both been discussing for years. Until now he had been too busy building up the business to start on it. They were going to put out portfolios of lithographs of Albert's river sketches.

At least that much of the story Albert already knew about, he thought ruefully—he wondered what his old friend would think about their sharing the place together. "It'll be a lot more convenient if I'm living over there too. We'll fix it up and be as snug as two bugs in a rug."

Patrick was overcome with remorse. "Tom, I didn't mean nothin of what I said."

"I know you didn't, son. I've enjoyed sharing the house with you, but it's high time I made a change."

Elizabeth went around to embrace him. "You mustn't go, Tom. Why, whatever would we do without you?" She had tears in her eyes.

"Now, now, my mind is made up. Anyway, I'll just be a few blocks away." He patted her gently.

Patrick reached over impulsively and took his father's hand. "I don't know how ya ever put up with a son of a bitch like me. I'm the one who should be leavin around here."

The kitchen door was pushed open and a beaming Veronica came in carrying the gateau, which she put down on the table, dowsed with brandy, and set aflame.

That night, Tom went up to his room on the third floor, morose over have to leave this house where he had been so content since Patrick moved in. But what hurt most was having seen how quickly and with what obvious relief his children had accepted it.

23

Tom Endicott's printing shop had become well known for the quality of its work. He and Albert often went directly to the clipper ships to choose the best papers brought back from the Far East. This attention to detail paid off—from all parts of the city people brought in special jobs.

One winter day, a conservatively dressed gentleman of about thirty came in with a short story to be printed up in a small edition as a gift to family and friends. He had written it himself. His address was one of the grand old houses on Washington Square still occupied by some of the city's more patrician families, at a time when the newer rich were building mansions up Fifth Avenue as far as Central Park.

This was something Tom knew would interest Elizabeth and his poet daughter Veronica when he saw them next. Going to Sunday dinner at the house on Perry Street had become a regular thing since he had moved out a year and a half before. His particular joy was his little granddaughter Alicia, a golden-haired angel of two, who still called him Papa.

Everything had turned out better than anyone could have expected. The Coopers no longer found the young couple such a novelty and let them alone—even Veronica gave up monopolizing the kitchen. At last Patrick and Elizabeth were living their own life.

When Tom went over that Sunday, the house was in its usual happy turmoil. Alicia dropped her doll and ran to grandpa for him to pick her up, while the family spaniel Cicero danced around barking. Smells of goose and mince pie wafted up from the kitchen. Patrick shouted hello from the study—he was on the floor repairing the sewing machine with the parts strewn around him.

In front of the blazing fire, Elizabeth and Veronica patted a place for Tom between them on the sofa. His granddaughter climbed onto his lap and played with a wooden printing block he brought her, as he told them about his well-dressed customer from Washington Square and the story he was printing up for him. It was called "The Passionate Pilgrim" and was so fancily written he was having a devil of a time proofreading it.

"Henry James!" Veronica cried, when her father told her the writer's name, and begged him to let her see a copy of the story. Not only had she heard of the writer but she already knew several of his stories from magazines—she considered him one of the most talented young writers in America. Though it was uncharacteristic of her, she talked a blue streak about him all through dinner and kept begging Tom for every detail of their meeting.

A few days later when James came back to the shop to pick up the copies of his story, he surprised Tom by mentioning his daughter's poetry. Apparently in the intervening week Veronica had sent him several of her poems, though she had never let anyone else see them before—certainly not her family. James said he found her style remarkable. In fact, he went on about it in such a complicated fashion that Tom could hardly follow. The one thing that was clear to him was that this was the first man who had ever expressed the slightest interest in his daughter. Even without having met her, James seemed enthralled.

When the writer asked him to convey his high esteem to such a talented poetess, Tom took the bull by the horns and invited him to join the family for dinner the following Sunday. He told James his daughter was an admirer of his work and would take great pleasure in hearing the words from him directly.

James had a kind of New England formality about him and it was hard to imagine him in the unpretentious environment of Perry Street, but then Veronica had much the same kind of reserve herself. She had never shown the least interest in getting a husband and at thirty-one seemed perfectly content to settle for spinsterhood, but there was nothing to lose by bringing them together.

Elizabeth was even more pleased than Tom, when he told her about

James coming to dinner. She agreed he had done exactly the right thing by inviting him. But Veronica was aghast at the prospect of meeting the writer face to face. He was a superior being to her. What if he should comment on her poems in front of everyone? At the most she had hoped for a note. Now she wished she had never done such a foolish thing as send the poems to him. He would feel obliged to say nice things about them and she would die of embarrassment.

Elizabeth pointed out to her sister-in-law that James wouldn't have accepted the invitation if he wasn't impressed with her work. There was nothing to worry about. She would invite her parents over to join them—they would be suitable dinner companions for a literary guest. She would see to it that the conversation stayed on agreeable topics, and Veronica wasn't to worry that Patrick would talk about public transportation. She knew how to handle him.

When Elizabeth explained the situation to her husband that night, he agreed good-heartedly that it was Veronica's show and he wouldn't put his clumsy foot into it. He would only open his mouth to ask for the butter. Besides, what did he have to say to "artist types" anyway? They gave him a pain.

As she kissed him, she thought, sadly, how true this was. Though once she had hopes of bringing him around, since their marriage he had obstinately refused to Be interested in anything to do with the arts.

This was not to be an ordinary family Sunday dinner. It was Veronica's first and only chance. Overriding her sister-in-law's complaints that she was making far too much of the whole thing, Elizabeth marched her off to A. T. Stewart's and got her to buy a new dress.

On Sunday, all were in a festive mood—except for Veronica, who was laying out the silverware on the damask cloth in a state of panic. The floors and woodwork had been oiled, the rugs beaten, and Alicia and Cicero banished to Albert Cogswell's care for the afternoon.

As Elizabeth rushed about with her mother and the hired girl to finish last minute preparations in the kitchen, the men were drinking hot buttered rum upstairs in the parlor, while waiting for the guest.

Leaning on the mantelpiece Professor Cooper was joshing his son-in-law about Bill Tweed, the Tammany boss. The politician had finally been caught with his hand in the till. "Even with your admiration for the rascal,

Patrick, you have to admit ten years is still letting him off easy."

Boss Tweed was an old bone between them and Patrick grinned. "How can I contradict a college professor? I'm too busy puttin up elevateds to worry about the crooks catchin the crooks."

His father-in-law clapped him on the back. "Just promise you won't put an elevated up Perry Street."

"Okay, if ya promise me you'll get Albany to let us build our subway."

"Isn't that up to the voters?"

"What's the good?" said Patrick. "The railroad big shots buy off any governor ya put in office."

Before James arrived, Elizabeth and Mrs. Cooper saw to it that Veronica came up from the kitchen with them to join the men and they were determined not to let her sneak away. The hired girl knew what was to be done, and if there were any problems with the dinner Elizabeth would see to them herself. She wanted Veronica to make the most of her opportunity to get to know this writer she admired so much.

How well Veronica looked this afternoon. The wedding photographs had shown Elizabeth what a mistake she had made overdressing her as her bridesmaid in that fussy velveteen gown with the flounces. The simple mauve taffeta she had chosen for her this time was far more becoming. Her hair was severely brushed back from a center part into a loose bun at the nape of her neck. Elizabeth decided her sister-in-law had a look of classical refinement—even an ethereal quality like her poor mother.

She saw how right she had been to insist Veronica look her best when a few minutes later Henry James arrived. Dressed in the best English tailoring, he bowed over Veronica's hand as if he were about to kiss it. "Miss Endicott, this is indeed an honor...."

He had pale patrician features and his colorless hair was too precisely parted, but Veronica's flush of pleasure showed that she found him to her liking.

Patrick winked across at his wife, but she sent him a look reminding him of his promise to behave himself.

James bowed just as formally over Mrs. Cooper's hand and then Elizabeth's own, when Tom presented him. Patrick and Professor Cooper were distinctly put off by his limp handshake and murmur of civilities, instead of the hand-pumping and effusive greetings they were used to.

Elizabeth was about to offer Mr. James a hot toddy when the bell for dinner rang. The hired girl had gotten it wrong—she had been instructed to wait half an hour before calling them down to the dining room. But under the circumstances, Elizabeth was just as glad. Considering how formidable the guest appeared to be, it might be easier to get things going over the table.

She had planned the dinner spcially for someone from the high-toned world of Washington Square—canvasback duck stuffed with oysters. Old Mrs. Saltonstall had told her often on their trip to Europe that it was a favorite of the best society.

In the dining room, when James pulled out Veronica's chair for her in a courtly manner, her sister-in-law's timid smile at him made her almost pretty. He took the chair beside her, laid his napkin across his lap without shaking it open, and leaned toward Elizabeth with a thin smile. "I was just telling Miss Endicott how unusual your centerpiece is," he said, referring to the arrangement of gourds and pine-cones on a carved alabaster pedestal she had brought back from Italy.

The hired girl was ladling around the terrapin soup—without splashing, for once. Elizabeth had put her into starched cap and apron especially for the occasion.

Reaching over to fill James' glass with an Alsatian hock he had bought for the dinner party, Tom said that he hoped James' family and friends liked the booklet he had printed for him.

The author sipped the wine, reflected, then pronounced it first-rate, before replying. "It was an excellent job you did, Mr. Endicott. You know, I'm getting some very creditable reactions to my little tale. The curator of special editions of the New York Society Library has asked for five copies for the collection." James looked immensely satisfied with himself.

He was conceited as well as pretentious, Elizabeth decided, but she was pleased that Veronica seemed to be drinking in every affected syllable. She smiled across at her handsome husband who was being good as gold, not even slurping his soup as he ordinarily did.

"Are you by any chance of English origin, Mr. James?" Mrs. Cooper asked, impressed by his meticulous way of speaking.

"For some reason, people always seem to think that," he said. "Actually, I was born right here in New York in the same house I still live in with my family, but I've visited London frequently since I was a child, so I suppose it's possible that one could pick up a trace of the accent. The day after tomorrow, in fact, I'm departing again on the Britannia for an indefinite stay."

"I do so wish we could afford it," Elizabeth's mother said. "I'd like to study the effectiveness of their child labor laws. My daughter was in London six years ago...."

The kitchen door opened and the girl brought in the brace of canvasback ducks on a platter, with glazed carrots, cranberries, and oyster shells filled with whipped potatoes.

"Bravo!" said James with his tepid smile.

Patrick was bored out of his mind by the stuffed-shirt guest and was only too happy to devote himself to carving the roast fowl.

"It would be of interest to me to hear your impressions of London, Mrs. Endicott," James said, turning to Elizabeth when they settled down to the main course.

His formal courtesy was not without its charm, she thought, and told him about seeing Queen Victoria pass by in her barouche on The Mall. But her greatest thrill had been the Gothic art at the British Museum.

"How extraordinary you should say that," said the author. "Very few Americans give a hoot about the Middle Ages. They're all obsessed with the Renaissance. Why can't any of them even begin to understand the subtleties and complexities of European civilization?"

"How true," cried Veronica, who until now had been too awestruck to say a word.

James turned to her and asked if she had observed this herself.

She flushed. "I'm afraid I've never been to Europe," she said, "but it's always seemed to me that those very subtleties and complexities you speak of must make life so much richer there." She looked surprised at having spoken out. She was not used to speaking her private thoughts at all.

James gave her a lofty smile. "As a poet, Miss Endicott, your concerns are hardly those of most Americans, I'd say."

She returned his smile shyly.

"I've read your verse with great pleasure, Miss Endicott. You are a lyricist of some power and originality."

"Oh...," Veronica gasped, looking like she could fall through the floor.

"I warn you though," said James, "your odd rhymes won't be a simple matter for publishers to accept. And using dashes instead of punctuation—definitely unconventional, but rather effective, I think."

"Oh, mercy, Mr. James...I'm embarrassed." She gave a flustered look around, as if expecting the others to be laughing at her.

James patted his lips with his napkin, enjoying the effect his words were having on his admirer. "Very well," he said. "No more about poetry just now. But I won't be put off, I insist on a talk with you privately after dinner."

As Veronica squirmed, Elizabeth exchanged a conspiratorial look with Tom who was following the little scene as avidly as she was. Things were going even better than they could have hoped.

Then her father threatened to ruin everything. Professor Cooper asked James what he thought of Disraeli's new bill in Parliament giving the vote to factory workers in England.

"For heaven's sake, Papa!" Elizabeth said, ready to strangle him. "No politics, please!" She turned quickly to the author. "Tell us how you found London the last time you were there."

"It's still the most compatible city in the world," James replied, as he deftly sliced bits of meat from a wing with knife and fork. "The only thing I disapprove of is that ghastly means of public locomotion they have installed underground. I made the mistake of taking a ride on it."

To her horror, Patrick's forkful of mashed carrots and duck stopped halfway to his mouth. "Did I hear ya say, Mr. James, that ya took a ride on the London underground?" He was alert and quivering like a pointer on the scent.

James seemed to look for the first time at her husky, black-haired young husband at the head of the table. "Why, yes, I did, Mr. Endicott! My brother William insisted on it. But I confess I loathed the entire experience. I got off at the first stop."

Patrick was tensed, as if ready to leap into the air. "It was the smoke drove ya out, I bet."

Oh, dear God, no, Elizabeth prayed. Don't let him go on.

"Why, indeed, it was the smoke," said James. "It was abominable."

Patrick was almost panting. "Electric locomotives will cure that. We're workin on them here."

Veronica was mutely appealing to Elizabeth. She tried to cut him off. "I'm sure Mr. James doesn't want to hear about subways, Pat dear." She gave him a hard look.

He grinned back. "It wasn't me brought up the subject, now, was it, darlin?" He winked and bent his head dutifully over his plate to stuff his mouth with oysters and mashed potatoes.

But James was not ready to let it go. "May I ask, Mr. Endicott, are you somehow involved with subterranean railways?"

Pat looked at his wife, begging for permission.

"Personally, who wants to ride in a hole in the ground," said Tom, looking around brightly, but no one paid any attention to him.

To Elizabeth's annoyance, James persisted. "Do you intend to build one of those railways here?"

This, Patrick could not be expected to let go by. "I wish we could, but the boys in Albany won't let us...."

Elizabeth tried again to rescue the situation. "Well, no one may agree with me, but I for one have no interest in...."

James overrode her. "Why won't they let you build it, Mr. Endicott?"

"Can't be done, they say. It's solid granite down there."

"Granite? Are you implying it's not impenetrable?"

Elizabeth looked so disapproving that Patrick couldn't ignore it and said, "Darlin, I'll just answer the gentleman's one question, okay?" And without waiting for her permission, was off and running. 'There's nothin to it. It's the shipworm gave me the idea, see?" And he was into the story she knew every word of, as James leaned on an elbow, engrossed—or pretending to be, the pompous ass.

She was in despair. Why did her husband have to look so attractive, his generous features alive with energy, his curly hair already mussed, jabbing his fork into the air to illustrate how he would get through the granite as easily as the shipworm bored through wood. There was no stopping him now. Her heart went out to Veronica who, with downcast eyes, wilted in her chair, as the afternoon collapsed around her.

Once again, they all had to hear about that silly shipworm with a digging shell in its nose and how it passed the wood pulp back through its body, mixing it with the lime in its gut—she saw Veronica cringe at the vulgar anatomical reference in front of her literary idol—to pave the walls of its tunnel behind it.

"...so what's to stop us, Mr. James, from doin the same thing? We got a team of men with chisels and pickaxes, followed by masons cementin up the walls, see, and we got ourselves a subway tunnel." He looked around proudly like a retriever dropping the quarry at its master's feet, wagging its tail, waiting to be petted.

Elizabeth could kill him. Veronica was sitting lifeless in front of her untouched dinner. They were not going to stay here another minute listening to him blabber on. She rang the bell sharply for the girl. It might not be customary, but they would take dessert in the parlor with the coffee, where she would make sure Pat didn't get near James.

But this, too, failed miserably. The change of plans threw the hired girl into a tizzy. She couldn't cope with serving the chocolate mousse in the parlor, and Elizabeth had no choice but to go into the kitchen to show her how to do it. She also had to help her prepare the goblets of mousse with whipped cream, and the coffee things. Then, taking the silver ewer herself, hurried upstairs, leaving the girl to bring up the tray.

But of course it was too late. By this time Patrick had James pinned to the fireplace. "Don't ya see? It's not just passengers we'll carry, but freight as well. No more of them delivery vans cloggin the streets...."

And poor Veronica standing beside the Coopers and Tom in her mauve dress, forlorn as a wilted violet. In a pique, Elizabeth poured out the coffee. What on earth was making him carry on like this? She had never seen him go on for so long—and with an "artist type" he had scorned a short while before.

With one eye on her impossible husband and his victim, she handed cups around, but Veronica shook her head miserably.

So long as Pat got the slightest encouragement he always went on propounding his schemes. But why was James pretending to be so interested? He could see perfectly well she was serving the coffee, but he never looked away from Pat for a moment. He had nothing in common with her practical-minded husband. He was a snob. It didn't make any sense.

She handed around cream and sugar. James was hanging onto Pat's every word as if it were Emerson, himself, lecturing on transcendentalism. He was even egging him on with idiotic questions. Answering him, Pat's voice had the Irish lilt it always had when he was carried away by his favorite subject, as he emphasized his points forcefully with his square hands.

She stood sipping her coffee, watching. James was laughing much too appreciatively. Why, he was flattering Pat to death!

Could it be?

Elizabeth had heard about such things. Winifred had even pointed it out in Paris. But here in the village of Greenwich? In her own parlor? The possibility intrigued her. She had always been amazed at how her husband had the ability to charm even the sourest old prunes, but this was something different. Why, poor Mr. James looked ready to get down on his elegant knees and lick his boots—or whatever they did.

To think that all that stuffy pretension hid a shocking secret. How difficult it must be for him to put on such an act all the time.

And dear Patrick, carrying on as if it was municipal transportation that so fascinated his listener. Wait till she told him, the innocent. But on second thought, she wasn't sure she would tell him. He might not be up to such "subtleties and complexities." She had to smile.

A door closed behind her. Her parents and Tom were chatting away oblivious, but Veronica had slipped out of the room.

Veronica was shaking as she locked herself in her bedroom. If she had stayed there another minute she would have started shrieking. She was ready to die of shame.

When the guests had departed, Patrick came up, begging her to open the door, trying to explain tlrrough the crack that he hadn't meant to monopolize Mr. James, it was his blathering tongue ran away with him.

Without opening the door she told him in an unsteady voice that it didn't matter, it wasn't his fault and please to go away. But a few minutes later when Elizabeth knocked, Veronica opened to her, and with Elizabeth's arms around her, wept on her shoulder. "Can you ever forgive me for running out like that?"

"I should never have put you through it," Elizabeth said. "We're all miserable. Pat feels totally responsible."

Veronica broke away and sat down on the bed. "That's not it, he could have gotten away from Patrick if he'd wanted to," she said bitterly. "I thought he was going to talk to me about my poetry. You heard him say so yourself, didn't you? But he didn't look at me once." She put a hand to her mouth to stifle her emotion that was threatening to get the better of her again.

Elizabeth sat down on the bed beside her. "You mustn't blame Mr. James altogether for acting that way. He's a more complicated man than we knew."

"Don't excuse him," Veronica said with a spark of anger. "There's no excuse for such rudeness. I just can't believe he's the same man who writes those beautiful stories...that one about the old maid...with her widowed father...." A sob escaped her before she choked it off.

"My dear," Elizabeth said, taking her hand, "great art has nothing to do with being kind."

Veronica blew her nose. "You're right, of course. I am naive. The man's a perfect boor."

"I think he may have a sensitive side."

"Was it sensitive of him to make me feel so worthless I had to run out of the room with my tail between my legs?"

"Naturally, you don't understand," said Elizabeth. "I didn't either. I thought it was all Patrick's fault too, taking him over like he did. But then I started watching what was really going on. . . ." She told the story to her unworldly sister-in-law without mincing words, trying to keep her voice as level as she could, considering how bizarre the whole thing was. "So you see, dear, if I'm right, it was really nobody's fault. We were defeated before we began—but I hope it won't make you despise him the more."

Veronica was quiet for a little. Finally she said. "How naive I am. I thought things like that only existed in classical mythology." She started looking almost cheerful and gave a wan smile. "Isn't it funny, dear sister, you did your best to snare him for me, but it was Patrick who snared him."

Elizabeth, giving her a kiss good-night, said that Patrick knew nothing about such things and she thought it best that they not tell him.

The lamp in Veronica's room at the top of the house was not turned down that night until she had written a letter:

> *Dear Mr. James,*
>
> *I do hope you'll forgive my sudden departure after dinner, but I'm occasionally struck by a migraine. I want you to know how much I admire you and your work. Although I doubt that we will meet again, I believe deeply that the greatest bonds are spiritual, and that is more than enough for me.*
>
> *I wish you a bon voyage and all good fortune. I know the brilliant literary milieu of London will make a place for you.*
>
> *I remain,*
>
> *Yours respectfully, V. Endicott*

At the time of the dinner for Henry James, Elizabeth was pregnant again, and she gave birth to her second child, a boy, on July 4, 1876—two weeks early—while the rest of the family was up in Central Park for the Centennial celebration.

When the stupendous fireworks display over the Hudson ended that night and Patrick returned, the midwife put the tiny infant into his big hands. Tears filled Patrick's eyes and ran down his cheeks. His son couldn't have been born on a better day if they had ordered it! "And a fine christenin at St. Aloysius's my boy is goin to have," he said, kissing Elizabeth soundly on the cheek.

It had been such an easy delivery that she was already sitting up in bed with her hair brushed and falling around her shoulders. She reminded him that he no longer attended St. Aloysius but she would have no objection to having the baptism there if he that's what he wanted.

He grinned. "A slip of the tongue, darlin. St. Luke's it will be, and just as fine too."

They named the baby Thomas John after the two grandfathers. But from the start he was Jack, Pat's all-American boy, robust and happy—and the whole family revolved around him.

24

Winifred Beaufort had gone on working for Will Kennedy in his down-at-the-heels music hall on Fourteenth Street. Her songs had earned her a small measure of success in the several years she had been there. But as the city's entertainment center continued to move northward, the audience was dwindling.

Will Kennedy adored her. He had made that clear from the start. But whenever he tried to get serious, she kept him at bay with a barrage of smart talk, letting him know as delicately as she could that she was not interested. She liked him—he had given her a job when no one else would—but it was impossible for her to take him seriously. His sights were not set high enough for her. Much as she tried to make him listen, he stubbornly refused to understand that theater could ever be anything more than his cheap revues catering to the lowest tastes. Though she was glad for the meal ticket, she was still waiting for the break that would put her before an audience who appreciated the full expression of her talent.

Her young painter friends from Tenth Street still came to see her devotedly, and it was in their company that she felt most at home. After the show, they often took her down to a tavern across from Jefferson Market on Sixth Avenue called Gridley's, where they bought her suppers of chowder and fried chicken. She was sometimes the only woman there. Except for those who didn't give a fig for their reputations, women didn't set foot in taverns. But she was not about to be held down by New York's provincial definition of a woman's place, which was a far cry from the freedom she had known in France. Among her artist friends—their conversation laced with French expressions—she was able to relax and forget for a few hours how unsatisfactorily things had worked out for her in New York.

Joe Gridley, the proprietor, liked the lively young painters who made his tavern a gathering place, and he let them hang their canvasses on the walls. Artist cafés were popular in Paris, but in New York they were almost unknown. The tavern even began to attract a few blue-bloods from Fifth Avenue, glad to escape the stifling formality of New York society.

But the elegantly dressed young black woman in the midst of it all made Gridley uncomfortable. He was uneasy about what some of his customers thought about her flamboyant presence, though no one had objected so far.

Winifred's friends were always urging her to sing for them, even in the tavern. In Europe a singer often performed spontaneously in a restaurant or café when asked—at Gridley's, where there was only some occasional drunken bawling around the piano, she resisted.

But one night, when she had been reminiscing about singing in a café on the Left Bank, she surprised them by going to the piano. Every sound in the room stopped as she made her way between the tables, a dark queen in a magenta gown, her hair pulled up in a tight psyche knot fastened with a rope of pearls. Sweeping up her skirts on one arm, she arranged herself on the bench. Then, as her fingers danced over the keys in a gay waltz tune, she began to sing in her husky voice a song about the Paris streets.

When she finished, the patrons burst out in shouts and cheering, some of them even standing up on their chairs. After a few more French songs she returned to her friends in triumph. A group of young swells in evening clothes even sent over a bottle of the wretched house wine.

Gridley's reservations about her evaporated. He had never been abroad but he knew good business when he saw it. Why not try to reproduce a little of the atmosphere of Gay Paree in New York since it seemed to meet with such favor? Amidst the laughter and toasts of her friends he proposed to Winifred that she come to work for him. He couldn't pay her much to start, he told her, but if she brought in business—and by her reception tonight it looked a good possibility—she ought to be able to make a living at it. Of course, she would have to adapt her performance to local custom—not so much shaking of her bosom, and showing the ankle, and tone down that ooh-la-la business. He was all for people having a good time, but he didn't want to get the reputation of one of those places over on Greene Street.

Winifred was exultant. It was exactly what she had been waiting for. She calculated the possibility of finding herself broke again if it didn't work out, but of course it couldn't fail. Look at the effect she had had on the audience tonight!

Her artist friends were just as excited as she was. They immediately began planning her new career as "New York's only genuine continental chanteuse." They bestowed on her an exotic pedigree. She would be, as in her solo at Will Kennedy's music hall, Guadeloupe-born, the daughter of a French planter and a beautiful Creole mother.

"Win! What's got you up so early?" Will Kennedy threw down his racing form and swung his high-laced shoes off the desk to pull up a chair for her close to him. "Have some coffee." He poured from a pot on a kerosene burner into a battered crockery mug and pushed it across to her. Even in a fawn-colored street dress and cape which subdued her naturally extravagant proportions, Winifred Beaufort was dazzling. Her perfume made him squirm in his trousers.

Waving the coffee away as she pulled off her gloves, Winifred swept over to the grimy window and tried to think how she was going to tell him. She had anticipated this little scene for a long time, but now that it had come she couldn't stand Will Kennedy being so nice. He had taken her in when every other door in New York was slammed in her face.

"Okay, let's have it," he said, puzzled that she was not already tearing into him about something in the show. Her gripes were continual—drunks in the audience, the pianist who didn't keep up with her, the girls chattering backstage during her number.

She still remained silent, digging the tip of her closed parasol into a crack of the floor planks.

"I know," he said, "I bet you want another raise."

She shook her head, making her spangled earrings glitter.

Her silence was worrying him. He wanted somehow to goad her into her usual sass. They had a routine between them. Sass was all he ever got from her, but it was something. "Don't tell me you're finally going to come across?"

"No." The look of mock impatience that always signaled her usual comeback was not there.

"Is it the costume again? If you lost five pounds you'd stop splitting the seams." He could almost feel his hands running over her, though whenever be actually tried she pushed him away.

Still without looking at him, she said quietly, "I'm quitting, Will."

He leaned back in his chair, puffing up a cloud of smoke from his cigar. "So you got an offer from the Garden? Tell me another."

With her figure outlined against the window, unattainable as Cleopatra, she told him about Gridley's offer.

"Who you kidding?" he said when she had finished. He tried to detect a glimmer of the usual mockery with which she fended him off, but the eyes looking back at him under the long lashes were serious. He tossed his cigar into a spittoon and shuffled through a mess of papers on his desk, pulling out some sheets covered with his wild scrawl. "Here it is, my new revue. You're gonna be the lead."

She didn't listen. "No, Will, it's too late. I'm going to sing what I want the way I want. It will be like the Left Bank."

So it wasn't a bigger part in the show she was after. He began to get worried. "This is New York, remember, honey? Nobody will go for that here."

"How do you know? You think the only thing I'm good for is Blackbirds."

He took a swig of her coffee and wiped his mouth with the back of his hand.

"You're forgetting one thing. There's no audience down there at Gridley's. The only place to go in this town is Twenty-third Street. That's where the money is."

"Big uptown spenders? That's not what I'm interested in. You've never understood anything about me. I'm a chanteuse. I need an intimate atmosphere." What had made her think she ought to feel the least twinge of guilt about leaving the show? He was making it quite clear that he didn't give a damn about losing her.

"And you think down at that cheap saloon you're going to find this special audience?"

"I've already got an audience."

"Your handful of nancy-boys? Don't make me laugh." He took another cigar out of his vest pocket and, with maddening coolness, clipped the end off and ran a wet tongue over it to keep the leaf sealed.

He was deliberately trying to get her goat. She walked up to the desk, hands on her hips. "You know as much about art, Will Kennedy, as a pig's ear!"

Lighting his cigar, he blew out puffs of smoke. "Who needs art? There's no money in it."

"Some people think about other things than money."

"Well, Gridley better think about it. He's sure as hell going to lose his shirt if he puts you on. This isn't Paris, sweetheart. A colored girl can't set herself up as a solo act in a tavern. Not in New York she can't."

"Why can't I? All that's been worked out. I'm being presented as a Creole from the islands. I'll have a French accent."

"Creole from the islands?" He gave her a horselaugh. "You got any idea what those Greenwich rednecks will think about that?"

"That I'm an uppity nigger you mean?"

"I didn't say that."

"Well, you're right." She jerked a thumb at her gorgeous bosom where inset garnets winked from under the cape. "But this here is one smart uppity nigger, and I know when a good thing comes my way."

"You'd be better off staying with me."

She sat down on the edge of his desk and began to pull on her gloves. "Sorry, but I'm not wasting any more time wiggling my ass for a bunch of two-bit drunks who come in to sleep it off."

He came around and put a hand on her shoulder. "Ah, Win, at least take a look at the script I worked out for you."

"Sorry, Will." She got up, adjusting her cape and gathering her skirts. "Can't you get it through your head it's been a dead end for me here?"

He stared at her, his neck swelling as he went red. "Then go on, you crazy bitch!" He stood up and banged the desk. "You think you're too good for me but I'm the one who took you in off the streets. Somebody's going to bring you down off that high horse one day, and when it happens don't expect to cry on my shoulder. I wash my hands of you for good."

"That's okay by me," she said, going through the door. "Thanks for the charity." Her heels echoed down the corridor.

By the time he decided to go after her and beg her to stay, the outer door slammed. He swore and kicked his boot hard against the desk, spilling coffee over the script of the new show he had written especially for her.

Winifred was an immediate success. Within a few weeks Gridley was persuaded by her devoted following to rename the tavern "Café de Paris." Business doubled and he was able to give her a decent wage.

Elizabeth pleaded with Patrick to take her there, but he wouldn't hear of it. He wasn't interested in anything that had to do with Winifred Beaufort, and a tavern—no matter what fancy name they called it—was no place for his wife.

Furious at his obstinacy, she set about wheedling her parents into taking her. The Coopers, although they were fond of Winifred, were almost as dubious as their son-in-law about going into such a place. But Elizabeth insisted that cafés like this in Europe were perfectly respectable for women as well as men. If her parents claimed to have liberal views, it was their duty to help break down the social restrictions in New York.

As usual, they couldn't resist their determined daughter whom they had brought up, after all, to have a mind of her own. Professor Cooper asked Patrick if he would mind them taking Elizabeth just this once to see her friend perform. Patrick muttered, as he tinkered with a model train for his infant son, that if they wanted to waste their money that way, it was their business.

As she and her parents sat over coffee at one of the small, crowded tables, Elizabeth was enchanted with the Café de Paris. Gridley had done little to change it from the simple neighborhood tavern with sawdust on the floor it had always been, except to move the piano to a more prominent spot. But with the artists' canvases on the wall and the animated crowd under the gaslights, it was transformed. Besides Elizabeth and her mother, a few other well-dressed women were present. She had to pinch herself to believe she was in sedate Greenwich, where nothing ever went on.

In a red satin gown and egret feathers in her hair Winifred appeared and seated herself at the piano under a hanging lamp that bathed her in a pool of light. She introduced each song by translating the lyrics in an exaggerated French accent that made Elizabeth giggle. When she finished her songs, she acknowledged the enthusiastic reception with deep curtsies like a diva.

Then, as if she had just spotted Elizabeth and her parents—even though they were sitting practically in front of her and she had been throwing them looks throughout the program—she held out her arms to them dramatically. *"Mes chers amis*, but how *délicieux* that you have come to see my little show!" She sat down with them and, putting on a deep southern accent, whispered not to give her away or everyone would walk out.

They all laughed, and Professor Cooper ordered a bottle of imported wine.

25

The leaves were beginning to turn yellow and red when a telegram came for Tom at the print shop. It was from the Bloomingdale Asylum.

Leaving Albert to run the shop, Tom took an elevated train up to the gloomy, red brick pile by the Hudson that he had grown to hate.

There he was told his wife was dying. He had been expecting it. On his visits over the years he had watched Fanny deteriorating physically as well as mentally. At first, she had appeared almost herself whenever he and Veronica went to see her. They had sat on the veranda of the asylum and walked through the grounds above the river. Out there, away from the occasional screams of the patients, it had seemed to him almost a pleasant retreat. The asylum stood in open countryside beyond the city. But New York's inexorable northern march had leveled the hills and laid out streets, until almost at a gallop, buildings filled in the fields right up to the asylum grounds.

Both Fanny's parents had died shortly after she was incarcerated, and unexpectedly she was left a share of the inheritance along with her brothers and sisters, none of whom had ever had anything to do with her.

The money had been helpful. Invested in railroad bonds, the income paid for her care that grew more expensive as her condition worsened.

Though the doctors kept telling Tom not to lose hope that his wife might recover, he knew better. After a while, the times when she was able to recognize him became rarer. Eventually, she was confined—with the other hopeless cases—to a ward, wearing only a gray smock, listless, no longer caring he was there.

The last few years it had become dreadful. In addition to her dementia, she developed consumption, and soon became hardly more than a skeleton wracked with coughing.

Tom was at the asylum gates before it occurred to him that he had not let Veronica know about the telegram. It was probably just as well. Lately, she seemed increasingly shaken after each visit to her mother. Though Patrick and Elizabeth were unaware of it, he knew how his daughter felt living off the crumbs of other people's happiness. It was better to spare her this last painful confrontation.

Fanny had been moved from the ward to the hospital wing. Even before Tom went into the room, painted an institutional green, the smell hit him. He was nauseated as always, and then guilty over it.

He could hardly bear to look at her. What had that poor wretch in the bed to do with him? Under the sheet she was shrunken to the size of a child, the only evidence of life a harsh breathing in and out of the toothless maw that had once been her pretty mouth. Her eyes were closed, the thin blue-veined skin of the lids like a newborn, featherless bird.

"Fanny, dear…." He took a chair by the bed. It was obscene to apply that name to this wasted being who bore no resemblance whatever to the delicate girl he had once loved.

She didn't move or open her eyes. Only that ghastly hawking in of air through the open mouth.

"Fanny, can you hear me?" he tried again in a voice totally false. The truth was he felt nothing but revulsion.

She seemed unaware of him as he sat there, when unexpectedly there was a stirring under the sheet and a talon of a hand emerged clutching a scrap of paper. She was conscious after all! Though he hated himself, he was sorry—he wanted to be done with it at last. Gingerly, he slipped the scrap of paper away and the clawlike hand fell like a puppet with the strings broken.

This past year, since she had been unable to speak, she had scratched notes to him several times. Just a few words, almost illegible—pitiful pleas to take her home. Only once had she said something else. She had asked how Elizabeth was, which made him think briefly that, incredible as it seemed, she might actually be getting better. But the next time he came she didn't even know him, screeching when he tried to talk to her, until it had ended in a coughing fit.

Putting on his spectacles, he saw that her writing was more legible this time. Instead of a plea to take her home, the words "MY WILL" were printed at the top. Under it was written "My money to Veronica" with "Promise" at the bottom heavily underlined. It was her share of the Slocum inheritance she was referring to, the money from her parents.

When he looked up, he was alarmed to see her head turned toward him, the eyes open, huge and unblinking, waiting.

"But, Fanny dear, this isn't necessary," he said automatically. "You're going to get well and come home."

Her head tried to lift off the pillow in her effort to say something, but it was too much for her and she fell back in a fit of coughing. When he started to pour her some water from the bed stand, her bony fingers clutched his wrist, holding him back and forcing him to look at her ghastly face.

"I promise!" he said, in a panic not to be touched. "She'll get the money."

The fierce eyes watched him for a moment and then dropped shut again. The coughing had stopped, but sputum trickled from her open mouth. The breathing, always noisy, changed into a gurgle.

He ran out to find a nurse, but by the time he got back the terrible breathing had stopped forever.

On the elevated going home, Tom stared out the window, hardly seeing the solidly built-up new blocks of the city. His sole feeling was relief that he would never have to go back to that hellish place again. No matter how tranquil his life had been these last years, Fanny had always been in the background like an apparition, and hanging over his head, the monthly visit.

The girl he had loved so long ago had nothing to do with that poor wretch he had taken leave of with a final kiss on the cold brow. He tried to remember the strange, delicate girl who had once nestled against him in a sunny bay window, as they read together their poem, the poem that was her—

For the moon never beams without bringing me dreams
Of the beautiful Annabel Lee.
And the stars never rise but I feel the bright eyes....

He shuddered, still seeing those vulture eyes fixed on him with their unmistakable message of hatred and accusation. In his fist was the crumpled note with the words "MY WILL," and he remembered his promise.

When he showed Veronica the will, she broke down in tears all over again. It was proof, she told him, that her mother had never forgotten her. Even in the asylum and ill as she was, she must have known how inconvenient it had become for her daughter, living on in the house with Patrick and Elizabeth and their growing family, where there was less and less privacy. And now the bequest would allow her to live out her life as an independent woman.

Veronica made immediate plans to settle in a cottage in Sands Point on Long Island where she had friends from school, a pair of unmarried sisters, and she began going through her things, filling trunks and boxes.

26

After Winifred Beaufort's initial success at the Café de Paris, things took an unexpected turn. Though her following remained faithful to her, there was some local muttering that a colored woman had stepped out of her place and set herself up as if she were as good as white. Unpleasant things began to happen. One evening when she was singing, there were catcalls from some louts at the bar. Gridley had them thrown out and Winifred laughed it off, dismissing them as riff-raff.

But next morning the word "nigger" was chalked on the door of the cafe. Then a few nights later a brick crashed through a window during her performance. The audience began to stay away.

Distressed, she offered to quit, but Gridley would not hear of it. When he complained to the police, demanding better protection, they told him that some of the workers on the new elevated line being put up there on the avenue were hanging around the neighborhood after work hours. They persuaded him to hire a bouncer.

For a while there was no more trouble—and then it happened.

One night after the café had closed, Winifred left with a couple of her young actor friends from the boarding house. Heading home, they turned up an empty street, dimly lit by a single gas lamp. They were in high spirits, singing the chorus of a new song she had introduced that night, and their voices echoed from the sleeping facades of the houses.

They were halfway up the block before Winifred became aware that they were being followed. Out of the corner of her eye she saw the three men behind them. She knew that they had followed them from the café.

Gripping her friends' arms, she tried to keep herself from walking faster. "Don't look around," she whispered. "They're following us."

"Come on, we'll run," said one of her friends.

"No!" Winifred said, gripping their arms tighter. "Just keep going."

Ahead were the lights of Seventh Avenue, where a few night owls were still strolling about.

Just a little further.

But the men were coming closer.

"Run!" she cried, picking up her skirts.

Her two friends did their best to pull her along, but she was hindered by her high-heeled boots and petticoats.

"Get the nigger!" shouted one of the thugs.

From a building across the way, a window was thrown open.

The men were on them in a flash. Winifred's two friends tried to shield her, but were kicked and beaten to the ground. She screamed as a thick arm gripped her around the neck and she was dragged into an alley.

"Goddamned drunks," said a voice from the window, and slammed it shut.

In the pitch black, Winifred tried to fight back, but a fist smashed her in the face and she sank to her knees. A hard kick and she crumpled onto the cobblestones. She lay there, half-conscious, as the three men threw themselves on her in turns, their hoarse breathing the only sound in the alley.

When they were finished with her, they ran off into the night, whooping and hollering.

"Winnie?" One of her actor friends staggered into the alley, calling into the darkness, "Winnie, you there?"

Groping forward, he stumbled against a garbage can. Then his foot touched her. "Winnie!" He dropped to his knees, felt the tumble of skirts, the blood. His voice shook, "Don't be dead...."

His hand found her hair. He thought he heard something. He bent forward, leaned down close.

Her words were just audible. "...those bastards...."

The next morning a boy brought Elizabeth the news. She left the baby with the hired girl and went as fast as she could to the boardinghouse, two blocks away, where Winifred lived. She found her in bed, bruised and suffering, lips almost too swollen to talk.

Tending to Winifred, she was late in getting back for the baby's noon feeding. The hired girl had taken little Alicia with her while she did the marketing, and when Elizabeth came in, she found Patrick, who was home for lunch, trying to calm a fretting baby Jack.

"Where the hell ya been?" he said. "He wants to eat."

Putting a towel over her shoulder, she took the baby and told Pat what had happened.

"Too bad," he said, "but she asked for it, didn't she, puttin herself on show like that? Anyway, I got to get back to the job." He grabbed his hat and was gone.

"Patrick!" she called after him, unable to believe his callousness, until Jack set up a wail and she gave him the breast.

In the days that followed, she spent most of her time with Winifred, coming home only to nurse the baby. She could not forgive Patrick for his attitude. Using her preoccupation with Winifred as an excuse, she slept in the spare room and hardly exchanged a word with him.

Patrick was working on the section of the elevated line passing Jefferson Market, supervising the construction of a station above the avenue with iron stairways leading down to the sidewalks. Gridley's café was just across the street, boarded up now. He was furious every time he looked at it, thinking of Winifred Beaufort, who he was convinced had caused all this trouble between him and Elizabeth.

He didn't understand why his wife was carrying on like she was, acting like it was his fault. It was a damn shame what had happened, but why did that woman have to push her way in where she wasn't wanted? She had damn well asked for it. Every time he looked across at Gridley's, he wanted to tear it down with his bare hands.

A week later when he passed the tavern on his way home to lunch, several young laborers were standing around the tattered poster that once had announced Winifred's nightly appearance. A big fellow was scrawling something on it with a hunk of charcoal as the other two sniggered.

He recognized them. They were on one of his work gangs, though he didn't know them personally. He had seen them lately at the Hell Hole bar, where he liked to stop in for a beer after work.

All his boys were hard drinkers and he sometimes had to send them home to sleep it off. A week before, this same trio had shown up in the morning with pints of whiskey in their pockets and already three sheets to the wind. He didn't like the way they looked at him when he told them to go home and sleep it off. Though it was nothing he could put his finger on, they were not the kind of good-hearted lads he liked to have a beer with.

There was something queer about the way they were carrying on over there by Winifred Beaufort's poster. He stopped and asked the biggest of them, who was called Smitty, if he had ever gone to see her sing.

"Not exactly," Smitty said, as his pals sniggered.

"Ya know her then?"

Smitty said, "Well, ya might call it that." They all laughed again.

"She's a real tomato, huh?"

"Not bad for a jig, wouldn't ya say so, lads?" And they broke into guffaws.

He saw what Smitty had scrawled across the poster: NIGGER BITCH GOT IT GOOD.

The rest of the day Patrick couldn't get the three hoodlums out of his mind. The morning they had showed up drunk was the morning after the rape. It might be a coincidence, then again it might not. But even if he told the police, he knew they wouldn't do anything, not over the rape of a colored woman. Besides, he had no proof.

He wanted to talk to his wife about it that evening but she was away at Winifred's, and after a silent dinner with Veronica he went to the Hell Hole, hoping for the gang to show up.

Waiting in the shadows at the far end of the bar, he was about to give up, when Smitty and one of his sidekicks came in and began washing down whiskeys with beer. About midnight the sidekick, very drunk, staggered out, but Smitty stayed on. He was the size of an ox and apparently unaffected by the amount he was drinking.

It was nearly two in the morning by the time Smitty left. Patrick followed not far behind through the dark streets near the riverfront, a slicing wind blowing dead leaves into drifts. When Smitty stepped into a cul-de-sac to take a leak, Patrick waited until he was through, then challenged him, "I'm goin to beat the shit out of ya, Smitty."

The thug whipped around as if he might be about to draw a knife, but recognizing Patrick, grinned. "Oh, it's the boss! Ya scared the bejesus out of me. I thought it was them wops from Hell's Kitchen."

"I know what ya did to that woman," Patrick said, moving toward him.

Smitty sized up his stocky but much shorter opponent. "Ya had too much to drink, boss. I wouldn't want to have to hurt ya."

Patrick's fist caught him hard on the chin. Smitty barely flinched, and then moved in, expecting his size and weight to finish Patrick off in a jiffy. But Patrick had a rage in him that no size was a match for, as his fists smashed into muscle and bone.

He left the hooligan a bloody heap in the alley, and walked away, exhilarated.

When he got home, Elizabeth was waiting up for him, nearly out of her mind with worry. But when she saw his bruised fists and disheveled clothes she was furious. "I don't believe it," she cried, smelling the liquor on his breath. "You're just a mick after all, drinking and fighting and staying out all night! What about your children? What a disgusting father they have. I wish I'd never married you."

He didn't answer. He went up to the bedroom and stripped to his long johns. Only after he had doused his head in the washbasin did he turn to her, his black curls dripping. "I thought ya cared for your friend Winifred."

"What has that got to do with it?" She faced him, flushed with indignation.

"I got one of them bastards, that's what."

She was quiet as he told her what had happened. Afterward, she pressed herself against him, begging him to forgive her. His arms went around her. Victorious in battle, he had reclaimed his wife again.

Gridley had decided not to reopen the café for the present because of continuing threats. In any case, Winifred was in no state to go back to work. For weeks she kept to her room, long after her bruises healed. It was not that she lacked friends. The boardinghouse she lived in was full of theater folk, a sympathetic breed. The painters from Tenth Street even took up a collection to pay her rent.

Elizabeth spent as much time as she could with her. She understood the tremendous shock her friend had suffered. That Winifred had fallen into despair was natural, but that it should last so long was frightening. It was as if the most vital person she knew had stopped wanting to live.

Elizabeth pleaded with her to let her contact Will Kennedy. Will was devoted to her. He had a right to know. But Winifred was adamant. Under no circumstances was Will ever to hear what had happened. She was not going to crawl back to him on her hands and knees.

Since the attack Winifred had missed one menstrual period, which the doctor ascribed to shock, but after missing a second, it was discovered that she was pregnant. She collapsed all over again.

"I don't want it!" she wailed to Elizabeth. "Not like that! I'll kill myself first!"

When she calmed down, Elizabeth suggested the possibility of having a medical intervention. Although it wasn't talked about openly, abortion wasn't illegal, even if lately certain organizations had started to campaign against it. But abortionists still advertised freely. Curiously, they all had French names, Madame This and Madame That. Elizabeth had seen their ads in the back of Demorest's Ladies Magazine describing their services euphemistically as "correcting menstrual irregularities."

With Winifred's approval, she chose a Madame Restelle because of her address nearby on lower Fifth Avenue, and went to see her. As she paid the cabman, she knew from his look that he thought she was going for the notorious procedure herself.

From the outside, the address appeared to be a fine town house among other palatial establishments lining the avenue where the city's wealthiest lived. A butler admitted her, just as if she were a rich young matron making a social call, and led her through the ornate foyer to a reception room.

When a rear door opened and a gray-haired woman came in, Elizabeth caught a glimpse of a brightly-lit hospital corridor beyond, with white-aproned nurses going about their duties.

Madame Restelle, despite her exotic name, was stout and capable looking and introduced herself without a trace of French accent as they sat down at her desk. If she was not French, it was with French directness that she stated her price right off, three hundred dollars.

Praying she had come to the right place, Elizabeth told her the story of the gang rape.

Madame Restelle shook her head in sympathy and agreed that an abortion was absolutely justified, advising that for safety's sake it be performed as soon as possible. She got out an appointment book and, taking up a pen, asked the victim's name.

Elizabeth hesitated.

"You don't have to worry," said Madame Restelle. "I wouldn't be in this profession long if I weren't discreet. Many of my clients are from the best social circles."

Reassured, Elizabeth gave her Winifred's name.

"But wasn't she the singer down at Gridley's? I think she had a perfect right!" The woman dipped her pen briskly into the inkwell. "I'm putting her down as Mrs. W. Smith."

Elizabeth arranged to bring Winifred the next day, but when she was walking back to the hack stand where the steaming horses were stamping hooves metallically against the cobblestones, she asked herself where they were going to find the three hundred dollars. Winifred didn't have a penny. Pat might be able to borrow it, but after what he had done already she couldn't ask him for so large a sum. Though she handled the family finances, she was annoyed that wives didn't have bank accounts of their own.

Her father couldn't help. Professor Cooper was away at the University of Virginia as a visiting professor for a term. Winifred's friends would do anything for her, but they were all poor as church mice.

Will Kennedy. He was the one to ask.

Of course, there was her promise to Winifred never to contact him. But what was breaking her word against Winifred's entire future?

That evening, cloaking herself in a mohair pelerine with the hood up, Elizabeth went to the music hall on Fourteenth Street and asked at the box office for the manager. But the ticket seller said the show was already on and the boss was entertaining a party in his box. She would have to come back the next day.

Without missing the breath she bought a ticket and, brushing aside the usher, marched straight into the box at the rear of the orchestra, interrupting Will Kennedy, who with a group of cigar-smoking sharpies was watching the show. Onstage, to the thumping of a razzle-dazzle band, chorus girls in blackface were kicking up their legs as amused patrons threw coins. The girls were encouraging the pandemonium by raising their skirts to slip the money inside their rolled-down striped stockings, while barmaids rushed about with drinks for the patrons.

Will saw at once that something was wrong and led Elizabeth out into the corridor.

"Serves her right for running out on me!" he said, when he heard what had happened. "Come on." He took her arm. "I'll get a cab."

If Winifred's outbursts had alarmed the other boarders on numerous occasions, Will's roaring at her entertained them greatly as he charged into her room.

"You crazy, know-it-all bitch, didn't I tell you...?"

She was lying on the bed in a faded wrapper, so changed—the eyes that had once blazed with life were dull.

"Oh, Win...." He got down beside her and stroked her hair. "Why didn't you let me know, Win? Did you really think I didn't care?"

As Elizabeth stepped back into the hall, Winifred was sobbing in his arms.

It was Will Kennedy who accompanied Winifred to Madame Restelle's the next day, and when she was well again, took her to stay with him in his rooms behind the music hall.

The following week, appearing totally restored, she visited Elizabeth wearing a lime-green street costume with a large fox fur muff. Will was closing the music hall, she said, and they were opening a gambling club on West Twenty-fourth Street in the Tenderloin. She was going to be the hostess.

"But won't the police cause trouble?" Elizabeth asked, observing the flashy beaded fringe on her friend's cape and the heavier rouge on her cheeks.

There was nothing to worry about, Winifred said. Will had already fixed it up. They were going to rake in more than enough to pay off the cops.

When Elizabeth asked about her singing, her answer was just as smooth. "Green stuff is all I care about now, honey. If you got it, nobody can touch you, even if you're colored."

Her cynicism gave Elizabeth a turn, but considering the ordeal she had gone through, how could it be otherwise? Winifred had never been a shrinking violet, and anyway she was as beautiful as ever and with all the old spirit back again.

Elizabeth said she would give anything to see her as a gambling queen, and Winifred said, Why not? She'd get Will to sneak her in for a look some night and Patrick would never have to know. They laughed together and it was like old times.

Her friend was truly a phenomenon, Elizabeth thought when Winifred had gone, leaving a scent of frangipani in the air. Of course, the face paint and the gaudy trimmings were excessive, but ostentation was acceptable in that world, as she knew well enough from Paris where all the women in theater and the arts painted. She did so want Winifred to have a little happiness after her hard life.

The one thing Elizabeth regretted was that her friend seemed to have given up her singing altogether.

Elizabeth had never been happier with Patrick, their marriage having weathered its first serious crisis. But Winifred's unconventional life was a reminder to her that she had never wanted to limit herself to being just a wife and mother. There were aspects of living she meant to explore, even if Pat was unwilling to follow. Having her own ideas and keeping a part of herself separate from him only made her feel more of a person in her own right, and even their lovemaking was better for it.

She and Patrick were both relieved, though they didn't admit it to each other, that Veronica was going to leave Perry Street and move to a home of her own on Long Island. Her trunks were called for, and on the morning she left they said good-bye at the cab in front of the house. Elizabeth hugged her sister-in-law and promised they would be out to visit her the following weekend.

It was only after lunch when she went up to air out the empty room that she found the note stuck in the bureau mirror.

With the open window letting in the brisk March air, she read Veronica's message—she had sailed at noon on the Franconia for England where she was going to make her home, *"because it's the ideal place for an old maid who writes poetry....You have both been kind to put up with me for so long, and I will always be grateful...."*

Tom came over for dinner that night. They were all in a state of shock around the table as they discussed Veronica, wondering if there wasn't something they could have done. Elizabeth blamed herself for not paying more attention to her lately, having been so preoccupied with Winifred. Patrick remembered that when he had offered to make any needed repairs at her new home on Long Island, she had been evasive. In fact, she had refused to allow any of them even to see the cottage.

Tom recalled how taken she had been with the young writer, Mr. James, who had also gone to England to live. Was it possible the poor girl was still smitten, and had run off to throw herself at him?

"I do hope not," Elizabeth said. "I know for a fact that he never answered her letter." She put a hand to her cheek. "But how awful it would be, if...."

Tom said that whether or not that were the case, it was probably better that Veronica go off to find a life for herself at last, now that she had independent means. "Fanny and I were so wrong for each other, our children didn't have much chance," he said gloomily over his coffee.

The hired girl brought in Alicia and the baby to say goodnight, the spaniel at her heels, and as Patrick held baby Jack in the air, Alicia called out "Papa" and climbed into grandpa's lap.

1886

27

In June, Alicia Endicott had her thirteenth birthday party, the first family celebration after the period of mourning for Elizabeth's mother, who had died the year before. For the party, the portieres between the parlor with its green brocade walls and the plum-papered study were thrown back, and the room was festive with crepe paper strung from the chandeliers, which had just been converted from gas to electricity.

Six of Alicia's school friends were invited over. Alicia, in white pinafore and ruffled pantaloons with long golden curls, was the prettiest of all. They were playing charades, taking turns acting out book titles for the others to guess, while Elizabeth sat with the mothers, chatting over punch and birthday cake in a row of chairs along one wall. In front of the bay window, the hired girl was at a buffet table serving the cake and a bowl of fruit punch.

Patrick was on his hands and knees with nine-year-old Jack astride him in an Indian headdress, whooping and kicking for his horse to buck harder. At thirty-nine, Pat had put on some weight, but his black hair was as thick as ever. Through the war whoops and the girls' laughter and clapping at each other's antics, he was managing to hold forth to Professor Cooper about the horse cars on tracks that were at last replacing the old stages on Broadway.

"Just ya wait until they're electrified," he said, pausing to wipe the sweat from his forehead. "We've got an electric engine in the works already."

"Personally," said his father-in-law, "I'm still partial to the horse."

"Giddy-up!" Jack yelled, bored with his lazy steed.

"In fifty years there won't be a horse left on the street," Patrick said, bucking lackadaisically. "I predict...." A disturbance in the hall cut him off.

"Hey, Paddy!" yelled a drunken voice. "What in hell's goin on here?"

He looked around to see his brother-in-law Billy Yates, who had barged in through the parlor door without even taking off his cap. Billy had never been to the house before, though he and Nora had been invited for dinner several times—they always had an excuse to get out of it. He must have belted down a few to get up his nerve.

Patrick untangled Jack and got to his feet. "What is it then, Billy?"

"It's them wops I'm talkin about." His face was flushed and his eyes blazed.

Billy was a foreman of a work gang on the el.

"Ah, don't get so riled up now." Patrick took his brother-in-law's arm and tried to get him out of the room, but Yates shook him off.

"Listen to me, Paddy, them bastards are tryin to make trouble on the job and I'm not takin it any more."

The girls in their paper birthday hats had stopped in the middle of their game and the mothers stared.

Alicia had always been ashamed of her Irish relatives and now her party was being ruined. She yanked at her father's sleeve and, stamping her foot and shaking her curls, demanded he get Uncle Billy out of there.

Patrick, pleased at his highfalutin daughter's display of low-class Irish temper, devilishly pulled her around and held her in front of him. "Ya remember your Uncle Billy, don't ya? He's here to wish ya a happy birthday, aren't ya, Billy?"

"But I didn't invite him!" the girl cried.

Elizabeth came up and put a firm hand on her shoulder. "That's enough, young lady. Now go bring Mr. Yates a piece of cake."

Ignoring his sister-in-law, Yates lurched over to look up at the chandelier in the middle of the ceiling. "So it's electric light ya got, Paddy? Gettin too fancy for your relations?"

Patrick tried to move in on him. "Come on now, Billy, we can talk better outside." But again he slipped away, having spied the punch bowl.

"Ain't ya goin to offer your brother-in-law a cup of cheer to toast the little birthday girl?" He looked around with a drunken smirk.

"It's not the kind of punch ya go for, Billy."

But Yates was already dipping the ladle into the bowl. As Alicia and everyone else held their breath, he slurped it up straight from the ladle. Then screwing up his face, he spewed it out all over the table. Pulling out a shirttail, he hawked and spat into it. "What kind of pizen is this to give a man?" He staggered toward the row of flabbergasted matrons.

As little Jack jumped up and down and laughed, Patrick gripped Yates by the arm and marched him past a pouting Alicia and her wide-eyed girlfriends out of the room. "Off we go, Billy. We'll talk it all over at the Hell Hole where we can get ya some real stuff."

Patrick did his best to keep him headed in the direction of the bar, but Yates stopped and poked a finger into his chest. "Listen Paddy, them wops was pesterin me why shouldn't they do the weldin too. I tried to get it through their heads that weldin takes experience. I told them real nice, but get this"—again Yates's finger poked him—"one of them wops pulled a knife on me! Honest to God, Pat, pulled a fuckin knife on me! It was that Benny Alfano…."

"I hear ya, Billy," Patrick said, getting him moving again, "but let's have a drink."

As he pushed him across Hudson Street, Yates carried on. "Paddy, I knocked that knife out of his hand, and told him to go collect his pay. And if he ever showed his face around there again I'd wipe the floor with him—personal. But I'm not kiddin, if those other dagos hadn't pulled him off, I'd be pushin up the daisies now. Ya got to do somethin, Paddy. We can't go on workin with them."

Patrick stopped his brother-in-law from lurching into an iceman crossing from his ice wagon at the curb, balancing a chunk of ice on his shoulder with a pair of tongs—he was delivering to all the ice boxes on the street.

Patrick pushed Yates on. "Aren't ya forgettin, Billy, twenty years ago they talked the same way about us micks?"

Yates spat into the gutter.

He pointed out that with New York growing so fast there was enough work for them all, but Yates was not interested. "Don't kid yourself, Paddy, they're animals. Ya see how they look at our women? They don't have no morals."

Patrick stopped and pulled him around. "Now get this, Billy, they're Catholics the same as you. And now, goddam it, there's not enough micks to do the work and if you or any of the other lads don't like it, ya can damn well quit." Billy looked bewildered by this. Patrick put a hand on his shoulder and said, "I got my job to do, the same as you. Ya see that, don't ya?"

Yates scratched his head under his cap. "Okay, Paddy, if ya say so, we'll give it another try."

Patrick put an arm about his shoulders and moved him on toward the Hell Hole. "Attaboy. Let's have a drink on it."

"Wait a minute," said Billy, holding him back. "'What are we goin there for? Nora's heart is breakin that ya don't come around any more. Come on home and have a whiskey with us."

It was true, he hadn't been by to see his sister in months. He decided Alicia's party could wait a while longer.

By the time they set off down Greenwich Street in the shadow of the el, Yates had sobered up a little. A train rattled by deafeningly overhead, and they stepped into a doorway to avoid the coal cinders and sparks raining down from the locomotive.

"That's why we got to electrify," Patrick yelled over the din as they brushed off their shoulders.

The smell of cooked cabbage hit him even before Billy opened the door to the flat. With five children still at home, the rooms were as crowded with bedsteads as ever.

His sister Nora, still in her early thirties, was already spreading into middle age. "Patrick! I didn't know you was comin. The place is not to rights." Her fingers picked at a spot on her apron. She was self-conscious in the presence of this well-dressed brother from another world.

"Ah, Nora," Patrick said, giving her a hug, "I'm not a stranger, am I? With family ya don't have to make a fuss."

But the children stared as if he really were an outsider. Tinted engravings of Jesus, Mary, and all the saints judged him from every wall.

"What are ya waitin for, woman?" Yates cried, pulling Patrick over to sit with him at the table. "Get your brother somethin to drink."

She brought in a pitcher of beer and mugs for them and was about to sit down when Yates stopped her. "Get Paddy some of that corned beef ya fixed for supper, why don't ya?"

Patrick said that he wasn't hungry and not to go to any trouble.

"You're an Irishman, ain't ya? An Irishman is always ready for corned beef and cabbage."

As his sister set heaping plates in front of them, Patrick wanted to feel the way he used to about the food of his childhood, but it didn't taste the same as he remembered, and it was only by swilling the beer Billy kept pouring out for him that he managed to get it down.

The children soon got used to him and were running all over the place, screaming and jumping up and down on the beds. When Yates yelled at Nora to shut them up, she doled out bowls of molasses pudding for them.

"She's got more than me!" a boy yelled. He was wearing a raveled turtleneck sweater as though it were winter.

"I have not!" screamed his little sister, putting her arms around her bowl. She had blue eyes that reminded Patrick of his mother.

"It ain't fair," the boy said.

"Just shut up now, Colin," Billy shouted, "or you'll get the back of my hand." He stood up and drained his mug. "Paddy's throwin a big birthday party today for that daughter of his," he told his wife, and flopped down on one of the beds. "Electric light they got now...." The words faded away and in seconds he was snoring.

Nora sat down in her husband's chair and watched Patrick eat. He forced a last bite of corned beef and cabbage down, embarrassed he had not invited them to the party. "Ya understand, Nora, Alicia just had some friends in."

Nora gave a little smile, partly awkward and partly wanting to make him feel better. "We couldn't have come anyway, Pat, none of us. Billy had to work, and I got to keep poppin over to the Jews down the street on Saturday to tend their cookin. Ya know, they ain't allowed to lift a finger on their Sabbath day."

Her children were playing on the floor now, building a house with odd scraps of wood.

"Ya got a good heart, Nora," Patrick said.

She looked at him with moist eyes. "Billy tells me how patient ya are with the men on the job. I'm glad it's turned out so well for ya, Pat."

As he got up to go, she gave him a holy medal, explaining that their brother Timothy had sent it from Cork, and she'd like him to have it.

That night, as he lay with his arms around Elizabeth, the balmy air billowing out the bedroom curtains, Patrick told her about his visit to his sister. "I felt like a stranger with her, can ya believe it? I don't fit in there any more. And over here, my daughter's ashamed of me. Where do I belong, do ya think?"

Elizabeth covered her mouth as she yawned and told him that Alicia was at her most sensitive, overcritical age. All children went through it and it would pass. She knew how hard it had been for him to go from one world to another, but what a good job he had made of it. "I'm so proud of you," she murmured sleepily.

As he pulled her closer and turned down the bed lamp, he whispered against her ear that he couldn't have done it without her.

On the other side of Greenwich, in the Italian section near Washington Square, Benno Alfano and his wife were also awake. He had been fired that day by the foreman, Bill Yates. Their children were asleep in another bed in the tenement room whose windows looked out on the elevated tracks where they curved from Sixth Avenue onto Third Street.

"What's the matter?" his wife asked, for Benno had turned to the wall instead of to her as he always did.

His voice muffled in the pillow, he said he couldn't think about anything but losing his job.

She made him turn back and pulled his head against her breast. "Ya gotta take it easy, *caro*," she said. "We think of something."

But Benno wouldn't be comforted. He raised his head, tears wet on his cheeks. "I only showed him my knife. I want him to know I make it myself, I know about steel. But my English no good. That bastard, he don't give me a chance. Why the hell can't we do the welding too?" His voice was getting louder. "We got families just like them."

"Shhh," his wife whispered, reminding him of the sleeping children. She stroked his back. "It's okay."

"It's not okay! We already late on the rent."

She kissed the tears from his eyes and told him she had an idea. Her brother Tony had a vegetable pushcart on Bleecker Street and was doing fine. Even if they didn't get along so well together, maybe he could help Benno out, rent a pushcart, something like that. "What you want to work with steel for anyway? I worry. You just get hurt." She caressed him under the covers.

Responding, he leaned over her, slipping a callused hand into her nightdress to cup a breast, but she cautioned him to be quiet about it. "Mario's not a child any more. He's a man already, big like you, Benno. I saw."

A screeching of iron wheels on tracks came from outside, rattling the window frames, as an elevated train made the turn onto Third Street. The beam of the steam engine's light flashed across the room and for a moment they saw their thirteen-year-old son Mario's curly head, as he lay asleep between his younger brother and sister.

28

One day in October, when Patrick was working on a trial project to electrify a section of track on the el, he took his son along. Jack loved to go with his father to his job. He knew all the men and took a keen interest in everything that was going on.

Jack was in his Sunday best, a navy-blue sailor suit with short pants and a round boater on his head with red midshipman ribbons hanging down behind. Just past his tenth birthday. He was a sturdy boy, the image of his father.

Up on the platform near a group of Irish workmen eating their lunch, Patrick was explaining to his son how the generator would send electricity through the third rail to power the train. A prototype engine was expected to be delivered any day now, though it was still in the experimental stage.

Jack, who caught on to such technicalities as quickly as they were explained to him, asked if there wasn't any danger of the iron wheels grounding the electricity and shorting the whole thing out.

"Better watch out, boss," one of the workmen yelled out, "if ya tell the lad too much, he'll be takin over your job and you'll be back with us on the gang."

"That's okay with me," Patrick said, putting a proud hand on his son's shoulder. "I'll step aside for him anytime."

An engineer came out of the construction office at the end of the platform and called over to him. There was a problem with the blueprints and they wanted to consult with him about it.

"Will ya look after my boy, Mike? They can't get along without me for a minute."

Jack ran over to the workman, who was an old friend.

Inside the office, it was Patrick as usual who found the mistake that was causing the other engineers the trouble. They joshed him about being too smart for them, but on his way out he heard two of them arranging to go rowing with their families in Central Park the next Sunday.

It was always like that. No matter how well they liked him on the job, friendship ended at quitting time. In the first years he had been too busy catching up to notice, but eventually he got the message that these men were never going to forget the difference in his background and theirs.

When he came out, Jack wasn't where he had left him. Mike said he was down the platform. To his dismay, his son was sitting in the middle of a group of Italian workmen who were sharing their lunch with him. One of them was playing a mouth organ and they were all laughing and urging him on, as Jack buried his face in a big sandwich stuffed with meatballs. The sauce was all over his chin and sailor suit.

Keeping his temper down, Patrick went over and reminded his son that it was time to go home. The boy was still munching the sandwich as his father led him away and the workmen waved goodbye. But as soon as they were on the stairway going down to the street, he pulled the greasy mess out of Jack's hand and, ignoring the howl of protest, threw it on a pile of trash.

On the way home, the boy was still peeved and wouldn't talk to him, until a sudden downpour caught them and they had to run for it. By the time they got to the door, they were both soaked through and laughing together.

The boy was shivering as he chattered to his mother about the trip to the worksite. Elizabeth made him take off his wet clothes and wrapped him in a blanket, scolding Patrick, then poured them some hot chocolate in the kitchen.

That night Jack developed a high fever and within twenty-four hours was dead of diphtheria.

In her first shock, Elizabeth could only think it was the drenching that had brought it on. Patrick, still not believing it had happened, raged about the "filthy wop food." But the doctor told them diphtheria needed at least two days to incubate, so both their ideas were wrong.

Patrick's joy in living disappeared overnight. He went about the house like a sleepwalker. Elizabeth hardly had time to mourn, she was so concerned over the change in her husband. He no longer touched her and he hardly spoke to anyone. As much as she tried to interest him in life again, he returned home from work each day to sit dully waiting for dinner, not even looking at the newspaper or his engineering manuals. She wished he could find a way to express the grief bottled up in him, go out and get drunk even—anything to bring him back to life.

After a period of hysterical weeping over her dead brother, Alicia recovered and threw herself into music lessons, announcing she was going to become a concert pianist. But the atmosphere in the house remained so gloomy that she spent most of her time after school at her grandfather's place over the printing shop or practicing piano at her music conservatory.

Not long after the funeral, Professor Cooper took a leave of absence from New York University to join a Quaker group out west, trying to do something to stop the senseless slaughter of the Indians. It was a painful decision to leave his only daughter and her family, but he had been so depressed after the death of his wife—and then the terrible loss of his grandson—that he wanted a complete change. Before leaving, he turned his house over to a realtor to rent for him.

Patrick, who ordinarily would have scoffed at his father-in-law's idealistic scheme to save the redskins, was too miserable to take any notice. Only when the house next door was put up for rent did he emerge come out of his lethargy enough to show some concern that Italians might move in—already they were spreading up along Bleecker Street from the area south of Washington Square. Elizabeth dared to hope that his mutterings against them meant he was coming back to himself, but it was soon clear to her that not much had changed.

Patrick was relieved when a couple named Ashmore moved in next door—until he got a good look at them. Fleming Ashmore was a painter just returned from several years in Paris. He was tall and lean with a vandyke beard and sported an odd costume of smock and beret. The first weeks, having gotten permission from Professor Cooper, Ashmore busied himself cutting out the walls on the top floor and putting in a skylight— creating a studio, so he said, like the one he rented in Paris.

His wife, Corinne, who set herself up to do Parisian dress-making for the women in the neighborhood, turned out to be a genuine Frenchwoman. She had garish orange hair piled on her head, and her buxom shape was stuffed into overbright dresses with too many ruffles and bows. For a woman well past thirty she had a girlishly flirtatious laugh and manner that got on Patrick's nerves. He had heard what they said about French women, and when he saw her with a cigarette drooping from her lip one day as she was pinning up a dress on Elizabeth, he knew it was all true.

Desperately unhappy herself about her dead child and her grief-stricken husband, Elizabeth welcomed the arrival of the colorful pair next door. It had been months since Patrick had taken any interest in her and at least they were a distraction. She didn't mind that so many of the old families were leaving Greenwich and moving to newer neighborhoods uptown. She liked the immigrants coming in with their European ways, and the trickle of artists like the Ashmores attracted by the low rents. Even the genteel shabbiness that was settling over their village she found artistic, giving it the air of a bohemian quarter.

One of the few things that gave her any respite at all during this bleak period was her friendship with Winifred Beaufort. Over the years since Winifred moved uptown with Will Kennedy, the two women had seen each other less frequently, attributing this to the different paths their lives had taken. But the truth was that the rape had opened their eyes to a problem they had been unwilling to face before. New York just wasn't an easy place for interracial friendships.

When they used to meet at Elizabeth's house or in public, there were forever little unpleasantnesses both pretended not to see—hostile stares from neighbors, whistles and remarks from men on the street, rude treatment by waitresses, or worst of all, the assumption that Winifred was her maid.

Though as flamboyant as ever after her recovery, Winifred became more cautious going about by herself. On the occasions they did get together, it was Elizabeth who usually went up to Winifred's rooms over the gambling club in the noisy entertainment area behind Madison Square Garden in the West Twenties. Of course, Patrick never knew anything about these visits—he would have been furious to hear that his wife sometimes alighted from a cab in front of a gambling hall where sporting gents made indecent proposals as she passed by. But she found these little escapades a welcome antidote to her domestic life and enjoyed keeping them secret.

Once inside Winifred's upholstered boudoir, both friends could forget that any color problem existed. Winifred regaled her with stories of life in the gambling casino, how she paid off the police, how she enlisted prostitutes into the club to keep the customers spending, and how afterward, the girls took the johns out to hansom cabs where they tipped the driver to shut his eyes to what was going on in back, as he drove along.

Elizabeth, who until Jack's death had found monogamy blissful, was both fascinated and shocked by her friend's casual love life. She found it hard to believe Winifred's claim that Will Kennedy didn't mind her carrying on whenever the mood struck her. There had been a railroad magnate, once even a cabinet member, and always there were men she just liked the looks of.

One afternoon in June, still dressed in mourning, she mounted the familiar carpeted steps on West Twenty-fourth Street. It had been seven months that she had been a wife in name only, and as she and Winifred settled themselves on a pair of blue velvet sofas facing each other in the cozy little boudoir with its scents of talcum and rosewater, she was grateful for her friend's diverting chatter. Diamond Jim Brady, it seemed, had been into the club that week and dropped a cool fifteen hundred dollars without batting an eye.

In her mid-thirties, Winifred was remarkably handsome. Uncorseted in an embroidered Japanese kimono, she was heavier than she used to be, which she did her best to camouflage by wearing what looked like all her jewelry, including a diamantine choker more usual in a ballroom than a boudoir. "You should have seen those white bitches drooling over Diamond Jim," Winifred said, as she reached for a box of Turkish cigarettes, the sleeve of the kimono falling away from her plump, brown arm.

Elizabeth accepted a cigarette, a thing she would never do anywhere else.

Winifred scratched a phosphorous match across a claw leg of the sofa and they both lit up.

For Elizabeth, this was the world of the living again. She leaned back and crossed her legs under her black voile skirts, exhaling a stream of smoke. She was cheered up at the very idea of what her neighbors on Perry Street would think if they saw her, a proper Greenwich matron, with a cigarette between her lips in a boudoir above a notorious gambling establishment.

Everything about the intimate room was designed for its impact on men. Even the quilted yellow satin walls were chosen to set off Winifred's chocolate beauty.

Elizabeth asked if Diamond Jim Brady resembled his pictures in the newspapers.

Winifred took the cozy off the teapot and started pouring. "Honey, he's got a gut and a big red nose like Santa Claus. If he didn't have money, nobody would look at him. But you ought to feast your eyes on my new gentleman friend."

Elizabeth laughed. "Not another new gentleman! What does this one do?"

"What doesn't he do!" Winifred lay back against the sofa, her cigarette in the air. "He's a piano player. Plays rag like you never heard, and honey, he's blacker than me. I didn't think I'd ever meet a colored man again who could stand up against Rafer."

"You never told me about any Rafer." Elizabeth was enjoying herself. This was exactly what she had come for.

"Didn't I?" Winifred kicked off her fancy slippers and put her feet up on the cushions, giving a glimpse of green silk chemise under the kimono. "I was only thirteen. He was a field hand, nineteen years old, the most beautiful man I ever saw. We used to meet in the pecan orchard. Had three months of it, until that white family took me off to Paris. It nearly broke my heart."

"Your life's been so exciting, Winnie."

Her friend caught the wan note in her voice. "I can make it sound good when I want to. Things no better for you, huh?"

Elizabeth confessed that nothing had changed. "I'm just going to have to wait until Patrick wakes up"—she sighed deeply—"but I'm beginning to doubt he ever will."

Winifred refilled their cups. "When are you going to do right by yourself like I been telling you? If one man don't do it for you, get yourself another."

Here we go again, thought Elizabeth. That was Winnie's one solution for everything—a love affair. She sat back to wait out the sermon.

"You wouldn't have any trouble, honey. You've aged a lot better than I have. Sure, I get plenty of attention. But it's the way I fix myself up. A complexion like yours doesn't come out of a jar, and that hair and figure aren't a bit changed from the first time we met."

Elizabeth looked away as if bored.

"Why is it," Winifred said, putting the back of her fist to her forehead in exasperation, "when you're trying to help somebody, you want to kill them if they don't listen?"

Elizabeth came over and sat beside her. "I'm sorry, Winnie. I know you're trying to help, but I really can't see another man as the solution."

"There are other possibilities," Winifred said, looking at her.

Elizabeth couldn't imagine what she was talking about. "A new hobby?"

"You might call it that."

Elizabeth laughed. "Thanks, but making birch bark playing cards wouldn't take my mind off my troubles."

Winifred kept her eyes on her, exhaling smoke. "I'm not talking about that."

Elizabeth shifted uneasily on the sofa. Her friend's world always went slightly beyond her own imaginings. Of course, that was what attracted her. "Well, what are you talking about then?"

Winifred carefully examined the high buff of her nails. "How about trying a woman?"

Elizabeth stared.

"If you're not getting any romancing from your man, a woman might do the trick—while you're waiting."

Elizabeth was still taking it in.

Winifred stretched out her arms along the top of the divan, an orchid with trembling tendrils. "I find a woman makes me feel real good when men are getting me down."

Elizabeth tried to laugh it off, but couldn't. A musk was in the air that made it hard for her to sit still.

"We all need to step outta line from time to time, honey. Mosly a man fills the bill, but once in a while it can be a woman."

"You mean, like those flamboyant women at the Café Select in Paris?"

Winifred gave a raucous laugh. "Honey, they weren't women, they were men."

"Were they!" Elizabeth puffed at her cigarette, but it had gone out. "I've read about women with women of course, but this is the first time...."

"Well, honey, there's always a first time, isn't there?" Winifred struck a match to light Elizabeth's cigarette, but instead leaned forward and kissed her full on the mouth.

Elizabeth had been kissed by women all her life—friends, relations, pecking her on the cheek—but that a woman could kiss another woman... the scent of frangipani nearly made her swoon. She jumped up and started arranging her hair in front of a gilt-framed mirror with a garland of snowdrops incised around it. Her face was burning.

Winifred blew out the match and brushed ashes from her lap. "I guess I scared hell out of you, didn't I?"

"Certainly not!" Elizabeth said, furious that her voice was shaking. "You've given me a lot to think about."

Winifred stood up, retying the sash of her kimono. "Well, let me know sometime what the verdict is." She went over to sit down at her vanity table. Removing her choker, she began to cream her throat, watching her friend in the mirror.

Elizabeth couldn't keep herself from chattering on inanely. "I accept all behavior as natural, of course. It's the principle of my life. I can't stand puritans. I'm entirely open to the unconventional, but...."

"...you're a woman who needs a man?" Winifred started rubbing a rosy tint into her brown cheeks, getting ready for her evening stint at the club downstairs. "I agree with you completely, honey. That's what I been telling you for a long time."

All the way home in the hansom cab, Elizabeth squirmed. Of course, Winifred would always be dear to her, but living in the demimonde as she did, she couldn't be expected to understand that if you really loved a man, you wanted to be faithful to him. It didn't have anything to do with Winnie, but it was just that with all her frustrations over Patrick she was ready to scream.

At home she tried to settle down with a play by Oscar Wilde, which she had been reading. She was up to the scene where Salome was performing a lurid dance, holding the severed head of John the Baptist by the hair. When the dusky princess kissed the dead mouth, which might have amused her two hours before, now it made her uncomfortable, as if those frangipani lips were stifling her. She got herself a glass of sherry, but she was so agitated she couldn't calm down.

At her wit's end, she slammed the book shut and hurried around to the printing shop. Spending time with Tom and Albert as they did the technically exacting work of making their lithographs always soothed her. Though it was after five, Patrick wouldn't be home for two hours since he had deliberately taken to working late, and she had already prepared a cold supper for him. She didn't have to worry about Alicia, who was practicing the piano at her music school for hours every day.

In the months since her estrangement from Patrick, she and her father-in-law had drawn closer together. They had long talks. They read each other letters they got from Veronica in England. He even encouraged her to participate in making the prints, where her artistic eye could be useful.

When she got to the shop, the two pressmen had already left for the day. She went past the printing presses to the back where the engraving and lithography were done. Albert Cogswell was working by himself, his graying hair falling around his bearded face as he lay a sheet of paper over a flat lithography stone on the worktable. He told her that Tom was over at the Brooklyn docks picking up a shipment of rice paper from Shanghai, and she turned to go.

"Hold on a minute, Lizzie," Albert said.

She winced at the nickname.

"I'm about to pull this proof. I want to see what you think of it."

The lithographs Albert and Tom had been turning out were selling briskly to art collectors. Currently they were working on a portfolio of prints entitled "The Legend of Greenwich Village," a Canarsie Indian tale. The rough sketches for it were tacked upon the wall. Elizabeth had helped them write the text for the story that was to be inserted in the folder.

Albert noted her flushed cheeks as she waited impatiently while he aligned the paper with the crossmarks on the corners of the stone. This had to be done exactly so that each successive color printed over it would fall in the right place.

Albert Cogswell was aware that he didn't fit her conception of what an artist should be—he was too homegrown and folksy in his style. She would have preferred that he paint impressionist landscapes as they did in Paris. "Did I ever tell you how they invented this process, Lizzie?" he said, as he ran the hand roller over the paper. "This fella sat down on a stone one day where a farmer had just painted his acreage markings, and when he stood up it was printed on the seat of his britches." He peeled off the wet print and held it up to her. It showed the earth god waking up after the sun goddess was shot out of the sky by a warrior's arrow.

For no reason at all, the lithograph struck Elizabeth as ridiculous. What looked like a hirsute hermit with a bare behind was in the act of mounting a naked Pocahontas sprawled on the ground. She broke into a peal of laughter that ended in a hiccup.

What was the matter with her, Albert wondered? Elizabeth Endicott wasn't the kind of woman to be easily shocked, no matter how ladylike she acted.

"I'm sorry, Albert," she said, holding a handkerchief over her mouth to control herself. "I don't know what's wrong with me today. It's not funny. I think you caught it exactly."

"No," he said, studying the background of the print, "the Jersey shore is all wrong."

"Jersey shore?" For some reason, this seemed even more hilarious to her. Tears were streaming from her eyes.

He started wiping the picture off the stone with a turpentine rag.

"Stop!" she cried. "You mustn't!"

"Oh, it's not you. That one was just for practice." He cleaned his hands off on a towel. "You must have had a merry time of it today."

"It hasn't been that at all," she said, getting hold of herself, but she began to titter again at the thought of the hairy behind in the lithograph.

"Looks like something's got into you. Look here, Lizzie, I'm knocking off for the day." He put on his jacket, pulling his gray locks out of the collar. "How about I give you a cup of coffee? Maybe that will calm you down."

"I feel a perfect fool," she said. But now it struck her as comic the way he took the stairs two at a time ahead of her to open the door—and he was sixty-six years old!

In the loft overhead that he shared with Tom, he pulled up a chair for her and went to get the coffee pot from the stove.

The place was spartanly furnished with a table, two plain wooden bedsteads, Albert's watercolors tacked to the walls, and the iron stove that served both for heat and cooking. Every time she thought of the litho of the bare-bottomed hermit and the naked Pocahontas she couldn't hold back her giggles. When Albert poured a dollop of liquor from a medicine bottle into her coffee, explaining that the Shinnecocks brewed it from wild cranberries, she shook with laughter again.

Something was certainly eating her. Albert couldn't be sure what it was but he had a pretty good idea. "You sure caught the laughing bug," he said, sitting across from her on the stool with a glass of the red liquor in his hand. "Are things all that hunky-dory between you and Pat?" His eyes were twinkling.

At once, she burst into tears, covering her face with her handkerchief as she wept.

He waited until she was finished without taking his kindly eyes off her.

"Forgive me, Albert. I don't know what came over me. I've never done that in my life before—at least not in public," she said at last. She wiped her eyes.

"There's nothing wrong with crying," he said quietly.

She had never talked intimately with Albert Cogswell. They had never even been alone together before, but she began to tell him how much Patrick was still suffering over little Jack's death. "I'm so concerned. He's miserable and I don't know what to do."

"Seems to me with Pat treating you that way, you must be goddam mad at him."

She was about to protest that it wasn't so, then she caught herself. Actually, she told him, though she hadn't admitted it to herself until now, she was mad at Patrick—mad as hell.

Albert said that the women he knew, Indian women mostly, were more in touch with their feelings and acted more natural with their men. "They let everything out right off—if you get what I mean."

"But we're from different backgrounds," she protested. "Women in my world have to act the way we do. Men wouldn't want us otherwise." She was filled with gratitude to him for making her see this.

"Not me," Albert said. "I've never gone after that kind of proper acting woman. Too much horseshit to get through."

His using the obscenity so naturally, as if he were talking to another man, pleased her. She considered using it herself casually in her next gossip with Winifred—and reddened at the thought of what had happened that afternoon.

"But to be open with you, Lizzie," Albert was saying, "I've never believed that you were near as high-and-mighty as you act."

"Albert! I've never been high-and-mighty, and you know it! Women who act that way bore me out of my mind."

"Oh, yes, you are. You walk around in your fancy duds talking that Vassar College accent, but you don't fool me. I know the woman you are underneath."

She had to laugh with him. This homespun philosopher knew more about women than dear Tom ever did. He obviously had a lot more experience. Maybe she had been pouring out her troubles to the wrong person all this time. "You're making me feel so much better," she said, holding out her cup for more coffee.

"That's because you're real like me, Lizzie. You've got too much marrow in your bones for anything to keep you down for long." He chuckled and splashed some more cranberry liquor into her cup without even a gesture toward the coffeepot.

"Please don't call me that dreadful name. I'm not one of your squaws."

He roared. "You're wearing a lot of flossy clothes instead of deerskin, but they can come off just as fast."

She turned scarlet. "Don't be vulgar."

"You'll go off the rails without love, Elizabeth. You're a woman who needs it"—his voice was husky—"and I love doing it." He drew his chair up closer.

She gave a nervous laugh. "But I've never…Patrick…no, it's absurd."

"You think I can't cut the mustard just because I've got myself a belly now?" He raised a shaggy eyebrow.

"I didn't say that…." Her voice was shaking. She couldn't breathe. The vigorous man sitting in front of her with his legs spread was someone who had never lived by any rules. He was an artist who had painted his pictures in the wild, lived with his women in the wild—women who were not bound by convention as she was. He had taken them in shacks, had run them down in the fields, in the woods….

Her heart pounded as he got to his feet, his eyes shining into hers. He had caught her and she couldn't run any longer. He understood, and wanted to help. She let him take her hand and pull her to her feet. Then she fell into his arms and turned her mouth to his.

She walked home past the playground where, on the warm June evening, children were still squealing on the slides and swings, the hurdy-gurdy carousel, and the pony ride. A street sweeper was singing as he raked a twig broom over the cobblestones.

She was inordinately pleased with herself. With all the talk these days about women's rights, it was high time she had an affair. She had been a dutiful wife long enough, sitting by while her husband moped his life away.

True, there had been Jean-Paul in Paris, but she had not let it go this far, and it didn't count. Albert was a dear for going along with her. He was a little rustic on the surface—she would never tolerate that "Lizzie," but she certainly understood how all those women had fallen for him. If it weren't for Tom living there, who knows, she might even consider continuing it. It was so French, after all, not to have to be in love with your seducer.

Seducer. The word thrilled her.

She looked around at the passersby, the women with their children in the playground, most of them middle-class wives smug in their stereotyped "virtue." Wouldn't their eyes pop if they knew that half an hour before she had been lying with a strange man in a bachelor's studio!

Turning on to Perry Street, she realized with a guilty start that she had been humming all the way.

At the breakfast table next day, sitting across from Patrick, she glanced at herself in the wall mirror behind him to see if it showed, then looked at her husband to see if he had noticed anything. But as usual, she didn't exist for him. He sat eating his porridge and reading his newspaper as he had done for months.

Albert had told her she was angry and had a right to be. Well, she was, she was furious. Where were Pat's instincts? How could he not sense the fulfilled womanhood radiating from her every pore this morning? If she had hoped the incident with Albert would provoke him into a reaction— anything—it had failed dismally. She was so annoyed that she was on the verge of announcing what had happened and damn the consequences, when he folded his newspaper and, without even a glance at her, left the room.

He was unreachable in his self-pity and she was sick of it. If he thought she was going to sit around passively waiting for him to wake up, he had another guess coming. She was not going to deny herself any longer.

That afternoon she did her hair in a softer style, recklessly sprayed on her Worth perfume, and changed from her ordinary black mourning dress into a purple sheath under black lace. When she set off for the print shop, she knew that she had never looked better.

But today, in the bright light of day, everything had changed. The shop was a beehive of activity—the pressmen noisily running off handbills, and in the back, Tom and Albert, two old men fussing over another litho in "The Legend of Greenwich Village" series, the sun goddess soaring back into the sky, her raiments rekindled.

When Elizabeth left the shop again, if she'd had any idea that an affair with Albert would solve the problem, it was apparent to her now how impossible it was.

She had to find an outlet for her restlessness. Not knowing what else to do, she threw herself into social work the way her mother might have done, counseling immigrant mothers at a settlement house on Barrow Street.

The infant mortality rate among the poor was alarming, and she lectured them on proper infant diet and health care, advising the Irish mothers not to put whiskey into the baby bottles with the milk and the Italian mothers not to give them wine. She also warned them not to leave their babies alone in their tenement rooms when they went out, but to take turns looking after each other's children, and not to overswaddle them but to allow them freedom of movement.

As she had hoped, this outside activity helped. Although she was supposed to be the teacher, she was touched by the outpouring of maternal concern these women showed her, their solicitude about her life, asking her to tell them about her husband and children.

When she said she only had one child, a daughter, the Italian women wagged their fingers at her and said she was young and healthy. She ought to be having many more *bambini* for her husband.

"*Figlio*," they chorused, "you must give your husband *figlio*."
A teenage Irish mother who was nursing her baby, laughed and said that the word was "son" in American.

"Yes, yes," said the others, "you need a son!"
Moved by the concern of these simple women, Elizabeth broke down in tears. Immediately, they clustered around her to comfort her. "Why is the pretty lady crying? She is so young, she have such a good life."

Unable to control herself, she sobbed out that her son had died.

She was showered with caresses and exclamations of sympathy. "You must have new son. That make everything good."

She confessed that her husband didn't come near her any more, he missed Jack so much.

But it's up to the wife, they said. "Don't be such a grand lady. Where does it get you?"

"I don't understand," she said.

"It's easy, *Signora*. Us women always on top, no matter what the men think. They dumb. They slaves to that little bird in their trousers. All we got to do is make the birdie sing and they crawl after us on their bellies, don't forget it."

Up-to-date as she was, Elizabeth felt herself blushing.

A short, plump, dark-eyed woman pushed up to her. "*Signora*, tonight in bed, don't wait for him to come to you. Go to him. You make him feel good there where he likes it. Take his little bird in your hand, kiss it, make it a rooster again. The cock crows, your husband wake up, make you a son—you see!"

Elizabeth put her arms around the little woman and pressed her cheek against hers. No one had ever spoken so frankly or made so much sense. All the women laughed and nodded at each other in approval. The young Irish mother was laughing so hard she had to put her baby down on the table to keep from dropping it.

In no time, Patrick was in love with her all over again. But she had already missed her period and knew she was pregnant by Albert Cogswell. She was aghast at first, then in the euphoria pregnancy always brought her, it came to her that there was no reason not to pass the child off as Patrick's. When the time came, the child would be "premature," and he would love it in any case and never question its paternity.

She waited a few weeks before telling him she was pregnant. As she had expected he was exultant, convinced that another son was on the way.

29

Fourteen-year-old Alicia began neglecting her piano to hang around the studio of Fleming Ashmore and his Parisian wife next door. Elizabeth was amused that her snippy daughter, who had always been indifferent to boys, had developed her first crush on the debonair painter more than twice her age—and a married man at that! She would end up with a broken heart, no doubt—and no doubt recover just as fast. But it would be a good introduction to the world of art to which Elizabeth herself had always been so attracted.

For his part, Ashmore, who painted in the style of Renoir, was charmed by Alicia's pubescent sparkle and asked her if she would like to pose for him—with her mother to chaperone, of course. Overjoyed, Alicia rushed to beg for permission.

Elizabeth was gratified that Ashmore was taking an interest in her difficult child whose airs had always got on Patrick's nerves. When he sketched his conception of Alicia in a summer dress holding a parasol—still a child but with just a hint of approaching womanhood—she looked at her daughter with new eyes. Evidently Alicia didn't appear to the rest of the world the way she did at home.

But when Elizabeth told Patrick about it, he wasn't keen on the idea at all. He didn't like the looks of that fancy pants of a neighbor, he told her, or that redheaded floozy of a wife of his, either.

"But he's an artist, and it will he so good for Alicia. She's been so pouty lately and this could be the best remedy. I know you don't think much of it, but do remember, it's all right for a girl to be interested in art."

"She ought to be out with her school chums," said Patrick. "Sittin up there with a middle-aged man, I don't like it."

"She won't be alone. I'll be there too. I admire his work tremendously and it will be an experience for me as well. Please, Pat."

Her pregnancy just beginning to show, his wife at thirty-eight had never looked so lovely to him and he was more passionately drawn to her than ever. With all his misgivings, he was too happy about his coming son to say no to anything she wanted.

Elizabeth was nearly as thrilled as Alicia when they were in the studio and Ashmore began the portrait. She adored the smell of turpentine and the stacks of canvases, the couch with the oriental rug covering it and the paint-spattered easel set up under the skylight. She had to admit that her daughter with her lambent eyes and masses of blonde curls was a perfect Renoir child, as she posed with awkward grace on the platform in a light frock and parasol.

For a few weeks Elizabeth sat with them every afternoon from three to five. But Ashmore was such a perfectionist he was forever wiping out in a moment what he had been working on all day. As her pregnancy developed it became harder for her to sit up, and she began to long for an afternoon nap. Winter was approaching and it was chilly in the studio, even with the potbellied stove. No amount of heat could warm up that barn of a place with the drafty skylight. Even in her mittens and shawl her bones still ached, and it seemed like the portrait would never be done.

Ashmore's wife, Corinne, who broke off her dressmaking to look in on them regularly, bringing tea and cookies, saw Elizabeth's discomfort and suggested, to her relief, that it wasn't necessary for her to come every afternoon. She herself would always be around and make sure her husband did not get so wrapped up in his work that he forgot to give Alicia regular rest breaks.

Ashmore seduced Alicia the first day Elizabeth stayed away. It was done expertly, while his wife kept judiciously out of sight downstairs, presumably finishing up a rush order. He put down his brush and went over to arrange his young model's dress, saying he was dissatisfied with the pose, tilting her chin, putting a hand lightly on her waist and another at her back to turn her gently into a "more paintable stance." The schoolgirl was transported by the sensitive hands of this magnificent being she was infatuated with.

Later, as he lay next to her on the couch in the studio, his long johns unbuttoned and a hand resting on one of her ripening breasts, he asked her if he had made her happy.

"Oh, yes!" she said, overwhelmed. "But what about Corinne? I like her so much, I don't want to hurt her."

"Don't worry about that, angel. She knows I'm an artist." He ran a finger under her petticoat along her inner thigh.

"But what if she should find out?" she said, trembling from the exploration of his fingers.

"Corinne and I are above all that" he whispered, as he leaned over her again.

As soon as Alicia was again posing with her parasol, Corinne came in with wine for them both, and seeing Alicia blush, made a point of going over to kiss her tenderly, saying, "Nothing to worry about, dear child."

The next day, Ashmore told her he no longer saw her as the Renoir child in a garden of innocence. If she would agree to it, he had a whole new idea for the painting, this time portraying her as a young "Diana Fleeing the Storm." He put her into a diaphanous shift, draping it to reveal one of her newly formed breasts, as if the wind had blown it aside as she ran.

Moving her hand away from her breast, which she had covered in modesty, he assured her that when the painting was finished and her mother saw how beautiful his new conception was, she would approve completely.

This time, the painting progressed like a dream. Ashmore declared he had never had such an inspiring model to work from and he felt renewed in his art. The painting was going to be his masterpiece.

Pretending to be running was a difficult pose to hold, even for a healthy young girl like Alicia, and Ashmore often had to put down his palette to massage her limbs on the couch, which led inevitably to love-making.

Even Corinne was caught up in the excitement of Ashmore's artistic enterprise, as she discreetly slipped in with little snacks of bread, wine, and cheese. Alicia often stayed to have supper with them after the posing session. Corinne liked the effect of this sweet child on her temperamental husband. No matter how hard he had worked, Ashmore always revived when his foot touched that of his young model under the table.

On the day in February the painting was finished, the three of them went to celebrate at a little restaurant on Washington Square that was a favorite of the Ashmores. It was a frosty night as they set off, Alicia between them, through the narrow Village streets, until they came out at busy Sixth Avenue, where new electric streetlights made everything as bright as day.

Under the elevated, a chestnut vendor in a worn greatcoat left over from the Civil War was stamping his feet to keep warm. The pan of chestnuts roasting over the charcoal sent up billows of pungent smoke. Fleming held Alicia's arm tightly against him as they plunged into the clattering traffic, dodging hooves and wagons and avoiding the fresh horse-droppings. She felt as though she was almost one of the grown-up ladies with their escorts in the passing hansom cabs.

When they were nearly across the avenue, a stallion pulling a wagonload of firewood was practically on top of them before the driver reined the beast in. It reared up with a powerful snorting, gusts of steam coming from its nostrils, almost upsetting the cart. Alicia fell back against Fleming who held her close as the wagon clattered past them.

Walking on toward Washington Square, Fleming's arm still tight around her, he told her about the artists moving into this neighborhood, not just those like himself back from abroad, but from all over America. "I first heard about Greenwich Village in Paris from an extraordinary woman who used to live right near here. Averbach her name was. She was my first patron. We were very good friends."

"Very, very good friends," Corinne broke in with a laugh.

He ignored her. "Adele told me, that when she lived here years ago, this section below the square was called the French Quarter. That was before the Italians started moving in."

The restaurant Ashmore took them to was on the south side of the square and was called Le Chat Noir. The silhouette of a big black cat was painted on the door. It was a noisy little place with red-checkered tablecloths and candles stuck in wine bottles. After they had squeezed into a table, Corinne went off to the ladies' room and returned with her orange hair fluffed out and her lips painted orange to match. She lit a cigarette and passed one to her husband.

Alicia was astonished at her transformation. Corinne was like something out of a picture in a magazine of Parisian life. Other women were fixed up in the same extreme manner. The place had a raffish atmosphere she knew her mother would love, the noisy patrons refilling their glasses from jugs of wine, and steaming platters of spaghetti held high in the air by waiters weaving between the tables.

The owner, a heavy woman with eyebrows plucked to a thin line and scarlet cupid's bow lips, stopped by to greet Fleming and Corinne. She kissed them on both cheeks and they all chattered away in French.

"*Enchantée, mademoiselle,*" she said, when Alicia was introduced. "She's charming, Ashmore."

"Isn't she? She's my Diana Fleeing the Storm." He looked at his model fondly, thrilling Alicia to her toes.

When the owner had moved off to other tables, Fleming told Alicia that she rented out rooms upstairs.

Corinne snickered. "She's in the beds as much as she's making them up."

A heavy-set man with a walrus mustache and a ring in one ear came up to them and Fleming introduced him as a sculptor named Augustus Saint-Gaudens. Not only did he kiss Corinne's hand, but to Alicia's amazement, he kissed hers too. In a loud voice that rode over the uproar around them, the sculptor invited them to stop by his studio to see a new bronze he had just finished, an Artemis ten feet high that had been commissioned for the top of the new Madison Square Garden.

What a coincidence, Fleming said. He had just finished painting a Diana himself, and here she was. He laid a hand on Alicia's shoulder, making her blush.

The sculptor appraised her with a professional eye. "She's indeed a young Diana, isn't she, Ashmore?" he said with a wink at her that made her blush even more.

When he was gone, Fleming told Alicia that Saint-Gaudens had a certain talent, but he had been getting so many public commissions, he was selling it down the river. "And don't be fooled by that hand-kissing or his name. He came over on the boat from Dublin."

The waiter appeared and Corinne ordered a meal of snails, onion soup, and frog's legs. And when a bottle of champagne arrived and Ashmore popped the cork, Alicia was floating on air.

The next day, she arrived breathless at the studio at her regular time to find Fleming Ashmore with a new canvas on the easel, a cornucopia of fruits he was painting—persimmons, late apples, and a mandolin—set up on a table before him. He waved her away with his brush. "Your painting is finished," he said. "I've got a commission now to do a still life for an important collector."

"But what about me?" she asked.

He dabbed a silver highlight onto an apple and started mixing ochre into the red on his palette. "Your painting's done, can't you understand?"

She stood there unable to speak. But when he refused even to look around at her, she turned and ran down the stairs.

Corinne, who was on her knees in the parlor pinning material to a dress form, called her in before she got to the front door. Fleming Ashmore's wife had been through this scene many times before. It was never easy. She stuck the pins in a cushion, got up, and went over to take both the child's hands. "It's not much fun now, I know," she said, with a sad smile, "but you had a sweet moment, didn't you?"

She doubted the girl was hearing her, but she went on anyway.

"You were the painting to him, don't you see? He always makes love with his models. It makes the work so much better. It's all for his art."

She couldn't bear the uncomprehending eyes any longer and turned back to her work. "It may sound cruel now, *chérie*, but nothing is forever in life. You're still young, you'll get over it. I had to go through it myself."

When the front door closed, Corinne Ashmore gave up trying to work and poured herself a brandy.

In the next few days, Elizabeth, who was heavily pregnant, noticed that Alicia had stopped going next door to pose and seemed in a worse sulk than usual. She asked if the painting was finished, but her daughter was evasive.

She was out on the stoop getting a breath of fresh air when Ashmore emerged from his house, obviously not pleased to see her. When she asked him about the painting, he told her he was still completing the background and thought it bad luck to let anyone view it until it was done.

But Alicia's sulk continued, which had her mother mystified. Patrick irritated his wife with his I-told-you-so attitude. "Ya see, it's what I said all the time. Those artists you're so crazy about didn't do her a bit of good. Now admit it," he said, patting her big belly.

Elizabeth had grown so large nothing fit her any more and a few days later, when Corinne was over measuring her for a new robe, the dressmaker said, "Poor little Alicia, I hope she's feeling better by now. It's so hard when these things come to an end."

The innuendo, especially after Ashmore's excuses, disturbed her. Later, when her daughter came home, she confronted her and Alicia sobbed out the whole sordid tale.

The next morning, Elizabeth waited until she saw Corinne go out to the market with her string bag. Then, walking carefully, she went next door and, holding tight to the bannister, puffed her way up the three flights of stairs to Ashmore's studio. Still breathing hard, she made her way right by the astonished painter at his easel over to a large painting covered by a cloth against the wall. She tore off the cloth and gasped at what she saw.

It was even worse than she expected. Instead of the Renoir child in a garden she had been imagining all these months, her fourteen-year-old daughter was painted with a bare breast, and little else hidden by the diaphanous shift. What had happened was plain for all the world to see. Outraged, she tried to scratch at the canvas, determined to destroy the obscenity.

"Stop!" Ashmore leapt over and pulled her away. "What do you think you're doing!"

"You're a...a moral degenerate!" Elizabeth cried, shaking off his hand.

"Please spare me the bourgeois indignation," Ashmore said, turning back to his easel.

She reached out for the back of a chair to steady herself. "You had no right to take advantage of her! She's only a child!"

He picked up his brush and started to mix some colors on the palette. "You know as well as I do that she wasn't hurt in the slightest. Sure, she's young, but she's tasted life and she's going to be the better for it."

Elizabeth was fighting for her breath. "If you don't destroy...I'll take you to court...."

"If it's any of your business, Mrs. Endicott, which it is not, you have nothing to worry about. I have no intention of sharing the painting with the public. It's much too precious." He dabbed the color on to the canvas. "I intend to keep it for my private collection."

She held on to the back of the chair, watching him. "How can I believe you?"

Cleaning the brush with a rag, he gave her a smile. "My word as a gentleman."

"I'm probably a fool to trust you." Elizabeth started for the door.

She opened it and was about to go out, when he called after her, "I admire you, you know."

She half-turned and saw his cool artist eyes appraising her.

"Under that conventional veneer, there's something special about you. I'd really like to paint you, just as you are, passionate, heavy with child."

"Don't be absurd!" Elizabeth said.

As she made her way carefully down the stairs, she had to face the bitter truth—art did not necessarily come out of noble souls. She knew Fleming Ashmore was immune from any moral consideration beyond the necessity of his painting, however much she longed to bring him down.

That evening after dinner, while Patrick massaged her back with witch hazel as he did every night now in her final months, she told him that she had seen the painting and was thoroughly disappointed. It looked nothing like Alicia. "You were right," she said. "I shouldn't have encouraged her to sit for him. It was a waste of time."

"Ah, who gives a hoot about it, anyway?" Patrick said. "It's all over, so let's forget it." He pressed his strong thumbs into the flesh of her lower back where he knew she needed it most, and Ashmore faded from her mind.

Elizabeth persuaded him to let Alicia spend a few weeks with a girlfriend on the Jersey shore, even though it meant interrupting the school year, using as an excuse that the child's moodiness was just too much for her to put up with in her condition.

The day after Alicia left, while Patrick was at work, she took a cab to the family lawyer. Since her father had given her power of attorney, she instructed the lawyer to notify the Ashmores that their lease on the house was being terminated because the property was up for sale. They were to vacate the premises by the end of the month.

Crocuses were already poking through the earth in March of '88, when New York was hit by a blizzard, preventing even the hired girl from coming in. The city was at a standstill, paralyzed by the worst snowstorm anyone could remember.

Patrick was terrified that night when Elizabeth went into labor "a month early," though she did her best to calm him down, knowing perfectly well the baby was right on time and nothing was wrong.

There was a telephone in the house—Patrick had installed it, he claimed, for "transit emergencies," and it was the first one on the block. But now with the biggest emergency of all, he couldn't get through to the midwife at St. Vincent's Hospital. Though he cranked away for the operator, it was no use—the lines were already down. He plunged out into the pitch-black night and fought his way through mountainous drifts toward the hospital.

He was no sooner gone than the electric light went out. Between contractions, Elizabeth managed to get a lamp lit beside her bed, and with the storm howling at the windows, gave birth by herself to a little girl.

It was hours before Patrick made it back to her, nearly berserk from having been away so long. But by then she was all right. She had dealt with the whole mess herself, and the baby, wrapped in one of his flannel shirts, was in her arms.

With the snow melting off him in pools, he fell to his knees beside the bed, holding his wife's hand to his heart, and wept. She ran her fingers through his thick hair and saw that it had gone gray.

Although he had wanted a son so badly, it was love at first sight between Patrick and this tiny girl with wisps of reddish hair. They named her Polly.

And amid all the fuss after the birth of the baby, Elizabeth paid little attention to the Ashmores moving out next door. But when Alicia came back from New Jersey, her old self again, though with a wistful look in her formerly innocent eyes, Elizabeth thanked God for having had the power to get rid of them.

A year and a half later when Elizabeth was again pregnant, her father-in-law came by for supper with some startling news. Albert Cogswell had run into Fleming Ashmore in an art supply store, and Ashmore had invited him to a show he was having at the gallery in A. T. Stewart's on Broadway. The major work was the portrait he had done of Alicia, entitled "Diana Fleeing the Storm." Albert had gone to see it, and, though he didn't care for that studio type of painting, thought it was the best thing Ashmore had ever done.

Elizabeth listened aghast, but Alicia, who hadn't mentioned Ashmore's name once since coming home, went on eating as though the news meant nothing to her.

Patrick put down his knife and fork and looked at his wife. "You didn't tell me they were going to show her picture in public."

"I had no idea…," Elizabeth stammered.

"We better go over and take a look at it," said Patrick.

Elizabeth begged him not to. It wasn't worth all the fuss. But it griped him that Ashmore had put a picture of their daughter on public view without asking for his permission. He would not be put off from going, no matter what his wife said, and the next day she was forced to accompany him to the exhibition, praying that she could deal with what she knew was coming.

They had no trouble finding the painting. It could not have been more prominently displayed. It was hanging on the wall opposite the gallery entrance and a crowd was around it. When Pat saw that it was Alicia almost in the altogether, he roared, "Why, that son of a bitch!" He broke away from Elizabeth and pushed through the gallery patrons, determined to pull the picture down off the wall and smash the canvas and its elaborate gold-leaf frame to smithereens. But the guards got hold of him just in time and hustled him off, with Elizabeth following along behind, clutching his bowler hat which she had rescued from the floor.

Hauled before the immaculately-suited gallery director, Patrick wrenched himself free from the guards and demanded that the picture be removed at once.

The director reviled him icily for having dared to lay a hand on such a masterwork. Didn't he know the painting had been purchased by the Smithsonian Institution? Emboldened by the presence of the guards, the director added that if the gentleman ever showed his face around there again, he would not hesitate to have him arrested.

Finally, they were allowed to leave, and Elizabeth moved a steaming Patrick toward the exit. Outside, he shook his fist in the air and, to the astonishment of passing shoppers, shouted that he was going to cut Ashmore's balls off.

The next day the telephone rang. When Patrick heard Elizabeth exclaim indignantly into the mouthpiece, "What are you talking about!" he grabbed the receiver.

It was the gallery director again. He had communicated with Mr. Ashmore, the director said, and the artist wanted Mr, Endicott to know that up to this point he had not revealed the identity of his celebrated Diana. But if Mr. Endicott were to make any more trouble, the newspapers would learn quickly enough who she was.

Patrick went straight to their lawyer, who eventually made him see that, much as he had moral right on his side, his legal rights were less clear. Moreover, a court trial would certainly be more humiliating for the family, and expecially for his daughter, than the painting's brief exposure at A. T. Stewart's, before being consigned to the obscurity of the Smithsonian Institute. Unfortunate as the whole thing was, the lawyer thought it best to drop the matter.

1891

30

Alicia was at the piano playing arias from *La Traviata*. It was an April morning. The front windows were open and a breeze was riffling the pages of her music. From the street came the shouts of children at their games and the occasional clatter of a horse pulling a tradesman's wagon

At seventeen, Alicia's coloring was more delicate than her mother's and she had light gray eyes like her grandfather's. She was as ethereal as a ballerina in her clinging pleated skirt and shirtwaist blouse with high collar that emphasized the graceful way she held her head aloft at the piano.

But however lovely she looked, Alicia was not happy. She knew how much her mother worried about her, the way she kept to herself, spending long hours playing the piano. She was too quiet, she hardly laughed and didn't seem to enjoy herself the way other girls her age did.

It was not exactly that she was unhappy either. It was more like she was numb. She didn't feel much of anything any more, not since what had happened. Her mother had never once mentioned it, so Alicia knew, on some undefinable level of her being, that her shame was irreparable. It separated her from everybody else, and it would prevent her from ever having the kind of life her schoolmates chattered about.

As her agile fingers followed the score, she saw herself in the doomed heroine of *La Traviata*. Sometimes Alicia wished she too could be carried off by consumption, the way Marguerite had been. It would be better if she were Catholic, Alicia often thought. Then she could become a nun. At least that would give a purpose to her life.

Caught up in the melodies she was playing, she scarcely heard the cry of a vegetable vendor outside, "Baby carrots, new peas, strawberries, and bright red cher-reez!" When she began playing her favorite theme, Alfredo's love song to Violetta, suddenly from the street a glorious tenor voice floated in through the window singing the aria *"A quell' amor."* Without missing a beat, she accompanied it to the end of the song, as it soared through the tricky passages scarcely missing a note, and held the high D long after the piano chords faded away.

She jumped up and ran to the window. But it was not a prince outside declaring his love for her, it was a street boy with curly black hair and a swarthy face, standing by his pushcart. "Hey, miss," he called out to her, "how about some strawberries?"

For a second she was disappointed, but when he flashed her a dazzling smile, she heard his soaring voice again and he was transformed. He repeated his question and she nodded shyly and went out to him. While he filled a horn of newspaper with strawberries from a basket, she asked him if he was studying singing.

He furrowed his swarthy brow. "Me study? Who needs to study? I'm Italian." His dark eyes were so intense she had to look away.

His wagon was crudely but brightly painted over with all the fruits and vegetables of the four seasons. She asked him who had done that.

He told her he had painted it himself.

"But you're so talented!" she exclaimed.

"You never met an Italian before?"

They both laughed.

He handed her the cornet of strawberries, but when she reached into the pocket of her skirt she discovered she had no money with her. She blushed, saying she would go get some.

"Never mind," he said. "I'll be by this way tomorrow. You pay me then."

His name was Mario Alfano, and the next day when she went out to pay him, she found herself inviting him to come over on his afternoon off and she'd accompany him on the piano.

Elizabeth was up in the nursery helping the hired girl with three-year-old Polly and her new baby son, Eugene, who had arrived the year before. Despite Patrick's often-announced wish for a son to replace Jack, he did not take particular interest in Eugene, having already given his heart to little Polly, a pixy-faced child with red hair who did not resemble him in the slightest.

But for Elizabeth, it was different. Eugene was the first baby she felt special about. Though she couldn't have explained it, it was as if he needed her more than any of her other children had, this child who had arrived when she was past forty.

She had just finished nursing him, when she was surprised to hear an operatic tenor voice reverberating through the house. Handing the baby over to the hired girl, she went downstairs and was even more surprised to find her normally reserved daughter playing the piano for the swarthy youth who sold produce to the neighborhood and who was singing like his heart was breaking.

After he left, Alicia couldn't stop talking about how talented the pushcart boy was and she couldn't wait for next week when he was coming over.

This spirited girl was an Alicia she had not seen for years. Smiling, she agreed with her daughter that he was indeed beautiful and talented. But the baby started to cry just then, and as she went back upstairs, she heard Alicia back at the piano playing the aria the boy had sung, this time embellishing it with elaborate arpeggios.

Alicia and Mario were quickly in love. He took her to a caffé in Little Italy where they ate spumoni and listened to singing waiters mangling their favorite arias. She took him to the Metropolitan Opera House where from cheap seats in the top balcony, with the stage half-obscured, they listened to *La Traviata* with Emma Calvé and Jean de Reszke.

"They weren't so bad, even if they're not Italian," Mario conceded, entwining his fingers in hers as they walked out under the brilliant electric lights of the marquee and started down the avenue for the Village, too alive with the music to take the trolley.

"You're so lucky, Mario," Alicia said. "Why don't I have any exotic blood in my family?"

He reminded her that her father's side was Irish.

"Oh, that's not the same thing at all," she said. "It's so low class."

"Whaddya talking about? You think Italians ain't low class? Maybe I'm too low class for you?"

She reassured him with a kiss on the cheek. Looking around to make sure no one could see, Mario pulled her into the shadows and pressed hard against her. Giggling, she pushed him away and ran off down the street with him after her.

One day, after they had been to the San Gennaro street fair, celebrating the patron saint of the Italian neighborhood south of Washington Square, he took her to his family's for dinner.

The Alfanos had long since moved from the room by the elevated into a tenement over on Carmine Street. Benno, Mario's father, having lost his construction job on the el, was now in the vegetable business with his brother-in-law, and Mario worked for them. There were several more children and an old aunt crowded into the railroad flat.

Two tables had been pushed together and were loaded with platters of Italian food and a big bottle of red wine. Alicia sat in the midst of the noisy family, taking it all in. On one wall was a tapestry depicting the sunset over the Bay of Naples, and on the other side, candles burned before a statue of the Virgin. Above the fireplace were framed oval photographs of the grandparents in Italy. The grandfather with a big walrus mustache and the grandmother in black with a cameo brooch were both staring into the camera, morosely.

All the Alfanos made a fuss over Alicia, refilling her wineglass and teasing her with sly allusions about her being Mario's girl. But the mother, carrying plates back and forth from the kitchen, watched her narrowly.

"Such beautiful hair she got," shouted the old, deaf aunt sitting next to her. "Her people from the North? Milano?"

Mario tried to correct her. "No, aunty, her name's Endicott. En-di-cott."

The old lady didn't get it. "What kind of name is that? She go to St. Anthony's or Our Lady of Pompeii?"

The younger children snickered. Mrs. Alfano set a dish of cornmeal with tomato sauce and cheese before the toothless old woman to shut her up.

"Is no problem," Benno said. "Father Pellegrino give her instruction in no time. She be good Catholic girl for Mario."

Alicia was about to say that she had no intention of converting to Catholicism and was not planning to marry anyone, when she caught Mario's dark, velvet eyes on her from across the table. She got his message not to let his family upset her, they were only teasing, and the two of them would be alone soon.

The next evening after dinner, Alicia carefully introduced the subject of the San Gennaro street fair to her parents. It was like a carnival, she told them.

The whole street was blocked off and there was music and dancing and food, and it was only a short walk away. It was amazing that none of them had ever been there before. She thought they might enjoy it too.

Elizabeth looked up from a letter she was writing to Veronica, took off her glasses, and tried to catch her daughter's eye.

Patrick muttered from behind his newspaper that he had to deal with them on the job and that was enough for him.

"But they're such warm people, papa, so spontaneous, so beautiful."

He lowered his paper and looked at her grumpily. "You don't work with them. They stink of garlic, and if ya try to tell them anything, they pull a knife on ya. They been here for years and don't even try to speak English right." He went back to his paper again.

"How can you say that?" she cried. "You act as if you're better than them!"

"I don't know about the ones you know, but the ones I know spread disease."

Turning a page of the paper, it crinkled and he slapped it flat.

"Alicia, dear...," Elizabeth warned.

But she was not going to stop. "Why don't you ever listen to me, papa! You've never cared about anything I like. At least try to understand. Do you always have to be so bigoted?"

"Young lady, you shut your mouth!" said Elizabeth sharply.

Her mother had never spoken to her that way before. Alicia was mortified and ran from the room.

Sighing, Elizabeth put aside her pen and capped the inkwell, and told Patrick she had better go see what was wrong.

On the second floor landing, before going on up to Alicia's room, she cocked her ear at the half-open nursery door to make sure the baby hadn't been awakened. Eugene was so sensitive to noise since he was weaned.

She found her daughter lying across the bed with her head in her arms. Shutting the door behind her, Elizabeth said, "I'm sorry I spoke that way, but why in God's name did you have to bring that up? You know how your father is."

Alicia turned to her with wet eyes. "You only care about him. What about me? I've been so miserable since...you know what I'm talking about." She covered her face with her hands.

Elizabeth was taken aback. Never had her daughter alluded before to what had happened with Ashmore. Her own guilt in the matter had kept her from ever speaking about it. She sat down on the bed beside Alicia and stroked her hair. "I know you've been unhappy, darling, and I've wished we could talk so many times, but I just kept hoping you'd put it behind you."

Alicia turned to her mother. "I thought nobody would ever want me again," she wiped tears away with her fingers, "and now that I've got somebody, a perfectly wonderful boy, you and papa are against him because he's Italian and poor."

"Of course, I'm not against him. I'm happy you have a friend. It's just that your father...."

"I'm going to marry him, mother."

Elizabeth gasped. "Marry?"

"With or without papa's approval. I'm starting to take instruction at Our Lady of Pompeii next week."

Elizabeth searched her daughter's shining eyes. "You're sure this is what you want?"

"I feel alive again, mother, really alive! This time it's right!"

Elizabeth felt the barrier between them since the Ashmore business falling away. She pressed her hand. "Then I want it too."

"Oh, mother!" Alicia threw herself into her arms. "Thank you, thank you!"

Elizabeth walked slowly down the stairs. It wasn't going to be easy for her daughter marrying into poverty, but the boy was charming, and as for his family, she didn't know them yet, but she was sure they would love Alicia too.

How strange life was. She'd hoped and prayed for so long that Alicia would recover from that dreadful experience with Ashmore. Now it was happening, in a way she never could have imagined. But hadn't she herself married a boy from the slums? Patrick.

It was going to take awhile, but he'd just have to accept it.

Alicia began taking instruction at Our Lady of Pompeii. The wedding date was set and the banns were posted.

One afternoon when Mario picked her up at the church, they walked to nearby Hudson Square Park and sat in a secluded corner in the cool, green shadows of old chestnut trees. They were out of sight of the boating pond and the promenade, where ladies with parasols pushed spindly perambulators past benches filled with immigrant mothers in shawls with children playing around them.

Mario was upset because his cousin had gotten into trouble with the police the night before. The cousin and some of the other *goombas* on the block had fought off an Irish gang who had come over to Carmine Street to break windows. The police had only picked the Italian boys up and his aunt had to go to the precinct house to get his cousin off.

"Them mick cops talked fresh to my aunt," Mario said. "They hate us. They act like we don't have no right to live here too. Who the hell they think they are?"

Alicia said not all the Irish were like that. She had Irish relatives on her father's side. She didn't know them very well but they were respectable people.

Mario slumped on the bench. "Your old man don't like us either."

Alicia put her head on his shoulder. "Your family is being so understanding, making the wedding. I can imagine what they're saying about my father. He just makes me sick!"

"Hey!" Mario bounced up in his seat and put an arm around her. "When your old man sees how good I'm gonna be to you, it'll be okay." He leaned close. "And Mario is gonna be very good to you."

She brushed away the fingers slipping under the collar of her blouse. "I know things are going to work out. It's just that sometimes I worry."

"You'll see. We got two nice little rooms all our own right across the hall from my family. You sure it don't bother you living in such a little place?"

She smiled at him. "Of course not. I love your family. Anyway, it'll only be for awhile. With your voice, it's only a matter of time until you're singing at the Met."

He kissed her on the cheek. "You and me, we can't lose!"

"You're right. Life is going to be splendid, I'm sure of it. I can't wait for us to be married."

She snuggled closer, and he pulled her to him, his hand sliding over one of her breasts.

She removed his hand. "Please, Mario, we're not married yet...."

"You're gonna be my wife, why should we wait?"

She scuffed the toe of her kid boot in the gravel. "It's very important to me. I just can't explain it."

Mario grinned. "You know what? I think you're paying too much attention to the priest. You're gonna be as holy as my Aunt Rosa!"

"You don't like me any more?" she said coyly.

His dark eyes looked into hers. "You're just the kind of girl I want."

On the day Alicia was received into the church, she and Mario Alfano were married in a side chapel of Our Lady of Pompeii, attended by the Alfano family and a single representative of the Endicotts, the bride's grandfather, Tom. The bride's mother was not there, because of her husband's unyielding opposition to the marriage,

When the boisterous party got back from the church, there was a blue banner over the door of the railroad flat across the hall that was to be the newlyweds' home, with *"BUONA FORTUNA"* painted on it in gold lettering.

Tom brought Elizabeth news of the wedding, although his old legs had not been up to climbing the five flights to the Alfanos' for the celebration afterward. But a couple of days later while Patrick was away at work, Alicia visited her and told her all about it. She had never been so happy, she said, and longed for her parents to come see her new home.

Elizabeth waited for Patrick to relent, but days passed and her obdurate husband showed not a sign of dropping his ridiculous pride and accepting the marriage as a fact.

One night, when she came downstairs after putting the babies to bed to find him blithely whistling away as he glued together some broken toy of Polly's as if his older daughter didn't exist, she had had enough. Instead of delicately pussyfooting around the subject, she brought the whole thing out into the open. After two weeks he had no excuse any more not to give his blessing to his own daughter and her new husband, she said.

Instantly, he scowled. "I'm tellin ya for the last time, Elizabeth, I'm not goin to see her and I don't want her settin foot in this house."

She was seething. She had taken his feelings into account and had even missed her daughter's wedding. She was sick of being reasonable. "What you're doing is vile. She's your own daughter!"

"What kind of daughter, I'd like to know? She was always ashamed of me. And now look what she's done, disgraced us all by marryin into wops, no better than niggers."

"Shut your filthy mouth! Those people are as good as you are!"

"Oh, are they, Miss Smart Ass? Now you listen to me." He caught her arm by the sleeve and wrenched her up close so that drops of saliva spewed into her face. "I want ya to swear to me that ya won't go there."

He had never laid hands on her before. "I'll cut my tongue out first!" she said.

Breaking free, her arm flung out, slamming him across the chest. She staggered back against the side table, causing a Dresden figurine to shatter to the floor. "I hate you!" she shrieked.

The color drained from his face. He stood there stiffly, as if her words had turned him to stone. Then, gasping for air, he groped around for something to hang on to.

For a moment she didn't understand, until she realized that something was terribly wrong. She got his arm around her neck and helped him to a chair. "Darling, be calm. I'll call a doctor. Just be quiet. Only a moment." Her cheek felt the cold beads of sweat on his brow.

"Swear to me," he gasped. "Swear ya won't go." His hand gripped hers like iron.

"Of course, I swear," she said.

Patrick had suffered a mild heart attack. The doctor explained that it was not so unusual, even for a man still in his mid-forties and in such good physical shape. There was no special cause for worry. It was merely a warning. Of course, he mustn't go on swinging from the girders of the elevated and jumping across from track to track like a monkey any more.

He recovered quickly, but continued to act as if Alicia didn't exist. While he got a kick out of baby Eugene, who was taking his first steps, it was three-year-old Polly with her red hair and freckles who remained the apple of his eye. She was his girl as Alicia had never been. He would bounce her on his knee while she screamed with joy.

Unhappy as she was over the situation, Elizabeth didn't bring up Alicia's name again. She kept her promise never to go to Carmine Street, though she didn't see any reason why she shouldn't meet her daughter on the outside.

In the ladies' tea shop at A.J. Stewart's, Alicia told her how happy she was with Mario, but as the weeks passed she complained that the reality of living in such close confines with his family was not so pleasant. All the Alfanos ran in and out of their flat whenever they felt like it, and Mario didn't see anything wrong with it—he thought that was the way it was supposed to be.

Elizabeth was sympathetic and told her about her own experience when she first got married, with Tom and Veronica in the house and her parents right next door and never a moment of privacy.

If she had her piano, Alicia said, it would be more bearable. But in any case, there was no time for music because her mother-in-law expected her to spend most of the day with her, learning how to become a good Italian wife. It was as if Mrs. Alfano was a drill sergeant who saw it as her duty to her son to train this ignoramus of a daughter-in-law, not only in the kitchen but haggling in the markets too—besides having to go to Mass every day with the other women. At such close range, the world of the Alfanos didn't seem so colorful to her any more, with all of them talking at the top of their voices.

Elizabeth said, lamely, that it was sure to work out in time. The important thing was that she and Mario had each other, even if things were a bit difficult just now. But Alicia's face showed that these hopeful words didn't mean much, and though Elizabeth wanted to offer something more practical, she didn't have any ideas.

It wasn't until her daughter told her she was pregnant that Elizabeth saw the way to help. Her father had settled permanently in California and the house next door was still being rented—at present, an elderly couple was living there. But why shouldn't Mario and Alicia take it over? That would solve everything—a better street, a backyard, plenty of room for a growing family, and blocks away from the Alfanos.

Alicia loved the idea, but reminded her mother about her father's opposition.

"But don't you see, dear, your baby is the answer to that!" said Elizabeth, unwilling to admit any obstacle. "Your father can't resist babies."

"Oh, mama, do you really think so?" she said, with the same trusting look that had once made her so vulnerably appealing to Ashmore.

But as the months passed, Alicia grew more hopeless. She had entered marriage anticipating her life with Mario would be carefree and full of music, not this reality of being heavy with child in a five-flight walk-up next door to a domineering mother-in-law. Elizabeth couldn't think what to do in the face of her daughter's unhappiness and waited impatiently for the baby to be born, so that Alicia could move with Mario into the Coopers' house where everything would be better.

She asked her son-in-law to send for her as soon as Alicia went into labor. But in the spring, when Alicia began a difficult delivery in the Carmine Street flat, Mario was so distraught he forgot all about letting her know. Mrs. Alfano did not bother, because she considered Elizabeth to be an unnatural mother for not having put on—or even attended—her own daughter's wedding. But when it was clear that Alicia's life was in danger and the priest had been sent for, she told her husband Benno to go telephone her.

Fright made Benno's usually broken English almost incomprehensible over the line, but Elizabeth understood. She felt no obligation to keep her word to Patrick in such an emergency. Trying her best to hide her panic, she begged him to go with her. He turned pale, but shook his head without a word, nor did he try to stop her as she hurried out.

By the time she came into the humid little bedroom with its single window facing the wall of the next-door tenement, the midwife had been working for hours. The woman's sleeves were rolled up to the elbow and she kept pushing her hair back from her sweating brow. In a flood of Italian and graphic gestures she made Elizabeth understand that Alicia was built too narrow, and after so many hours of labor was worn out and not trying any more.

Elizabeth bent over her barely conscious daughter and, laying a hand on her damp cheek, said, "I'm here, darling...."

Alicia opened her eyes and saw her mother. As another contraction came over her, she began to scream.

Elizabeth shoved a towel between her daughter's teeth. And as the contractions got more severe, she ordered, "Push from underneath. Push into it. Push!" Elizabeth glimpsed the baby's head beginning to emerge. "It's coming, darling! Try again, once more...."

In a gush of blood and fluid, a tiny, dark-haired infant slipped into her hands.

It was a boy, and as it began to squall, Alicia faded away before her mother's eyes.

Mario, who had been waiting just outside, threw himself across his young wife's bloated and discolored body, sobbing uncontrollably, and the priest intoned the final blessing and slipped a rosary into her hand.

Elizabeth handed the infant to a broken and lamenting Mrs. Alfano, wiped her arms on her petticoat, and quietly left the room.

She walked down the dark stairs of the tenement that reeked of cooking and came out into a bright, noisy street with kids yelling at stickball, pushcart peddlers shouting their wares, women calling from window to window where lines of laundry crisscrossed the street.

No one took any notice of the American woman, pale and exhausted, walking away.

Two days later, a funeral Mass was held at Our Lady of Pompeii. The casket heaped with flowers rested on black velvet before the ornate altar. The cavernous church was nearly empty except for the Alfano family in the front pew, Mario shaken by sobs throughout the Mass.

In the back of the church, Elizabeth sat with Tom. Tears ran down the old man's cheeks for his lost granddaughter, but Elizabeth was dry-eyed. She was struggling with a terrible guilt. Some words of Albert Cogswell tormented her—that she was the kind of person who pushed others to take chances she would not risk herself.

How true that was. How true.

Some part of her, some ugly part, had set all of this in motion. First, there had been Ashmore. That had been her own doing, no way of avoiding the bitter fact. She saw now how that had led directly to this. She had been swept away by the tawdry romanticism of a daughter defying her father to run off with a street boy with a silver voice. Then, she had knuckled under to Patrick's orders and had all but abandoned her child, when she most needed her mother.

Now, Alicia lay in her wedding dress in that satin-lined box, her eyes closed forever. How could she, a supposedly mature woman, have allowed her daughter, already so fragile from what had happened with Ashmore, to make such a mistake, marry into a world so different from their own?

With the tinkle of the sanctus bell and the censer sending out clouds of incense, it was the choir that brought the first tears to her eyes, the high, sweet innocence of the boys' voices.

As the priest went on intoning the Latin Mass, she began to weep. This alien rite, awesome in its ancient grandeur, taking place before an enormous crucified Christ dripping with vermilion jewels of blood, spoke to her of ages of women accepting their losses as the will of God.

With a veil drawn over her face, she and Tom followed in a hansom cab a short distance behind the rented carriages of the Alfanos and the glass-sided ebony hearse, flowers obscuring the casket, pulled by a pair of horses draped in funerary capes, black plumes waving. The funeral procession made its way across the city to the East River and over the bridge to Long Island, where beyond the tree-shaded streets and modest frame houses lay St. Mary's graveyard.

There, amid a jumble of statuary and baroque mausoleums, they stood apart, Tom leaning on her arm with a cane, watching the group at the graveside. They did not go up to Mario, surrounded by his family, his tiny newborn son wailing in his grandmother Alfano's arms.

When, finally, the casket was lowered into the ground, Elizabeth closed her eyes and said a prayer. Alicia's child was in loving hands. She didn't know how she was going to do it, but she would find a way to stay in her grandson's life and watch him grow, even if Patrick never came around.

31

Patrick remained unalterably opposed to going to see his new grandson, Dominic, but Elizabeth did not keep from him her own regular visits.

If Pat showed his disapproval at home, it was no easier for her on Carmine Street where Mrs. Alfano treated her like an interloper. One day when Mario was there and saw how his mother was acting, the Alfanos had an argument over it in front of her. Even though they were speaking Italian, Elizabeth knew what it was all about—she made out her name and the gist of it with no trouble. What kind of a mother was this anyway, Mrs. Alfano wanted to know, never having come to see her own daughter? Mario defended her, insisting she had a right to visit her grandchild.

Several weeks after Alicia's death, Patrick was going over a report on the feasibility of a subway system for New York City that he was devoting much of his time to these days, while Elizabeth was getting lunch ready downstairs. An organ grinder came down the street singing a Neapolitan song as he cranked out a rackety accompaniment.

In the kitchen, she was humming along with the music, when she heard Patrick yelling out the window so the whole block could hear, "Get that goddam thing out of here, will ya? Can't ya understand English?" He slammed the window shut.

It made her sick. He wasn't getting over it, he was worse. And there wasn't a thing she could do about it.

She called him down to lunch, but he didn't come. "Patrick!" she called again from the foot of the stairs. Still no reply.

His heart!

He was so robust, she was always forgetting. She raced upstairs.

He was slumped in his chair, his head in his hands, sobbing.

She knelt and embraced him. "Won't you go with me to see the baby, dear? It would make everything all right."

Without taking his hands away from his face, his big frame still heaving, he shook his head again and again.

Patrick began going over to his sister Nora's more frequently, sometimes taking little Polly with him. He didn't feel awkward there any more—his grief over the deaths of his children returned him to his own. It was a solace to be reminded of his boyhood when he and Nora and Timothy had all lived together with their mother in Shamrock Alley—until the raid on the tavern had ended everything for her, for all of them.

Nora's rooms were cozy, with sagging furniture and an old afghan of his mother's on the sofa, horsehair bursting out of the upholstery. He felt at home with the souvenirs of the Yates family outings to Coney Island, dusty palm fronds from the previous Easter, lace curtains and antimacassars that Nora crocheted endlessly, and a rubber plant grown leggy reaching for the light above the elevated tracks out the window. Though he wouldn't have given up the electric light in his own house, the gas wall brackets at his sisters', if they were not the candles and kerosene lamps of his childhood, shed a glow of an earlier time.

Most of Nora's children were grown and away. He seldom saw any of them when he was there, except for the youngest, a boy named Dennis who was Polly's age, and her two teenagers who were in and out. Occasionally one of his nieces stopped by with her own children.

He and Nora were easy with each other again. It didn't matter what they talked about—or if they talked at all. Each time he came, he told her she was to make no fuss over him. But just the same she was in and out of the kitchen on her swollen legs, fixing him Irish coffee and bringing in treats like the raisin pudding his mother used to make for them. Nora was younger than Elizabeth, although she looked much older. But it was just her shabby, unreproachful presence that comforted him.

It was a relief to get away from Perry Street where he was continually reminded of what had happened, and especially of the grandson he had never seen. He couldn't bring himself to talk to Elizabeth about it—he didn't know why, maybe out of some kind of Irish stubbornness—but kept the pain inside.

One evening as he was leaving with his brother-in-law to have a beer before going home to supper, they heard a commotion on the next block. Around the corner they found themselves in the midst of a noisy brawl in front of St. Aloysius's Church.

He saw immediately what was going on. Some Italian roughnecks had come over to beat up the local Irish lads. It was nasty. Yells and curses filling the air, they were all bashing one another with fists, sticks, chains, anything they could get hold of, and stomping and kicking whoever fell. A rock went wild and hit a horse hitched to a delivery wagon by the curb. The beast lurched off at a gallop, bottles of seltzer tumbling from the wagon and smashing on the cobblestones behind.

"Jesus, Mary, and Joseph, there's my boy!" Billy Yates cried, pointing at two young hooligans going at it. He and Patrick waded into the melee to separate them.

"Scrap, will ya, ya little bastard?" Billy said. "And after ya promised your ma?" He got a grip on his redheaded son who was cursing him and trying to get free.

Patrick hung on to the other boy, who was shouting that he was going to kill that son of a bitch. For a skinny kid, who couldn't have been older than twelve, he was a tough little number. It was only when a priest came out of the church that the fighting broke up. The gang scattered in all directions, except for the two boys Billy Yates and Patrick were holding on to.

"What are them Italians doin over here, Billy?" the priest called, coming down the steps of the church.

"Damned if I know, Father. But don't worry, we got it under control," said Billy, loosening his grip on his son who was momentarily chastened by the cleric's appearance.

"Better get that wop out of the neighborhood," the priest said to Patrick. "Our lads will make mincemeat out of him if they catch him." The priest turned and went back into the church.

Billy Yates gave his son a cuff on the head and pushed him down the street, kicking and cursing him as they went.

Muttering away to himself, the Italian kid tucked in his torn shirt and dusted his trousers off with his cap, as Patrick led him off. Several Irish lads loafing under a lamppost opposite a candy store eyed them narrowly as they passed, and the boy stuck closer to Patrick. Without his gang around he wasn't so cocksure.

But he had a filthy mouth on him just the same, cussing out the "dirty micks" coming over to his block to break the windows and turn over pushcarts. And just when his gang had begun to give them a taste of their own medicine, they were stopped. "But don't think, mister, we won't be back. We're goin to leave those bastards with their heads shoved up their fat asses."

Patrick was reminded of his young rascal of a brother, Timothy, who once hung around these same streets. This little punk didn't look anything like Tim, but he was every bit as tough, with the same infernal chip on his shoulder. "What's the point of all that bellyachin, I'd like to know?" he said, softening a little. "Those lads have it no better than you."

"The hell they don't!" The kid took in Patrick's good clothes with a sneer. "But you wouldn't know anything about it, mister."

"Oh, wouldn't I now?" Patrick's eyes twinkled. "Are things that tough for ya, then?"

As they waited for a wagon to pass, the boy looked up at him in the light of a street lamp. "You don't know the half of it." He told Patrick about the day labor he did, unloading freight wagons in the wholesale market.

"You're a little small for that kind of work, seems to me."

That wasn't the problem, the boy said. There was no money in it. But he had a plan. He stopped and fished a wrinkled cigarette out of his shirt. Striking a match on the heel of his shoe, he lit it up and took a drag. "I'm goin into the Black Hand."

"Are ya now? The Black Hand's got a reputation for bein a bunch of crooks, don't it?"

"Lemme tell you something, mister," said the boy. "They take care of you when nobody else gives a damn. They got their eye on me. They're gonna call me one of these days."

Patrick was about to ask what sort of jobs he thought he'd have to do for them, when the boy stopped in front of a tenement.

"Here's where I get off. You didn't have to walk me, you know." He flashed an unexpected smile, skipped up the steps, and was gone.

Patrick looked after him. What a little devil he was! Into the Black Hand he was going, was he? He certainly had a lot of spunk in him.

Slowly, he started back for home. At a restaurant table on the sidewalk, a man and woman eating spaghetti stared at him.

He was in Little Italy.

This was one neighborhood he always avoided, but he had been so caught up in the lad's blarney, he hadn't paid any attention to where they were heading.

The sign on the lamppost read Carmine Street. He caught his breath. This was Alicia's street. How many times had Elizabeth begged him to come here.

He started to go on, then changed his mind. With his heart pounding, he turned and walked down Carmine Street to the end, before going home.

That night as they were getting ready for bed, he asked Elizabeth for the first time about their grandson Dominic.

His wife had been waiting for this for three years. Watching him in the mirror as she brushed out her long hair, she said that Mario had remarried a young widow with several children of her own, who was good to Dominic. The little boy was talking a mile a minute now, Elizabeth told him, and had started asking her about his grandpa when she took him out to the park for the afternoon to play with Polly and Eugene. She cautiously suggested that Patrick come with her one day. But he got into bed and turned away without saying anything.

The next evening when he came home from work, Polly and Eugene jumped up from the rug in the parlor where they had been playing blocks and ran to him calling "Papa!" He took them both in a bear hug and kissed them loudly. Then he saw the little boy with brown velvet eyes staring up at him from the middle of the rug.

Patrick stooped over and picked him up and held him out in front of him. "And what might your name be, little man?"

"Dommie."

"Dommie, is it? That's a fine name."

Elizabeth walked in from the hall just in time to see her husband down on the floor helping his little grandson build a house with the blocks, while Polly and Eugene looked on.

After that, Mario often brought the child and left him for the day, before going off to work at the family vegetable store. Sometimes, Patrick walked the little boy back to Carmine Street, and even managed to exchange a few polite, if awkward, words with the Alfanos at their door.

32

On a night in February, Elizabeth was leafing through a copy of The Yellow Book, an arts magazine that Veronica had sent her from England. Her graying hair was upswept and she was wearing a high-necked, rose-colored dress in the long, slim style made fashionable by the illustrator, Charles Dana Gibson. Although it was cold outside, it was stifling in the parlor. Besides the hot air pouring in from the central heating registers, Patrick had installed a gas log in the fireplace. She would have preferred a wood fire, but he was so happy with his "improvements" she couldn't say anything.

Beyond the portieres, in the study, he was tinkering with wires and batteries, improvising a bell system to connect the children's room on the second floor with the kitchen. He had some idea that it would save her steps in calling them down to meals. Dominic was staying over for the night and the three children were playing upstairs until it was time for bed.

In the magazine on her lap, she studied a drawing by Aubrey Beardsley with its elegant peacock design. Then, as she toyed with a gold pin at her throat—a scarab that Mme. Averbach had given to Claude long ago—she looked around critically at her own fashionably-cluttered sitting room.

She had chosen the carved horsehair furniture herself, the velvet draperies festooning the windows, and the dark Flemish landscape paintings in their rococo frames. She had always been complimented on her displays of coral and old porcelain, as well as the Belgian rug with the millefleur pattern, rescued from her father's house next door at the time it was sold. She felt now there was something wrong with it all, though she couldn't put her finger on it exactly.

How glaring the light from the chandelier, which had been converted from gas, and the flame-shaped electric bulbs in ornamental sconces on the walls! Worst of all, the dust catchers around the ormolu clock on the mantelpiece—birch bark and pinecones and seashells from family vacations at the Jersey shore and in the Adirondacks!

She had always believed in Ruskin's axiom "simplicity of design results from vacuity of thought." Well, the room couldn't be in better taste—she knew that. But after these Beardsley drawings in the magazine, it all looked a hodgepodge. And she was sick to death of it. It lacked a theme, a motif that would better express her own mature sensibility.

What if she were to sweep away the accumulation of twenty-five years and completely redecorate? But how?

She was about to ask Pat what he thought of the idea when the ormolu dock chimed eight and she lay aside the magazine to go upstairs and put the children to bed.

In the back bedroom on the second floor, Polly, who was eight, was initiating a new game. She, her six-year-old brother Eugene, and Dominic were sitting in a circle on the floor with their underpants pulled down. Playing "doctor," she reached out a hand for Eugene's peepee and said, "What have we here? I'm afraid we're going to have to operate." With two fingers she scissored away at it.

Dommie giggled.

Polly told Eugene that it was his turn to be doctor and stick his finger in her peepee hole to make it well.

Eugene said he wouldn't.

She insisted.

He pummeled the floor with his hands and feet. "I don't want to!"

She turned to four-year-old Dominic. "You do it then, Dommie. You be doctor."

She snatched his hand, which he made into a little fist, and tried to pull a finger loose.

"I don't wanna," he said, starting to snivel.

"Okay, you asked for it." She picked up a floppy-armed Topsy doll. "I'm going to give you an enema, you little crybaby, and it won't be any fun."

Elizabeth came to the half-open door just as Polly pulled Dominic over her lap and started pressing the arm of the rag doll between the bare, little cheeks of his bottom. It tickled and he shrieked with delight.

Elizabeth stepped back out of sight so as not to make the children self-conscious. Pretending to be just coming up the stairs, she called out that it was time to get ready for bed.

When she came downstairs again, Patrick told her that Tom had called on the telephone and was on his way over to tell them something. He had refused to say what it was, but he sounded very lively.

They both agreed that it must be about the sale of the print shop. Tom was nearly eighty and still lived in the loft over the shop, although Albert Cogswell had left a few months before to go stay with one of his children who ran a saloon in San Francisco. The printing business had long since fallen off to a trickle of old customers, and Patrick and Eliizabeth had been urging Tom to sell out and move back in with them, but he had always refused, saying he would have nothing to do with himself if he gave up the business. As much as he enjoyed his grandchildren, he said he didn't want to be in the way—and besides, he was used to taking care of himself.

But since Albert had left, he was feeling differently about it. It was harder than he thought to manage by himself. He had put the shop up for sale at last and agreed to come live with them when it was sold.

A few days before, a couple of offers had come in and he had asked their advice. One was from a real estate developer who wanted to demolish the building to put up a seven-story apartment house on the site. The other was from a young printer who had the ambition of publishing books on the side. The real estate developer was offering cash, while the printer could only afford to pay out the purchase price over a number of years.

When Tom had come over to discuss which offer he ought to accept, Elizabeth and Patrick had gotten into one of their classic wrangles.

Naturally, she had plumped right off for the young printer.

Pat said it was Tom's decision, not hers, then went on to argue that the shop had been erected in 1818 and ought to be pulled down along with a lot of the other old eyesores in the neighborhood.

She was furious. The young publisher, in her view, was just what Greenwich needed. She liked it that the Village was being passed by while the rest of the city was in a frenzy of rebuilding. Why not keep it just as it was with its old houses and quiet streets?

He had dismissed this as sentimental hogwash. Money was the only consideration. That printer with his harebrained schemes sounded like a poor risk to him.

It had gone on like that, and by the time Tom left he had been so upset by their bickering that he said he wasn't going to sell after all, and he was damned if he was going to come back to live with them!

That had been a few days before, and as Patrick and Elizabeth waited for him now, they promised each other that they were going to keep their opinions to themselves, no matter which offer he had decided to accept. The important thing was that he was retiring at last—long past the age when he should have—and moving back home with them where he belonged.

Tom came right in without ringing the bell, even forgetting to stamp the slush off his boots on the doormat. Though arthritic and getting more feeble, he was chuckling away to himself, as Patrick helped him off with his coat.

When he was settled in a chair by the fire with his cane beside him, Patrick assured him that they would be happy whichever offer he had accepted. Elizabeth sat at his feet on a Moroccan hassock and said they were thoroughly ashamed of themselves for the way they had acted.

"Well, before you two start spatting again," he said with twinkling eyes, "let me tell you what I came about. I've made up my mind I'm going to live with Veronica."

"Holy Mother!" said Patrick.

"In England?" said Elizabeth, repressing a smile. They exchanged a look. The old man couldn't make it by himself over to New Jersey, much less across the Atlantic.

Tom chuckled. "I thought that would surprise you two."

He had it all worked out, it seemed. Veronica was alone and he was alone. She had a nice little house by the seaside. She had been after him for years to come over to England, and now they would be able to take care of each other. He would be no trouble to anyone that way.

"But, Tom, dear," said Elizabeth, taking his hand, "whoever said you'd be any trouble? You belong with us."

He didn't hear her. "I'll be off just as soon as I straighten out my papers. I've never seen the world and Veronica will show me London town. I should have made this trip years ago."

"What about selling the shop?" said Patrick.

Tom looked uncertain, as if he had forgotten all about it. "Oh, yes, I suppose I will have to do something about that, won't I?"

"What I think we need is some coffee," said Elizabeth brightly, jumping up.

But the old man shook his head and gripped his cane, preparing to get to his feet. "No time for that, I'm afraid. I've got to start packing."

"Aw, don't go yet, Tom," said Patrick, moving his chair closer. "If it's London you're goin to, maybe you'll get yourself a limey wife."

Elizabeth watched them as Pat went on gently humoring his father, who said he was already thinking about a trip with Veronica to Constantinople, and maybe even Samarkand.

Poor dear, imagining he was going anywhere at all. But those place names! How thrilling it would be to travel again. She fingered the gold scarab at her throat, remembering London and Paris and Rome. So many years ago. She hadn't been farther than Saratoga since.

Her eyes dropped to the Moroccan hassock with its gold-stenciled design of minarets in the red leather.

All at once she understood what was wrong with the room.

It was the image of stodgy married life. It lacked any sort of mystery, romance, or adventure—all the things that hassock stood for and she believed in.

She would redesign the whole room around the hassock. She envisioned her windows filled with plants. It would be like an oasis—not just those tired ferns in their wicker planters, but spiky palmettos in pots to filter the sunlight. And at night, paisley shawl drapes that would enclose the room like a seraglio, the eyes of peacock feathers gleaming in nacreous vases, a Turkish carpet with all the arabesques of the East, and fringed lamp-shades suspended from the ceiling, casting rosy pools of light. Patrick would do all the rewiring. She couldn't wait to get started.

"I take it you're pleased about what I'm going to do, Elizabeth," said Tom, misinterpreting her smile.

She had forgotten all about him. She went over and kissed his cheek. "I think it's wonderful, Tom. Now you really must stay and let me make some coffee."

He considered. "Maybe I'll just do that. I can start my packing in the morning." He settled back in his chair, hardly able to keep his eyes open.

Elizabeth was thoughtful as she went downstairs to brew the coffee. Redecorating the parlor would have to wait. There was something more important to do first—the children had to be moved to the top floor so that a room could be made ready for a tired old man.

1900

33

Tom Endicott was resting on a lounge chair in the backyard. It was not cold but his granddaughter Polly had put a shawl around his shoulders, and when he asked for it, covered his legs with a robe. It was May, and the ailanthus trees were in bloom.

Tom had a letter in his hand that Polly had already read to him. It was from Veronica. He had never gone to England after all. Elizabeth and Patrick had taken him in to live with them, and shortly afterward he had become an invalid.

Now, with his eyes closed, the thin sun warm on his brow, he was remembering the days when he first lived here on Perry Street with Fanny, and little Veronica and Claude played in this same yard.

The slamming of the front door roused him. The family was back from the ground-breaking ceremony at the Battery for the subway that was about to be built. The start of the subway construction was a personal triumph for his son Patrick, and Tom couldn't have been prouder.

He heard Elizabeth telling the boys to set up a picnic table. That would be Eugene, who was already nine, and his best friend, Toby, from down the block, along with his great-grandchild Dominic, a chubby little boy of seven. Tom perked up as the boys charged out the back door and started to put together some sawhorses and boards for a table, the three of them exclaiming about the ships they had seen in the harbor and how much cake and ice cream they were going to eat.

Oblivious to the activity in the yard, Polly was lying on her bed writing in her notebook when her father came upstairs to change his clothes. She was wearing a pinafore and leggings, and the spectacles on her pug nose gave her freckled face an owlish look. She was twelve and, at the moment, dedicating her life to poetry.

Just when she was searching for the perfect rhyme to end her "Ode to Spring," her father walked right in without knocking, fumbling with his cuff links.

"How's my little monkey?" he said, smacking her on the bottom and sitting down beside her. He had pulled off his jacket, and his shirt, stretched across his big chest, was wet in the armpits and along the suspenders.

"Oh, papa, don't call me that," she said, slipping her notebook under the pillow. "And I've told you to knock. I'm not a child any more." But she had to smile when she saw her helpless father holding out his starched cuffs for her to undo. She jumped up and, giving him a kiss on the cheek, bent over the cuff links.

"I'm sorry ya had to miss all the fun, monkey," he said, beaming at his daughter. "Was grandpa any trouble?"

With her tongue between her teeth, she worked the mother-of-pearl cuff links out of the stiff buttonholes. "I've been so busy I forgot all about him."

"Better not spend all your time writin that stuff. You'll never get a boy to pop the question."

She pushed up his chin and began to work on his collar studs. "I don't care. I'm going to be a poet like Aunt Veronica."

"Your aunt would have chucked all that nonsense fast enough if any man had ever given her the time of day."

Polly wrinkled her nose. "That's not true. A lot of girls decide not to get married." Deep down she was convinced no one would ever want to marry her. She was much too homely. She didn't take after her beautiful mother or her handsome, black-Irish father.

But like Trilby, the heroine of her favorite novel, one day she would discover a world of artists and writers where there would be a place for odd girls like her.

Down in the backyard, the boys were squabbling as they cranked away at the wooden ice cream freezer.

"Lemme do it too!" Dominic's voice whined.

"It's Toby's turn now," yelled Eugene.

"That's no fair!" The smaller boy began to cry.

Patrick called down to them through the window, "Let Dommie take a turn, boys."

"He just did, pa," Eugene said, and started giggling at something his inseparable friend, Toby, was telling him.

Patrick took a long breath of the spring air, pungent with the aroma of the ailanthus blossoms that were shedding over everything. Polly's room overlooked all the backyards of the block, each divided by a sagging board fence. The foliage was sparse because the houses and trees blocked most of the sun, but here and there was the yellow explosion of a forsythia bush, and daffodils and tulips glinted among the scraggly patches of grass.

It was one of the best days of his life, the culmination of years spent fighting for the subway, working on planning commissions, submitting estimates to legislators, getting preliminary bids from contractors.

Patrick came down to the yard, slipping on an old striped flannel jacket over his shirt. "Ya should have been there, Tom," he said, interrupting his father, who was trying to tell the boys from his lounge chair how to get the top off the ice cream freezer.

"Oh, there you are, Patrick!" The old man waved his letter at him. "Where have you been all day? I've just heard from Veronica."

It always upset Patrick to see how daft his father had become. At breakfast the old man could talk of nothing but the subway ground-breaking, and now it was as though he had never heard of it. And that damn letter—it had come a week ago, yet he went on making a fuss over it every day as if it had just arrived.

Patrick bent down to tuck the robe under the old man's feeble legs. "Veronica, is it, Tom? How is she this time?"

"What would you say if I told you I was thinking of making a trip over there to see her?"

Elizabeth, who had come out with a layer cake, looked away. She couldn't bear to listen to any more of that babbling. But it was not just her father-in-law. Truthfully, this change of life she was going through had made the whole day a nightmare. She wasn't going to put up with anyone, not the way she felt.

While Tom rambled on about how he was going to treat Veronica to a sight-seeing trip all around England, she took a dust cloth and flicked the soot from the two iron filigree garden chairs drawn up to the table on one side and from the old wooden bench on the other. How dirty the city was, and all this construction making it even dirtier and more unlivable. She told Eugene and Toby to stop squabbling over the ice cream and bring out two dining room chairs for her and Pat—and right now!

Patrick lined up the seven plates in front of him as if dividing the cake were a technical problem to be solved, and called out to Polly to come down. "It was a grand occasion, Tom," he said, deftly slicing the cake. "The mayor was there, and the governor, and all the big railroad boys—the lot of them standing around actin like the subway was their idea all the time."

Polly slipped in at the bench beside Toby, and was gazing up at her father adoringly with her bespectacled eyes.

Elizabeth had never seen her husband looking more glorious. At fifty-three he was still dashing, and more than ever today, basking in self-satisfaction. It was unfair, just when she was feeling so rotten, so unattractive, so old. The boys were making so much noise kicking each other under the table, while Eugene served up the ice cream, that she could scarcely hear herself think.

"Twenty-five years ago when I started pushin for a subway, those bastards wouldn't have none of it." Patrick flourished his spatula like a sword against the infidel.

"Pat, the children want their cake," she snapped. She never wanted to hear another word about that damn subway again. The first thing that morning, instead of asking her how she felt, he had started right in about it. He hadn't shut up since. Not once had he complimented her on her hair, dressed in the fashion of Mrs. Patrick Campbell in "Lady Windermere's Fan." A hot flash came over her and she felt as if she were suffocating in one of those damn subway tunnels. She gripped the edge of the table. Her corset was soaked through with sweat and he could care less.

"... but once we got those electric engines," Pat was saying, "they couldn't hold out against us." He plopped a piece of cake onto a plate and handed it to Dominic to take to his grandpa. "Of course, they're still not lettin me do it the way I want. We ought to tunnel through the granite, but this surface diggin method will work, even if it makes a mess of the streets for a while."

"For heaven's sake, Tom doesn't want to hear about that," said Elizabeth.

"Oh, yes I do," said the old man, taking the plate from Dominic and putting an arm around the boy.

"Honestly," she said, holding a hand to her throbbing temple.

Patrick paused in mid-sentence to ask, "Is anything wrong, darlin?"

"Nothing at all." She forced herself to taste the ice cream Eugene had passed to her.

He missed the sarcasm and gave her a happy grin. "The only thing I'm sorry about is we're goin to have to detour it around Greenwich. All these damn crooked little streets. Not one big avenue for us to dig under."

"I don't think we need a subway," Elizabeth said, reviving somewhat from the ice cream. "We like our neighborhood just the way it is."

"We're goin to have to put one through here one day. If they won't tunnel down the way I want them to, then we'll just have to cut an avenue right through. It would only mean tearin down a few old houses."

"Patrick, have you taken leave of your senses?" she cried. "That would mean destroying the heart of the Village!"

He slurped his ice cream and said that things had been going downhill around there for years, and it might be just the ticket to bring business back and get things moving again.

She wiped ice cream from Dominic's chin. "I'll tell you one thing, people would never stand for it. There'd be a revolution."

Polly, holding a piece of cake on her fork, peered at her father through her spectacles. "Do you really think they might put an avenue through here some day, papa? How spiffy!"

On the other side of her, Toby reached over and took a big bite of her cake while she was turned away, rolling his eyes at Eugene.

When she turned back and saw the small piece left on her plate, Eugene giggled out of control at what his hero had done.

"That will do, Eugene," Elizabeth said, as her freckled-faced daughter glared at the two boys. Again, she was struck by how much Polly resembled Albert Cogswell. She had always had his coloring, but because of how close Polly and Patrick were, Elizabeth seldom thought of her not being his blood child, the same as Eugene. Polly was such an earnest little thing with her plans to be a painter one day, a poet the next. Since being caught up in the Trilby craze, she had talked of nothing else but living a bohemian life in a garret. But how plain she was. Things were not going to be easy for her.

"Grandpa," said Dominic, pointing.

A plate clattered on the flagstones behind them.

Tom's head had fallen forward. For a moment they thought he had dropped off to sleep clutching his daughter's letter, with the ailanthus blossoms falling across him like snow.

BOOK II

1909

1

On a late winter afternoon when only a few patches of dirty snow remained in the gutters, Polly Endicott got off a double decker motorbus at the corner of Fifth Avenue and Eighth Street with a portfolio under her arm. She was returning from her art school uptown. A block down, the sun glinted off Washington Square's triumphal arch that put a classical finale to the sweep of Fifth Avenue.

Polly hurried down Eighth Street because she was meeting a friend at a tea shop and was late. They were going to see The Great Train Robbery at the bioscope. Even if she had been pretty it would have been hard to tell, for she was wearing the plain garb of young Greenwich Village women who considered themselves "emancipated"—a severe coat and skirt of coarse hopsacking, with brown stockings showing at the ankles. Her thick reddish hair was cut short under a wide-brimmed felt hat.

Many of the houses along the street now sported skylights, for their attic rooms had been turned into studios for artists. Polly preferred this side of the Village to where she lived on Perry Street over by the river. She'd been trying to talk her parents into taking off the old-fashioned high stoop of the family house and moving the front door down to street level, as these houses on Eighth Street had done. Although her father liked the idea, her mother had put her foot down. She said their house was perfect just as it was, even if some people no longer appreciated its old-fashioned Dutch stoop.

Her mother had too many fusty ideas about the Village and had even formed a Village Preservation Society to keep the streets exactly as they were, which Polly thought ridiculous. To her mortification, her mother had insisted that she and Eugene help her collect signatures on a petition against a proposed avenue to be cut through the Village. Her father had scoffed at this hairbrained crusade, and predicted that, like all the others, it would fail. Much as they loved her, her mother was sometimes difficult to put up with.

Polly crossed the street to turn down MacDougal, dodging between a horse-drawn delivery wagon and a motor taxi that blared its klaxon at her. She passed a mews where the stables were being converted into more artists' studios. When she was a child, Greenwich Village had been an ordinary New York neighborhood, but during the past few years it had been changing. New people were moving here to pursue the arts—or pretend to—while living it up in the heart of the city that was too busy growing taller to interfere. The change had suited her entirely. If men were paying no attention to her, she was making a very satisfactory life for herself with her painting classes at the Art Students League and being caught up in the ferment of ideas all around her.

On Washington Square, with its bare sycamore trees and black iron railings, several motorcars and a horse and carriage were parked in front of the elegant old brick houses. Blocking off the far side of the square were the gray, unaesthetic buildings of New York University. She preferred Judson Church on the south side with its golden Florentine bell tower, designed by Stanford White, who had shot his rival over a Ziegfeld girl several years before.

Across the square she entered the Italian neighborhood on MacDougal Street, where everyone walked in the street as casually as on the sidewalks. Some teenage boys on a stoop jeered at her because of her short hair and glasses. What oafs, she thought, to be so set against the revolutionary changes going on all around them! There were more emancipated women with bobbed hair like her every day.

She went down some steps into a tea shop called The Pirate's Den. It was a favorite for her friends because it was just below the Liberal Club, where people discussed the latest radical ideas. She had been there the night before to hear the anarchist Emma Goldman.

Her girlfriend Helene, who worked as a life model at the Art Students League, was waiting for her at a corner table. Polly was vexed to see that she had a man with her. Helene was always making plans to get together, but with her face and figure men never let her alone.

Polly had no such luck. She hated to have to sit with Helene and one of her pickups while the two of them flirted. No matter how much she tried to hide it, she always felt left out. Sometimes it seemed that the only man in the world who could really like her was her father. They had always adored each other. She wasn't so close any more to Eugene who was going to Columbia and had no time for anybody but his girlfriends. And Dominic they hardly saw since he had gone to work in the Alfano family restaurant.

She would have turned around and walked out, if her friend hadn't already seen her and waved her over. Putting on a bright face, she sailed up to the table and, to hide her awkwardness in front of the man Helene was with, made a show of scolding her for not coming with her to hear Emma Goldman the night before. The young man barely gave her a look, too busy entwining his fingers in Helene's curls. He had the kind of insipidly handsome face she abhorred. Helene was always telling her the details of her affairs, and she would hear all about the ecstasies of this one tomorrow.

Taking the young man's hand out of her hair, Helene wanted to know if Emma Goldman had brought up Free Love. Polly shook her head and, leaning her art portfolio against the leg of the table, made another show of imitating Goldman's Russian accent and incendiary style—she was a whiz at mimicry. "Women, there is only one word on our banner,"— she paused for effect—"R-r-r-revolution!"

Helene laughed, but the young man stared at her as if she were nuts.

"Much as I adore Emma," Polly said, loathing him as she slipped into a seat at the table, "I was sorry she didn't come out in support of scientific sexuality."

Helene turned to her boyfriend with a giggle. "Polly is our high priestess of Free Love."

"Emma is the high priestess," Polly snapped back. "The rest of us are only vestal virgins, even if you're trying to make it otherwise, Helene." She took a dim look at the insipid young man.

Helene clapped her hands and even the young man laughed.

Polly sat back, pleased with herself. Men might not be falling all over themselves for her, but she was at least clever enough to get everyone's attention when she wanted to with her clowning.

She had given up on poetry. When she was eighteen, she had had a booklet of her poems, called *Quintessence*, printed up privately. Nothing had happened and, except for a few copies given away, it was still stacked in her room. Though she had thrown herself into her painting since then, she was beginning to suspect that enthusiasm and willpower were not enough to make up for lack of talent. But growing up in the Village, and with her handsome mother talking as if art were the only goal in life, there seemed nothing else to do—especially since men remained distessingly indifferent to her, except as a pal.

The waitress set an order of milk toast in front of Helene. Bland though it was, it was a specialty of the tea shop. Helene began to feed the young man with a spoon, to their mutual absorption and Polly's disgust. She swore to herself that if Helene subjected her to this once more, she would never go anywhere with her again.

She looked around at the crowded tables. She didn't know anybody there and hated them all. And those posters of avant-garde Paris art shows on the walls! She saw no point to the distorted figures with three eyes and two noses.

"Goldman has to push for revolution, she's too ugly for love." A skinny kid with lanky hair at the next table was talking to her.

"I beg your pardon?" she said, dismissing him.

He pulled his chair around to face her. "No one would ever want to make love to that battle-ax."

"Men adore Emma," she said snippily, pretending to be studying the menu card through her thick glasses. "If you had the soul of an artist, you'd see how beautiful she was."

He laughed and pulled his chair closer to her. "I am an artist, and an artist sees with his eyes. Let the philistines keep their little souls." His protuberant Adam's apple wobbled unpleasantly.

"Don't be horrid," she said. "Everyone has a soul." He was wearing a heavy sweater and a shabby green velveteen jacket with what looked like a red firecracker embroidered on the breast pocket.

"Okay, I got a soul if you say so," he said, grinning and waving his strong. long-fingered hands, "so long as it doesn't get in the way while I'm painting."

Oddly, he made her feel as if she was being looked at by a man for the first time. It was like a bird being hypnotized by a snake.

Helene interrupted to ask when the picture show was starting. While she and Helene were discussing how much time they had, the young man started rifling through her portfolio. He held up one of her paintings, a simple study of Central Park. She blushed scarlet and tried to snatch it away from him, but he kept it out of reach.

"Wait a minute. It's not so bad, for Impressionism...."

"Give it back please!" She tried to grab it.

"... but the trouble is, it makes New York look like Paris."

"Give it back!" She was near to tears.

"Impressionism is no good for skyscrapers and ash cans," he said flatly, slipping the canvas back into her portfolio. "It pretties things up too much."

She slid the portfolio to the other side of her chair and glared at him. "But the purpose of art is to make things beautiful."

"Bunk!" said the youth with the prominent adam's apple. "The purpose of art is to show things the way they are."

He flustered her. She didn't agree at all with what he was saying. "But what about the Old Masters? They didn't emphasize the seamy side of life."

"And there was no Industrial Revolution back then, either."

"Well, I don't want to paint factories."

"You don't understand very much," he said, resting a leg on a chair, showing long red underwear under his trouser cuff. "You ought to take a look at my work. It'll put you on the right track."

And in which gallery might his work be seen, she asked snidely.

He laughed and said the galleries were all as old-fashioned as she was, but his studio was just down the street. She could take a look now if she wanted to. He stood up, waiting for her to come with him.

She hesitated.

"John Sloan says I'm the most promising undiscovered painter in America."

Polly had to smile. "You expect me to believe that?"

The young man grinned back, "Okay, so I'm a liar. But it doesn't mean I'm not a great painter. Why don't you see for yourself?"

She looked back at Helene who was snuggling with the insipid young man and appeared to have forgotten all about her.

She got up and followed him.

"Poll, what about the Bioscope?" Helene called after her.

"I'll be right back," she said. "Keep an eye on my portfolio."

She followed the artist who bounded up the steps. Out on the street, he took her hand, pulling her along after him.

Polly had visited artists' studios before, always with other students from the League. This studio turned out to be a shabby loft over a machine shop with a screech of lathes audible from below through the floor. It was chilly, and the young man poked up a coal fire in the potbellied stove. The room didn't have much more than a cot and an easel, but it was not the meager furnishings that held her attention. The walls exploded with huge canvases of slaughterhouse scenes, slabs of raw meat hanging on hooks, dripping with blood. It was sickening.

With his foot up on a chair and an elbow on his knee, he gave her a cocky smile and asked her what she thought.

"Well," she said, trying not to betray her nausea, "they're certainly unusual. You must have read *The Jungle*." The muckraking novel about the Chicago stockyards had been discussed at the Liberal Club.

"I don't get my inspiration from books," said the young painter. "I paint from life. That's what your stuff lacks—real life."

She looked again at the starkness of the room, the unmade bed, all the violence on the walls. What was she doing here? If this was real life, it made her uneasy. "I think you're trying too hard to shock," she said, moving toward the door.

"Wait!" He skipped over to grab her hand and pull her back. "I want to show you something else." He made her sit on the cot while he squatted down to pull out a pile of canvases from underneath.

His arrogance was unnerving. She wanted to get out of there. She didn't want to see any more of his work. He jumped up and sat beside her, holding up one canvas after another in front of her. She didn't like them much, certainly not these grim scenes of street life under the elevated—a saloon with drunks, streetwalkers, a police wagon hauling away derelicts.

"This is the way I see New York," he said, "raw and gutsy."

She was alarmed by his sitting so close, but she made herself concentrate on the canvases. His bold brushwork and harsh colors did have a certain power. She was on the side of the masses as much as he was, but it looked to her like he was deliberately exploiting their misery in his work. She wished his knee wasn't pressed against hers.

While she was trying to concentrate on a painting of an all-night diner, he leaned around, took her glasses off and kissed her with wet lips. She made a little struggle to get up but he held her fast. For a moment she was in a panic, but as he kissed her again she told herself that this was life. She talked Free Love and liberation, but Helene was living it. It was time she gathered up her courage and exposed herself to it. She could always stop before he went further then she wanted him to.

His kisses got more insistent and his tongue went into her mouth. It was disgusting, but she closed her eyes and told herself submit. Then she felt his hand beginning to unbutton her coat. "Don't do that," she said.

"But I want to," his voice was husky.

She closed her eyes again, telling herself she was plenty old enough, far older than Helene had been. It was different than in her mother's generation. Girls today were giving themselves to men of their own free will. Indeed, to prove that they were advanced, they were supposed to. She tried to think of Emma Goldman.

When he uncovered her breasts she was embarrassed. "They're so small," she said, in a weak voice.

"I like them. They're beautiful," he whispered, leaning over to mouth them.

She tried not to feel what was happening down there. He was the first man who had shown any real interest in her, and she could always stop him when she wanted to.

But when he pushed her back on the bed and she felt his weight on top of her, everything was suddenly wrong. His breathing was harsh in her ear as he forced her legs apart,. She tried to get him off. It was not the way it was supposed to be. He was a stranger who didn't care anything about her.

"Please, don't!" she cried, struggling, but he pushed harder against her. This was hideous, like those slaughterhouse carcasses spreadeagled from hooks, staring with lidless eyes from the walls.

When she felt the sharp pain of his thrust, she screamed. But he didn't stop, and her scream was lost in the noise of the machines from the floor below.

When it was over, he raised himself and looked down at her crying in the pillow. "Damn it! Why didn't you tell me you were a virgin?"

"I tried to," she whimpered.

"But you talked so big back there."

"What am I supposed to do?" she cried, furious and ashamed. "Everyone thinks because I was born in the Village I invented Free Love. Anyway, I didn't know it was going to be like this."

He sat on the edge of the cot, buttoning up. "What was wrong with it? Nobody's ever complained before. Maybe there's something wrong with you." He leaned over and tried to wipe her tears with an end of the dirty sheet. "Gee, I wish you wouldn't cry, but you got me so hot, damn it, I couldn't stop."

She shoved him away and made him turn around while she limped over to the water tap and washed hastily, straightening her rumpled clothes.

He went on apologizing, sounding much younger than before. "I really am sorry. I couldn't help it, but you should have told me."

"You don't have to say that any more," she snapped, her face blotchy. "You got what you wanted, didn't you?" She yanked on her coat and walked painfully out, down the iron steps, past the open door of the machine shop where workmen looked up from behind their goggles, and onto the street.

When she got home the family was at dinner, and she was able to sneak up to her room. She was still in pain and prayed she wouldn't have to call the family doctor. He was such an old fuddy-duddy. It would be horrible.

She was in a panic and there was no one she could talk to. She would die before confessing to her perfect mother. Eugene would only pity her. He was already an expert with girls—he and his friend Toby spent all their free time chasing after them. If only she could put her head against her father's chest and cry her eyes out.

She wondered if what that bastard had said was right. Something had to be the matter with her. All the girls she knew who boasted about their conquests had never reported anything like what she had gone through, not even the first time. From what they said, it was divine all the way, not painful and odious.

When she was calmer, she took down her Havelock Ellis from the shelf where it was wedged in between Freud and Oscar Wilde, and looked up the section on Female Sexuality, Disturbances Of. She was sure she had found what her problem was when she read an exact description of it, Vaginismus, defined as "painful penetration." The case study, a Miss L.B., had never been able to engage in satisfactory sexual congress with anyone without experiencing acute pain. She had made the rounds of doctors and psychiatrists, but no cure had ever been found for her disorder.

Polly didn't call the doctor, and when she woke up the next morning she felt no different than before. She took a grim satisfaction in the fact that she was no longer a virgin, but she knew it was only a technicality, because even if by a miracle another man were ever to pay attention to her, sex would never work.

She had held to the principle that sexual fulfillment must be the basic requirement for any liberated woman, but to tell the truth she was relieved she would never have to go through the hideous act again.

As much as she wanted to push out of her mind the thought of the boy who had seduced her, she couldn't forget what he had said. It was as if he had turned a powerful searchlight on all her pretensions. He had revealed to her that she was a fraud. She had to face the fact that she was never going to be an artist—any more than she had been a poet. Her work at the League was a pale echo of Impressionism—the style of a genteel age, it now seemed to her, that had lost its energy. She had been clever at following her art teacher's instructions. But she had no ideas of her own. It was clear that real art took a boldness and daring she lacked, the same as Free Love did.

"Frigidity" might not technically describe her condition, but it was right nonetheless. "Love goddess" indeed! She was sick of the act she had been putting on with Helene and the others, talking a fast line and implying she was as physically liberated as they were. Just because she had grown up in Greenwich Village, she had assumed she was supposed to be something that wasn't in her nature to be. Her father, who had always ridiculed her attempts at painting, understood her better than her perfect mother who had pushed art down her throat. But much as she needed him now, she didn't feel so free with him any more. His strength, which she had always seen as her bulwark against the world, repelled her. She couldn't say why.

In the days to come, her classes at the Art Students' League became increasingly meaningless, and one day she tore up all her drawings and canvases. On the way home, she threw them into a trash bin on Madison Square and never went back. Helene and her other girlfriends telephoned to find out what was wrong, but she put them off with an excuse about having to take care of her invalid mother. It was such a preposterous fib, her mother being the last person in the world who could ever be described as an invalid, that after she hung up the phone she ran up the stairs and threw herself on her bed in a fit of giggles—until, unaccountably, she dissolved into tears.

Having quit the League and her Village activities, Polly was in a quandary about what to do with herself, when one day she saw an article in her mother's Atlantic Monthly about young women who were taking jobs in business offices and even living on their own for the first time away from their families—"bachelor girls," they were called.

Although she would have scorned such a life before, now it seemed to her just the solution—a world where girls did not have to prove themselves in bed or in the art studio. She liked the idea of herself settled into her own little apartment and making her own money. That was a kind of liberation she had never thought of before. Going each day to an office and working at a typewriter didn't sound half bad. And however conventional the business world might be, she would be spared any further test of her sexuality. Nor would she be forced into displays of artistic creativity she had no talent for.

Her ears burned as she remembered again the young artist's ridicule of her pallid little study of trees in Central Park. That bastard! Well, he had taught her a good lesson. She supposed she ought to be grateful to him.

Whatever the magazine article said, it was highly unusual for unmarried children, especially girls, to move away from their families. Her father, Polly knew, would be miserable when she moved out, he depended on her so, but she was sure she would be able to talk him around. He never refused her anything.

The next Monday she went to an employment agency on Forty-second Street and, because of her high marks in mathematics in school, immediately got a job as a clerk in an insurance company on Lexington Avenue. They told her that once she started work she could attend free evening classes in typewriting, which would qualify her for one of their better paid secretarial positions.

Exhilarated by getting a job right off, Polly set out to find a place to live.

2

"Your friend likes his music loud, doesn't he?" said the rather serious young Barnard girl sitting beside Eugene Endicott on the couch, as the ragtime piano jangled from the Victrola horn. "That is, if you call that music."

"But it's Scott Joplin," Eugene said. "Joplin plays the hottest piano since Paderewski."

The girl, whose name was Clare Marshall, looked at him impatiently. "Now whoever told you that?"

She could have been pretty, Eugene thought, if it weren't for the severity of her expression. "Well as a matter of fact," he said, good-naturedly, "Toby said it."

"I thought so." Her tone was superior. "I was pretty sure it was your friend's idea."

Across the living room, Toby Harris in a red-and-white, striped blazer and bow tie was showing off, dancing with a girl named Effie, a busty blonde who couldn't stop giggling at his antics. The two girls were cousins. In contrast to Clare's tight braids pinned in a coil at the back of her head, Effie's plump little body was swathed in a dress of chiffon veils, and her golden curls were held with a sequined band across the forehead.

It was Toby who had found the girls. He had picked up Effie on the Columbia campus, though she wasn't a student. She was only in town for a few days from Cincinnati staying with her cousin Clare at Barnard— Barnard was the women's college affiliated with Columbia across Upper Broadway. The girls from Barnard often took classes at Columbia and Effie was waiting for her cousin to come out of her biology lab.

When Toby asked Effie for a date—he never wasted time—she said she'd love to but she'd have to bring Clare along. After all, Effie was staying with her in her dorm room.

Toby had sized Clare up as a cold fish as soon as he met her—she was a sociology major, for God's sake. But the winsome little blonde from Cincinnati had lit a fire inside him and he asked Eugene, as his best buddy, to come along and take care of the bookworm.

Toby and Eugene had brought the girls down to the Village from Barnard to see a play by someone named O'Neill or O'Hara or something like that, that was being performed in a cellar on Cornelia Street. It had been Eugene's idea—he had heard the play was scandalous. But it didn't turn out to be scandalous in the way they had hoped. It was full of heavy silences and long speeches, and at the end of the first act, when the family in the play discovered the mother was a morphine addict, Toby called out in a loud voice that it was "a stinker." While the audience shouted for them to leave so the play could continue, Effie giggled at the uproar, but Clare, who was taking a course in abnormal psychology, wanted to stay and told Eugene that Toby a perfect boor.

It was only nine o'clock when they got out to the street and Clare wanted to go home and study, but Effie insisted they couldn't refuse Toby's invitation to go to his parents' apartment nearby to dance. He had all the latest Victrola records, and his parents were out for the evening, which made it even better. Eugene, who had hopes that he might loosen Clare up once she had a little wine in her, finally got her to agree by promising to see them back to the dorm before curfew.

But as he sat with Clare watching Toby impudently tickling the little blonde in the ribs while dancing—Toby always said the easiest way to weaken a girl's resistance was to keep her laughing—Eugene was beginning to doubt that he was going to get anywhere with Clare at all.

Ordinarily, he didn't mind going along as the partner for the obligatory girlfriend of the girl Toby was hot for—he usually enjoyed himself anyway. This one, though, didn't want to dance, and she had hardly taken a sip of her wine.

"I'm afraid I don't agree with you," Clare was saying. "I find your friend's taste in music not only low level, but his behavior in the theater was inexcusable. You may find it amusing, but to me it was simply juvenile."

Eugene was taken aback. No one ever said anything against Toby. Everyone liked him. In their first semester at Columbia his friend had already made the sculling crew, was a promising welterweight on the intercollegiate boxing team, and was being unofficially rushed by every fraternity on campus, though rushing wasn't supposed to begin until the start of the second term.

Across the room, Effie was screaming with laughter as Toby, dancing so close his knee was pushing between her legs, quick-stepped her around a library table. Things always worked out for Toby, girls were crazy about him from the start. Eugene wished he had the same effect on them. He slipped an arm across the back of the couch behind Clare and moved a little closer. Toby always said let them feel the heat of your body, it was sure to drive them wild. But Clare went right on talking.

"...Of course, it doesn't take much to impress my cousin, she's so boy-crazy." The record ended, and Clare called over that it was time they were going because of the curfew.

Effie pouted. "Oh, Clare! Don't be a killjoy. The party's just getting started."

"You betcha, honey," Toby said, winding up the Victrola.

"I'm sorry, it's too late," Clare said, starting to get up. "It'll take us an hour to get home."

Effie pouted again. "Have a heart, Clare. What if we don't make the curfew. We can get in through that window. You showed it to me yourself."

Toby slipped another record out of an album, put it on the Victrola, and dropped the needle into the groove. As the quavery strains of a tango began, he caught up the willing Effie, and holding her tight with his cheek pressed against hers, swept her away in a long glide, before halting abruptly, and taking off in the reverse direction.

"Who does he think he is, the Sheik of Araby?" Clare said to Eugene, and turned away from the dancers to look around critically at the expensive new, varnished oak furniture.

Since the time Toby had lived down the street from the Endicotts, his father had made a lot of money and the Harris family had moved into a modern French flat on Washington Square. They were on the seventh floor of an elevator building with a living room three times the size of the Endicott's parlor, and with big windows that looked out over the treetops.

"What does his family do?" Clare asked, suggesting that the spanking new grandeur must imply something illicit.

Eugene said that Toby's father was a lawyer for J. P. Morgan. "Toby's going to be a lawyer too. He's taking pre-law at Columbia."

Clare smirked. "He looks more like Phys Ed to me." Toby was bending giggling Effie almost to the floor in an exaggerated back bend over one arm, while passing his other hand over his slicked-down hair like an apache dancer in a moving picture show.

"Look here," Eugene said, exasperated at Clare's continual sniping at his friend, "why are you so down on Toby?"

"Did I say I was down on him? I just don't like show-offs." She turned to Eugene. "I'm really surprised that you two are so chummy."

"Why shouldn't we be? We've known each other since we were kids."

"But you don't look like you have anything in common. She held a forefinger to her chin as she studied him. "It's obvious you're an introvert."

Eugene laughed. "I'm a what?"

"It's nothing bad. It only means you don't throw your wares in everybody's face. Personally, I prefer introverts to extroverts."

"If you'd stop analyzing everything," Eugene said, feeling flattered, "maybe I could get you to dance."

Clare smiled for the first time. "That's my problem. People always say I have a tendency to be too intellectual. I really ought to enjoy myself more. But why do men expect a girl to stop using her brain when they go out together?"

They were looked at each other openly, when they became aware that the music was over and the needle was scratching around in the groove.

"Where are they?" Clare said, with the edge back in her voice.

Eugene looked around. The dancers were gone. He settled back with a grin. "I guess they went out for a walk." He moved his arm down over her shoulders, but she pulled away.

"Listen!" She was on the edge of the couch. "What's that?"

"What's what?" said Eugene, who heard perfectly well the sound of Effie's muffled giggles coming from down the hall.

Clare was up, starting out of the room.

"Oh, shit!" Eugene said under his breath. "Come back!" He ran after her. Damn Toby! Why did he have to get so carried away that he forgot to shut the door?

Clare was staring in disbelief into the bedroom. It couldn't have been worse. On the bed, Toby's head was hidden under Effie's skirt, which was bunched up, showing a bare, white thigh above the stocking, as she moaned, her head flung back on the pillow.

She let out a scream. The thrashing halted. "Effie," she cried, "how could you!"

"Oh, for God's sakes!" Effie said, struggling free. "What's the fuss?" She got off the bed and straightened her dress.

"I can't believe this...," Clare said, as she dragged Effie past an astonished Eugene in the doorway, "I just can't believe it!"

"Oh, come off it," said Effie. "We're leaving, that's what you want, isn't it?"

Toby stumbled out into the foyer, holding up his pants. "Wait! Where the hell you going?"

"She's got to get back," Effie said, furious, as her cousin pushed her coat at her.

Toby held on to his pants. "But what about us?"

"I'm sorry, Toby," Effie cried over her shoulder, as Clare pulled her out the door. "I guess you'll just have to visit me in Cincinnati."

"What about tomorrow?"

"I'm leaving in the morning," she called back from the stairs, and they were gone.

Letting his pants drop, Toby yelled down the stairwell after them. "Go to hell, you bitches!"

Eugene, who was thinking of the neighbors, maneuvered his out-of-control friend back into the apartment and shut the door.

Toby opened another bottle of wine and started swigging it down. "Boy, did she leave me hanging off a cliff. Did you ever see such a hot piece, Gene? I'd almost go to Cincinnati for that. If it wasn't for that fourteen carat gold-plated virgin of a cousin, I'd have made it. I got to apologize for setting you up with her."

Eugene said he really thought he ought to go see the girls home.

"Forget 'em. They're not worth it." Toby put down the bottle and said he was still so hanker he had to go to the Turkish bath and sweat it out.

Eugene had never been to a Turkish bath before, and he was amazed to discover that Toby knew all about it. His friend was always surprising him.

They spent an hour sitting in the steam on wooden benches among other towel-wrapped figures who had been out on the town, drops of water falling on them from the tiles of the domed ceiling. When their names were called, he and Toby followed an attendant through the vaulted passage to a row of massage cubicles, echoing with the slaps of masseurs pounding the flesh of their clients.

Then he was lying on his stomach on a marble slab in a tiled cubicle next to Toby's, a partition between them, while a bald masseur with a big belly kneaded his muscles. Lulled by the steamy air, the echoing noises of clogs on tiles, the banging of pails, the continuous dribbling of water, his thoughts kept going back to Clare Marshall. If only her nitwit cousin hadn't ruined everything. What was it Clare had called him? An introvert? She had interesting ideas, not like most girls he knew. He wished they could have gone on talking.

It was typical of Toby to leave the bedroom door open. Toby never worried about anything. He went ahead and did whatever he wanted. That's why girls liked him so much.

With Eugene things weren't that simple. He wasn't so good at meeting girls himself. It was Toby who got them dates and he depended on Toby's antics to keep things going. It had always been that way. It was Toby who got him into that trouble when he was fifteen and the girl's irate father—he was a plumber and they lived over by the docks—had come to the house in his workman's overalls to demand that Mr. Endicott punish Eugene for trying to seduce his daughter.

As if it had been his fault! The girl had asked him in after they had double-dated with Toby, assuring him that her parents were dead to the world upstairs. They had been necking on the couch and he had just put a hand on her breast, following Toby's instructions, when the lights went on and her dad stood there in his bathrobe.

Gene knew he was in for it when his father ordered him into the study and shut the door. His father was in such a temper, he confessed he had only gone out with the girl because he wanted to get rid of his virginity. Toby had already lost his—and besides, Toby had already had this girl. And he had taken the precaution, on Toby's advice, of bringing along a French letter. But no matter what the girl's dad claimed, he never actually did anything to her.

"Then what's that son of a bitch coming to me for?" his father raged. "But you were messing with her, goddamit. Whether or not you got your prick into her." His father said he would let him go this time, but if anything like that happened again, he sure as hell wouldn't get off so easy.

Eugene was almost out the door, when his father stopped him. He turned, expecting another blast.

"Next time, son, don't get caught." And to Gene's amazement, his father had winked.

From the next cubicle he heard Toby's laugh as he kidded around with his masseur. Toby got along with all kinds of people. Even if he wanted to, Eugene wouldn't have been able to think of anything to say to the old man, who was kneading his back and shoulders.

His father might have been happier with a son like Toby. Eugene always felt uncomfortable when his father walked in on him and his mother having one of their long talks about books and other things they were interested in. But Gene had always been as bored as his mother was by his father's obsession with those damn elevated trains and subways.

His father was just as bored when his mother couldn't stop talking about Gene's winning the American Legion contest for a patriotic essay the year before. Ironically, his subject had been his father's rise from the slums to civil engineer.

On the other side of the partition, Toby was giving loud yelps as he was being pummeled.

After the trouble over the girl, it was Toby who had found the solution to the problem of his virginity. He arranged a date for him with a woman he knew who was being kept in the Village by a Park Avenue banker. She was always free in the afternoons and told Toby she liked nothing better than inexperienced young men. It had actually been pretty awful, but afterwards he'd felt so relieved, even victorious....

As Eugene lay on his stomach, his own masseur was working on his thighs and buttocks, and with the strong fingers squeezing and massaging his flesh, he began to be aroused, yielding to the pleasure. He could have gone on like this forever, when, without warning, to his mortification the masseur flipped him over onto his back. He had a boner. He shouldn't have been thinking of that woman. But the old man appeared not to notice anything and switched to kneading his scalp—after all, it must happen sometimes, and the curtain was drawn over the cubicle. Eugene closed his eyes and relaxed, as the masseur's fingers worked away at his shoulders.

Girls put out for Toby most of the time, though Gene had never gotten any of his dates to come across—like tonight. But it didn't upset him all that much when nothing happened, not like it did Toby.

The old man had worked down his body to his abdominal muscles, and an arm accidentally brushed against his boner, making him tremble. He kept his eyes shut, unable to resist the sensations that flooded him. The man's arm kept brushing against his erection as he worked, but he didn't seem to notice, and Gene couldn't make it go down.

He was trying not to breathe too noisily, when he became aware of Toby's hoarse breathing in the next cubicle. Suddenly his friend gave another yelp that subsided into a long sigh.

Eugene couldn't help himself—he shot off too, the most powerful orgasm of his life.

But, as if nothing had happened, the old man washed him from head to toe with a soapy sponge and doused him with a bucket of warm water.

"That's it, buddy," he said in a businesslike tone, helping Eugene off the table, and with a slap on his rump sent him to a dormitory down the hall.

Toby was grinning, as they lay, wrapped in sheets, in the rest lounge. "Nothing like a massage, when the skirts have let you down, eh, Genie boy?"

Eugene tried to sound casual, "You mean that always happens?"

"Sure, if they see you need it, they help you out. Why the hell not?" Toby looked over at him. "Felt good, didn't it?"

Even if what Toby said was true, Eugene still felt funny about it, and he was relieved to put it out of his mind in the excitement of rush week that was about to start. All through high school he and Toby had looked forward to joining a college fraternity together. But on the night they were invited to a smoker at Sigma Chi—the most prestigious fraternity on campus and the one Toby wanted most to pledge—Eugene felt completely out of place. He hated the over-heartiness of the fraternity men, but Toby loved it all. And when he did his imitation of a woman wriggling out of her corset that everyone howled at, Eugene was unaccountably nauseated.

Later, when they and several other freshmen were invited into the trophy room to pledge, Toby was the first to accept, but Eugene said he wanted to think it over.

He had avoided Toby's puzzled look, and on the way home when his friend slung an arm around his shoulders and asked him why the hell had he done that, he muttered something about his grades, aware that Toby knew as well as he did that he had a B+ average. Unlike Toby, he enjoyed his studies, even thrived on them.

Toby said that didn't make any sense. If it was grades he was worried about, didn't he know the frat kept a file of term papers and even copies of exams?

Eugene mumbled something about maybe joining next year. Fraternities didn't ask you again and they both knew it. Toby said he was crazy and Eugene went home half-convinced he was right.

3

Eugene was slumped in his chair in the Low Library reading room, Milton's *Paradise Lost* open before him.

It was early May, and the sun lit up the stained-glass panels in the library windows. Around him students were preparing for end of term, consulting piles of research materials and writing papers at the long tables under green-shaded electric bulbs. Others picked up books at the check out desk, stopping to whisper a few words to friends as they passed.

Lulled by the echoing hall, Eugene was thinking back over the semester since Toby went into the fraternity and their lives had gone in such different directions. He had followed his instincts not to join the fraternity himself, though at the time he had not been at all sure he was doing the right thing.

He enjoyed his college classes, and a world of serious thinking was opening up to him—the history of the English novel, the philosophy of Hegel—but after Toby moved into the frat house he had keenly felt the loss of his easygoing friend. It had been a surprise to discover how much he depended on him to fill up his life.

Going home to Perry Street every night had seemed so dismal in those early weeks of the semester. His sister Polly had moved out, and after years of squabbling about one issue or another, his parents were hardly talking to each other. His mother, who had always been his confidante and ally, was obsessed with her latest campaign, to stop Seventh Avenue from being extended through the Village, and his father was just as determined to get the avenue slashed through so that his precious subway could be put in underneath it.

He and Toby had planned to see each other often, but either fraternity activities prevented Toby from showing up, or—as he explained on the phone—being a pledge meant he had to be at the beck and call of the brothers at all times of the day and night.

Actually, they had only gotten together once, and after six weeks of not seeing each other, both had been a little awkward as they sat in the noisy student hangout just off campus at 115th Street and Broadway. Over their beers, they had tried to pretend that everything was the same.

Toby covered the gaps by telling him all about his life at the fraternity house, the top athletes who belonged, the beer-busts with girls sneaked into the bedrooms. His social life was so active—not to mention his sports practice—that Eugene could tell he hadn't been able to give as much time to his studies as he ought to. But Toby assured him that the fraternity was arranging for the tutoring he needed to keep up the required C average.

Eugene didn't talk about his own life because he knew it was nothing that would interest Toby—his discovery of philosophy and literature and the great minds of the past. Once he caught his friend looking around the bar as if hoping for some distraction, and when they left they promised to get together more often, but Eugene hadn't seen him since.

Now, drowsing in the cavernous reading room, he slid down to rest his head against the back of the chair with his legs stretched out in front of him under the oak table.

To fill up some of the free time he no longer spent running around with Toby and Toby's girlfriends, he had attended some meetings of the college literary society. Because of his growing interest in English Lit, he expected to have something in common with the society's members, but they turned out to be a bunch of affected snobs who made him feel stupid with their talk about things he had never heard of, like the Symbolists and Futurism.

It was in the middle of March, when he had just walked out on a literary meeting in disgust, that Toby had passed him. Toby was so busy talking away with a couple of fraternity brothers, he appeared not to see him, but as Gene pushed through the glass doors of McManus Hall on his way to a philosophy class, he caught the reflection of Toby's group going around the corner and, at that moment, he saw his old friend turn and look back at him.

It was only a flash, but he remembered that look. Something about it had troubled him. Was Toby as satisfied with fraternity life as he made out? Maybe he missed hanging around with Eugene too. As long as they had known each other, they had never really talked seriously. Toby didn't like to be serious about anything. But he didn't have to be. Things always worked out for him, or at least that's the way it seemed.

Eugene wanted to ask him if everything was all right, but he didn't want to sound nosy. Besides, he couldn't just go and ring the bell of the frat house.

His sister Polly had known Toby as long as he had and he wondered what she would think. He hadn't seen Polly much since she had moved uptown to take a job in an office. She was living in a boardinghouse for young working women in the east forties.

But when he had telephoned her, the atmosphere had been all wrong for any personal talk. The phone at her boardinghouse was in the hall and he could hear girls calling to each other, doors banging, mules clattering as they ran through the halls. One girl was even yelling at her to get off the phone, she was expecting a call.

He hardly had a chance to open his mouth anyway, his sister was so busy talking nonstop about her new job in an import-export house and how busy she was with evening classes in shorthand and a new man she was going out with. As a matter of fact, she said, she was getting ready to go to the opening of the new George M. Cohan musical at the New Amsterdam Theater. Had he read the reviews? They were raves! She was sorry she couldn't talk any more, she had to run.

When she hung up, he was depressed. The two of them had nothing in common any more. Just like Toby, she had thrown herself into a social whirl that had nothing to do with him.

But Toby's face reflected in the glass stayed with him, and one day he got up the nerve to ring the bell of the porticoed fraternity house.

There was so much noise going on inside that nobody heard the bell and he finally opened the door himself and walked into bedlam. A row of pledges were bent over baring their naked bottoms, submitting to the thwack of paddles from bellowing upper classmen. Toby was not among them. In a lounge off the hall he found one of the members reading the sports pages, and asked if Toby was around.

The fellow squinted up at him over the top of the paper. "You want him for something?"

Eugene said he was a friend.

"Your buddy really pulled a fast one," the frat man said. "He's in Cincinnati. Sent us a telegram. He eloped with some girl he knew out there."

Eugene had been pretty sure he knew the identity of the girl, and a phone call to Toby's mother had confirmed it. It was that plump little blonde Effie with the giggle Toby had run off with, throwing up at one stroke college, fraternity, and all the athletic triumphs everyone expected of him.

Slumped in his chair, Eugene pulled over *Paradise Lost* and propped the book on his stomach against the library table in front of him. The whole situation was clear to him now. Toby had never been cut out for college. It had only been an excuse for more social life and it was a sure bet he would have flunked out anyway—he must have known that. Marrying Effie was probably the right thing for him to do.

How could he ever have felt that Toby was such a superior being all those years? He had been fun to run around with—Eugene had learned a lot from him—but he was just an ordinary fellow, why shouldn't he marry an ordinary girl?

He was thinking about how Toby's elopement had put the finishing touches to a whole period in his own life, when he became aware that a girl sitting across from him was trying to get his attention.

"Would you mind moving your legs?" she said crossly. "My shins are black and blue."

As he straightened up with an apology, he thought there was something familiar about her. She had gone back to taking notes from a thick volume of charts, graphs, and statistics—the kind of thing he never could make head nor tail of. He looked more closely. It was the girl Toby had got for him on the double date with Effie—Clare Marshall, the cousin. The same serious face with braids wound around the top of her head. She looked better than he remembered, that night she had stormed out with Effie after catching her in the act.

She must have felt his eyes on her because a moment later she looked up. Then she recognized him too and smiled. He didn't remember that she had smiled at all at Toby's.

A little later they were sitting over lemonade in the student cafeteria with Gothic windows looking out on a baseball diamond where a team was practicing. The dark paneling of the walls was decorated with crossed school pennants, and plaques celebrating athletic victories, and framed photographs of the winning teams from way back.

"That's exactly how I always felt about Effie," Clare said, when he told her of his changed attitude to Toby. "I've never told anyone, I was ashamed to, but can you believe it, I was envious of her ever since we were little girls? She was always the popular one—boys swarmed around her. That's why I got so upset when I caught her with Toby. I was awful, wasn't

I?" She blushed charmingly. "As you say, he's got all the good looks in the world, just like Effie. But she doesn't have a brain in her head either. They really deserve each other."

They both laughed.

"They're just perfect specimens meant for breeding," Eugene said, and was delighted at her reaction to his sassy quip. Beyond her, on the ball field out the window, a batter hit a pop fly and one of the outfielders leaped up, catching it in his glove.

Clare was pleased to hear he had refused to go into the fraternity. He was simply not the type, she said. She hadn't even considered a sorority herself. She was majoring in sociology and minoring in psychology, and she felt just as he did that the most exciting thing in the world was the intellectual adventure of higher education.

Eugene agreed completely. "I had plenty of running around in high school," he said. "It seemed fun at the time, but looking back on it, it was just a lot of meaningless promiscuity." He had never spoken the word before, but it rolled off his tongue easily. With this bright, approving girl across from him, whom he had once scorned as too intellectual when he was under Toby's shadow, he felt able to talk about anything. He wasn't sure the one time he had actually made it with a girl qualified him as promiscuous, but he had never felt so much a man with anyone before— Clare's hands were so small, and her shoulders under the polka-dot blouse so fragile.

A trace of the old seriousness settled over her face. "Dr. Bieler, my psychology professor, has interesting ideas about that. He says that sexuality is only justified in the context of a responsible relationship." She went on as if quoting a recent lecture. "Giving in to one's random impulses is the cause of all the unhappiness in the world."

"Well, I'm not sure it's the same for a man as for a woman," Eugene said uneasily, shifting his gaze out the window again. On the ball field a batter hit a home run and as he trotted around the diamond, the basemen patted him on the behind in congratulations. The memory of the naked male asses at Toby's frat house popped into his mind. He jumped to his feet and suggested they go down to Riverside Park and walk along the Hudson. "Do you have time?"

"Let's!" Clare picked up her books and hugged them to her. "We'll play hookey!"

For the final weeks of the semester, Eugene Endicott and Clare Marshall were inseparable. As they walked around the city holding hands, everybody smiled at them. Eugene loved the feeling of having a girl of his own, of being like everyone else.

He was always wanting to spoon with her, but he was just as glad she held him firmly in check. Whenever he went too far, she explained to him that she had her sexual needs too, but she was willing to wait. Still, she always kissed him passionately when they said good night on the steps of her dorm.

On the last night of the term, sitting with him in the visiting lounge of the Barnard dorm under the strict eye of the housemother, Clare said she would be seeing the newlyweds when she went home to Cincinnati, and asked if he had anything for her to tell Toby. Toby had found a job out there selling automobiles and he and Effie were living in an apartment near her parents' house.

Eugene thought hard, finally said to tell him "Best of luck," and they both laughed, and agreed once more how stupid it was to get married so young and give up your education.

Clare regretted that she had committed herself months before to do settlement house work in Akron with slum children for the summer.

Eugene said he didn't know how he was going to get through the long, hot months without her.

"Why don't you come with me and get a job too?"

"To Akron? Where would I live?"

Clare studied her hands folded in her lap. "If we got married, there wouldn't be any problem."

"Married?" Eugene was thrown for a loop by the enormity of the idea. He hadn't envisioned marriage for years, not until he was finished with college, in a profession, settled in life at some distant time.

"And as for that silly rule students aren't allowed to marry," Clare said, "if that's what's worrying you, I've already talked to Dr. Bieler about it and he's promised to clear it with the administration."

"I don't know...," said Eugene. He tried to picture the reaction of his parents as he stood before them and announced that he was getting married.

Clare was already moving on. "And when we get back in the fall, we'll find a room for ourselves, walking distance from the campus."

Eugene tried to cover up the queasy feeling in the pit of his stomach with a grin. "Well, I guess...you've got it all worked out."

Clare smiled. She put her arms around his neck and under the disapproving eye of the housemother, sealed their engagement with a kiss.

4

Doesn't anybody but me care at all about these lovely streets? Elizabeth Endicott asked herself on that day in September, 1911, which ever afterward she considered to be either the worst or the best day of her life.

She was driving back home from City Hall in the family's Franklin automobile, negotiating the narrow streets of the Greenwich Village she loved, which was about to have an obscene swathe cut through its middle, so that an extension of Seventh Avenue and, ultimately, Patrick's subway, could come through. It was going to necessitate bulldozing dozens of the handsome old Federal houses that were becoming more unique and precious with the passing years, as the mad building craze continued. New York City insisted on obliterating its past to make way for "business" and "progress," two words she had always hated. They were the enemies of everything she valued—tradition, beauty, charm.

For years she had been fighting against the cut-through, trying to alert other Villagers to the danger to the community, but the forces she had rallied had been so pitifully inadequate—only women. She couldn't interest any men at all. Not all of them were as blindly obstinate as her husband, but saving an old neighborhood was considered somehow a female cause, something unworthy of even the most intelligent man.

Even the artists whom she had counted on most to rally to her side had shown scant interest. They were willing to take advantage of what the Village offered—studios they rented for a song, the freedom to live as they chose—but they couldn't see that they had to fight to preserve these old streets for themselves, if not for posterity.

"Elizabeth Endicott's suffragettes," her little group of civic-minded ladies was dubbed in the popular press. Any woman who tried to do anything at all was labeled suffragette nowadays.

Already, houses in the path of the new avenue were being condemned and boarded up, and wreckers were starting to demolish them—why, they even planned to slice buildings in half! It would look grotesque. Elizabeth and her handful of supporters had gone down to City Hall to picket the office of the mayor, the one man who still had the power to stop the whole thing.

They had started at eight in the morning when the streets in the Foley Square area were full of people on their way to work and could see them holding their placards, SAVE GREENWICH VILLAGE, DON'T RIP THE HEART OUT OF THE VILLAGE. But people had only stopped to jeer—and not just men. "Suffragette" had been shouted at them repeatedly like an obscenity.

When finally they were allowed in to City Hall to leave a deposition, Elizabeth thought they just might have a chance. But it was not the mayor who received them, it was a minor official, and he hadn't even bothered to hide his complete lack of interest, and had looked at them like hysterical females.

She turned the Franklin onto Sixth Avenue, honking at a dog that ambled across the street unconcerned.

The whole thing had been a fiasco. She had tried everything and failed. She gritted her teeth as she drove past Washington Place and Waverly Place that now lay in shadow, even on this brilliantly sunny September afternoon, because of the elevated that Patrick had helped to put up in the name of "progress," turning a once pleasant avenue into a near slum. The people passing by, including an artist who had set up his easel to paint the busy street scene under the el, were totally unconcerned that the city's new bulldozers were about to move in and carve out the heart of their neighborhood.

The automobile skidded off the unused trolley tracks still embedded in the cobblestones, causing a horse pulling a delivery wagon to shy, and all around her was the squealing of brakes, klaxons blaring, and wagon drivers reining in their teams.

Elizabeth wanted to cry at the injustice of it all. If Patrick had been defeated on some issue he cared about, he would be bawling his head off—he could always cry so easily when he was hurt, like a child. It was in his blood to cry like that, get all his pain out of his system at once and then bounce back newborn, ready to leap into the fray again with the same blind energy. She rarely wept and it had been so long ago, she wasn't sure she still knew how.

At Ninth Street across from Jefferson Market and the Courthouse, she passed an ice cream parlor that years before had been Gridley's bar where Winifred Beaufort had sung for that brief time. How she wished she could talk to Winifred, who had been the one person in her life she could reveal her innermost self to. But Will Kennedy had been arrested in a vice cleanup and sent to prison the year before. His gambling casino had been wrecked in the raid. Winifred rescued what assets she could and had gone back to New Orleans, the place she had left years before as a slave. She was running a school for colored children while she waited for Will's eventual release.

Elizabeth turned off in the direction of home. She wasn't eager to get there. Not just because of today. The house on Perry Street had become a place where she was treated as a stranger by her husband and had been deserted by her children. For the life of her, she couldn't remember what she had ever thought she had in common with any of them.

She was so distracted that she had to slam on the brakes and blast the klaxon to keep from running down some children playing in the middle of the street. As she shifted into third gear, the car bucked, and she drove on cursing under her breath at the difficulties of life—even driving the automobile, which normally she was a whiz at. Driving was something that gave her a feeling of being in complete control, of being obeyed by a powerful machine.

Her daughter Polly had been the first of her children to disappoint her. She had thrown up her art studies for no reason at all and taken it into her head to play at being a "bachelor girl" and work in a business office.

Elizabeth hated offices. She had been in and out of so many these past two years, trying to cajole hardheaded bureaucrats, who treated her like an escapee from a lunatic asylum. As she drove past St. Vincent's Hospital where Patrick's avenue was to begin cutting through to the south, she had the wild notion of chaining herself with her small band of supporters, wrist to wrist, in front of the handsome old brewery building that was soon to go. She could imagine the conventional reaction of her daughter, who sided with her father on everything. Why, Polly's real father, Albert Cogswell, was the most unconventional man she had ever known. It distressed her most that Polly had turned out to be such an ordinary person. How she hated the ordinary!

Even more disappointing was her son Eugene's unexpected marriage. She had disliked Clare Marshall from the first time she set eyes on her. Such an opinionated priss, who was leading her son around by the nose.

Eugene had it in him to be a writer—she had always counted on it— but now he was planning on becoming a technical editor, of all things. Clare—how she loathed the name—had talked him into it because it would lead to a well-paying career. A technical editor! She had done her best to raise her children with high ideals, but what could she do? Always there had been her philistine husband to counteract her every effort.

Since she had begun fighting to save Greenwich Village, it had become clear to her that she and Patrick had no interests in connon. They lived in the same house, the world considered them man and wife, but they had long ceased sharing the same bed. Though they scarcely said a word to each other any more except when other people were around, there was mockery implicit in his every look. His loathesome subway meant more to him than she ever had.

As she slowed down in front of the house, her husband was waiting for her on the stoop, along with their grandson, nineteen-year-old Dominic, and Polly, her papa's darling, who were over for dinner. Patrick had the same smirk on his face when she left the house that morning. With his insufferable knowledge of the way men ran things, he knew she didn't have a chance at City Hall.

She felt their eyes on her as she parked the big automobile at the curb and turned off the motor. Well, they weren't going to get the best of her. Before getting out, she took off her motoring veil that held her ostrich-plume hat in place and tucked in straying gray hairs. She drew herself to her full height and walked toward them.

At sixty, Elizabeth knew herself to be a handsome woman. She was heavier than she had been, but she bore her weight with a Junoesque grace. Without looking at either her husband or her daughter as she came up the steps, she focused on her grandson. A plump young man with a round face and glasses, he had none of his father Mario's looks, or any of his personality, for that matter.

"Dominic, dear," she said, giving him a kiss. "I'm so glad you had some time for us." He was about to leave for a year in Italy to study at a cooking school.

Patrick broke in. "So His Honor gave you the keys to the city, Elizabeth?" He had on his outlandish striped shirt that she had told him a million times clashed with his checkered trousers and made his beer belly twice as big as it already was.

"We thought you wouldn't get here in time, mother," Polly said. "Dommie can't stay long. He's got to do his packing."

As usual, she was echoing her father—even to the point of implying that what her mother had been trying to do at City Hall was of no importance. With Albert Cogswell's pug nose and freckles, how could she wear that unflattering grey jacket and skirt combination, that was the uniform of every spinster working girl in the city? Those wire-rimmed spectacles made her even more anonymous. At least she'd let her hair grow out again after that horrendous bob.

Ignoring her daughter, she smiled at Dominic. "How I envy you your year in Italy. You're going to love Florence."

"I don't know, grandma. To tell you the truth I'm not much of a traveler."

She reassured him that he would soon change his mind, but it was like trying to set fire to damp kindling.

"Wait a minute before ya rush off, Dom," Patrick said, getting to his feet with the ease of a younger man—he was in his mid-sixties. "I've got a little treat for ya."

As Elizabeth heard him opening the roll-topped desk in his study, she told Dominic again what a revelation Italy had been to her. Of course, it hadn't been the boy's idea to go to Italy. It was his father, Mario, who had enrolled him in the cooking school, foreseeing for his taciturn son a future as a chef in the family restaurant he had started after Alicia's death. But even sailing tomorrow on the Vulcania, something she would have given her eyeteeth for, was less appealing to him than a trip to the wholesale market to buy produce for the Alfano restaurant. She sometimes doubted that her grandson had a single opinion of his own, or a passion for doing anything except boiling a potful of spaghetti She was relieved when Patrick came back outside, presenting him with a brand new hundred-dollar bill and she was able to escape to the kitchen.

She wasn't up to fixing more than a cold supper tonight. As she took some coldcuts out of the icebox, she heard Patrick on the steps outside, letting the whole street know how he was expecting Dom to fix him a first-class ravioli dinner just as soon as the boy got back to the States.

A man on top of the world, gloating over his foolish wife. Who was she to try to influence the mayor? Cutting that ugly swathe through was going to be the best thing for the Village since he had put up the Greenwich Street el. She hated him for winning. She knew him well enough to know that he wasn't about to let her suffer her defeat quietly. He was going to keep on rubbing it in.

And he did, that night at the table.

His sister, Nora Yates, had also dropped in for dinner, as she was apt to do without an invitation, to read them one of their brother Timothy's letters from Ireland. Nora's husband, Billy Yates, had been killed in a subway accident and Patrick was forever going on about how they must do all they could for the poor woman since times had been so hard for her—with never a thought for what his own wife was going through! Nora, still in black long after the year's mourning period, brought over every one of Timothy's boring letters, even though he had ceased to exist for any of them except as a dull echo from the past. The young hoodlum Patrick had put on the boat so long ago was no longer recognizable in the bigot who condemned everything with the narrowest interpretation of church dogma.

Patrick, who had appeared to be giving his rapt attention to his sister's laborious reading aloud of the letter, an especially gloomy one about the sinfulness of the young, suddenly turned on Elizabeth and asked what his honor the mayor had had to say that afternoon.

She was caught off guard and blurted out the flimsy lie that her appointment with the mayor had been postponed because of an emergency City Council meeting.

"City Council meeting, was it?" He winked at Polly across the table and sat back complacently in his chair, arms folded behind his head. "As ya may have heard, Nora," he said with a wicked grin, "my wife's been wagin a heroic battle all on her own against the forces of capitalist exploitation who are out to wreck our precious Greenwich Village by cuttin Seventh Avenue through."

Sister Nora, who was well aware of the conflict between husband and wife, gave a nervous giggle.

Elizabeth clutched her hands so tightly under the table the tendons stood out. Keeping her voice level, she said the Village was perfectly livable the way it was.

Patrick was still enjoying himself too much to let her off the hook. "Well, your daughter didn't find it so livable down here any more. She had to move uptown. Isn't that so, Pol?"

"Oh, really, papa," Polly said, pretending to scold him.

Elizabeth's hands were numb. "You refuse to understand, Patrick, that a beautiful neighborhood is not improved by slashing a highway through it."

"But haven't ya been tellin us all for years about them boulevards they cut through Paris, and I thought that was supposed to be the most beautiful place ya ever seen."

Elizabeth took a quick breath. "This isn't Paris! It's the Seventh Avenue Improvement Association, for God's sake!"

"Ah, Elizabeth," Nora piped up, "the Improvement Association has our best interests at heart, I believe. We need them to raise the tone. Lemme tell ya, when I go to early Mass, there's bums still carousin on the streets from the night before."

"You're right about that, Nora," said Patrick. "Greenwich Village is not what it used to be, not by a long shot." While his wife had her head in the clouds, he said, trying to save a few old streets nobody gave a damn about, she failed to see that things were falling down around their ears.

Elizabeth was ready to explode, when to her relief, Nora's policeman son Dennis stopped in off his beat. He had come to escort his mother home. Her youngest nephew had a blarney tongue and natural good spirits that made him irresistible to everyone. He took off his high-domed copper's helmet, and holding it under his arm, bent over to kiss her, his favorite aunt, before going over to his mother.

The way Dennis looked, sturdy in his blue uniform, with his swiped back, sandy hair, always made Elizabeth's heart skip a beat, though she was not only his aunt, but nearly forty years older than he.

"What's this you're sayin about the Village not bein safe then, Uncle Pat?" the young policeman asked. He reached for a toothpick to diddle between his fine white teeth as he sprawled in a chair, his legs in blue serge stretched out in front of him.

Patrick turned to his nephew, confident of another supporter in his ranks. "You're an officer of the force, lad, ya know what I'm talkin about. It's all these artist types my wife is so crazy about who've seen fit to come and set themselves up in the neighborhood as if they owned the place. Ya can't walk down into Sheridan Square in even the brightest daylight without them floozies who claim to be artist models givin ya the wink and lettin ya know what their real profession is fast enough, not to mention all them nancy boys mincin by. It's a disgrace to decent women and children, having to put up with that. When Seventh Avenue and the new subway spur is put through, we'll get some more respectable folk down here again."

"That's utterly ridiculous," Elizabeth said, not looking at him. What a prig he had become, stuffy, hypocritical! How had she put up with his shanty Irish morality all these years? She turned back to her nephew. "My husband would like this neighborhood to be as dull as any other in the city. I keep trying to tell him it's just the people who are out of the ordinary that give it its wonderful flavor, don't you see?"

Dennis laughed. "These queer characters we got around here sure give it a flavor all right, Auntie."

His blue eyes twinkled back at her. He liked her. Patrick's eyes had once looked at her like that, bold, mischievous, ready for anything. Flushed, she turned away to her sister-in-law to ask if she wanted any more coffee.

Patrick was disappointed at Dennis's lack of support and growled that this element they liked so much was actually dangerous.

Aware of her nephew's approval of the high color in her cheeks, Elizabeth said, "Because people are out of the ordinary doesn't mean they're dangerous."

Patrick ignored her and snapped at his nephew, "If ya kept your blue eyes open when ya was walkin your beat, Dennis, ya wouldn't talk like that."

"Don't get so hot under the collar, Uncle Paddy," Dennis said, unbuttoning his policeman's tunic and hooking his thumbs under his suspenders. "Aunt Elizabeth isn't so far off at that. I can tell ya for a fact there's less crime here than there is in a lot of the other precincts in this town. Hell's Kitchen, for one, and them chinks is always cuttin each other up down on Pell Street."

"Praise God for the finest," Nora exclaimed, apropos of nothing, her eyes beaming at her last born whom she saw as single-handedly saving them all from being murdered.

With Dennis on her side, Elizabeth gave her husband a triumphal smile. "There, you see?"

Polly banged down her coffee cup. "Well, I for one think you're absolutely right, papa. I know the artists in Paris may have been different in your day, mother, but these people who call themselves artists here are just out to take advantage of us all any way they can."

Elizabeth couldn't believe her ears. "Polly! Have your months of living uptown banging away at a typing machine made you lose all your senses? You're being irrational...and stupid!"

Polly turned red, as if she had been slapped.

"What the hell are ya sayin to her?" Patrick said. "Pol, your mother didn't mean it."

Elizabeth knew she had gone too far. Holding her voice down, she said, "I'm only saying that artists are citizens too and have as much right to be here as we do."

Polly pushed back her chair without looking at anyone. "If you'll excuse me, I've got to get back to my stupid uptown life." She hurried out of the dining room and up the stairs to the front hall.

"Ah, come on back, Pol." Patrick had flung down his napkin and was already on his feet. Going up the stairs after her, he said loudly enough for them all to hear, "Your mother's all hot and bothered because she hasn't got anywhere with her looney scheme, that's all."

Even nephew Dennis could find nothing to say to cut the deadly silence in the dining room, as he and his mother and aunt sat listening to Patrick pleading vainly with his daughter at the front door.

When Polly had gone, Patrick returned with a scowl on his face. The young policeman jumped up, making a feeble joke about needing to get his mother back early through the dangerous streets, and took her home.

The moment they were alone, Patrick burst out, "What ever possessed ya? I wouldn't talk to a dog like that, much less my own daughter."

Elizabeth was noisily stacking the dirty plates. "You're always worrying about that precious daughter of yours."

"I never thought I'd be sayin it, but you're a cold mother," he said.

She elbowed past him with the pile of dishes. "Well, I can't bother to understand her little quirks. I've got my own problems."

Patrick was right on her heels. "Ya don't understand her because she's nothin like you are. There it is, pure and simple. Thank God, she takes after me."

Elizabeth had reached her limit. She turned at the kitchen door and the words flew out, "What do you mean, 'takes after you'? She's not your daughter at all. Her father was an artist!"

Patrick stopped dead. "What's that ya say?"

In confusion, she got the dishes to the sink before she dropped them on the floor. She couldn't believe those words had come out of her mouth. It was unthinkable. She was tottering on the edge of a precipice. "Don't listen to me," she pleaded, trying to erase those terrible words. "I'm not making sense any more, you've got me so upset."

She felt him behind her, staring, struck dumb.

"Oh, leave me alone, can't you? Why are you paying any attention to me anyway?" Her voice was shaking, as she held a plate under the water tap, leftover cold cuts falling into the sink. "The day's been hellish…and you and Polly and everyone all ganging up on me.…"

He wrenched her around. The dish in her hand clattered to the floor. "What is that you was sayin, then?"

She clutched her forehead, she was going to faint. "How do I know? It was just gibberish. I never should have gone through that awful dinner." She tried to pull away. "My head is splitting, I'm going up to bed."

But his fists held her. "Look at me, woman! Pol is my daughter! She's mine!" He shook her hard. "Isn't she?"

She was crying now, as her words tumbled out helter-skelter. "I didn't mean anything. Of course, she's yours. She's more your daughter than mine. She adores you. For God's sake, let me go.…"

"Who's the father then?" Patrick said. "Tell me before all the blood pours from my heart. Tell me before I fall dead at your feet!" When she didn't answer, he slapped her. "Tell me!"

She shrieked. "Don't make me! Please don't!"

His grip on her tightened. "Tell me or I'll break every bone in your body, so help me God!"

The pain was agonizing. "All right!"

He let go of her and she dropped into a chair, holding her throbbing arms.

"Who, then?" He stood over her.

Her voice was remote, almost like a child's. "I wasn't ever going to tell you," she began. "I didn't want to hurt you, but I guess now there's no help for it.…" Relieved to unburden herself at last, she told of her single infidelity so many years before, the secret she had planned to take with her to the grave. She tried to explain to Patrick that it had happened when she felt so abandoned because of his inconsolable grief after little Jack's death.

But put into words made what she had done sound so tawdry, so shameful. As long as Patrick didn't know, she could feel justified, it had even seemed a miracle, because at the time it had been the means of bringing him back to her. But now that he had dragged the story out of her, she knew her life was over.

"So that's the truth of it," he said afterward.

"Yes."

He turned and walked upstairs to his room.

For a while, she was too dazed to move. Then the enormity of what had happened struck her. She jumped up and rushed after him.

He had closed his door. Her first fear was that he had suffered another heart attack, and it flashed into her mind that she would have to hurl herself against the door. But when she turned the knob, it opened.

He was sitting on the bed, staring out the window into the gathering darkness.

She spoke from the doorway. "I'll go away. Polly will never know."

When he didn't answer, she thought, sickeningly, that that was what he wanted. But then he said, "Ya don't have to do that."

She moved around the bed, intending to throw herself at his feet and beg for forgiveness. Instead, she sat down beside him.

They had not shared the same bed in years. Not once in that time had he tried to touch her. But now he did. He reached out and pulled her roughly against him. He threw himself on her, as violent in his lust as a young man. At first, she let herself submit as if it were punishment deserved for the hurt she had done him. But when his mouth fastened on hers and his fingers gripped her breasts, not caring that he was hurting her, the old feelings broke through. She started to fight back, taking her pleasure just as selfishly as he, her nails digging into the flesh of his buttocks as she pulled him into her.

It was ruthless, and swift—a coupling of two people whose passion had supposedly ended, who had not understood or even liked each other for so long. It had nothing to do with liking or understanding—nothing to do with the illusions of love. Patrick and Elizabeth were rediscovering sex for themselves, this time as a battlefield, with no rules to guide them.

Afterward, he did not stay with her, but went downstairs to his study where he sat alone in the darkness. When he came upstairs again, in the cold hours just before dawn, it was not to his own room he returned, but to hers, the room they had shared when love still bound them.

Though they never spoke again about what she had told him, in the years that remained to them he slept with her and made love to her until the day he died.

5

Polly was standing with a girlfriend, Gladys, on Bleecker Street in the falling snow, as their dates, two out-of-town salesmen named Will and Clarence, whom Polly had met in her office, were struggling to start their stalled motor car. The boys, both in evening clothes and driving cloaks, their patent leather pumps soaked through in the snow, were taking turns cranking the engine, with no luck.

They had all been out to dinner at the Astor Hotel and, when the boys learned that Polly had grown up in Greenwich Village, they had insisted on coming down for her to show them the wicked life among the artists.

Finally, Gladys, clutching her thin evening coat around her, screamed at them to give up on the car, she was frozen stiff. It occurred to Polly that they were only a few blocks from her parents' house, but she wouldn't dream of letting her mother meet these out-of-town rubes. Her mother would see them as loud and superficial, everything she couldn't abide— and they were. Instead, Polly guided them toward Sheridan Square where she remembered a restaurant from the old days.

Each man shielded his date from the falling snow with his cape, using the weather as an excuse to get in some cuddling. There was nothing wrong with Clarence, Polly's date, except that he was bland, simple-minded, and grinned. It might make him a top salesman of farm machinery, but, except for the flat midwest accent, he was a carbon copy of all the men she'd been going out with the past four years, since she had moved uptown.

She was fed up with all of them. They didn't have an idea in their heads except getting their hands on her, when the time came for petting at the end of the evening. She could usually keep them from going further than she wanted. Occasionally, she felt sorry for one of them and let him go all the way, but she always regretted it—it was as unpleasant as the first time.

It gave her a peculiar sensation to be walking through the streets of the Village again. Once, she thought she was going to have a brilliant art career and had talked so glibly about "women's rights." That girl was dead as a doornail. But, she wondered ruefully as Clarence's arm tucked her tighter against him, who was the girl who had replaced her?

"Where are all the sex fiends I've been hearing about?" Gladys's young man asked, as they trudged through the falling snow along the empty street.

"Is that all you're interested in?" Polly snapped. "Then what did you bring me down here for?" She was cold and these rubes were even more banal than usual. And as far as that nitwit Gladys went....

Just ahead of them was the wasteland, where the streets had been torn out to make way for the extension of Seventh Avenue. Some houses were half demolished. The snow had settled over the surviving walls and the rubble, and in the pale light of the street lamps the eerie desolation seemed to stretch into infinity.

"Hey, we got here too late!" Polly's young man laughed. "Why didn't you tell us they were tearing the place down?"

Polly, who was surprised herself at the extent of the demolition, suggested that they look for a place to warm up closer by. Gladys spotted the glow of a crackling fire through the window of a cellar tea shop called The Teaspoon, and they all trooped down the steps and inside.

It was a snug little place after the cold and the snow—a typical Village hangout with checkered tablecloths and candles stuck in wine bottles and, tacked to the wall, caricatures of the regulars. Two men bent over a chessboard in one corner, and a gaunt man with long hair was making a charcoal sketch of a waif-like girl with big eyes. At another table, some students were arguing loudly over the latest issue of a small radical monthly called The Masses, which was being passed around.

As they rubbed their hands in front of the fire, the salesmen joked about coming all the way from Indianapolis to Greenwich Village only to end up in a tea shop. Polly, holding down her irritation, let them know that gypsy tea shops in the Village were very much the place to go.

When the four sat down and the one called Will ordered a bottle of wine, a bored waitress in kerchief and hoop earrings examined her fingernails and said, "We don't serve wine, beer, or spirits."

"Why the hell not?" Clarence said in a loud voice.

A plump woman with orange-dyed hair eased the waitress aside. "I am so sorry, gentlemen," she said in a heavy accent, "but if you were looking for a bar, there is one around the corner." Rouged lips clashed with the orange hair, emphasizing the ravages of what must once have been an attractive face. But her lidded eyes, Polly could tell, missed nothing as she surveyed them.

After they settled for coffee with whipped cream, the proprietress suggested that maybe the nice people would like to have their portraits sketched and beckoned to the gaunt-faced man with long hair, who left off drawing the waif-like girl to bring over samples of his work.

Gladys squealed over the sketches he spread out on the table.

"Hey, this fella's good!" Clarence said. "Ever see a better likeness of Teddy Roosevelt?"

Polly thought it looked more like Abraham Lincoln, but she kept her mouth shut.

The artist assured them that he could do a likeness of each of them in just five minutes and they could pay him anything they wanted.

As he began to sketch Gladys and the boys watched, absorbed by his quick, skillful strokes, Polly gazed into the fire, wishing she were anywhere else.

The proprietress with the orange hair came over, flopped down on the bench beside her, and lit up a cigarette. "You're not having much fun, *chérie*, are you?" the woman said. Under eyebrows plucked to a thin line, those hooded eyes gave her a look of immeasurable sadness that her brisk manner denied.

Polly gave a bitter laugh and the woman laughed with her, as the others carried on inanely about the sketching.

The woman raised an eyebrow in the direction of her friends. "But they look like charming boys."

Now they were exclaiming over the artist's sketch of Gladys, which flattered her shamelessly.

"They bore me to death," Polly said. "I'm absolutely disgusted with myself for getting into situations like this."

The woman flicked her cigarette ash on the sawdust floor. "Why do you do it, then?"

"I don't know any more. I'm not sure I ever knew."

The woman examined her with her lidded eyes. "How old are you, twenty-two, twenty-three? You sound like you don't expect any more surprises in life."

Polly looked over at Gladys and the salesmen. "With them, there aren't any surprises."

A service bell sounded. She looked up to see four steaming coffees on the serving counter, and in the kitchen behind them, a swarthy man with a thick, black mustache grinning slyly at Corinne.

The proprietress tossed her cigarette into the fire and stood up. "Why don't you tell them to go to hell, then?" she said.

Polly followed her with her eyes. The woman was extraordinary. She had grasped at once her whole stagnant situation. As she sipped her coffee, Polly mused that there must have been people like her in the Village all the years she had lived down here, but she had been too self-absorbed to notice.

She gave only perfunctory attention to the sketch Gladys showed her— she was watching the proprietress and the swarthy man in the kitchen. The woman must be at least twenty years older than him, but it was obvious from the way he bent over and nuzzled her cheek that there was something between them.

"What's going on here, you trying to clip us?" Clarence yelped. He was hopping mad.

The artist's face was impassive. "Not at all, sir," he said, "but twenty-five cents is not even in the realm of payment."

Clarence slipped his change purse back into his pocket. "Well, it's all you're going to get from me. You think what you're doing is work? Why don't you get a real job!"

"Oh, Clarence, don't be such a piker." Polly said, opening her hand-bag.

"Darn it, Polly, no!" Clarence said, and reached over to snap her bag shut. "This fellow thinks just because we're from out of town he can take us for suckers."

"I assure you, sir," said the artist, "you're wrong on that count."

Suddenly, the man working in the kitchen was there—up close, he was big, his dark eyes fierce. He yanked Clarence up by the collar. "Pay up, cheapskate, or get out!"

"What did I do?" the salesman said, changing his tune in a hurry.

Gladys screamed, clinging to her boyfriend.

"Out!" the cook said. He gave Clarence a shove toward the door.

"Maybe we ought to get out of here," said Will.

"You're damn tootin'," Clarence said, straightening his coat. "Come on, Polly, we're going."

She stayed where she was.

"Polly, what's wrong with you?" cried Gladys, grabbing up her things. "They're out to scalp us!"

Watching the scene unfold with increasing detachment, Polly heard herself saying, "Go on ahead. I'm staying awhile."

Her riled-up companions argued with her, but she wouldn't budge. Finally, dumbfounded at her behavior, they left.

The cook slammed the door after them and headed back to the kitchen. Polly was already getting into her coat, intending to follow them after all.

"You stay!" he ordered, but there was a glimmer in his dark eyes.

"But I really ought to...."

"No arguments!" he said, and disappeared into the back.

"This will do you good, *chérie*."

The orange-haired proprietress poured out two cognacs and sat down across from Polly, who still couldn't get over what she had just done.

"I'm sorry if Milos was not so nice to your boyfriend, but sometimes one needs a strong man around, *comprenez*?" The heavily-shaded eyes looked fondly in the direction of the burly cook who was rolling out pie dough in the kitchen, singing lustily about a girl named Corinska. When he saw his employer looking at him, he threw her a kiss.

"Are you Corinska?" Polly asked, starting to relax.

"That's his Hungarian embroidery. Actually, my name is Corinne." She raised her cognac to Polly and drank it down.

When Corinne learned that Polly's last name was Endicott, she asked if, by any chance, her family lived on Perry Street.

"You know them?"

"But of course! This is extraordinary!" Corinne recounted how she and her ex-husband, Fleming Ashmore, had once lived next door to the Endicotts.

Polly was amazed to hear that this remarkable woman and her painter husband had been her family's neighbors. Her mother had never said a word about them. That was strange. Polly felt close to her already. She began telling Corinne about her childhood on Perry Street, how out of place she felt growing up in Greenwich Village. Even when she moved uptown, it was the same story—she simply didn't fit in there either. And, moreover, she couldn't advance in her jobs because she was a woman.

The proprietress nodded. "The only solution for a woman is to start her own business." It was the same problem she had faced, she said, when Fleming had dropped her after he became a success and started chasing after the society women he painted. "That big bear in the kitchen," she nodded toward the cook with the bushy mustache, "he was having trouble with his wife, and my husband left me, so we clicked. *Eh, voilà!* Of course, he's a couple of years younger than me." She winked.

Polly said she would quit her secretarial job in a minute if she had an inkling of what to do with herself.

The older woman looked at Polly with an appraising eye. "If you like, you could help out here while you're making up your mind about it. I could use someone like you. The one I've got now is useless."

Polly glanced around the cozy little place with the fire blazing merrily. Being a waitress was nothing she had ever remotely considered, but she suddenly liked the idea. The trouble was, she didn't want to move back with her family.

As if reading her mind, Corinne added that there was a free room upstairs. "You could live there, and you'll have your meals down here with me. But you'll have to put up with that wild man in the kitchen." The Frenchwoman smiled.

Polly moved in at the end of the week, and Corinne dressed her in a gypsy tearoom costume like her own with a purple bandanna, hoop earrings, and a lot of beads. The customers were entertaining, and soon she knew them all by their first names. They expected her to live through their creative agonies and the complications of their love affairs, and sometimes stake them to a meal or even loan them a little money. They always swore that they would pay her right back, but both knew they never would, because people who lived on the margins forgot about such details. Whenever they got too much for her, Corinne reminded her to be glad they weren't running a lunch wagon in Yonkers.

Milos was always there in the kitchen if she needed him. He seemed never to sleep except for five-minute naps when business was slow, lying flat on his back on the counter with his hands folded across his big chest. But always, when Polly called in an order, he leaped to his feet and returned to the stove. At least once, whenever she was on duty, he would disappear for twenty minutes upstairs to Corinne's apartment and return livelier than ever.

While he was gone, Polly had to do his job too, preparing the omelets and sandwiches and salads they served. But she had always hated to cook, and was glad when he returned, ordering her out of his kitchen.

He never failed to pinch her behind whenever she came into the kitchen, but Corinne told her not to mind, it was just his nature. "What do you expect, *chérie*, he's a lot younger than me, he's got energy to burn."

It was not the job Polly could see her perfect mother approving of, and she let a week pass before stopping by Perry Street. She was relieved that her mother wasn't at home. But before she could tell her father about the tea shop, he started railing against Elizabeth's latest cause, some zoning law to keep the Village brownstones from being converted into businesses. He warned Polly not to mention Eugene to her mother. Her brother was a sore point ever since they had gone up to dinner at Eugene and Clare's little apartment near Columbia. The two of them were about to graduate, and Elizabeth had learned that instead of Eugene becoming a writer, as mother and son had talked of, Clare had persuaded him to take a job, at least for awhile, so that she could fulfill her own ambitions and go on to graduate school.

"Your mother barely kept her mouth shut until we got out of there," her father said, "but once we were on our way home, Pol, you should have heard her." And he went on about how her mother was not as young as she had been, and less reasonable than ever. She hadn't even kissed Eugene when they left and hadn't stopped talking since about how that opinionated daughter-in-law had made their son into a lapdog and a mollycoddle. "I got nothin against that girl myself, she's Gene's choice after all—though it's true I prefer a lustier woman, like your mother."

Polly had never been so acutely aware that her father was getting older himself, and her mother, when she came in, didn't give her any chance to speak either, hardly bothering to say hello, in her anger over the latest news about the Seventh Avenue Improvement Association. After having made such big promises about beautifying the new avenue through the Village, someone had absconded with the funds appropriated for the project, even before the avenue was put in. "Nobody paid the slightest attention when I warned that the whole thing was a disaster. Boulevards of Paris, indeed!" Her mother flashed a look of scorn at Patrick.

Then her father complained that it was wrong of her to hold it against him. If he had got his deep-bore method through, they wouldn't have had to tear down a single house to put in the subway. "But they wouldn't listen to me, either," he said. "Did I ever tell ya, Pol, about the shipworm?"

When Polly was finally able to break in and tell them about her new job at the tea shop, her parents showed little interest. "You'd both love Corinne. She's so generous. She even gives out free soup to regulars who are down on their luck, 'starving artists' stew' she calls it. And the most amazing thing is, she was once our neighbor."

Her mother came to life. "Really? What did you say this woman's name was?"

"Corinne Ashmore. Don't you remember her?"

Her father's face turned deep red.

Elizabeth's voice was cold. "I thought she and that husband of hers had left town years ago."

"Oh, the husband's long out of the picture. He ran off with another woman."

Polly couldn't understand her parents' reaction, and when her mother was out of the room, she asked her father about it.

"I think ya better ask your friend Mrs. Ashmore that question," he answered without looking at her, and she couldn't get anything else out of him.

"*Eh, voilá*, that is the story," said Corinne, as Polly sat with her the next morning in the nearly-empty tearoom. "You are shocked, *hein?*"

"I'm stunned...," said Polly, her tea gone cold in front of her. Until now, Alicia, her long-dead sister had been little more to her than a faded portrait in the family album.

The proprietress sighed. "When Fleming cast her off so brutally, I should have been kinder to her, *pauvre enfant*. That I will always regret. But as for my abetting the little romance, that I do not regret for a moment.

Of course, I understand your mother's point of view. But I believe it is never wrong for a girl to be initiated into *l'amour* during her most impressionable years. Instead, in your puritan society, a girl is taught to be afraid of pleasure, close herself against it."

"You're so right!" Polly said, thrilled to hear the exact description of her own sexual problem. "I do wish something like that had happened to me when I was fourteen!"

The older woman studied her through the smoke of her cigarette. "Why do you say that?"

"Oh, I don't know. Things might have turned out so differently...," Polly said.

"Tell me," Corinne said.

Never in a million years could Polly have told her mother, but this Frenchwoman did not make her feel a fool, and she was able to talk about her experience with the young artist over the machine shop, and how, ever since, sex had been just as painful and humiliating, and she was afraid love was not in the cards for her because of her vaginismus.

"What nonsense are you talking?"

Polly gave her the clinical description from *Psychopathia Sexualis.*

Corinne lit a fresh cigarette with the stub of the old one and blew out the smoke. "Vaginismus they call it? Ridiculous! Men think women are a terrible complication. We're not so complicated."

"But, Corinne, I know what I feel! It's excruciating. It kills me!"

"Yes, *chérie*, I don't doubt it, but...." She looked around as Milos came up with a bottle of cognac and three glasses. Plunking them on the table he pulled out a chair.

Corinne's eyes flashed. "Shoo!" she said, waving him away. "We want to be private."

"Ah, only ladies!" Grinning, the muscular cook picked up his bottle and glasses and sat down at another table, where a bearded young man was writing away in a notebook. The young man looked up, annoyed.

"This bothers you?" Milos scowled, pouring out cognac and shoving the glass over to him.

Corinne watched him fondly. "It's a pity you've never known a man like that one, *chérie*," she said, taking Polly's hand.

On drizzling Village afternoons, when a drowsiness was in the air in the tea room, Polly and her employer had long talks about her sexual predicament. Only now, nearly twenty-four years old, was she beginning to learn the ABC's of it. Although she saw no solution to the problem, she began to feel less desolate about her life.

Meanwhile, she was meeting new people. A little acting company that performed in a loft nearby often came in after rehearsing, and one day one of them asked her if she'd like to help them out. Soon, her free time was taken up with painting sets, and pasting up announcements of their shows all over the Village, and even playing an occasional walk-on part.

6

Eugene and Clare graduated from college in June, 1912. The joint ceremony for both Barnard and Columbia was held on the steps of the Low Library overlooking the Common where the guests were seated on folding chairs, the ladies holding parasols against the morning sun.

Clare's parents had come by train from Cincinnati. Seated nearby between Patrick and Polly was Elizabeth in a wide-brimmed straw hat trimmed with damask roses. Though pretending to be in a festive mood, Elizabeth was annoyed, because her daughter-in-law, whom she knew to be nowhere near the intellectual equal of her son, was awarded a degree summa cum laude.

Clare was going on for a master's degree, while Eugene had a job as a copywriter with an advertising agency, arranged for him by his father-in-law, who was a college chum of the agency's president. It was agreed by everyone except Elizabeth that, given his literary bent, this would be an ideal job for Eugene, and at the same time he'd be getting in on the ground floor of a booming new profession.

But though the job turned out to be easy for Eugene and his superiors liked him, it didn't interest him very much, and with Clare spending most of her time in the college library, he found himself increasingly bored with nothing to do in the evenings.

One night when he'd gone down to the Village to have dinner with his parents, he and his mother got to talking about his writing again. Since he had so much free time on his hands, she suggested why didn't he try to write a magazine article on his late uncle Claude and the notorious Madame Averbach and her circle, back in the sixties. Eugene was enthusiastic.

"What do you want to do that for?" Clare asked, when him told her about it over breakfast the next morning. "They like you so much at the advertising agency. Why, if you put all your energies into it, you'd rise to the top in no time. Remember how everyone loved the copy you wrote for the Arrow shirt ad in Metropolitan Magazine? I wish you'd talked it over with me first, Gene. There was no need to go to your mother."

"But that's not it," he said, wanting his wife to understand, "it was really my idea. I've been thinking of free-lance writing for a long time. It was just that talking to mother reminded me of it."

"But why write about some uncle? Why do you think anyone would care?"

"I care! It's not just that he was my father's half brother, he was a colorful character. When you think about it, Uncle Claude was in at the start of the whole bohemian thing down in the Village."

She shook her head as she spread some toast with raspberry jam. "Honestly, you do sound just like your mother. Why not write about somebody who's really doing something with his life—Jack London, for example? Or William James?"

"Everybody's writing about them," said Eugene. "But this was my uncle. I can get all kinds of background from my mother."

"I'm sure she'll have lots to tell," Clare said, popping a piece of toast into her mouth.

He ignored her sarcasm. "Before my uncle died, he told her everything about his affair with a fantastic woman who got him addicted to opium. And I'll be able to work on it while you're studying."

His punctual wife began gathering up the dishes—her first class was in half an hour. "You should have told me before I started that you resented my going on to graduate school."

"Don't be silly. You know I'm glad you're going. This will keep me out of mischief nights, that's all."

"Well, I don't want to fight about it." On the way out, she pecked him on the cheek. "You have been understanding about my education. And I suppose it is important for a man to have a hobby."

Eugene began his project immediately. While Clare was off with her books, he started going down to the Village to record what his mother remembered about Claude Endicott and do research. Even though the local library on St. Luke's Place was in some disarray, with part of the building having been sliced off because it was in the path of the new avenue, he found scrapbooks of clippings in the archives from the middle of the previous century.

Walking around the streets where he had grown up and that had been his uncle's milieu so long before, he was struck by the numbers of odd-looking people who now lived in the area. In an attempt to appear artistic, men sported all kinds of costumes, with beards, capes, berets, and alligator-headed walking sticks. One young man he saw even went around dressed in an Elizabethan court jester's outfit with a lute over his shoulder.

Their girl friends were just as bizarre. They shadowed their eyes heavily with kohl, and their hair was cut shorter than the men's. Some of them painted their lips like prostitutes and wore fringed Spanish shawls with tight skirts showing their ankles. From his mother's descriptions, he could imagine these same women in other costumes at Madame Averbach's salon, a half century before, embodying the fantasies of Edgar Allen Poe.

He located the house where Madame Averbach had lived south of Washington Square. It had gone downhill. It was now inhabited by several Italian families, and the ground floor had been converted into a live-poultry market. He had to step around crates of squawking chickens on the sidewalk, and a vat of boiling water where a woman was plucking feathers. The paint on the window frames and cornices was flaking, but the battered front door was still flanked by elegant colonettes, and the fanlight over the entranceway, though cracked, proclaimed an earlier grandeur, as did the tall French windows on the parlor floor, even though they were now hung with laundry. Eugene tried to imagine his morbid young uncle who looked so much like Poe first taking to the opium pipe here.

But though his interest in the research continued, as he absorbed the atmosphere of the old Village on his free evenings, a disturbing presence began to make itself felt. At first, he couldn't put his finger on just what it was. It was as if digging up the old foundations of the demolished streets, where Seventh Avenue was being bulldozed through, had exposed to the glare of the streetlamps a certain kind of inhabitant that until now had been invisible.

He had heard these men joked about, but they had never impinged on his world before. They were almost indistinguishable from everyone else, yet now that he was aware, he wondered how he could have missed them. These men seemed to be everywhere, on every street, lurking in every shadow. They had the stark fascination of something every fiber of his being was repelled by, but no matter how hard he tried, he couldn't keep from looking at them. And yet it was those outcast eyes that made him so uneasy. Why were they looking at him?

He found himself loitering on his way back to the uptown el station on Fourteenth Street, falling into a slower step as if waiting for something to happen, he didn't know what. And then, one night, he stopped himself just in time from going into one of their bars.

He went home in a sweat of self-disgust, sick over his morbid curiosity about such things. Clare was already asleep. Without bothering to wake her, he threw himself on top of her in his need to empty himself of the images that throbbed in his head.

He was through before his wife was fully awake. She was frightened and bewildered by his irrational behavior. He felt dirty, dishonest, as he muttered something about not being able to control himself when he saw her sleeping there. She looked at him uncertainly—she had never gotten such a compliment from him before. But his agitation was too visible to deny, and she pulled his head awkwardly to her breast and said what an impetuous boy he was.

Six weeks later, when there was no doubt that she was pregnant, she was furious that he hadn't withdrawn early, the method they had always followed. She didn't want a child now. She wanted her Master's degree first.

But Eugene, though outwardly shamefaced, was reassured about himself. It was a confirmation of the manliness he had begun to doubt. He had awakened from a nightmare, and was grateful that he would be kept busy in the future by the needs of a growing family.

In spite of the disruption of pregnancy, Clare went on with her studies, determined to get as much credit as she could before she was forced to take a maternity leave. But Eugene, much as he wanted to settle down to writing the piece about his Uncle Claude—he had all the notes he needed by now—was drawn back against his will to the night streets of Greenwich Village. No longer fooling himself with any illusion that he was gathering material, he stayed out later and later roaming the darker byways, his eyes covertly seeking out this strange brotherhood. But when one of them met his eyes, he quickly looked away. They had chosen a life that cut them off from all respectable society. He would never do that.

One night, as though he had been waiting for something to happen, he was on Greenwich Avenue heading for the elevated, when a man not much older than himself—without any of the obvious signs like red tie, wristwatch, too dandyish clothes—passed him from behind, then a little way ahead stopped at a drugstore window. The man pretended to be studying a display of liniments, but as Eugene went by, glanced back at him. With thudding heart, Eugene stopped at the next shop window and saw in the glass the man's reflection walking slowly past him, before stopping at the next window and looking back again.

At the last window before the elevated stairs, where Eugene feigning interest in a collection of men's hats, the man came up beside him and pulled out a cigarette. "Got a light?" he said, his eyes holding Eugene's.

For a moment, Eugene was rooted to the spot, then turned and fled up the grimy, iron staircase, dropping a nickel in the turnstile with a shaking hand, not breathing until he was on the train, the doors shut, roaring northward through the night.

When he got home, again in a panic, he threw himself on his sleeping wife, who once more took his desperation for passion. But before he came, he froze, realizing he was imagining the young man in his arms. Sickened, he turned away and began to smash the pillow with his fists, breathing hard through clenched teeth.

"Gene! Stop it," Clare cried. "What are you doing?"

He fell into the pillow, his voice muffled. "I'm sorry...I'm sorry...It's got nothing to do with you."

He was ashamed to tell her what was wrong, he said. It was unspeakable. But Clare persisted, reminding him that she had studied psychology and that all problems, no matter how dreadful they seemed, could be solved.

"But it's contemptible! I hate myself!"

His wife was wide-eyed. "What on earth have you done?"

He hadn't done anything, he said. It was what was in his mind,

Clare was obviously relieved. If he hadn't done anything, she said, there was nothing to worry about. What was in his mind was only imagination. He could tell her. She was his wife. She would understand.

Finally, he sat up on the edge of the bed and began to talk, revolted at the way it must sound to her—what had been going on, and that he was afraid he might be like them.

"I knew this whole writing project was absurd!" she burst out. "Why did your mother ever put you up to it!" But she immediately controlled herself and moved over to sit beside him, taking his hand and making him look at her. "I realize you've been under a strain, Gene, and I blame myself. I've been too busy with school to give you the attention you need. I don't think it's so terrible. It's normal for a man to go through a crisis when he's going to become a father. You're taking on a great responsibility, and those morbid people your mother suggested you write about, it's led you in the wrong direction."

His voice was barely audible. "Please don't talk about my mother. She's not to blame for this."

"Of course she isn't." His young wife put her arms around him. "I am. What you need is all the love I can give you. That will drive those silly thoughts out of your mind."

He looked around at her abjectly. "You mean you don't want to leave me?"

"Of course not, you dunce! You've done nothing to be ashamed of and you never will. Let me make us some camomile tea."

Later, when they lay in bed at dawn, listening to the clop of the milkman's horse and wagon in the street below, and the clinking of the bottles as he dropped them into the wooden boxes at the front door, Clare suggested to him that if he was still concerned he might talk it over with Dr. Bieler, her psychology professor and graduate advisor, who would convince him that he had blown this thing up out of all proportion.

But while Eugene was relieved at how his wife had taken it, he knew she wasn't facing up to the seriousness of the problem. Bringing it out in the open had made it more real to him, and although he did not go down to the Village all the next week, neither could he bring himself to touch her.

The following Friday was his twenty-fourth birthday and Clare made a point of staying home from her classes and fixing a special dinner. He was uneasy from the moment he opened his eyes that morning and she greeted him with a tender birthday kiss.

All day at the advertising agency, he dreaded the evening to come. They ate by candlelight with champagne afterward, but though she made a show of light-hearted banter, he felt her eyes were watching him.

Later, she changed into a new nightdress—it was peach colored with ruffles and made him nauseous—and she smiled at him from the bed, her hair carefully tumbled about her on the pillow.

He was beyond sorrow as he got into bed, switched the light off and mumbling good-night, turned away from her. He lay there listening to the ticking of the clock, wondering how long she would wait.

"I've tried, Gene," she said, snapping on the light at last, "but I really don't think it's all my fault." When he didn't answer, she let him have it. Not only had she given him plenty of time to pull himself together, but he hadn't even made the least effort. He hadn't gone to see Dr. Bieler when she'd made a special appointment for him, and for days he had treated her like she wasn't even there, knowing the pressure she was under, wanting to do everything she could to help. He hadn't given her a chance. Not once had he reached out.

When he didn't respond, she went out of control. She didn't know him any more. Where was she supposed to fit into all this? Was he doing it just to defy her? And just when she needed him most to take over while she was having his baby. What kind of a man was he? The baby needed a father who was a real man, not a pansy.

When he still kept his back to her, she yelled, "Well, I'm fed up! I'm going home to Cincinnati if you don't want me."

"Maybe you ought to," he said quietly, not caring. He had known it was coming. He had listened to everything and it had made no impression. His marriage was dead to him. He wanted it to be over.

Clare stopped and caught her breath. "I didn't mean that. I don't want to leave." She was waiting, wanting him to take it back. But he didn't—it was too late. "You really want me to go then?" He had never seen her so close to tears before.

Sitting up, he told her that while she was waiting for the baby it would be the best thing. In a few months, she wouldn't be able to climb the four flights of stairs anyway, and it wasn't a bad idea for her to be with her mother during this time. It would be better all around. Once the baby came and she was ready to come home, he'd have a larger apartment waiting and he would give up the writing project and do whatever she wanted.

"All right," she said in a small voice, as she sat on the bench of her vanity table, looking at him through eyes full of tears, her hair in disarray around her thin shoulders in the ruffled peach peignoir. "When you're ready for me you can find me out in Cincinnati with my mother." She smiled at him bravely, but it was evident to both of them that her studies in modern psychology had not given her all the answers.

7

As soon as Clare left, Eugene gave up the little apartment near Columbia and moved back in with his family on Perry Street. He explained to his parents that it was Clare's decision to have the baby at her mother's, but the more reasons he gave to explain her departure, the less credible it sounded to him.

His father raised his predictable objections that his grandchild was going to be born so far away, and what were these newfangled ideas that a wife had to be separated from her husband just because she was having a baby? But his mother, who had listened in tactful silence, gave his father one of her looks and said she thought it a perfectly wise thing to do under the circumstances, and refrained from making any other comments at all.

With his mother there to talk it over with and to encourage him whenever he ran out of steam, Eugene finally was able to start writing the article about Madame Averbach and his Uncle Claude. As the piece took shape, his identification with his long-dead uncle grew—it became clear that Claude was just as confused about life as he was. He even started to let his hair grow like Claude's in an old daguerreotype and wore a flowing tie which, considering some of the odd outfits to be seen on the streets of the Village, attracted no attention. But at the advertising agency the long hair and the tie aroused some disapproving looks. He just didn't care. He disliked the job and knew his days there were numbered.

He felt that this temporary separation from Clare was exactly the right thing and their correspondence was frequent and friendly. Clare wrote him from Cincinnati that she, too, thought it was for the best. From a distance, she had gained some perspective and saw that her overinvolvement in her graduate studies had become obsessive, which in itself would be reason enough to make him feel neglected. Although she was looking forward to motherhood—her mother was fixing up an extra bedroom as a nursery— she couldn't wait until the baby was old enough to travel and she could come back to him, and the three of them would all be together to begin a new life and make a real marriage.

As Eugene worked into the late hours in his old room on the third floor, he had never been more sure of his love for her. Although he had made an appointment to see her Professor Bieler right after she left, when he started working on the article he felt his problems flying away, and he canceled the appointment. Putting everything he had into his writing was exactly what he needed, he wrote her. Even this period of celibacy was a necessary factor, so that all his energies could flow into his development as a writer. He told her that he no longer had any curiosity in exploring the depravity of the Village streets. He wondered now how he ever could have given two cents about it.

When his essay was finished, his mother found it remarkable and insisted he show it to his old English advisor at Columbia. The professor thought the piece had real merit and passed it along to the editor of The Masses, whom he knew from Harvard. Stunned, Eugene read and reread the note that came from Max Eastman accepting the piece for the magazine. It would fit perfectly into the issue they were currently putting together, the editor wrote.

Gene had heard of The Masses—it had something to do with the Liberal Club and political protest—but he had never bothered to read it. All he knew was that its circulation was small. His mother said that wasn't the point—the magazine represented the avant-garde in the world of ideas and the arts, and it was a greater tribute to him than if it had been taken by The Saturday Evening Post.

He went to their offices over on Charles Street, met Eastman, and readily agreed to some minor changes in grammar and construction.

It was his sister Polly who was the first to see the article in print. At that time, she had a one-line part in a play called "Hobohemia," written by a member of her little theater company named Sinclair Lewis. The director of the play turned out to be a proofreader in his spare time for The Masses, and he had brought her a set of the galleys. She rushed over to her parents' house and read it aloud from beginning to end to the family at the dinner table. Eugene listened in awe to what he had created. It sounded completely professional.

After the magazine came out, he didn't know what he expected to happen. But when nothing did happen, as if that particular issue of the magazine had dropped into the sea without a ripple, his mother said he mustn't expect immediate acclaim, and the best thing to do was begin another article at once. Why not try a piece on Henry James? His late aunt Veronica had practically had a love affair with him.

But her advice was no consolation. He felt like a failure. He didn't want to write anything else. The more he thought about it, he didn't even want his wife to come back. His job at the advertising agency became more meaningless than ever, as he sat in the office trying to think up a reason anyone would want to drink Dr. Dooley's Sarsaparilla.

The next day, along with the usual fat letter from Cincinnati, his mother handed him a stiff, gold-trimmed envelope with his name and address written in purple ink in a flowing hand. Inside was a personal note.

> *Dear Eugene Endicott,*
> *Max brought me the latest issue of The Masses and I read your illuminating piece. You made that period come alive for me. I had no idea there was anyone in the Village like Madame Averbach back then. By coincidence, I have a few people in myself on Thursday evenings.*
> *Won't you do us the honor of joining us this Thursday? I'd love to meet you.*
> *With my warmest regards, Mabel Dodge*

His mother was ecstatic. She knew all about Mrs. Dodge, whose Thursday salon was reported in the papers. She was a wealthy hostess from Buffalo, who lived on lower Fifth Avenue across from the elegant Brevoort Hotel and entertained not only people from the arts and literary worlds, but political radicals and even members of high society. Her lover was reputed to be the hotheaded radical writer, John Reed, years younger than she was.

For Eugene, the invitation was like a trumpet announcing a change in his destiny. Mrs. Dodge thought it a coincidence that her evening was the same as Madame Averbach's, but in his new identification with his Uncle Claude, he saw it as inevitable that he should find his own Madame Averbach.

When he left the house on that first Thursday evening in early September, his mother gazed after him mistily, as if he were indeed the reincarnation of Claude and he were setting out to continue the life of the romantic young man who had died too soon.

And when he entered the drawing room and saw the hundred twinkling candles in the famous chandelier with brightly-enameled birds perched all over it, it was as if he were stepping back into that earlier salon in 1864. Even if it was really 1914 and the guests were in modern dress, it made no difference.

A panel discussion of some sort had just broken up and chairs were being pushed back against the wall. People were arguing about a silk workers' strike in Paterson, New Jersey—a man even jumped onto a table and started haranguing everyone to get out on the picket lines and show some solidarity. Servants were maneuvering through the guests with trays full of champagne, and a glass was put in Eugene's hand.

For a while, he was cornered by a woman with bitten fingernails who talked of nothing but the war that had just broken out in Europe, and told him that unless he agitated against it, he would be prime cannon fodder.

It was his editor, Max Eastman, who rescued him, telling him he must meet his hostess. Eastman was bald with steel-rimmed glasses, and though Eugene didn't know it, he could have passed for Claude Endicott's chubby guide in outrageous red velvet jacket back at Madame Averbach's salon.

People called Mabel Dodge The Sphinx, Eastman said, as he led Eugene over to her circle. She had incredible intuition, he would see for himself.

And then Eugene was before her. Mrs. Dodge was a majestic woman, big-boned in flowing draperies, but it was her eyes Eugene saw. Though they were small and shrewd, they were painted like an Egyptian queen's, extended with black lines and shadowed with purple and green.

"Here's a riddle for The Sphinx," Eastman said, pushing him forward into the center of the group surrounding her.

"Don't tell me,"—Mrs. Dodge smiled, taking both his hands—"you are Eugene Endicott." She spoke in a straightforward midwestern accent that lacked the cultivated tone he had expected.

"Mabel, you amaze me," said Eastman. "How did you know that?"

"I know many things about Mr. Endicott." She turned on Eugene an expression which, even more than her exotic eyes, made him understand why she was called The Sphinx. Running a finger around the line of his jaw, she said, "I knew from the way you write you had to be beautiful."

Eugene had never been called beautiful. He would never think of himself that way—if the word could be applied to a man at all. People like his friend Toby were beautiful, people with classical features and athletic bodies.

Mrs. Dodge said she wanted him all to herself, and sent Eastman away to cheer up "that poor little waif in the corner. Her name's Fanny Hurst. She writes sentimental little stories in the magazines. Dreadful!"

The other guests who had been standing around her turned away to talk among themselves, leaving Eugene alone with his hostess.

As her eyes, which the cosmetic paint seemed to enlarge into hypnotic moons, encouraged him, he told her how he had come to write the article.

She couldn't help feeling a certain kinship with that Averbach woman, Mrs. Dodge said, though Adele was a great beauty and Mrs. Dodge didn't pretend to be any such thing. When he tried to protest, she said she wasn't fishing for compliments. She wasn't ruling herself out by any means. She had her work too—to create a stimulating ambience for the arts and for the exchange of ideas. That's what her get-togethers were for, to create an Athens on the Hudson. When she asked what he was writing now, Eugene told her about the Henry James essay and, stimulated by her luminous attention, became excited about it for the first time himself.

Other guests competing for her attention soon gathered round and Mrs. Dodge had to relinquish him, though not before she gave him orders to circulate and meet all her special people.

And meet them Eugene did, though he couldn't forget her and kept looking back to catch sight of her—not a steel butterfly like Madame Averbach, but there was steel in her, and mystery too, as Eastman said, behind that robust personality.

He was introduced to the novelist Theodore Dreiser, who told him that the best advice he had for a young writer like him was to apply the seat of his pants to the seat of his chair, and not get into a rigamarole like that pantywaist Henry James—just tell his story straight out.

Across the room, a giant of a man with an eye patch, was flirting with a gaggle of young women around him. Eugene recognized him from his picture in the papers. He was Big Bill Haywood, the famous union leader, founder of the "Wobblies," the International Workers of the World, who was described in the press as a mad anarchist out to destroy everything America stood for.

Not far away, John Sloan, the leader of the notorious Ashcan school of painters, was hotly defending avant-garde French artists, names Eugene had heard of, like Marcel Duchamp, Braque and Seurat, who had been shown for the first time in America at the Armory show. The show had been a year ago, but they were still being ridiculed in the papers.

People around him were discussing all kinds of things that were not mentioned in polite company—abortion for one. Eugene overheard Margaret Sanger, a harmless-looking little woman who had been thrown into jail several times, asserting every woman's right to birth control. Another firebrand was loudly condemning the munitions makers who were trying to drag America into the war that had just broken out in Europe.

Eugene recognized the man who had written the play his sister Polly was in, though he didn't remember his name. He was red-haired and not much to look at with his acne scars. The man recognized Gene immediately, reminding him that his name was Sinclair Lewis. He told Gene that Mrs. Dodge had lived ten years in Italy where she had entertained Europe's aristocrats and bohemians at her villa in Florence. When Gene asked about her husband, Lewis laughed. "Dodge? She devoured him long ago. That's her current guy, Jack Reed. He's a real climber." Reed was at least twenty years younger than Mrs. Dodge, Eugene noted, intending to tell his mother later on, but he was devilishly good-looking, and from the way Mrs. Dodge kept bending toward him with total adoration, Eugene suspected that Reed was quite a lover.

Later, as he was saying goodbye to Mrs. Dodge, she clasped his hand with both of her own, fixing him once more with her remarkable painted eyes. "I'm so sorry we haven't had more time to talk, Eugene," she said. "You're a talented, beautiful, young man. You must promise to attend all my Thursdays from now on—I won't take no for an answer."

On his way home, the eyes of the woman they called The Sphinx pursued him. It didn't matter that he had babbled so foolishly about his pitiful essays to her, someone who knew the greatest writers of the time. She had asked him to come back. And she had called him talented. And beautiful.

He went again on the following Thursday and on the Thursday after. Mabel Dodge had already become the most important person in his life. In the evenings, while he worked on his James piece, his mother and father downstairs reading under their fringed lamps, he looked out over the moonlit ailanthus trees in the backyard, thinking about her, just as Claude must have thought about Adele Averbach, fifty years before—the pressure of her hand each time she greeted him, the way she always found a few minutes for him alone no matter how besieged she was by her illustrious company, the interest she always took in the progress of his work, her eyes that the theatrical makeup made luminous. She was the kind of woman he should have married. He believed now that it was an older woman he needed, just as Claude had.

One glorious autumn night, filled with the sudden possibilities of his life, he left off his writing and walked over to the Hudson river, wanting the freshness of the air, the solitude of the deserted waterfront. Along the river the covered piers were silvery in the moonlight. He walked out onto an open pier and gazed across the water at the lights of a ferryboat crossing to the Lackawanna ferry slip on the Jersey side and, farther up the river, the glittering lights of Luna Park with its roller coaster and Ferris wheel. He smelled the salt air of the Atlantic coming in with the tide from beyond the distant shapes of the Wall Street skyscrapers.

The headlight of a little tugboat putt-putting in to the pier to tie up for the night swept across the water and the weathered planks. It was the final touch, turning the night into a seascape by Albert Ryder. A seaman threw a rope onto the pier, then jumped across and looped it around the bollard closest to him.

"Looks like we're in for a cold snap," the seaman said to him, taking his pipe out of his pocket and hunkering down on the pier while he filled it.

Eugene went weak in the knees. He mumbled something and started walking away as casually as he could.

The lit windows of a diner across the street from the pier was a beacon in a night suddenly turned threatening. But the strong, black coffee he gulped down did not steady him. There was only one person he could think of who would hold back the night.

He gave the waitress a nickel to use the wall telephone, cranked for the operator who seemed never to come on, and when finally he had given the number, it rang for a long time before the voice of the butler answered.

Mrs. Dodge was with guests at dinner, the butler reported. If the caller left his name, he would give it to her later. But Eugene would not be put off and said it was an emergency.

"What is it, Eugene?" He heard the slight irritation in her voice.

"I've got to see you."

There was silence at the other end of the line. Finally, she spoke. "Very well." But he musn't come until eleven-thirty after her guests were gone.

He lost count of the number of cups of coffee he drank in the noisy cafeteria on Sheridan Square, waiting for the time to pass. Simply her telling him she would see him was enough to hang on to. The all-night cafeteria was a seedy place—the light bulbs hanging from the molded tin ceiling glared over the greasy marble tables and the floor was covered with sawdust and bits of spilled food. But it was crowded and anonymous and that was what he wanted. Occasionally, local characters stopped to pester him to buy a poem written on a napkin for a cup of coffee or simply to ask for a handout. But his eyes never left the hands of the clock on the wall.

When he arrived, Mrs. Dodge was still not free. As he was led across the foyer past the open doors of the drawing room, several of the guests in their formal evening clothes looked up curiously.

It was after midnight before she came into the library in a vivid, orange gown, apologizing for the delay.

Without waiting for her to arrange herself on the gilt settee, he started spilling out his writing plans, realizing that he had told it all to her before, but unable to stop. She was his inspiration, his goddess, he said—he could do nothing without her.

Mrs. Dodge, who listened as always with exquisite patience and tact as though she had never heard any of this before, protested that he was giving her far too much credit, that he was a gifted young man who would make his own mark quite as well without her encouragement.

No, Eugene pleaded. Without her nothing would be possible. She was the only woman in his life who mattered.

"But what about your wife?" she reminded him. "Max told me you were married."

That had nothing to do with it, he said, jumping up and going to the window to look down at the busy sidewalk café of the Brevoort Hotel across Fifth Avenue. His wife didn't appreciate the literary experience. She didn't understand anything about him. He had left her and was never going back to her.

He turned around to face Mrs. Dodge. Since writing the piece about his uncle and Madame Averbach, he said, he seemed to be reliving his uncle's life. The first time he walked into her drawing room he felt himself to be Claude.

"But don't carry it too far, Eugene. I'm not Madame Averbach."

"I know you're involved with someone else," he said, "but that doesn't matter. I mean...don't you see that I worship you. I think I'm in love with you!" He was shaking. The words that came out were just what he was feeling, though he hadn't known he was going to say them.

Mrs. Dodge smiled sadly. "Come sit beside me, Eugene."

Apprehensive, he did as he was told. As he sat with her on the settee, she seemed to loom larger, her essence filling the room.

"I'm perfectly willing to offer you the spiritual stimulation you need," Mrs. Dodge said, "but as to the physical, you don't love me that way at all, and I hope you're not confusing the two."

"But I'm not!" Eugene protested. "I mean I do need you, in every way. You're the only one who can help me!"

"Yes, of course," Mrs. Dodge said, "and I want to help you the best I can."

Eugene's flicker of uncertainty disappeared. "I knew you'd feel that way." He reached for her hand, but she gently withdrew it.

"I hope we'll always be friends, Eugene, but I'm going to speak frankly, even at the risk of losing your friendship."

He started to object, but she told him to pay attention. "I don't think anything I'm going to say will surprise you, though you may be shocked to hear it put into words. I've known a lot of young men like you, though very few as gifted as you are. You see, my dear, you don't want me in the way you imagine—and I don't think you want any woman that way."

He began to stammer, What was she saying? It was a lie, but she took his hand and held it firmly.

"Listen to me, Eugene, I know these things in my bones." And she told him there was nothing wrong with him, that people tormented themselves over such things unnecessarily, and the world was cruel about it. But there were many paths of love, and he had been trying to deny his. "Haven't your dreams been telling you what you really want?" she asked.

Panicking, he looked around for escape, but she held on to his hand and lifted his chin, forcing him to look into her eyes. "I'm right, aren't I?"

When he refused to answer, refused almost to listen to her—his mind rejecting the words—she told him that if he was going to develop as a writer or even just as a man, he had to accept all sides of himself. Of course it was tough, she said. He was going to have to fight the whole world, but there was nothing wrong with what he felt, and he would make himself sick over it, if he went on denying it.

Eugene kept his eyes on the floor, waiting for her to finish. Why was she going on this way, tearing apart the last shreds of his pride?

"And remember, it's not just men who feel these things," Mrs. Dodge said. "Women do as well. I've had some beautiful experiences with women myself."

He looked up in alarm, trying to connect her with what he had seen on the streets, those predatory eyes everywhere—he was revolted. And she was speaking about it as if it were a great adventure in self-exploration—as if it were something noble!

"You have to have the courage of your own way. There really are no rules in love, no matter what the world says." She laughed and her voice became more flat and midwestern. "I'll tell you this though, you're lucky to be living here in New York and not in Buffalo where I grew up."

He sprang to his feet. "You're all wrong!" he shouted, hating her, and stumbled his way to the door.

"Gene, dear!" Mrs. Dodge called, starting up after him, but he was already down the hall, passing the startled butler, and out the front door into the night.

In October during an early cold snap, Eugene was down in the cellar adding coal to the furnace, when the front door chimes sounded. There was no one else at home, so he banked the fire and went back upstairs.

It was the electrician, who had been working on the antiquated wiring in the house, come to install new fuse boxes. Eugene let him in and, leaving him to his work, went up to his room to get back to his Henry James piece. But however much he tried to concentrate, his mind kept flashing back to the humiliating interview with Mrs. Dodge, and he was relieved when he heard the electrician calling from downstairs. He jumped up and went out to see what the workman wanted.

"Would ya mind trying the lights up there?" the voice called from below. "I wanna see if I got it."

Eugene switched the lights in his room on and off. "Afraid they're not working," he called down.

"Shit!" came the electrician's voice. "Lemme turn off the juice, and

I'll be right up."

A moment later he was up the stairs, bending over to examine the light switch on the wall in Eugene's room. He was sturdily built in his overalls, with tools hanging from a leather belt. "Jesus, wonder this hasn't burned the house down," he said, looking back at Eugene. "When was it put in?"

"Must have been about thirty years ago," Eugene said. "Dad did all the wiring himself."

The electrician straightened up and took a pack of Lucky Strikes from his shirt pocket, shook one out, and stuck it between his lips. "We got a safety code we gotta follow now." He struck a match on the sole of his boot and cupped the flame to his cigarette. "I'd say we gotta change all the switches. I could start up here, ya give me the word."

"That's up to my dad," said Eugene. "I don't know anything about that stuff." He wanted to get back to his desk, but the man just stood there, looking at him.

"Expect him back soon?"

"I'm not sure. He's down at City Hall."

"No problem. I can fix you up some light meanwhile."

But the electrician seemed in no hurry, and exhaled a slow stream of smoke. Eugene didn't know how to tell him to get on with the job.

The man looked around, taking in the desk covered with Eugene's papers and an empty coffee cup. "This your room?" Now the man was looking at him again.

Eugene gave a nervous laugh. "It's kind of a mess, isn't it?"

"You some kind of professor?"

"Actually...," Eugene swallowed, his heart pounding, "I'm trying to write a piece for a magazine. Not getting very far...."

"You a magazine writer, huh?" the electrician said. "That takes brains. Me, I'm only good using my hands."

Eugene swallowed again. The man was just standing there.

"You're a nice looking kid, you know that?" He was grinning.

Eugene couldn't get out a word. He saw the stubble on the unshaven jaw.

The man leaned around to stub his cigarette out in the empty coffee cup on the desk. He turned back. "How about me closing the door?"

In the years to come Eugene relived what happened next a million times. It was all over so fast, and then the man was gone. They had done little more than fumble clumsily with each other, but it had transformed his life forever.

In his room afterwards, he didn't know what to do. He flung himself down on the bed, jumped up again, looked at his startled, disheveled self in the bureau mirror, went over to throw up the window sash and leaned out to take in gulps of the cold air. It was the most tremendous thing that had ever happened to him! He longed for it to happen again, but he was sure it never would.

Two days later, when the electrician was back in the cellar finishing up the job, Eugene sat in the living room, forcing himself to sit still as he pretended to read, but trembling with every sound that came from below. His mother knitting across from him asked if he'd mind going downstairs to put some more coal in the furnace. He stared at her, wondering if she was reading his mind. He got up too fast, made himself walk normally to the door.

Going down the cellar stairs, he kept his eyes on the furnace. His face was burning when he opened the furnace door, but it was more than the reflection of the fire. He shoveled in some coal, then turned back to the stairs.

"Your lights okay up there?" The electrician was grinning at him, over by the fuse box.

Eugene made a move toward him.

"What about your ma?" The man's voice was husky.

"She's not coming down," Eugene said, and this time, he was the one who reached for the man.

Through the mica panel in the door of the furnace, the coal was crackling as it caught fire, shooting hot steam through the tangle of pipes throughout the house.

The blood was pounding so loud in his head, he didn't hear the footsteps in the hall above, the opening of the cellar door, but suddenly a shaft of brilliant light shot down on the two men at the bottom of the stairs, their clothes torn open.

Patrick was about to call down to ask how the job was going, when the words froze in his throat as the light illuminated his son and the electrician doing something that turned his stomach.

For Eugene, the next few minutes were a blur. Somehow he got up the stairs, past his father who was rooted to the spot, and on up to his room. He scrawled a note for his mother, grabbed his wallet and his jacket, and was back down to the hall again, heading for the front door.

His mother was in the door of the living room, a skein of wool unraveling from her hand. "Eugene! Whatever in the world…?"

But he was already out of the house and down the steps to the street.

At the corner of Hudson Street, he shouted for a motor taxicab, and as one chugged over to him, he leapt in, even before the vehicle had come to a full stop.

In Montreal, bleary from a sleepless all-night train ride up from New York, he enlisted in the Royal Canadian Ambulance Corps. Before he left on the troop ship for France, he wrote to his wife that he had come to a decision for a divorce and explained why, wishing a good life for her and their child soon to be born.

He sent one more letter, to his sister.

8

Polly was just about to open the envelope with the Montreal postmark, when there was a crash from the back of the tea shop. As if things weren't bad enough already since Corinne had left, she ran back to the kitchen to find pancake batter all over the floor and the new kitchen boy trying to shovel it up with a spatula.

She pushed him aside, telling him that she could do it better with one hand behind her back, and started cleaning it up herself, as the boy stood by apologizing. He didn't know the first thing about working in a kitchen, though when she had hired him he swore that he had been a short order cook back wherever the hell he came from. She mopped the floor, furious at herself for being so gullible.

The boy had practically begged her for the job. New to the city, just in from the corn belt, his name was Larry Mathews and he claimed to be nineteen, though he looked younger—a wholesome, corn-fed kid, a little too anxious to please. He had come to New York to become a painter, or so he said, and showed her some not-very-good pen-and-ink sketches. She had briefly considered the possibility of training him to be her cook. Well, that little illusion was knocked for a loop.

Polly had never wanted to take over running the tea shop. She had liked things the way they were, with Corinne in charge and the mad Hungarian keeping the kitchen humming—if that was the word for it—leaving her plenty of time for her little theater group, which had become more important to her. At the time Corinne left, Polly had been offered her first real part, not the usual walk-on, but she had to turn it down.

It didn't matter that Milos and Corinne, one as temperamental as the other, brawled in front of the customers. They always made it up and for a while went around twittering like lovebirds. It was only when he began to stay away from The Teaspoon after their fights that things had gotten bad. There was another woman, Corinne told Polly. Corinne had always known about her. The woman lived somewhere over in New Jersey, but as long as he only spent an occasional night there, it was of no concern to Corinne. When Polly looked shocked at this, she had laughed and said there was plenty of Milos for her and the other woman, plenty for a dozen women in fact.

But Milos's visits to New Jersey grew more frequent, as the summer heat drove the temperature up in the airless cellar tea shop. As the "coffee breaks" up in Corinne's room got rarer, the fights got worse. Several times, Polly was awakened in the middle of the night by the two of them yelling at each other. Corinne swore at him in French, while he let loose a string of Hungarian expletives before storming out, declaring she was a bloodsucking capitalist and he was never coming back to such an exploiter.

Polly, feeling sorry for Corinne, who was showing the strain, got up her nerve and told Milos one day in the kitchen that he wasn't being fair. He turned on her and called her a bourgeois pig and what did she know about it anyway, and then had announced, so everyone in the restaurant could hear, that all any woman wanted was his cock, half the world would crawl on their bellies for it. And his hearty laughter filled the tea shop.

He began staying away for days at a time. Polly asked Corinne how they were going to manage with him gone so much. But her employer, whose orange frizz of hair was tied back with a ribbon as she dripped oil into the egg yolks she was beating for mayonnaise, told her he'd be back, *chérie*, he always came back.

And he did come back, right in the middle of the noon rush, wearing a fitted velvet jacket with a brocade vest and bowler hat, looking like a dashing confidence man. Putting on his apron, he shoved Corinne aside and, with a wink, said he'd been away on monkey business.

Finally, his visits upstairs stopped altogether and he was hardly ever at the tea shop. Corinne still carried on as if nothing was wrong, saying he was a selfish oaf but he needed her as much as she needed him. But Polly saw her go up to the street now and then to look for him. Corinne even took the ferry over to New Jersey one day, saying she had paid him a month in advance and wasn't going to let him steal from her.

To Polly's surprise, she actually located him and brought him back. He stayed for a time, grudgingly, and the fights went on. Every customer felt the sting of his contempt. But the visits upstairs were not resumed. Even with all her face paint on, the dark circles under the Frenchwoman's eyes could not be hidden.

One day after one of their fights, Milos shut off all the burners on the range, threw his chef's apron on the floor, and said, "I take no more of this shit!"

Corinne said she wouldn't give him a cent if he walked out on her without notice. They argued in front of the patrons, until he pushed her out of his way, took some bills from the cash drawer which he claimed she owed him, and started out. In a fury, she hung on to his arm, screaming "*Cochon!*" and that she was calling the police. It had been the worst ever. She clawed at his face, he grabbed at her red frizzy hair and, to Polly's horror, it came off in his hand, a wig, leaving her like a plucked chicken with only some wisps of gray hair, the paint she covered her face with ending abruptly at the hairline.

Even Milos was mortified and tried to put the wig back on her head, but she got it away from him and tried to hit him with it. Polly put her arms around her and she started to cry.

"I good cook. I good man," the cook said, "but she want slave." And he walked out for the last time.

After that, Polly watched helplessly as the Frenchwoman let herself go, not bothering to wear her corset, giving up on the face paint, haggard. Corinne spent most of the time in her room, and every morning there was an empty cognac bottle thrown out in the trash. Polly had to manage as best she could with a succession of temporary cooks, because Corinne still had a glimmer of hope that Milos might come back.

It was the news of the outbreak of war in Europe and German troops crossing into France that rallied her. Corinne bought a new red wig, made herself a stylish traveling suit on her old dress form, and with pins in her mouth told Polly she was going home to take care of her old mother and sister in Armentières. Until the war was over, Polly was to run the shop for her and send her money every month. Polly was going to be on her own now, but she was not to forget what Corinne had taught her, that where men were concerned, she must always think of her own pleasure first.

The last thing Corinne said on that crisp autumn day, before they hugged good-bye on the pier, was that there was no need for Polly to worry about her at all. In France, a woman of her age was not considered garbage, like she was in this lousy country.

As the French liner full of anxious Europeans returning home pulled away from the dock, Corinne waved confidently from the rail, looking years younger in an extravagant cartwheel hat with a saucy plume, ready to defy all the armies of the night.

After she finished cleaning up the spilled pancake batter, Polly sent the apologetic young Larry Mathews out to wait on tables and took over the cooking herself.

She closed the tea shop early that evening because she was exhausted. If she were going to open up for breakfast she had to get some rest. She was just about to turn out the lamp beside her bed, when she remembered Eugene's letter and retrieved it from the pocket of her dress.

She was relieved he had written, because he had run off so unexpectedly the week before. All the note he had left behind said was that he was going to Canada to enlist in the war.

It had made no sense at all—not that she'd had much time to think about it. Just when things seemed to be going so well with him after having broken into print. He had given up the advertising job he hated and was devoting all his time to his writing.

She had never seen her father so stricken. What's more, he refused to talk about it, even to her.

The letter from Montreal began innocuously enough. He was writing to her, Eugene said, because she was the best one to explain to their mother about it. But when she read what her father had had to witness in the basement, Polly was so aghast she could hardly make herself read on, as her brother tried to justify himself. The only possible explanation was that he had gone berserk. Actually saying he had known for some time what was wrong with him, but hadn't been able to admit it to himself!

Why, he was nothing at all like those people! She saw them in the tea shop all the time. She knew them in her acting group. They could be fun, the way they carried on—hilarious even—but they were freaks! Eugene was nothing like that. He was her brother. Besides, he was married, and he was about to become a father. It had to be some kind of temporary aberration, something he would get over.

She flopped back on the pillow, crumpling the letter in her hand.

But how could he have done it to them? Their parents were getting old now—her heart ached for her father. No wonder he hadn't mentioned Gene once since that dreadful moment. With his heart condition this might kill him. And Gene expecting her to tell their mother, as if it was just some schoolboy prank?

Polly snapped off the lamp and tried to settle down, but sleep was impossible.

Invert. Nancy-boy. Fairy. The ugly words mocked her through the sleepless hours.

As she flicked impatiently at the bric-a-brac on the mantelpiece with a feather duster, Elizabeth repeated for the hundreth time in the last week, "Whatever made him go off to that horrible war without even a word?"

Patrick, who was sitting in his chair doing absolutely nothing, muttered, as he had been doing all week, that it was the best thing he could have done.

She tossed the duster aside and turned to face him. "Will you stop saying that? He is your son!" But she couldn't get another word out of him and, exasperated, went upstairs looking for more work to do.

Polly hadn't opened the tearoom that morning and had sent young Larry Mathews off to the Metropolitan Museum for the day. Coming in the front door of her parents' house, Polly called out hello, but got no answer. She found her father alone in the living room. When she saw how bewildered and old he looked hunched over in his chair, she leaned over and put her arms around him. "How awful for you, papa," she said.

Hearing about her letter from Gene, he looked away and said it wasn't fit for a girl like herself to hear such things, let alone to have such a brother.

It was better she did know, she told him. She didn't want him to have this burden all to himself. She asked him to wait for her downstairs while she went up to talk to her mother.

"What do you mean he sent you a letter?" Elizabeth snapped. "Why on earth hasn't he written to me? I'm his mother. Not a word, not a single word. What's got into him?"

"I'm trying to tell you, mother, if you'll give me a chance."

Elizabeth stopped, hearing the authority in her daughter's voice. Until this minute, she had never thought of her as a grown woman. She listened as Polly told her the gist of the letter, not saying a word.

"It's some kind of rebellion against papa," Polly said, "some horrible insanity. It's heartless."

Elizabeth didn't hear her. She sat with her hands folded. "My poor boy," she said at last, almost to herself.

"How can you say such a thing?" At that moment Polly loathed her mother. "What he did was vile, absolutely vile. If I weren't—"

The postman's whistle interrupted them and Elizabeth, coming alive, hurried downstairs to intercept the mail. "Maybe he's written," she called over her shoulder.

When Polly followed after her, Elizabeth was standing with a letter in her hand, calling Patrick to listen. Polly's first thought was that Eugene must have written to her mother after all and the foolish woman meant to subject her father to it, in spite of what he'd already gone through.

But the letter was not from Eugene. It was from Cincinnati. Clare's baby had been born.

"It's a boy," said Elizabeth, her eyes blinking away the possibility of tears, "and she's naming him Seth." She forced a brave smile. "Oh, dear God, if only Eugene had stayed long enough to hear this."

As Polly took her father's arm—she could feel him trembling—she was furious thar her mother was taking her usual unrealistic attitude, as if that miserable baby's arrival at such a time was anything to celebrate.

9

The spring day in 1916 was cold, raw even, but as Patrick strolled back from Sheridan Square in his formal clothes, the crisp air invigorated him and he filled his lungs with it. That morning, he and other pioneers of city transit had been honored at the ceremony to inaugurate the opening of the new IRT subway station in the Village. After being presented with the Knickerbocker Medal by the Mayor, they sat back in their top hats on the dais, tolerating with amusement the self-congratulatory speeches of younger engineers, who addressed the gathering as if the old-timers had never existed and the subway had been their idea all the time.

Patrick was seventy. He had officially retired five years before, but that hadn't kept him away from the subway construction site on Seventh Avenue during that time. It was his baby after all, and they needed a man of his experience around, even if they weren't always smart enough to take his advice. He had had the idea of a New York subway before any of them were dirty thoughts in their papa's minds. It might have taken them a while to get around to it, but finally he had gotten some recognition.

"Oh, Mr. Endicott, you were the handsomest man on the platform," said a buxom neighbor lady in the dispersing crowd, "but don't tell Elizabeth I said so." She had the look in her eye that made him know she meant it.

He certainly wouldn't tell his wife—Elizabeth couldn't abide the woman. "Ah, ya mustn't turn my head now, Caroline. A fine-lookin woman like yourself is in danger if ya give me such ideas." He was sure he detected a trace of a blush in her cheek.

As he continued his walk up the street, he felt the appreciative glances of everyone he passed. He knew he made a fine figure of a man in his morning suit with the striped trousers rented for the occasion. The spats were his own. Cleaned up, they looked as new as ever, though he had bought them for Tom's funeral, sixteen years before.

With his walking stick he nudged an old dog snoozing in the middle of the sidewalk. The dog stared up at him reproachfully with its one good eye before waddling out of his way.

Patrick had the girth suitable to his dignity. The suit hire had to let out the trousers, but there still wasn't an ounce of fat on him. Even with his beer belly, he was as solid as he had been when he first went to work for the elevated. He was randier at his age than other men at thirty. Elizabeth still got skittish every time he looked at her.

He knew she had been truly happy for him today. They'd had their little tiffs over the years—with her crackpot ideas about wanting to keep the neighborhood stuck in the nineteenth century. But when the Mayor called him "one of the visionaries of municipal transportation" and presented him with the medal, he could see tears in her eyes. After the ribbon-cutting ceremony at the subway entrance, and after he had come back up from the subway platform where the official party had welcomed the first train through the new station, Elizabeth told him to forget all their differences over the subway, she was so proud of him, and she had sent him off to Jack Delaney's bar with several of his colleagues who had been honored with him. There, between toasts, they had recalled the old days when they were putting up those first els, trying to make practical sense out of the muddled blueprints, and finally doing it their own way.

All along the street, neighbors and friends kept stopping him to shake his hand and congratulate him. With the new subway, the neighborhood was sure to revive, they all told him, and they had him to thank for it. He walked on, feeling like he had never retired at all.

It had been a good life, a few vicissitudes along the way—they came to every man—but all in all he hadn't done so bad for a lad from Shamrock Alley, born without a pot to piss in. He had worked at the profession he wanted, and succeeded at it—not every man could say that. He was married to a superior woman. And his children? Well, they took ya up and they took ya down, but who said it was supposed to be any other way? On this superb spring day, all the sorrows were forgotten, and he thought back pleasurably to the time he had taken little Jack to visit the elevated, when they were putting it up on Sixth Avenue. Now there was a smart kid for ya, smarter when he was ten than some of those younger engineers who had been shooting off their mouths today. And snippy little Alicia at her birthday party, when Billy Yates came in drunk that time, the divil. And Polly, the little monkey, with her freckles and red hair, crawling all over him.

He turned on to Perry Street. That was some cock-and-bull story about old Albert Elizabeth had tried to sell him when she was peeved that time. He gave a lamppost a whack with his walking stick. Oh, he'd put all that behind him years ago. He supposed every man had mixed feelings about his children once in a while. Except for baby Seth, his one child who was a complete pleasure to think about—his grandchild, he meant. He shook his head at his absentmindedness. It must be those whiskeys he had at the bar with the boys.

He and Elizabeth had gone out to Cincinnati to see their grandchild Seth the previous fall. Seth had taken to his grandpa right off. Patrick smiled happily at the recollection of how the little pisser had climbed right up on his lap as soon as they met. By the end of the two-week visit, Seth was already saying his first word—Grandpa. And now he and Elizabeth were going out there again next month, and the mother was going to let them bring the little lad back for a visit here. Seth had inherited his own Irish eyes and curly black hair, his one child—grandchild—who had come out as Irish as he.

"Hey, Pat, you all right?" someone said, touching his arm.

"Perfectly fine, Bill." Patrick was so preoccupied, that for a moment he thought it was his sister Nora's husband, but Billy Yates was long dead, "Oh, it's you, is it, Ben?" he said, recognizing his doctor's boy. "I was off on a cloud, ya might say. It's been a big day for me, I guess ya know."

Patrick squared his shoulders and walked on slowly. His legs seemed a little mixed up. He remembered how he used to visit his sister Nora with her kids in that railroad flat under the el on Greenwich Street, and then he thought about Shamrock Alley. It was gone now, torn down, and a big, red brick office building covering over the whole space.

He thought about his Irish mother then, always cheerful no matter how hard life was, so fine and healthy he remembered her, until the drink got her.

He was in front of his house, his hand on the iron gate while he caught his breath, looking down the steps to the kitchen where once, oh so long ago, his mother had worked as the housemaid. He was thinking of his mother, and Timothy and Nora and Shamrock Alley all in a jumble, when the pains struck him and his strong, thick fingers that had never failed him before slipped from the black iron railing, and clutched at his chest.

It was the biggest moment of Polly's life at her little theater group, finally to get a chance at her first real part after all those walk-ons—and in the most significant play the Players had ever done.

They were meeting at the Liberal Club bookshop as they always did for rehearsals, sitting on their coats on the floor among the bookshelves. The dregs of cold coffee in innumerable cups testified to the hours they had been arguing over the play since early that morning.

Polly had arrived late, after attending her father's subway opening. She was chalking the names of the actors on a slate board to make herself useful to the director, as he chose them for the roles, not expecting anything for herself, when out of the blue he handed a script over to her. It took her a moment before it sank in that he meant for her to read for the supporting role of the companion to a spoiled rich girl, traveling on a freighter. The companion comes upon the girl at the moment she is being raped by a stoker in the hold and tries to rescue her.

The director had already chosen the rich girl, a dazzling newcomer to the group with chestnut hair and luminous eyes named Edna St. Vincent Millay, who had just come down from Maine after winning a national poetry contest.

He explained to Polly the significance of her part. She, the traveling companion, was the symbol of Puritanism struggling with the elemental sexuality of the stoker over the soul of America, the rich bitch.

It was a new play by Eugene O'Neill, shocking in its realism— completely different from the vapid theater of Broadway she despised, with its farces and costume melodramas. The dialogue was so frank, it might even get them raided by the police.

The director wanted her to read the climactic scene where she interrupts the rape. She was waiting for her cue, trying not to squint without her glasses and shaking with nerves, when the phone jangled outside in the hall. The man who ran the bookshop broke in to say it was an urgent call for her.

She could have screamed. As she went to the phone, she could hear the director already asking someone else to read the part.

By the time she got home, her father had been carried upstairs and was lying in the center of the great Victorian bed. He was ashen as he fought for breath, his barrel chest heaving under the sheet. The doctor had told them that after such a massive coronary attack, he wasn't really conscious any more, even if his eyes were open, and it was only a matter of time. There was nothing more to be done.

But her father's eyes looked so natural, a little perplexed as if he couldn't understand what was happening to him. He might not be conscious, but his body refused to give up.

The doctor had gone outside in the hall where a neighbor had brought up coffee. To Polly's annoyance, her mother, kneeling beside the bed as she wiped her husband's damp forehead with a towel, was trying to get him to talk, as if she thought she could actually jolt him out of his coma.

"What is it, Patrick, dear?" she kept calling to him. "Tell me, what are you trying to say?"

Her mother interpreted his pitiful gasping as an attempt to speak. He was struggling, as he fought for breath, but it was certainly not to speak, didn't she see that? Her mother couldn't seem to get it through her head that papa couldn't even hear her.

"He's not trying to say anything, mother," Polly hissed at her. "Leave him in peace, can't you?"

"Be quiet!" her mother said, not taking her eyes from her husband. "I know he's trying to tell me something." She was guarding him like a tigress. She leaned closer to the dying man, her ear almost at his lips. "You want something, Patrick, I know it...."

"Please, mother, let him breathe." Polly came around the bed to make her give him room, but her mother blocked her with her arm.

"I understand, Pat!" She lifted her head, her face lighting up almost demonically. "It's a priest you want. A priest, isn't it?"

"What are you saying?" Polly was furious. Her father hadn't said a word. And even he were able to speak, he'd never want a priest.

"Call St. Aloysius!" her mother commanded.

Polly raised her voice, forgetting where she was. "He doesn't want a priest!"

"Are you going," her mother said, "or do I have to go myself?"

Polly stood firm.

"Damn you!" Her mother pulled herself up and rushed out of the room.

Polly stared after her in disbelief. She heard the footsteps clattering downstairs and the cranking of the telephone. At the one moment her mother should be most calm, most clearheaded, she had lost her mind.

Polly dropped down beside her father and took one of his hands. "Don't worry, papa," she said, forgetting in her turn that he couldn't hear her. "I won't let her force that on you. I won't let her do anything you don't want." Helplessly, she had to watch the dying man struggle for breath, as he tried to suck air into lungs already filling with water. Why must he fight so hard to the very end?

But even dying, he was beautiful. Her father had always been beautiful, of course, the only one who had ever really cared for her. She remembered how he used to break in on her with his irresistible grin, while she was writing her silly schoolgirl poems, holding his arms out like a big helpless baby for her to unhook his cuff links. Her wonderful papa. And now there was nothing she could do—nothing anyone could do. And the final, precious minutes were ticking away.

Footsteps behind her. And her father's eyes, so wide and confused until now, were calm.

A priest was in the room.

Standing beside her mother, Polly was forced to witness, as last rites were given and her father's fingers gratefully curled around a rosary, before he closed his eyes.

She felt betrayed, as if her father had kept this secret from her deliberately, as if she had never known who he was.

On his deathbed, he had shown himself to be a stranger.

10

In the tea shop, Larry Mathews was whistling as he set the chairs back on the floor from the tables. Polly was upstairs in her room, getting dolled up for a midnight bash he was taking her to—or rather, she was taking him. It was being held in the studio of the artist John Sloan, and her little theater group had been invited. John Sloan was practically as famous as Toulouse-Lautrec!

Larry had already cleaned up the tea shop kitchen, and before he took off his apron, he sprinkled fresh-smelling sawdust on the newly-mopped floors to keep them dry, with everyone tracking in slush from the winter streets.

He'd spent most of his childhood in an orphanage outside Des Moines. He hadn't known what he wanted to do with his life back then, but one day, when he was thirteen, he found a book of Toulouse-Lautrec's paintings in the local library.

In his two years in New York, he had become Polly's full-time assistant at the Teaspoon. Not only that, but he had his own studio upstairs and was starting to paint in oils. If only Polly would take him seriously. But she went on treating him like a kid brother. He might be only eighteen, but he looked a lot older. Growing up in an orphanage made anyone mature pretty fast. The truth was that he was crazy about her and had been ever since he first saw her.

He gave a final look at the spanking-clean tea room and put on his jacket. Tonight, at this party, he'd find some way to make her see that he was the right man for her.

The trouble was that every time she took him to one of those Village places, he got more tongue-tied than ever. Everyone seemed to know everything there was to know about the arts, and made him feel like a hick. What he really wanted was just to be alone with Polly, and hold her hand and tell her how he felt about life. She was always telling him all about herself and she was the first and only person who had ever been interested in him, but it was like he was scared to open his mouth.

He went upstairs to change his clothes. He had bought his suit secondhand down on the Lower East Side. It was double-breasted, dark blue with a pencil stripe, and made him look older and more citified.

When he first got to New York, he was prepared for everyone to be suspicious and unfriendly, but when he had walked in off the street to ask for a job, Polly hired him without question. And then when she discovered he didn't know anything about cooking, instead of letting him go, she had started teaching him the ins and outs of the job. She had even encouraged him to break through the wall of the apartment she had put him in—it had belonged to the former owner of the tea shop—to create a real painter's studio for himself, while Polly stayed on in her smaller quarters next door. She had actually taken him seriously when he told her his ambition was to be a fine artist, and had led him off to Gertrude Vanderbilt Whitney's little gallery-museum on Eighth Street, which featured American artists, to hear John Sloan talk about his work.

Larry was proud to be her escort tonight, even if he was pretty sure she had only asked him because she didn't have anyone else to go with. She was always taking him to interesting places—or had, until her father's death. It had been a real blow for her. This was the first time she'd wanted to go out since then, and he was determined to make the most of it. If he got his nerve up, he was going to tell her more about why Toulouse-Lautrec meant so much to him, how he had been a hunchback cripple and, even when the whole world scoffed at him, he found a world for himself among the low-life of Paris. That's why he, when he got out of the orphanage, had hitch-hiked straight to Greenwich Village, because it sounded like the kind of place a kid who'd never had a family would fit into.

It was not easy for him to make friends here either—New Yorkers had no time for an ignoramus from out of town—but he had found Polly. Even if he couldn't open up to her, he knew that she understood him. That was why she told him everything about her life.

He was fascinated. Her family was nothing like what he had imagined family life to be. Her father sounded like everything you could want in a dad. But even growing up like that, he felt she was almost as lonely as he was inside, especially since she lost her father.

On his deathbed, her father had asked for a priest. It had been a shock, Polly said. She had never thought of him as a Catholic, though they all were Catholic on his side of her family. But the way Polly had come to terms with it, it was her father's way of joining his Irish mother again in the afterlife.

It had been an even worse shock for her, discovering about her brother. She blamed Eugene for their father's death, and she resented her mother for taking Eugene's side. Polly knew a lot about Freudian psychology and said it was her dominating mother who had made her brother that way. Larry wasn't so sure about that, not that he knew that much about it. In the orphanage, plenty of kids used to climb into each others' beds at night and nobody ever cared beans, if the matron didn't catch you.

Every time Polly went to see her mother she came back all worked up. According to her, Mrs. Endicott only had two subjects—first, her zoning law that had just gone through, which she kept praising for having saved the old Village from being torn down for skyscrapers. She'd never admit, Polly said, that it was the Seventh Avenue cut-through she'd fought against that had raised the value of Village real estate and got her precious zoning law passed.

But what got Polly riled up even more was her mother's other subject, Eugene and the war—her poor, darling boy risking his life in the trenches for all of them. Polly said it was outrageous that her brother was getting away with that hero stuff, after what he had done to her father.

As Larry pulled on the trousers of his suit, he could hear the water from Polly's bathtub gurgling through the big pipe in the corner of his room, and he imagined her standing in front of her steamed-up oval mirror, dusting herself with lilac talcum. He buttoned his fly and swore under his breath as a button popped off.

He couldn't get over it that she didn't think of herself as pretty. She was twenty-nine, it was true, but she didn't look any older than he did. She was always making cracks about her freckles and pug nose and how she was no threat to any woman. One of her psychology ideas was that her problem with men came from being too close to her father, but Larry didn't see anything wrong with missing someone if you loved them. Anyway, if she would only let him, he would show her that she had no problems, and that she was as pretty as any woman around.

She was always comparing herself to the leading lady in her acting group with the flaming red hair. Polly saw her as everything she wasn't. Edna St. Vincent Millay had won a prize for her poetry, wrote plays that were actually put on, and she had all the men she could handle. She even called herself Vincent, a man's name, just like George Sand, and sometimes wore trousers to make herself notorious.

It was Vincent Millay, in fact, who had gotten the Provincetown Players invited to John Sloan's studio party tonight. Sloan was painting Millay's portrait, and Polly was convinced they were having an affair. Larry wasn't looking forward to the party much, even if he had never been inside the studio of such a famous artist.

But he never got to see Sloan's studio that night. When he and Polly got there, a note on the door said to meet at the arch in Washington Square. On the note, Sloan had drawn a caricature of himself astride the arch, holding a wine bottle in the air. Polly said it did seem bizarre on such a cold night in February to hold a party outdoors—they weren't dressed for it. Did Sloan think they were Eskimos?

But they went anyway.

When they got to the arch with its two cold granite statues of George Washington grimly guarding the entrance to the park, no one was in sight, but they heard voices coming from somewhere. Someone called Polly's name, and looking up, they saw people on top of the arch. With much waving and pointing, they were directed to a service door in the side of the arch, which they had never noticed before. As he kept lighting matches in the pitch black, they giggled their way up the iron stairway.

They came out on the roof of the monument, where people were whooping it up in the frosty night with bottles of wine being passed around. Some were snuggled under heaps of blankets to keep warm while, in one corner, around a bonfire, a crowd was toasting marshmallows and singing to a mandolin.

Larry recognized John Sloan from the lecture at the gallery. A tall, bearded man in tweeds, the artist was standing up on the balustrade holding onto a flagpole with one hand, while energetically leading the singers by the bonfire in a popular song from the war about "knocking the Kaiser on his heinie."

It was even colder up here in the wind, and Polly, saying she was about to freeze her fanny off, pulled him along and found a place for them in a pile of blankets and bodies, and next thing he knew, she was snuggling up against him to get warm.

He stopped giggling fast enough, when he found himself under a rug with the girl he was in love with, looking up at the tiny, frosty stars and sliver of moon, listening to the crackle of the fire and the occasional backfire of a passing automobile below. It seemed a long way off where John Sloan was leading the singers to the strumming of the mandolin and some wild figures cavorted in the firelight.

He felt like walking around the balustrade, balancing high over the park, as Polly told him how much fun it was to have him with her in the tea room, and how it was too bad he hadn't known the Frenchwoman, who ran it before her and who still owned it really, and what an exciting life Corinne now had, working in a hospitality center for the troops in Paris. Polly wondered if she ought to send Corinne's address to her brother, so that he could look the Frenchwoman up if he got to Paris, but she sighed and said she guessed she wouldn't.

He was in bliss, and snuggled up closer. But when she felt how aroused he was, she pushed him off with a laugh. "Oh, Larry, you're the limit!" she scolded. "Behave yourself!"

It was all so perfect, more than he had ever hoped for.

But suddenly, everything went wrong. She was being pulled away. Someone on the other side of her under the blankets, someone he couldn't see, had pulled her out of his arms, away from him.

"I don't believe it!" Polly's voice was loud, ecstatic. "Milos!"

Larry listened, struck dumb. She and Corinne's cook were whispering under the blankets, giggling, as if he didn't exist.

Polly had been feeling perfectly peaceful with Larry, when the large head emerged from the blanket near her shoulder and fleshy lips in a bush of a mustache against her ear gave a low growl, "Hello, hunky-punky."

She turned away from Larry and started to raise herself, asking Milos what he was doing there, but with a big, soft hand he shoved her back down. "I'm here on monkey business, what else?" he said, and gave his familiar laugh.

Surprisingly, it seemed to her perfectly natural in that unnatural setting to have Milos turn up like that. She tried to make him be serious, to find out what he had been doing since they had last seen each other two years before, but all he said was, "A little of this, a little of that. You know us gypsies." He pinched her cheek.

She had to laugh.

"I don't make you cry?" He was hovering over her, his old outrageous self, making her feel like a child. He began to nip at her earlobe.

Across from them, a sheet painted with a skull and crossbones was run up the flagpole at the balustrade, and the painter John Sloan called for everyone's attention.

"Stop it, won't you!" She couldn't help laughing as Milos nuzzled up to her. "I want to listen."

"What are you afraid of me for? You still virgin?" His dark whiskers smiled over her.

Aware of Larry behind her, she tried to extricate herself. "That's none of your business."

"Doesn't matter," he said. "You been waiting for me to make you woman, yes?"

With the skull and crossbones fluttering in the breeze against a backdrop of the darkened Rhinelander mansion and the sweep of lower Fifth Avenue, John Sloan on the balustrade was shouting that they would never support the European war, even if the rest of the country was stupid enough to get into it, and therefore he was proclaiming Greenwich Village an independent republic.

All the celebrants on top of the arch erupted in cheers.

"Do you hear that, world?"—John Sloan seemed to Polly bigger than life, as he shouted out over the skeletal trees of the Square in the direction of Wall Street—"The glorious republic of Greenwich Village says No to your fucking war!"

Everybody cheered again, and the beautiful chestnut-haired poetess of the theater group, Vincent Millay, jumped onto the balustrade to hug him, and then with an arm around his shoulders, began to recite in her theatrical voice, "We are the music makers, we are the dreamers of dreams...."

Polly had never been so comfortable in a man's arms before. For a moment, the thought of him and Corinne crossed her mind, but Corinne was gone, and she was vaguely aware that Larry Mathews had slipped off into the night.

Then Milos began kissing her.

She hadn't known that a man could be so gentle, so playful. But my God, what was he doing with his hand!

"Stop!" she squealed, tightening up. He was ruining everything. The old despair came over her.

"I help you," he whispered into her ear, and his head was gone, under the blanket.

"Stop! The people...."

Suddenly, his lips were nibbling her down there, and as she felt his tongue exploring, her back arched involuntarily.

Then his face was over her again.

"We mustn't," she begged.

"You don't like it?"

"They'll see us!"

"Nobody looking," he growled. "You're so beautiful." He was hard against her.

"I'm afraid...."

"Come," he said. "I make you woman."

And she opened to him.

The crowd on the arch, the bonfire, the speeches, even an awareness of where she was, faded, so overcome was she by her own pleasure, as she took him all the way into her.

All that remained was the night, and the million stars in the sky.

In the days that followed, Larry had never seen Polly so happy. It tore him apart as she told him everything. She talked about nothing else. She wasn't being cruel, not deliberately, he knew that. He understood in his misery that it was the natural exuberance of a woman who had thrown off fetters that had always bound her.

But it wasn't all sweetness and light for her. One of the Hungarian's little surprises turned out to be a wife and children. He announced to Polly one day that he had to go to his son's high school graduation in Teaneck, New Jersey. For awhile, she was ready to break off with him, but he only laughed and called her a bourgeois goose, and when she thought it over, she told Larry, and realized that much as she adored him she wasn't in love with him that way, she decided she was being silly not to be grateful—after all she was almost thirty and had never had anything like this before.

The situation at the tea shop became so painful for him—most of all when he heard the sounds of lovemaking through the wall, night after night—that when America entered the war in April 1917, he was in the first shipload of recruits to sail for France.

1918

11

Following the armistice in November, the whole country clamored to bring the boys home by Christmas. Not all the troops made it in time, but on a late Friday afternoon in mid-December aboard the USS Grover Cleveland were two thousand lucky doughboys who did. Eugene Endicott was one of them.

As the troopship moved slowly up the Hudson River, tugboats tooted and a fireboat sent long streams of water into the air. The shouts of the welcoming crowd on the pier at the foot of West Thirty-Fourth Street all but drowned out a brass band struggling through "Stars and Stripes Forever," as the ship was guided into its berth. Children, perched on shoulders, waved tiny flags and snatched at colored streamers spiraling down from the decks.

Polly Endicott, in a large hat trimmed in red fox with matching neckpiece and muff, waited beside her mother, trying not to feel goose pimply. It was so obvious, she told herself, how they concocted this kind of emotional atmosphere—anyone who knew anything at all about the theater could see that. It had nothing to do with how she felt about her brother, whom she had by no means forgiven.

In the three years Eugene had been gone, she had tried her best not to think about him, though, no matter what was being talked about, her mother seemed always to bring his name up at least once. When, the year before, the United States had entered the war, he had transferred into the American Expeditionary Forces, and had spent most of his time pinned down in the trenches on the Marne. He had written them that once, on leave, he had bumped into Corinne Ashmore at the hospitality center for Allied troops in Paris. Poor Corinne, she heard later, had been killed in a bombardment, while visiting her family in Armentières.

It was ironic that of all Polly's friends and acquaintances, the only one who had been killed in the war was a woman and a civilian. Every one of the boys she knew who had gone to fight had survived, among them her cousin Dennis Yates, and Cpl. Larry Mathews, already back home in Iowa.

And now, Eugene.

Polly tried not to look up at the masses of wildly yelling soldiers jammed at the ship's rails, as the hawsers were dropped around the moorings and the gangways were pushed into place. She didn't want to spot him among all those faces. She was only here because her mother had begged her to come. It was pure sentimentality.

She wished she had gone instead with Milos to see some of his Hungarian friends in Brooklyn—there was always food and music and turbulent political argument. Milos had come by to get her, and when she told him she couldn't go with him, they had a terrible fight. That meant she wouldn't see him for a week. It was the same story as with Corinne—after the least tiff he disappeared over to New Jersey, until he got bored with whoever was consoling him there. The Slavic lunacy that made him irresistible also made him the last man any woman could ever count on. But at the Red Cross hospitality center on Times Square, where she fox-trotted with soldiers and sailors twice a week, Polly had learned that other men besides Milos found her attractive.

How she wished she had never come today. She could even have gone to the little theater on MacDougal Street and helped paint sets for the next production of her acting company. The Provincetown Players was actually attracting a few critics from uptown, with experimental productions of Village playwrights. She was still running the tea shop, but it was really only her acting she cared about. Although most of her parts were small, for a whole month she had been understudy for the role of Anna Christie and had prayed every night that the lead actress would fall through a trap door and break her neck, but it never happened.

She was brought back to reality, when the military band struck up "Yankee Doodle Dandy" and the troops began marching off the ship, shouldering their packs. Non-coms did their best to form them up into ranks in the big shed below, but the crowd pressed forward and turned it all into chaos, anxious to reclaim their returning heroes.

"There he is!" Her mother gripped Polly's arm, waving her umbrella at the farther gangway.

"Mother, please, my arm!" She tried to feel some irritation, but her heart was pounding, too, as her mother pulled her along, jostling her way through the milling crowd in the vast shed. For two weeks her mother had talked of nothing else but Eugene's homecoming.

"Oh, just look at him!" Elizabeth said, loudly, using her umbrella and her elbows to prod her way through the people who stood between her and her son. "He's a man now!"

Polly saw her brother standing in the midst of a hastily-formed platoon in his campaign hat and puttees, and kicked herself for having come.

She was not going to forgive him—ever.

Eugene was miserable, as the other soldiers, who had nothing to fear, were welcomed back by their delighted families. He was hoping against hope that neither his mother nor Polly would come. If only this homecoming hoopla would get over with, they could all be loaded onto the waiting trucks and taken over to the camp in New Jersey, where in a few days they would be officially discharged.

He would not telephone his mother until he was out of the army and settled in a furnished room somewhere. They'd meet in a quiet place, where things could be talked out unemotionally. She had alluded to nothing in her letters, but he knew she knew, his father had to have told her, and he dreaded the awkwardness between them.

He didn't want to see his sister at all. She had made it all too clear how she felt about him—she had never written a line. His mother tried to give the impression in her letters that Polly was much too busy with her many activities, but he had seen right through it. He knew she wasn't devoting herself to knitting socks for the troops. Polly had always sided with her dear papa in everything. The one thing Eugene was relieved about was that he would never have to face his father again. The whole time he had been off to the war, no matter the horrors, what had happened on that day in the cellar and what his family thought about it was never entirely out of his mind. If only they wouldn't show up....

Standing over his pack nearby, a soldier named Hymie Liebman was burned up that it had to be a Friday night the ship got in, so his family couldn't come over from Brooklyn to meet him. They were Orthodox Jews, and Friday sundown being the start of the Sabbath, they weren't allowed to carry money, not even a nickel for the subway.

But Hymie was so charged up about being back home in New York, he could hardly stand still. His bright eyes darted around everywhere, taking in all the emotional reunions in the noisy, echoing shed, when his attention was caught by a pretty shiksa with a turned-up nose and freckles, accompanied by her mother, approaching an infantryman. The doughboy looked like he was waiting for a firing squad instead of his mother and his sweetheart. The sweetheart didn't look so happy either, but was she dressed for the occasion! The fox skins around that doll's neck his furrier father wouldn't turn his nose up at.

While the band segued into "Glory, Glory Hallelujah," Elizabeth held her son at arm's length for a moment, looking at him. Then she pressed him to her with her eyes closed. Stepping back at last and dabbing at her eyes with a lace handkerchief, she turned to Polly. "He's home," she said. "Our dear boy is home."

Polly faced her brother at last. Determined not to let anything show, she put on an artificial smile, wondering if she ought to peck him on the cheek. But Gene's obvious misery made it suddenly all too absurd. She couldn't go on with her little act any longer and threw her arms around him. "Bless you for coming home to us, Gene," she said, biting her lip.

He patted her back awkwardly. "That's all right, Pol."

It was the most undemonstrative welcome Hymie Liebman had ever seen. This jerk was just back from hell with poison gas and crab lice and Big Bertha blowing everybody's brains out, and they acted like he was coming home from a Boy Scout jamboree. Hymie's own family, when he saw them, would go hysterical. They'd have to hold his mother up to keep her from collapsing, and his sisters wouldn't stop crying as they held on to his sleeves, and even his strict, old father would blubber like a baby, hugging him again and again.

If these women didn't show much, the guy was even worse. Didn't he have any balls? Any girl deserved a better welcome than that. Hymie shoved back his campaign hat, trotted over, and moved Eugene aside. "Buddy, if this doll were my sweetheart, this is how I'd do it." And, sweeping her into a bear hug, he gave her a kiss she wouldn't forget so soon.

The three Endicotts stared at him as if he were a wild Indian. Then, to his pleasure, they all came to life and burst into laughter, explaining to him that the "sweethearts" were brother and sister. Hymie, who wasn't the least put off, winked at Polly and said he hoped she'd excuse him. It was just that he'd been away so long he couldn't help himself, and a knockout like her shouldn't be left within reach of a doughboy, who hadn't seen an American girl or a bagel in over a year.

Pleased with himself, he returned to his knapsack, but he couldn't take his eyes off the pretty *shiksa* with her red hair and little turned-up nose, and when the troops were lining up to get into the trucks for the camp in New Jersey, he ran back and asked for her address.

12

Life had seemed empty to Elizabeth Endicott since her husband's death, in spite of her many volunteer war activities. But her spirits revived with Eugene's return. Christmas was the perfect time for it, the house filled with the smell of pine from the tree in the front room—their first Christmas tree in years. They unearthed the boxes of fragile, Victorian ornaments from her childhood stored on the third floor, including the prize of the collection, the Venetian glass angel that symbolized for her the magic of Christmas.

It was so long since they had been together, and now, she and her son were having their wonderful talks again. Mornings, she brought him up a breakfast tray, and then sat on his bed for hours. They went on talking in the kitchen, as she rolled out dough for mince pie. She was glad that she had thrown out Patrick's old gas log in the fireplace, so they could sit before a real wood fire, sipping eggnogs. They talked about many things—Polly, who was so sophisticated now, with her eccentric Hungarian—her grandson Dominic, still under his father's thumb at the family restaurant—and always Eugene's writing, though he didn't show much enthusiasm when she spoke of his getting back to the old Henry James piece. It was understandable, considering what he had gone through—the newspapers were full of advice about returning soldiers needing to be handled with care, but on the whole, Gene still seemed like his old self.

They had their own little world again, though she was careful not to bring up anything she thought might be even mildly upsetting, after all he had gone through in the war. She didn't dwell on his father's decline after Eugene had gone off so precipitously, ending in the heart attack. She described for her son, instead, his father's triumph, that last day, when he was given recognition as a pioneer of the city's subway system, and most of all, his pleasure in seeing his new grandson—the son Eugene had never seen—on their trip to Cincinnati shortly before he died. She ought to have known it was premature, showing Gene the Kodak snapshots of his little boy, when he was just off the boat. Why, he still had the mud of the trenches on his boots! But she was so anxious to have him reconciled with his wife and child again, that a grandmother's bumbling could be excused.

For Eugene, it was an unexpected joy, his homecoming. Not in a million years had he thought it would be so easy. But why did his mother have to keep bringing up Clare and the baby, when she knew he had asked Clare for a divorce?

On the long boat trip back to the States over the wintry North Atlantic, leaning on the rail at night with a cigarette, he had thought about what he was coming back to. While he was at the front, he was able to bury this thing in himself that he didn't understand, especially since his one attempt to give in to it had ended in the horror of his father's discovery. But even in the trenches, with the constant proximity of male bodies, thrown together, even unwashed and smelling, there were times when it was all he could do to keep from reaching out. But he hadn't—the penalties outweighed the temptations. Soldiers were court-martialed for it, and once he had seen a soldier bashed almost to death behind the barracks.

Going off to the war had been a solution for his predicament, but it was only a temporary one. Still, he was determined to avoid any discussion of it with his mother.

But it didn't turn out that way.

It was while they were trimming the tree, his mother sitting by the fire, pulling apart tinsel into strands, with him on the ladder tying on the antique ornaments, that she started in again about Cincinnati, and how well Clare looked, and how four-year-old Seth kept asking her about his daddy.

He was about to place the Venetian glass angel on the top of the tree, when she asked one more time had he given any thought to going out there for a visit before settling down? With the angel still in his hand, he turned around on the ladder. "Mother," he said, careful to keep his voice steady, "Will you please mind your own business?"

She looked up, removing her glasses. "I didn't mean anything...."

He couldn't stop. "I'm sorry, but Clare and I are getting divorced. That's all there is to it, period."

His mother bit her lip. "I know....But it's just...your little boy...."

He smashed the angel to the floor and climbed down from the ladder. Alarmed, Elizabeth had jumped up, clutching the tinsel against her.

There was no turning back. He was going to suffocate if he didn't deal with it. But she looked so fragile, so afraid of him. He put an arm around her and sat her down with him, taking her hand. "Look, mother, it's hard, I know, but there's something we're not talking about, and I think it's time we did."

"Oh, all that fuss about nothing." She fiddled in her pocket for a handkerchief.

He touched her chin, forcing her to look at him. There were tears in her eyes. "It isn't nothing," he said. "I know it and you know it."

She was still fighting him. "But you're an artist...you're my son... you take after me!"

"It's not about you," he said. "It's about him."

"But you were always spatting with your father." She dabbed at her eyes. "That didn't mean anything." Patrick had been limited in so many ways, she said. It was hard for her too. He musn't torment himself over it any more. She leaned down, taking up the tinsel again. "In any case, it only happened once, and that was a long time ago."

Eugene was in despair. His mother's avoiding the issue made it all hopeless. He felt that his feelings were being swept under the rug, when it was something that was driving him wild. He snatched the tinsel from her hands and threw it into the fire. "If it doesn't bother you," he said, "the rest of the world doesn't take it so lightly. And look what I did—my father went to his grave because of me."

She protested it was heart trouble that had caused Patrick's death.

"And it's not just him," he said, not listening. "Look what I did to Clare! And my son—God, what if he's inherited it!" His voice was shaking. "It's horrible! My own father hated me, and I hate myself worst of all!"

"Stop that, Gene! In the first place, your father did not hate you. I'll admit he couldn't understand...."

His voice went quiet. "It broke his heart to have a pansy for a son!"

Elizabeth was stunned. It wasn't the word, but the way he said it that brought home to her, finally, the depths of his wretchedness.

For the first time in her life, she was at a loss for words.

The single idea she clung to was that he had to get back to his work. He was meant to be a writer—his published article had proved it to the world. But for the four years of the war, he had been cut off from his writing. With no outlet, his fertile imagination had somehow created this morbid phantasmagoria he couldn't deal with.

The next day, she did not bring him his breakfast in bed, and when he came down to the kitchen for coffee, she got up from the table and kissed him. "I've been doing a lot of thinking, dear, and I think I know what to do." She told him that it had finally occurred to her that what he needed most was a special place of his own where he could get back to his writing. So, if he agreed, she was going to call in workmen to convert the ground floor of the house into a separate apartment for him. She would be just upstairs whenever he felt like seeing her. That way he could get right back to his unfinished Henry James piece.

Eugene had to smile. His indomitable mother. Full of her plans for him, for the two of them together, she looked twenty years younger. In spite of not understanding the first thing about it, she had come up with one of her "sensible" solutions that was supposed to take care of everything— even arranging it so that she would still be hovering over him—as if there was anything that she could do.

But he, too, had done some thinking in the night. Bringing that word out into the open, applying it to himself for the first time in public, however repulsive it was, had made a change in him. A part of him wanted the safety of wife and child, the comfort of mother, but that would only be running away from himself. One thing he was sure of—he'd never find out who he was, so long as he stayed here. The very walls of this old house he had grown up in watched him, made him feel guilty.

There were no guides ahead, no books of instruction. All he had ever seen were a few ambiguous items in the papers about arrests and scandals—the way Mabel Dodge had talked was up in the clouds. He was as baffled as ever how he was going to live with it, but he felt able to take the first step.

He told his mother as carefully as he could that the Henry James piece belonged to an earlier period of his life. What he had to write about now, he didn't know. It was something he would have to discover for himself, and that meant he had to move out of the house. He had to be on his own. His mother said she understood—but how old she looked to him then.

As Eugene talked on about finding some kind of part-time job, behind Elizabeth's show of encouragement she couldn't help wondering if what he needed to be on his own for was more than just writing—and she was afraid.

13

Polly's on-again off-again affair with the turbulent Hungarian, Milos, had taught her a lot, but he had never been the right man for her. With Hymie Liebman it was different. From the moment of his flamboyant embrace at the troopship, she knew he was the one. When he took her phone number before he jumped on the army truck, she only waited for his call. She told herself she couldn't hope to hear from him before the next weekend after he had a few days with his family in Flatbush in the far reaches of Brooklyn. But it turned out better than that—three days later, the minute he got in to the city from the army separation center, even before catching the el home, he phoned her from Penn Station and came down to see her at the tea shop,.

She had just set an omelet before a customer, when she saw him, bounding down the steps and through the door. Then he stopped, legs apart, knapsack hanging from one shoulder of his open military overcoat, taking her in with his bright eyes.

She waited for him to say something.

He just stood there, looking at her.

At last she spoke. "You're here."

"Yeah."

He was the soldier from three days before. Dark, stocky, intense. But already there was a difference. With his discharge in his pocket, he had thrown over the last pretense of conforming to military regulations. He was still in uniform—he had nothing else to wear until he got home—but he was hatless, and his thick, black hair, already growing out, was falling over his brow.

"Hey, what am I standing here for?" He grinned, dropping his knapsack on the floor and, fishing around in it, came up with a bottle of perfume. "This is for you. From Paris." He held it out to her.

"I can't take that. You probably bought it for your mother."

"My mother wouldn't know perfume from chicken soup. Besides, I got a cuckoo clock for her." He shoved the perfume into her hands, his eyes twinkling. "Take it!"

With any of the men she'd met before Hymie, she would have quipped, "Give your mother the perfume, I'll take the cuckoo clock." But for once she didn't try to be funny.

At thirty, Polly considered herself a late starter to have fallen in love for the first time. But since she knew she looked younger than her age and Hymie was only twenty-three, she saw no reason not to let him go on thinking that she was her brother Gene's younger sister.

When he came by the next evening, the doughboy of the previous day was transformed. Sporting a brand-new, blue, pin-striped suit and snap-brim fedora, his black hair slicked back with brilliantine, he thrust a bunch of violets into her hand. Her mother might have found him a trifle vulgar, but to her, this dark-eyed, alert young man from Brooklyn was glorious.

He asked her where she would like to go that night, the sky was the limit. Without thinking, she said dancing at the Peacock Court of the Plaza. Some buyer from out of town had taken her there during her secretary days and she couldn't think of anywhere else that sounded fancy enough, considering how he was dressed.

Hymie Liebman laughed, and said he had just spent his last two bits on the flowers. "Will you take a rain check on the Plaza and settle for the Staten Island ferry instead?"

It was freezing on the deck of the ferry, crossing New York harbor. From the shelter of a warm-air vent they watched the skyscrapers of lower Manhattan vanishing into the fog. They listened to the plashing of water against the hull, the blasts of the ferry's horn, the chiming of buoys.

Hymie was full of plans for his future in real estate. Before the war he had worked for an uncle who had a realty office in Brooklyn, he told Polly, but his sights were set on Manhattan. There were two or three neighborhoods where a sharp real estate man could make a killing, and, though no one but him had caught on yet, Greenwich Village was the most promising of the lot. "With the new subway down there, Pol, it's virgin territory. And lemme tell you, it's gonna be a gold mine for the guy who gets in there first."

"But it's got such a bad name," Polly said. She told him about an article in the Saturday Evening Post that called Greenwich Village "a nest of freaks and perverts."

Hymie wasn't fazed. "That's just what we want! Those weirdos are free publicity, don't you see?" He leaned back with his elbows on the rail, the wind whipping his hair on his forehead. "The war's over, people are ready for a good time. They'll flock down to ogle the freaks and perverts."

"I hate that word," said Polly.

"Huh? What word?"

"I can't say it." It was on the tip of her tongue to tell him about Eugene. "It's so...I don't know...ugly."

"Okay, if you say so." He grinned wickedly. "Come here, you little pervert." He gave her a hug.

She pushed him away. "Stop saying that, won't you?"

"Pervert, schmervert, who gives a good goddam. In the Village you can do anything you want, and that's what I'm going to sell. We're a new generation, Pol. We're not gonna follow the rules of the stuffed shirts any more."

"I didn't know you were an idealist."

He grinned. "Sure, I am. But who says it's against the law to make a buck. I'm going to sell so many houses in the Village, those real estate schmucks uptown aren't gonna know what hit 'em!" He picked her up and whirled her around on the deck, until she was laughing so much, she begged for him to stop.

She envied him, she said, when he let her get her breath. He was moving so fast, the way he talked, and she was stagnating. "I've been stuck at that tea shop"—she stopped herself just in time from saying "—for six years," and giving her age away. He made her feel a million years older than him.

"What do you do it for?"

"I don't really know." For a long time, she told him, she had to stay there because Corinne Ashmore had left her in charge. After the news of Corinne's death, when she had taken over the lease, she had thought about giving it up and going on the professional stage. "But I don't have that much experience and…"—she couldn't tell him that it was a little late to begin a stage career at thirty—"besides, I don't think my face is right for Broadway."

"What are you talking about? You're gorgeous. Why don't you sell that tea shop you hate so much and give it a try?"

"What's there to sell? It's not like I owned the building. Only some old tables and chairs and an iron cookstove."

"You've got a going business, a regular clientele, a reputation. It's worth a bundle."

They were so busy talking about so many things that, when the boat pulled into the Staten Island terminal, they didn't get off, and when it arrived in Manhattan again, they stayed on. They rode back and forth all night until dawn broke over the skyline, dispersing the last wisps of fog.

As they walked up lower Broadway through the canyons of the deserted financial district, the windows of the towers reflecting the red streaks of the sunrise, Hymie made up a song for them.

"We were so jolly, we were so merry,
   we rode all night back and forth on the ferry."

"You're a poet, too!" Polly said.

"I can do a lot of things," he said, pulling her close.

At the end of the last century, waves of immigrants poured into the country, expecting to find the streets paved with gold. Many of these arrivals came from other places than those who had come earlier. They were swarthier people —Mediterraneans, Slavs, Jews, with unpronounceable names. But instead of finding gold, they were packed into slum tenements, and blocked on all sides by a white Protestant society that was determined to hold the barriers against them. Yet the children of these immigrants went off to the war just like the scrubbed sons of the "real Americans"—and went through the same nightmare.

The war that blew up their buddies also blew to smithereens the old barriers that kept the immigrants down, and those who returned were lean and hungry, no longer willing to accept crumbs, while others got the pie.

One of the hungriest was Hymie Liebman. He had been waiting his whole twenty-three years for his chance, and after the Armistice he shot out into the post-war world like a cannonball.

Hymie was the first Jew to be hired by the Darby & White Real Estate Agency on Eighth Street, that specialized in Greenwich Village properties. He wouldn't have gotten the job if they had known he was Jewish. But after having the door slammed in his face too many times because, in the euphemistic language of the employment agencies and want ads, he wasn't "clean cut," he got smart and gave a fake name.

"If I'd caught them looking too hard at my schnozz, I was ready to tell them I had a Spanish grandmother in the woodpile," he told Polly, jubilantly.

Passing as Henry Lambert didn't bother him one bit, if it would get him a foot in the door. When they heard his ideas, they'd soon see he was worth triple the peanuts they were going to pay him.

In the opinion of Darby & White, the Village was next thing to a slum, and they had little interest in keeping it from deteriorating further. In the new, post-war world, no one wanted to buy old houses anyway which, unlike the Endicotts' house on Perry Street, were mostly either dilapidated, had inadequate plumbing and wiring, or were teeming with roomers, insect and human. There were plenty of impoverished artists and their camp followers flocking to the Village for cheap rooms and studios. But even if the agency did a brisk business renting to them, rents were so low that the commissions were, as Hymie quickly learned, pitiful.

Still, it was clear as day to him that real estate in the Village was ready to take off in a whole new direction. The old gentility was out of date. He'd show them how to sell the bohemian angle, instead of pretending that it didn't exist, and people with money would flock, because it was titillating to live there. Now was just the time for Darby & White to invest in some of those crumbling, old buildings off Fifth Avenue that had turned into rooming houses, and renovate them. All they'd have to do is rip out the old plumbing and makeshift wiring, cut away the low-class brownstone stoops, and fix them up as elegant, one-family town houses.

But when he showed them how he would do it, the old boys he worked for failed to share his enthusiasm. They had the *goyish* idea, he told Polly, that doing business with caution and dignity—the way they always had— was more important than trying something new and going after the big money. It was going to take him a while to get through to them. They weren't used to a live wire like him.

But time was just the thing they didn't have. If Darby & White didn't do it, somebody else would. If he could only lay his hands on a little capital—a couple of thousand, say—he'd tell them to go to hell and do it himself.

Hymie shocked his old-world parents by leaving the family in Flatbush and moving to the Village.

Polly insisted on him showing her his new place right away. When she saw the rooms over a noisy bar on Christopher Street, for a moment she remembered the artist's loft above a machine shop. But when Hymie called her "my own shiksa" and took her into his arms, she forgot everything else. They fell on the bed.

"Come to your Jewboy," he whispered, and pulled her over on top of him.

She was taken aback.

"You say it, doll," he was nuzzling her neck, "tell me."

She tried to turn her face away, but he forced it back. "Go ahead, say it." He was moving under her, kissing her all over. "Say 'my own Jewboy'."

The words were so ugly. She felt herself tightening up in the old way.

"Please…," He was breathing hard.

"No…," she wanted to escape "…I can't."

"Please…."

Finally, in spite of herself, she closed her eyes and got it out.

Once spoken, the words had a dramatic effect. Rather than disgusting her, instantly she was alive. Her hips moved to meet his, opening up to him.

As they made love, the words were part of it, "My own Jewboy… Jewboy…," to his answering "shiksa…shiksa…."

Afterward, propped on an elbow, she studied his nakedness. The coils of black hair on his chest. Wondering at his circumcision.

"You look like something out of the Fourth of July." He grinned, running a finger over her pert, freckled, little nose. "You're the cutest thing I've ever seen."

"You're not getting so much in this department." She cupped her breasts and giggled.

"You're nuts," he said. "I don't go for big Jewish boobs." Taking her hands away, he kissed them.

She was late for her shift at the Teaspoon. As she wrenched on her clothes, she told Hymie she wished she could douse the place with gasoline and set a match to it once and for all, she hated it so.

"It's a damn albatross. If you got rid of it like I told you, you could do what you want for a change."

"How could I?" she said, impatiently. "Who'd buy it?"

"Didn't I tell you I could sell it for you?" he said, lying back with his hands behind his head, watching her. "I'm a real estate genius, even if Darby & White don't know it." He grinned.

As she put a foot on a chair and pulled up her skirt to roll down a garter, his eyes took in the display of white thigh above the stocking top. "Why don't you let me try? I'd get a kick out of it and you'll be free to become a star in the moving pictures. You're a lot cuter than Lillian Gish."

She made a face. "It takes a while to become a star, you fool, and I don't much want to move back with my mother while I'm waiting."

"No problem. Move in here with me—this place could use a woman's touch." He waved at the bare room with unpacked boxes stacked on the linoleum floor. "We can live off my salary until you make it."

"And then we'll take the loot we get for the tea shop," she said, buckling the strap of a shoe, "and go on a spree!"

"We'll blow it on the Peacock Court!" Then he sat bolt upright. "Wait a minute! Why didn't I think of it before!" He threw off the sheet and jumped out of bed, naked. "That's how I'll get the cash I need!" He told her that with the money from the tea shop, he could buy one of those run-down houses on Tenth Street, fix it up, and get their money back twice over. "I don't need those old farts at the agency. We'll be on easy street."

When Polly saw the possibilities of the scheme, even with no head for business, she was so caught up in the prospect of being free to do what she wanted, that she grabbed the key to the tea shop out of her pocketbook and ran to the window, ready to throw it as far away as she could.

"You nuts?" he said, grabbing it away from her. "How we sell the place without this!"

The following night, after lovemaking, they were lying cosily together on Hymie's narrow bed and Polly started to tell him about her affair with Milos—she didn't want any secrets between them, she said.

"Great idea! Then I'll tell you all the details about the mam'selles I had in France, okay?"

"You're not taking me seriously," she said, slapping at him.

But if she was disappointed that he was not interested in mutual confessions, still, the problem remained, what to do about Milos. She knew there was no reason to feel guilty—the Hungarian disappeared all the time to beds in New Jersey and elsewhere—but it was not going to be easy to tell him it was all over between them. Impossible as he was, he could be such an angel.

She hadn't seen him since he had walked out in a rage, the day of her brother's homecoming. But sure enough, one day, the big man with the mustache waltzed into the tea shop all hearts and flowers again. "Hello, beautiful," he said with a wet kiss. He looked at her with his Valentino eyes. "How's my little pancake?"

Wishing he weren't making it so difficult for her, she said she had something to talk to him about. He paid no attention but tried to pull her upstairs, in front of the customers. It was like getting untangled from an octopus, but she managed to get him out the front door and around the corner to Chumley's bar where they could sit in a quiet booth.

She couldn't bear to think of him being out of her life, but it wasn't fair to Hymie to go on with him.

"Did my little pancake miss me? What a pile of shit Milos is. I promise I never walk out on you again."

He was making it even even more difficult for her. She said she didn't mind his walking out—he had a perfect right to. They had agreed always to leave each other free, and that's what she wanted to talk to him about.

He snuggled closer. She was so edible, he said, and began to nibble her ear.

She pushed him away. "Will you stop it! I'm trying to talk to you." And she got up to sit across the table from him.

Keeping his big hands that were exploring under the table from going up her skirt, she told him about Hymie and her plan to sell the tea shop and move in with him. She was sorry, but she and Milos had to break it off.

When he appeared not to have heard and went on trying to get at her under the table, she asked if he was listening. She was only sorry she wouldn't be seeing him, because she did think of him as one of her best friends.

"So you got a new boyfriend. So what? You and me can still be friends, can't we?" He was next to her again, snapping his fingers at the waiter for champagne.

When it arrived, he looked in his wallet and then told the waiter to put it on Polly's account. Clinking glasses, he said he hoped she was going to be very happy and, added that if the new boyfriend was not good to her, he'd tear him limb from limb.

Putting his cheek against hers, he looked up with his smouldering eyes. "How about we do it too from time to time?"

He was such an adorable clown. She put her arms around him. He gave his rumble of a laugh and let her rock him against her breast.

14

Polly had scrubbed off her makeup, so that her freckles showed and her snub nose was shiny. She looked with approval at her reflection in the mirror. She could pass for a teenager. Not that she liked her gamine face any more than she ever had, but at least now it was going to be good for something. She had an audition that afternoon uptown at the New Amsterdam Theater on Forty-second Street to try out for the part of the kid sister in a play called Lilac Time.

The tea shop was gone. Hymie had sold it for her to a woman who claimed to be a Hungarian countess, but who Milos said was as much Hungarian as he was Filipino and it took a real Magyar to sniff out a fake.

Polly was living with Hymie now, and with his encouragement was going after parts in Broadway plays. He didn't see any future for her in the semi-amateur, experimental theater company in the Village she had been fooling around with, and she agreed with him.

Since she felt at least ten years behind her real age anyway, and looked it too, it was simply being more realistic for her to try out for character juvenile roles—older actresses with her kind of looks were always cast in them. Before Hymie, she had done nothing with her life that meant anything, except for her affair with Milos, which had been the merest beginning. She was only starting to do at thirty-one what other people would have done ten years before.

Hymie had used the money from the sale of the tea shop to buy up one of the old rooming houses off lower Fifth Avenue, and he was in the process of turning it back into the handsome town house it once had been. He said he would be able to buy two more old houses with what he would make from the sale of the first one. It would be a start. He still had his job at the real estate agency, but he was going into business for himself as soon as the deal paid off. Polly had already typed up the prospectus for him to show buyers. He had swiped a list of gilt-edged customers from the files at Darby & White's. He didn't feel any loyalty to those prejudiced bastards, he told her.

In front of the mirror, Polly tied her hair back with a big bow like a schoolgirl and, with a towel on her shoulders to protect her middy blouse, powdered over again a kiss mark on the side of her neck. She hoped it wouldn't show under the work lights at the audition.

Hymie was a powerhouse in every way, never wasting a minute. He always brought home from the office a briefcase full of papers to study. After losing so much time to the war, he said he had a lot of catching up to do, if he was going to be a millionaire by the time he was twenty-five.

And when he wasn't working, he was always ready for a lark, like them sneaking into the Ziegfeld Follies at intermission when they were broke, or going over to Hoboken on the ferry for steamed clams. Once, at midnight, they even took off their shoes and stockings and splashed in the august fountain in front of the Plaza Hotel.

Her mother adored Hymie, of course. She could never hide her attraction for young men, and basked in his shameless flattery, like telling her she looked like Lillian Russell. But whenever Polly asked him about his own parents, he was evasive. What did she want to meet them for, he said, they lived way out in Flatbush. It was so obvious that he didn't care to talk about them, that she let it drop. She suspected that he might not be on such good terms with them, since they hadn't come to meet him at the troopship. Perhaps he was ashamed of them—they probably spoke with an accent and lived in a tenement. It must be because they were immigrants and old-fashioned. He was a fanatic about being up-to-date on everything.

He was also fanatic about his appearance, whether at work or play. When they were out together, he was a walking brilliantine ad, the pants of his pin-striped suit pressed to knife-sharp creases, his pointed, black oxfords polished like mirrors. Women couldn't keep their eyes off him. Polly gritted her teeth, remembering the time they'd run into Edna St. Vincent Millay, when they were having coffee at a sidewalk table at the Brevoort. The red-headed vamp of the Provincetown Players had become even more successful as a poetess than as a playwright, and her appetite for men had not diminished either.

"What a surprise!" Vincent cried, pretending to be overjoyed to see Polly, whom she scarcely spoke to at the theater. But the big, green eyes were drinking in Hymie, whose own eyes were almost popping out of his head. "You sell houses!" she exclaimed, after Polly had introduced them. "How divine! You must take a look at mine. It's an absolutely darling little house on Barrow St. Just nine feet wide. Polly knows it, don't you, love?" The green eyes barely flicked in Polly's direction, before locking on Hymie's again. "I'm dying to know how much you think I could get for it—that is, if I ever decide to sell. Would you be interested in coming over some time?"

"You bet I would," said Hymie. "Give me a call." He whisked out one of his business cards and handed it over. "Any time!"

"How lucky I am to have run into you!" Millay gave him a brilliant smile, as she slipped the card into a beaded handbag. "I really must dash. Toodle-oo." She sauntered away through the tables, giving him a view of her pert behind.

Hymie grinned. "Quite a dish! You never told me about her before."

"Is it any wonder?" Polly said. "She practically seduced you across the table."

"Come off it, doll," he said, "she only asked me to look at her house."

"Don't play dumb. She'd have you in bed in five minutes."

He touched a finger to her turned-up nose that he was so crazy about. "You don't have to worry about competition from any high-powered maneater like her. Cross my heart."

"Well, you certainly ate up her goo-goo eyes."

"Hey, don't I put up with Larry Mathews making goo-goo eyes at you?"

"Don't be mean. I'm so worried about him." Since Larry Mathews had come back to New York, Polly had hardly seen him. They'd only run into him once. As far as she knew, her ex-assistant had no friends and spent all his time painting in some furnished room over by the river. In one way it might be a good thing, after the pressure of what he had been through, but in another she felt he was running away from life. She sighed. "The war must have been ghastly for him."

"Hey," Hymie said, "I was in the war, too. Don't you feel a little sorry for me?"

Polly laughed, and kissed him. "Of course, I do. Why do you think I got mother to invite you to dinner tonight?"

Finishing her preparations in front of the mirror, she checked her watch. She still had plenty of time to get to the audition in midtown.

It still worried her, that meeting with Larry. She hadn't thought of him in weeks. He'd looked so forlorn. She should have asked him for his address.

Larry Mathews had been fired from his latest job as a sign painter. He walked home along the busy Hudson waterfront in the middle of the afternoon, not really caring. He had hated all the jobs he'd had since coming back from the war. This time, his boss had said he didn't have the right attitude. Of course, he didn't have the right attitude. Who wanted to be a sign painter.

He turned onto West Thirteenth Street and went into the tenement building with the rusty fire escapes down the front, where he had a room. The landlady's door opened and, as if she had been waiting for him, Mrs. Kaminski looked out.

"I was hoping to see you, Mr. Mathews. I've got some clothes of Melvin's think might fit you."

Not responding, Larry headed for the stairs. The landlady was a widow who had lost her son in the war. She never let up on him.

She called up after him, "Like to take a look at them?"

"Sorry. Don't have time." He just wanted to be let alone. He walked down the hall to his door.

His small room was musty and he opened the window a crack. Next to the iron bedstead, an easel was set up. For a while he gazed at it, then at the stack of unfinished paintings against the wall. He had sweated over each one of them, before giving up.

He made himself set the first one back on the easel. It was a sketch of one of his old subjects, a barn and a silo at the edge of a wheat field he remembered from before the orphanage. He picked up his palette, blowing away some flecks of soot, then tried to squeeze out some ochre paint from a tube. But he'd left the lid off and the paint had hardened.

He tossed it onto a pile of debris in the corner and, at the sink, washed down two barbiturate tablets the army had given him.

He stretched out on the unmade bed, looking up at the cracked plaster of the ceiling. He hated this room, he hated being back in New York, but what else was there to do?

Polly Endicott was the only one he could think of he'd like to talk to, but he'd run into her with a new boyfriend, and hearing that they lived together, he knew she had no time for him any more. The tea shop, where he'd been with her every day, was gone, everything he remembered from before was gone.

He felt his lids heavy and, before he knew it, he was sinking into blessed sleep. But instead of the oblivion he hoped for, he was back in the trenches, the air filled with the exploding shells of the howitzers, the frightful cries of "Gas!", the men being blown to bits around him, and then he was falling into the mud, the mud covering his face, suffocating him....

He sat bolt upright, wide-awake, shaking, terrified.

Someone was pounding on the door. Mrs. Kaminski.

"You okay in there? You been calling out!"

He didn't make a sound, waiting. Finally, he heard her muttering under her breath, walking away, back down the stairs.

He twisted his face into the pillow, grinding his teeth.

Ready at last for the audition, Polly smoothed her skirt and straightened her middy blouse over it, promising herself that she would try to find Larry and cheer him up. She had a fund of stories about making the rounds, and, hopefully, she'd have good news if she got the part today.

She struck a pose in front of the mirror with her hands on her hips and a grin on her face, as if she had just made a wisecrack to big sister. She was a perfect character juvenile, and this audition was her big chance.

But as she was putting on her coat to head uptown to the theater, her stomach went into a spasm, and she ran to the sink and threw up.

When the nausea didn't stop, she went to the doctor, who confirmed that she was pregnant.

The following evening, she and Hymie had plans to go to a new speakeasy on Eighth Street, but now a raucous atmosphere was the last thing she wanted. She cajoled him into taking her on the Staten Island ferry again, using the unlikely ploy that it was the eleven-month anniversary of their meeting.

The ferry! he said. Was she nuts? It was November, and cold out there on the water. But she said it wasn't that cold. She was feeling sentimental, and the ferry ride was exactly what she was in the mood for.

Hymie grinned. "Since when are you so schmaltzy?"

"There are a lot of things about me you don't know," she said in her character-juvenile voice.

But as the two of them stood against the rail at the back of the boat watching the towers of lower Manhattan recede, the nostalgic mood she was hoping for didn't materialize. Hymie kidded her that the eye shadow she had put on to hide the ravages of a sleepless night made her look like Theda Bara.

She waited until they were out in the middle of the harbor, and were reminiscing over their first date on the same ferry, before she sprang her surprise. Taking a deep drag on her cigarette, she exhaled and said in an offhanded manner, "Now don't laugh, but what if we just got married?"

Hymie was taken aback. "You kidding? Don't I already have enough problems?"

She looked out over the dark-roiling wake of the ferry to the lit-up Statue of Liberty across the water. Still trying to keep her tone light, she said, "You're going to make all those buckets of money and I want to be sure I get my share."

He didn't laugh as she hoped. Why change anything, he told her? Weren't things just fine the way they were?

"Of course. I just thought it would be fun, that's all."

Puffing fast on his cigarette, he looked out toward the distant lights of Ellis Island, where his parents had landed a quarter of a century before, just in time for him to be born in America. Then he dropped the cigarette on the deck, grinding it out with his shoe. "You're serious about this, aren't you, Pol?"

"I just think it would be fun," she said too brightly, but sensing it was not going right. "We could play house for a while, and if we get tired of it, we could always get a divorce—everybody's doing it these days."

But the more she pushed, the more remote Hymie became, chain-smoking one cigarette after another, until at her wits' end, she dropped the last of her pretense. "What's wrong with us getting married, for God's sake? Don't tell me you have a wife, too!"

He was still looking off over the dark water, smoking restlessly. "If that were the problem, it wouldn't be a problem. I don't know if I can make you understand." When he turned back to her, he was frowning. "It's my family."

"Your family! What do they have to do with anything!" He hadn't even let her meet them, she said. How could he be so sure they wouldn't like her?

It wasn't that, he said. It was just that his family still believed in the old traditions. "Look, Pol, I may have a trim haircut and drink bathtub gin and even eat bacon and eggs with you every Sunday morning, but a part of me has still got invisible earlocks flapping."

Polly was exasperated. "What in hell are you talking about?"

"This is going to be tough," Hymie said, "but give me a chance...." He sat her down on a bench, and explained that his parents were strict Orthodox Jews, and if he married a Christian girl, they'd go into mourning for him as if he were dead and grieve for the rest of their lives.

Polly said that was ridiculous, if they cared about him so much, why the hell hadn't they come to the troopship to meet him when he came home from the war?

"It was a Friday night!" he said.

"What's that got to do with it?"

He explained about Friday night being the start of the Sabbath, when religious Jews were forbidden to travel.

She jumped up and turned on him. "I've never heard of anything so utterly absurd!"

"That's what they're always telling us." He gave a sad smile. "I think it's a little meshugganeh myself...." But his religion was five-thousand-years old, he told her, and after what they had gone through to hang on to it, they weren't going to drop their customs just because they seemed out-of-date.

Polly wanted to shake him hard and tell him she didn't care about all that, he had to marry her, she was pregnant, didn't he understand that? Pregnant, and unmarried! But something held her back. This man she had fallen in love with was far more complicated than she imagined—almost alien. Much as she hated to admit it at this moment, maybe it was this unknown part of him that had always attracted her the most.

"So you see, Pol," he said, putting his arms around her, "getting hitched just wouldn't be the right thing for us. We're okay the way we are, aren't we? You know I'm crazy about you and always will be."

Polly was defeated. She wound her scarf around her neck against the chill and said, keeping the quaver out of her voice, that maybe it was all right as they were.

His arms still around her, he sang his corny song about being very jolly and very merry and riding all night back and forth on the ferry.

But this time they didn't ride all night on the ferry. They went back to the Village to the new speakeasy on Eighth Street, where she drank too much gin, and when they came home and he tried to make love to her, she told him she wasn't feeling well, and lied that her period was coming on early.

It wasn't hard getting the name of someone. A woman Polly knew, who ran a pottery shop across the street, had used the man several times already, and took her to the ordinary apartment house out in Queens. As she lay waiting on the makeshift operating table, the man who claimed to be a doctor said there was nothing to worry about, she'd be as good as new in no time. But no sooner was it over and she had just laid her head back and closed her eyes in the "recovery room," the "doctor" told her friend from the pottery shop she had to get Polly out of there, he wasn't running a rest home. Somehow, her friend got her to her feet and, with her friend supporting her, she stumbled downstairs. In the cab back to Manhattan, Polly covered her face with her hands, hating Hymie, herself, the whole mess.

During the first couple of days recuperating at her mother's, she was determined to give Hymie up. She knew most of her women friends would support her on this, agreeing he was a selfish bastard. But on the third night, she dreamed about Corinne Ashmore. She awoke the next morning feeling the Frenchwoman's presence still in the room. "You would throw passion away over a convention like marriage? Don't be a fool, *chérie*. Marriage has nothing to do with love. It is a contract based on other concerns. He doesn't give you the ring? But that is no reason to give him up. You get from him something more important. Something that women have just as much a right to as men." And here Polly felt on her the wise, lidded eyes she remembered so well. "But one last bit of advice, *hein*? Do not be a silly goose again and forget to take the precautions...."

Polly's resolve was shaken. Maybe Corinne was right. It was true Hymie gave her something no man ever had. She'd never love another man like this. But if she did go on with him, she would follow Corinne's advice. Hymie had never used a condom when they made love. She had been too embarrassed to say anything, but why the hell hadn't she? She was the one who had to spread her legs on the abortionist's kitchen table. It was her own damn fault playing the innocent twenty-year-old, when she was a thirty-one-year-old woman. If Hymie was irresponsible, she couldn't afford to be.

Before going back to her lover, she turned around the gold birthstone ring her father had given her, so that it resembled a wedding band, and went to the Margaret Sanger birth control clinic to be fitted for a diaphragm.

With the diaphragm in her purse, she followed an impulse and stopped off at a hairdressing salon to have her hair bobbed and marcelled. Everybody had been talking about this new hairstyle, since the rotogravure pictures in the papers of Frenchwomen at the Armistice celebration in Paris. It was an extreme thing to do, but she didn't want any trace left of that pug-nosed, freckled-face little daddy's girl. Her old act revolted her.

But when she came out from under the hair dryer, prepared to see herself transformed into a woman of the world, she got a surprise. Reflected in the mirrors of the salon, her short hair pressed into finger waves around her head made her look even younger than before.

On New Year's Eve—it was 1920—as she and Hymie toasted their first year together with champagne cocktails at the Peacock Court of the Plaza, he said they hadn't seen anything yet. The new decade was going to be a roller coaster ride like never before, and the two of them were going to take it all the way to hell and back together.

How adorably innocent he was, how maternal she felt. My love, she thought, as she looked into his eyes and they clinked champagne glasses, I'm mad about you and can't live without you, but I won't fly off into the blue any more. You can have your dreams and I'll be there for you all the way, but I'm looking after myself from now on.

15

On a warm evening in September, the lights of the Casa di Mario, the Alfano family restaurant, blazed, and a sign on the door read, "Closed For Private Party." Through the open windows, passersby marveled at the glorious tenor voice belting out *"Addio mi bella Napoli…,"* the Neapolitan song once heard by young Alicia Endicott through the open windows on Perry Street.

In the restaurant kitchen, Dominic Alfano stopped whipping cream for the dessert to listen to his father serenading the guests out in the restaurant. It was Dominic and Rosalie's engagement party, but as the restaurant's chef, Dom was proud to cater the dinner, content to let his affable father bask in the limelight as usual.

The song his father Mario was singing always made him nostalgic for the Naples of his grandparents. Though he adored his grandmother Elizabeth, Dominic had been raised mostly by the Alfano side of his family, and he never felt totally at home in the Endicotts' world. This conflict in him had always made him feel somewhat out of place—except when he was cooking. Now that he was engaged to Rosalie—all the relatives and friends were gathered to celebrate it—he was sure things were going to be easier for him from now on.

Just before he finished whipping the cream, he added a few drops of liqueur. Late that afternoon, busy as he was, *Nonna*, his Neapolitan grandmother, pleaded with him as a special favor to make for dessert his *zuppa inglese*, although he had already baked anise-and-pignole cookies, and a spumoni was in the icebox.

"…Addio mi bella Napoli…." His father's voice soared above the accordion and violin accompanying him. Even the children had stopped yelling and running around among the tables.

In his year in Italy at the cooking school, Dominic had visited Naples, even taken the little train around the slopes of Mt. Vesuvius and the *vaporetto* out to Capri—it was all very picturesque. But listening to the sobbing for a lost Naples in his father's bel canto voice, it was not a place it made him long for, but something else, something he had never had, something he hoped to find with Rosalie.

In the cooking school he had gotten to know a girl he wanted to marry, a blonde girl from Holland, like the pictures of his mother who had died at his birth. But his father had discouraged it, and made him see that it was better that he marry a girl from home.

After he got back from Italy, he had been too busy helping his father in the restaurant to give a thought to marriage. But once he had settled in, his father asked what was he waiting for, it was time for him to start a family.

When the cream stood in peaks, he set it aside, and took down from the cooling rack the large pan holding the cake of egg batter and candied fruits, and soaked the cake with rum before swirling the whipped cream over the top.

The kitchen was the place he was at his best, but when he was a schoolboy, he had resented having to work there after school and on weekends, because it had cut him off from his late mother's family, especially his grandmother Elizabeth. She and Polly and Eugene were at his engagement party today, even if Nonna wasn't happy about it, but his father had shut her up. Nonna was always talking against the Endicotts.

Prohibition had come in at the beginning of the year, but it hadn't been a problem. Casa di Mario had a regular clientele who liked the food and the wine they made themselves in the cellar. They didn't need bootleg liquor to make a go of it. A bocce court ran along one side of the restaurant, where neighborhood men bowled on a packed earth floor. His father had painted the walls with sunflowers and olive and lemon trees, and on the ceiling, fat cupids among rolling clouds. For the party today, they had made it even more festive, with crepe paper rosettes and streamers and silver cutouts of Punchinello and Colombina.

As a final touch to the *zuppa inglese*, Dominic sprinkled over the whipped cream a handful of crushed pistachio nuts and another of chopped candied cherries, and decorated the pan with a fringe of gold paper. Lifting the dessert onto his shoulder, he pushed his way through the swinging door into the dining room and waited behind a marblized pillar, as the glorious voice washed over him.

There he was, standing at the front table, his bald, roly-poly father gesturing with his pudgy arms, and wiping with a red handkerchief the sweat glistening on his brow. Ever since Dominic could remember, his father had sung at family events. He loved to be with people so much, how could he help but be the center of attention? It was almost as if his papa were the one getting engaged to Rosalie.

Dominic's dark-haired fiancée was gazing up at her future father-in-law entranced, her full lips parted as she listened to the song. In a beaded, pink dress, she had the air of a Titian madonna he had seen in the Turin cathedral, and with the same hint of a blush on her face. *Che bellissima.* It was only in Italian—the language he had learned from his Nonna before he knew English—that he could describe her, his *promessa sposa.* She was just out of the convent school of St. Joseph on Sixth Avenue, educated by nuns the same as in Italy. Her father was a wholesale butcher, and the restaurant got its meat from him.

Rosalie was ten years younger than Dominic and they hardly knew each other, but she would make a good wife. He had so little experience with women, but of course, if he needed any advice, his father would always be there for him.

Rosalie was going to work in the restaurant with the family, and Nonna would train her. His grandmother Alfano, though she was almost eighty, still supervised making the red wine they served, even though it had become illegal since Prohibition. But there was nothing to worry about. The Casa di Mario wasn't a speakeasy and the cops knew it. How could you eat Italian food without wine?

Most of the other restaurants in the Village had already turned into speakeasies. They were nothing but ginmills, his father said. The food didn't matter any more. He didn't want to have anything to do with liquor or the bootleggers who supplied it. When the hoods came around threatening trouble if Casa di Mario didn't sign up, his father told them to go to hell—he wasn't afraid of anybody.

Dom didn't like them either, they scared him, but he wasn't so sure a restaurant turning into a speak was all bad. It wasn't just the bootleggers making money. Several other families with restaurants in the neighborhood who went along with them were making so much money it was falling out of their pockets. They owned brand-new Cadillacs and bought fur coats for their wives.

"*...Addio mi bella Napoli....*" His father's voice sobbed out the final refrain. Among all the Italian faces in the room, his three Endicott relatives stood out. His handsome grandmother Elizabeth, in a big hat swathed in veils and a lavender suit, was sitting between Eugene and Polly at a table on the side. It was hard to believe that she was almost as old as Nonna, who was wrinkled and bent over and always in black.

It was lucky the Endicotts didn't understand Italian because of the awful things Nonna always muttered in front of them—Elizabeth a widow and not dressed in black, for example. When he defended Polly's bobbed hair because she was an actress, the old woman said it was the same thing to being a *puttana*. Half the Protestant women were.

He didn't care what she said. He loved his grandmother Elizabeth, and Polly had always been nice to him. It was harder to be with Eugene, but then Eugene was a college graduate and a writer, and he himself had such a stupid tongue. His Nonna didn't have a good word to say about Eugene either—hadn't he left his wife and child and gotten a divorce? To her, there was no good in any of the Endicotts, and she was always warning him that he had to watch out for their bad blood in his veins.

The song ended. His father held out his arms in triumph, the sweat glistening on his bald head, as everyone shouted and applauded. Then he caught sight of Dominic waiting with the cake pan, and called out, "Dom, where you been? You come over here and sit down by your sweetheart, where you belong."

His pudgy father trotted over and, as the room burst into laughter, took the *zuppa inglese* from him, balancing it in the air with one hand, and with the other pushing Dominic over to the chair beside the blushing girl he was going to marry.

With the jokers in the room teasing him, Dominic was too shy to look at Rosalie, but he was dizzy from the scent of her long, dark hair. Even her skin smelled as fragrant as orange blossoms in Naples. Was this vivid creature really going to share his bed? How could he wait the months till June? Now that they were engaged, he hoped that they wouldn't have a chaperone every time they were together.

The violin and accordion struck up a traditional Italian dance, and his father, his cheeks flushed with wine, called out, "Hey, Dom and Rosalie, what you two lovebirds waiting for?" Everyone started clapping in time to the music, urging the engaged couple to take to the floor. But Dominic was afraid he'd fall over his feet and Rosalie would be ashamed of him—he could never catch the rhythm—so he made a comic show of hiding his head under his arms.

Everyone roared. His father drained his wine glass, wiping his lips with the back of his hand. "If he don't want to, Rosalie, I guess we got no choice!" He held a hand out to the delighted girl and danced her off around the floor with amazing agility.

Everyone exclaimed what a perfect couple they made. An uncle called out to Dominic that if he didn't watch out, his old man was going to carry off his bride. His grandmother Alfano, having drunk too much, hollered that that was the kind of girl her son Mario should have married in the first place and, turning to Dominic as she kept time with her old, gnarled hands, said that with Endicott blood in him, no wonder he couldn't dance like a real Italian.

"Ah, grandma, you're crazy," he said, as he clapped to the music along with the rest.

His father, in spite of his weight, was still as light on his feet as a boy, and after whirling Rosalie around the room, he delivered her back to the table. Her cheeks were flushed, and the tight armpits of her pink satin dress were wet. As she sat down, she glanced at Dominic, then looked away quickly—she was still so shy with him. That was the way a virgin should be, his father had said, like a sleeping princess, and it was up to the husband to wake her up.

The musicians were playing a medley from *La Traviata*, and everybody joined in singing the drinking song. But when Alfredo's aria *"A quell' amor"* began, his father's soaring tenor took over and he turned to sing it especially to Dominic and Rosalie. But he wasn't singing for them. It was as if the music had carried him away, as if he were thinking of something long past—and listening, Dominic felt a stab of the old longing in his chest.

Before the final verse, his father moved across the room to stand in front of grandmother Elizabeth. His hand on his heart, he sang to her alone Verdi's anthem of an impossible love. And though her expression betrayed nothing, Dominic felt that the song held some great meaning for her in the past. Whatever it was had never been spoken about, but he knew that what he was homesick for was a world that had disappeared before he was born.

As his father came to the final note of the aria, his chest expanded and his voice rose to a heart-stopping high C, holding the note for what seemed an eternity. When, finally, it faded away, the audience sat in stunned silence. His grandmother Elizabeth, visibly struggling to control her feelings, raised a glass to his father in a gesture of thanks, as the bravos and stamping applause burst forth.

Then, everything happened so fast, Dominic was never clear about it afterward. Everybody who was there that night gave different versions to the police.

His father walked slowly back to Dominic and Rosalie's table in an exalted mood and, smiling broadly before them, banged a spoon against a glass for silence. "My dear family and friends," he said, "join me in a toast to my beloved son and his beautiful bride-to-be."

He had never looked so happy, his father, so full of love, so full of life, when without warning the front door of the restaurant was kicked open and three men with tommyguns, their faces behind the lapels of their overcoats, the brims of their hats down to their eyes, stood in the doorway and opened fire.

His father's body fell across the table in front of him and, as the room erupted in screams and pandemonium around them, Dominic stared at the blood, spattered onto the bosom of Rosalie's pink dress.

16

In the years following her husband's death, Elizabeth Endicott fell into the habit of spending Sunday mornings in bed reading the Times. On a wet Sunday in the spring of 1921 she was propped up on pillows wearing a rose-colored bed jacket, her still-ample gray hair in a net, the paper in sections around her on the coverlet. Beside her on a chair was her breakfast tray—the shells of a soft-boiled egg, the crumbs of a corn muffin, an empty orange juice glass. She was going to be seventy-three her next birthday, but she felt better than she had twenty years before.

Getting cold on the bedside table was a pot of coffee. Eugene always came by for coffee around nine, but it was well after nine and he hadn't shown up yet.

She examined a photograph in the women's pages of the modernized interior of a house in the neighborhood with stark white walls, low, block-shaped furniture, and cubist pictures in metallic frames. It looked like an icehouse. She couldn't imagine living in such a place.

There were always stories about Greenwich Village in the papers stressing its eccentricity. Hymie Liebman, of course, would be highly pleased with the piece. In the past year, since he had left the real estate office to set up on his own, he had been quite successful cashing in on the growing reputation of the Village as a place to live in Manhattan. He was doing so well with those renovated houses on Tenth Street. What a blessing that he was rescuing them from decay.

Polly was spending most of her time these days doing his secretarial work, but Hymie was such a charmer, who could blame her? Since they were living together openly, Elizabeth would have been more pleased if they had gotten married. But Polly declared that marriage was the last thing she cared about—it was the twentieth century, after all, and women were emancipated. To her daughter, anyone who still remembered Queen Victoria was a fossil.

Elizabeth poured herself a cold cup of coffee. She wouldn't wait for Eugene. She still had her community activities during the week—the fastest way to turn into a fossil was not to keep busy. She saw enough examples of that in the volunteer work she did, visiting the elderly and shut-ins in the area, reading to them, doing little chores, trying to keep their spirits up. But it was an uphill struggle, and she was getting tired of it. She herself had never been sick a day in her life! She saw no reason for anyone to sit around all the time like a vegetable.

She got up and went to the window to see if Eugene was coming. He was living such an interesting life now, and knew so many of the arts people in the Village. He made his living working as a bartender nights at 86 Barrow, a charming, little bistro, and during the day he helped put out a literary magazine that had already published a couple of his stories.

He'd introduced her to the editors of The Little Review, Margaret Anderson and Jane Heap. they two of the most formidably intellectual women she had ever met. They shared a bizarre, little apartment on Fourteenth Street where they edited the magazine, and rented a room to Eugene on the floor above. Their living room had gold wallpaper and a sofa suspended by chains from the ceiling. They were publishing that Irishman's unreadable novel, Ulysses, in installments, and causing a scandal. Every other issue of their magazine was impounded by the post office, and they had gotten into so much trouble over it, they were talking about moving to Paris.

Eugene made her laugh so much, telling her about the oddball characters who came into the bar where he worked. He seemed in fairly good shape, but there was an anxious look in his eyes, that others might not recognize, but that she could detect. Thank God, he was finally going out to Cincinnati to see his son—Seth was already seven years old. His ex-wife, Clare, was about to remarry and he was going to the wedding. Of all people, she was marrying Eugene's boyhood chum Toby Harris, who was also divorced, and doing very well, with an automobile dealership out there.

Eugene had read her his ex-wife's letter, which said she ought to have married Toby in the first place. She claimed she had always been attracted to Toby, though she hadn't realized it, and went on to say she and Eugene were much too alike ever to have made a go of it.

How absurd! The opposite was true. That woman had never understood the first thing about her son—their interests were entirely different. That was what had been wrong from the start.

Clare said she was convinced that Toby would be a good father to Seth, who already looked up to him, and Toby had added a postscript seconding the invitation to the wedding.

Gene going out to meet his son at last was just what Elizabeth had hoped for. He needed to have the boy in his life. It would make up for all the unhappiness he had gone through.

Out the window, Perry Street was deserted in the wet. It had changed so little through the years, except for the parked automobiles. The old houses still looked exactly the same. A horse and wagon clomped along, and stopped to deliver milk. The milkman's assistant, a dark-haired young man, ran down the kitchen steps of the house across the street and, as he came back to the milk wagon, happened to glance up at where she stood in the window. Her heart contracted—he was the spitting image of Mario when he first met Alicia. It had been six months since that ghastly night at the Alfanos' restaurant. Suddenly weary, she went back to bed.

Elizabeth hadn't understood why the Alfanos had rushed the wedding, until Dominic told her that Rosalie was pregnant. It had not been a joyous affair—the ceremony had seemed to her more like a wake than a wedding mass.

Dominic's world had always centered around his father, but after the murder, it had fallen apart. He wanted to quit the restaurant, but his Nonna and Rosalie wouldn't hear of it. They kept after him, arguing that what had happened to Mario was not just because of the mob, but it was God's will, and with a child on the way, he just couldn't walk out. It wasn't as if selling liquor was a sin, everyone did it—and the only thing to do was follow the way all the Village restaurants were going.

Elizabeth had to agree that Prohibition was a foolish law, but she wasn't so sure that Dominic didn't have the right idea about getting out of the family restaurant, considering the painful associations it would always have for him. Still, wife and grandmother were too much for him, and he submitted. It was clear that the vacuum in her grandson's life left by the death of his father was going to be filled by his new wife. At the New Year, the Casa di Mario reopened as a speakeasy.

Elizabeth had spent so many nights agonizing over the monstrous killing of Mario. It would haunt her forever.

The doorbell rang. Eugene must have forgotten his key. She got up, slipped off her hairnet, and put on a robe. They would talk over what he was writing, all stream-of-consciousness prose she couldn't make head or tail of, and he would distract her from that awful memory.

But it wasn't Eugene at the door. It was her nephew Dennis Yates in civilian clothes. He was a lieutenant on the police force by now, but he still dropped by to visit her. He had married only after the death of his mother, and she thought at first that he must be coming to thank her for the birthday gift she had sent his little boy, Timothy.

But Dennis was here for something else, something he was having difficulty telling her, that filled her with foreboding.

"It's about Gene, Aunt Elizabeth."

"Eugene!" she cried. "He's been in an accident!"

"It's not that," said Dennis, his brow furrowed.

"Well, what is it then? Tell me!"

Her nephew didn't meet her eyes. "I'm afraid...he's in jail."

Elizabeth sucked in her breath. "Oh, dear God! What's he done?"

Dennis was twisting his hat in his hands, looking miserable. "I don't exactly know how to put it to you, Auntie."

Elizabeth saw that she must keep calm and take charge of the situation, if she was to get out of him what this was about. Taking his arm, she led him to the sofa to sit down beside her, assuring him that whatever it was, she was capable of understanding.

It was several moments before her nephew raised his eyes to her. "You know about Eugene, Aunt Elizabeth...."

Her stomach fluttered. "I think I do," she said, keeping her voice under control. "Now tell me, please."

It was worse than she expected. It turned out, Dennis told her, that Eugene had been arrested several times over the past year, always blind drunk and in situations that Dennis couldn't bring himself to describe to a lady. Until the night before, he had always been able to get Eugene off. Once, the judge at night court had been a personal friend and he had dismissed the case as a favor to Dennis. Another time, he got the arresting officers to release Eugene with a warning, instead of booking him. But this time he couldn't do anything. They were having a crackdown on vice in the Village—all the publicity about it in the papers, orders from higher ups—and the only thing to do was to get a lawyer who would pay off the judge and the arresting officers. That was the way it worked.

"How much will it cost?" Elizabeth asked, without flinching.

"Two hundred dollars, I'm afraid. I could chip in twenty, Auntie— that's all I got on me."

"I have the cash." She went over to Patrick's old rolltop desk where she kept money for emergencies. Handing it over, she asked, "They'll let him off now and that will be the end of it?"

Her nephew said that Gene would definitely be released that afternoon, but he couldn't promise her there wouldn't be more trouble in the future. Even if Gene kept his nose clean, in every vice case from now on he'd be an automatic suspect, and be picked up. "I just can't figure, Aunt Elizabeth, why he goes on this way? In the name of God, doesn't he have any self-respect?" Dennis's good-natured face screwed up. "He couldn't have had a better mother than you. If you ask me, he'd be better off if you put him away."

Elizabeth said she was grateful for all he had done, but as she saw him out the door she noticed that his once trim frame was thickening and, for the first time, she was annoyed with him and his limited policeman's way of looking at things.

While she waited to hear from Eugene, she suffered over the humiliation her son must be going through. Now she knew why he had so often seemed drawn and nervous. Why hadn't she done something? She was to blame for not having been able to admit to herself what was wrong. Now that it was out in the open, they would have a more honest relationship. She would see to that.

But when she hadn't heard from Eugene by five that afternoon, she went to the room where he lived on Fourteenth Street.

It was twilight when she got there. She knocked, but there was no answer. The building super told her that he was there, he had seen him come in earlier.

Elizabeth was frightened and she knocked louder, calling out his name. Eventually, there was a sound and the door opened. In the glare of the hall bulb her son was haggard, his face unshaven and bruised. He had a black eye.

"What did you bail me out for?" he said, and looked away.

She walked by him and over to the lamp to turn it on. The pull-down bed with its tumble of bedding nearly filled the room. She quickly straightened it and pushed it back up into its niche in the wall. Then she went to fill the pot at the washbasin for coffee.

He was still standing by the door, not looking at her. "You can stop playing the understanding mother," he said in a belligerent tone. "I'm not going to apologize."

"I'm not asking you to." He was in no state to listen to anything. Lighting his hotplate and setting the pot on, she clutched at the one idea that would help give him back some self-respect—the trip he was going to make out to Cincinnati to see his son Seth. He was a father, after all. Being reunited with his child might save him. She would have to look for a way to introduce the subject.

It was when he told her she shouldn't have come, he was going to go away, that she saw her chance. "Of course, you're going," she said brightly. "You're going to Cincinnati." He might even make his train reservation sooner, she added. She could do it for him.

"You making a joke? I couldn't look that kid in the eye."

"Nonsense. You'll feel differently after you get some rest. And you'll see Toby Harris again. Clare wants to see you too, and she says little Seth has been talking of nothing else."

Eugene told her to stop pushing him, he was not going to see his son. He was just going to get on a bus and keep moving. He just wanted to go away.

"But you've got to go somewhere." A plan began to take shape in her mind, while she scrambled him some eggs. She understood now that it was impossible for him to go on with his life in the same way. He'd get into even worse trouble than he was already in—Dennis had made that quite clear. But was there any point in bringing up such brutal facts at this moment?

After she made him sit down and got a few bites down him, she said, as casually as she could, that if he wasn't ready to visit his son just now, might not Paris be an idea? "Going to Paris made a big difference in my life once, maybe it can do the same for you. You'd get away from all this unpleasantness, and it would be a fine place to go on with your writing."

She was heartened to see a spark of hope in his eyes, but immediately the resentful look was back. He said that he had no money, and if she was going to offer to pay his way, to forget it. He was past thirty, and he had messed up his own life beyond repair, and no well-meaning, old mother was going to rescue him.

His using the word "old" gave her a momentary start, but she covered it with a determined smile. "You could live for very little over there now, from what they tell me, and it won't be any sacrifice for me to advance it to you, dear." When he still remained adamant against the idea, she reminded him that so many young artists were going to Paris since the war. He had told her himself, hadn't he, that his two friends in the building, Jane Heap and Margaret Anderson, were transferring The Little Review there?

"I'm finished with all that," he said, shoving back his plate. "What good is it?" He looked out morosely at the lit skylights and back windows of the studios across the way. A violinist was practicing double stops, and somewhere a typewriter was clacking.

There were times when only brutality worked, and she laid it on the line. "Listen to me, Eugene, I don't think you have much choice. Dennis tells me that just because he got you off again doesn't mean you won't be picked up every time they're looking for someone."

She saw that this hadn't occurred to him, and he collapsed into a chair under the weight of his predicament. He said that even if the law kept punishing him for the way he was, he was stuck with it.

It didn't look good to her at all. He was so defeated by his wretchedness, he couldn't do a single thing to save himself. As they sat on in the drab hall bedroom, where the pages of a forgotten manuscript lay forlornly around his old Remington typewriter in the corner, she saw a way to get him to the boat. "What if I were to come with you?" He didn't look up, and she went on rapidly, "Not to be your keeper—don't think that. I mean just for a few weeks of museum-going, while you get set up." He was still slumped in the chair, but she knew he was listening. "I know what a joke it's been in the family, me always talking about Paris, but I've wanted to go back for so long. Your father would never hear of it, of course, and now, here's my chance."

Her son, who had been keeping his battered face turned away from her, looked around and let her see the gratitude in his eyes. "You don't give up on me, do you?"

Elizabeth turned the house on Perry Street over to Polly and, a week later, she and Eugene sailed for Le Havre on the Ville de Bordeaux.

17

Polly stepped off the train onto the sunny platform of the Sixth Avenue el a few blocks from Hymie's office, but as she descended the stairs, the seedy, leftover-midnight feeling in the shadows under the tracks better reflected her mood. The audition she was coming from had turned out to be one of those cattle calls, where everybody and his grandmother showed up, and the producers hadn't gotten around to her until nearly noon. Her knitted, nile-green suit and cloche hat she had bought especially for the part of the young aunt, only to be told even before she opened her mouth that she wasn't the right type! She was fed up—too old to be an ingenue, wrong for leading lady, too young for character woman. What the hell was she supposed to do while she waited?

A long, open touring car pulled away from the curb, belching exhaust fumes in her face. An elevated train roaring by overhead powdered her new, nile-green outfit with soot. And her father had predicted that electrifying the trains would end the dirt problem—the poor innocent!

She was ready to call it quits with the acting. Since Hymie had gotten rid of the tea shop for her and she had started making the rounds, she had had exactly four acting jobs, two of them walk-ons, another as an extra in a D. W. Griffith one-reeler shot out in Astoria, and another demonstrating potato peelers at Woolworth's.

When she had left the apartment that morning, Hymie, with his usual optimism, swore she would knock 'em dead at the audition and promised to keep the decks clear for a celebration lunch—he was going to lock the office door to the world and catch up on paperwork all morning. She needed that lunch and a couple of drinks, even if there was nothing to celebrate.

Hymie's storefront office on West Tenth Street was between a Chinese laundry and a tattoo parlor. It wasn't much, but it was a toehold. The couple of Village houses he had fixed up and sold had brought in enough capital for him to speculate on several other modest properties. Real estate in the Village was booming, but he was facing a lot of competition from other small-potatoes operators like himself, and even from some of the big boys who were moving in. He was way over his head in debt, but he wasn't worried—he told her that was the way business worked now. Polly didn't understand all the details, but it astonished her how slickly he operated—the way he conned his clients, his indifference to living in the red.

He had finally managed to pay her back the money from the sale of the tea shop, and had invested it for her in the stock market. She saved him the price of a secretary by doing his office work. It filled in some of the time she had on her hands from all the roles she wasn't getting.

She wondered why her own ambitions never seemed to come to anything. Hymie believed in what he was doing, maybe it was as simple as that. And even if he believed in what she was trying to do, too, she had to admit that she had never been more than lukewarm about the theater. But it didn't make her any the less furious when she was turned down and treated so shabbily, like today. It was a pick-me-up to know Hymie was waiting for her. What would she do without him?

But when she got to his office, he wasn't waiting for her with the consolation she needed. He was holed up with a customer, giving him his spiel about a listing on Charles Street.

She leaned against her desk in exasperation, waiting for him to finish. But he was too busy spinning a fantasy about the property being a perfect example of the Greek Revival style of the 1860s to even give her a glance. She knew the house he was talking about—it sagged so badly, the floors sloped. She cleared her throat several times trying to get his attention, but he was in the middle of dispelling the client's doubts based on newspaper accounts of gang warfare in the neighborhood between the Irish and the

Italians.

"Take my word for it," Hyme said, "the papers are making a mountain out of a molehill. With the values going up down here, the locals are selling out as fast as they can. I'm not kidding, a year from now you won't be able to touch a house like this at double the price." And, knowing full well that she was waiting for him, he had the nerve to suggest that he and the client walk right over and take a look at it.

Her heart sank—there went the lunch.

Her hopes revived when the client still expressed doubts about the neighborhood. But that bastard Hymie wouldn't give up, and insisted the house was just around the block, and it wouldn't take more than twenty minutes to look at it. What about her? Was she supposed to go and have a hotdog at a lunchwagon? Not caring what the client thought, she went over and planted herself in front of Hymie's desk. "In case you've forgotten, Mr. Liebman, we have a lunch date, and I for one am starving to death!"

The client stared at her open-mouthed, but Hymie, unfazed, jumped up and put an arm around her. "Pol, why didn't you let me know you were here?" he said, with a feigned innocence that made her want to throw up. "You know how I am when I'm hot about a property." He winked at her, and without missing a beat, turned to the client and smoothly introduced her as the famous painter, Pauline Endicott.

What in hell was he doing? Did he take the client for an idiot? But to her surprise, the man looked at her with fascination, and said that he and his wife were both interested in art.

She was about to disillusion him in no uncertain terms, but Hymie shut her up with a torrent of words, inventing for the client's benefit an instant career for her, with reputation, shows, and rave reviews.

The client was completely taken in, even asking for the name of her gallery.

Damn Hymie for getting her into this! She wasn't going to play along with the silly charade another minute. She told the man she had quit her gallery and had given up painting. Let Hymie deal with that one!

But he was undaunted. He laughed and asked her how many times she had threatened to do just that, but her collectors would never stand for it. And then he told an even bigger whopper to the gullible client—that her studio was in the same block as the house he wanted to show him. And moreover she wasn't the only artist who lived around there—there were at least a dozen other well-known painters and writers in the radius of a few blocks. "Isn't that right, Pol?"

"Yes," she said, beginning to enjoy the game, "and every goddam one of them is eating lunch now, except me."

The client seemed only more entertained by her display of "artistic temperament" and, before he departed, Hymie had talked him into bringing his wife to see the house on Charles Street the next day.

Hymie was jubilant when he came back from showing the man out. "You clinched it, Pol! I didn't have a hope in hell of selling that guy on the house, until you said you were a painter. He was drooling over it."

"When he finds out I don't have a studio on Charles Street, or anywhere else, he'll sue you for misrepresentation."

"The hell he will," he called from the storage room in back, where he was washing up. "He'll probably screw his wife tonight, thinking of you."

As they headed out to lunch, Hymie still chortling about Polly wowing his client by posing as a famous painter, not getting the part didn't seem so important to her any more. In fact, she wasn't sure any more that she wanted to go on with the theater. She needed to find a new direction.

18

Rosalie Alfano was sitting behind the cash register at the Casa di Mario. Her first child Stefano was not even a year old and she was already heavily pregnant again. Her ankles were so swollen, she could hardly walk.

She watched her stolid husband showing a party to a table across the room. Dominic didn't know how to joke with the customers like Mario, his late father, had, but most of the people who patronized the Casa di Mario cared about only one thing now, booze—Canadian Club or Seagram's Seven smuggled in over the border from Canada, or rum and scotch from some ship anchored beyond the three-mile limit—and they were willing to pay plenty for it.

Old Angelina, the grandmother, had got Dominic to cut out the fancy food he used to spend so much time preparing in the kitchen. That wasn't where the profit was any more, she told him, but for awhile he had been too thickheaded to see it. Spaghetti and meatballs with a little tomato sauce would satisfy the uptown customers—when they wanted any food at all—and the people around here would come anyway for Angelina's wine and to sit around the bocce court in back.

The Casa di Mario had been a speakeasy for a year and a half, and if it weren't for having to pay off the mob and the police, the Alfanos would have been on easy street. The restaurant was dominated by a magnificent, new mahogany bar with a large, cut-glass mirror behind it. The curtains at the front windows were never opened, even on sunny days, and the front door had a peekhole, so the customers could be checked out.

Rosalie straightened her blouse coyly, so her breasts would look good. One of the men in the party across the room had his eye on her. She was glad she was sitting down and he couldn't see her belly. She used to think she was pretty, but she hadn't had much attention from men since her marriage. It seemed to her that she had been pregnant and unattractive the whole time.

The man was still ogling her. Even if he was an old goat, she was pleased. The women with him at least weren't bad-looking and were smartly dressed.

Filippo, the waiter, who was a cousin of Dominic's, was showing her a fifty-dollar bill the local ward boss had left on the table without waiting for change, when Dominic came up to tell him to get back to work. Not a word or a look at her from him—her own husband—as if she weren't even there. It wasn't much different when they were upstairs together in the apartment. Even when the old woman wasn't there babbling away about how they should do this and how they should do that, he had nothing to say to her. He carried around his father's death like a sack. Dominic still took it so hard that he didn't even want her to mention his father's name. She sometimes wondered if that life-loving man, who had taken her breath away dancing her around the room at the engagement party, could actually have been his father. What a dummox she had been, thinking the son would be anything like him.

She couldn't even get Dominic to show any interest in their baby. Whenever he had any free time at all, he never relaxed with his family. He just wanted to keep busy, going over his accounts or finding things to do in the restaurant. Even at dinner he stayed just long enough to get the food down. How could you live like that?

She was no more to him than the cash register in front of her. When the lights went out in their bedroom, he climbed on her without a word and went through the act, without a thought for her. Being a good Catholic girl taught by the Sisters, she had no other experience of it, but from her married girlfriends, she knew there was more to it than that. Their husbands were passionate men, whispered beautiful words in their ears, wanted them to be passionate too. But whenever she started to let herself go, Dominic always lost interest, and turned away.

What kind of life was it? She wasn't even twenty-two, with a husband who acted like a lump, and old Angelina always on her back about something, no matter how hard she worked.

Sitting at the cash register night after night, Rosalie felt as if she were behind a glass wall, with the customers getting drunker and noisier, and the man she was chained to for life gloomily taking the orders and writing out the checks, and without an ounce of pleasure in his bones.

Her eyes met those of the bouncer on his stool beside the front door. Luciano his name was—such a beautiful name, when she whispered it to herself while she was out in the hall lavatory, the only place she could be herself. Dominic hated him, of course. Luciano they had been forced to hire. He kept an eye on things for the mob, and made sure nobody else tried to muscle in. Every night he took the mob's cut with him, when the black Packard came to pick him up. Even old Angelina upstairs, who saw dealing with the mob as strictly business, didn't have a good word to say about him.

But every time the bouncer looked at Rosalie behind the cash register—he had gray eyes, so unusual in a swarthy face—she felt herself go weak in the knees. They never spoke. Dominic and the grandmother, both, had forbidden her to say a word to him. But though she didn't tell any of her girlfriends, and there was nothing to tell the priest at Confession, Luciano kept her hope alive. He made her feel she wasn't totally defeated yet.

She risked another look at the bouncer, but he had gotten off his stool and was sizing up some new arrivals through the peekhole in the door before admitting them—there was always the chance that, even though the cops were paid off, there could still be a raid.

A party of two couples came in. To her annoyance, she saw that one of the women was Polly Endicott, her husband's relative. Dominic went over to greet her, for once with a smile on his face. Rosalie hardly ever saw him come alive for anyone—and that woman had the nerve to kiss him on the cheek.

As usual, she was dressed fit to kill in a coral print dress, showing no bosom and with the waistline around her hips—it must have cost a fortune. She was all painted up, with plucked and penciled eyebrows, and her bobbed hair looked suspiciously blonde. She was with her real estate boyfriend, and made a big show of introducing him and the other couple to Dominic. There were several empty tables, but to Rosalie's disgust, her husband had to seat them at the one closest to her at the cash register.

Polly recognized her and flashed a phony smile, but Rosalie pretended not to see. She knew the Endicotts hated her and she hated them back. She always found it hard to believe that Dominic was related to them in any way.

Why was he playing up to that stuck-up bitch like that, snapping his fingers for Filippo and telling him to give them anything they wanted? Polly waved a cigarette holder and said, in her high-falutin way, he was a perfect angel. It made Rosalie's stomach turn.

When she got the chance, she asked Dominic what were they doing there. Polly hadn't been around since Stefano was christened. He whispered back to please stop glaring at them—Polly and her boyfriend were just showing some people the Village.

Rosalie wasn't glaring, she was just taking in that long string of jade beads she would have given her eyeteeth for, but that hair was bleached to a frazzle—and who did Polly Endicott think she was kidding with all that paint on, she still looked every minute of thirty-five. And she went on waving that cigarette holder and swinging those beads, as she prattled away about her "studio" and her "painting." She had a nerve—she was no more a painter than an actress!

Her cigar-chomping boyfriend was laying it on just as thick, telling the suckers they were with that Polly wasn't the only artist there, and as Polly made a show of waving to some friends at another table, Rosalie heard him letting the other couple know they would be part of the "arts world" too, once they moved down here. It was all a lot of hooey, but the couple seemed to be eating it up, rubbernecking around the Casa di Mario, as if it was a sideshow.

While the boyfriend went on yapping about what a kick he got out of living in the Village, Polly pulled Dominic over, and stopped guzzling her booze long enough to ask, "Remember, Dommie, when we used to play upstairs with Eugene? No, of course you don't, you were too little." And she burst out laughing, as if someone were goosing her.

What nerve, acting as if Dominic had ever been one of the family to her. But her gullible husband infuriated Rosalie by saying, of course he remembered, and laughed along with her, forgetting the Endicotts had dropped him like a hot potato years before, although Rosalie reminded him often enough.

The final straw for Rosalie was when they asked for the check and Dominic told them it was on the house, like a big shot.

She kept quiet until after closing, when she was in the kitchen with him, counting the cash drawer, and he told her Polly had moved back to his grandmother Endicott's house on Perry Street, and had asked them for dinner.

"Over my dead body!" Rosalie said, putting a rubber band around a bundle of tens. "I wouldn't cross the street to see her. They all think we're dirty wops."

"What are you talking about?" Dominic said. "I told you how we grew up together. She's my family. You'll see."

"What I see is she's a stuck-up bitch and you're some kind of chump to fall for it."

Her husband tied up the bag containing the day's cut for the mob— the bouncer was outside at the bar waiting for it. "Why are you always carrying on about her? You and Nonna, both of you nagging at me. It's all on my shoulders. You're just jealous of her, that's all."

She slammed down the lid of the cash box. "What's on your shoulders? If you were half the man your father was...."

Dominic put down the bag, slowly, his usually expressionless face changing. "I told you before, never mention him. You're not good enough to kiss his ass."

He had never spoken to her like that. She knew she had gone too far. "I didn't mean nothing." She pouted, picking up the pencil and turning back to the account book. "It's just her putting on her hoity-toity airs. It gets me mad, that's all."

But when she went upstairs, where the old woman was looking after the baby, Rosalie still heard the edge of menace in her husband's voice, the rough language he had never used before—and she liked it.

19

Breakfast time at Rikers on Sheridan Square was the busiest time of the day. On one side of the horseshoe counter, customers freshly dressed for work, some of them reading a folded-back New York Times, downing their coffee and bagel before plunging into the subway. Facing them, at the opposite counter, the denizens of the night—haggard in the merciless light of day—swilling black coffee before moving on home to collapse.

The two countermen in between never stopped, as they took the orders and filled coffee cups. One of the countermen was Larry Mathews, who had been on the job for nearly a year. He had given up trying to be an artist, once and for all, dumping those accusatory, unfinished canvases and his dried up paints and brushes. His depression was pretty much under control—the job left him with much less time to think about himself.

And he'd even found a solution to the nightmares, better than the pills the hospital gave him, that left him a near-vegetable. Riding the subways, as he often did when he was unable to sleep, one night he ended up in a Harlem bar. The girl on the stool next to him started getting friendly. He always felt safer with whores, and ended up telling her about the nightmares that were making his life a hell. She knew all about it, she said, and knew just what to do. He had followed her outside into an alleyway, where she put a pinch of white powder on the back of her hand, and holding one nostril shut, she had showed him how to sniff up the powder into the other.

After his first sniff, he felt better immediately. The girl had been right. Cocaine had made his nightmares all but disappear. And it was easy to get. It was for sale all over the Village. Wherever there was jazz there was coke.

It was several hours later, mid-morning, when the crush was over and Larry had just lit up a cigarette, when Polly Endicott came in. She was with a friend, a short, plump girl, with the pretty face so many fat girls had.

When he brought them their coffee, Polly introduced her. She was Stella Banks and was studying voice at the Mannes Music School. Polly had hired her to be a life model in the sketch classes she was setting up in her mother's house on Perry Street.

Her mother had written from Paris that she had decided to stay on awhile with Polly's brother Eugene and, meantime, Polly and Hymie

Liebman could move in if they wished. Polly was helping out at her boyfriend's real estate office, but to earn some extra money, she had the idea of turning the parlor floor of the house into a space for artists, with evening sketch classes to start.

"Mother would die if she could see all her precious furniture piled up in the bedrooms, with all those hideous knick-knacks." She laughed, then said, "I know you've sworn off it, Larry, but I'd love to have you come by and help launch the class."

"That's all over, Polly. I sling hash now. It's okay."

Polly put an arm around Stella. "But you'll never have as pretty a model as this," she said.

As they got up to leave, the smile the girl gave him was indeed pretty, with dimpled cheeks, blue eyes, under her cap of short, blond hair. "I'd really like you to come tonight," she said.

Through the plate-glass window, he watched them walking away, and in spite of himself, he felt his hand itching to draw the line of her buttocks.

That afternoon, when his shift ended, he stopped off at an art supply shop, and bought a drawing pad and some charcoal pencils.

At six that evening, he was one of fifteen, artists and would-be artists, at Polly's sketch class. Each had paid two dollars at the door to work from a nude model. He was at one of the half-dozen easels she had set up in the emptied-out room that had been her family's parlor floor, with others on straight-back chairs with their pads in their laps. The plump girl from the coffee shop posed before them against the drapes. Big breasts, big hips, and a delicious, blond nest between plump thighs, she was young and fresh, surprisingly curvaceous for her weight.

At his easel, Larry was enchanted by her, but things went wrong from the first. Trying to put what he saw on paper, he tightened up as he always had, and what came out was academic. It was art student hackwork. It disgusted him.

When Polly called a rest period for Stella, who slipped behind a screen, he wanted to sneak out. He put his charcoal pencils in his shirt pocket, but before he could close his sketchpad, Polly was beside him.

She took the pad from him and glanced at his several attempts. "Larry, these aren't so bad! For someone who hasn't put a hand to paper for ages, you're doing very well."

He took the pad from her and closed it. "It's crap, Polly, and you know it."

"Don't be so hard on yourself." She laid a consoling hand on his arm. "You're going to get there." And she moved on to another artist.

He was seething. She was putting on a big act, trying to encourage him out of pity. He felt humiliated, crushed.

It was too late to escape. The naked model was coming out from behind the screen, slipping out of her kimono.

But this time she took a different pose. Leaning her elbows on the back of the chair, she bent over, exposing her fleshy behind to the class. Instead of just arousing him, it fueled the anger that Polly's condescending tone had set off.

He grabbed a charcoal pencil out of his pocket, and without a thought about what he was going to do, something extraordinary happened. He began to express his rage on the paper. This time, his drawing was not academic, the way he had always done, the way he thought it should be. He slashed lines across the paper, letting his hand do whatever it wanted without his brain getting in the way. He was plumbing the cesspool of his consciousess, daring to bring some of it out. He watched in a kind of grim satisfaction as his hand delineated not only the model, but the fantasies of his troubled mind. Finishing one sketch, he began another, stopping only to turn the page.

It was better than coke.

In bed that night, he was too excited to sleep, even to think of sleep. He had become an artist again, but this time his art would express everything he had gone through. He saw his mistake in clinging to his conventional thinking from before the war. In the morning he was going to go out and buy paints and canvas, and as soon he was off work at three, he would start a painting from the sketches. This time, it would not just be a model posing in a studio, it would be something never conceived before, something entirely his. People were sure to hate it, call it ugly, but he didn't give a good goddam.

It was that girl, the model, who had made it happen. Stella, her name was.

Her beautiful, unbelievably beautiful, ass.

He was about to come off, and after he did, he sank into his most untroubled sleep since the war.

The first sketch class had been a great success. After the session was over, most of the artists had stayed on, talking into the night, fueled by wine from Dominic's restaurant. Stella was declared the perfect model and she basked in all the admiration.

Everyone was having such a good time, but Polly only wished that Larry Mathews were there. He had rushed off after the class without a word. She'd go by the next day and make sure he was all right.

She spent the next morning straightening up the parlor floor and, after lunch, helping Hymie with some correspondence. It was after four when she arrived at his building. He ought to be back from the coffee shop by now.

She climbed the stairs as quietly as possible, not wanting to alert the busybody landlady. She was about to knock on the door of Larry's room, when she heard the sounds within. Could that be Stella? She pressed her ear against the door. It *was* her…she was calling out Larry's name…not calling, gasping…and Larry…he wasn't saying anything, but she heard him…oh my God, yes…it couldn't be anything else….

She backed away from the door, suddenly aware this was no place for her. Turning, she rushed back down the stairs.

On the street, she slowed her step, trying to get her breath. It was unbelievable, but how marvelous!

"It was a complete surprise to me, too," Stella said to Polly, as they sat at the counter in Bigelow's Pharmacy. "I mean, at your life class he looked so unhappy. But the way he makes love…. Of course, I have nothing to compare it with, but it's overwhelming." He confessed to her that until her, his sex life had consisted of one-night stands, mostly with prostitutes.

Stella was especially pleased that Larry didn't mind her weight. "He says I'm Rubenesque, can you believe it?" But she didn't see anything Rubenesque in the painting he was making of her. In fact, she couldn't see herself in it at all. "But it's modern art. And he seems happy with it, so why not?"

There was only one thing about him that bothered her, she told Polly, the whimpering in his sleep. It went on and on. She'd asked him about it, but he dismissed it. He never remembered his dreams, he said, and it didn't mean anything. "He's not the kind of person who opens up easily," Stella said.

"I know," said Polly. "I think it might be the war."

"But that's years ago!"

"He's a very sensitive man," Polly said. "I'm so glad he's found you."

The sketching sessions continued. Word got around and more painters showed up, glad to be able to draw from a live model for a modest fee, and learning from each other, especially from the older members. And there was always wine afterwards from Dominic.

Stella continued to pose for the class, while Larry was going on with his painting at home. Polly tacked up sketches of her artists on the walls, giving the room more the look of a working studio. They let her know how much they liked what she was doing for them and how much they appreciated having a gathering place in the neighborhood.

It was an easy step to letting them hang their work, not just the sketches they did, but their paintings too, whatever they wanted, and after the classes, friends began to drop by to look at their work. None of them had galleries yet, only a few would ever make it uptown, but their work was having a chance to be seen.

Polly liked the way things were developing. She was finished with any idea of making it in the theater. She would never be much of a painter either, but this way she didn't have to be. She was finding a new role in the arts. And the more she thought about it, there were other things she could do—hold lectures, discussion groups. The house could become a Greenwich Village center for painters.

When she told Hymie what she had in mind, he thought it was a fine idea, but it needed to be put on a paying basis. "You gotta charge something for that stuff, Pol. I bet you some of those starving painters of yours aren't as broke as you think."

Polly laughed. "They're poor as church mice."

They pay you for the sketch classes, don't they? People don't value anything that's free."

Polly thought it over, and after the sketch class that night she sounded them out about what she had in mind and asked if they'd be willing to pay a modest membership fee. She didn't tell them she would need a little more money, but she'd face that later. They were all more than supportive, and by the time they left, the idea of a village art center was born.

They would inaugurate it with a group show, and she asked everybody to bring in a painting for it.

On the day of the show, on her way back from Hymie's, there were two letters in the mail. One was from Eugene in Paris and the other, addressed to Eugene, from a Mabel Dodge Luhan in Taos, New Mexico. She dropped her handbag on a chair in the hall and ripped open Gene's letter—he wrote so seldom. He was talking about his novel…it was going well…he saw his way to finishing it in the not too distant future. Then he came to the point. Their mother had suffered a couple of small strokes. He emphasized that the doctor had stressed the "small," and, luckily, there had been no damage, physically or mentally. She was taking it easy, that was all, and he was looking after her. Polly slipped the letter back into the envelope. Was he holding something back? No, she decided, if anything were seriously wrong, he would have been forthright.

She glanced again at the other letter. Mabel Dodge. Of course! It was the wealthy hostess who'd befriended Gene before the war, the woman who had the famous Thursdays. Luhan must be a new husband.

Before going on with her preparations, she dashed off a note to Mabel Dodge, telling her that she was forwarding her letter to Eugene in Paris where was writing a novel. Knowing of Mabel Dodge's interest in the arts, she couldn't help adding a note about the opening of the art center, and hoped that the next time Mrs. Luhan was in New York, she would stop by and say hello.

The Village Art Center at the Endicott house on Perry Street opened on June of 1925. The members hung their paintings on the parlor floor, jockeying for the best spots, with Polly as final arbiter.

She had posted notices at all the artist hangouts in the neighborhood, and the show attracted a crowd, friends and partners of the artists, other Villagers, and even a few uptowners, including an art-loving cousin of Hymie's in the garment trade.

There was plenty of controversy about the pictures, especially around Larry's frenzied distortions of Stella. A few claimed to see something in it, but most did not. A number of canvases were sold—Polly knew most of the buyers were friends and relatives. But the bombshell was when Larry's painting was sold to Hymie's art-loving cousin.

The show was supposed to end at eight, but at ten, people were still there. The wine was long gone, but bottles of bootleg booze mysteriously appeared. At Elizabeth's old upright piano, pushed out into the room again, Stella Banks accompanied herself singing Broadway show tunes. Her classically-trained voice had a bluesy informality, that brought the room to silence. When she belted out "The Man I Love" from the current Ziegfeld Follies, Polly saw Larry across the room, fidgeting and uncomfortable.

When the evening was over, Hymie took Polly into his arms, pressing her close. "Pol, you're one fantastic broad."

Another letter arrived from Mabel Dodge Luhan in New Mexico. This time it was addressed to Polly. In addition to the letter there was a check for $5000.

> *My dear Polly,*
>
> *Please accept my small contribution to help with all the expenses I know you're having at the new center. I long to see it and most certainly will on my next trip to New York.*
>
> *Thank you so much for forwarding my letter on to Eugene. I've heard from him this morning, a lovely letter, telling me how content he is writing his novel, how well his life is going. He was only a boy when I knew him, but I know it is so right for him to follow his own special destiny. I do think he is very fortunate to have you as a sister, and such a remarkable mother.*
>
> *I do look forward to visiting the Village Art Center, but most of all, meeting you in person.*
>
> *With fondest regards,*
> *Mabel Dodge Luhan*

As Larry walked home from his evening shift at the lunch counter, he was not anxious to see Stella. He was losing interest in her as a subject for painting. She had been the catalyst for his breakthrough, after a couple of years of total frustration. Selling his first portrait of her at Polly's show had been wonderful, but after using only her as his subject for weeks, it was starting to feel like a dead end. He wanted to recapture that initial burst of energy that had brought him out of the doldrums. But he didn't know how.

He crossed Hudson Street toward the river, and the area became darker. It always made him a little nervous here, sensing his nightmares lurking in the shadows. He felt easier seeing the outline of a woman standing in a doorway, smoking a cigarette.

"Want to party?" Her voice was almost a whine.

He walked faster, then stopped, turned back. In the darkness, her head was skull-like, repulsive, but something about it attracted him.

"I'll pay…I mean, I don't want sex, but could I paint you?"

The woman took a drag on her cigarette, studying him. "You pay, it's okay by me." She tucked her purse under her arm and fell in beside him.

In the light of his furnished room she was older than she looked on the street, but there was still that death's head quality.

He set a fresh canvas on the easel and selected a brush, the woman sat on the edge of the bed, crossed her knees and looked at him. "Please, would you mind taking off your clothes?" he said, squeezing out a large amount of carmine paint on the palette.

"Cost you more," the woman said, pulling her dress over her head. She was naked underneath, except for stockings rolled down above her knees, and he told her to leave them on and lie back on the bed.

She got a cigarette out of her purse, lit it and, looking at him oddly, sat back against the headboard, her legs crossed at the ankles.

Something wasn't right. He remembered a painting he had seen at the League in a show of German Expressionists. "Would you mind spreading your legs a little?"

She did as she was told, but something was still wrong. He went over and crooked one of her knees, exposing her cleft. She reached for him to pull him over her.

"No…I'm sorry…but I really want to paint you."

"Suit yourself." She leaned her head back and blew a smoke ring.

Her sulky look was just right, like one of Toulouse-Lautrec's working girls.

He set to work furiously with his brush, sketching her out in the carmine paint on the canvas. The inspiration that had been diminishing the last couple of weeks with Stella was back. His brush had a life of its own, sketching not a likeness of his subject, but broad exaggeration, even wildly distorted, and with the garish colors he would use, would express the nightmare that was inside him, the nightmare he had brought back from the war.

"Spread your legs wider! Wider!"

As she did as she was told, in his excitement, his brush ground into the canvas, smearing the thick paint across her face.

He paid her off and as she pulled on her flimsy clothes on, he washed his brush off in turpentine and wiped it on a paint-stained rag.

"Easiest job all week," she said, heading out the door, her heels clicking on the stairs.

He unbuttoned his fly and cleaned himself off, then stepped back and took a look at his work. This was going to be the best so far, in a style that could express far better than words what he had gone through.

When it was finished, he would go out and find another woman, and then another. He felt newborn, powerful, and best of all, not afraid.

In September, Polly and Hymie attended Stella Bank's first-night performance at the Birdcage on Eighth Street. She had been hired as a result of her impromptu singing, accompanying herself on the old upright at the Village Art Center. Unbeknownst to her, the funny, little man with the bald pate next to the piano, mouthing the lyrics of the songs, was the owner of the piano bar. He offered her a job on the spot.

But there was bad with the good. Stella had told Polly the affair with Larry was over. He had been spending most of his time at her place, when he wasn't working at Riker's or painting in his room. But then, he began to lose interest, she didn't know why. He increased his hours of painting after he got off work, often spending whole nights at his studio, sometimes not even coming back to her before going off to work. When she tried to find out what was wrong, he was uneasy, uncommunicative as always.

Finally, she made an unannounced visit to his studio. When she opened Larry's door, he had leaped up from the bed, stark naked. And on the bed was a naked woman. The canvas on his easel told the rest of the story—painted in his new expressionist manner, the woman's body was dissolved into a series of brushstrokes. The one element you couldn't miss, she told Polly, was the woman's vagina, a slash of red in the middle, the inner lips highlighted with lurid vermilion.

After the woman had gone, Larry, keeping his back to her, said he knew he was a shit, but maybe it was time they called it quits.

Like all clubs in Prohibition New York, the Birdcage was not lit up on the outside. When they rang the bell of the unmarked door, a panel was pushed back and a bouncer gave them the once-over. The place was full up, he said. Polly pushed Hymie aside and insisted they were friends of the singer and he damn well better let them in. He disappeared briefly, then returned and grudgingly let them in. In the tiny foyer, a spot lit up a poster of a smiling Stella with a chic new hairstyle, announcing her New York debut, direct from a triumphal engagement on the West Coast.

"What the hell's wrong with that gorilla," Hymie said, as they were led through the darkened room to a table. "He think we're cops?"

When they were seated and Polly looked around, the mystery was solved. The dimly-lit club was filled with young men, not a woman among them. She thought of her brother. Eugene could be in a place like this tonight in Paris. The waiter brought them the usual watered-down gin. Then Stella was in a pool of light at the piano, her ample body swathed in pale green chiffon, sparkles in her hair. From the first number she belted out, "Get Happy," the audience erupted in shouts and applause, won over by her big voice and warm smile. But it was her last song, a heart-tugging performance of "The Man I Love," that left them spellbound. Polly knew that the tears that glistened on Stella's face were real.

Polly and Hymie wanted to congratulate her afterwards, but it was impossible to get near her. Surrounded by adoring young men, Stella was chattering away and laughing, her tears forgotten.

It was clear to Polly that she would survive, but she wasn't so sure about poor shell-shocked Larry.

One afternoon on their way home from Hymie's office, they ran into Edna St. Vincent Millay again. Her poetry was fast making her a national figure and she looked more striking than ever in a sealskin coat and elegant fur hat atop her flaming red hair. But Polly saw that when she looked at Hymie, she had the same old predatory look in her eye.

Vincent told them she was on her way to a cocktail party at the Plaza Hotel and invited them to come along. Polly said they were awfully sorry, but they had dinner reservations and were on their way home to change.

"What a bore," said the fiery redhead, looking at Hymie. "The party's being given by someone you might know. Dave Lauterbach."

Hymie almost wet his pants. "Dave Lauterbach! He put up half the skyscrapers in New York." He turned around quickly. "Look, Pol, lets go with Vincent for just one drink. We can change the reservations."

She knew wild horses couldn't keep Hymie from the chance to meet the real estate tycoon, but she wasn't about to walk into any room with Vincent Millay and feel like an ugly duckling again. Smiling sweetly, she told him to run along and have his drink. She'd soak in the tub, until he got back to take her to dinner.

But long after time for dinner had passed, Hymie still hadn't come back. She called the Lauterbach suite at the Plaza, but whoever answered couldn't hear her, because of the noise of the party, and besides was too drunk to take her seriously. When she tried again later on, she was told by the hotel desk that the party was over. To keep her spirits up, she made herself a drink and ate some crackers and cheese.

It was nearly midnight, when it occurred to her that he might have stopped by his office on the way home and, as he sometimes did, lost all track of time. She walked over, hoping to find him there.

His storefront office first appeared to be dark, but the streetlight lit up the interior well enough for her to make out the sealskin coat thrown across his desk, and then she saw the light under the door of the back room where the daybed was.

Hymie came home an hour later, jubilant about his meeting with the building tycoon. "Lauterbach is crazy about me, Pol. He wants me to come up to his office next week and talk to him, can you believe it?" He threw himself on his back across the bed. "What wouldn't I give to get even the crumbs from the Lauterbach Corporation."

She smelled the heavy, lilac perfume. "Did you go out with him to dinner?" she asked, making herself sound as if nothing were amiss.

Hymie sat up and snapped his fingers. "Holy Moses, our dinner date! Sweetheart, will you ever forgive me? I guess it just went to my head, meeting this guy."

She asked him again if Lauterbach had taken him to dinner. "Me? Are you kidding?" He leaned on an elbow with his head in his hand. "I got stuck with Vincent Millay. You were right about her, she is a man-eater. It took me all this time to shake her, if you want the truth!"

Polly tried to stifle the jealousy that was tearing her apart. Though they had never made a contract not to sleep with anyone else. "Was she a good lay?" She hated herself for her eyes filling with tears.

"Honey," he said, getting up on his hands and knees on the bed to kiss her, "I didn't sleep with her. I told you I don't go for her."

"You mean for the past four hours you've been sitting around with her playing Parcheesi?" Her voice came out shrill.

"That's right. I mean, not Parcheesi, but I told her I had to pick up some stuff at the office and she insisted on coming back with me. You know how it is, Pol. We sat finishing a bottle of gin we copped from the party. Can that dame talk your ear off! Even recited some of her poems. I don't know where the time went."

"In the back room?"

"What back room?" Hymie looked blank.

"The back room of your office." In spite of herself, her voice was shaking.

"So? We couldn't drink in front of the window, could we?"

"Was that all?"

"We made up poems."

"For hours?"

"Well, she started telling me about her favorite romantic places in the city, so I told her the ferryboat poem, remember? 'We were jolly, we were merry.' She loved it!"

"Our poem?"

"I guess I shouldn't have told her, but she was reciting poems about her love affairs...."

Polly couldn't miss his equation of their love affair with Vincent's notorious one-night stands. But he was answering her doubts so innocently, it made her feel like a grand inquisitor. If only she could believe him. "You really mean it, you didn't sleep with her?"

He took Polly in his arms. "I didn't even kiss her goodnight when I left her in front of her house." He swore again that absolutely nothing had happened and apologized for telling their poem, but Vincent was a famous poet after all and it wasn't like telling it to just anybody—she liked it so much she even wrote it down in her notebook.

But afterwards, after the lovemaking, when he fell asleep beside her, one leg over hers, Polly lay awake. Even if he had slept with Vincent—and she would never know for sure—it could only have been a totally naive mixture of business and pleasure. She knew that meeting the construction tycoon Lauterbach had meant far more to him than any casual adventure. She gazed at her peacefully-sleeping lover beside her. She'd never be able to trust anything he said to her—he was the greatest con man in the world. But the passion he had for her, that, she knew, he would never have for another woman.

Hymie was especially considerate the next day, though Polly suspected that he was having a hard time keeping off the subject of Dave Lauterbach. That night, he was taking her out to dinner, and this time, he said, even the Marines couldn't stop him. He even insisted on walking her to her hairdresser's in the afternoon, where she was going to have her hair bleached a shade lighter. When he left her at the door, he told her with a wink that he'd be stopping off at the jewelers on his way back to the office. Sitting under the dryer, she dared to hope he had gotten over his traditional ideas at last and was getting her an engagement ring.

After a candlelight dinner at their favorite bistro, he took her again to the little club where Stella Banks was singing her torch songs. They were drinking mint juleps, waiting for Stella to come on, when a waiter delivered a note for Hymie.

Polly bent forward. "What's it say?"

Hymie grinned. "You won't like it."

She snatched it away and read the message penciled on a cocktail napkin: *Get rid of the bitch and meet me outside.* Startled, she looked over at the dark bar with it's cluster of anonymous young men, then back at Hymie, and they both burst out laughing.

When Stella began her husky interpretation of "Can't Help Lovin' that Man of Mine," Hymie took Polly's hand, and with that easy giving-in to sentimentality that was so much like her father and so alien to her mother, he said, "I'm on my way, Pol, but I couldn't have got to first base without you." He reached into his pocket. "I'm a shmuck for not telling you often enough how much I love you. I've never said that to anyone else, will you believe me?" His eyes as bright on her as the first time he spotted her at the troopship, he put something into her hand.

But it was not the ring. It was a string of pearls.

Much as the episode with Edna St. Vincent Millay had shaken her, Polly couldn't deny that meeting Dave Lauterbach had turned out to be the opportunity Hymie was waiting for. The real estate tycoon not only liked him, but was in agreement with his idea that Greenwich Village was prime residential property, and was already planning to put up several modern apartment buildings there. He gave Hymie the job of buying up properties for the building sites. To make up a large enough parcel of land for each of the apartment houses, Lauterbach needed him to negotiate with dozens of house owners and clear the titles.

If some people thought these big buildings were out of place in the Village, Hymie repeated Lauterbach's argument that this was the only way to preserve the historic neighborhood, because it would bring in a better class of people. So even if they had to tear down a few old houses to clear the sites, it was necessary to sacrifice them to save the rest. Lauterbach wasn't forcing out the Irish and Italian poor. The money he was paying for their run-down properties would give them the chance to escape to newer neighborhoods in Queens or Brooklyn, which they considered more "American," anyway.

House sales and rentals became less important to Hymie, as he began devoting more time to Lauterbach. He often didn't get home for dinner because of conferences at the corporation's Madison Avenue headquarters. Frequently, Lauterbach invited him on to dinner at his Park Avenue apartment afterwards. Over brandy and cigars, the tycoon liked to tell how at first, being a Jew, he had not been able to rent an apartment for his family on Park Avenue. But he had licked the Park Avenue Association's anti-Semitic restrictions by buying a parcel of land through a front and building his own apartment house there. He even had a tougher battle getting himself his estate out on the North Shore—years of litigation cracking restrictive zoning laws in the face of the whole pack of snobbish Anglo-Saxon blue bloods. Now he was fighting the country club and the private schools.

Polly was soaking in a bubble bath, after a long day downstairs at the Art Center, when Hymie came home to announce that Lauterbach had invited them out to Oyster Bay for the weekend.

"Me too? Sweetheart, how thrilling!" she said. Then she sat up in the bubbles and looked at him, wising up. "Are you sure he invited me, too? I thought I was just supposed to be your secretary!"

Hymie perched on the rim of the tub and squeezed water from a sponge over her back. "Well, not exactly, but it'll be all right, you'll see."

Polly tried not to give in to the soothing trickle of the water on her skin. "You mean I just show up, and you're willing to take the chance he'll accept me as your weekend floozy?"

"Cut it out, Pol. I didn't mean it that way."

She stood up, dripping bubbles, and reached for the towel. "I'm not going," she said flatly. She waited for him to say if she wouldn't go, he wasn't going either, even to the fabulous, Long Island retreat of his millionaire patron.

But he didn't. As he took the towel from her and patted away the exploding bubbles, he said that maybe she was right not to go after all. He and Lauterbach would be talking business most of the time anyway, and she'd be bored to death. Next time, he'd make sure Lauterbach invited her personally.

It was obvious to her that he was relieved—she was a complication he wasn't ready to deal with.

She went with him to Bloomingdale's to find suitable clothes for his country weekend. As he tried on tennis whites, she thought that for someone who came from immigrants and had never worn such things, he looked like he was born to them. She picked out a monogrammed weekend bag for him and when he left the house in his blazer, striped tie and panama hat, he looked like a young lawyer just out of Yale.

Hymie was away at Lauterbach's estate most weekends after that. She never went with him—no invitation from Lauterbach was ever forthcoming—but Hymie told her about the lavish grounds and the pool, horseback riding with the family, and when the weather was warm enough, swimming at the private beach on the Sound. It was clear that Lauterbach had taken him under his wing, even talking about sending him down to Washington to work on getting government contracts. Though mostly occupied with Lauterbach Corporation business, he continued to handle a few Village listings and tried to find buyers.

It was a relief to Polly when, occasionally, he found time to turn up for a drink with her artists after the life classes.

Before anyone showed up for the afternoon life class, Polly was attempting a cubist still life of apples and a chianti bottle, set up on a table in front of her easel. Not that she had any hopes of becoming a serious painter, anymore, but just because it was fun. She often did this now. Without other artists around, looking over her shoulder, she didn't feel her old self-consciousness.

She had turned the round shapes of the apples into a cluster of rectangles, feeling pleased with the effect, and was about to add the finishing strokes, when the front door opened. A girl appeared in the hall doorway. Expensively coiffed and dressed, but with a warm smile.

"Am I allowed to come in and look around?" She was interested in possibly signing up for a life class, she said.

Polly caught the accent of an Ivy League women's college. "We have one starting in half an hour," she said. "I'm almost through here, but, meantime, why don't you sit down and I'll give you our brochure."

The girl came into the room, the scent of Patou cutting through the turpentine smell. "I'm not much of an artist, I'm afraid. Perhaps I can just sit in today?"

The girl took the brochure Polly handed her and sat down on a sofa pushed against the wall. "But please go on with your work. I didn't mean to interrupt."

Polly took another look at her still life, feeling the girl's eyes on her. What the hell had she come for? "I'm through with this." She began to clean her brushes.

The girl tossed the brochure aside and came over to look. "But that's awfully good, Miss Endicott," she said. "My art history prof at Smith said the female brain doesn't understand cubism, but I think you do."

The compliment was excessive. "Well, I don't know about that," she said with a faint smile, dropping onto the sofa, and taking out her cigarettes.

The girl sat down beside her, refusing a cigarette. "Your center is such a marvelous idea."

"I think so," Polly said, lighting up. She didn't look much older than twenty. Whatever she was here for, she was definitely not the usual arts lover. Even when they had money, they seldom had her class. That was a Chanel she was wearing, and alligator shoes. "Do you live down here?" she asked.

"Actually, no. I live on Park Avenue, I'm afraid. Does that disqualify me for membership?"

"Of course not. Everyone's welcome. Even Park Avenue."

The girl leaned forward. "I must apologize. I didn't come here for the life class. I came here to see you."

"I'm afraid I'm mystified...."

She put a hand on her arm. "I'm Miriam Lauterbach, and I've been dying to meet you."

Polly was speechless.

"I really hope you don't mind," Miriam Lauterbach said. "Hymie doesn't know I'm here, but I've heard so much about you." When Hymie was visiting at her father's house in Oyster Bay, she explained, he had intrigued them all with his description of the art center his assistant had set up. "And without your help, he couldn't run his office."

Polly wondered if the girl suspected anything, but she seemed so genuine, without guile. In spite of herself, Polly couldn't help liking her.

As the Lauterbach heiress went on about how Hymie left them all in stitches over lunches and dinners, Polly watched her, fascinated. So this was the "little" Lauterbach daughter Hymie had mentioned. From the way he talked, Polly had assumed she was about ten. Those croquet matches on the lawn, the romping in the pool! And here she was, the picture of marriageability—cultivated, feminine in a way that made Polly feel gawky and boyish—obviously only a year or two out of college, when Polly felt every minute of her thirty-five years. And worst of all—and here she remembered bitterly the night on the ferryboat when Hymie had refused to marry her—Miriam Lauterbach was Jewish.

He knew as he came home that he was in trouble, when "You're not sore, are you, Pol," he began, wondering how he was ever going to prove his innocence. "She made me let her come. She's just a spoiled kid who gets everything she wants."

"That's obvious," said Polly, in a voice that made him feel charged, tried, and convicted. "Why didn't you tell me about her before?"

"I did. I told you about Lauterbach's kids."

"The little daughter? You made me think she had braces on her teeth and pigtails!"

Hymie was carrying a bouquet of anemones, as he ran up the stoop at Polly's. Thanks to Lauterbach, he had just made the biggest sale of his life, to a rich client the real estate tycoon had steered his way. To celebrate, he was going to take Polly out on the town—dinner at the Plaza and, afterwards, orchestra seats for Showboat.

In the front room artists were setting up easels for a sketch class. He didn't see Polly around so he headed up the stairs to her room.

He found Polly sitting in a boudoir chair staring out the window, a drink in her hand. That was odd. He always fixed them a drink when he got home. But his news would cheer her up. He put the flowers on her lap, kissing her on the cheek. "I've got a surprise for you, doll face."

"I don't want another surprise." Her voice was tight.

The theater tickets in his hand, he was stopped cold. "What did I do?"

"You lied to me!"

"Huh? What the hell you talking about?"

"Your little girlfriend." And she told him about Miriam Lauterbach's visit that afternoon.

"Oh, shit!" He sat down on the edge of the bed.

She took a sip of her drink, finally looking at him.

He leaned forward, his hands on his knees. "I know what you're thinking, but there's nothing between us, I swear to God." Lauterbach's pampered daughter had been a problem from the start, he told her. She was a royal pain in the ass, but he couldn't afford to offend her. Lauterbach doted on her.

"And not a word to either of them about your shiksa girl friend!"

Hymie was miserable. "I couldn't do that, Pol. Look at today, biggest deal I ever made, thanks to him." He told her about the big sale.

"Who cares about your sale," Polly said. "You led me to think she was some little kid with braces on her teeth, the little brat with pigtails"

"You saw her, she acts like a kid just out of high school."

"High school!" she corrected him acidly. "She's just out of Smith College."

"Don't let that fancy way she talks fool you, she's still spoiled rotten."

"Does Lauterbach tuck the two of you into bed at night?" Polly took a long swig of her drink, hearing the bitchiness in her voice and knowing it was making her ugly.

"I sleep in the guest room, Polly!"

His reasonable tone drove her berserk. "I'll bet you do! I should have known all along," she cried, and her voice broke into a yell, "and I'm just your shiksa whore."

"Pipe down, they can hear downstairs…"

"What the hell do I care!" she screamed.

And on it went, louder and even uglier. It was the first real fight they ever had—and it ended with him going back to his own place that night.

After Hymie went off, hurt and perplexed, Polly threw herself on the bed, sobbing. She was sick at the way she had acted. He could sound so innocent, like with Vincent. Maybe it was true that he saw that calculating husband-hunter as a kind of kid sister and didn't really take her seriously. But it was Lauterbach who called the shots and he'd picked out Hymie for from the first.

Nothing was right between them after that, even though Hymie made a special point for her sake of turning down most of Lauterbach's weekend invitations, to prove to her that his relationship to the tycoon was strictly business. As the weeks passed, though he never mentioned her, Polly felt Miriam between them, poisoning her every minute. Still, there was nothing she could do about it without wrecking his chances—it was inconceivable that she demand he break off with Lauterbach. What she and Hymie had together was built on air, on the dreams of youth, on romance. The real estate tycoon was offering him a substantial life, something he could build on. She saw that Hymie was not happy either, much as he put on his bright face, and began to feel that she was in the way of the inevitable.

Still, she hung on, not knowing what else to do, until the day in June when the cablegram arrived from Eugene.

Their mother had had a major stroke in Paris and he wanted her to come. She was almost relieved. It was as if she had been waiting for something to set her in motion.

The cablegram came on a Friday and, since it was the beginning of the summer rush, Polly was lucky to be able to book passage on a transatlantic ship sailing that Monday. Without calling Hymie, she went to get out her valise and there, stacked in the back of the closet, was her book of poems, *Quintessence*, which she had had printed years before. Since her hopes for the book had come to nothing, she had never looked at it since. But now she opened it at random, and the poems seemed prophetically to speak to her present situation. Forgetting her packing, she sat down on the floor and read the volume through. She had thought she had become a different person altogether since then—knowing the answers, without illusions— but this heartbroken voice from the the past was immediately recognizable as hers. It was as if at the threshold, she had written the book of her life.

She knew she ought to start getting her things together, packing, but instead, with the minutes ticking away, she sat there, dreading what was awaiting her in Paris and, most of all, knowing what the separation would mean for her and Hymie.

Darkness settled in, the book still in her lap.

It was after eight when Hymie came in, flipping on the light switches, and, not even questioning why she was sitting there in the dark, he announced he had gotten a commission check from Lauterbach and he was taking her to Provincetown for the weekend to celebrate.

"Right now?" she asked,. Her spirits were picked up immediately. Could she postpone telling him about having to go to Paris?

"Why not? I got a car outside. We'll be there by morning. How does a swim before breakfast sound to you?"

As if he were on top of the world again, he hugged her tight and told her everything was going to be different now. She couldn't tell him about the cablegram then either. She even forgot about it herself as she let herself be carried away by his enthusiasm.

He had borrowed a Stutz Bearcat, and with their valises strapped on back they sped up the old Boston Post Road in the warm night, singing and laughing. Then out along the winding Cape Cod road, roaring through sleeping villages, and as dawn broke, they came out into a world of sand dunes and cranberry bogs along the bay, with gulls wheeling high over the sea, and filled their lungs with the salt air.

They turned a bend and ahead of them in the morning sun lay the isolated little fishing village strung along for a mile on the furthest curve of the Cape, with its piers and clusters of fishermen's sheds. Fishing boats had already returned with the night's catch, and the Portuguese fishermen who made up most of the town's inhabitants were unloading it and tossing worthless bait fish to circles of flapping, caterwauling gulls. They passed the pier where the Provincetown Players performed in an old fish-processing shed. The troupe was about to open another summer season with a repertory of gloomy O'Neill plays, that the critics from New York would make the long trek up to report on.

Narrow Commercial Street was slippery with cobblestones and the tracks of the little trolley that ran all the way out to the public beach on the ocean, where the lighthouse of the neat, white Coast Guard station warned vessels away from the point. Hymie was immediately full of plans to buy up all the fishermen's shacks along the harborfront and fix them up as studios for summer rentals. Artists and bohemian types were already coming up, and he saw its possibilities.

Polly laughed. "Let's not tell anybody about it. It's perfect just the way it is."

He grinned. "You're right. No more real estate while we're here. I'm going to devote myself to that button nose and those freckles." His hand squeezed her knee.

If the cablegram existed at all, Polly thought, it was fiction. This was reality.

Just beyond the village, hidden away from the road by dunes tufted with beach grass, they found the cottage he had rented, hardly more than a shack of weathered boards with fishnet curtains at the windows. And beyond a tangle of bayberries, a wide beach leading down to the sea.

With the waves breaking on the white sand, even after the all-night drive they were too excited to be tired and got out their bathing suits. Hymie snatched away her itchy wool suit, and handed her a box with a Lord and Taylor label.

It was a clinging tank suit of black jersey. "I'll be thrown into jail!" she gasped.

"Scared?" Already into his belted trunks and white top, he watched appreciatively as she wiggled into the brief, form-fitting bathing suit.

They spread a blanket in the sand dunes, and with the pearls he had given her around her neck, she paraded like a mannequin for him, until he tackled her down and they made love under the open sky.

Still naked, they lay drowsy in the morning sun, miles from the city, on the blanket among the dunes, and Polly saw the boat on Monday sailing off without her, and she didn't care. The cablegram from Paris was unreal.

Hymie was tickling her belly with her strand of pearls, as he told her that this was the turning point for them. The hard times were over and there would be all the money they could dream of from now on.

Silly man, talking about money now. She lay with her eyes closed in the warm sun and she drank in his voice like a faraway lullaby.

There was something he wanted to ask her about, he said. It wasn't anything he was going to do, he just wondered what she'd think about it.

She heard the raucous cry of a gull high overhead, somewhere above the pounding of the surf, but she didn't open her eyes.

She knew, didn't she —his deep voice was like a caress—that he would always love her? It would never be this way with anyone else. When he was with her, it was always perfect...

Beach grass was scratching her and she swiped it away, but the wind kept blowing it back.

...Lauterbach was very pleased with his work, and saw no reason why he shouldn't go right to the top in the corporation, "and he's already treating me like one of the family." He gave a nervous laugh. "It's making me uncomfortable..."

Wide-awake, she raised herself on her elbows. He was a blur in the white glare of the sun. "He wants you to marry her, is that what you're saying?"

He kept his eyes on the pearls he was running over her thighs. "He didn't say it in so many words, but essentially those were his terms."

She pulled her leg away and started brushing off sand. "What are you telling me this for?"

"Don't get sore. I don't want that, it's just that I have to deal with him. It wouldn't have to mean any difference with us." He spoke more quickly. "Miriam's nice enough. She's really not so spoiled when you get to know her, but it still wouldn't mean anything....I mean, it's you I love. It would just be an arrangement...."

"Is that what you brought me up here for?" She was on her feet.

"No, of course not!" He threw a handful of sand hard against the blanket. "Forget I ever said it. I'm not marrying anybody. I was a shmuck to bring it up."

She was standing, legs spread, facing him with the sun behind her head, radiating spokes like an avenging angel in her golden nakedness. "Liar! You wouldn't have brought it up unless you wanted to. I don't believe anything you say. You've never given me a goddam thing but shit!" She grabbed the pearls from him ran down toward the ocean.

"Hey, wait!" he hollered, hopping on one foot as he pulled on his wool bathing trunks. "Pol!"

But before he got to her, she flung the pearls out as far as she could over the water, the sun glinting off them before they plopped into the swell of a wave.

He jumped in as the wave broke, scrabbling about with his hands in the roiling foam.

"You son of a bitch," she screamed at him.

He grabbed her arm, shaking her. "What the hell you do that for? You know what they cost?"

"Is that all you think about, you dirty"—she tried to think of what would hurt him the most—"you...."

"Jew?" he yelled back. And though every ounce of her denied it, his eyes were cold points, looking at her. "I always knew you'd get around to that in the end." He turned and walked back up the beach.

The wind beat at her face, and her crying was blown away to sea.

Polly insisted on returning to the city immediately. On the endless drive back, Hymie tried to apologize, denying he was going to marry Miriam. She's got it all wrong. If it's in Lauterbach's mind, it wasn't in his. There was no way he was going to marry that bitch.. He was sorry he brought it up. Polly said she was sorry too—she shouldn't have thrown away the pearls, she'd regret it the rest of her life.

But when they got back to Perry Street in the middle of the night, deathly tired from the drive up and back and no sleep, she said she needed a little time to get herself together and asked him if he would mind staying at his own place.

"You're sure you're not still holding it against me?" His eyes were sad and searching.

"Sure." She looked away.

Under the streetlamp she watched him get back into the car in his new sports clothes, the plus fours, the jaunty cap. At the wheel of the expensive sports car, he shifted gears expertly and roared off down the empty street.

She packed the next morning—it was Sunday—and sent her trunk on ahead to the boat for the Monday sailing.

Around noon the phone rang for ten minutes. She didn't answer. She knew it was him. But when it rang again half an hour later, she was afraid he might come by—he had his own key—and she didn't want that. To avoid any chance of seeing him, she was going to spend Sunday night in a hotel, before catching the boat the next morning. On the way out, she tacked a notice on the front door—she'd already let Stella know—Village Art Center Closed Until Further Notice.

1927

20

It was with a mixture of fear and elation that Eugene Endicott stood at the ship's rail, trying to make out the New York skyline in the cold fog that shrouded it, as if symbolic of his uncertain reception. He hoped America had changed during his years abroad. The two things that gave him confidence were the letter in his pocket from the publisher accepting his novel, and his sister Polly's promise to meet him.

His mother had died in Paris two years before. It had been a tranquil death. She had slipped away without a word, as he and Polly were at her bedside in the American Hospital at Neuilly. In death, her face had the translucent elegance of an ivory carving. They buried her in the old Montmartre Cemetery under chestnut trees in the Parisian drizzle.

He would always thank God that his mother had shown him in his darkest time that writing would be his salvation. And he had applied himself to it since her death, to the exclusion of almost everything else. In her last days, they had long talks about the novel he had started—the story of a group of expatriates like himself, whose lives America had shattered in various ways and forced into exile.

But no matter how well his writing went, he didn't feel at home in Paris. New York was never far from his mind. He had left, defeated and humiliated, holding on to an old woman's skirts. But when Tortured Souls was taken by the publishing firm of Boni and Liveright it had seemed to him the sign he was waiting for. It was time to return to the country where he was born, where his roots and traditions, so necessary to a writer, were.

He had cabled Polly from the ship his time of arrival. His sister was his only real family now. After their mother's death, Polly had stayed on for a few months. Meanwhile, in New York, their mother's lawyer settled the will and arranged for a mortgage on the Perry Street house, investing the money in the booming stock market. This and the remainder of their mother's estate gave both Polly and Eugene a modest income.

On her return, Polly had not reopened the Village Art Center. No longer dependent on Hymie, she opened a small art gallery in the Village. While she was still in Paris, she had spent a lot of time making the rounds of the galleries, studying up on all the schools of modern French painting from Cubism to Surrealism. Some of it reminded her of the kind of art Larry Mathews and other painters she knew at home were doing. It was the art of the future, she told Eugene, but no one was taking it seriously in America, and it was going to be her job to make them swallow it.

From New York, she regularly sent him reviews of the shows in her new gallery. The critics, the few who came, jeered and she wasn't finding many buyers, but it was becoming the center of avant-garde art in the Village.

Polly wasn't at the pier to meet him. After he got through customs, he looked for her everywhere beyond the barrier, where the flashily-dressed crowd waited to greet the arrivals. The noisy shed was almost identical to the one he had disembarked into from the troopship nearly a decade before, and he felt himself a stranger now, just like then. The baggage handlers wheeling great stacks of luggage jostled him as he carried his bags through passport control and out into the street in front of the pier. He was trying to find a free cab amidst the welter of vehicles coming and going, when Polly leaned out of a cab window, calling his name.

He was relieved, but the bleached blonde in the cloche hat he saw stepping out of the taxi, with her narrow skirt above her knees and wearing too much makeup in the raw daylight, didn't look much like the sister he had last seen in Paris two years before.

"I bet you're ready to kill me," she cried, pecking him on the cheek. "I know I promised to meet you. I really meant to, but I got so involved in hanging my new show, it completely slipped my mind." She stepped back to take a look at him, raising a penciled eyebrow. "My God, still wearing a beret—and a mustache, too! Don't you look like a fugitive from the Left Bank!"

Her artificially bright manner was jarring enough, but to ruin everything completely, she poked her head back into the cab and called, "Don't just sit there, you big lug. Get out here and say hello to my big brother."

A husky kid, who looked like a prizefighter in a leather jacket and paint-spattered denims, slid out grinning sheepishly. "Hey, Polly's big brother," he said, extending his meaty hand.

Eugene mumbled something. The boyfriend wasn't more than twenty-five, whereas his sister was pushing forty.

She tucked her arm under his. "Gene, you're going to be amazed when you see Jock's show at the gallery. He's going to knock the critics on their asses. He's the best surrealist painter in America, and I found him." She looked up at the muscle-bound kid proudly, as if he were a prize possession.

As the driver strapped Eugene's luggage onto the rack, Polly pulled him into the cab beside her, directing her prizefighter boyfriend onto the jump seat facing them. "You're going to kill me, sweet," she told Eugene in a voice that cut through the noise of the shifting gears as they set off, "but I'm going to have to drop you off at the house. The Villager critic is coming and we're hoping for some more, so I have to get Jock back to the gallery in time. You only have to see him"—she ran a blood-red fingernail over his thigh—"to know how talented he is."

Mr. Muscle's sheepish grin again. It was depressing.

The cab headed down to the Village, bouncing over the cobblestones past the waterfront warehouses and tenements. Polly's chattering didn't let up for a minute. Eugene had only seen her so wound up once before. That was shortly after their mother's death in Paris, when a friend sent her the clipping from the Times about Hymie Liebman's wedding to the Lauterbach heiress. Polly had already told him that she had thrown Hymie over, but he had been repelled at her tone, as she read aloud in a mocking voice about the extravagant wedding on Long Island's North Shore—the guest list that included Guggenheims, Lehmans, a Rothschild, and even Mayor, Gentleman Jimmy Walker himself, the month-long honeymoon cruise to South America, the house in Larchmont, a gift of the bride's father, and the bridegroom's plan to open offices in the Lauterbach Building. "Look at that shit-eating grin," she had said with a loud laugh, that grated on his nerves even then, holding out the picture of Hymie with his bride. "He's pulled off the biggest business deal of his life!"

And now, as the cab turned into the maze of familiar Village streets where Eugene had grown up, that he hadn't seen in six years, she refused to shut up, and the same strident voice blocked out anything he might feel, but irritation. Arriving at the house, while the driver unstrapped his bags from the back of the cab, Eugene's only wish was to get into his own room and shut the door. But she even loused that up. Through the cab window, she called after him that she had forgotten, but he couldn't stay in his old room, she was using the whole top floor for storage. "Take the room next to mine, okay?" Without even noticing his dismay, she turned back to the muscle-bound boyfriend, as the cab drove off.

Only the outside of the house was the way he remembered it. Throughout the entire parlor floor the wallpaper and woodwork had been painted over dead white, and the front room had nothing in it but stark, tubular-steel chairs around a mirror-topped coffee table and huge, garish oil paintings on the walls.

Polly had taken over their mother's old room on the second floor and it was a mess, with discarded clothes draped over everything. A silk stocking dangled from a ceiling fixture. Even if he had wanted to, he couldn't move right into the smaller room next to hers. A suitcase was open on the unmade bed and a pair of trousers hung over a chair. She had someone staying there and was so dizzy she forgot. And just as she'd told him, the whole upper floor where his room had been was chockablock with their mother's old furniture from downstairs.

It wasn't much of a welcome. Glumly, he carried his suitcases down to the dining room to sleep on the daybed in the corner, wishing he had never come home.

It seemed to him, those first days back with Polly, that she was forever bringing artists or hangers-on home from the gallery. And more people would drop in and, inevitably, someone put a jazz record on the Victrola, turned up loud. He never seemed to be alone with her. She was always talking to someone he didn't know, waving a cocktail glass in her hand, in perpetual motion.

Even when he moved into the extra bedroom after the guest was gone, he couldn't escape the noise of the partying downstairs. And when finally that was over, there was no way of not hearing through the wall her wild transports with muscle-bound Jock. And within a week there was a new "Jock," this one introduced by Polly as "the best Dadaist painter this side of the Atlantic."

Though the house had been left to both of them, and she had written him that she wanted him to come back and share it, he ought to have realized that she'd had it to herself a long time, and he couldn't expect her to adapt to his less frantic way of life. And he certainly was never going to accustom himself to hers.

He had to find somewhere else to live, and he went out to look. In the years he had been away, the Village had changed for the worse. Many blocks were scarcely recognizable. On Greenwich Avenue, the ornate Jefferson Market had finally been torn down and was being replaced by a monolithic women's prison overshadowing the once-elegant clock tower of the old courthouse, now looking forlorn with its gothic windows boarded up. Several blocks in the south Village had been razed as well, to make way for traffic ramps leading to the entrance of the new Holland Tunnel under the Hudson. Around Washington Square, so-called artists hawked oil paintings on black velvet, of gauzily-draped lovers kissing in the moonlight and galleons under full sail. Tour buses rumbled down narrow side streets with megaphones blaring nonsense about "artists and bohemians," while the tourists aboard gaped.

The noise level had risen everywhere. Undaunted, Eugene turned in wherever there was a For Rent sign. He looked at all kinds of rooms and cold-water flats but, even when they were tolerable, always there seemed to be noise coming from somewhere—from other apartments, from the courtyard, or from speakeasies right below—as if nonstop parties were all anyone had time for, floors shaking from the Charleston and the Black Bottom. New York was said to have thousands of speakeasies and, it seemed to him as he walked the streets looking for a place to live, that at least half of them must be in the Village.

Trying another tack, he stopped into the drugstore on Sheridan Square, where he used to have breakfast years before, hoping to run into a familiar face, someone who might steer him to a decent place to live. Once, there had been a bulletin board, where people put up notices of neighborhood rentals. But the bulletin board was gone, the counter where he used to have breakfast was torn out, and even the old druggist was a younger stranger.

He returned home discouraged that evening, dreading to find the usual party going on. But for once, the house was quiet and Polly was in her room, at her vanity table, painting her nails. Relieved to be alone with her, he told her about his day, searching for a place to live. "By the way, I almost forgot, I saw Hymie's name in the World-Telegram."

She looked up at him in the mirror, almost spilling her nail polish. "What's it say about him?"

He told her Hymie was a member of an investors' group, that was erecting a luxury apartment building uptown on Beekman Place.

"Is that all?" Polly said, blowing on her nails. Hymie was always on the business page, she told him. It was such a bore. Was she ever glad she had finished with him. "Thank God, I'm not his hausfrau stuck up in Larchmont." She reached for her bag, and knocked it to the floor.

Gathering up the contents for her, Gene came upon the picture. It was a snapshot of a boy in a scout uniform. No one had to tell him who it was.

Since coming home, he hadn't had the nerve to ask Polly about Seth. He knew that she corresponded with his ex-wife but, guilty as he felt about the son he had never seen, he had tried to put the whole subject out of his mind. Now, seeing the snapshot of the boy with Patrick's Irish grin, Eugene was filled with a confusion of feelings. Polly started to tell him what news she had of the Harrises out in Ohio—Clare and Toby had two other children of their own in addition to Seth—when up the stairs came a couple of her loud friends who had barged in as usual without ringing. She jumped up, her abrasive self once again, calling for them to come meet her famous brother who was having a novel published, and did they want a drink?

Eugene fled the house, out into the night. As he walked toward Sheridan Square, barkers tried to pull him into strip joints and drag shows. Everywhere people filled the streets, looking for what the papers were calling "Sodom on the Hudson." The speaks were packed, and even louder and more unruly than during the day. The bar where he once had worked, 86 Barrow, which had catered to the literary crowd, now was jammed with loud uptowners in paper hats and tin horns. This new Village seemed to him as tawdry and commercial as a carnival midway.

Then, a block beyond the square where it was already quieter, he heard the faint tinkle of a piano. It was coming from a small, neighborhood bar. He stopped to look at the picture of the girl singing there. Not the usual type—too chubby, with a good-natured smile. Then he could make out her voice along with the piano. A husky voice belting out "Someone to Watch over Me." On an impulse, he rang the buzzer and was let in.

As he already knew, it was a queer bar. Since coming home, considering what he had gone through before, he was determined to avoid such places. But he ordered a drink, trying to ignore the men around him.

The singer, who was accompanying herself at the piano, had the pretty, doll-like features fat girls often have.

Won't you tell him please to put on some speed,
follow my lead,
oh, how I need
someone to watch over me....

In a full, yellow gown with filmy sleeves that did little to disguise her plump arms, she was giving herself completely to the sentiment of the lyric, as she belted out the song to the rapt patrons. Nobody was talking or even lifting a glass. His anxieties were falling away. Since his return from Europe, he had hardly had a moment of peace. Beyond the simple-minded lyrics of the song, something in her voice gave him courage—something that said, in spite of all the humiliations, you could go on. When she finished the song, he joined the group of admirers around the piano and waited his turn to thank her.

She gave a broad smile when she saw him. "Don't tell me, you're Polly's little brother!" She jumped up and gave him a hug.

He was mystified, until she told him that she was an old friend of Polly's, and her name was Stella Banks. Linking her arm through his, she led him over to a table on the side and ordered drinks. She dabbed at her damp forehead with a cocktail napkin, then, opening a compact, powdered her nose. Snapping the compact shut, she gave him a friendly bump with her shoulder. "I couldn't miss you. Polly showed me snapshots from Paris. She said you were back."

He smiled. "I'm not sure I'm going to stay. Her shindigs are driving me crazy."

"Me too. But luckily I work nights." They clinked glasses, and sipped their whiskey sours.

A couple of young men came over, inviting her to an after-hours party, but she begged off, fibbing Eugene was her long-lost cousin. "They're all adorable and I'm grateful to them forever," she said, turning back to him with her sweet smile, "but tonight, I'm giving all my attention to you."

Although the two women were entirely different, she was the first person since Mabel Dodge he could open up to.

They stayed together until time for her next set. Stella told him that she had sung in several little clubs around the Village. She had been at Blue Notes for nearly a year, longer than anywhere else, and had developed a following. He told her about Paris and his novel that was about to be published, which, of course, she knew all about. They couldn't begin to tell each other everything they had to say. At her next break—after a set opening with "Button Up Your Overcoat" and concluding with "He's Just My Bill," that brought tears to the eyes of everyone—to his joy, she came straight back to him.

She was sympathetic when he went on about his problems living with Polly. "She can be a terror, all right. You don't have much chance of getting any writing done there, much less sleep, that's for sure. But I've got an idea." She was living in a tenement on Weehawken Street. It was a quiet block over by the Christopher Street ferry. An old man on her floor had just died, and they hadn't cleaned the place out yet. Two perfectly good rooms, and she'd love to have him as a neighbor. She could speak to the janitor and it was his.

It turned out to be a cold-water flat, three flights up, with the toilet in the hall and a high-legged washtub in the kitchen for bathing. It was still a mess, but it was next door to Stella, and there wasn't a speakeasy on the block.

Gene paid the janitor a month's rent, and he and Stella spent a week cleaning out the old man's junk. They had to rip up several layers of rotting linoleum, and after they put a fresh layer of paint over everything, the last traces of musty smell were gone.

To keep out the draughts, Stella helped him stuff the worst gaps in the window frames with newspaper, and putty the chinks in the panes. There was only an old gas kitchen stove to heat the place with. Even with the oven door open and a pot of water inside to cut the dryness in the air, it wasn't very warm, but it was an improvement over the frigid, little maid's room he had lived in in Paris, eight flights up under the mansard roof. For a good part of his time there, he sat at his typewriter, keeping on his sweater and overcoat, with only a smelly alcohol burner for heat.

He brought over some of his mother's furniture from Perry Street, and the janitor found him a folding, iron camp bed in the cellar. On her mother's old Singer, Stella ran up bright, patchwork drapes for the windows out of her bag of remnants—she had to make her own clothes, because she couldn't get dressy-enough gowns in her size for her act. They went on expeditions to the Lower East Side finding whatever else he needed.

Polly, in a new cloche hat with a feather, surveyed the results skeptically, as she perched on the table next to his Remington typewriter. "It beats me why you think this is better than having the whole top floor at home to yourself. If you'd just given me a few more days, I'd have had it cleaned out." She slipped another cigarette into an ebony holder, and lit it with the butt of the old one. "I've been trying to get Stella to move out of this dump for years, but if you two want to do your *la vie bohème* thing, it's okay by me." She tossed a long, knitted scarf over her shoulder and sailed out, wishing him lots of luck.

But the place suited Eugene to a T, and the next morning when he was having breakfast with Stella, the mailman brought up a package for him, the first piece of mail in his new home. It was the galleys of his novel to correct.

In Paris, when he had gotten the letter from Boni and Liveright, the prestigious publishers of Sherwood Anderson and Willa Cather, accepting Tortured Souls for publication, he had been so exhilarated that he went to his regular café in Montparnasse, the Select, and blew the remains of his quarterly dividend check on drinks for everybody, including the waiters and the *patron*.

Recognition as a writer was oxygen to his shaky ego. It was going to be his passport back to respectability. Ever since his mother had picked him up out of the gutter and taken him off to Europe, he had given himself over to his writing with a single-minded determination. If his life had led him down devious paths that brought him scorn and ridicule, the publication of the novel was going to redeem him. Just the writing of it had done a lot to heal his psychological wounds. The theme of the book was exile, after a man had all but destroyed himself, but the ending promised rebirth through the discipline of art and, bowing to convention, a woman's love—and now, with his book about to appear and Stella in his life, it seemed to be coming true.

And always in the back of his mind had been the hope that something would make him worthy of the son, who was growing up in the Midwest without knowing him, the son he was too cowardly to contact. Once the novel was in print and he was a published author, Seth would be able to think of his father as something more than an outcast. At least, so he hoped.

But when the proof sheets of Tortured Souls were spread out on his desk for him to go over, and he actually saw his words in print for the first time, he squirmed at his self-exposure, imagining the world's ridicule when it came out. What had seemed to him a serious book, while it was still in manuscript, now looked embarrassing. He had an impulse to tell his publishers that he had changed his mind about the book being published, and catch the first boat back to Europe and anonymity.

Through the wall he could hear Stella at her upright piano, working out an arrangement for a medley of Gershwin songs. He hated to interrupt her, but he felt so panicky that he gave three raps on the wall, their signal when they wanted to talk.

He couldn't bear to go on correcting those damn proofs, he told her, as they sprawled in her overstuffed armchairs, Stella comfortably mussed in her housecoat, with a hairnet holding her marcel wave in place. He bemoaned the self-exposure the book would bring. Everything was all wrong since he had come back—the Village, his sister, and now his book.

"I know what you're going through, sweetie. Believe me, I get it too whenever I go into a new club. First-night frazzle, I call it."

"It seems so personal," he said. "Even if it's fiction, everyone will know it's about me."

Stella shook her head. "The book is marvelous. I love it, and the world will too. But if you're nervous about the exposure, why don't you use a pseudonym?"

"Like what?"

"Let's think…." She was studying the face of her watch. "What about Elgin?"

"Okay. Elgin what?"

"I dunno, something poetic….I've got it, Elgin St. John!"

He laughed. "Doesn't sound much like me."

"But that's just it! You don't want anybody to know it's you."

"Elgin St. John," he said, "sounds like a pansy…."

"So?"

They both laughed. She jumped up and gave him a kiss. "We'll start on the proofs this afternoon."

Eugene pronounced the syllables slowly, "Tortured Souls by Elgin St. John…." He shook his head. "Polly will howl."

"Give her time, she's really proud of you," Stella said. "Don't let that tough act fool you. It's just since Hymie."

Eugene wasn't so sure. He'd run into Hymie—they had a beer at the White Horse—and heard something about the breakup. "I'll never get over that sister of yours, Gene," Hymie had told him. "She really threw me a curve when she walked out on me."

Stella brought him a cup of coffee. "Hymie's a charmer, but he's also a born salesman and he throws a good line. The truth is, he dumped Polly." And Eugene heard for the first time the story of Hymie's mercenary courtship of Miriam Lauterbach, and how he expected Polly to settle for back-street wife.

"Why the hell didn't she tell me?" Eugene said. Maybe that was why she acted so bitchy nowadays.

"Acting tough is just her way of looking after herself," Stella said. "same as me."

"You're nothing like her! You're the most lovable person I know."

"Don't be fooled, sweetie," she said. "I'm just a fat girl compensating with a laugh-a-minute personality." She put sugar into her coffee from a Riker's sugar bowl left by Larry Mathews. "Polly's lucky. I never had a great love. Men lay me and leave me, it's the story of my life." She sighed.

"Life's not much fun," Gene said.

"It's not easy, I know."

They were silent for awhile. Then, suddenly, he was telling her what he had never told anyone—how it had begun with the electrician in the cellar and ended with him being driven out of the country. Well, not exactly ended, he corrected himself. "I hold off until I can't stand it anymore, but it's a lottery. Even if it's not a cop, or some guy who wants to beat the shit out of you, it's like you said, when you want to see them again, you never do."

"We're a real pair, you and me," she said. "Love ought to be easy and nice, and everyone for the asking—if there were only a kind God in the sky."

"But you have your singing," Eugene said.

"And you have your writing." Stella jumped up. "Come on, Elgin St. John! Let's get started on the galleys."

As he read the proofs aloud to Stella, correcting the printer's errors and making minor textual changes, Tortured Souls didn't sound so bad. In fact, it sounded as good as it ever had while he was writing it. It made all the difference having Stella there.

They completed the job in a week, and Eugene delivered the galleys to the publishers himself. The novel would be out in a couple of months, they told him, but Stella wouldn't hear of him waiting around for the big day, and sent him back to his typewriter. Whenever his confidence flagged, she made him talk through his writer's block.

Usually, in the evenings, he walked over to Blue Notes to meet her, when she finished her stint at one in the morning. On the way home together, they enjoyed themselves, speculating, whenever a man was coming toward them on the sidewalk, about which of them he would give the eye to as he passed. On her nights off, they went to concerts with half-price tickets from her old music school, and on days there were matinees, they watched Broadway plays from the top of the balcony. They went to rallies around the city to save Sacco and Vanzetti from the electric chair. Often, after he walked her home from the club, they sat up for hours over a bottle of chianti, telling each other their life stories. Inevitably, she made Eugene see the comic side of all the things that had tormented him.

She also joked about her own past—how she had been a homely, fat girl in high school, never having a boy look at her, and having to content herself with her thinner girl friends' stories of their dates, until she went to music school and fell in with the queer boys, and never sat home alone again.

Polly was giving Larry Mathews his first one-man show. Her new gallery, on Greenwich Avenue, had been a spaghetti maker's shop before she took it over, and had a crude peacock painted on the window. Instead of scraping it off, Polly had added the words Peacock Gallery above it in multi-colored letters, that stood out against the tangle of green house plants in the window, also left from the previous tenant. She hardly changed anything in the place, except for one dramatic effect—she painted the walls black, including a pasta-making machine, that loomed up like a strange cubist sculpture. She even left up the old noodle-drying racks at the rear, and pinned watercolors and drawings to them like clothes on a line.

Larry Mathews's unframed canvases on the walls looked almost like paintings of tangled strands of multicolored spaghetti. He had moved on from his expressionist phase. In front of one of the canvases, Polly, in a coral dress with no waist and a dipping hemline, was waving her long cigarette holder as she explained the painting to a bespectacled man in a business suit. "It's like modern music, don't you see? It embodies all the harsh, jangling colors of the machine age....It's American to its fingertips...."

"Look at her," Stella said to Eugene. "Isn't she something?"

He had to admit it. This avant-garde art she was showing had no support from any recognized authority. In fact, the magazines were full of cartoons ridiculing it. If she seemed aggressive, how else to get people to accept what was being done today? Stella was right—it had to be shoved down their throats.

In a smart, new suit and a polka-dot bowtie Polly had picked out for him, Larry Mathews was looking uneasy as the focus of so much attention. As people came up to congratulate him, many of them declaring that his work was so original, it did not escape Eugene's notice that others were raising their eyebrows at the bizarre canvasses.

One of the paintings, at least, had been sold, with a red star next to it. But Stella had told him that Polly bought it herself, letting Larry think that some collector bought it, to build up his confidence. "Poor lamb, he looks like a fish out of water. I'll just say hello," Stella said.

He didn't look any happier when Stella threw her arms around him. "You're on your way, darling. I'm so proud of you!" she cried. "I never saw you in a suit before! I adore it…," and on she went. Larry was squirming. It had been years since their affair, but Eugene knew he was still the love of her life. Only when a group of her young men from the club came up and got her attention, was Larry able to slip away.

A middle-aged waiter was circulating with a tray of coffee.

Eugene started to refuse.

"It's not coffee," the waiter said, smiling shyly. "It's Nonna's wine."

"Dom!" His relative blushed with pleasure. Eugene hadn't seen Dominic since Mario was shot. But how he had changed! Dom had never been handsome, but now his cheeks were much fuller and his thinning hair was going gray—and he was two years younger than he was. When Gene had gone with his mother to Europe, he'd been too caught up with his problems to say goodbye to Dom or any of the Alfanos.

Dominic was waiting with his shy smile for him to say something.

Eugene clapped him on his shoulder. "Polly tells me you have a couple of boys now." It sounded to him like something a stranger would say, but Dominic broke into a real smile and happily told him about his family—his son Steve was six and Frankie was four-and-a-half, and he and Rosalie were about to move out to Long Island, where he was buying a little restaurant."

"What about Carmine Street?"

"I think maybe out there is a better place for the boys to grow up."

Eugene said he might be right, and promised to come by the next day and see Rosalie and the boys.

Then, Polly was with them—the old Polly again—slipping her arms around their waists. "I'm glad you two have reintroduced yourselves. We were all a family once, remember?"

As the people in the gallery milled around with their loud voices and laughter, Dom, Polly, and Gene sipped their wine quietly, feeling as close as they had when they played together as children—until Dominic had to move off to refill empty cups with Nonna's wine from a percolator.

"This came today," Polly said, putting an envelope in Gene's hand. "I almost forgot." She was watching him carefully.

The envelope had a Cincinnati postmark. It was from his twelve-year-old son, Seth, whom he had never dared to communicate with—and it was addressed to him.

21

The Casa di Mario had changed with the times—mirrors covered the old bucolic scenes Mario had painted on the walls. The court in back where men used to play the game of bocce had been floored over and more tables squeezed in. In the roseate glow of the modern lamps it looked warm and intimate, though by daylight, when the doors were opened to let out the stale smoke, the tables and chairs were battered and the marbleized columns were yellowed.

On a gray February morning, Dominic dragged out the overflowing garbage cans to the curb for pickup. But instead of going back inside to get out of the bitter chill, he stood on the sidewalk in his maitre d' jacket and soiled apron, ignoring the cold, looking down deserted Carmine Street.

Rosalie had left the restaurant the night before and hadn't come back.

And now, in the cold light of dawn, he knew she wasn't going to. He gave an involuntary sob and tears ran down his face.

She hadn't given any indication she was going to leave him—and certainly not the way she had done it. He knew he had infuriated her by buying the lunchroom out on Long Island against her will, but his cousin Filippo and his uncles had all said that if he went ahead with it, Rosalie would not be able to do anything about it—she would have no choice but to go along. She was his wife.

Ever since the murder of his father, he'd wanted to get rid of the restaurant. In fact, leaving the city altogether was the only thing he had been living for. He wanted to raise his boys somewhere decent, a place where Rosalie would stop thinking of herself as a hostess and settle down to being a wife and mother. Here, he was paying off the Mafia and the cops, playing along with the stinking system his father had given his life to stay clear of. Even if the bootleg liquor did bring in money—more than they ever could have made before Prohibition—it still made him feel a traitor to his father.

Worst of all was what it had done to his wife. Rosalie hardly paid attention to the kids, Stefano and Franco, leaving them to his grandmother, who was too old now to take proper care of them, so they were running wild in the streets. Rosalie hadn't gotten pregnant since Frankie was born five years ago, and Dominic sometimes suspected she was doing something to prevent it. Maybe that's why she had gained so much weight. She had long before gone against his wishes and had her hair bobbed, and insisted on wearing skimpy dresses, that showed only too well how she was going to fat. It looked cheap the way she used so much makeup, and heavy powder always seemed to be sprinkled on the collar of her dress. He knew the customers liked her, yet it humiliated him to see her carrying on with the men the way she did, sometimes stopping to have a drink with them, and with a few drinks in her, talking back to him with a filthy mouth like he wasn't her husband.

Standing at the curb on the empty street, he began to shiver with the cold.

His grandmother was always complaining to him that Rosalie was shirking her duties as wife and mother, and though he agreed with the old woman, Rosalie was still his wife and he had to put up a show of defending her. She was an American, he told *Nonna*, and didn't she know women here didn't have to hide away in the house like they did in the old country? His grandmother had never understood American life—she had been over here fifty years and still couldn't speak English.

"When do I have time to learn English?" she said in her Neapolitan dialect. "I too busy taking care of my own kids, then when your poor mama die, I take care of you—and now your kids, because your wife won't. What do I need English for? I'm not a *puttana*."

Whenever he tried to put his foot down with Rosalie, she told him to go to hell. She had to be friendly with the customers, she said, because he didn't know how to. It was good for business. Besides, she liked people, even if he didn't.

But the way she behaved, it was more than just being too friendly with the customers. He had to fire a couple of waiters for getting too chummy with her, and once even the bartender.

And now this.

He was freezing in his light jacket, and jammed his hands deeper in his pockets. The lunchroom in the old house with gas pumps in front was exactly the kind of place he had wanted for years. It was on the highway on the South Shore, within driving distance of the city, where families could come for Sunday dinner. The ocean was nearby, and it was a healthy, law-abiding community where Frankie and Stevie could grow up honest men. Rosalie would come around. He was sure she would see how much better it was out there for all of them.

The elderly couple who owned the lunch counter were retiring, and the price they were asking was low enough for him to buy it outright. It would be a relief to get the cash out of the house—he couldn't put it in the bank or the government would get it. He had taken Rosalie out to see the place, explaining to her how he saw them expanding the lunchroom—which he agreed didn't look like much now—into the rest of the ground floor of the house to make it a real Italian restaurant. And there was plenty of room above it for them all to live. There were other Italians living out in Bellmore, family people who had already left New York. He had tried to explain to her that, as soon as summer came, all the trees would be green and full. They'd have a backyard with grass and fruit trees and a rock garden—just like in magazine pictures.

Rosalie listened without saying anything. When he was finished, she said, "Over my dead body!" and was silent the whole way back into the city.

On the advice of Filippo and his uncles he had started negotiations for the purchase anyway. Last night, when he got up his nerve and told her, instead of throwing the fit he was expecting, she didn't say a word. She went on fixing her hair, and went down to the Casa di Mario as usual. That had worried him. Whenever they disagreed, she always blew up at him, accusing him of never doing anything to make her happy.

Dominic had put up with her flirting with the customers for years, knowing there wasn't much he could do about it. But this time, she started carrying on more brazenly than usual with a big, blond guy from out of town, who had been coming in for several nights in a row. Laughing at everything the guy said to her, she kept touching him on the shoulder. Filippo had come up to Dom at the espresso machine to tell him that maybe he ought to do something, she was making a spectacle of herself.

But Captain Dennis Yates had shown up for the weekly payoff, and he'd had to turn his attention to him. Ordinarily, he liked listening to the Irish cop. They were related through the Endicotts, and besides, he was grateful to him—payoffs or no payoffs, Dennis was the main reason the Casa di Mario had never been raided. The one time the Feds had come around, Dennis had warned him in time, so that they were able to get the liquor lowered into the cellar through a trapdoor, and when the Feds showed up everyone was innocently eating fettucine and drinking seltzer.

It was just after Dominic had slipped the envelope of cash to Dennis, that he noticed Rosalie was no longer with the blond guy at his table. She wasn't anywhere around. At first, he thought she must have run upstairs to the apartment, as she sometimes did, but more customers came in and he found himself doing everything at once. He kept watching for her through the side door from the hall. Finally, he got Filippo to take over, and started to go up and get her, relieved to see the blond guy paying his check.

His grandmother was sitting at the kitchen table. She always stayed up after she put the boys to bed, listening to an Italian language broadcast on the radio and often dropping off to sleep in her chair. When he asked her about Rosalie, the old woman, keeping her ear to the speaker, shouted back she didn't know where she was. She had come up and grabbed her coat, scooped some things out of a drawer, and left.

Dominic had panicked. He had run down to the street and saw her halfway down the block, leaning into the open window of a car, talking with the driver—he knew it was the blond guy.

He shouted her name, and started to run toward her. She told him to go to hell, and ran around and jumped into the car, and it drove off. The last thing he saw in the glow of the taillight was a Florida license plate.

He had gone back into the restaurant, finally. But busy as he was, he kept watching the front door every time it opened. She was just trying to get even, he told himself, making the guy drive her around the block a few times to scare him. But the minutes passed. Then it was an hour. It crossed his mind that she might have sneaked back up to the apartment through the hall entrance. He checked upstairs several times. But she wasn't there.

Standing in front of the Casa di Mario, Dominic shivered in the frozen, early-morning light. He remembered his wife, soft in bed beside him, the outline of her breasts as she reached for dishes on a high shelf—even her tantrums didn't seem so bad—and again, tears ran down his face.

Rosalie Alfano walked slowly homeward through the Village streets. She was wearing only a light coat—she hadn't been expecting to come home at all. But she didn't feel the cold. She hated having to face up to what she had done, but there was nowhere else to go.

Last night, she had been so angry at Dominic, when he told her he had actually bought that piece of shit property out in the middle of nowhere, and expected that she was going to go live there. If she ever did move out of the neighborhood, it would certainly not be out to the sticks to some filling station-diner. Maybe some roadhouse-type place in Sheepshead Bay or Coney Island might be okay, someplace that would attract big spenders, be lively, exciting. That was what she needed to put up with her dull husband.

So when she heard he had actually bought the run-down lunch counter with the gas pumps in front without a word to her, she had nearly gone out of her mind—that was the only way she could explain what she'd done, as she walked through the chill, deserted streets.

It had been a nightmare in the hotel room in Newark. That wasn't what she wanted. When she had been kidding around with that slob, rubbing Dominic's face in it to get even, it wasn't that she really fell for his line about taking her off to Miami Beach, where he claimed he was in the hotel business, and showing her a good time. Miami was the place for a full-breasted woman like she was, he said, so full of life. All she knew was that he had made her feel like somebody, feel desirable—and she had gotten reckless. But she never would have jumped into his car, if Dominic hadn't come out just then and yelled at her to come back, like she was his dog.

Tears filled her eyes as she turned onto Carmine Street, partly from the cold and partly from fear, knowing what she was going back to.

She had tried to get out of the car, but the man had only laughed and told her to pipe down, hadn't she told him she wanted a good time? Then, in the hotel in Jersey, drunk and slobbering, he had come at her. She had fought him off. He had started beating her, and her screams brought the night clerk. Then the police had come and she had escaped. Somehow she had gotten herself to the ferry back to Manhattan.

He had never actually gotten all the way, but in the eyes of God, as well as the world's, she was just as guilty as if she had gone through with it. And she had to admit, that in her fury at her husband the night before, part of her had wanted that man.

Now her life was over. She was coming back only to take her punishment. She had once seen a movie, where all the men of a Sicilian village were stoning an adulttress to death, as the villagers watched—and she knew that was what she deserved.

When Dominic saw her coming down the block, he was filled with joy. Then he saw her bruised and battered face, and he felt sick. But only for a moment. He remembered what she had done. He was her husband. She had dishonored him.

As she came close up, he kept his eyes turned away. To look at her directly in her humiliation seemed a violation.

She walked past him and turned into the building. He followed her up the stairs, knowing what he had to do—what every husband would do in the circumstances, what his father would have done. He was glad his father was dead, would never have to know.

Inside the kitchen, she waited with her back to him, her head down. *La Nonna* was not up yet to start the fire in the stove and, for the first time, he felt the chill. He saw that the green enamel paint on the walls, only recently applied, was already beginning to peel, not hiding the swollen places in the old plaster underneath. A cockroach ran down the wall and disappeared under the open edge of the linoleum on the floor.

"I didn't do nothing," she said in a flat voice, still turned away.

He didn't speak.

She turned to face him. "I know what it looks like, but I didn't do nothing, I swear it."

Dominic scarcely heard the words. Instead of rage, he felt only desolation for the years of their loveless marriage. For her always looking at him with contempt, as if she thought him worthless. For her never smiling at him as she smiled at the customers.

He knew he ought to hit her. He wanted to.

"Go ahead!" she cried out. "I got it coming!"

He did nothing.

"What ya waiting for?" she taunted him, her eyes flashing. "Hit me, for the love of God, hit me!"

A door opened. The old *Nonna* stood there, the two little boys clutching her nightdress, their eyes saucers.

It became even more hideous. Rosalie went on taunting him to hit her, the children were screaming, and the old woman kept croaking, "Kill her, Domenico! Kill the *puttana!*"

They were all at him at once—the old lady like a witch, the boys orphans like he was, and most of all, the woman who was supposed to be his wife, drawn up to the size of a howling fury, whom he could never satisfy, who made demands on him he could never meet, who had done this thing that the heavens cried out for her to be punished for.

It was too much for him. He slumped onto a chair. Why couldn't they all shut up? Even if she had done it, he couldn't hit her. That wasn't why he was so unhappy. It was because the way he had set up his life had been shattered. This life was all he had—the only thing he cared about.

If only his father was still alive.

Rosalie saw that he was not going to beat her up, and her fear evaporated. He didn't even have the balls to tell her off. With different eyes she looked at the man she was married to, slumped before her. He had always been a coward, but now she had total contempt for him. She didn't have to be ashamed of herself, whatever had happened. She was still the wife, and that was a lot more important than being some man's whore in Miami Beach, running after will-o'-the-wisp schoolgirl dreams of God-knew-what. None of that meant anything and she had been a fool to think it did.

Until now, she had misunderstood everything about marriage. Now that she saw how weak men were—and all men were weak, not just her husband, but drunken, two-bit salesmen who promised the world as well—it came clear to her how powerful and satisfying the role of wife could be. What a sap she had been, waiting for her husband's smiles and approval. He was waiting for her to take charge of his life. They all were. The strong woman was at the center of everything.

She looked at her husband crying, the old witch in the doorway who was cursing at her with her gums, and her boys whimpering because their father was weak and their mother, with her stupid hopes for something better, had never paid attention to them. Hanging up her coat, she told the old lady to shut up and light the stove. She kissed both her crying children, wiped their noses, and sitting them down at the table, peeled them each a banana.

When he saw that she was taking charge, Dominic pulled himself to his feet. "I better go down," he said. "It's Filippo's day off." But at the door, he waited, as if for permission.

"Maybe you better," she said, all anger gone.

"Will you be down later?"

"When I get the boys off to school."

He went down the stairs, and she washed her face at the sink, moving the old woman out of the way to fix the kids' breakfast herself.

She knew that, bad as things might be, there would be no more talk about moving out to Long Island, or anywhere else for that matter—not unless she said so.

22

Eugene read and re-read the short letter from the son he had never seen. The boy told him all about his activities at the junior high school he attended, his paper route, and all the fun he had going fishing with his stepfather. But it was the end of the letter that gripped Gene the most. "Maybe you could write me back sometime and tell me about what you're doing too. I'd really appreciate it." It was signed, "Very truly yours, Seth Harris." And he added in parentheses, "(Endicott)."

Hearing from his unknown son set up an even worse conflict in Eugene. He wanted to see him, but knowing that he would have to hide so much of himself, how could he look him in the eye? On Stella's advice, he wrote the boy a friendly but noncommittal note, and in another letter, to his ex-wife, sent in care of her husband's office, asked how she felt about his coming out to meet Seth. Clare let him know by return mail that she was in favor of the boy meeting his real father, but for a number of reasons she thought it wiser that Eugene not come out to Cincinnati. She had another idea. Since she, husband Toby Harris, and Seth were planning to take an automobile trip through New England and would stop off for a day in New York, staying at the Brevoort Hotel near Washington Square, where Eugene could meet his son.

The night before their arrival, Eugene was so jumpy he didn't think he could go through with it. What did he have to offer his son after all this time?

"No, sweetie, that's not what's wrong," said Stella, when he came over for supper. "But you have nothing to worry about. Some of my boys at the club are fathers too, just like you, and I can assure you it doesn't rub off on the children."

"Am I that transparent?"

"You forget I'm an expert on the subject. I have been since I was a pimply-faced teenager at music school. All the sons turn out straight as an arrow. It must be some kind of natural law."

Eugene said he wouldn't know what to talk about when they were face to face.

"Give him a present. That will get things going."

The next morning, with Stella along to bolster him, he went to Wanamaker's to look for one. Toys were out for a twelve-year-old, of course, and when he was that age, he had hated gifts of clothes—it was never what he wanted. Finally, in the sports department, he settled on a fishing reel.

The Brevoort, on lower Fifth Avenue, was no longer the center of international bohemia that it once had been, when people like Caruso stayed there, but it was still the best hotel in the Village. Mabel Dodge, who had held her evenings in her town house across the street and once had seemed the most important thing in Eugene's life, had long since moved on to Taos, the arts colony in the Southwest.

As he stepped through the ornate doorway into the Brevoort lobby, his stomach in a knot, he remembered Mrs. Dodge's advice never to hold back from the adventure of life. This was an adventure all right.

Clare opened the door with a wide smile he didn't wholly believe. "Gene! I don't believe it! You look younger than ever!"

"You too, Clare," he said, taking her hand. But it wasn't true. Her rouge and lipstick were over-bright and she had peroxided her bobbed hair. Her floral patterned dress reached just above her knees and a rope of beads round her neck hung over her bosom. She was only thirty-three, the same as he, but if he had to describe her in a word it would have been 'matronly.'

"Seth and Toby will be back soon," she said, taking his arm. "Meantime, you and I can do some catching up." She led him into the sitting room of the hotel suite, where they sat opposite each other, he on a chair, she on the sofa, a coffee table between them. "How do you keep from getting older like the rest of us?" She poured out two sherries from a decanter on the coffee table and handed him one.

His confidence faltered. Was she implying anything? It occurred to him that she might have planned it this way to make sure that he wasn't too much of a freak before exposing him to Seth.

"I thought we ought to have a few minutes together before you meet our son. I hope you'll be pleased with him. Toby and I have done our best...." Eugene felt her scrutinizing him as she talked on about raising Seth. Toby was a good stepfather, she said. Naturally, there had to be some trauma when the real father is not there. Even though she lived out in the Midwest, she had kept up with the latest psychological theories and had come to the conclusion that it would be healthier for Seth to confront his feelings about it, before any trouble developed later on. "So when Polly wrote that you were in New York again, I thought it might be a fine idea if Seth wrote you a letter. It was for his own good."

Eugene was taken aback. "You mean it wasn't his idea to see me?"

"Well, not exactly." She fingered her beads. "But he loved the idea when I suggested it. He's dying to meet you." On she went about the very comfortable home she and Toby were providing for Seth and their two younger children. Toby had the Pontiac franchise for the southern

Ohio area, and Seth had every material advantage, while she saw to it that important things like books and good music were not neglected in his education, either.

Eugene only half-heard. All he kept thinking was that the letter was her doing, and the boy had no interest in seeing him, and that it was a mistake to have come.

A door slammed, and he heard voices in the hall.

"Here they are!" said Clare, brightly, standing up.

A more portly version of Toby Harris in a business suit stood in the entranceway, but Seth was not there. "Gene, you old son of a gun!" The portly Toby rushed to pump his hand. He had altered as much as Clare. "It's been a coon's age!" He saw Eugene's eye on the entranceway. "Seth had to go take a leak. He had three orangeades at that Nedick's on Eighth Street." His eyes darted over to Clare, then back to Eugene. "I hardly recognize it around here any more. It's really changed." He sprawled in a chair and reached for his cigarettes. "I guess we've all changed, huh, Gene? You'll have to tell me about your war experiences. Goddarn it, my flat feet kept me in the Quartermaster Corps in Fargo, North Dakota, you believe it?" He held out his hand and Clare put a drink into it. "I do envy you guys who saw action. Sethie's a real bug on the war."

A door banged somewhere in the back, and Eugene's heart pounded. But nobody appeared.

"Hey, Babe Ruth, what's holding you up?" Toby yelled out.

After another moment, a boy wearing a scout shirt and knickers was standing in the entranceway. He looked as nervous as Eugene felt. With his dark, curly hair, he bore an uncanny resemblance to a photograph of Eugene's father Patrick at the same age.

"Come in, dear, and meet Gene," Clare said in a mothers' club voice, picking up her bag. "I have to go down to the lobby to see about theater tickets. Tonight's our only chance." She tapped her husband's shoulder. "Come on, dear."

"Great idea!" Toby leapt up, as if that were the prearranged signal, and followed her out.

The boy remained standing just inside the room, avoiding his eyes.

Eugene grabbed the decanter of sherry to refill his glass. "Care for any?" he said without thinking. "No, of course not....There must be something around here...."

"No, thanks."

"Too much orangeade?" Eugene tried to laugh.

Not a muscle moved in the boy's face. Patrick's face.

Eugene made another attempt. "Too bad you're only here for today. Not much time for sightseeing." He knew how false he sounded. "I've lived in New York all my life, but I've still never been to the Statue of Liberty, can you beat that?"

The boy sat down on the edge of a chair. "You don't have to try so hard," he said. "This is my mom's idea, not mine."

It was like a slap in the face. He never should have come. "Your mother told me," Eugene said, "but when I got your letter, I was just stupid enough to think maybe you'd want to meet me."

"Because you're my real father?"

"I guess something like that...."

"But I've already got a father. Toby's my father."

The boy wasn't going to come around, why should he? And there was nothing he could do about it. "You're right. Sorry I barged in." He got to his feet.

"Take it easy," the boy said. "It's no problem. My folks said you were going to tell me about the war."

Eugene was confused. Had he been misreading him? "You want to hear about the war?"

"Dad told me you were at Château-Thierry. But if it's hard to talk about...."

"Why sure I'll talk about it!" He sank back into the chair. "Some of it's pretty gruesome, though."

"I can take it!" The boy was already on the sofa across from him, his face alive.

"Okay, let's see now. In 1914 before we got into the war, I went up to Montreal and joined the Royal Canadian Ambulance Corps...." Responding to the boy's hanging on to his every word, he laid it on thick—the screams of the wounded in no-man's-land—running, head down, under fire, to pick them up on stretchers and carry them back. Then, in '17, when America came in, he had transferred to the A.E.F., and there were the mustard gas attacks—the stink of the trenches—even the long stretches of boredom—and always the shells, his buddies getting blown up around him.

The boy was absorbed, leaning forward, his chin in his hand. "Gosh,

Gene, you were a hero!"

Hearing his son use his name for the first time, Gene felt his eyes smarting, overcome by a rush of feeling. He took a breath and shifted in his chair. "Now it's your turn. What are you up to?"

The boy shrugged. "I haven't done a goddarn thing."

Eugene tried to come up with a question. "That's a scout shirt you've got on, isn't it?"

"Yeah, I was initiated just before we left," he said. "You don't want to hear about that...."

"Sure I do!"

"It was a lot of fun!" Seth grinned. "After the scout oath, they tossed me up in a blanket." Then they had all stood in a circle around the campfire and sung the scout anthem.

Eugene was transfixed by this happy boy, telling him about his family life, his younger brother and sister, his school, the track events he'd won, the American Legion speech contest, and going fishing with his dad in Upper Michigan.

"Oh, shit, I have a new reel for you, but I forgot it. What a numbskull I am! I'll have to send it to you."

Seth grinned. "Don't bother. The one thing I don't need is another reel. Dad buys me a new one every time we go fishing."

They laughed, and by the time Clare and Toby came back, they were on the sofa together, huddled over the family album Clare had brought along, as Seth pointed out the pictures of a vacation the family had taken the previous year to Yellowstone National Park.

Eugene hurried back to report to Stella how well it had gone with Seth. But she wasn't home, so he went over to Perry Street to Polly. For once, he was the one to monopolize the conversation, ecstatic over his meeting with the boy.

Seth looked so much like their father in that old, faded photograph, he said, and told her how, when he left, the boy rode down in the elevator with him and walked with him to the corner, promising to write him all about the science museum in Boston. "And this never would have happened," Eugene said, "if it weren't for you."

"What are you talking about?" she said, concentrating on painting red varnish on her long fingernails. "I had nothing to do with it."

"Don't kid me! I know you twisted Clare's arm to get her to give in."
Polly smiled, blowing on her nails. "So wasn't it about time after
twelve years that you two got a look at each other?"

He leaned back in his chair, throwing his arms behind his head. "God,
Pol," he said, "I feel like a million dollars!"

23

Eugene Endicott's first novel appeared in the spring of 1928. The
cover was maroon, with Tortured Souls by Elgin St. John in flowing green
script. He gave copies to Stella, Polly, and several others, and sent one to
Clare in Cincinnati, who thanked him, saying that, when he came out to
visit, he must write a special inscription for Seth. Polly gave a dinner for
him with a few friends at Chumley's.

After the first week, walking past bookshop windows to see his book
displayed alongside Sinclair Lewis's Elmer Gantry ceased to be a novelty.
Only a few mentions of it appeared in the press. On the day of publication
the Times gave it a listing under "New Fiction," and in the Telegram's
fictional roundup, the reviewer dismissed it, saying that, while it had some
first-rate passages, he was fed up with one more novel about the so-called
Lost Generation. Boni and Liveright, his publishers, gave it no publicity,
and all his editor said over lunch was that they liked the book and looked
forward to seeing his next.

It was quickly apparent that it was not going to earn Eugene more
than his modest advance. He had had big ideas about what would happen
when Tortured Souls came out, but though he was disappointed at the lack
of interest, the book actually was sitting there on the shelf, proof that he
could do it, and in his mind's eye he saw the shelf filled with his Collected
Works.

He was having trouble settling down to his writing again, when out
of the blue a literary agent got in touch with him, telling him she could see
Tortured Souls as a play. She'd like to handle it, and suggested he build it
around the book's secondary plot—the hero's involvement with a married
woman, who gives him back his self-respect. The agent's conviction that
the play would be a saleable property sent him back to his typewriter.

But no sooner had he started work on it, than the first heat wave of the summer descended, and even with the windows in his room wide open and the door ajar, there wasn't a breath of air. The city was blanketed in a suffocating haze. The river half a block away might have been made of molten glass—only the stink of the pig farms from the Jersey flats wafted over.

He tried to get started by telling himself that writers must have always written in the heat of the city, like Melville, who worked at the customhouse just a few blocks to the north. But with the sweat trickling down his face and dripping onto the sheet of paper in the typewriter, with nothing more than "Act One" typed on it, his mind refused to care about the problems of the artist as a young neurotic on the leafy avenues of Paris.

One evening in the middle of June, instead of working, Gene sat there wishing he could talk to Stella. She was home, but she was with a man on the other side of the wall, a dull family man from Valley Stream. It was always the same. He took her out to dinner, then came back to her place for an obligatory tumble. Her bed knocked against the wall in mechanical repetition, and he imagined all that flesh of Stella's bathed in sweat on the soaking sheet, and how bored she must be putting up with it.

"You're absolutely right, sweetie…," Stella said, next day, as they sat together on the end of a nearby Hudson River pier, hoping for a breeze. She wore a straw sunshade hat and a flowered wraparound she had made for herself, and had fixed them a thermos of lemonade spiked with gin. But even out over the river, the heat reflected off the glassy surface of the water, where an occasional used condom floated by among the debris. "Ed's a perfectly nice little man, but, poor dear, adultery is just not in his line. I think I'm the only girl who's ever really come across for him in the twenty years he's been married. I try to give him other ideas, but all he does is pump away at me. It's better than nothing, I tell myself, and he's hardly the first man who's used me as a filling station, but in this heat sex takes a lot out of you, and if I'm going to put out, I'd like something more for my money."

Stella was glum because the club was closed for the summer. With the onset of the heat, most of the clientele had moved off to cooler places like Provincetown and Atlantic City. "I guess I'll have to get a job in a hash house to pay the rent. The only thing that might make it bearable is a real love affair, but I'm not getting any younger, sweetie, and Prince Charming hasn't come along yet, so I'm not too hopeful."

Eugene told her that, if he was still fool enough to be looking for Prince Charming, it wasn't bothering him so much any more. He had been nervous, coming back to the States, considering what had happened before, but having her in his life was the perfect antidote. Besides, there was nothing like throwing yourself into your writing to take your mind off your frustrations. "It's very puritanical, I guess, like taking long walks or cold baths to overcome temptation. At least, most of the time." He laughed.

"We sound like St. Francis and St. Theresa justifying why we're not having any fun," she said, pouring them out the last bit of spiked lemonade.

Eugene finally gave up making the effort to work at all in the sweltering heat, and he and Stella tried to cool off by trips to Coney Island, but with the long subway ride and the sweaty multitudes packed tight together on the sand, it was not much help. Hoping for a breeze, they rode on the open-air upper deck of Fifth Avenue buses, and lay inert on a blanket on the withered grass in Washington Square, listening to the pitiful dribble of the fountain.

One afternoon they didn't go out at all. They lay around in Stella's apartment, giggling, and snacking on potato salad, she trying to keep cool in an old Chinese kimono, he in a pair of walking shorts and undershirt. They got into a squabble, when he tried to force her to eat the last mouthful of potato salad and he found himself lying on top of her. Before he realized it, things had gone further than play. He hadn't had sex with a woman since Clare. He had been a kid then, and hadn't felt the slightest impulse in that direction since.

Stella caught his uncertainty. "It's okay, sweetie. Let's just hold each other. It's so comfy—two waifs in the storm."

And that's how it happened—not perfectly, but comfy, as she said. And afterward, when he tried to apologize, she told him that it was a lot better than married Ed banging away at her. "And my God, you kissed me after you came! And you're not even getting dressed now, saying you've got to catch a train!"

"Maybe I'd better catch a train," he said, with a nervous laugh.

"Don't think that this is going to change anything between us. A friendly fuck doesn't have to mean anything more, just another game to play when we're bored."

"You mean I'm not your Prince Charming?"

"I wouldn't dream of trying to cast you in that role, sweetie. I don't want to convert anybody. I'd rather stay friends." And she kissed his sweaty forehead, as she got up to go to the sink.

The city continued to bake in the heat wave. Stella couldn't rouse herself to go look for a job, any more than he could sit at the typewriter. It didn't cool off enough to sleep until about four in the morning, and most of the time it was easier to stay on over at her place and sleep there, and not as lonely. He wasn't as clumsy the next time they reached for each other.

They weren't in love. Neither of them had any illusions, Stella had slept with other men like him, and he wasn't the dumb kid he was when he was married to Clare. They were settling for what was possible, and it felt grown up. His whole being breathed a sigh of relief that he had escaped out of that land of fantasy, where in the shadows beautiful strangers turn into assassins.

Cries of street urchins diving off the pier into the oily waters of the river came through the open windows. Stella was giving herself a cold sponge bath in her kitchen washtub, when Eugene said why didn't they get the hell out of here and go to Cape Cod? She ought to be able to find some kind of summer job there, and he might actually get back to his play, if he could stop having to mop off the sweat.

On the day that the whole city was cheering Charles Lindbergh on his return from Paris with a ticker-tape parade up Broadway, they slipped away and took the bus to Provincetown. The little fishing village, where the love affair between Polly and Hymie had come to an end, was the favorite summer gathering place for Greenwich Village bohemia. Stella and Eugene found a room for themselves on Commercial Street in a guesthouse, whose split-cedar shingles had curled from the salt air, and turned to silver. They had to share the bath with the other roomers, and the fuses blew whenever Stella tried to iron one of her bright wrap-arounds for an evening out. But a cool breeze always wafted in the open windows from the bay, and from Eugene's worktable he looked out at the pier in back, where the fishing boats unloaded their catch each day to be trundled across to the processing shed.

He had no trouble getting back to adapting his novel as a play, and

Stella found a job at a lunch counter from eight to three. When she got off work, he left his typewriter and they took their rented bicycles and rode out to the beach. Sometimes, they stayed on after dark and grilled hot dogs over a fire, and Stella sang her songs to him.

For Eugene, living with Stella was perfect, because it didn't have to be anything it wasn't. They weren't newlyweds filled with expectations of never-never bliss—Stella was hardly the young, pretentious Clare with opinions of how things ought to be. And besides, it was a practical solution to his sexual dilemma. When they went back to the city in the fall, they were going to put in a connecting door between their rooms to make one big apartment. It would be a real home for both of them, a home where Seth could come visit them.

But the screeching of the gulls that announced the return of the fishing fleet always broke into his reverie over the typewriter. He began to look forward to it each day and, abandoning his writing, leaned out to watch the boats coming in through the breakwater, chugging across the bay. He could make out the fishermen, mostly of Portuguese descent, bright in their sweaters and dungarees, lounging on the decks, and one young fisherman in particular in a ribbed maroon pullover, always the first to leap off his boat to catch the lines and secure them to the pilings.

One day, Stella asked him to go buy a fish for them to grill on the beach. He went over to the pier where the boats had just tied up, filling his lungs with the salt air and pungent smells of fresh fish, as the screeching gulls circled overhead. The catch was being unloaded and he could have approached any of the fishermen, but he delayed. He had almost given up, when he saw the young man in the maroon pullover coming out of the hold of his boat, holding a large silvery fish by the gills.

"Any chance of you selling me that one?" Eugene called over to him. The fish was far too big, but he didn't care.

The fisherman leaped across to the pier. "Striped bass don't come cheap," he said, grinning. Under his watch cap he had curly hair bleached from the sun, and black, shining eyes. "Cost you a dollar."

Eugene agreed, and the fisherman squatted down on the edge of the dock to scale the fish, the spray of scales from his knife glinting in the sunlight. He slit open the belly, pulling out the guts to throw to the hovering gulls, who flapped down, practically seizing them out of his hands with rapacious beaks. He wrapped the fish in an old newspaper. "Good eating there," he said, and handed it over, stuffing the dollar bill Eugene gave him into his dungarees. Then, he rinsed his knife off in a bucket of water.

Eugene stood there, racking his brains for something to say. "Maybe you can tell me, where's a good place to get shellfish around here?"

The young man wiped the blade casually on his thigh. "If you want to get the best clams, you gotta get them yourself. Same with crabs...." He explained that you could catch the biggest crabs at the mouth of Sconset Creek, where it emptied into the bay just outside town.

Eugene said that let him out, he wouldn't know how to begin.

"Nothing to it." The fisherman sloshed the bucket of water across the dock where he had gutted the fish. "I'll show you, if you want. I'm out there almost every night." He jumped down into the boat, then turned back to Eugene. "Come on out anytime," he called, and disappeared into the cabin.

The sun was going down across the bay the next evening, as Eugene bicycled out along a dirt road, looking for Sconset Creek. He had begged off going with Stella to have drinks with a couple of her fans they had run into on the beach that afternoon. Along the way, he had to stop at two saltbox cottages to ask directions, but finally, in the twilight, he came to the bridge where the creek emptied into the bay, and heard the sound of flowing water beneath.

He got off his bicycle and leaned over the wooden rail, peering into the shadows, flickering with fireflies. Below the bridge along the creek were clumps of thick bushes and reeds, abuzz with night insects, but no one was visible. The fisherman must have finished his crabbing already and left.

It had been too much to hope for.

Eugene was about to get back on his bike for the long slog home, when he heard a splash underneath the bridge. "Hello?" he called out tentatively.

"Down here!" came the fisherman's voice from the dark. "Good you came. The big ones are out tonight."

When Eugene scrambled down the bank, he found him under the bridge. In rubber boots in the water, he was using a flashlight to spot the crabs as they scuttled away from shelter, and scooping them up with a net. A gunnysack on the bank was already a moving heap.

It was hard to make him out in the dark. Eugene really didn't get a good look at him until they were seated on the bank in front of a small fire, and the young fisherman was showing him how to roast crabs.

His name was Manuel Silva, but he said everyone called him Manny. He was twenty-two. His brothers and sisters were older and married, but he still lived with his widowed mother. He was halfway engaged to a local girl—the families had been pushing it for years, but he was in no hurry to get married. "I haven't been around much. Actually, I've never been further than the state of Maine. I'd like to see a little of the world first...."

Eugene sucked out the crab legs and tossed the shells off into the sand. It sounded to him like the boy had never had anyone to talk to before.

...Everyone in his family, from way back in Portugal, had always been fishermen, Manny said, and he had worked on his brother's trawler since grade school. But there were other things he wanted to do. Lots of things....

Eugene had never been happier. Propped on an elbow, he watched Manny Silva across the burning coals. The young fisherman was leaning against a log, one hand on a raised knee, his voice blending with the night sounds of crickets and frogs, and waves slapping on the nearby gravel shore.

"I don't know what it is I want to do exactly, but one thing is I like to read...." It turned out Manny had read all of Jack London, one of H.G. Wells' books, and even Melville about the white whale. He was impressed to hear Eugene was a published writer. "God, Gene, I sure am glad we ran into each other." His dark eyes shone in the firelight and there was a silence between them, before he jumped up and started stamping out the coals. And Eugene got up reluctantly.

After Manny Silva chugged away in his boat, Eugene cycled home under the great sweep of stars, the lights of the little fishing town strung out ahead along the bay.

And when he got back, Stella was there and he told her about Manny. She was glad for him, and over the next nights encouraged him to go crabbing again. She had plenty to do, working on her songs, she said, and had any number of boys from the club to go out with.

He felt guilty, but he went. Nothing could have stopped him from pedaling out to the creek.

And it was on the third night that it happened. It was all so natural.

The crickets were already filling the air with their evening chirruping, along with the wash of the surf. He got off his bicycle, scarcely able to walk, his need was so desperate, and visible. And Manny was standing across the creek looking at him, manly and vulnerable.

And Eugene knew…he just knew.

For the first time, he was not afraid. There was nothing to fear. He waded across the stream, the current sloshing against his pants legs. But as he came up to the young fisherman, waiting motionless in the dark, Eugene hesitated, overcome by a sliver of doubt.

It was Manny who reached out, took his arm and pulled him closer….

They never got around to crabbing that evening. Or the next.

After a month of this, in mid-August, Stella told him that she had decided to go back to town early after all. She wanted to look for some new songs for the fall, and it would be easier for her to work them out without his being there to distract her.

He said there was no reason for her to leave.

"No, sweetie. Stay on and have me always here to remind you you're not free as a bird, just as we always agreed?"

"I'm just like all your other men," Eugene said, with a stab of guilt.

She put her arms around him. "I'll never put you in that category, I swear."

He saw her off on the bus, but neither of them mentioned anything about when he was returning to the city, or if he was coming back at all.

24

The last years of the twenties were a blur for Polly. After openings at her Peacock Gallery, she often threw open the Perry Street house for riotous parties, the floor shaking with people doing the Charleston and loud jazz echoing down the block. All kinds of people showed up—artists and would-be artists, and Village personalities like the baroness with the shaved head who hung sardine cans from her breasts, masquerading as the spirit of Dadaism. And the poet, Maxwell Bodenheim, who was always being pursued by girl would-be poets and their irate fathers, making headlines in the tabloids. Even Jimmy Walker, the city's fun-loving mayor—a Villager himself, living only a few blocks away on St. Luke's Place—sometimes dropped by. The mayor told Polly he didn't give a damn about art, but he came for her bathtub gin, and the chance that one of the artists' models would take her clothes off.

No matter how late these bashes went on or how boisterous they got, the neighbors seldom complained, because several speakeasies had opened in the hitherto sedate neighborhood, and automobiles jammed Perry Street into the wee hours. When someone did call the police, nothing happened, since the captain of the Sixth Precinct was Polly's cousin, Dennis Yates.

Sometimes, a wealthy art collector took them out on the town. They all piled into taxis and went up to the Cotton Club in Harlem or to one of the notorious drag balls there, where Park Avenue socialites as well as Villagers danced with the flamboyantly-dressed Harlemites.

More often, they went on to a club in the Village. After her big Futurism show, which included two paintings by Larry Mathews, Polly and a crowd from the gallery ended up at a dive called the Bunny Hug. They only went to the place because the muscular young painter Polly was currently sleeping with was a part-time barman there, and they didn't have to pay the cover charge. But from the way they were being clipped for their drinks, she suspected her boyfriend was getting a cut. Sex with him was more impressive than his painting, and in soberer moments she had to admit that she had let this affect her judgment. Generally, she was more particular about the work she showed at her gallery.

The drinks at the Bunny Hug were flagrantly watered, and the floorshow a broken-down comic with stale routines that were funny only to the drunks, who wanted an excuse to stamp their feet. Her muscle-bound boyfriend was looking more asinine to her by the minute, as he flirted with a girl at an adjacent table, assuring her that he knew an art gallery he could get her paintings into, if she was nice to him. Polly was trying to focus on something Larry Mathews was telling her, but when she overheard her boozed-up boyfriend tell the girl that he had the dame who ran the Peacock eating out of his hand, she slugged down her drink, stood up, the long fringes of her black silk dress shaking, and called him a no-good bastard. She never wanted to see him or any of his idiot paintings again.

The scene got uglier. The numbskull boyfriend yelled back that he wouldn't show his pictures at her cheesy gallery if she paid him. Everyone knew about the junk she showed, and all she ever wanted him for was his big meat. He shook off the club's bouncer, grabbed the floozy he'd been making time with, and left.

"Let him go," Larry said, as Polly tried to get around the table to follow. "He's a worthless son of a bitch. You're well rid of him."

"You bet your life I am," Polly said, bitterly. "There's plenty more where he came from," and, black fringes shimmying, she tottered back to the powder room.

The "powder room" was only a single toilet, and the door was locked. She waited outside in the dank hallway, furious at herself for having built up that punk's ego, when she should have told him right off to dump his canvases and get a job house painting. What really galled her, though she hated to admit it, was that the girl he had walked out with was years younger than she was. His own age.

"Don't let it get you down, Pol."

Hymie Liebman was there in the hallway, how she didn't know, but his familiar arms were supporting her. He had been across the room with a party, he said, and he had seen it all.

Humiliation and self-pity washed over her. "Don't look at me," she said. "I don't want you to see me like this…." She began to cry.

He wiped her running mascara with a handkerchief from his breast pocket, holding her until she could get herself together, then said he would take her home. They'd slip out the back and she wouldn't have to say good-bye to anybody.

Their cab zigzagged through the crowded nightlife streets. Still not sure where Hymie had come from or even where she was, she clung to him in the back seat, feeling his arm around her, the familiar flesh of his body under his clothes. It was as if the years since their breakup had never been.

Her living room was a tumble of spilled drinks and overflowing ashtrays, left from the party earlier in the evening, and Hymie took her up to her room. He poured them drinks from a bottle, questionably labeled Gilbey's, on her bed table, and handed her one of the glasses. She clutched it, needing it, but knew she'd had more than enough.

His glass clinked against hers. "Here's to old times, Pol," he said, and drank it down.

Throwing caution to the winds, she did the same. She felt a rush of blood to her head and sat down on the rumpled coverlet. To her surprise, her head actually seemed to clear, the gin burning away the resentments and defenses she had built up over the years. They were together again, just like it was in the days when life was beginning for both of them.

She watched him pour them another drink. "You really are impossible, you know," she said, feeling even better. "You never come to my gallery."

He pulled over the stool from her vanity table, and sat down. "I know I'm a shit, Pol, but you know how it is, never been so busy in my life, don't even have time for my family any more."

"I know how it is," she said with a wry smile. "The critics don't bother to come either...." She emptied her glass.

"Fuck the critics," Hymie said. "They don't know their asses. You've always been a damn gutsy little trooper and I'm proud of you." He leaned forward and squeezed her knee.

"Same old soft soap," she said with a hiccup. "Tell me more."

He grinned back and moved over onto the bed beside her. "You always fell for it, didn't you? Would you believe me if I said I've stayed away because I was afraid of what it might lead to? I'm still a sucker for freckles," he touched her face, "and turned-up *goyish* noses."

"You son of a bitch," she said, turning to kiss him. He put his arms around her and they fell back on the bed.

Afterwards, perfectly content, she told him she wanted to take back everything she said that time on the beach in Provincetown. She had been such a fool then. She wanted him on any terms now, back street, back stairs, behind the barn, whatever he wanted—they could work it out.

Hymie looked away, and said that might not be so easy.

But why shouldn't it be, she said, raising herself on the bed to look at him. They could work it out, couldn't they? It was wonderful what they had together, wasn't it, just like always?

He reached for his pants and said sure it was, but there was his family. It made a difference, even if it would never be the same with his wife as with her.

She sat up. Why did he let this happen then, she asked, the old despair coming over her again. Did he think that guy she was with tonight meant anything to her? Did he think any of the men meant anything? She hadn't cared for anyone since he left her.

"That's not true, Pol," he said, avoiding her eyes, as he tucked in his shirttails. "Your life is all different too. We both got our feet on the ground now."

"You may have. You think this hardboiled act I put on is real? If I let it go for a minute, I'd crack up. You can't walk out, not again."

"Pol, don't," he said, buckling his pants. "You think I want to leave either?"

"Then, don't!" She jumped out of bed, naked, and thrust the phone at him. "She can get along without you for tonight. Call her. Tell her the car broke down."

"I can't. Miriam's pregnant again. She's going through a bad time. It wouldn't be fair."

"Fair?" She tried to stop him from putting on his suit jacket. "She has you every night, is that fair? If you go now, I'm afraid what will happen."

"I'm sorry, Pol. I can't." He moved her firmly aside and started away.

"No!" She clutched at him, but slipping his arms out of the sleeves, he escaped down the stairs in his shirt, leaving her with the jacket in her hands.

.

She didn't stay in that night. She went out to a speakeasy and got even drunker. The next afternoon, when Larry Mathews found the gallery closed, he went to her house to look for her and found her passed out on the sofa, still wearing her clothes from the night before. He helped her get herself together.

"Larry, angel, what would I do without you?" she said, trying to laugh it off, as she made up her face. "That cheap gigolo I've been wasting my time with wasn't worth going on a bender over." She splashed some gin into the orange juice he had fixed for her.

He eased the bottle away from her. "I saw Hymie at the club," he said.

"I guess I don't have to tell you what happened then." Her puffy eyes, that the makeup couldn't hide, watched him put the bottle in the cabinet.

"No."

"Don't worry, I've gotten that bastard out of my system, once and for all," she said, drinking off her spiked orange juice with a grimace.

But she hadn't.

She went to the gallery in the afternoon, after assuring Larry she'd be all right. But that night she made a round of the speaks again, and the next day the gallery didn't open. This time he found her passed out in her slip on the floor.

She started going out drinking every night, and no matter how much he tried to get her to see what she was doing, she wouldn't listen. At first, he stayed with her at the bars as long as he could take it, watching, helpless, as she belted them down. He had never seen her falling apart this way. She had always been the strong one, the one he could rely on, and suddenly it was all reversed.

Finally, the only thing he could do was to go out in a cab in the early hours of the morning and check all the speakeasies she frequented, until he found her and she was ready to let herself be taken home.

"Why are you doing this?" she said angrily, one morning, when he was helping her into a cab. "Why don't you just let me go to hell like I want to?"

"Maybe because I think you're worth it."

"You innocent kid."

He gave a wry smile. "Pretty big kid by now, aren't I?"

"You'll always be a kid to me," she said, settling back in the cab and switching to a boozy nostalgia, "the kid who came into the Teaspoon and told me all about Toulouse-Lautrec, remember?"

"I'll never forget." He hugged her to him. It was a moment of sanity in a sea of madness, and he was grateful.

By the time he got her home she appeared to have sobered up a little, and he told her he was scared for her and asked her what he should do—he wanted to help her, but he didn't know how. He was nearly crying.

She put her fingers to his lips. "You can help me by dancing with me," she said, and, refusing to listen to anything else, wound up the victrola. With her arms around his neck and pressing up against him, she insisted on stumbling through a fox-trot. "You can go as far as you like," she told him, laying her head against his chest. "I'm not very hard to get any more."

"It's late," he said, heartbroken, trying to work her toward the stairs. "Don't you want to open the gallery tomorrow?"

"Good boy," she said, patting his face. "Good, good Larry. Everybody's so good. Except bad, bad Polly."

She didn't open the gallery the next day. He couldn't get her up at all. And after that, the gallery seldom opened. She railed at him if he even suggested she go, and yelled at him to get out of the house. Or, she locked the door to him and he knew she was drinking at home.

Finally, there came a night when Larry couldn't find her, though he hit all her favorite haunts. She had let herself be taken by some drunken pals to a saloon over on the Bowery that featured a Gay Nineties floorshow for slumming uptowners. At the bar, titillated tourists had the opportunity to rub elbows with bums, invited in off Skid Row by the management.

One of the bums was cadging a drink from Polly, who was on a barstool trying to figure out where she was, her beaded bag open on the bar in front of her. She fished out the change for him, and when he had his boilermaker, a shot glass of whiskey with a beer chaser, in front of him, he put his arm around her, said she was a real nice tootsie, and called some pals over to join the party.

25

Larry was waiting back at the house when, at dawn, the telephone rang. A bartender had got Polly's number from her bag, and told him to come and get her. He found her, passed out in a booth at the rear, where a number of the regulars were slumbering in the sawdust and vomit. Her stockings were loose and her panties were on the floor.

It was the next afternoon before she woke up in her bedoom, still in her rumpled clothes—she had been so out of her head, he hadn't been able to undress her. Her lipstick was smeared across her face and on to the pillow.

He was sitting beside her bed, wondering if he ought to call a doctor, but when he saw that she was awake, he came alive and rushed down to get her some coffee.

After cleaning herself up and changing into a nightgown, Polly crawled back into bed, ashen without her makeup, looking as if she were in the throes of a long illness. She took the coffee with shaking hands and told him she didn't remember anything about the night before—and didn't want to. "But I can guess how it was for you," she said. "I don't know why you go on doing this." She couldn't meet his eyes. "How I must disgust you." She gulped her coffee. "I wish to God I could make up for what I'm putting you through."

"You can," he said. "Marry me."

She tried to laugh it off, until she saw that he was serious. "Don't kid me, Larry, I'm just a drunk."

He took her hand. "Polly, I know what hell is. God, don't I know. That's why we can help each other." Didn't she see that no one understood her like he did? He loved her, he always had, she had to know that. But even if she didn't feel the same about him, they could make it work. It would give them both the stability they needed. They weren't kids any more. Would she be willing to take the chance?

She listened and began to believe. A drunk had to believe in something, and even if it was only a straw he was offering her, she was going to clutch at it.

Once she had made up her mind, she couldn't wait. Still hung over, her head splitting, she got out of bed and dressed, insisting he call Grand Central Station to get the train schedule to the first town in Connecticut, where they could find a Justice of the Peace, who would marry them without any waiting period.

On the train she didn't stop talking, planning their glorious future. Using his artistic talents, Larry would get a job as a draftsman, doing architectural drawing—maybe on the new Rockefeller Center complex, that was going to transform the whole midtown area. They might even move out of the city to one of those places where married people lived, like… it was on the tip of her tongue to say Larchmont, but she remembered that Hymie lived there, and substituted White Plains. She'd give up the gallery and devote herself to being a housewife and, ignoring the fact that she was forty years old, she talked about the children they would have. Larry might even become an architect like the Bauhaus architects in Germany, who believed that art should put itself at the service of industry. Life would be transformed for both of them. Over and over, she said she could never express how grateful she was to him.

When they got to Stamford, he bought her a bouquet of violets—the first of the year—at a florist in the station, before they got a cab to take them to a Justice of the Peace.

They had to wait for the judge to finish marrying another couple, and, getting nervous, it was on her mind to say maybe it might not be a bad idea to go for a drink before the ceremony. But just then, the other couple came out, and they were called in.

When the judge got to the part about the ring, they didn't have one, and he brought out a tray of rings he had for sale. Larry picked one out and, holding her still-shaking hand, tried to slip it on her finger, but it didn't fit, and he had to try three more before he found one that did.

She was still nervous and would have liked to stop off to celebrate—even a little ginger ale. After all, they weren't going on a honeymoon cruise to Bermuda. But Larry insisted on them getting back to the station, and she made a joke about him being such an eager bridegroom.

On the train returning to New York she was suddenly exhausted, and when they got home, she had such a bad headache she had to go right to bed. But the minute she lay down, she started getting the shakes.

Frightened, Larry leaned over her.

She looked up at him with a weak smile. "Not much of a wedding night, is it…."

"I'll get you some aspirin."

"Aspirin never works." She clutched herself when another spasm of shaking came over her.

Desperate, Larry looked around the room, trying to think of what to do. Then he thought of the pills in his pocket. Army pills he'd been taking off and on since the war.

"Take these." He put two pills on her tongue and held a glass of water to her lips until she swallowed them.

It was heavenly. She sank away into a deep, untroubled sleep, the first real rest she'd had in days.

Something was wrong, pulling her out of her heavenly sleep. She heard screaming. It was Larry, having a nightmare.

She forced her eyes open. He was sitting up in bed, looking around panicky, until he saw her. He sank back, throwing an arm over his eyes.

She was still so groggy, but she knew she ought to help. "Larry…?" She tried to reach out a hand.

She heard him from far away, trying to tell her something in a shaky voice, about being too scared, running away…. If he was in some kind of trouble, she couldn't keep her eyes open.

She caught a few more words—being blindfolded…rifles…a captain giving the order….

His words came and went, incoherent. Whatever was going on with him, she couldn't rouse herself....

Then, he was leaning over her, gasping out the words, "I was a deserter, they said! A coward! A traitor!"

"Poor Larry...," she heard herself say, drifting away.

Then he was raging, "Why won't you listen! I can't stand it any more!"

She heard his fury, his despair, in the distance.

It was only when he threw himself over on his stomach, his fists pounding, crying into the pillow, that she came awake. His sobbing went on and on, until, at last, he sank into an exhausted sleep.

By this time, she was curled into a ball, beginning to understand he was as crippled as she was. He had fallen apart, the one man she had counted on to rescue her. But he couldn't do that to her, she needed his strength. That was the only reason for getting married. He had to get himself together. Somehow. Some way. If he didn't, she didn't know what would happen to her.

In the morning, he seemed to be his old self. In fact, he didn't seem to remember what had happened. She didn't bring it up either—the way she felt, she couldn't cope, even if the splitting headache was gone.

He came with her to the gallery, she knew in his watchdog capacity to keep her off the bottle. But after last night, he needed looking after as much as she did, maybe more, and even if they had gone into the marriage too hastily, maybe they could still make a go of it.

When she saw the tired paintings on the walls that had been left up for weeks, she instantly knew what to do. She would put Larry up there. It was the perfect time for him to have a second one-man show—it would give him a boost. She made him help her get out all his paintings from the storage racks and decide where to hang them.

That night, though her stomach was still queasy, they went out for a wedding supper—just the two of them. She didn't want to be with any of her friends just yet. She kept up a flow of talk about the new life they were starting together, and though she was able to eat most of her chicken marengo—no wine, of course, Larry the old stick-in-the-mud was adamant—she couldn't keep anything down and threw up in the ladies' room. But she wasn't in the least interested in going home after dinner—it was a celebration, wasn't it?—and dragged him off to the Loew's Sheridan to see Al Jolson in The Jazz Singer. As soon as the lights went down, in spite of the novelty of hearing a live voice from the screen, she promptly dropped off to sleep on his shoulder.

Then, when they got home, feeling the emptiness of the house like her own emptiness, she was in a panic and clung to him fiercely, begging him to respond to her the way she remembered from all those years ago before the war, that night on the Washington Square Arch when, under the bearskin rug, he had pressed up against her with his boyish ardor. She was desperate to feel married, to feel safe.

But though she did her best, she failed to arouse him. He tried to explain. It was the war. He'd been in this predicament on and off ever since he came home. It was embarrassing. If she could just bear with him. Maybe not now, but she would see, things would work out. "Please, Polly,"—his voice shook—"just be a little patient."

Poor Larry. She kissed him gently. She told herself it didn't mean anything. They had been like brother and sister until now. It wasn't easy to see each other in this new way. There was no rush. They were married. They had their whole life. She held him, whispering that he wasn't to worry.

But the next night was the same, and with her demons ever closer, it was harder to be sympathetic. She listened as tolerantly as she could to his protestations about wanting her more than anyone else in the world and having dreamed of her for so long. Knowing he was lying awake beside her, she mulled over the problem—impotence was not that unusual, especially knowing the horrors he had gone through, and the worst thing she could do was to push.

Then it occurred to her what might be wrong. In the years since the war, his art was the one thing that had kept him going. The next morning, she told him that his looking after her through her troubles, grateful as she was, had kept him away from his painting for too long. But she was all right now, she didn't need him at the gallery. She had more than enough to do planning the Art of the Twenties show for the fall. He had to get back to his work.

But without him there to watch her, she kept a bottle in her desk. She didn't go too far, just a nip now and then to keep the panic away. And Sen-Sen for her breath. She had her drinking under control now. She knew where it could lead.

But no matter how patient she was, Larry's repeated sexual failures became her failure. His anguish and endless apologies only made things worse, and her tippling became more necessary. She kept another bottle at home in the bathroom clothes hamper for the nights.

One night, after the usual fiasco, she suggested that a drink might do the trick. Just because she was on the wagon didn't mean that he had to be on it too. He didn't say anything when she brought in the bottle from the clothes hamper and poured him a shot. He swallowed it down and she poured him another, this time pouring herself one too. She ought to have thought of this before, she said. One drink made her feel like Cleopatra, how about him? He laughed and said it made him feel like Antony. But though there was a flicker of the old ardor, it ended in the usual way.

In a flash, the shreds of her patience snapped and she let him have it. He didn't want her. He had tricked her when she was down and would have fallen for any man's line. Who the hell was he to think he could help anybody? He was nothing but a basket case. She jumped out of bed, telling him he was never going to get himself together and she was sick of it. As he lay across the rumpled sheets, his eyes shut, his face immobile against her onslaught, she said she was going out to get a real man and have a real honeymoon for herself.

She fled the house into the night, unclear about what to do, except to find someone, something, anything….

But the liquor she drank in the hours she was away, expecting to get some jazz riffing in her head, only played back the scene in the bedroom. It was Larry she had said those things to. He was her friend. He was as wounded as she, maybe more so. She didn't want to hurt him, but what had she done—she had been vicious, my God, she had castrated him. She would go back, get down on her knees, beg his forgiveness, beg him to forget what she said, she didn't mean it. Everything would be all right. She'd make it all up to him. She'd make him tell her about Toulouse-Lautrec again…how he found the book in the library in Iowa…how it led him to the Village, to her at the tea shop….

But when she got back to the house, he was not in the bedroom. There was only the rumpled bed, his clothes on a chair, the whiskey bottle on the floor.

Then she heard the faucet running in the bathroom sink. "Larry," she called, pushing open the door, expecting to see him washing up, turning around with his shy, farm boy smile. Forgiving her....

But he wasn't at the sink.

He was hanging by a belt from the water pipe on the ceiling, his body still swaying after kicking away the stool, his unseeing eyes open and staring at her....

And, like a final irony, sticking out through the gap of his pajama fly, an erection, the proof of the manhood she had ridiculed.

26

Eugene came down to New York to take his sister back with him to Provincetown, where he was still living. It was nearly a month before the tourist season on the Cape began, and the fishing port, which later on would be bursting, not only with the influx of summer people, but with ferry loads of tourists down from Boston for the day, offered the tranquility he hoped would help her.

In the year since first going up there with Stella Banks, he had moved out of the rooming house on Commercial Street to a fisherman's shack around the bay, that belonged to Manny Silva's family. It had been fixed up for rental to summer people—Manny had done all the work on it himself, shingling it and putting in a kitchen and bathroom—and when Eugene needed a place to live, Manny had rented it to him.

Eugene gave Polly the bedroom that opened on to a wooden porch, sunny in the morning and shady in the afternoon. The first weeks, she lay around most of the time hardly responding at all, not even looking at him. Except for the few times when they were kept indoors by the lashing of a late spring squall, she would lie outside for hours in a beach chair, while he revised his play at a weathered table, where he could keep an eye on her.

Beyond the clatter of his typewriter, the only sounds were the distant putt-putt of a motorboat in the bay and the cries of the gulls. Although her eyes were closed and she wasn't making a sound, from the trembling of her body he knew that she was crying. It seemed to him that she cried in her soundless way for hours. Sometimes he tried to talk to her, but she only turned away. He saw to it that she ate at least something every day. He was with her all the time. There was nothing else that he could do. His friend, Manny, stopped by to bring whatever provisions they needed from the town.

After a while, he got her to go on walks with him along the bay, and tried to interest her in shells and driftwood he picked up. Sometimes a dog from the town joined them. The dogs always took to her, and once when a friendly little mongrel was leaping up, trying to lick her face, she bent over and held it in her arms.

Another time, they came upon an abandoned dock of a boathouse that had long ago washed away in a storm. He gave her a hand up, and they walked out to the end where they sat on the rough planks, letting their feet dangle above the water, and watched schools of minnows flash by in the sun. It was there, after a long peaceful silence, that she said out of the blue, "Isn't it funny, Gene, I always thought that of the two of us, you were the unhappy one."

It was the first time she had made a real comment about anything since she had been there. She was coming alive. But much as he wanted to tell her that things wouldn't always be so bad, he knew it was too soon for that. So he simply said that things had worked out pretty well for him up here, and, smiling, added he was glad she had noticed.

She looked at him affectionately. "I think Manny's awfully nice. You don't have to send him away so fast when he brings the groceries, just because of me."

So while he had thought his sister was isolated by her grief, she had understood about his special friendship. He started telling her about Manny, at first so as to have something to talk about with her, something to take her outside herself, and then because he wanted to. He hadn't had a chance to talk about it to anyone before, and he was surprised how it poured out of him.

It had been a kind of healing, he said. Until Manny, he had never believed it possible to find someone he could feel so close to, a real friend. The age difference—the fact that he was close to forty and Manny only twenty—didn't seem to matter. In many ways Eugene felt himself the younger one. Manny approached life with a physical joy that was an revelation to him. And the boy had a mind that had developed without any outside stimulation. It was a miracle that anyone who grew up here could have escaped a narrow, small-town outlook. All on his own, he had accumulated a vast knowledge of the natural world, and he hadn't even finished high school. Eugene often considered what his young friend might be capable of, if he were to have a real education. Of course, Manny only scoffed whenever he brought up the idea of going to college. He still worked on the fishing boat, participated in all the family events, and went on taking his girlfriend to the movies every Saturday night. The incredible thing, Eugene told Polly, was that Manny saw nothing out of the ordinary in their connection, and would have been surprised if he were to bring up the subject at all—there was nothing to talk about. And as far as the world knew, Manny was just his landlord.

After that, Polly wouldn't hear of them leaving Manny out of things, and from then on, whenever he wasn't off with the fishing fleet, they became a threesome. Manny thought up all kinds of excursions. One day, he rowed around in a skiff to their landing and took them out on the bay to fish for mullet. He baited the tiny hooks with balls of dough, explaining to Polly they were vegetarians, with little mouths.

Another time, he came by in an old jalopy belonging to one of his relatives, and they drove down the Cape to Wellfleet to see a Buster Keaton movie. After bringing over fish from the day's catch, he usually stayed for dinner, and showed them how to make his grandmother's Portuguese chowder with lots of garlic and chunks of bread soaking in the sauce. And once after dinner, with Manny mending a casting net on the floor, Eugene read aloud the play he had adapted from his novel. He was calling it "The Weak and the Strong," which Polly agreed sounded less melodramatic than "Tortured Souls." His literary agent had already sold an option on it to the Greenwich Village Playhouse on Sheridan Square and a tryout was scheduled for that winter.

"If you like," he said to Polly, "maybe I can get you a juicy role in it."

She shook her head. "I gave all that up long ago. I have a gallery to run, have you forgotten?"

"Of course, I haven't," he said, offhandedly, but he could have shouted for joy. Until now, she hadn't mentioned having any life to go back to.

By August, when the town was full of summer people, she began going with Eugene and Manny to the plays at the Provincetown Theater on the wharf. She was even confident enough to go to the beach with them, the three of them hanging on outside of the packed little trolley that wound its way along the length of the town's main street.

One day at the end of summer, they took a picnic basket to the beach, but the wind was too strong and blew sand in their eyes. Manny, who knew the whole tip of the Cape like the back of his hand, led them to a secluded inland area, where there were cranberry bogs among the dunes. He found a sheltered hollow in the sand above a pond with redwing blackbirds whistling in the reeds.

After they had gathered driftwood for a fire, Manny rolled up his dungarees and went down to the pond to dig up shellfish for chowder. Eugene was trying to get some dry reeds burning to ignite the damp wood, and Polly, slicing vegetables into an old kettle, said that she wished their parents could have known Manny.

Blowing on the reeds to encourage the flame, Eugene said he was just as glad their father never would. "We didn't exactly see eye to eye, to put it mildly."

These last days, brother and sister had been talking about their growing up on Perry Street. It seemed to be the subject Polly was most comfortable with. It was so long ago, there was no pain in it for her.

"Papa wasn't as much of an ogre as you think," she said, "and mother was hardly the innocent one of the two."

"Come on, she was okay."

She turned from the pot. "Do you realize that she went to Vassar, but never even considered the idea that I might also want to go? The subject didn't even come up."

"I never thought of that."

"What a circus it was, that house, all those years,"—she sprinkled salt into the pot—"you taking her side all the time and me taking his."

"They had a real death grip on each other," he said.

"And with us two brats egging them on. Doesn't it give you the creeps, them sharing the same bed all those years when they hardly spoke to each other?" She actually giggled! "Do you think they ever had sex?"

"Sure," he said, overjoyed to see her coming to life, "four fucks—Alicia, Jack, and you and me."

They were both laughing when Manny came back up from the pond, with his burlap sack full of clams and crayfish.

"I've got something for you," he said, squatting down beside her and holding out his fist.

Polly giggled. "Will it hurt?"

"Uh-uh. Give me your hand." Manny was seeing the old Polly for the first time. "But be careful, don't let it get away."

She closed her eyes tightly like a child, her hand out.

Into it he placed something cold and wet, and when she looked, it was a tiny emerald frog, its yellow eyes blinking, its wet belly pulsing against her palm. She shrieked, and the frog leaped out of her hand and down the slope, hopping into the pond.

They all laughed, and Manny began opening the clams with a knife, and Eugene silently blessed him for doing so much to bring Polly back to the world.

27

After Labor Day, Polly returned to the city to reopen the Peacock Gallery. She didn't have to face living in the house alone, because Stella Banks was there. Stella had come up to spend a few days with them on the Cape, and when Polly heard that she wanted to get out of Weehawken Street by the river because the neighborhood was getting too rough, she invited her to move into the Perry Street house, which had plenty of room for the both of them.

There was no question of Polly returning to the old life of parties and speakeasies, or touching liquor again. She had nothing to run away from any longer. The horror in the bathroom had divided her life like a cleaver into a Before and an After. Everything before it was dream. The other deaths—her mother's, her grandfather's, and Mario's, gruesome as it had been, even her father's—had scarcely touched her like Larry's. She knew now that until his suicide she had been in some state of unreality, living out childhood fantasies of escape. But his death had been like an alarm clock jolting her awake, and there was no more escape from pain and guilt. She was paying for that blinkered innocence she had clung to until now.

Whatever she had left to give would be devoted to the gallery. Her work, at least, would never cause pain to anybody. She threw herself into assembling her Art of the Twenties show that she had begun planning in the spring. It was to be a survey of all the avant-garde movements American art had embraced since the war. During this period, the Peacock had been alone in showing such controversial art by Americans, rather than the better-known European avant-garde artists the bigger galleries showed. Since she originally expected to have the whole summer to work on the show, she had to put in long hours to meet her October opening date, and she was relieved not to have time to think of anything else.

The news of the show had gotten around and she was astonished at the number of artists working in the most original styles, who brought their work in for her to consider. She also made the rounds of Village studios to see sculpture and canvases too large to bring in. Then there was framing to supervise—she had to keep a sharp eye out to be sure they gave her the simple frames she wanted.

Thanks to her lawyer's investments, she was making an unbelievable amount of money from the stock market—more than enough for both Eugene and her to get by comfortably—so she didn't stint on her catalog, even to a full-color reproduction on the cover of a Picasso-like African mask. If she was right that Art of the Twenties was going to have, in its own way, the impact of the Armory Show back in 1913, the catalog would become a collector's item. She wrote the introduction herself, and included not only prints of some of the works in the show, but manifestos by the artists and photographs of them as well.

She had timed her opening to coincide with the opening of the city's first permanent Museum of Modern Art, which was to occupy a converted brownstone on West Fifty-Fourth Street and was getting all the publicity.

"That place is just a socialites' plaything," Stella said, as she helped her write out invitations. "What do the papers think you've been doing down here all this time? They don't take Villagers seriously, whatever we do."

Polly reminded her that her gallery and the new museum were not competitors. The Museum of Modern Art was going to specialize in European art. "It always takes critics a hell of a lot longer to appreciate what's homegrown," she said, "but this is going to be one show they won't be able to overlook."

But if Polly Endicott expected Art of the Twenties to knock the art world on its ear, it never had a chance. On October 29, ever after known as Black Thursday, the bottom fell out of the stock market, and two days later the art opening that took place at the Peacock Gallery was more like a wake. In the middle of things, two homegrown bolsheviks walked in and pronounced the art on the walls a symptom of the decadence of the capitalist system that had finally collapsed from its inner rot.

Stella told Polly they were just crackpots, but with the newspapers and radio blaring about bank failures, mass layoffs, and tycoons jumping out of windows, it seemed to Polly a fitting epitaph. The canvases in the show that had seemed so significant to her two days before had become irrelevant, superficial as the boom times that were now bust. She remembered with a bitter detachment Hymie's New Year's toast at the start of the decade. They were going on a roller coaster ride to hell and back, he prophesied then. Well, the part about the roller coaster into hell wasn't wrong, but that's where the ride ended.

After the Crash, the gallery became a luxury Polly could no longer afford. She had to let it go. She couldn't even pay the framing and printing bills she had run up for the show. Her quandary was simply how to survive, with the Perry Street house heavily mortgaged and no way to keep up the payments, not to speak of the taxes.

With the bank threatening to foreclose, she swallowed her pride and went up to Hymie's office. She told herself that the enormity of the financial debacle affecting everyone made his betrayal of her, however painful it had been, inconsequential. He was the only person she knew who might be able to find her a buyer for the house, so she could rescue something out of the mess.

But it was impossible to get in to see him. The secretary was unsympathetic—she had strict orders to admit no one. Couldn't Miss Endicott comprehend what a businessman like Mr. Liebman had to deal with because of the Crash? He was working around the clock trying to pick up the pieces.

Polly sat down and waited anyway, and an hour later he came out talking a blue streak to a bunch of worried associates. Her heart gave a lurch at seeing him, but she stifled the onrush of feeling.

When he saw her he broke off with the men he was with, and hurried over and took both her hands. For a moment his touch stopped her cold. But she had rehearsed what to say and was about to speak, when he stopped her. He told his secretary to cancel his meeting, he was taking Miss Endicott out to the Casa di Mario for lunch.

In the cab going downtown, sitting close to her, he said that what had happened to the market was a lousy, stinking shame, but it couldn't last long. Schmaltzy as it sounded, he was still hanging on to the idea that this was America, land of opportunity and all that. He had just about lost his shirt himself, though he had hopes he might be able to rescue his shirttails. Everyone was in the same boat, but he felt a special responsibility to her.

His physical presence might be overwhelming, but she told herself their relationship was on a different level now, and she knew she had done the right thing by coming to him.

The Casa di Mario was nearly deserted. Although it was the height of the lunch hour, business had dropped off. Since the Crash, uptowners, long the Casa di Mario's mainstay, were not coming down to the Village. But Dominic Alfano's normally glum face lit up as it always did when he saw Polly. His wife Rosalie gave her a barely perceptible nod from behind the cash register, but Polly wasn't in any mood to care.

At their table, as Hymie broke chunks off a loaf of Italian bread, smearing them with butter, Polly said she didn't mind so much losing the gallery, it was having to sell the house that bothered her. It had been in the family for nearly a century. But she and Eugene had talked it over on the phone and both had agreed there seemed to be no way out of it.

"I don't want to let you down hard, Pol, but you couldn't find a buyer now. No one has the money. Anyway, the mortgage is bigger than that old house is worth."

They were interrupted by Dominic with their plates of spaghetti, and she managed a smile for him. "Thanks, Dom, it looks lovely."

He beamed. "Special, in your honor," he said. "Lots of fresh basil."

She waited until her Italian relative was out of earshot. "But what am I going to do if I don't sell the house? With my stocks worthless, I haven't a cent."

"There's gotta be some way…," Hymie said, as he set to twirling the long strands around his fork. "There's going to have to be a moratorium on foreclosures, or everyone will be out on the street." Between mouthfuls of spaghetti, he told her about the fix he and Miriam were in over his late father-in-law's house out in Oyster Bay—forty rooms, it really was a white elephant. There was no selling it, either, in the current situation. The only possibility was to tear it down and cut up the estate into lots, but the tight-ass neighbors weren't going to like that. He was just about to take another mouthful of spaghetti when he put down his fork. "Wait a sec, how does this strike you? Maybe I could get the bank to hold off if we made the house an income-producing property."

"But who's going to rent it now?" she said. "And besides, where would I live?"

"You're not getting me, kid. You could stay on. We'll cut it up into furnished rooms. It'll be a rooming house. Loads of people are looking for a cheap place to stay." He explained how it would work, as she did her best to take it in. He was sure he could get her a second mortgage to pay for converting the house into furnished rooms. That way it would generate enough income to take care of her and pay the bank too. He stopped, seeing her knitted brows. "You don't think much of the idea, huh? I wish to hell there was something better I could offer. Forgive me for being blunt, Pol, but you don't have a pot to piss in. Even to raise this much capital for you won't be easy."

"Was I looking unhappy?" Polly said, breaking into a smile. "Actually I was just thinking it's not a bad idea at all. Running a rooming house might be a lark. But I wouldn't have the remotest idea how to go about it."

Fired up by her approval, Hymie told her she had nothing to worry about—he'd handle the whole thing himself. He'd round up the workmen—they'd be happy to have the job.

She listened to him elaborating his plans for partitions, washbasins, secondhand beds and mattresses, thinking how she could never hold any rancor against him for long. With all she had gone through over him, he always came through for her.

After they finished the zabaglione Dominic insisted they have, she told Hymie over coffee about seeing his wife Miriam's picture on the society page of the Times, proud of herself for being able to talk about something casually that once would have killed her. But she wanted him to know that she had gotten past all that.

Hymie told her he hadn't seen his wife or kid in a week, he was so busy trying to untangle the mess his business was in. He'd barely had two hours sleep since this thing happened. But she had never seen him looking better—clearly he was flourishing on the challenge of the crisis. When he pulled out a gold watch on a chain across his vest, she saw his impatience to get back into the thick of things and said she didn't want to take up any more of his time.

He told her he always had time for her, and out on the street he even offered to walk her home, for old time's sake, but she countered that she didn't quite feel up to the temptation. His eyes gleaming mischievously at her, he said that probably it was just as well.

Before Hymie kissed her on the cheek and got into a cab, he told her to keep her chin up and he'd send a man down on Monday to get things rolling.

Polly walked back home in an altogether more hopeful frame of mind than before, even passing the stacks of newspapers just thrown off delivery trucks, with their headlines about new financial disasters and the latest suicides. Already the streets of the Village seemed quieter, more deserted, even grimier. Some stray tourists called to her from a car and asked her where Greenwich Village was. A prematurely cold wind was blowing leaves and litter down the street, and she wrapped her alpaca coat with its luxurious beaver collar more snugly around her—it was the last expensive present she would be able to buy herself for a long while, but what did it matter?

At the corner of Christopher and Bleecker, in a store window with a For Rent sign, she caught her reflection and stopped short. She hadn't taken a real look at herself in ages. Was that face under the burgundy cloche hat actually her? Could it just be age that had done that to her? She was only forty-one.

1937

As far as the outside world knew, the great bohemian era of Greenwich Village appeared to be over. More than ever, the lament was heard, The Village is not what it was." But this time even a lot of Villagers themselves sadly believed that it might be true—so many of their friends had left and the old haunts closed down. In the artist hangouts that remained they went on reminiscing about the plush times before the Crash—Edna St. Vincent Millay, Eugene O'Neill, the Peacock Gallery openings, Gentleman Jimmy Walker, speakeasies, and bootleg gin. All had receded into mythology.

Those who stayed on had a far harder time keeping their heads above water, or justifying themselves at their easels and typewriters, when panhandlers and the unemployed filled the streets of the Village just like everywhere else. Not that young people still weren't drifting in from all over the country, attracted by the old reputation, even if they seemed to put their energies as much into political causes as the arts. But they were much less visible than they had been before, and sometimes it almost seemed as if Greenwich Village belonged to the Irish and Italian residents again.

28

Rosalie Alfano, a hoover apron around her lumpy body, her hair stringy from a grown-out permanent, was sweeping the sidewalk in front of the Endicott house on Perry Street. Her fifteen-year-old son, Frankie, sprawled on the stoop, was rolling his shirt-sleeves up over his skinny arms, admiring incipient biceps.

Rosalie stopped her sweeping to glare at a woman down the block, whose fat, little dog was hunched over in the middle of the sidewalk, trying painfully to pass a hard lump. "Look at her, she's letting it crap right on the sidewalk," she announced in a loud voice, as Frankie snickered. "It's people like that make this street a pigsty."

The woman, embarrassed, dragged away her pet, it's little claws scraping in protest over the sidewalk.

"They think I like coming out here six times a day to clean up after them?" Rosalie muttered, half to herself, as she began to raise a cloud of dust on the same patch of sidewalk in front of the house she had been sweeping for the past half hour. Actually, she preferred being outdoors to being shut up in the kitchen all day with Dominic, making ravioli to order for local Italian restaurants.

"You scared the hell out of her, ma," Frankie said from the stoop. "She's running away like she's got a poker up her ass."

Rosalie turned on him. "You shut your filthy mouth! You can talk profanity with the bums you go around with, but your mother you respect, hear me?"

During the depression years of the thirties, Rosalie's life had not improved, but whenever she complained, Dominic said they were lucky to have a roof over their heads and enough to eat. Let him be satisfied with that, she never would. At least when they had owned the Casa di Mario on Carmine Street, she was still part of the world, even at the end when they were hardly making out. But after the repeal of Prohibition in 1933, a little bar like theirs couldn't survive, with the old Casa di Mario crowd able to get liquor anywhere, and even when they had gone back to being a real restaurant again, the neighborhood people couldn't afford to eat out any more. Finally, the city marshal had sealed the place for unpaid taxes.

Things had gotten to the point where they were about to be evicted from their upstairs flat, when Dominic's Endicott relatives, the hoity-toity Polly and her brother Eugene, offered them the lower floor of their house, where the kitchen and dining room were, to live in until they got on their feet again. Though the old grandmother was dead, Rosalie and Dominic and the boys—almost men now—hardly had room to turn around, all jammed in together.

Rosalie hated taking charity from the high-and-mighty Endicotts, and she and Dominic worked day and night making the ravioli for a restaurant supplier on Grand Street, so they could save up enough to start another place of their own and get out of here. But even working their asses off, after three years they were barely keeping their heads above water. It was the emptiness of her life that got her, the endless rolling out of the thin sheets of pasta dough, mixing the ricotta filling, and then separating the bulging raviolis with the perforated cutting wheel, while the boys helped out packing and delivering. Looking back, her life when the Casa di Mario was a speak seemed like a lost paradise.

She hated being away from the old Italian neighborhood, here on a street of private houses where people didn't get to know each other, not to speak of the bums who lived upstairs in the furnished rooms. It wasn't good for the boys. Her oldest, Steve, who was sixteen, didn't have any friends and didn't seem to want them. He was too serious—like his father. Whenever he wasn't working or going to school, he was alone with his books. No good for the eyes. And Frankie, having to go blocks away to hang out with boys their own kind, and she didn't know what he was up to most of the time.

She stopped sweeping, as Steve came out of the basement kitchen door and up the steps to the street, carrying a stack of flat boxes of ravioli for delivery. He was taller than his younger brother, light-haired, and already filled out. As he opened the iron gate with one hand, he balanced the boxes on the other.

"How many times I got to tell you don't carry them that way?" she snapped, not caring that she was being unreasonable. "You drop them and we got a mess all over the goddam street."

"I got it all under control, ma," Steve said. "Nothing to worry about." He tied the boxes on the rear carryall of his bike leaning against the iron railing, and wheeled it into the street, before throwing his leg over the bar and pedaling off.

Rosalie knew perfectly well that Steve would never drop the ravioli. She didn't know why he irritated her. He worked hard and got high marks and everybody praised him. Not like Frankie, who was always getting notes from school and being left back.

"What you looking at, big eyes?" she said to him, taking a swipe at him that he easily ducked. "You ought to be more like your brother, that's all I got to say. You wouldn't get into so much trouble."

"I'm not looking at nothing. What you hitting on me for?" Frankie went on combing his thick dark hair, training in the sleek pompadour at the front.

He was her favorite. His cocky attitude—the way he wasn't afraid of life, wasn't afraid of anything—was exactly her own. He wasn't going to settle for making ravioli all his life like his loser of a father. Not this one.

He took after her—he didn't think it was a crime to want to have some fun once in a while.

Sometimes, when the four of them were at the table in the crowded kitchen, with Dominic bent over his plate never talking, never interested in anything, she could tell from the way Frankie looked at him, that he shared her contempt. But she enjoyed being hard on the kid to see how he fought back. It was like a game between them. He was the only one with balls in the family.

"Don't you have anything to do but run that comb through your hair?" She was about to send him down to help his father in the kitchen, when at the top of the stoop the front door opened and one of the roomers came out. Mother and son watched, as a girl with her long hair pulled back tight ran down the stoop, barely giving them a glance. It was Norma, who called herself a modern dancer. She lived on the top floor, where Manny Silva, Eugene's so-called friend, also had a room.

Rosalie glowered after the girl walking away down the street, swinging a canvas satchel with her leotards and dance slippers. "Doesn't that one think she's the cat's meow? You can bet your life she's on her way to turn some two dollar tricks."

"She's got a trick right upstairs," Frankie said, trying to sound nonchalant, as he watched the movement of the girl's shapely buttocks.

Rosalie glared. "How do you know? You been hanging around up there again?" The dancer claimed Frankie had been bothering her, and Eugene and Polly Endicott both had made a stink to Dominic about it—as if either of them had any right to complain about anyone else's morals.

Frankie leaned back, his elbows on the step. "Didn't have to, ma. I was coming home last night, and the colored guy's window was open on the second floor, and I saw her in there with him."

Rosalie gave him her full attention. "Go on! You trying to kid me? They hate each other's guts."

A few nights before, the whole house had been awakened, when Lenny deKnight, the black saxophone player, who lived directly beneath the dancer, started banging on her door because of her stomping over his head all night, practicing her dancing. Rosalie had trooped upstairs in her bathrobe along with everyone else. The black musician was yelling through the door that, if she didn't stop that thumping and playing her victrola while he was trying to get some sleep, he was going to break every record she owned over her head. The dancer had opened her door, just as furious as he was, and told him she wasn't going to stop rehearsing for him or anyone else, and what about his goddam saxophone when she was trying to sleep? Then she slammed the door in his face.

"I seen her in there with him, ma," Frankie said, enjoying his mother's disbelief. "They finally pulled the shade down, but I saw the shadow of the two of them going at it."

As much as the news outraged Rosalie, and though she knew she should slap him silly for snooping, still she saw the lust in her son's eyes, and it held her. "The dirty tramp," she said, her cheeks on fire. "It's hard enough bringing up my kids decent with all the nutcases those Endicotts got living in this house, and now it's not only a looney bin, it's a whorehouse!" She couldn't help going on to excite her adolescent son further. "The dirty whore!"

She turned, ready to repeat the phrase so the whole neighborhood could hear, but stopped short. Coming up the block was Polly Endicott, accompanied by a balding man with glasses, homely as sin.

Rosalie was not about to give that one another chance to lord it over her—Dominic and the ravioli were easier to take. She opened the wrought-iron gate and started down to the kitchen, yelling at Frankie to come on and get the orders packed.

The boy lounged back on the stoop and said he'd be in in a minute.

She took a step back up toward him, a hand raised. "Now, I said!"

Reluctantly, he got up and slouched down after her.

"Isn't she a snake in the grass?" Polly said to her painter friend, as she closed the front door behind them. "Did you see her sneaking away so she wouldn't have to say hello to me?"

Paul Miller glanced through steel-rimmed glasses at the handwritten notices tacked up in the front hall. *Night owls coming in late requested to keep noise down, no smashing furniture during vitriolic discussions, friends of tenants' not permitted to take baths,* and in bold letters, *RENT DUE EVERY FRIDAY, NO HARD LUCK STORIES.*

"That woman infuriates me," Polly said, unlocking the door to her room at the back. She pulled off her tam, ducking to arrange her hair in the mirror. She didn't lighten it any more—the gray in it naturally toned down the red she once hated. "I'd like to give her the boot."

"Then why don't you?"

She was rummaging in a drawer for the key to the empty room upstairs that she was showing to Paul. "If only it were that simple. She's a relative. Anyway, it's her husband who's my cousin…I mean nephew…oh, it's too complicated."

Polly's room was her father's old study with the bay window looking over the backyard. It had been partitioned off from the parlor where Eugene was living. After selling off most of the family's old Victorian furniture, she had stored as many smaller items as she could in her room, and still leave enough space for a bed. The other rooms had been cleared out for the tenants and refurnished with cheap second-hand beds and dressers.

"I can't figure you out," Paul Miller said, examining an antique Tiffany lamp she had saved. "You've got Italian relatives in the basement, you tell me your father dug sewers, you have to rent rooms—yet you're a gold-plated bourgeois."

"Don't try to fit me into any of your lefty pigeonholes," she said, as she led him upstairs, showing him the bathroom, before unlocking the door of the vacant room at the rear that had once been hers.

After the house was converted to furnished rooms, Polly Endicott had realized that she would still have to get a job. She couldn't live off the rent from the rooms alone, not with all the bills—mortgage, taxes, gas and electric and the rest. Moreover, a lot of the tenants were unreliable. She never knew how long any of them would stay on, in spite of what they told her at first. They often left without notice, not to speak of several who had disappeared owing weeks of back rent.

After months of looking, her gallery experience had finally landed her a job. It was in the Village office of the Federal Arts Project, set up by Roosevelt to provide work for unemployed artists, part of the WPA. It didn't pay much, but it helped.

It was there she had met Paul Miller, who brought his artwork in one day to try to qualify for the program. She was on the selection committee. The subject matter of his paintings— factory workers, smokestacks, and social themes—wasn't much to her taste. But Paul was a competent painter, and she saw it was the kind of thing that would do for the murals they were assigning artists to paint in post offices and other public buildings around the city.

When she opened the door of the vacant room, Paul was taken aback—

zigzag orange and purple stripes covered the walls and ceiling. "Looks like a lunatic lived here," he said.

Polly laughed. "Worse. The jerk skipped out owing me four weeks rent. I can tell you're not very excited, but my brother and his friend will be repainting it this weekend."

Paul pushed up the window and looked out over the backyard, where the trees were flowering. He breathed in deeply, then turned around. He was smiling. "Did I say I didn't want it?"

"You mean you'll take it?"

"Sure! Where I'm living on the Lower East Side, I look out on garbage cans."

Polly flicked a lamp on and off to see if it was working. "Maybe you'll stop painting garbage cans and paint something beautiful here." She looked at him impishly. "A great poet wrote in this room, you know."

"Who was that?"

"Me! Didn't I tell you I once had a book of poems published? They're mildewing down in the cellar."

"You mean this was your room once?"

She told him about growing up in this house, the way her parents had wrangled on the other side of the wall, and how her brother Eugene had come back from Provincetown after the Crash wiped out the income the two of them had been living on, and how curious that, after all these years, Eugene and she and their nephew Dominic were forced by circumstances to live together.

"Boy, you've really got it tough," Paul said, checking the mattress on the bed. "You each have your own room and plenty to eat and a nice backyard to look at. And you're bitching?"

She laughed. "If you look at it like that, I suppose I am a little spoiled."

He stretched out on the bed, his hands folded behind his head. "My ex-wife was something like you. She had it up to here with the Party. That's why she left me. I'm not sure I blame her, actually."

Polly sat on the windowsill and asked him about his marriage. It was a dull story, he said, but she persisted and heard for the first time about his life after the war. He had been active in the Wobblies, the radical labor organization. When, during the Red Scare, he had been branded an anarchist and kicked out of his job as a high school art teacher, his wife, who saw it as his own damn fault, got a court order preventing him from seeing their children.

Polly was completely absorbed. "Where are your children now?"

"No more of your questions," he said, swinging his legs off the bed and sitting up. "I'm late for my meeting."

"I'm impressed," she said, simply. She had admired his quiet idealism, but she had never suspected he had gone through so much for it. He was a far more complex man than she knew.

He was on his feet. "If you're so impressed, why don't you come with me to the meeting then?"

She made a face. "I hate politics."

"But it's for Spain, to raise money for the Republicans. Tell you what—if you're bored, we'll go out afterward for a bite."

"I'd like that," she said, as they left for the meeting.

He was certainly an unassuming little man, nothing to look at with his spectacles, big nose and not much of a chin. And that dreary corduroy suit that seemed to be all he had. But in a curious way, she found him quite appealing. Since Larry, there had been a couple of men, nice enough in their way, but her feelings had been untouched. With Paul she felt safe, comfortable. She had to smile—if there was nothing much romantic about him, at least, he was going to be an untroublesome tenant.

There were a dozen people around the table at Romany Marie's café discussing ways of raising money to help the Spanish Republic in its fight against Franco. In 1937, the Spanish Civil War was the hottest political cause in the Village since Sacco-Vanzetti. At subway stops and all around Washington Square, volunteers shook canisters for contributions for the Abraham Lincoln Brigade.

They weren't all radicals like Paul at the meeting. Polly recognized a woman she knew from the New Deal Democrats and another from the League of Nations Association. Various ideas were being proposed on how to raise money—street-corner speakers, writing letters to prominent people, fund-raising dinners with Broadway actors. Everyone was very sincere, but when the group had all but decided to hold a hootenanny with fiddlers and square dancing, she couldn't keep her mouth shut and spoke out to say that she didn't think a hootenanny was a good idea at all.

What was wrong with folk music, someone asked. It was wholesome and progressive, wasn't it?

Nothing was wrong with it, Polly said—if you were a hillbilly. But since it was the Village, she thought they ought to do something a little more sophisticated.

Like what, for instance?

Well, she improvised, what about a ball—an arts ball? People could invent their own costumes. It would be like the old days. It would be reviving a tradition.

Before she knew it, she was put in charge of organizing the arts ball, though she protested that she hadn't meant to put herself forward. "I'm not even a member of the committee," Polly said.

Beside her, Paul Miller raised his arm. "I propose we make Polly Endicott an honorary member."

"I second the motion," the League of Nations woman said.

And by a unanimous vote, she was made a member on the spot.

"Paul, you're outrageous!" she said, "I never would never have gone with you, if I knew I'd get into all this." The two of them were sitting at a delicatessen on Eighth Street over corned beef sandwiches and egg creams.

"I did it on purpose," he said, with a wink. "Now I can sneak some of my ideas into the entertainment. Maybe we can do an agit-prop theater piece to show how the boss class exploits the workers."

"Oh, no you don't," she said, "we're going to have fun."

She was already full of ideas. There would be posters plastered all over the Village announcing the Artists' Costume Ball For Spanish Relief, featuring nude models, celebrity guests, rumba and ballroom dancing contests, prizes. It would be a nostalgic revival of the great days of the Village. And best of all, nobody would have to feel guilty, in spite of the hard times, because it was all in a good cause.

29

After Manny Silva finished his classes at City College—it was usually nine or ten in the evening by then—he worked all night at an outdoor wholesale produce market. When he graduated he would be qualified to teach in high schools, but that was still at least a year off, maybe two. Going to college in the evenings was a lot looser than during the day, which meant he could take as much time as he needed to get a degree.

It was hard to make his family on Cape Cod understand what he was aiming at. Fishing or maybe a factory job was all they knew. Nobody went to college up in Provincetown, except occasionally a son from one of the better families off to Boston U. or a daughter to Marymount. His family had even discouraged him from finishing high school—what did he need it for? He had had to make up the missing high school credits the first year he was in New York, before he could enroll at City College.

The Depression had hit Provincetown like a fall hurricane that broke the boats from their moorings and washed them away to sea. The radio kept saying the hard times were only temporary, and for a while, after Eugene had to go back to New York, Manny and his brother had tried to continue with the fishing boat. But as the Depression dragged on into the thirties, the fish processing plants closed down and only a few summer people showed up for rentals. They had finally dumped their fish back into the sea and given up the boat, and his brother had gotten a county job on the roads.

It was then that Eugene gave him the idea of going on with his education. Fishing wasn't to be counted on, but teachers were always needed. Gene suggested that he might just as well complete his high school credits in New York, and then be eligible to go on to City College, which was free. He could live in one of the furnished rooms in Gene's converted Perry Street house. Manny immediately took to the idea. He didn't have to worry about running out on his family—they would never starve, with the sea to live off and their vegetable garden, and in the years he had been in New York, he always got back for Christmas and other holidays, hitchhiking if he was short of cash for the bus.

His fiancée was getting a little tired of waiting. She was nearly twenty-four, and didn't see why they couldn't get married if they both worked. But Manny came from a family of seafaring men who didn't let women tell them what to do. A lot of the men joined the Merchant Marine and got married years later, when they had saved up a nest egg. Even if his fiancée wasn't happy about it, he could only see settling down to start a family when he had his degree and a steady job. He loved kids, and he couldn't imagine not having a lot of them someday. Kids liked him too. Everybody liked him, he was lucky that way.

His greatest piece of luck had been meeting Eugene Endicott that summer in Provincetown. It had changed his life. He was improving himself living down in New York City. There was a lot to learn from Gene and Polly, and even from the other tenants—there were always all kinds of odd ducks living in the house, and even a refugee professor from Germany had just moved in across the hall from him next to Norma the dancer, and told him all about Hitler and the Nazis taking over. Manny's family felt uncomfortable around educated people and, when he went home, were always kidding him about becoming a brain.

The City College campus was on the fringes of Harlem and, sometimes, carrying his gym bag with his books and work clothes, he would walk down to 125th Street to have a beer, before taking the long subway ride downtown to work. Usually, he was the only white face in his favorite bar next to the Apollo Theater. He liked the colored people of Harlem, and never got tired of the diversity the city offered.

The produce market he worked in was below Canal Street in an area of warehouses with loading platforms, where fruits and vegetables for the city were trucked in from the New Jersey farms during the night. He helped unload the trucks along with several hundred other men, who, while waiting to be called, stood around fires blazing in oil drums. Later, there was more work loading the pickup trucks and station wagons of the buyers from restaurants and food markets, who came to get the day's provisions—crates of lettuce, oranges, tomatoes. You could make enough to live on if you were called out regularly, and he always was, because he was strong and cheerful and got along with everybody. Then, there was the extra bonus of food to take home from broken crates, that didn't always get broken accidentally.

But even while waiting around to be called, he liked the bull sessions with the guys, as they tossed pieces of crates to keep the fires going in the barrels against the chill. Most of the men were drifters who had lost their regular jobs years before, and left families behind all over the country. They might be college professors, executives who had fallen on hard times, even jailbirds—and a lot of them were alcoholics. Because of the Depression they had all ended up on Skid Row.

He was always telling Gene about them and even got him to come down and listen in. Gene found the market interesting in a literary way.

He saw everything as material for his writing. Manny liked to kid him about it, but he was flattered that the hero of Gene's new play was a lot like him. It was even set in a produce market, though he was nowhere near as good-looking as that guy in the play. There was a chance it was going to be put on. A theater group in the Village was interested in it. Gene knew the director, a man named Dubinsky, from the twenties when he was going to put on his first play, The Weak and the Strong. But then the stock market collapsed and that had been the end of that.

Sometimes, Manny felt he was getting more of an education working at the market than from his classes. He liked the way his life was divided up in New York, using his brains at school and his muscles on the trucks. Ever since he was a kid he had done heavy work, scraping down hulls, hauling in nets, fixing engines. Now, spending his nights lifting crates of fruit and vegetables kept him in shape, and besides, there was a whole world of good-natured roughhousing. He and the other men sometimes wrestled with each other just for the fun of it. They had plenty of time between jobs in the long night hours to catch forty winks stretched out on flattened cardboard cartons behind the crates or to go off for a beer together.

Sometimes the roughhousing got a little raw, the same as it had on the fishing boats, when they were out to sea for days at a time. Just because he was a kid, the fellas here also tried to fool around. Plenty of them had been in jail, and even hoboing around the country, it was mostly a life without women, so any young guy like him looked pretty good to them. He went along with it sometimes, but he never felt so good about it after. It wasn't like that with Gene. Gene and he had a real friendship. They had respect for each other, and when they were together, it seemed right. But it wasn't something the world had to know about. It was just between them.

After a hard night's work, it always felt good coming home to Perry Street at dawn, with the city still asleep and the air fresh and the light so clear, and his gym bag full of food he had snitched from the market. He looked forward to breakfast with Gene, and then up to sleep in his little room at the top of the house, that he kept shipshape, like the cabin of the fishing boat.

In front of the house, he checked to see if any windowpanes were broken and needed replacing. He didn't like the messy look of underwear hung to dry in the windows, or the bottles of milk and food the tenants kept out on their windowsills, but Gene told him they couldn't make too many rules or the tenants would leave. Still, Manny enjoyed the communal life of the rooming house, with all the running up and down stairs, the loud conversations on the telephone in the hall, the hubbub of radios in the rooms. He sat in on long discussions over what was wrong with the country, and about endless schemes for making a buck. Some of the tenants brought in women. Others had affairs with each other, and it sometimes seemed that none of them slept in their own rooms.

From the top of the stoop Manny leaned across and tapped his key against Gene's window to wake him up. After another tattoo on Gene's door, his friend would come to let him in, tying on his bathrobe. Then Manny opened up his gym bag, took out the eggs, oranges, and bruised bananas, and made them breakfast. Gene liked his banana omelets that Manny called "Portugee tortillas." They always finished off, sharing a reefer, which left him ready for bed and Gene able to face a day at the office.

Gene worked days at the uptown office of Polly's old friend Hymie Liebman. His job was to put together the real estate catalogs and dream up flowery descriptions of the properties for sale—in order, Hymie said, to "snare the suckers." Even though Gene griped about the work, it was the first to make any use of his talents after a series of dismal depression jobs—running an elevator, taking inventory for a paint store, or typing bills in a bookkeeping office.

Because of their different hours, he and Manny hardly saw each other during the week, except for breakfast. But on weekends they got together and had time to do repair work around the house. Gene had never done this kind of thing before. Manny had had to show him everything, from how to put a new plug on a lamp cord or tar over a leak in the roof, to unclogging the toilet with a wire snake, when Norma, the dancer, tried to flush down a sanitary napkin, in spite of the notice about it.

With him and Gene working together, the house was in much better shape than when he had come down from Provincetown to find the furniture falling apart and half the windows cracked. Gene felt a lot better about the house now than ever before. He said it was something like a person you took care of. Manny could understand that, like keeping the boat in shape, burning off the old paint and sanding down the hull—it became part of you.

Best friends as they were, he never got over how different Gene was from him, the way he talked, the way he handled people, even the way he ate his breakfast. Manny always wolfed his food down, ravenous after working in the open air all night—he sometimes felt a little crude next to Gene. His friend had something that it took more than a college education to get. He could see Gene as best man at his wedding, godfather to his children. Because he was still going to marry Anita back in Provincetown, but he was determined to finish college first. When he said he wanted to be best man at Gene's wedding too, Gene gave a little smile and said he'd been through all that, but now his writing was all he cared about—plus Manny, of course.

Manny studied his friend across the breakfast table, his face so alive as he talked about his new play.

Suddenly Gene shut up. "You're not listening to a word I say, are you?"

"I don't have to," said Manny, grinning. "I just like looking at your ugly mug."

Gene leaned over and tried to get smoochy.

"Hey, cut it out," he said, pulling back. Then, seeing Gene's hurt, he pulled him over. "I'm sorry. You're one heck of a guy…."

Manny lay on the daybed, blissfully drifting away with Eugene's head on his belly, when Gene opened his eyes, noticed the time, and bolted off the bed to get dressed for his job. Before he left, Manny reminded him that it was Friday and, the next day, they had to paint the room on the floor above for the new tenant Polly had found.

He started upstairs to his own room, feeling pleasantly sleepy. The house still had that early morning quiet, except for the racket Rosalie Alfano made, getting breakfast for her family down in the kitchen. He'd never get used to the way these city people slept so late. In Provincetown, by this time, the fishing boats were already out to sea.

On the second floor, the bathroom door was locked when he tried the knob, but a female voice yelled she'd be right out. It was Norma Lucas, the dancer, whose room was across from his, upstairs. Things had been pretty tense for awhile, before Norma and the colored sax player below her had settled their noise fight and gotten together.

The toilet flushed and the door opened. "Oh, it's you!" Norma said, coming out in a cloud of feminine cologne.

"Who'd you think it was," he teased her, "your little friend, Frankie?" He knew how the fifteen-year-old Alfano boy drove her crazy.

"Thank God it's not," she said, tying the sash of her flimsy robe in a way that showed off the cleft of her breasts. "He looks at me like I don't wear any underwear."

"Well, do you?" Manny grinned.

"That's for you to find out, handsome," she said over her shoulder, as she went upstairs, doing everything but bumps and grinds.

Norma was something else. She was always complaining that nobody ever took her seriously as an artist. Though Manny would never say a word, he was afraid with a shape like that no man was ever going to see her as anything but a sex pot.

He went into his room, shut the door and threw open the window to the morning air. A blue jay in the backyard was squawking at a squirrel running through the branches. There was that special scent given off by the sun on new leaves.

When he first moved down to New York he felt cut off from nature— the city seemed all concrete and asphalt. But as time passed, he began to appreciate these little Greenwich Village backyards with their plants and trees. He had written a term paper in botany comparing the adaptation of the plant life in the city to the flora of the sand dunes of Cape Cod. He got an A for that one, though he had only done average in his other courses. There was too much going on in his life to spend as much time with books as he should—he was content just to get by.

After taking off his sweaty work clothes, he threw himself down on his bed in his shorts and dropped off to sleep. He never had any trouble sleeping during the daytime, or waking up either, for that matter. He had an inner alarm that would get him up in time to study for a math final that evening.

He thought at first his own snoring had awakened him but, as he came to, he heard voices in the hall outside. Norma yelling at someone and a male voice protesting. He looked out.

It was Frankie Alfano, and the dancer in a black leotard was letting him have it.

"This kid is driving me out of my mind," she said, when she saw

Manny.

He asked what the trouble was. According to Norma, while she was doing her exercises in her room, she heard something at her keyhole. She yanked her door open and Frankie practically fell on his face.

"She's full of baloney!" Frankie held his ground, a tough, little street kid with a teenage pompadour and ragged corduroys with the cuffs rolled up.

Manny couldn't blame him for jacking off over the bosomy dancer in her tights. All you thought about at that age was pussy.

"Okay, what were you doing up here then?" said Norma, not letting up on the kid.

There was a phone call for the new guy, Frankie said.

"The new guy! Professor Weiss you mean?" Norma said. "You know damn well he's away at work, you slimy little pervert!"

"And you're a whore!" Frankie shot back.

"Hey!" Manny put on his robe and came out into the hall. "That's no way to talk."

"Oh, yeah?" the kid said, looking around with a sneer. "What do you know about it?"

Manny put a hand on his shoulder. "One thing I know is you don't talk to girls like that."

The kid shook him off. "You're full of shit. You're a fairy!"

It was unreal. Norma's mouth fell open in astonishment. Manny reached out and grabbed the kid by the shirtfront. "What was that?"

"You heard me," said Frankie, not quite so tough.

"What did you say?" Manny repeated, gripping him tighter. As the accusation sank in, he felt something boiling up inside him.

"Maybe we all ought to cool down," Norma said, but Manny paid no attention.

"You little bastard!" he said, and began slapping the boy back and forth across the face with his other hand. "Who the hell you think you're talking to? You wouldn't know how to put your dick in a woman if you had the chance." It wasn't the boy in front of him he was punishing. It was something nameless, unclear, threatening from the edge of his consciousness, and he had to beat it back.

"Stop!" Norma was screaming, trying to protect the frightened boy, who was holding his arm in front of his face to ward off the blows. "Stop,

Manny! Please stop!"

He came to and saw the frightened, cowering punk in front of him. "Oh, Jesus God…," he said, shoving him away.

"Beat it, Frankie," Norma said, quietly. "You're not hurt."

"He's crazy!" the boy sniveled, and escaped down the stairs.

Manny was leaning his forehead against the wall with his back to her.

"Are you all right?" Norma asked.

"I wanted to kill him," he said, aghast at himself.

"He deserved it," she said.

But Manny could tell she was as stunned as he was at his loss of control. He had never hit a kid before. "I hate people who beat up kids. It's like hitting a woman."

She came over and put her hands on his shoulder, making him turn around to face her. "It's all right. He knew where he was hitting you." She stroked his face maternally. "You're just a man, that's all. Any man would have felt the same way. Why don't you go get some sleep?"

Manny tried to get back to sleep, but he lay on his bed listening to the noise of the traffic from the avenue, the yelling in the backyard, a telephone ringing. He hated losing control like that. Frankie didn't deserve it. The kid didn't even know what he was saying. He called everyone names.

But he was so wide awake he threw on his clothes and went downstairs. In the kitchen, Dominic told him Frankie was out on a delivery, so he went outside to sit on the stoop to wait.

The boy was looking at him warily as he rode up on his bike. "You don't have to worry," Manny said, standing up. "I want to apologize."

"What for?" Frankie Alfano leaned the bike against the iron railing, but kept his distance.

It made Manny sick to see the kid shrinking away from him. "I guess I lost my head," he said. "I didn't mean to hurt you."

"You didn't hurt me." Frankie was still over by his bike.

"Then why don't you come here and shake?"

"Forget it," the boy said, opening the gate down to the kitchen.

"No, I mean it, I want to make up," he said, keeping his hand out.

Poker-faced, Frankie reached over and gave it a quick shake, then dashed down the steps to the kitchen.

But the handshake Manny thought would settle it left him dissatisfied.

30

The arts ball in June to raise money for the Spanish Republic was the biggest event in the Village since the Depression had laid its pall over the euphoric twenties. It took place at Webster Hall on East Eleventh Street—the owner himself was a fervent opponent of Franco.

Polly's instinct that Villagers were ready for a good time again—as long as it was coupled with a worthy cause—proved right. The crowd packed the place, dancing beneath a giant banner, proclaiming VINCEREMOS! LONG LIVE SPANISH DEMOCRACY, to the music of a swing band on the stage at one end. Lenny deKnight, the colored sax player who had the room above Eugene, had put the band together from a group of his out-of-work friends. There was a steady traffic between the tables around the dance floor and the cash bar set up along one side, where Dominic Alfano, a red cummerbund around his middle, supervised the volunteer staff.

Times might be hard, but Villagers had turned their talents to good advantage, concocting costumes of whatever came to hand—old clothes, papier-maché masks, even out of newspapers showing the headlines. It being the Village, nearly-naked artists' models with surrealistically-painted bodies were everywhere, and Tarzans in loin cloths, men dressed as women, and women dressed as men.

Eugene, in the garb of a poet of the 1860s, danced with the saxophonist's girlfriend, Norma Lucas, who was impersonating Marlene Dietrich in a tuxedo and top hat. Out of the corner of his eye, he watched Manny cavorting with a series of scantily clad girls, who couldn't get enough of the good-looking Portuguese-American in his tight fisherman's dungarees and blue-and-white-striped pullover, and a single gold earring that Eugene had suggested for a pirate touch. Some men, defying the law, were dancing together, and Eugene had a fleeting impulse himself to cut in and dance with Manny. Just then, a centaur with a floppy rubber erection that kept getting in everybody's way cut in on Eugene and danced Norma off.

He was leaving the crowded bar with a drink when he heard a deep voice call, "Gene, baby, wait up! I got some news."

A six-foot Shirley Temple, her mop of curls accentuating a five o'clock shadow, pushed up to him. Eugene recognized his director friend, Dubinsky, in drag. He had started a new acting company that was putting on plays at the Cherry Lane Theater, and was considering a production of Eugene's new play.

"Good news, I hope," Gene said. "Are you going to do my play?" He had had no luck with his writing for years and, deciding finally to change his style to fit in with the realism the times demanded, had worked up a raw drama of drifters and laborers, set n the wholesale vegetable market where Manny worked.

"Not the new one," said Dubinsky. "I'm talking about that old play of yours, "The Weak and the Strong," remember? We're going to give it another chance."

"You're kidding! Isn't it a little dated, Lost Generation in Paris and all that?"

"Not if we give it a different slant." Dubinsky said he saw the play as a contemporary "Cherry Orchard," which also took place in a decadent society about to collapse. The company would be rehearsing the play over the summer, and he hoped Eugene would sit in and give them his ideas all the way through.

Eugene let his play about the wholesale produce market drop into the ocean without a regret. "The Weak and the Strong" had been written from his heart, but when the earlier production had been canceled at the time of the stock market collapse, he had put it away in a drawer, never dreaming that the Depression might give it a meaning it hadn't had in its own time. Dubinsky was smart enough to see that.

After so long with nothing to look forward to, Eugene felt like a writer again. He went looking for Manny to give him the news. A slowly-rotating mirrored ball on the ceiling, colored lights reflecting from its facets, played over the crowded dancefloor. He found him on the other side of the room in close conversation with a Pocahontas leaning voluptuously against a pillar. Gene tried to break in, but all Manny had to say when he heard about the play was, "That's swell, Gene," and turned back to his Indian maiden, whose breasts were splendidly displayed in a fringed bra.

Eugene moved off to look for Polly, telling himself that Manny was still a kid, after all, and had a right to enjoy himself. But his friend's lack of enthusiasm made the news seem less important.

At the stroke of midnight, Polly, decked out as a Greene Street madam of the Gay Nineties, announced the start of the cabaret program. She was wearing a moth-eaten, green satin dress of her mother's, jet pendants at her ears and ostrich plumes in her hair. After the usual screeching noises from the loudspeakers, as she adjusted the microphone on the stage, she introduced a good-looking young actor from the Group Theater, Jules Garfinkle, who was going to read a poem by the anti-fascist Spanish poet, Federico Garcia Lorca. Suspected of being a homosexual, the Spaniard had been hideously murdered by Franco's soldiers by having a gun fired up his anal passage.

As the dancefloor went still, Garfinkle recited Lorca's famous poem about a bullfighter's death in the arena, with its ominous refrain, "*at five in the afternoon.*" The audience was stunned, understanding that the bullfighter in the poem stood for Spain and the bull that gored him to death was Franco's Falangist army. Before the thunderous applause died away, on came a group of flamenco dancers, castanets clicking and shoes tapping.

With the Village audience all but ready to lay down their lives for Spain, Polly's friend Paul Miller seized the microphone to appeal for donations. The band took up the hypnotic beat of Ravel's "Bolero," as he exhorted the crowd to empty their pockets, and the dancer from Perry Street, Norma Lucas, in an elaborate evening dress and elbow-length gloves, appeared on the stage with a hand provocatively on one hip.

"Five bucks!" a man shouted from the front, as Polly had set him up to do, and Norma unpeeled one of her gloves, swinging it like a professional stripper to the rhythm of the drums, before tossing it out to him. The audience caught on with a roar of approval, and the pledges came in loud and clear, as Norma shed ever more intimate items of her clothing against the hypnotic beat of the music in the background. She took off her bra for fifty dollars. Her panties went for seventy-five. The crowd went mad, as the bidding began for her G-string.

Behind the bar, Dominic Alfano was splashing out Seagram's 7 into a row of highball glasses, tapping a foot to the music and keeping one eye on the doings on the stage. He didn't judge these artist types like Rosalie did—they were a different world from him—any more than he judged other people's politics. Rosalie thought he was crazy for volunteering to work the bar for Polly and getting mixed up with this kind of people. Who cared what was going on over there in Spain, she said. The American government wasn't taking sides, so why should they? Except for the President of the United States, according to her, Mussolini was the only one that knew what he was doing.

She had tried to stop him from taking on the responsibility of ordering the liquor from his old supplier. Those Commies were a bunch of bums who would never pay him back, she said. And then where would they be, saddled with another debt they could never pay, no matter how much ravioli they sold, and they'd end up at the bottom of the river in concrete shoes.

But Dominic wasn't worried about that. His wife would never understand that Polly and Eugene were his blood family. They had given them a place to live, when he and Rosalie and the boys were about to be thrown out on the street, and he would never forget it.

He was running short of seltzer. He looked around for his younger son, Frankie, who was supposed to be helping out, bringing supplies from the storeroom backstage. But the kid had sneaked away again. Dominic had already caught him finishing off the remains of somebody's drink. Rosalie let him get away with everything.

Dominic wasn't close to either of his sons, but at least Steve, who was helping with ticket sales at the door, was no worry to anyone. Steve was more like him. Though only a year older than Frankie, he took things seriously.

"The Bolero" was building toward its dissonant climax. Dominic caught sight of Frankie up near the stage, gaping at the almost-naked girl, who was keeping time to the music, her breasts shaking, as Paul Miller over the loudspeaker encouraged the crowd to up the bidding. He was holding out for one hundred dollars for the G-string, but much as everyone wanted to see the sequined patch yanked off, nobody had that kind of money, and to a collective groan from the audience, the dancer, still wearing her G-string, ran off the stage throwing kisses. But a couple of seconds later, as the Bolero hit its final notes, she bounded back to the center of the stage, whipped off her G-string, and twirling it aloft, ran off to thundering cheers.

Between acts, the bar got busy again. But when a men's chorus came on to sing songs of the Abraham Lincoln Brigade, Dominic had a chance to go backstage to get the seltzer himself. He was about to pick up a crate, when he heard the screams from inside the dancer's dressing room next door.

He rushed in and stopped dead. Norma, clad only in bra and panties, was struggling with an attacker. It was his fifteen-year-old son, and to Dominic's horror, the boy's erection was sticking out of his open trousers, as he grappled with her.

"Lemme," he was begging, "lemme do it!"

Dominic leapt forward and seized a fistful of Frankie's hair, pulling his head back, until the boy cried out from pain.

The girl backed away, white-faced and shaking. "...crazy...he's crazy!" She snatched up her clothes and ran from the room.

Dominic held his son's arms pinioned behind his back, as the adolescent kicked and howled.

"What's it to her? She puts out for niggers, why not for me?"

Frankie was totally drunk, Dominic could smell it. "Shut up!" he said, shaking him hard, until the boy finally stopped his tantrum and began to cry like a child.

Dominic let him go and sank onto a chair. "...like an animal, Frankie. Why....?"

His son turned his back and fastened his pants, still crying. "They call me a punk. They think I can't...."

"...like an animal," Dominic repeated, his voice shaking, "...out of control...."

"You can talk," the boy said, turning on him in a fury, his eyes still full of tears. "Ma says you're just a fucking patsy."

Outside, the chorus was singing some anthem from the banks of the Ebro.

Dominic shook his head over and over, exhausted, saying, "You did what you just did, and you talk that way to your father?"

"Norma?" The voice of Lenny deKnight, the black sax player, called from the hall. He looked into the room. "Oh, is Norma around?"

Dominic stared at the musician without speaking. In the middle of the room Frankie looked at the floor, face streaked with tears.

"Oh...." The sax player stepped back. "Sorry," he said.

"He didn't mean to do it," Dominic said after him, but the musician was gone.

Frankie had bent over and was vomiting in a fire bucket in the corner. When the boy was finished being sick, Dominic told him to wash up at the basin and then come help him. Still wet-eyed and sullen, Frankie followed his father outside and hoisted a crate of seltzer onto his shoulder.

Muted colors flickered over the dancers from the revolving ball overhead. The band was playing "Night and Day," and Polly was dancing with Paul Miller on the crowded floor. The cabaret show was over. It had all gone much better than she'd expected. Young Steve Alfano, collecting admissions at the door, had told her they had raised more than five hundred dollars, including the pledges from the striptease, and that wasn't figuring in the profits from the drinks.

"I'd never guess a man with all your principles would be such a good dancer," she said to Paul. She had removed the ostrich feathers from her hair so as not to appear taller than him.

"You mean dancing is the opiate of the people?" Paul chuckled. "Even us lefties believe in having a good time sometimes."

"I believe in having a good time all the time," Polly said. But the truth was that she hadn't enjoyed dancing this much in years. It still made her vaguely uneasy to have someone's arms around her, feeling the heat of another body. But her mother's Gay Nineties ball dress was made for dancing, and she let herself be swept away as the saxophone played the nostalgic tune.

When they were back at their table, Paul Miller said, "Ever since my wife left me I haven't had much of a personal life. I thought I could do without one." His hand brushed hers, as he flicked pretzel crumbs from the tablecloth.

His touch was more disturbing to her than if he had actually taken her hand. She liked him and she valued his friendship. She didn't want to have to hurt him. Carefully, she said, "I'm not so sure, Paul."

The shabby, middle-aged man smiled deprecatingly. "I know I'm not the pot of gold at the end of the rainbow."

"Don't be foolish, it has nothing to do with you," she said. "Things have happened to me, that's all." She tried to make a joke of it. "I have a past."

He was no angel himself, he told her. He didn't care how many men she'd had, if that's what she was worried about. Or if she drank a little too much once in a while—what the hell, so did he.

The hall was shaking with several hundred people doing the rumba. Some men in the middle of the floor were tossing a happily-shrieking girl into the air on a blanket.

"It's not that, Paul." She avoided his eyes. "Something happened...."

"We all do terrible thing in our lives."

His homeliness was reassuring. A man died because of her, she told him. She had effectively killed him. When Paul started to protest, she shook her head. "Not with a gun, I don't mean that. Maybe that would have been kinder...."

She had never mentioned Larry Mathews to anyone, not even that first summer with Eugene in Provincetown. She had never intended to talk about it—never thought herself able to—but on this bacchanalian night when everybody was letting go, with this kindly man who didn't judge her, she found it possible at last to tell the story. It even felt right.

"I'm sorry," he said, when she was finished, and put his hand on hers.

Tears wet on her cheeks, she sat with him, as the costumed dancers swirled around them.

It was when the competition for the best costume was going on that there was a disturbance at the door.

"What is it?" Polly said, trying to see over the sea of heads.

Paul Miller stood up on his chair. "Somebody's making trouble."

The people at the front were pushed aside, as a band of burly men broke into the room, yelling, "Commie queers!" and began overturning tables. The music stopped in the pandemonium. People were yelling and screaming, trying to get out of the way of the goons attacking in all directions.

"Fascist bastards!" Paul shouted.

"The money!" Polly cried, remembering Steve at the door.

Some of the costumed revelers were rallying and fighting back. In the middle of the melee, whistles shrilled and police charged into the hall, as if they'd been waiting for an excuse to break up the party.

"The money!" Polly said again, as bottles flew in every direction.

"I'm getting you out of here!" Gripping her arm, Paul started hustling her toward the alley door.

She had a last glimpse of Eugene ducking a chair and Manny wading in on the attacker with his fists, before she and Paul fell into the crowd outside that had been attracted by the noise and shattering of glass. Half a dozen paddy wagons were lined up, sirens were screaming, and newspaper photographers were already on the scene, flashbulbs snapping.

Back on Perry Street in the Alfanos' basement kitchen, Polly sat with Paul Miller and Dominic over coffee. Weary as she was, she felt closer to Dominic tonight than she had in a long time. They had spotted him in his red cummerbund outside Webster Hall, as they watched, helplessly, the police loading scantily-clad girls and men in drag into paddy wagons, to be hauled off to night court and charged with public indecency.

The three of them had rushed over to the office of Paul's organization sponsoring the arts ball, to see if by some miracle anybody had rescued the receipts. But just as Polly feared, nobody knew anything about it.

Although it was after three in the morning, Rosalie had gotten up and come out in her housecoat and was eyeing them sourly from the sink, where she was occupying herself cleaning spinach for the next day's pasta. Eugene and Manny had escaped with a few bruises, and the dancer, Norma, although picked up by the police briefly, had been released. Frankie had already gone to bed, but his brother Steve still hadn't shown up and they were worried.

"You'd expect this kind of thing in Nazi Germany," Paul Miller said. "Those cops are workingmen too. They should be on our side."

Polly, whose finger was worrying a rip in the skirt of her costume, asked Dom to try again to remember when he had last seen his son, Steve. Dominic thought he had caught a glimpse of him around the stage, but so much had happened he couldn't be sure.

"I told ya, you were a sucker to get mixed up in it," his wife muttered at the sink, as she shook water out of the spinach. "Now we're in hock up to our necks over all that liquor you signed for."

Dominic said not to bring that up now. Polly tried to say that she'd find some way to pay for it, but Rosalie ignored her, keeping on at her husband. "They just want to use suckers like you. I read in the News that it's the Commies behind all that Spanish crap."

Paul put down his coffee cup and turned to her. "Mrs. Alfano, I don't think it's quite as simple as the Daily News makes out," he explained, patiently. "All kinds of people are upset about what's happening over there, and are trying to work together to do something about it."

Rosalie angrily shook out her spinach. "Why collect money for them? There are plenty of poor slobs here in our own country."

Paul was still patient. "But if Spain falls to fascism, Mrs. Alfano,,,,"

Polly put a hand on his arm. "Don't bother, Paul."

"Nobody wants to hear the rotten truth," Rosalie said at the sink. "That's it, isn't it?"

"I didn't say that," Polly said, firmly. "We're all upset—it's been exhausting." She held her long skirt, as she got out of her chair. "I think maybe we should go upstairs, Paul."

Rosalie dropped her spinach and turned around. "Go on, have a good night's sleep. Who gives a damn about us? Thanks to you, we're bankrupt, and one of my boys is out there—maybe dead—and you ought to have seen the way Frankie was acting when he came in." She was building up a head of steam.

"Polly didn't have nothing to do with it," Dominic told his wife. "Why don't you lay off?"

"Lay off? You'd like that, wouldn't you?" she said, wiping her hands across the middle of her faded housecoat. "I been keeping my trap shut for three and a half years, cooped up in this basement—oh, so grateful we are to be here, and all thanks to your generous relatives." She looked Polly's fancy Gay Nineties dress up and down and pretended to spit.

"Come on, Paul," Polly said, as she gathered her skirts to go.

Rosalie was back at her spinach again, chopping it up on a board. "… us working our tails off down here, with a houseful of chiselers upstairs living off the government, and we're supposed to kiss her ass and say thank you for taking us in out of the gutter."

There was no stopping her, though poor Dominic kept trying to interrupt.

"I know you don't care for me, Rosalie," Polly said at the door. "These are hard times, but we've got to make the best of it."

"Best of it? The best of what?" Her knife went at the spinach faster, chopping it to bits. "It's easy for you to talk, with a regular paycheck, and raking in all that dough from those bums upstairs—whores and fairies, all of them."

Polly turned pale, hating the woman's fat evil behind at the sin as her vicious chopping continued. "Rosalie," she said, carefully, "You are full of shit."

Rosalie threw the knife into the sink, her eyes bright as she turned around. "Ah, so we're off our high horse," she crowed. "Now the Queen of the May is down here in the mud with the rest of us. The truth hurts, doesn't it?"

"You're vile!" Polly's voice was shaking. "You're so filled with hate, you're...."

Paul tried to restrain her. "Let's go, Polly."

She shook off his hand, already carried away. "You think I like having you here, you fat sow? You think I like seeing your ugly face blabbing to the whole street, every time I go out?"

Rosalie leaned back against the sink, reeling from the blast of the unexpected attack.

"...I'd throw you out right now if it weren't for Dom. You could go crawling right back to whatever hole you came from!" Polly stopped, breathing hard, aghast at what had come out of her.

Rosalie's bluster was gone. Nobody had ever talked back to her like this, not on her own terms. Feeling the other woman's contempt, she wilted and put her hand over her mouth, as she dissolved in self-pitying sobs. "They hate me here...everybody hates me." Tears smeared her contorted face. "I got no place to go. I'm trapped...trapped!" With her arm she swept the chopped spinach off the board, scattering it across the floor, and let out a wail.

Going over to her, Dominic tried clumsily to comfort her, telling her they didn't have to leave, but she cracked him across the face. "Get away from me! What kind of a life have I got? I want to be happy." She laid her head down on the bare table and cried.

Polly was wretched over having blown up at the unhappy woman, and tried to apologize.

While Dominic was hovering around his wife, making gestures to Polly that it would be all right, the gate on the sidewalk outside opened and they heard footsteps coming down. Rosalie lifted her tear-bloated face, curiosity distracting her from her performance, as her son Steve came in looking like the perfect student with his book bag and cap. He cast a quick look at his mother, who gave one last burst of sobs for the new audience.

"Don't worry, ma. I'm okay." He hung up his jacket, and tossed a copy of the early edition of the Mirror on the table with the headline COPS BUST COMMIE BALL.

"Where you been all this time?" Dominic asked, angrily. "We got back hours ago."

"Don't ride me, pop. I had a hell of a time getting away. I didn't want those goons to get me, so I had to lie low." He pulled open the flap of his book bag and dumped the contents out onto the table—a pile of coins and bills, the money from the dance.

As a jubilant Paul Miller questioned him about it, Steve told them he had been counting the take in the back when the trouble began, and he had managed to hide under the stage, waiting until the cops had cleared the hall and finished questioning the employees. With all the exits under police guard, he eventually shinnied through a window and got out over the roof.

Even Rosalie forgot her miseries, as Dominic got out a bottle of chianti and poured glasses all around.

31

Seth Harris lay awake in his upper berth in the Pullman car in anticipation of seeing his father again. The train was arriving at Penn Station first thing in the morning.

He and his wife Babs, who was in the lower berth, were taking a belated honeymoon to New York, and he thought the sleeping car porter had a wicked gleam in his eye as he showed them to their separate berths. Seth had connected with Babs after moving from Cincinnati to take a job in a department store in Cleveland. He was in a training program to become a buyer. He had once had ideas of becoming a civil engineer, but with his stepfather, Toby Harris, losing the auto dealership in the Depression, there was no money for Seth to go on to college—and he damn well wasn't going to stay in Cincinnati and sell cars. Whatever the economic situation was for some people, now that he was happily married and with a secure job, he himself didn't have anything to worry about.

Ever since his marriage several months before, he had been saving for this trip. Lulled by the rhythm of the train wheels rolling across upstate New York, he let his mind drift ahead. He and Babs had ten days to spend in Manhattan and were going to stay with his father and his aunt Polly, so there was no hotel room to pay for.

Since their first meeting at the Brevoort Hotel when he was a kid, Seth had only seen his real father a couple of times, the last time being at his high school graduation when Eugene had made the trip out to Cincinnati. He liked Gene, but even if he was his real father, they were very different. Whereas Gene's interests were primarily literary, Seth's went more toward science. At his graduation, Eugene had remarked that Seth took after his grandfather, Patrick—they had the same outgoing personality.

It was true, he had been popular in school and had a lot of success with girls. But none of them had been special until Babs. Before he knew her she had been a prom queen. In high school he had always pictured a prom queen exactly like her as he whacked off. He didn't go for the girls his mother tried to push on him, girls with four eyes and books under their arms.

Babs was only going to keep her job another year or so, until they had saved enough to move into their own house and start a family, instead of their apartment in a decayed old Victorian mansion on Euclid Avenue broken up into flats. He was looking forward to children—they were the next best thing in marriage to making love.

The motion of the train rocked him in his berth, and he thought of his wife's terrific breasts in the berth below. The sheet covering him rose like a tent. He and Babs had actually gone all the way before they got married. She had the same devil in her that he did, and since they had gotten married, life had been one long, happy screw.

"Babs," he whispered down through the curtains to the berth below, "you still awake?"

"What do you think?" his new wife whispered back, showing him her mind was on the same subject.

He laughed, and peeking into the aisle to be sure the porter was not around, he climbed down through the curtains into her berth. "Be quiet, dopey," he said to his giggling wife, as he slipped in beside her.

"But I want to play." She groped for the drawstring of his pajamas.

She was the sexiest little tease in the whole world. With her mouth over his throbbing cock, he lay back in absolute bliss, as the train whistle hooted through the night.

His father let them have his front room on the parlor floor, where they could look out on Perry Street and watch the Greenwich Village characters passing by. It was only a few blocks from Sheridan Square, with its clubs and bars and coffee shops that stayed open all night. Nobody ever seemed to go to sleep in this town.

Gene was temporarily staying in one of the smaller rooms on the top floor that belonged to a friend of his, who worked nights unloading trucks and slept days, so they could use the bed in rotation.

Before going off to their jobs the first morning, his father and Polly had breakfast with the newlyweds in the Alfano kitchen. Dominic and Rosalie had started serving cheap meals to the roomers to make extra money, and Polly assured him that he and Babs could eat there any time they wanted. It always struck him as odd that Eugene and Polly were actually Dominic Alfano's uncle and aunt, though they were about the same age.

Seth got to know the Alfanos for the first time. The older son, Steve, was a bit of a grind, but Frankie was a kid after his own heart, a real wise guy, and it tickled Seth to see the way the skinny kid's eyes popped, when Babs wore her cashmere sweater backwards without a bra. Seth couldn't blame him—with those tits his wife was the perfect sweater girl. She could give Lana Turner a run for her money, any day.

But his favorite of the Alfanos was Rosalie. They took to each other right off. They had the same sense of humor. When she asked him, with just a trace of a smile, what he liked to eat—canned pork and beans, maybe?— he was ready for her. "No, pasta fagiol'."

"Come on, you're kidding me," she said. "It's got to be something like apple pie!"

"I'm not kidding," he said, "my favorite is spaghetti and meatballs."

Rosalie was fat and had to be on the far side of forty, but she kidded around with him whenever he ran into her on the stoop. She was always there with her broom. From his room, he could hear her yelling to the whole neighborhood how the country was going down the drain, and it was the fault of the reds and queers. She couldn't pile his plate high enough when they ate in her kitchen, and wouldn't take any money from him. The trip east would have been worth it just to get to know her. Though when he told aunt Polly what a card Rosalie was, Polly said dryly that she had never seen Dominic's wife take to anyone so fast, and it must be because he was so good-looking.

This was the real Greenwich Village he had heard about, running into all the characters in the rooming house. There was Lenny, the sax player, a terrific guy, who told him right off that, anytime they wanted, he could get them in free to Eddie Condon's, the jazz club in the Village where he was playing. They went to see the modern dancer from upstairs rehearsing with her company in a peculiar work, where all the dancers made movements like the different parts of a machine. The dance was called "Assembly Line." Babs liked it better than he did, and signed up to take a dance class herself. She said it would be good for her figure.

Paul Miller, a friend of his aunt's, was a bug on unions and thought Seth was being exploited by the department store in Cleveland where he worked. Seth didn't take this seriously, and joked that he was hoping to become one of the bosses himself someday. Another tenant in the house was a refugee from Nazi Germany who lectured at the New School for Social Research, which was full of refugees from the Nazis. The professor and Paul Miller didn't believe in the Capitalism System, and were always talking together about setting things up in some pie-in-the-sky, idealistic way. Every time he went upstairs to the bathroom, he heard the two of them in Paul's room arguing about the Spanish Civil War. Everybody in the Village seemed nuts on that subject. You never heard about it in Cleveland.

Paul Miller never talked about women, it was always politics. Though Seth had noticed from the way Paul looked at his Aunt Polly that he went for her. Babs, with her feminine intuition, said that, if he did, he was out of luck, Polly was a gold-plated American virgin.

It was a pity, Seth thought, to be fifty and an old maid. His aunt had missed so much in life. He had only known her from a few brief meetings and letters and birthday gifts, but now she was coming alive to him as a remarkably interesting person.

The professor was German, the Alfanos Italian, the sax player black, and Manny Silva, whose room Eugene was using while he was off to his night job, was Portuguese. It was just like the League of Nations.

Gene said he wished he could spend more time with him and Babs and show them around, but a play of his was being put on and he had to go to rehearsals every night. It was opening at the end of the week, and he and Babs would be able to see it.

Seth wasn't particularly interested in going to rehearsals, but it would be a way of spending a little more time with Gene. They had never been together much. Gene was totally different from his other father at home, not an easygoing, hale-fellow-well-met like Toby. His real father had a way of taking things seriously that made Seth curious to know everything about him. Gene's life had followed none of the conventions—living in

Europe, not tying himself down to regular jobs, having a novel published. There were gaps Seth was anxious to fill in—the women in his father's life, for instance. Who were they? Gene was foxy about it, but now that Seth was grown up, he hoped they would be able to talk man to man.

The first chance he got, he asked Gene about the woman he had brought out to Cincinnati with him, when Seth graduated from high school. He had assumed Stella Banks was his father's lady friend then, and there didn't seem to be anyone else around now. Stella was still a dear friend, Gene told him, but she was working for the IRS in Philadelphia, and he didn't see much of her any more. When her club work had given out, she had taken a civil service exam and turned out to be a whiz at figures. When Gene said Stella would be at the opening of his play, Seth guessed they were still carrying on long distance.

At the time Gene and Stella came out for his graduation, it had seemed so sophisticated of his father to bring along his mistress, though now, thinking back, he couldn't get over how innocent he was then. He knew several men at the department store who kept mistresses, but the difference was, in Cleveland it had to be hush-hush. Horny as he was about Babs, he could imagine wanting some variety himself someday.

Before going uptown to the midnight stage show at the Roxy, he and Babs stopped off at the ramshackle little theater called the Cherry Lane in the crook of Barrow Street. Seth had taken a look at the script of "The Weak and the Strong." It was about the Lost Generation of the twenties, and he suspected it was based on Gene's life in Paris, years ago. He didn't see why the characters had to talk about their agonies so much, and it was hard to concentrate on it.

But sitting on the dilapidated seats in the empty theater with the bare bulbs of the work lights on the stage, and hearing the actors saying the lines, the play began to make more sense. It wasn't so morbid—parts of it were even funny. It was amazing how the director, a bald-headed man named Dubinsky, got the actors to sound so real by making them remember similar times in their own lives. Gene whispered to him it was called the Stanislavski Method.

Though Babs didn't really want to, he talked her into stopping by the rehearsal again with him the next night, before they went on to hear the sax player at the jazz club. He was curious to see how the director and the actors would do the rest of the play. This time he asked Eugene more questions about the Stanislavski Method. When Dubinsky saw how interested Seth was, the director asked him if he'd like to fill in during the remaining rehearsals, in a small part the director was going to play himself. It would be a big help to have someone else walk through the role, Dubinsky said, and leave him free to sit out front and just direct. It would only take an hour or two for the next few evenings, before the play opened.

Seth agreed to do the part, more as a favor than anything else, but it turned out to be something that changed his life. Not only being on the stage and saying your lines to the other actors, but listening to them answer as though they meant it, which made the situation seem real instead of make-believe. For minutes at a time, he even felt like the character in the play. Everybody, including Dubinsky himself, told him how good he was, and no one could believe he had never been on a stage before.

He knew Babs was bored, having to sit in the darkened theater all by herself, waiting for him to get through. But he cheered her up when they went home at night and he made love like a Trojan. She had to admit that being in the play had put extra lead in his pencil.

Seth was doing so well in the role that Dubinsky told him he would be happy to turn it over to him, if he would stay on in New York for the run of the play. Much as Seth was tempted, he didn't want to lose his job in Cleveland.

But even if he didn't play the role, the opening of "The Weak and the Strong," the Saturday night before their return to Cleveland, was the high point of the trip for him. As the audience poured into the theater, at least half of them seemed to know his father. Gene's boss, Hymie Liebman, and his elegant wife, Miriam, in evening dress were in sharp contrast to the rest of the crowd. "Isn't it marvelous, the whole Village has turned out!" said his aunt Polly, sitting next to him. But looking at the serious-looking audience, Seth was a little uneasy, so many of them long-haired types with papers and books under their arms, and short-haired women without makeup. Would they be intolerant of Gene's story of twenties decadence?

His father's girlfriend, Stella Banks, barely made it at the last minute from Philadelphia. In bright makeup and a flowered dress that didn't do much to camouflage her plumpness, she was just as he remembered her from his high school graduation. When the lights signaled everyone to take their seats, she popped into the empty place beside his father in the front row and gave him and Manny Silva a quick hug and kiss, before the curtain went up.

In spite of Seth's doubts, "The Weak and the Strong" was an immediate hit. Almost every scene met with applause. Seth wished he were up there. If it weren't for Babs, he was ready to give the boot to Cleveland and job, and take over his role again. And when the cast came out at the end for curtain calls, the high-spirited audience refused to let them go. The director brought Gene up on stage, then stepped back, leaving him alone in the spotlight. Seth swelled with pride as his father, bashful but happy, received the acclaim of the audience.

Seth told his aunt it looked like a terrific success. Yes, Polly said, if the critics had bothered to come—she indicated several empty seats on the aisle—but she was sure that word-of-mouth would pull them in.

Stella Banks, her arm through Manny Silva's, told Gene his play was such a relief after all that "depressing social realism" she was forced to sit through all the time. Hymie Liebman's wife, Miriam, kissed Gene and told him she had laughed and cried.

Dubinsky, the director, threw a party for the cast afterward at his loft on Eighth Street, with its nightclubs and bars and the Saturday night Village crowd hooting it up right below the windows. As soon as Seth and Babs pushed into the packed loft, Babs, in her best party dress and high heels, wanted to leave. This was not her idea of a good time—no music, no dancing, just people standing around, talking about things she cared nothing about and names she never heard of. She despised New York, she told Seth. She hadn't had any fun since they got here. Seth, on the other hand, was entranced by the Village gathering. All around him people were loudly debating the issues in his father's play, gossiping about Broadway, stage stars, things he knew virtually nothing about, but which he felt attracting him like a magnet. Babs was insisting that they go, when someone put a Dorsey Brothers record on the phonograph, and to Seth's relief a young actor from the play came over and asked her to dance. Babs's sulk vanished, as she was whirled away.

Seth was admiring his wifes's million dollar legs, as she expertly followed her partner's tricky routines, when he felt a hand on his shoulder.

"Just the fellow I've been looking for...."

It was Dubinsky, the director of his father's play. Dubinsky was filled with praise for Seth's acting in the small role when he'd filled in at rehearsals. Seth, flattered by the compliment, told him what a revelation the whole experience had been for him. He'd never acted before but he had loved it. Dubinsky suggested he look into the Cleveland Playhouse when he went back. He said it was one of the best community theaters in the country. "And while you're about it, you might enjoy reading Stanislavski on acting." Before Dubinsky moved on, he scrawled the name of someone he knew at the Cleveland Playhouse for Seth to look up.

Seth slipped the paper into his wallet and joined the group of friends and admirers around his father. He could imagine how it must feel to have this success after waiting so long. All the while Gene was accepting compliments, modestly explaining what he had attempted to do in the play, he kept his arm around Stella Banks—Seth was glad they were still together, even though her job kept them apart. Her dramatic eye makeup and extravagant gestures reminded him that she had been in show business herself. They were an ideal couple, Seth thought. He wished they'd get married. That would really make it all perfect.

He only half-listened to the talk around him, letting his eyes rove over the room. All these people celebrating his father's success—everyone, that is, except Manny Silva. Seth spotted him drinking in a corner by himself, not talking to anyone. He looked so unhappy. What was wrong with the guy?

He had never been so happy himself—in the middle of New York City, at a theatrical party, his father a celebrated playwright, and things opening up for him in a way he couldn't have imagined. He looked around for Babs, suddenly wanting her beside him, sharing this moment. But to his consternation, when he caught sight of her, she was dancing in the arms of another good-looking actor. It seemed to him that for the last hour she'd been dancing with one good-looking man after another. He felt a stab of jealousy. He knew she hadn't enjoyed going to the rehearsals, but what was this all about? She could at least spend a little time with him, even if she was bored to death.

He must have shown how upset he was, because Stella Banks said, "It's all right, sweetie. Those guys are nothing for you to worry about, believe me!"

A couple of men next to her laughed.

He was about to ask what the joke was, when they were interrupted by a drunk Manny Silva, coming up to Gene. "Sorry to interrupt your moment of glory, Mr. Bigshot," Silva muttered, "but I'm getting out of here."

Seth expected his father to laugh it off. Instead, to his surprise, his father looked like he'd been punched. As Silva turned toward the door, none too steadily, Gene started toward him. "Manny, you can't go! This is your party too...."

Seth couldn't understand what was going on.

"You don't have to work tonight," his father pleaded, following after Silva. "I thought you were taking the night off."

The whole room had stopped dead. All except Stella Banks who tried to cover the awkwardness by saying loudly that Manny always got drunk at parties and Eugene felt responsible, that was all. But no one was listening to her. Everyone was transfixed by the spectacle of Silva turning on his father with bloodshot eyes.

"You don't need me here. You've got them all at your goddam feet!" He waved an arm drunkenly.

Seth didn't hear what Gene said then, but his father talking to another man like that made him squirm. Babs shot him a quizzical look from across the room, but Seth couldn't meet her eye. He hadn't realized his father had been drinking so much.

Whatever Gene replied, it seemed to be the last straw. "Get your tentacles off me!" Silva shouted, shaking off Gene's hand. "I'm not your fucking wife!" And he slammed out the door, leaving his father standing alone and humiliated.

In the embarrassed silence that followed, Stella jumped to Eugene's side, slipping her arm through his. "Don't mind him, darling, he's just drunk," she said. "Come on now, it's time for the champagne."

Corks were popped and a pretense of normality was restored. His father appeared to pull himself together, even apologizing with a little laugh for interrupting everyone's fun. Dubinsky proposed a toast to Eugene Endicott, the new Eugene O'Neill of the American theater. But as Seth raised his glass to his father along with everyone else, it was hard to look at him.

Things weren't quite the way he thought they were. Stella tried to cover it up by suggesting—and later, Polly, too—that Gene had some kind of father-son relationship with Manny Silva, that his father had been impressed by the young fisherman's intelligence when they'd met in Provincetown, and had encouraged him to come to the city to finish his education. Naturally, since Silva had come to depend on Gene so much, it had upset him having to take a back seat when Seth, his real son, showed up.

Seth pretended to go along with them, but he knew the story was phony. He wondered what his mother would say if she knew. He wondered if she already knew.

"Sorry about the little scene," his father said to him, when the party was breaking up.

"The guy was drunk, that's all," Seth said, doing his best to sound natural.

"I hope you can forget it," his father said. "I wouldn't want it to spoil anything."

Seth muttered something and turned away.

"No," said his father, as if reflecting, "…maybe we better talk about it. How about us having breakfast in the morning, just the two of us?"

They fell silent, as they walked down the stairs to the street, Babs behind with Stella Banks, and Aunt Polly following. Seth was in a quandary. It was all more fucked up than he could ever have guessed, this mysterious father at the periphery of his life. He was glad they were going to have a talk tomorrow, and at the same time, he didn't know what he could say, his feelings were in such confusion.

Eighth Street was even livelier than it had been earlier in the evening, and it was a moment before they became aware that a fracas had broken out down the block on the other side of the street.

"Oh God, they're raiding The Main Street again!" Stella said, and hurried on ahead. As they followed her, his aunt told him that The Main Street bar was patronized by many of Stella's fans from her days as a cabaret singer. It was run by the mafia, like all those places, and they were always being raided by the vice squad.

A crowd was watching at the curb, as the police were hustling out the male patrons across the street.

Babs stopped, trying to see over the heads. "What are they going to do to those fairies?" she asked.

"Come on," Eugene said, pulling her by the arm, "there's nothing to see."

But Babs held back. An obstreperous customer was being dragged out of the bar, putting up a fight against four cops trying to control him.

The onlookers seemed transfixed at the sight of one of the men actually resisting, and actually spitting out obscenities under the flailing clubs.

"My God," Stella cried. "It's Manny!"

Eugene wheeled around. "Manny?" He shoved through the crowd of onlookers at the curb and jumped out between the parked cars, heading across the street at a run.

"Gene!" Polly screamed. "Don't!"

With a squeal of brakes, a delivery truck struck him, flinging him into the air and over on his back.

Stella shrieked.

Babs threw herself against Seth.

Across the street, the bar patrons, taking advantage of the distraction, slipped away into the anonymous crowd.

"I know I haven't been burning the midnight oil lately, Gene,"— Manny Silva was at Eugene's bedside—"but if I hit the books hard enough, I'll have my degree by next fall."

With Manny's head haloed against the sun pouring in through the hospital window, he looked the same to Eugene as the boy who had held up the fish for him to buy at the dock ten years before.

It was several days after the accident—Eugene wasn't sure how many—but he was able to receive a few visitors in the hospital. Manny had some bruises left over from his scuffle with the police, and told him he had paid a fine for disorderly conduct, but otherwise was okay. He couldn't stop telling Eugene how sorry he was for the accident. He knew it was his fault, the way he had been acting lately. He kept promising to make it all up to him as soon as Gene was on his feet again. Eugene smiled as best he could and said it might be a week or two before that happened.

Eugene didn't feel anything from the neck down and his body was covered with casts and bandages. Manny's voice seemed further away as he talked on about how they would get away from the city, and how he would get a job as a high school biology teacher, and Eugene would be able to do his writing, the way they had planned. Eugene's voice had given out, but he managed a smile. He was glad to see Manny so full of life and optimism, his calloused hand resting on the plaster cast around Gene's chest.

Manny asked him again if he could forgive him—as if there was anything to forgive.

When the nurse said it was time to go, Manny put on a blustery act, saying he expected to see Gene sitting up the next day or he'd pull him up himself. But as the friend who had filled the great gap in his life turned to leave, Eugene saw there were tears on his cheeks.

That night, Eugene Endicott died. Among his other injuries, his spine had been crushed—there had been little hope from the beginning. A funeral service was held at St. Luke's Church, although neither he nor his sister had been there since Sunday School as children.

Before Polly took Seth to the station to see him and his young wife off to Cleveland, he asked for something of his father's as a remembrance, and she gave him a watch fob Eugene had always treasured, that had been handed down from their Uncle Claude.

A week later, with Paul Miller's help, she was cleaning out her brother's room—his clothes and most of his things had already been disposed of. As she went over his manuscripts and put them into a carton, she and Paul were talking about Manuel Silva, who, the morning after the funeral, had packed his duffel bag to hop a freight train heading west, with no timetable and no destination. He had seemed so broken up. She was sorry he had gone off without giving her a chance to help him, as once he had helped her.

Paul, who was clearing off the mantelpiece and bookshelves, said she didn't have to worry. He had given Manny a list of contacts around the country.

"I hope not your Wobbly friends," she scolded him gently. "Manny's not interested in organizing farm workers."

Paul smiled. "I'm not trying to convert him. I thought he might need a free meal now and then."

As Polly went on sorting the manuscripts—so many more unfinished than finished—she thought about all the people that had been uprooted by the Depression, living in Hoovervilles, riding the rails around the country, looking for something, they didn't know what. Everything had fallen apart. People had to go on as best they could.

In her hands were the pages of a last novel her brother had begun. She dropped it into the carton with all the rest. Some day she would read it. She sighed. "Isn't it strange, Paul, how every member of my family is buried in some different place? Papa is over at St. Mary's in Queens, mother's in Paris, and now Gene's up at the cemetery in Westchester. It's as if we were all just waiting to get as far away from one another as possible." She bit her lip, trying to smile.

Paul had picked up the old-fashioned ormolu clock from the mantelpiece and was shaking it to see if it worked, before wrapping it up.

"Do you realize," Polly said, "if Gene had died a year ago before I met you, I'd be completely alone now? I wouldn't have a friend in the world." She looked at him mistily.

"I'm glad you finally recognized that." Paul was wrapping the clock in Eugene's last Sunday New York Times, that he never had a chance to read.

She got up and went to kiss him on the forehead. "I do, and I've never given you a chance."

When the parlor room was anonymous again, ready for the next tenant to come along, Paul carried the carton of Eugene's papers into her room and shoved it under the bed.

"You know, if you and I are going to start keeping company," she said, as she ran water into the percolator, "we've got to do something about our names. Polly and Paul, it's like the Bobbsey twins. People will howl."

"Keeping company?" He looked around at her.

She set the percolator down on the hot plate. "Well, won't they? Gene and I always went into hysterics reading The Bobbsey Twins." She turned to him brightly, and suddenly dissolved in tears. "Poor Gene…." Covering her face with her hands, she wept.

He went over and took her in his arms.

1941

32

When the Japanese attacked Pearl Harbor, the political controversies of the Depression evaporated, as patriotic fervor swept over Greenwich Village—few people had a sympathetic ear for the die-hard pacifists. Artists, who had never known anything but paintbrush and canvas, found themselves struggling to master the intricacies of assembling the M-1 rifle, cussed out by master sergeants from Iowa and Texas.

Frankie Alfano was among the first to enlist—in the Marine Corps—and his mother, Rosalie, after throwing a fit, gave him a big send-off party, and pasted a blue star proudly in her window to show she had a son in the armed services. His brother, Steve, who was studying business administration on a scholarship at NYU on Washington Square, wasn't drafted until he graduated two years later.

As the hordes of GIs poured into New York City on pass from nearby military bases, the Village hadn't seemed so full of life since the twenties. A few of the GIs seen regularly every weekend belonged to boys lucky enough to wangle cushy assignments at posts like the Brooklyn Navy Yard, the recruiting station in Times Square, or in the army headquarters near the Battery.

Greenwich Village was the one part of town where prostitutes lost out from the competition of eager Village girls, unencumbered by conventional morality. They couldn't do enough for the corn-fed boys from the hometowns they themselves had once deserted. If lonely GIs didn't score, they could always find consolation from sympathetic 4-Fs, glad to buy them drinks and listen to their troubles and even offer them a bed for the night.

Polly helped to set up a U.S.O. at Sixth Avenue and Eighth Street, the busiest corner in the Village. She spent most of her time there, seldom taking a day off, and though she was the age of their mothers, the boys quickly learned that nothing fazed her and they could talk to her about anything. With her easy sophistication, her savvy and her frankness, she wasn't like any woman her age they knew back home. Sometimes she took groups of them on tours of the Village, showing them historic sites and landmarks, never failing to point out coffeehouses and night-spots they might want to visit on their own.

Paradoxically, in spite of the congestion of the streets and the bursting bars and restaurants at night, apartments and rooms went begging as the local boys were drafted. Most of Polly's roomers on Perry Street were gone—the war effort sucked them up, as the unemployment of the Depression became a thing of the past. Paul Miller was directing an arts and crafts program at a military hospital in Maryland, and when he and Polly occasionally corresponded, it was as old friends, nothing more.

The German refugee from the top floor was giving anti-Nazi indoctrination lectures to German prisoners in a P.O.W. camp in Texas. Norma Lucas had quit her modern dancing, and was hoofing it in the chorus of U.S.O. shows from the Aleutians to the Philippines.

Lenny deKnight, the black sax player, Norma's old boyfriend, held out at first—he wasn't joining in any war as long as there were Jim Crow laws, especially not in a segregated army, and he wasn't going to kill any Japanese, another colored race. He was also bitter about the harassment he was getting from white southern GIs on pass in New York, who expected him to step off the sidewalk for them. When he talked like that at the rooming house, Rosalie, the mother of a marine already fighting in the Pacific, had to be restrained from smashing his head in with a frying pan.

But with the loss of Guadalcanal, even Lenny enlisted, and after basic training in a segregated unit, a postcard from him arrived from "somewhere in the Pacific." It went up on Rosalie's bulletin board, where she kept the letters from all her boys and her map of the war zones.

The war was Rosalie's great period. Instead of her litany of complaints while she swept the sidewalk, she endlessly recited to the neighborhood the military exploits of her boys. Then she surprised everyone by getting herself a pair of overalls, tucking her hair into a snood, and going off to a job in a war plant in Long Island City. She wouldn't tell anyone what she did—it was "a military secret."

Dominic also got a war job, at the Brooklyn Navy Yard, but what he took most seriously was his patrolling a four-block area around Perry Street at night as an air-raid warden. He was scrupulous about seeing that people drew their blackout curtains, as if a single chink of light would bring the Messerschmitts over.

But if the tenants were gone, Polly opened the house to GIs from the U.S.O. who needed a free place to sack out for the night, and the Alfanos made sure the boys got plenty to eat. Though Rosalie loved the houseful of boisterous young men who slapped her behind and called her Mama Mia, she wasn't so happy when she found out that some of them were sneaking in girls at night. Once, she even followed a sailor and his date upstairs and pounded on the door, screaming that this was not a whorehouse and they were abusing the privilege. But Polly pulled her away and told her to mind her own business, there was a war on, wasn't there? Rosalie glared at her, but she went back downstairs, and thereafter pretended not to know. On the stoop, she continued to proclaim to the neighbors or anyone else who passed that she couldn't stand slackers, who weren't giving everything they had to the war effort. She had two sons in the war, one fighting to take the Solomon Islands from the Japs—that was Frankie—and his brother, Steve, a second lieutenant, with Patton as an interrogator in the invasion of Sicily.

Seth wrote Polly that he was on the staff of the army paper, Stars and Stripes, in London, though because of his acting experience at the Cleveland Playhouse, he had hoped to be assigned to Special Services and do camp shows. He still wanted to be a professional actor. His wife, Babs, had always opposed the idea, but the marriage was on the rocks anyway— she had met somebody else and sent him a "Dear John" letter. Seth wasn't all that broken up about it—the marriage had been over for a long time. In London, he had met an English girl, and she had taken him to see John Gielgud play "Hamlet" on the West End stage. It had been a revelation. He was thinking of not going back to Cleveland when he got out, but trying his luck on Broadway.

Amidst all the reports of men killed and missing in action—Norma Lucas wrote from Guam the news that her old boyfriend, Lenny deKnight, the sax player, had gone down when his liberty ship had been torpedoed— the Alfanos got a long distance telephone call. Their son, Frankie, had been wounded, and was in the Bethesda Naval Hospital outside Washington D.C. Nothing could stop Rosalie and Dominic from fighting their way through the swarms of people in Penn Station to board a train for Washington, standing up all the way.

With a Silver Star pinned to the bandages that covered half his torso, they found Frankie basking in the fuss the nurses were making over him, giving a detailed description of how he had wiped out a machine gun nest single-handed, in the retaking of a South Pacific island. It was hard for him to keep quiet and listen to the letter Dominic read aloud from his brother Steve, telling about visiting their nonna's newly-liberated village outside Naples, where everyone seemed to be named Alfano.

In June of '44, Seth covered the Normandy landings for Stars and Stripes, and in August, sent a picture postcard of the Eiffel Tower to Polly from newly-liberated Paris. From Italy, 1st Lt. Steve Alfano went on to Germany, and in the spring of '45 was among the troops who shook hands with the Russians at the meeting of the two armies at the Elbe.

One night at the Village U.S.O., Polly was typing up the week's schedule of volunteer hostesses, when a serviceman stopped by her desk and asked her for a dance. Without looking up from her work, she told him she was busy, why not ask one of the girls? He didn't want to do that, he said, he had a yen for her. She looked up at the handsome, dark-haired man in Coast Guard uniform beaming at her, and gave a cry. It was Manny Silva. She jumped up and they threw their arms around each other.

He had just been home on leave in Provincetown, where he had married his long-suffering fiancée, he told her, and was working on his remaining college credits by correspondence from his Coast Guard base. In a corner of the service club they sat and talked for hours, filling in the years, remembering Eugene, until Manny had to catch his train at midnight.

1945

33

On V-J day, to celebrate the end of the war, it was open house on Perry Street. Polly had invited a lot of the GIs from the U.S.O., and they were spilling out into the street. An endless parade trooped down the stairs to the kitchen where the Alfanos were serving up spaghetti. There were cases of beer and gallons of wine, and the music of Glenn Miller blasted out the windows from the radio, interspersed with news bulletins.

Frankie Alfano, the war hero, was being made a great fuss over by his mother, Rosalie, and everyone else. He was strutting around with the Silver Star prominently displayed on his uniform, as if he had won the war single-handed. The only mistake America was making, he was telling everyone in a loud voice, was not to finish the job and clean up the Russkies while they were at it. Frankie's brother, Steve, was there too, but as far as his mother was concerned, it was only Frankie who existed.

"You musn't mind, Steve dear," Polly said, tapping his chestful of campaign ribbons, that showed he had been in major battles from North Africa to Germany. "Your brother's not the only hero here."

Steve chuckled. "Let him have his moment. I may be the quiet type, but I'll get mine in the end." He had plans, he told her, to go in with a buddy to open a store in New Jersey selling television sets. Television was the coming thing, and his buddy, who knew all about radar from the war, was convinced that if they got in at the start, they could make some real money.

Seth, who was staying at Polly's on temporary leave while waiting for his discharge, was dancing with a girl in the crowded hallway. He would have preferred to be with his English girlfriend in London, but that affair had ended when her husband arrived back from a P.O.W. camp in Singapore.

He was trying to decide whether or not to put the make on this girl, when someone cut in on him. Relieved, he pushed his way to the punch bowl set up in Polly's room, where his cousin Frankie, holding two fingers above his mouth like a mustache, was giving an imitation of der Fuhrer to loud laughter. Seth thought that if he were still writing for Stars and Stripes, Frankie, playing his Silver Star for all it was worth, would make a good subject for a story. Even the girl hanging on his arm was perfect. Not bad looking, with lively, dark eyes, but obviously still in her teens and trying to look older—and totally taken in by the loud-mouth show-off. They might both be morons, but they certainly made a good-looking couple.

His aunt Polly handed him a glass of punch. "For a man about to be discharged," she told him, "you don't look so happy. You're supposed to be having a ball."

"You mean like those two?" Seth nodded toward Frankie who was now jitterbugging with the teenager, with an admiring circle around them, clapping in time. He gave a wry smile and told Polly she didn't look so happy herself.

Rosalie was shrieking with laughter, as she carried on with a group of soldiers on the stoop outside.

It wasn't that she was unhappy, his aunt said, but now that the war was finally over, she was letting herself feel how tired she was for the first time in years. She was going up to the Cape to spend some time with Manny Silva and his wife. It would be a real rest. Did he remember Manny?

"How could I ever forget."

They were both silent a moment. People were filling their glasses at the punch bowl.

"What about Paul Miller?" Seth asked her. "Is he still in the picture?"

She laughed. "Oh, my heavens, no. That ended before Pearl Harbor." But she had just heard from him, she said. He had married again and was becoming a scenic artist in a movie studio on the Coast. "Can you imagine a lefty like him starting a commercial career? I think the war must have shaken up a lot of his old ideas."

"Well, I'm just sorry it wasn't you he ended up with," said Seth.

"You're sweet." She touched his cheek. "But love and marriage is not what I need any more. I had enough of all that business. It's your turn now."

Seth went out on the stoop with his punch to join the crowd for a breath of air. It was late afternoon and celebration parties were going on up and down the block. The street was full of people drifting from one house to another.

Down on the sidewalk, the indefatigable Frankie still cavorted for his admiring audience. A GrayLine Sightseeing Bus, drove slowly past, "Want some of this, ya fuckin rubberneckers?" he yelled, grabbing his crotch and humping away at them, to the delight of his buddies.

"How crass…."

Standing next to Seth on the stoop was the girl with the lively, dark eyes who had been jitterbugging with Frankie. Although she didn't look much more than fifteen, close up she was really quite beautiful—a more intelligent girl than he would have guessed his simple-minded cousin could attract.

"It's Frankie's way of having a good time," Seth said. "That's what we're all trying to do today, isn't it?"

"I suppose so," she said. "He really is pretty sweet."

Seth asked if she had known Frankie long, and she told him they had just met outside the U.S.O. on Sixth Avenue. She had pretended to be one of the volunteers there. She laughed. "I guess I didn't want to admit I came down from the Bronx with a girl friend to pick up a soldier."

Seth looked at her to see if she was trying to shock him, but she showed no self-consciousness as she watched Frankie hug his mother, who had come out to let everyone know, in case they missed the fact, that he was her son. The girl was just a kid, but her boldness attracted him.

"There's nothing wrong with liking soldiers," Seth told her.

"But it's already passé, isn't it?" The girl looked at him with her shining, dark eyes.

She had just told him her name was Susan, when Frankie came up the steps and grabbed her arm. "Hey, gorgeous, you playing hard to get? Gimme a break. I'm just a love-starved marine back from the war." He pulled her chin toward him and gave her a loud, wet kiss on the mouth.

Susan, Seth said to himself, his eyes following her as Frankie led her down to his group on the sidewalk. If he had met her when he was eighteen, even twenty, before Babs, how he would have gone for someone with her intelligence, her New York savvy. A pity Frankie had to be her GI experience. He was too much of a jerk for her. Seth drank off his punch and went in for a refill.

From Susan Schlesinger's reading of D. H. Lawrence, Frankie seemed to her the true natural man, the epitome of the "erotic force" Lawence was always talking about. Like the gamekeeper in the smuggled copy of Lady Chatterley's Lover passed around at The High School of Music and Art. A real woman didn't want an intellectual. Susan was also fascinated by the sexual theories of Wilhelm Reich. Though only sixteen and still a virgin, she believed in the ultimate importance of the cosmic orgasm that Reich preached, and with practice she was determined to achieve it, as well as everything else she put her mind to. At Music and Art she had been a brilliant student, but according to Lawrence and Reich, that was the wrong direction. She had to get outside her mind and more into her body.

She knew she was too much for the grandmother she lived with in the Bronx. She longed to get an apartment in Greenwich Village, share it with a girlfriend, maybe. Sixteen was perfectly old enough to live on her own, but her grandmother was old-fashioned and would never let her. She had just graduated from high school and was going to Hunter College in the fall. Unless a miracle occurred, she would have to continue commuting from the Bronx on the subway for another four years.

As night came on, Frankie told her it was time they got the hell out of there, and, with his arm tight around her waist, they left the house. The streets were a tumult, crowds shouting, car horns blaring, fireworks going off everywhere. Every bar and club was packed. She were plenty of underage girls like her around, but nobody cared—they weren't asking for proof of age tonight. Susan knew the Village. She had been coming down here with friends ever since going to Music and Art, using fake I.D.s to get into the jazz clubs, but Frankie had no interest in jazz.

With both his arms around her on one crowded dance floor after another, he nuzzled her with every part of his body, his hands cupping her behind—it was like being with a completely healthy animal. He was such a perfect proletarian. That, of course, was what made him just right, she told herself. There had never been any barriers to his fulfilling his animal nature from the start, while she was just beginning to explore her own. According to Frankie, he had lost his virginity when he was eleven.

Even if she had never gone all the way, the Village had always meant sex to her. But she had never seen it such a sexual marketplace as tonight. Couples in doorways were all but having intercourse, and behind window shades, she imagined people copulating in every position she had seen in a marriage manual passed around at school. It wasn't Rome burning, exactly, but it was just as historic an occasion, and people were commemorating it in the best way possible. She was determined to be a part of it. She would never tell her grandmother, of course, but someday she might tell a grandchild about how she had spent the night the Second World War ended—and about the man like the gamekeeper in Lady Chatterley's Lover she had chosen to spend it with.

With more drinks in him, her gamekeeper was getting sloppier in his attentions. If only he wouldn't open his mouth. He sounded so inane with his "Oh, babe, you got a gorgeous pair of knockers," or making loud sucking noises at her all the time. They ended up back at the Perry Street house where the party was still going on. But pushing aside his friends, he maneuvered her to the stairs. She caught a glimpse of his cousin, Seth, from Cleveland talking with a blonde girl in the hall. No more talking for her now, Susan thought, her heart pounding, as her gamekeeper pulled her up the stairs.

But in the darkened bedroom, lovemaking with this instinctual primitive failed to come up to the heights of ecstasy or the cosmic fulfillment Susan had read about. His body crushing her as he pushed into her, she tried to imagine she was Lady Chatterley. He was sweating like a pig, and she couldn't help thinking that thank God he had on a prophylactic.

After he finished and dropped off to sleep for a few minutes, he was at it again. It wasn't over quite so fast this time, but she still didn't feel anything. If only she could talk to him, tell him to go a little slower maybe. But he was already pushing to his ejaculation, and, afterwards, he kept her in a stranglehold and told her how crazy he was about her. He had big plans, he said. He had his pick of jobs—with his Silver Star everybody wanted him, all the big shots in the Village. He'd make lots of money and give his girl anything in the world.

"Now I'm really going to show you what I can do," he said, but before he could start in again, she slipped away and pulled on her bra.

"Hey, whatcha going for? It was terrif, wasn't it?"

She said sure it was, but her grandmother would kill her if she wasn't home by twelve, and explained about the long subway ride up to the Bronx.

Before she walked out the door, she looked back and gave a little wave. His brow furrowed, he was trying to comprehend how any female could walk out on him. But he really was the most visually perfect specimen of a man she had ever seen. If only, she thought, he had a brain to match.

"Frankie's got so many girls throwing themselves at him, he doesn't even notice I'm not there any more," Susan Schlesinger was saying to Seth at a table inside the Riviera Café. On such a beautiful October day it was a shame, Seth thought, that there weren't outdoor cafes to sit at, like in Europe.

He had hardly recognized Susan when she spoke to him on Sheridan Square, without lipstick, only heavily made-up eyes. It was the style he had seen in the cafés of the Left Bank.

Seth was out of the Army. He had already been to see his parents in Cincinnati, and come back in time to register for acting classes with Stella Adler, who had studied in Moscow with the great Stanislavski himself.

Susan smiled from across the table. "Frankie was quite an education for me. He got me over my fixation on D.H. Lawrence."

With her straight, long hair cut in new bangs, and the makeup emphasizing the pale skin and dark eyes, he liked her looks even better. He had to remind himself that although she looked so much older than she was, even worldly, he mustn't think of her as a woman—she wasn't. She was only sixteen.

She told him she had just started Hunter College, and he told her his hopes for Broadway, and about his marriage that had broken up during the war.

"You're a real *goy*," she said, "and you look the part perfectly."

He laughed. "How?" She might be a kid, but she was the first woman since his girlfriend in England, who was fun to be with, who was not just a quick lay.

"Well," she said, studying him as if she were analyzing a painting for an art criticism class, "your short nose, your proper tweed jacket—my God, how smooth, how professorial, and you can't be more than...." She waited.

"Twenty-seven," he fibbed, then smiled. "No, thirty."

"It's all right," she said. "I lie about my age too—the other way. And your manner, the way you act, so perfectly polite, so agreeable—not letting it all out, like people I know."

"I'm bland, you mean?"

"Not exactly," she said, enjoying their game as much as he was, "but I suppose over the long haul it might get that way."

"I'm not as colorless as you may think," he said, his elbows on the table, leaning closer. "I had an Irish grandfather, and I'm not always so agreeable—I've got some perverted impulses."

"Oh, goody!" Her eyes shone. "Tell me about them."

She was perfect New York, he thought, cool, nervy, smart. She was lovely. "For one, I wish to hell you weren't only sixteen, so I could make love to you."

She blushed like the kid she really was. "Don't worry, I've been taking care of myself for a long time." She told him about being raised by a grandmother, who hardly spoke English and who didn't have a clue about what she did out of the house.

He still wasn't convinced. "But I'm thirty—and divorced, to boot."

"You told me you were glad that your marriage was over—you were too young to know what you were doing."

"I was older than you are."

"You think I'd tell my grandmother and get the police on you?"

"But it's insane," he said, taking her hand.

"This isn't a movie," she said. "We don't have to conform to the Hays Office."

He argued what did she want him for, he wasn't any war hero. He hadn't seen action at all, he had spent the war at a desk, mostly. He didn't even have a Good Conduct medal.

She said, as they got up to go, not to be jealous. But she asked him please not to take her to his aunt's house, if that's what he had in mind. She'd rather not run into Frankie.

They didn't go back to Perry Street, but they made love that afternoon. This time, it still wasn't a cosmic orgasm for her, but what a relief to be with someone sensitive and intelligent, and afterward they went out for hamburgers and walked through the Village streets half the night, talking about orgone boxes and Jean-Paul Sartre and Seth's hopes of getting into a Broadway show—discovering all the things they had in common.

And he met her after her classes at Hunter the next day and rode up with her to the Bronx, where she introduced him to her grandmother who was horrified, not that she might get married at sixteen—the old lady had been fourteen when she got married in Russia—but that he wasn't Jewish, that's what put her off. But Susan explained that he wasn't the usual *goy*— he had a mind—and, looking at him with a mischievous gleam in her eye, she invented a Jewish grandmother for him and added that he was circumcised.

The little old woman looked at her outraged. "How the hell you know that?"

"I asked him," Susan said, avoiding Seth's eye.

She didn't tell her grandmother that he was going to be an actor and she would have to get a job to help him out, and if it was taking a chance, she was willing to gamble, and besides, she couldn't stand living up on the Grand Concourse any longer. Seth already had a little apartment lined up in the Village, not on Perry Street, thank God, and she didn't want to go to Hunter College any more, anyway.

Grandma eventually came around, but for her sake they had the ceremony at the temple social room.

His Aunt Polly was there, and stood with a lump in her throat as the wedding canopy was raised over the bridal couple, Seth in a top hat—the groom's head had to be covered—and Susan with a crown of pearls over her wedding veil, before the rabbi. Then, the ceremonial breaking of the wineglass, and the merry dancing afterward to a three-piece band, folk dances interspersed with waltzes.

Polly hadn't felt the pain of Hymie Liebman for years—the wedding that never was—until Seth, after the traditional waltz with his bride, came over and led her to the floor.

"There are tears in your eyes, dear Polly," Seth said, waltzing with her to the applause of the wedding guests, sitting around the decorated hall.

"Why shouldn't there be? I'm at my nephew's wedding. I'm so happy for you."

"I think you're hiding something."

"How the hell do you know?" she said, with a little tearful smile.

"Gene told me all about you and Hymie."

"I'm such a fool." She laid her head against his chest and cried softly, as they danced on, the grandmother happily clapping in time at the bridal table, a glass of schnapps beside her.

34

On a platform erected in front of the Church of St. Anthony, the South Village chapter of the American Legion was honoring Italian-American war heroes of the community. But the war had been over for more than two years, and the crowd strolling by wasn't much interested any more in patriotism or speeches. They paid little attention to the veterans, with decorations on their rumpled uniforms and non-regulation ducktail haircuts, and here and there a pair of plaid socks showing above civilian shoes. It was the street fair they had come for, and they paid more attention to the booths hawking sausage-and-pepper hero sandwiches and the greasy crullers called zeppole.

It was hot up on the platform, and Frankie Alfano loosened the collar and tie of his Marine suntans, once tailored for him in San Diego by a Mexican girl he was banging at the time—the uniform was too small for him already. He had drunk too many beers, the speeches were too long, and he had had his moment at the mike.

He felt like taking off. It wasn't as much fun playing the hero as it used to be. Two years ago in the postwar euphoria he was welcome everywhere—everybody bought him drinks, made him feel good. He was still ready for action, but there was no more action, no more excitement. He couldn't wait until the blowhards at the microphone finished their bullshitting and they'd all go back to the bar, even if he had to put up with their war stories he'd heard a million times.

His eyes drifted over the passing crowd, picking out the girls with bare shoulders, and even better, bare midriffs. The dark-haired chick he was following with his eyes turned her face and it was that Susan, from V-J Day. She was married to his cousin Seth now, and they were walking along licking paper cups of Italian ices.

Frankie swung himself off under the railing at the side of the platform, calling out to them as he pushed through the crowd. They were glad to see him, and Susan smiled that smile that had first hit him right in the nuts outside the U.S.O., as he explained why he was in his old uniform.

He had only seen them a couple of times since they had gotten married. He knew they lived over here in the south Village somewhere. He wondered if maybe they hadn't been around to Perry Street much because she was embarrassed to run into him again. He didn't feel that way—that was all past. They were family now. He wanted to be friends.

When Seth heard that he had left the platform just to catch up with them, he suggested that they all go back for the rest of the ceremony. But Frankie said it was just about over, and, anyway, those jerks would never miss him. He pushed between the two of them and took their arms, and, as they walked on past the various booths, asked where they had been hiding themselves so long. Seth said he and Susan were pretty busy these days. He was going to acting classes and had an evening job, and Susan worked for a fashion magazine all day and took classes at the New School nights.

They couldn't kid him—he knew what kept them so busy. He envied anyone having a girl as pretty as Susan, though he doubted that Seth was able to keep her all that happy in the sack, not after she'd had a real man like him. But Susan had class. Next to her, the bimbos he was screwing now were pigs.

But he didn't want to think of her that way. She was his cousin's wife—that was good enough for him.

He insisted they come and let him buy them an Italian dinner. It would be a delayed wedding present. But Seth said he had to work that evening. Then they'd have to let him buy them a drink, he said—they were all family now, wasn't that right? Susan smiled back her beautiful smile at him and said, of course, they'd have a drink with him, but it would have to be a short one.

Frankie took them into a local bar where they all knew him. "Did Seth tell you what kind of a crazy, mixed-up family you got yourself into?" he asked Susan, as they sat down. "It's not just wops like me, but half the micks in the Sixth Precinct too, you know that?"

He looked around the empty bar. "Why's it so dead in here?" He dropped a couple of nickels into the jukebox to liven up the place. The Andrews Sisters came on, singing "Boogie Woogie Bugle Boy from Company B." His fingers snapping to the beat, he asked them, "What'll you have?" It was natural to be a little stiff with each other, but they would all loosen up with a few drinks in them. "Whiskey sour, sidecar, gin fizz, you name it, it's on me."

Seth said beer for him and Susan asked for a Pepsi, but Frankie said this was a celebration, wasn't it? And he called over to the bartender, "Vinny, get off your ass and send over three Tom Collins!"

He grinned at both of them. "It's really swell running into you like this." He told them it sometimes it seemed like he hardly had a family any more since coming home from the war, with his brother Steve and his wife out in Jersey, and even his mother talking up Steve all the time nowadays and making him feel like a bum.

Waiting for the drinks, they talked about the new art gallery their Aunt Polly was opening on Waverly Place. She was calling it The Peacock again, like the gallery she used to have. Frankie didn't know anything about art, but his mother thought she was going to lose her shirt, and said the one business you couldn't lose on in the Village was a bar—but his mother was always talking about the good old days at the Casa di Mario. Did they know about the time his family owned a speakeasy and his grandpa got shot? He could tell them a lot of stories about that. He wiped the sweat from under his loosened collar. There were wet patches under his arms on his tight shirt.

Susan said it must have been hot sitting up on that platform. She was damn right, he said. It was no fun being looked over like he was a horse.

But wasn't it nice being honored that way? she said. His parents must have gotten a kick out of it.

He told her they couldn't make it. They were out in Verona at his brother's. They were going ape now that Steve's wife was expecting their first grandchild. He didn't blame them—everybody was fed up with war stories anyway. Sure, the war was over, but he thought it was chickenshit for the country to forget the guys who won it for them. "We were gung ho to go on and clean up the Russkies back then, but they didn't let us. It still pisses me off. They're all pinkos down there in Washington, you hear about it?"

But what were they talking about that for? He raised his glass and toasted the newlyweds, who smiled and leaned closer to each other.

It made him feel more left out than ever. "You know, my brother's doing great out in Jersey," he said. "Want to hear how he did it?" He told them that Steve and a couple of drinking buddies from the army got together to start up this business making parts for television sets. "You get in with the right contacts, you got it made. You don't have a chance if you're just a dumb ex-marine like me."

Susan said he wasn't a dumb marine, he had a Silver Star. And Seth said he heard that he was selling used cars at the big lot on Houston Street.

"That crappy place?" Frankie said. "I quit that lousy job long ago." All the big job offers, and just his luck to choose that one. He had put four months into it, trying to talk suckers into shelling out, but the boss turned out to be a shit. He had it in for guys who had been in the war because he had stayed out—flat feet, draft dodger—and kept riding him. "I told him to blow it out his ass!" Another job selling insurance hadn't worked out either. It wasn't his fault his sales quota was piss-poor. They were all a bunch of fat ass bums trying to cash in on his war-hero reputation, those mother fuckers, but he wasn't playing along any more. His brother wanted him to go into his television business, and he had just about made up his mind to give it a try.

Seth started to get up and said they really ought to be going.

What was he talking about? Frankie said, pushing him back and ordering another round of drinks. Had they heard that his brother Steve's wife was a college graduate? She even had her own white Buick convertible. They were living in a garden apartment now, but they had made a down payment on a split-level in Montclair. The television parts field was booming. He'd start out in the service department of his brother's business, but that was only to pick up the basics, and then the sky was the limit.

"Let's drink to that," Seth said, and Susan picked up her glass.

"Nah, let's drink to the three of us," Frankie said, feeling warm in their company. "I'm really glad we bumped into each other. We're going to see a lot of each other from now on."

Leaning against Seth's shoulder, Susan asked Frankie if any girl had caught him yet.

"You know me, dames keep trying, but Frankie-boy knows how to fight them off."

They all laughed, but he was thinking if he had the luck to run into someone like Susan now, he might be ready to settle down. He called out to Vinnie for another round of drinks, but Seth was already on his feet, saying he was already late for his job, they'd certainly have to do this again sometime. Seth even tried to pay, but Frankie wouldn't hear of it, slapping his money on the bar and snapping his fingers at Vinnie to hurry up with the change, so he could catch up with them going out the door.

"Wait up!" he called after them. "I'll walk you."

He took Susan's arm and steered them through the crowd, where a bunch of screaming kids were running around with colored pinwheels. As they came to the end of the street fair, he ignored their protests and bought them a bag of Coney Island taffy.

A few blocks away outside the building where they lived, Frankie shook Seth's hand and, holding on to it, said now that they had gotten together, he wanted to take them out to a nightclub on Third Street, where one of his buddies worked the door, and he could get them in without a cover charge. They'd get a kick out of it, real floor show, cha-cha-cha dancers, hot stuff, people came from all over to see it, he'd make sure they got a good table, everything the best.

He wanted to set a date right then, but Seth said maybe they'd better let him know because they were so tied up just now. Frankie said he'd call them, what was their number? They all searched for a pencil but nobody had one. Never mind, Frankie said, he'd get it from information, and call them first thing next week to make a date.

"Next week," he repeated, pumping Seth's hand again. "It really meant a lot to run into you." Then he put out his hand to Susan, who was looking at the ground as if she still felt awkward with him. But she looked up, smiling, and instead of taking his hand, leaned forward and kissed him on the cheek.

Frankie stood there awhile after they had gone in, sweaty in his old uniform that was too small for him, a sour taste in his mouth from all the drinks. But it was too early to go back to Perry Street. Nobody was home anyway. He decided to take the D train to Coney Island. He'd have a snooze on the beach, and then hang around the boardwalk and try to pick up a broad.

1951

35

Polly studied the wall of abstract paintings in their simple strip frames. She and her assistant had hung the show that afternoon for tonight's opening, and with the people about to arrive, she kicked herself for letting him talk her into putting the big, vacuous Rothko in the middle. The Jackson Pollock belonged there. It was a far better example of abstract expressionism.

She looked out the window to see if her assistant was coming back with the wine and paper cups. A student at Parsons School of Design, Frederick tried to tyrannize her with his automatic putdown of anything Art News wasn't raving about. Before he could catch her at it, she snatched the Rothko down and replaced it with the handsome Jackson Pollock that he had hung in a corner. Immediately the wall was right. It brought into focus the whole emerging abstract expressionist movement.

But then she started to worry about the paintings on the other side of the room—the realist painters from the thirties, in their conventional frames. Would they be overshadowed, look out-of-style? She didn't want that. She liked the realists as well. That was the whole point of the show and why she was calling it Dialogue. Later in the evening, after people had had a chance to look at the pictures, she was going to hold an informal discussion between the two factions, realists and abstractionists, and there were stacks of folding chairs waiting to be set up, so that everybody could sit down and have it out.

Frederick, her assistant, came back with gallon jugs of wine and the cups, huffing and puffing as if she were a slave driver making him carry blocks of stone up the pyramids. She sent him back to her cubbyhole office to retype the price list, instructing him to add a hundred dollars to everything and two hundred to the Pollock, and began to arrange the wine and cups herself.

She wondered if she should have bought some pretzels as well, but she had never tried to compete with the big galleries uptown, where champagne and canapés were served by waiters at the openings. Not only couldn't she afford such things—the new Peacock Gallery was turning out to be no more profitable than her old gallery—but if there was anything she had learned from her experience in the art world, it was that what brought people in was controversy, especially if it got written up in the papers. And she had spread the word that reporters as well as the critics were coming— and they would be, if her old contacts meant anything.

Frederick came to tell her that her nephew was on the phone. She finished uncorking the jugs of wine and told him to stack the pile of mimeographed announcements by the door next to the guest book, noticing with satisfaction his raised eyebrow as he spotted the replacement of the Rothko with the Pollock. She had her own way of paying him back for lording it over her in his fussy, narrow-legged Bloomingdale's suit.

Seth told her over the phone that an audition had come up and he couldn't make the opening. An after work audition—it had to be for another of those paltry little productions he was always trying out for, probably in some church social hall. If he got the part, she'd have to go—he always expected her to. God knew, his wife, Susan, wasn't so devoted.

She got up to look in the mirror, tucking in a few wisps of her gray hair that had come undone from the topknot she wore it in. At sixty-three, for the first time in her life she liked her looks in her dirndl dress and sandals, and not bothering with makeup any more or dying her hair. She hooked on her dangling earrings that her old friend, the mobile artist, Alexander Calder, had given her. They were a good luck charm. She wore them to every one of her openings, and never failed to sell at least one painting.

If only Seth could have a little luck in the theater. Ever since her nephew moved to New York after the war, it had been nothing but acting classes, semi-amateur productions, and dreary temporary jobs, with Susan having to work full-time to support them both. No wonder the girl always had that edge of resentment in her voice, as if she thought she wasn't getting her chance to fulfill herself. But then, what did she want to get married so young for?

Polly couldn't understand why the two of them stayed on in that horrid, cold-water flat in the south Village. But Susan had put her foot down against moving into the Perry Street house, when, a few years before, it had been remodeled into studio apartments—she said she didn't want to live with Seth in one room without a door to close between them. Maybe they weren't getting along so well, but the studios were perfect for a young couple. So there wasn't much space, but each one had a bathroom and kitchenette. Polly had never been so comfortable as she was in her snug studio, transformed out of her father's old study.

It had been Hymie's idea. He had persuaded her after the war to modernize the interior of the house. Young professionals would jump at the chance to move down to the Village to live in historic houses like hers, he said, as long as they had all the conveniences. What's more, the remodeling had freed the house from rent control, and it was profitable again.

She had made it perfectly clear to Seth that if he did the janitor work, which would take up no time at all with the new oil burner for heating, he and Susan could have one of the basement apartments rent-free. It would have been particularly convenient, because at the time of the renovation, the Alfanos, Dominic and Rosalie, had moved to New Jersey. Their son Steve's television parts company was doing so well, he had set them up in a little pizza parlor, where they could be near their grandchildren. Things were good for all the Alfanos, except for poor Frankie. He had trained as a television repairman, but he had no aptitude for it, and though Steve had tried to fit him in elsewhere in the company, he had quit in a huff and gone to Phoenix and married some girl out there. They didn't hear from him much, but Dominic had told her that things weren't going well for his younger son.

People were beginning to arrive for the opening, and Polly could already tell from the buzz in the gallery that it had been an inspiration to dramatize the feud between the two opposing camps in the art world, and that her Dialogue show was going to make a splash.

It was a bigger crowd than she usually got at her openings. She was talking to the critic from Art News, who was going to act as moderator at the symposium later on, when she noticed the handsome woman whose opulent mink coat stood out among the Village crowd. As far as Polly could tell without her glasses, she had never seen the woman in the gallery before. Probably a culture-vulture from the Upper East Side, who had taken an art appreciation course. The woman was holding a pair of glasses before her in one hand as she studied the Jackson Pollock. Polly could almost hear the voice of the instructor telling the art appreciation class to feel the rhythms in the splatters of paint, and not to look for meaning.

It was only later, when the woman in the mink coat moved closer and smiled at her, that she recognized, with a shock, Hymie Liebman's wife, Miriam. Polly hadn't seen her in years. Miriam had to be at least fifty now, but in the classic black dress from Bergdorf's and her expensive coiffure, she looked years younger. They only had time to exchange a word or two because the symposium was about to start, and people were setting up chairs for themselves around the room or settling down on the floor. She made sure that Miriam got a chair up front.

The discussion began better than she could have hoped for. The moderator hadn't even finished making his introductory remarks, before an artist she knew from the WPA Arts Project before the war jumped up and denounced the abstract expressionists for throwing over traditions in painting that went back to Leonardo. Then a young painter in button-down shirt, jacket, and jeans hit back, calling the realists "leftovers from the thirties," and declared what the abstract artists were doing was "art of the new American century." The war was on, and accusations flew back and forth across the room, the moderator throwing up his hands and letting it take its own course.

Polly sympathized with the realists, who were fighting to survive against the new wave of abstract art that was getting all the attention. It had become a situation like the cold war, where no coexistence seemed possible between the two camps. Though she remembered well enough back in the Depression, when the social realists had been equally as ruthless in suppressing the avant-garde work of the twenties.

She caught sight of Miriam Liebman leaning forward, absolutely enthralled by the goings on. From the way she looked, life with Hymie must have certainly been fulfilling—especially if you could afford a daily massage and beauty treatments. Miriam, her symbol of the woman with everything, had always made her feel so inadequate, from the time she had showed up at the Village Art Center.

The shouting of a wild-haired woman painter brought Polly back to the discussion. To the booing of some in the audience, she declared that this new, so-called action painting was "infantile self-therapy, throwing paint at the canvas, without even being able to draw." Others in the audience were jumping up, yelling back and forth, nobody listening to what anyone else had to say, several almost on the verge of blows. Polly's assistant, Frederick, in his Bloomingdale's pipe stem suit, was sending her alarmed looks with his eyebrows, but she sat back highly pleased, as words like "reactionary," "decadent," "philistine," "fascist," "fellow travelers," "McCarthyite hack," flew across the room. But what an irony it was that her artists could sound so much like those ridiculous politicians in Washington, who were so busy, these days, labeling everybody in sight a subversive!

When the discussion finally broke up, people were too agitated to leave and stayed around arguing. Polly moved from one group to another, overjoyed. How healthy it was, how American, that such an evening could take place! It almost justified her existence that she was the one who had set it up. It was the Village as she loved it, a center of controversy.

On her way out, Miriam Liebman came up to Polly and gushed that it was the most exciting art event she had ever attended, and the show itself was a triumph.

There was a write-up the next morning on the art page of the Herald-Tribune, and the gallery was busy, that afternoon, as people came in, attracted by the controversy. Nobody bought, of course—the realist painters were going out of fashion and the abstract expressionists were still something of a joke, but she had never measured success by sales.

She was exhilarated. She let Frederick handle inquiries out front, and went back to her cubbyhole office to fire off a sharp letter to the Herald-Trib, criticizing their version of the symposium, which favored the abstractionists. "Why isn't there room in the world for both schools of art," she was writing, when Frederick looked in. One eyebrow almost at his hairline, he whispered that there was a woman asking to speak with her, and she was wearing an emerald the size of a doorknob.

It was Miriam Liebman in a Chanel suit, looking as expensive as the night before.

"I couldn't sleep a wink thinking about that Pollock," she said, as Polly greeted her, "and I've decided to buy it." In the office, Hymie's wife wrote out a check for seven hundred and fifty dollars without a flicker. "Hymie will hate it, but I'll bring him around," she said with an amused smile. She was going to hang it in the living room, and if it clashed with her Renoirs, she was willing to take the chance. In any case, the Pollock would be a wonderful conversation piece. Miriam Liebman went on to say that she had been attending the art lectures at the Cedar Street Tavern, given by that young poet, Frank O'Hara, and even taken classes from the celebrated Hans Hofmann, though of course she was just an amateur. But it was the discussion last night at the opening that had finally got her to take the leap and start a modern collection. "You know, buying this painting feels like the most daring thing I've ever done. You live so adventurously, Miss Endicott, can you understand what I mean?" She smiled warmly and handed over the check.

Polly had made a big sale and it was cause for celebration, but more than that, she was surprised to learn how "the woman who had everything" saw her. Adventurous. Who would have thought it! She got out a bottle of cognac and, complimenting Miriam on her good taste in acquiring the Pollock, poured a little into two wine glasses, only pretending to join in the toast herself—she had been careful about alcohol ever since Larry Mathews' suicide.

Miram said how glad she was that she finally was having a chance to get together with her. She had always been so interested in Polly's life, which she only heard about in bits and pieces from Hymie. Polly was an independent woman who was out in the world, while she felt that marriage and family had limited her possibilities of self-expression. "But when was the last time we saw each other?" Miriam said. "I've been trying to remember."

"It was at my brother's play at the Cherry Lane," Polly said, liking her better. "I'll never forget how your evening dress stood out in that shabby theater."

"It did? The truth is I was totally miserable that night. I had just become pregnant again and I felt so ill. But I loved the play."

Polly was saying what a pity it was that the play had been withdrawn after Eugene's death, when her assistant Frederick came in, clearly bursting with curiosity to know what was going on, and when she told him to put a red star on the Jackson Pollock to show it had been sold, he nearly dropped his aquamarine cuff-links.

"I lead such a hopelessly conventional life compared to you," Miriam said, her eyes following with interest the departing figure in the pencil-thin trousers.

Referring to the emerald on Miriam's hand that had made such an impression on Frederick, Polly smiled and asked if that didn't make up a little for the conventionality of it all?

Miriam laughed and agreed the stone was far too showy, but it was Hymie's gift for their twenty-fifth wedding anniversary. "What an event that was—marquee on the lawn, Duke Ellington's band—it was lovely." Their house in Westchester was far too big for them, Miriam confided, now that their daughter was married and their older son was at Harvard. But they were planning to move back into the city once their thirteen-year-old son was bar mitzvahed. It was hard to believe, she said, how traditional her husband was, underneath it all.

"I know a little about that," Polly said, remembering the night on the Staten Island ferry, when Hymie had used the word "traditional" as his excuse for not marrying her.

Miriam smiled. "Of course, you do. I was never taken in by that story about you being just his secretary."

Polly felt herself on the point of blushing. "You knew?" How naive to have assumed this intelligent woman had ever been completely in the dark.

Miriam sipped her cognac. "I've sometimes thought if he had married you instead of me, it might have been better."

"I once would have agreed with you," Polly said, surprised by the woman's generosity. "But you were the only woman who could have kept him."

"I'm afraid he was never meant to be monogamous," Miriam said, and confessed to Polly that, though he had always been attentive to her and a good father to the children, for years she had known she was sharing him with other women. It had almost broken up their marriage several times. She was in such despair over the infidelities, she had even tried an affair of her own once to pay him back, but it had led to a nervous breakdown, and she had gone through a long period of seeing an analyst. When she finished therapy not long before, she decided, finally, to leave him, but he had cried so piteously and begged her to stay, she relented. She understood that he couldn't live without the security of the home she made for him. "What a masochist I used to be, but at least analysis cured me of that. At any rate," Miriam fingered her twenty-fifth anniversary emerald, "everything's all right with us again."

Polly suppressed a feeling of skepticism, remembering how easily she had fallen for his promises herself, and what they were worth. But she said nothing, and instead told Miriam about her own years of jealousy, and how stupidly self-destructive she had been because of it.

"I'm so sorry," Miriam said, placing a hand on her arm. "I wish we could have been friends through it all."

Polly smiled. "I'm not sure I was ready for it, until now."

They said good-bye out on the sidewalk, and Polly watched the handsome, immaculately-dressed woman get into her limousine, as the chauffeur held the door, disappearing back into her sheltered, elegant life.

There was a smell of burning leaves in the crisp air, someone clearing up their back garden. Her joining hands with Miriam Liebman, at last, had completed the circle. It was absurd that she had held on to any rancor toward her, or Hymie, or anything that had happened. It was so much better to be beyond the turmoil of youth. This was the age she always should have been, with passions and crises behind her.

Before going back into the gallery, she stopped to buy an afternoon paper for the art reviews. On the front page, below a scare headline of Senator McCarthy's latest accusations, her old friend Paul Miller's name popped up from a list of people, working in television, called to testify before the House Un-American Activities Committee.

36

Polly's first thought, when she got the subpoena, was that it must be a mistake. Her name was being confused with someone else. FBI agents had been snooping around the Village for months, questioning people, but nobody had questioned her and why would they? She had nothing to do with politics. Besides, neither she nor her friends spied for foreign governments or conspired to overthrow the government. Even Paul Miller, who was a homegrown leftist, had never had the least interest in anything like that.

She had talked to him when he stopped off in the city on his way to testify in Washington. The same, quietly determined man he had always been, he said he had made up his mind not to cooperate with the witch-hunters in any way, no matter how intimidating they were. He was going to take the Fifth—stand on his constitutional rights not to testify against himself—even if it made him look guilty.

But later, watching him being interrogated on television, Polly's heart had gone out to him, seeing the strain in his face from holding back his anger, when the committee badgered him and made ugly innuendoes about his radical past and his associates. She called him at his hotel in Washington, afterward, to tell him she understood what he had gone through, and that he had been magnificent. The only thing that had held him together during the ordeal, Paul said, was concern for his new family—he'd married a production assistant at the studios where he worked, and her two children were the joy of his old age.

But when she studied the legal document that ordered her to appear before HUAC, Polly decided that she had better talk to a lawyer about it first, and when she thought it over, she remembered that there was a lawyer in the family—on the Irish side. Policeman Dennis Yates had a son, Timothy, who was with a law firm down by City Hall. She'd never kept up with that side of the family, but she'd seen the posters all over town, promoting Timothy Yates for City Council. If he had any political connections at all, he might be able to get her excused from testifying.

Handsome, silver-haired Timothy Yates was delighted to meet her, and sitting her down across from him in his spacious office on lower Broadway, it took them a moment to work out that they were second cousins. When she explained about the subpoena, he said of course he would help her.

He was nothing like the other Yateses she remembered from her childhood. In his Brooks Brothers suit and Ivy League haircut, he might have been an ex-Harvard debater, though she had a vague memory of him winning a title as a wrestler at Fordham.

Her confidence in him was short-lived, however. When she insisted the subpoena had to be a mistake, he made a quick call to the Senate Office Building in Washington to check on it, then told her there was no doubt about it, she would have to testify.

"Well, I don't have the slightest intention of doing any such thing," she said, crossly. But Timothy Yates then had the nerve to tell her it wouldn't be wise not to cooperate, and she couldn't believe her ears when he parroted Senator McCarthy's line that communist subversives had infiltrated every branch of the government, and that the country was ripe for a takeover, if they didn't clean them out. He went on to say that if she answered the committee's questions fully, without holding anything back, she had nothing to worry about.

"Are you saying that they think I'm a communist subversive?"

He stood up behind his desk and looked at her with steely eyes. "If you have nothing to hide, you can testify with a good conscience."

"I can't believe you're saying that!" she cried, on her feet. She told him she was shocked that anyone as bright as he seemed to be would go along with this whole shameful business. If it was just to get himself elected to the City Council, it was cynical and disgusting, and she would manage very well without him.

She was breathing hard as she left, but she still had two weeks before she was scheduled to appear, so there was plenty of time to find another lawyer.

The show currently at the Peacock Gallery, paintings by an Indian artist from the Southwest, was not getting the attention it deserved, and Polly ought to have been working on publicity. But her mind was not on the gallery. It had snowed in the night, and to get rid of her nosy assistant, Frederick, she sent him out to shovel the sidewalk. Then, she went into her back office and dialed the American Civil Liberties Union, but their lawyers were swamped with civil rights cases as it was, and they couldn't take her on.

She was just starting to call Paul Miller in Los Angeles to recommend her a lawyer, when she heard the roar of a sports car pulling up out front. It was a brand-new, red MG with wire wheels, and getting out of it was, of all people, Hymie Liebman. He turned back to kiss the cheek of the attractive girl at the wheel, and Polly's first thought was poor Miriam—until she saw that the girl smiling up at Hymie was the image of a young Miriam. His daughter. A daughter she didn't even know the name of. They obviously adored each other. Of course, he would buy his daughter a splendid car like that.

On the sidewalk, Frederick held his snow shovel in midair, agog not only at the English sports car driving off, but at Hymie's expensive appearance in his homburg and topcoat with velvet collar, as he strode into the gallery.

"I hope you know what I'm giving up for you, Pol," Hymie said, taking off his hat. His bald head and gray sideburns emphasized his mischievous, dark eyes more than ever. "I've canceled appointments worth a bundle, but Miriam says I've got to see this show. Who's the artist, did she say?"

"Nobody you ever heard of," Polly smiled, and lifted her cheek for him to kiss, "and you're a hero for coming. Your wife tells me how you hate the new Pollock."

He went over and wrinkled his brow at a large painting of a cow skull, with a desert landscape seen through the eye sockets.

"What do you think?" she asked him, glad to get her mind off the subpoena.

He turned on her the old, wicked grin. "You're right, I'm a dumb schmuck when it comes to modern art." He put an arm around her. "I'd rather look at you."

"Suppose I fix us some coffee instead?"

"I've got a better idea. How about coming for a walk?"

"In the snow?"

"Let's enjoy it before it turns yellow from dog piss."

She laughed. "I'm supposed to be running a gallery."

"Can't junior outside mind the store?" He waved at Frederick, whose nose was practically glued to the window.

Scarcely giving her time to get into her snow things, tie a kerchief over her hair, or even advise Frederick not to spend the whole time on the phone, he led the way out the door, before she caught up with him and took his arm.

In the midst of her troubles, Hymie showing up out of the blue was just what she needed. She was grateful to Miriam for sending him down, whatever the reason. Out in the icy air, their footsteps crunching through the fresh, untrampled snow, she felt lighthearted, as if they were off again on another lark, like the old days. All the parked cars and fire hydrants were topped with snow, and dogs were frisking in the white fluff they couldn't understand, lifting their legs and already making yellow holes in it.

As they walked into Washington Square along an uncleared path, it was almost a Grandma Moses scene in the middle of the city. Sun glinted off icicles hanging from the branches of trees, and children belly-whopped on sleds, their scarves flashes of color in the black-and-white scene.

Hymie scooped up some snow and shaped it into a snowball. "What's this I hear about your commie past catching up with you?" He threw the snowball against the trunk of a sycamore tree.

Polly was taken aback. "How did you know about that?"

He patted her hand holding his arm. "Joe McCarthy tells me

everything. Don't you know I'm a big shot?"

"The whole thing's ridiculous," she said, remembering that her name had been listed that day in the paper. But it was buried in the back pages, and she was surprised anyone would notice it. "I can't imagine why they called me."

"You are one, naive dame. No wonder you never made a cent." It was plain as the Jewish nose on his face, he said, why her name was on the list. The whole point of the hearings was to get people to name names, and somebody had named her.

"Why would anyone name me?"

"You've spent your life with oddballs in Greenwich Village, so what do you expect?"

If someone had named her as a subversive, she couldn't imagine who it was, but she was annoyed with his flippancy and told him so. She let go of his arm and immediately slipped on an icy patch.

He steadied her and said he wasn't trying to be funny. "I know this is serious, Pol, and that's why I'm getting you the best lawyer in the business to see you through it."

To her surprise, she felt a tremendous sense of relief. He had always been there when she needed him. Why hadn't she gone to him in the first place and saved herself all that worry? With her arm tucked firmly into his again, they walked in the direction of New York University, ahead of the lengthening shadows of the apartment buildings behind them. He told her that when Miriam showed him her name in the paper at breakfast, he'd canceled all his appointments and come down to see what he could do. To tell the truth, he said, he didn't know whether she had ever been a commie or not, not that he gave a damn, and he didn't think those schmucks in Washington did, either. They were just out to hog the headlines, like all politicos.

She told him that she had been too shocked by the subpoena to be able to think straight. There was so much paranoia on both sides, and he was an island of sanity.

In spite of the gray hair, he still laughed with his old boyishness, and suggested that they go warm up at the Chock Full O' Nuts on the corner.

Sitting at the formica counter, his shoulder touching hers, as he liberally spread mustard on his hot dog, she thought how extraordinary it was that here they were, together again, after all these years. She breathed in the steam from the cup of coffee in her cold hands. "I think your daughter's lovely," she said, referring to the girl at the wheel of the MG.

He was chewing his hot dog, blissfully.

"You should have brought her into the gallery. I'd love to meet her."

He looked at her, a gleam of wickedness in his eye, as he licked mustard off his fingers. "Who says she's my daughter?"

With a flush, she realized her naiveté again. Poor Miriam with her emerald. He was back to his old tricks.

Whatever she expected to feel at the hearing in Washington—indignation, fear, humiliation—when the time came, she felt nothing. The massive government buildings, the officialdom engulfing her from the antechamber to the hearing room with its cameras, staged chaos, scare tactics—it was hard to believe any of it was real. And she felt most unreal of all, as if she were watching it on television herself.

She listened to them questioning her about her involvement before the war with the WPA. Arts Project…fund-raising for the Spanish Loyalists… signing petitions of all kinds, way back to Sacco–Vanzetti…and repeatedly asking her for the names of her friends. Whatever they said, she looked at them blankly, even when they called the Peacock Gallery a hotbed of subversion. She did what her lawyer advised her to do, each time repeating the odious words, "I refuse to answer on the grounds of my Fifth Amendment right against self-incrimination."

She still felt nothing, as she and the lawyer made their way through the crowd out to a taxi, newspapermen throwing questions at them and flashbulbs snapping.

It was on the train returning to New York that she came back to life, the consciousness of what she had been through flooding over her. She was furious and humiliated to have been treated so cheaply—used, violated in front of the whole country, before millions. And most of all, she felt alone. She longed for someone to talk to, someone who might understand how she felt, who could help her sort it out. Not Hymie—he would only try to distract her.

There was nobody—except for Paul Miller out in Los Angeles, who had gone through the same experience and also taken the Fifth, and everyone assumed he was guilty, just as they would her. Nobody understood that refusing to answer the committee's questions was the only way to avoid smearing people you knew.

As soon as she got home, she placed a long distance call to the television studio where Paul worked. When the receptionist didn't recognize his name, she thought for a moment the worst had happened and that he had lost his job, like so many others. Then, she remembered to tell the receptionist that he was a set designer on The Sid Caesar Show, and would she please check again.

There was a long wait before Paul's familiar voice came on. "I know how you feel, Polly, but it's over and they can't hurt you any more," he said. "You're lucky about one thing, you work for yourself and can't lose your job."

She told him how relieved she was to hear his voice, she was afraid he might have been blacklisted.

"It was touch-and-go for a while, but my lawyer says I'm okay," Paul said. Then, his voice changed. "What was so wrong with what we did back then, Polly? It was the Depression. I thought we were the good guys. They twist everything you do, and just when I was accepted into the union and had job security, doing sets, here where I wanted to be—I have a family now, Polly, two kids, you'd love 'em—they tried to ruin it all...." He broke off. "Did you hear a clicking on the line just now.

"I didn't hear anything. Why?"

"I gotta go, Polly," he said, fast. "I gotta get back to the set...."

"Wait, Paul! I want to talk...." She made a joke about the two of them being "uncooperative witnesses."

But he didn't laugh. He wasn't even listening. "I just want you to know, Polly," he said, almost in a whisper, "they got all the power. You and me, we got no choice...."

After he hung up, she puzzled over what she first took to be his lack of sympathy, his erratic talk, the uncompleted sentences.

And then it hit her.

Everybody knew about witnesses who took the Fifth, but afterward—behind closed doors—decided to "cooperate" to save their skins, their careers, their families. She wondered, sadly, if it were possible that the man she used to tease about his fuzzy-headed plans to reform the world, might have been the one who had turned her in.

37

In the years after the war, Polly's nephew, Seth Harris, tried to get somewhere as an actor, but nothing happened. In fact, as the fifties began, he had hardly progressed beyond a few TV walk-ons and some summer stock. Nearing forty and with gray in his hair, he saw his hopes for success in the theater fading, while his wife, Susan, at her fashion magazine, had already been promoted to special assistant to one of the editors.

Since Susan was making a good salary, they were no longer strapped for money, even though Seth managed to cover his own expenses with part-time office jobs. They moved from their walk-up on Sullivan Street to a smart three-room apartment on West Tenth, Susan paying for it all. She demanded a decent level of comfort for herself, she said, even if he was content to live in a dump. Seth hated the new apartment, and the newly acquired flair for interior decoration his clever wife brought from the job.

Everyone was impressed with Susan. He had married her when she was barely seventeen and he was fifteen years older than her, and already she had left him far behind. She never referred to his career, and he could tell by the way she avoided his eyes, whenever he talked about his plans for the theater, that she had stopped believing he was ever going to get anywhere.

He quit the latest office temp job, and went to work as a desk clerk at a run-down hotel nearby, just off Washington Square. His hours at the Earle were flexible, and the manager let him take off for casting calls and auditions. The only problem was that being turned down year after year was written all over his face, and he began to shrink from making the rounds, and putting on at auditions a confidence that he didn't feel. He sometimes pretended he had an audition to go to just to impress the hotel manager, but it was worse having to kill time at 42nd-Street movies. The hotel job had been only a means to an end when he took it, but after he moved with Susan to the new apartment, the Earle became the place where he felt most at home, where he didn't feel her accusing eyes watching him, impossible demands being made.

The hotel began to be the center of his world, as his acting hopes dimmed. On the outside, the building still looked a respectable place. Its ornate, carved-granite facade and the striped awning from the entrance to the curb gave tourists the idea that it must be a charming little place to stay in the middle of Greenwich Village. Yet, they no sooner came in to inquire about a room, than Seth saw them take in the linoleum floor of the lobby, the prominent Coke machine, the clump of wires in the ceiling where the chandelier had been. And usually there was at least one resident staring at a crack in the wall, lost in a heroin stupor. The hotel was full of the deranged and the aged, many of them ex-artists who had long given up.

Whenever he did go to try out for a part, the competition all seemed to be younger than he was, more aggressive, more talented. He showered and shaved and doused himself in aftershave lotion, but he still felt the smell of the hotel's clientele clinging to him, its reek of failure. Yet back on duty at the front desk, it was the same smell of failure, otherwise so repulsive, that began to fascinate him. The world he came from was middle-class and respectable, and if people had depraved habits, it didn't show. But in the hotel everything was in the open, and it couldn't be more sordid. He came to believe that he belonged to all this, more than to Susan's world of upwardly mobile, young professionals.

If he was not allowed to be part of the world of professional theater, then here was a theater of the lower depths that didn't reject him. And he— The Room Clerk—was at its center. Not just a spectator, but a participant, studying the undisguised behavior of the cast of characters for the time when he would portray them on stage.

When he and Susan were speaking—more often, nowadays, they were not—and when their hours at home coincided, he told her about the residents of the hotel. The scraggly-haired Beat poet who gave poetry readings in his room, ranting about his generation going insane from drugs and an insane society, to the accompaniment of a jazz clarinet. The audience listened glassy-eyed, calling "Go, man! Go!" to the verbal riffs that filled the room along with the marijuana smoke.

The hotel switchboard always lit up with tenants complaining about noise or heat or the plumbing, and it was Seth's job to go up to check. Some of the calls were from women. He didn't tell Susan about the women. He once got called upstairs by a resident, whose room, facing an airshaft, was stacked with her dusty oil paintings, and when he got there she was lying naked on her bed, her old, sagging body hopeful. He felt sick to see her there like that, the last shreds of dignity gone, but he couldn't forget how she looked, and the next time a woman called him to check on a leaky faucet, not much younger, but in a kimono that hid her used flesh, he stayed on five minutes, almost against his will, giving her what she wanted. After that, there were often similar episodes.

He found he didn't want to make love to Susan any more. When he did, after a fight that led to sex, which was their pattern, he sometimes thought he smelled other men on her—men from the magazine, from her new world of martini lunches at uptown restaurants.

One warm day, when sightseers were looking at the paintings lined up against the sidewalk railings in the annual Washington Square outdoor art show, and the front doors of the Earle Hotel were open to the street, the woman who made up the rooms came down to the lobby, needing his help. Later, that night, when Susan came home from the magazine, looking cool and immaculate as always, he told her every sordid detail of what had happened. He had gone upstairs with the maid and had opened the door of a third-floor room—it smelled of stale booze—to discover the old bum, once a famous poet in the twenties, lying on the bed, with his girlfriend snoring beside him. But the poet was not snoring. He was covered with blood and his eyes were open. One of their alcoholic cronies had stabbed him to death. There was a stab wound through an enormous, multicolored eye tattooed around his navel.

"Stop!" Susan shrieked, covering her ears. "What's the matter with you, anyway? You sound like you enjoy this whole disgusting mess you're in. You're sick!"

But it was incredible, he said. The man had been a great poet. Polly had known him and said women had once killed themselves over him. Then, the world turns its back and he destroys himself. Seth's voice rose, as he envisioned the dramatic possibilities. "Don't you get it? What a play it would make! I'd give anything to do the role."

He would never play anything, Susan said bitterly. He was a failure like his father, and she wanted out.

When he asked what she meant, she said the marriage was over, that's what she meant. She packed a bag and told him that, when she returned the next day, he'd better be out of there. It was her apartment. The lease was in her name and she paid the rent.

Seth's flimsy defenses began to crumble. Maybe their marriage hadn't been going too well, but if they broke up, if Susan left him, there was only the sordid life of the hotel. He got scared. "We could start over," he told her. "We'll go to Hollywood, where I can get work as an extra. I know some people out there. They'll get me in. I don't need Broadway."

But she only laughed—an ugly laugh—and told him he could go to Hollywood if he liked, to a nuthouse for all she cared, but she was sick to death of all his fantasies about what he was never going to do. She had her feet on the ground. In another year, she'd be editor-in-chief of the magazine. And she was not going to let him hold her back.

She left, and he began to shake uncontrollably. His fantasy of the theater had been dying for a long time, now she had demolished it—only her presence had kept him from falling apart. Terrified by the void opening up around him, he rushed out to look for her, to beg her to come back and put him together again.

But he didn't find her. Instead, a policeman found him walking barefoot up Eighth Avenue at four in the morning, raging to the world at the top of his voice that he never had a chance, that it wasn't fair, and blubbering like a baby. And when the policeman didn't smell liquor on his breath, he sent him to Bellevue.

They kept him there in a ward with bars on the windows, and attendants, who administered sedatives, every time he became conscious and started to cry.

They were going to send him upstate, commit him to a permanent institution. He heard them talking about it, a doctor and a couple of attendants at the foot of his bed, though he kept his eyes shut, feigning sleep.

His mind was immediately clear. He stole a dime out of the bedside drawer of the patient next to him and called his aunt on a public phone, and told her where he was.

Then, he was in a quiet room in St. Vincent's Hospital, the tumult of his emotions over, as he lay there, aware of the traffic on Seventh Avenue below.

Polly sat beside him. She came every day, bringing him tidbits to tempt him to eat, cottage cheese and ice cream and pieces of fruit, that an orderly removed every night, untouched. His aunt was looking older, tired, though she spoke brightly about his being discharged soon and coming to stay with her. She was trying her best to be cheerful, but he wasn't fooled. Life wasn't so easy for her any more, not since the harassment in Washington. The art critics had stopped coming down to her gallery after the papers printed the story. Her best painters had moved uptown to better galleries. The ones she showed now were getting old like she was, and their work was out of fashion, and nobody came to the openings but relatives and friends. And now, added to everything else, she had him to worry about, a broken down wreck at forty.

"It's quite a while since I've been connected to the theater," she was saying, as her hand fiddled with the clunky beads around her neck, "but I'm acquainted with the man who runs the Provincetown Playhouse on MacDougal Street. Of course, it's not the same theater I was with—that was torn down—but still, if there was something for you, it would be a showcase."

"Polly, stop it," he said, wishing she would go away. "I'm not an actor any more, can't you see?" He was determined not to unburden himself to anyone, yet her attempts to cheer him up got on his nerves. "I'm a total flop—I've failed at everything. Like father, like son."

"What are you saying?" she snapped. "You may think of yourself as a failure if you want, but your father wasn't. He was a brilliant writer, and his tragedy was only that he was cut down in his prime. Don't you remember his play?"

"No," he said, looking out the window, wanting to end the conversation.

"Of course, you do. You were in the rehearsals. You loved it."

He still didn't look at her. "I know you mean well, but I wish you'd give up on me."

She brought in the manuscript of "The Weak and the Strong" the next day. She told him she had kept it in a box under her bed with all his father's other writings. She was saving them for him. "Believe it or not," she said, reaching into her bag and pulling out the yellowed script, "I stayed up all night reading it over again, and I think you should read it too." She held it out, but he turned on his side, away from her.

"Don't you know I'm crazy," he said. "Crazy people don't read plays. They don't read anything. They don't give a good goddam."

Polly got up and leaned over him. "Stop that, do you hear? You're just feeling sorry for yourself?"

"It's not going to do any good," he said to the wall. "I'm just not interested...."

Polly sighed, heavily. "I'm going to leave the play here anyway." She laid it on the bedside table and gathered up her things. "Read it or don't read it, do what you want."

As soon as she left him, Seth rang for the nurse. He wanted a pill that would knock him out for the rest of the day, so he didn't have to face it. But though he kept ringing, the nurse didn't come. "Bitch!" He bunched up his pillow, trying to settle down, but without the pill he couldn't sleep.

Miserable, he opened his eyes and saw the manuscript on the table. He reached for it, looked at the first page. It made no sense. He didn't give a shit about it. He threw it on the floor, and pulled the sheet over his head.

"Well, well, we don't like the daylight, Mr. Harris?" The Sister pulled the sheet off his head. He loathed her smug face in her butterfly headdress with a heavy crucifix hanging around her bosom, but she was holding out the magic blue pill.

He gulped it down with a glass of water, and slipped away into blissful oblivion.

"You didn't look at it, did you?" Polly said, when she came back next day. She took the manuscript from the table and returned to her chair. "Will you listen if I read some of it aloud?"

"Aren't you ever going to give up on me, for God's sake?" Seth muttered into his pillow.

"No, dear, I'll never give up on you. You're the only close family I've got left. I'm going to keep trying. Now pay attention." She folded back the title page and began to read. He kept his eyes on the ceiling, tracing over ridges in the plaster. He wished she would go. The more she tried to get through to him, the guiltier he felt.

Polly looked up from her reading. "You're not listening. Please, dear," she pleaded, "just give it a chance."

He didn't answer. Why couldn't she see he was crippled, and no one was ever going to make him whole again?

"I'll go on, shall I?" His aunt waited for permission, but when he said nothing, she read on.

He was trying not to hear her, but as she kept on reading aloud the scenes in her determined voice, portraying each character so vividly, he began to be drawn in, in spite of himself.

Visiting hours were over and she had to leave, but this time, when he picked up the manuscript and continued reading where she broke off, the words were no longer meaningless. In his head, he heard the characters as if they were alive, and a world, his father's world, opened up to him.

"We're feeling perkier today, are we, Mr. Harris?" The Sister held out the pill with the glass of water.

He looked at the blue pill he'd been taking four times a day, the pill that had sent him off to merciful nothingness. "Leave it, nurse. I'll take it later."

She looked surprised. "Very well, Mr. Harris," she said, and put down the glass and the pill, giving him an appraising glance as she left.

He went back to the play. He had been a very young man when he saw it, his father's triumph, but he hadn't understood it, as he did now. What Gene had gone through, when he had ruined his life and had been banished to Europe. It was his father's story—and now, in a way, it was his own.

He had never felt so close to Gene before, the visceral connection to his father. There were differences, of course, factual differences, but the essence of the play's story was his, the odyssey of an exile coming back from the dead.

"What a role!" he said to his aunt, the next day. He was in his bathrobe, walking back and forth in front of the window. "I'd give anything to have played it. There are some dated references, the title's all wrong, but it's really good."

"Didn't I tell you?" she said, smiling.

He started acting out one of the scenes to her. Then, sitting side by side on the bed, they read through the play together, taking different parts, and the excitement of the production at the Cherry Lane, all those years ago, came back to them both. "It's got some of the atmosphere of Streetcar. I think it could almost go today," he said, when they finished. "Of course, it would take a brilliant director like Kazan, and the actor in the lead would have to be another Brando."

"We don't need Brando," Polly said, carefully. "You could do it."

"Oh, come on…."

"Why not? You're an actor."

"I was an actor."

"Nonsense! You're exactly right for the part."

"You're out of your mind...."

She took off her glasses. "Why don't we put it on?"

He had to smile. She was indomitable. "My dear aunt, you're forgetting a few little things such as," he ticked them off on his fingers, "producer and money, theater and money, director and money."

Polly refused to listen to any of this. Back in the days when she was a girl, working for the Provincetown Players, she told him, they hadn't waited for Broadway. They did it all themselves, putting together everything on a shoestring. "They ignored us for a while, but we got the critics to come down, finally. We gave them O'Neill. That made them pay attention!"

Seth shook his head. There wasn't any possibility of theater in the Village nowadays, he said, not real theater. It was all Broadway. That took big money and contacts, and he had finally faced it, there was no place for him in any of it.

She took his shoulder and pulled him around. "Never mind all that. If I get the money together, can't we put it on? At least for a short run."

He knew what she was doing. She was only encouraging him this way because she wanted him to be well again. But how full of energy she was all of a sudden. She looked years younger than her mid-sixties, like he remembered her after the war, when the Peacock was going great guns, and she was in the thick of the art world. She must have seen the doubt on his face, because she repeated, "We're going to do it. I can get the money."

And she did. She came back the next day to say she had it. She had gone to Hymie Liebman. He and his wife were living in a penthouse atop a high-rise building on Central Park West he had put up, with a garden on the terrace and a spectacular view of the Hudson. Much too elaborately furnished for her taste, she said—but never mind, the Pollock she had sold Miriam held its own.

Hymie had scotched her idea of taking out another mortgage on the Perry Street house—it was mortgaged to the hilt already. And as far as his sinking money into some cockamamie play to be put on in the Village or on Broadway, she must have more wires loose than he already thought.

But his wife, Miriam, told him to shush. She thought the play a splendid idea. It was something she'd always wanted to do. She said she was going to put up the money herself, and she and Polly would co-produce it.

Seth was afraid to believe her when she told him. But Polly brought

Miriam Liebman to the hospital to meet him, and he began to believe it. They read the play again, and he immediately saw how to make the necessary changes to bring it up-to-date—a new title to start with, then move it up from after the First World War to Paris in the late forties. And when he left the hospital, he showed the play to an out-of-work director he knew and they got a cast together.

The manager of the Provincetown Playhouse, who knew Polly, rented it to them for three weeks between scheduled productions, and Seth went to work.

Re-titled "Night Falls With The Sound of Guitars," the play opened on a September evening in 1955, eighteen years after its aborted first run in the Depression. As before, no critics showed up, but friends of the actors came, and some others attracted by the title. The first week, the audiences were sparse, until Walter Kerr, the critic from the Herald-Trib came the second week, and reviewed it favorably. The following night, the Times and the Post showed up. Their reviews were even better, and people who did not ordinarily go down to the Village came to see it.

At the end of the three weeks, the run was extended, the manager of the theater having canceled the play that was scheduled to follow.

Several theatrical agents had already shown interest in taking Seth on, when a scout for a Hollywood producer saw the play and got him to test for the lead role in a proposed film of O'Neill's "The Iceman Cometh." The part was made for him, a middle-aged man in a phantasmagorical world of derelicts and dreamers. When he was signed for the part, his picture appeared on the movie page of the Times over the caption, "An Actor's Life Begins at 40."

1975

38

From the open windows of the front apartment, a radio was blaring out minute-by-minute coverage of the helicopter retreat from the roof of the American Embassy in Saigon. Sitting in his usual place on top of one of the garbage cans on the sidewalk, where he could keep an eye on the whole of Perry Street, the super, Frank Alfano, chewed on his toothpick gloomily. It was a humiliating defeat for the United States by those little commie bastards. Hadn't he been saying for years to drop the fuckin' bomb on 'em? If they had listened to him, this never would have happened.

"Give us a break in there," he yelled over his shoulder to the bimbo who lived in the apartment with the radio. "Do we have to have our noses rubbed in it?"

But the tenant didn't turn it down. She was probably too stoned to hear anything except a phone call from one of her hippie boyfriends. Frank was always telling her that, if she'd seen him after the war in his marine uniform with his Silver Star, she'd have wet her pants over him, like all of the chicks. Shifting his overweight body on the garbage can, he groaned and rubbed his bad knee. He was sweating in his work clothes. The sun was hot for May.

The sanitation truck was coming down the street, and he got up and started lugging the garbage cans over to the curb. He was the only super on the block who did this for the sanitation guys. But he knew what it was like. He had worked on a garbage truck himself. That was before the car-wash job, where they caused him all the trouble. He had tried to make the judge see he'd only borrowed the fifty from the cash register to pay off a bill his last wife had stuck him with, when she ran off with that shit-head cop.

Polly was the only one who had written to him, when he was doing time in the road camp out west. He hadn't heard a word from his brother—him and his fat-assed wife out in Jersey, too busy living it up on all the millions from the electronics business. After he did his time, Polly had sent him a bus ticket home, and arranged for him to be the janitor of the Perry Street house, which included an apartment in the basement.

Lately, with her arthritis, Polly didn't get around so well, and he was glad to be able to look after her, to pay her back some for all she had done for him. She was the only one he cared about. It made him sick to think she was leaving New York.

The garbage truck stopped in front of the house and the sanitation man dumped the garbage in, as the grinder chewed it up. But instead of tossing Frank the empty cans to catch, as usual, the man shoved them back to him, scraping across the pavement.

"What'sa matter, too much pussy last night?" Frank kidded him, as he set the cans upright on the sidewalk.

"I don't get to sit around on my ass like you, Frankie boy," the sanitation worker called back from the running board of the truck, as it moved away.

Frank chuckled, and reassembled the battered cans by the iron railing in front of the house, replacing the lids. Then he settled down again with his toothpick, noting with disapproval the empty garbage cans and lids, littering the sidewalk up and down the street, in the wake of the garbage pickup. He was the only super who was on the ball.

With the Vietnam pullout still blaring from the front apartment, it was a moment before Frank heard his aunt's wavering voice calling him. Polly had come out on the stoop, needing his help. She'd been going through her things for weeks, sorting and disposing, getting ready to fly to California to live with her nephew, Seth.

"I thought you was taking it easy," Frank said, scolding her gently as he got up. "Everything's done. You got a long plane trip ahead of you tonight."

"I've found a whole carton of things I overlooked," Polly said. "It's under the bed and I can't manage." She pulled her cardigan around her, as she turned back into the house.

Frank's bad knee throbbed, as he climbed the stoop to follow her in. She moved carefully ahead of him down the hall toward her back apartment, a gnarled hand on the wall for support. Her ankles were bone thin and her white hair wispy. She was such a little thing. She could hardly weigh more than ninety pounds.

She turned to him, her eyes still lively behind her glasses. "Seth will be here before we know it. I've got so much to do yet."

"Aw, you got plenty of time," he said, in a voice made even more gravelly by his sadness over her departure. "Why don't you just take it easy?"

With her arthritis so bad, Polly couldn't take the cold any more, and that was the reason Seth had convinced her to come out and live with him and his family. Frank was no good with words and couldn't make her understand that she didn't need to move. He would take care of her when she needed it, he'd do everything for her. But she was stubborn as a mule. She had told him she didn't want to wake up some day and find herself in a nursing home, and just because she was old—she was eighty-seven, "such a ridiculous age"—didn't mean she couldn't start a new life in a warmer place.

In her room, she directed him to pull out the carton from under the daybed. "I was sweeping out just now, when the broom hit it. Heaven knows what's there."

Frank got down on the floor, his bad knee killing him, and pulled out the carton. He put it on the seat of the bay window next to her armchair. Even with the windows open onto the backyard, where the ailanthus trees were in new leaf for another spring, he still smelled cat in the room. She had two of them, and two cat carriers were beside her suitcases, waiting to go. The cats were hiding, Polly told him—they knew something was afoot.

It hurt him to see her apartment with the faded patches from the pictures on the walls and most of the furniture gone. The place already looked abandoned, and so small he wondered how she had ever crammed so much into it. Cartons filled with junk she was leaving behind were stacked by the door. She had made him promise to put them all out at least a day before the next pickup. They were the kinds of odds and ends that Villagers would enjoy going through, she said.

She had already given away many of her things to special friends in the building, the bimbo in the front apartment, and the long-haired faggot, who lived upstairs and came in at all hours of the night. Those two sometimes took his aunt out to the theater and art galleries, but it was Frank who did the hard stuff for her like cleaning and shopping.

Polly was running a dust rag over the top of the carton from under the bed. "I do hope none of this is anything I want to keep. There's not another inch of space in my luggage." She folded back the cardboard flaps.

"Need any help with that?" Frank stood by, feeling clumsy, as he always did around his indomitable little aunt.

She pulled an old book from the carton and her eyes lit up behind her glasses, as she started going through the pages. "I wondered what happened to this!"

Frank stood by awhile, but she seemed to have forgotten him, bent over the book with her tremor and her frail little body. He was afraid he might break down and bawl, and went back to sit out front.

In the light of the bay window, Polly caressed the copy of Eugene's novel. She had put it away at the time of his death and never looked at it since. Its maroon cover had faded, but the green lettering, Tortured Souls by Elgin St. John, was still fresh.

She admired the fine-quality paper and the handsomeness of the typeface. Gene's dedication to her on the flyleaf was a bit faded, although he had written it in purple ink—the color had seemed so appropriate in that long-ago time. They had thought of themselves as so decadent in those days.

Polly, dearest, here is the first of my little offerings—at
last! But no book I write in the future—and let's hope there'll be
a shelf of them—will ever come more from the heart.

Love, Gene

She smiled, remembering. Of course, she had to take this with her. She went over to put it in an open suitcase, but it was already chock full. On the very top lay a poster of "Timothy Yates for Mayor," that she wanted to show to Seth's family. Her lawyer nephew's face was pasted up all over town, still silver-haired and handsome, though now twenty-five years older than when they had their tiff at City Hall. Although they still didn't agree politically, she was sorry she was going to miss the excitement of the election. She'd have to repack the whole bag to get Gene's book in, somehow, without bending the poster.

Rummaging again through the contents of the forgotten carton, she came across a handful of theater programs for "Night Falls With The Sound of Guitars." Once, years after, Jose Quintero, the director who had been credited with founding Off-Broadway, had confessed to her that it was that production that gave him the idea of starting his Circle in the

Square Theater. The success of Eugene Endicott's play had shown him that audiences and critics were ready to come down to the Village again for serious drama.

But the birth of Off-Broadway had not been her reason for putting the play on—it was to restore Seth's faith in himself, and it had accomplished its purpose. She had always been thankful. It had given her nephew his chance at Hollywood, though he hadn't ended up acting in the movies after all. Just at the time he went out, the old studio system was falling apart, and "The Iceman Cometh" had never been released.

But the move to the West Coast had worked out well for Seth. He had become a producer in a company making TV commercials, and his wife, Anne, was a pretty, tanned California girl—well, not really a girl any more—who was fulfilled raising a family and taking care of his needs, a far cry from the restless Susan Schlesinger.

In the years since Seth, Susan had risen in her field, becoming editor of Harper's Bazaar. Jennifer, the free-lance artist in the front apartment, had caught sight of her several times when she delivered artwork to the magazine. Susan Schlesinger radiated charm, Jennifer said, but those eyes…. "Polly, that is one tough lady." But then, Jennifer wasn't interested in a big career. She was pure Village, in the old sense of the word Polly had always loved. She was always looking in on Polly to talk about her problems and the latest therapy she was trying.

Polly's other special friend in the house lived just above her. Danny was one of the young gays who had stood up to the police at the raid on the Stonewall Tavern, and didn't let anyone tell him how to run his life. He did street theater, worked as a waiter, and even made jewelry that he sold on the sidewalks. Often, when he got home in the wee hours and saw a light under her door, he would knock, and share his pastrami sandwich and coffee from an all-night deli with her. He wore his long hair in a head-band and a gold wire in one earlobe, and always cheered her up on her insomniac nights with his flamboyant talk about his nocturnal adventures. It was all so different for him than it had been for Gene. That was one way the world had improved, at least.

She began tossing various unimportant items from the carton into a box of trash. She was about to discard some old photos, when she caught sight of Larry Mathews' face. It was a wedding picture of the two of them, taken by the wife of the Justice of the Peace in Connecticut. She hadn't seen it since she put it away after what had happened. He looked so young and hopeful, Larry. Like he hadn't a care in the world. She gazed at it for a long time. Then put it with the other things she was going to find a way to take.

So many of her contemporaries were dead now—friends in the Village, in the theater, in the art world. She had outlived almost everybody. It seemed almost a lifetime since she'd given up the gallery, after that simple-minded Pop Art came in she refused to show. And even the collectors who were her mainstay threw their money away on it. They would learn their lesson. Most of that junk would soon be relegated to the basement.

Closing the gallery had not been the end. During the period of black voter registration in the South, she had gone on a Freedom Ride at age seventy-two. And then there was Vietnam and she was busy with the anti-war movement—read-ins, talk-ins, and teach-ins. One of the newspapers had written her up as "the little old lady who wouldn't quit." Thank God, the country was out of that mess, at last.

When Seth had urged her to move out to California, she hadn't really wanted to go. She couldn't imagine living anywhere else but New York. But this old house was always chilly. Until the last few years, the cold had never bothered her. And with her arthritis, the sun would feel awfully good, even if her mind did turn into mashed potatoes. Seth had pointed out all the advantages. The apartment attached to his house in Santa Monica would make more sense for her at her age—no steps to climb, no ice to slip on, no threat of a nursing home. She'd still be independent, and he and Anne would be there to help her whenever she needed them. And there were his two children, the son, a freshman in college and the daughter, going to private school, who adored her.

Seth's arguments all made sense. But some part of her just hadn't been able to make the decision. That was when she'd written to Hymie. He and Miriam were living in a retirement community outside Phoenix.

But it was not Hymie who answered her letter. It was Miriam. Hymie was not quite himself these days, she wrote. He was often confused, and his memory wasn't what it once was. The doctor called his condition Alzheimers Disease, but he was in reasonably good health and when, on his good days, they sat out on the patio to watch the sunset over the desert, he could be almost his old self. As to Polly's move to California, Miriam was sure he would approve. She thought of Polly so often with great affection, and best regards to Seth. It had been such a pleasure, working on the play with him, all those years ago.

The news about Hymie had taken awhile to digest. The man who had once been the center of her life, the most dynamic person she had ever known, didn't even know who she was any more.

Beneath the jumble of odds and ends, at the very bottom of the carton, she found a leather-bound portfolio of lithographs. Her grandfather had printed them back in the eighteen-eighties. She got the portfolio out of the box and opened it in her lap. The Legend of Greenwich Village.

She'd forgotten how striking the old lithographs were. An artist friend of her grandfather's named Albert Cogswell had done them. She remembered having seen an old photograph of him, and his kindly face had stayed in her mind. Her mother had always described him to her as "a bearded, homegrown Rousseau," and his bushy hair, her mother said, was as red as Polly's used to be.

No one in the family had red hair. No one but her. That had puzzled her. She'd read about genes and inherited traits…was it possible that her strait-laced mother…no, absolutely ridiculous!

Her two cats came out from under the bed and set up a racket beside their bowls. She had forgotten all about them. What was she doing, sitting here daydreaming, when they were hungry? She'd better give them something to eat right now, since they would be cooped up in their carryalls on the plane for hours, and she had all kinds of things left to do, before Seth would be here in the taxi to take her to the airport.

But when she was finally ready, she still had loads of time. She thought of asking Frank to take her for a short walk for a last look around, but even with her cane, there was the front stoop to cope with, and she musn't tire herself out.

She went back to her armchair in the bay window, with The Legend of Greenwich Village in her lap, intending to study Albert Cogswell's lithographs in the clear north light. Instead, she found herself gazing out on the small, sooty backyard that never got quite enough sun to flourish. All the extravagant flowers and greenery of the California lotus land would never mean anything to her, compared to this little plot of ground. Her eyes lingered on the ailanthus trees, the miracle of their delicate green clusters of new leaves, that never failed to fill her with joy.

And that was where Frank found her, when he came to bring her a container of coffee—in her chair, head fallen over, the portfolio of lithographs by her unknown father scattered on the floor.

After the ambulance had taken the body away, the police stayed behind with Frank to finish filling out forms. The girl in the front apartment wasn't at home. And the long-haired young man, who brought her pastrami sandwiches, had stayed out all night and wasn't back yet either. Two other tenants exchanged whispered words in the hall at the foot of the stairs about what a nice person the old lady had been, and how lucky it was she had died so quickly and without any pain, but they hadn't really known her and they had to get back to their own work. The two cats, spooked by all the confusion, had gone into hiding behind the waiting suitcases and the cartons of thrown-out junk, and didn't come out again until the strangers had left.

To keep himself busy until Seth arrived—he had called the hotel but couldn't reach him—Frank swept the steps and the front walk. He grumbled out of habit, as he went over to the curb to pick up a soda can that someone had dropped around one of the young trees the city had planted. Then, taking a handkerchief from his back pocket, he mopped his forehead and sat down in his usual place on one of the garbage cans. Down the block, a rock group was rehearsing. From one of the neighboring houses a typewriter was clacking.

As Frank waited for Seth, the sun dipped behind the row of houses across the way. But its glare still caught the windows above him, shimmering on the glass and giving the illusion of things that weren't there. For a moment, at one of the windows appeared a woman in a nightdress with tangled hair. She seemed about to cry out, then vanished with the last rays of the sun, leaving the old Endicott house in the deepening shadows.

THE END